YOU ARE READING THE LAST PAGE!

Start from the other side
and read this book from
right to left.

THE ART OF INUYASHA

RUMIKO TAKAHASHI

Translation/Stephen Ayres
Design/Zes Top
Editor/Ian Robertson

Production Manager/Nobi Watanabe
Managing Editor/Annette Roman
Editor-in-Chief/William Flanagan
V.P. of Sales & Marketing/Liza Coppola
Sr. V.P. of Editorial/Hyoe Narita
Publisher/Seiji Horibuchi

First published by Shogakukan, Inc. in Japan as "Takahashi Rumiko Genga Zensyu anime Inuyasha no Sekai".

Published by VIZ, LLC
P.O. Box 77010
San Francisco, CA 94107 USA
www.viz.com

10 9 8 7 6 5 4 3
First Printing, March 2003
Second Printing, July 2003
Third Printing, September 2003

Printed in Canada

INUYASHA

COLLECTION OF ORIGINAL ILLUSTRATIONS BY RUMIKO TAKAHASHI

The Art of Inuyasha

Shonen Sunday Vol. 40, 1997, color cover illustration

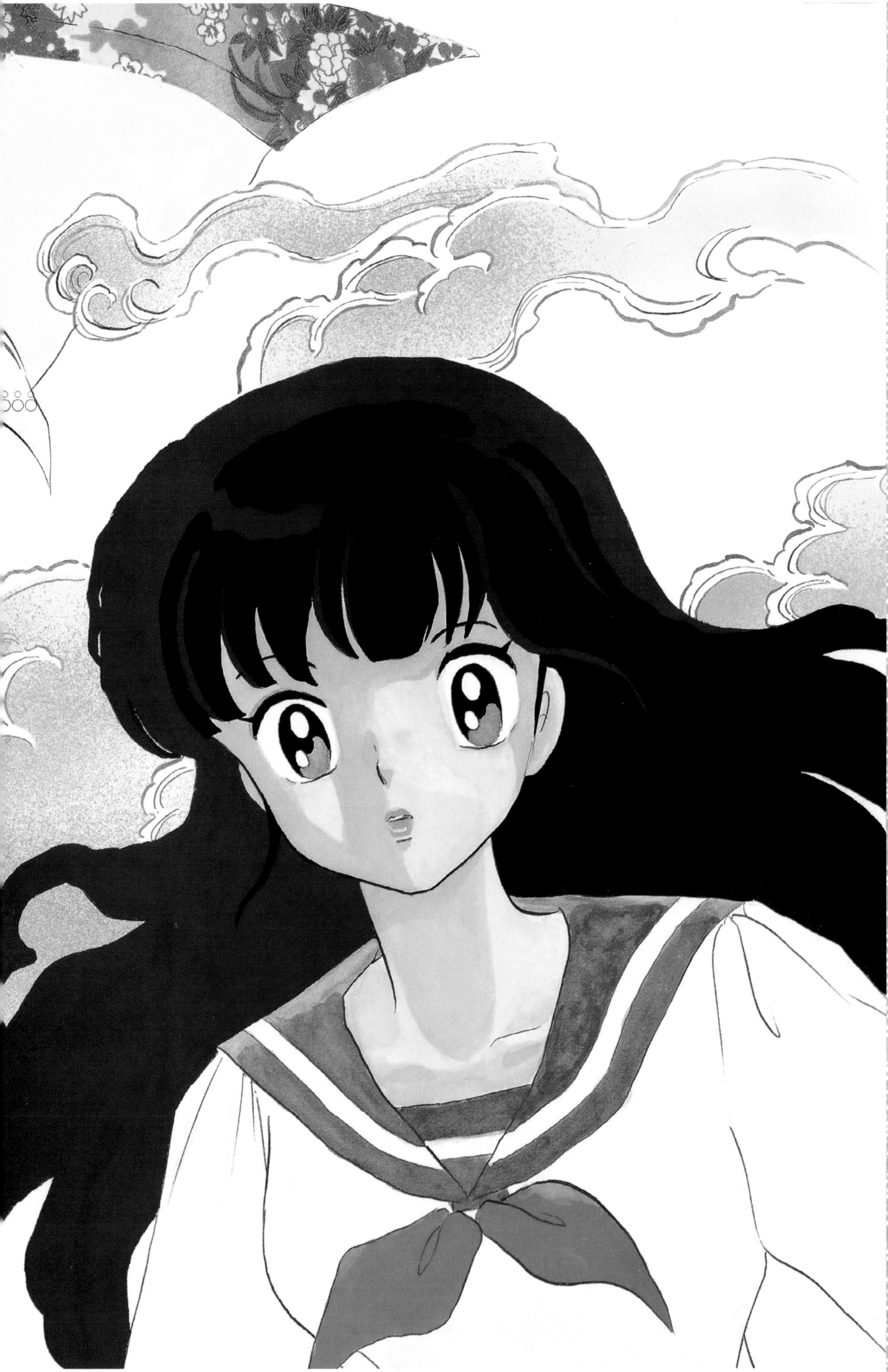

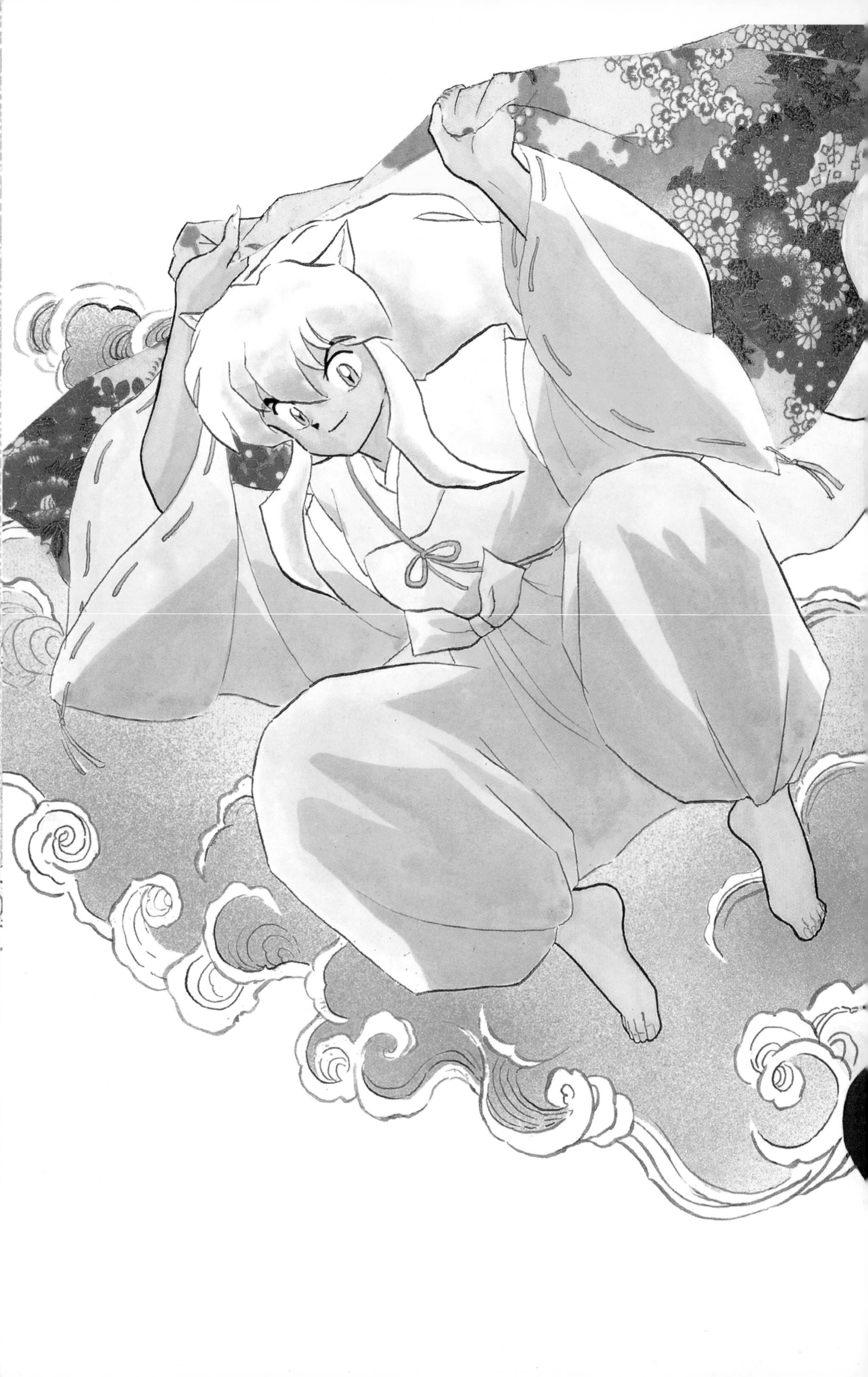

Shonen Sunday Vol. 50, 1996.
Fold-out page for Scroll 1

TABLE OF CONTENTS

Collection of original illustrations
by Rumiko Takahashi

The Art of "Inuyasha"

COMPARING COMICS AND ANIMATION

How are comics made into animation?
We'll learn the techniques of animation while we
compare the animation to the original story.

COMPARING COMICS AND ANIMATION

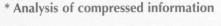

* Analysis of compressed information

Events that can be condensed in the comic must be expanded in the animation to provide detail. In the comic, the first two panels explain the scene of Inuyasha stealing the Jewel of Four Souls. In the animation there is a prelude to Scroll 1, The Accursed Youth, in which several quick cuts show the wild action, while providing a certain amount of explanation of the situation.

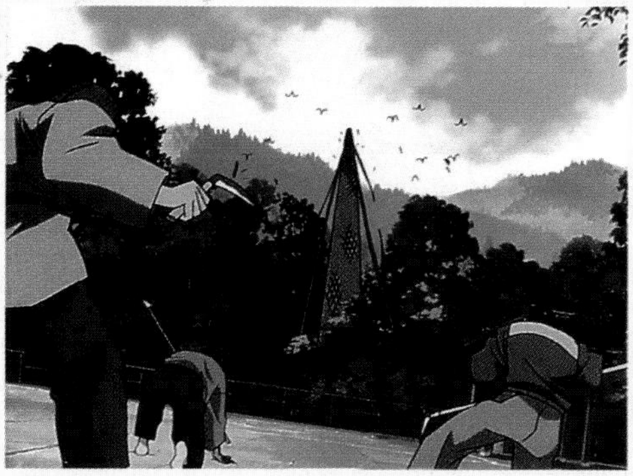

▲ A net rises from the ground as if to part the forest. This cut is replaced by another in which Inuyasha tears the net apart.

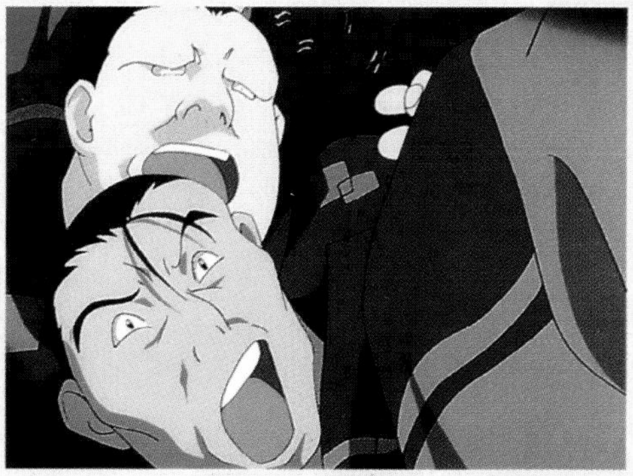

▲ After the distant view of the village, the viewpoint moves quickly to the foreground to capture the frightened expressions of the villagers.

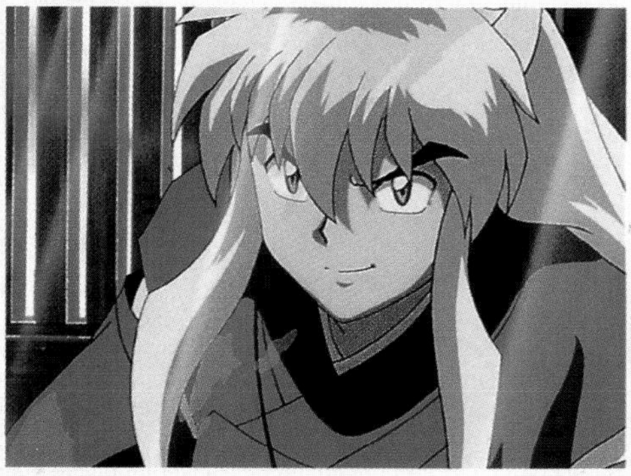

▲ In the shrine the Jewel is protected by its magical aura. To keep up the fast pace, several short cuts follow in sequence.

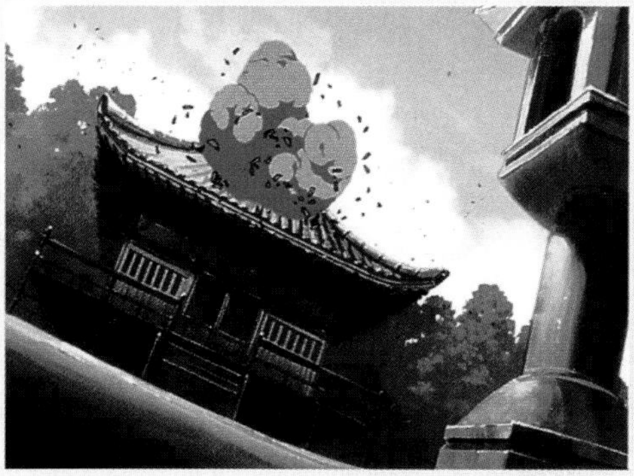

▲ The scene containing Inuyasha's invasion of the shrine to his capturing the Jewel is newly rendered for the animation.

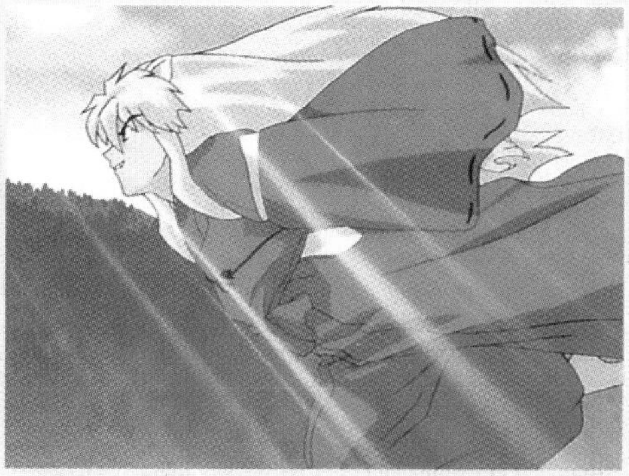

▲ The viewpoint pans to follow Inuyasha. The action with Inuyasha here is similar to the image in the first frame of p. 7 (in this book).

▶ Another up-tempo action scene with the villagers.

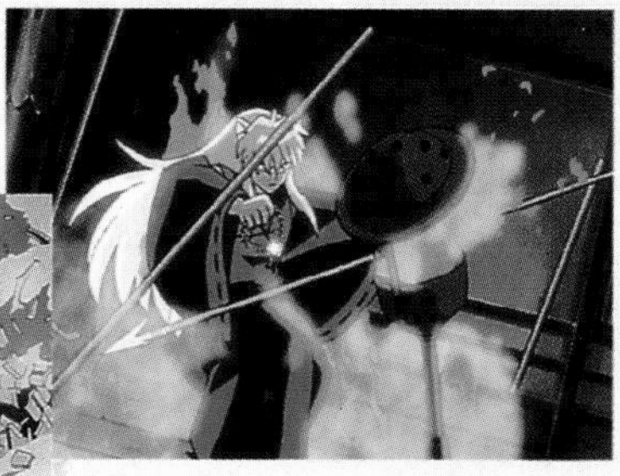

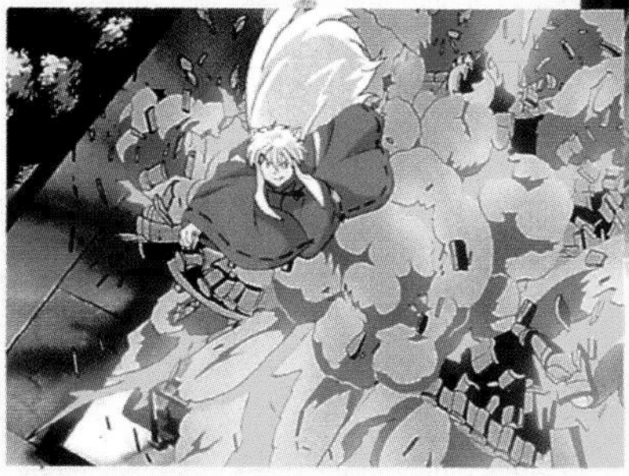

◀ The shrine explodes as though chasing Inuyasha, who is flying upward. Here the cuts begin to track those of the comic.

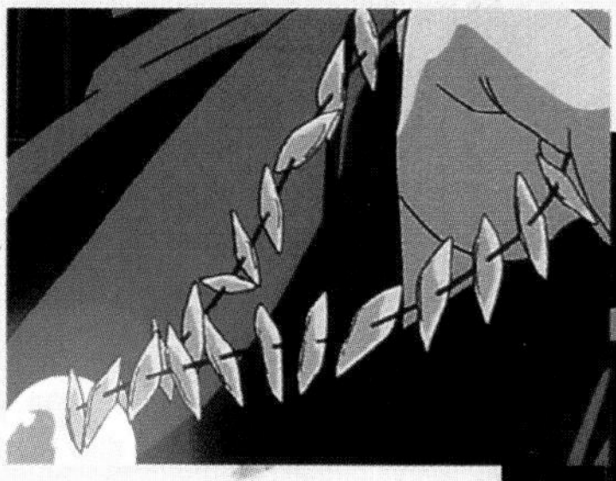

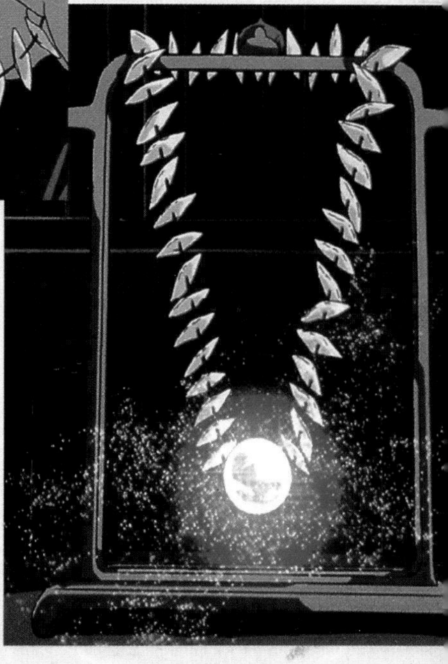

▲ ▶ Inuyasha's hand reaches out to grab the Shikon Jewel. The gleam of the Jewel is expressed by overlaying transparent light. The Jewel is seen for just a few seconds.

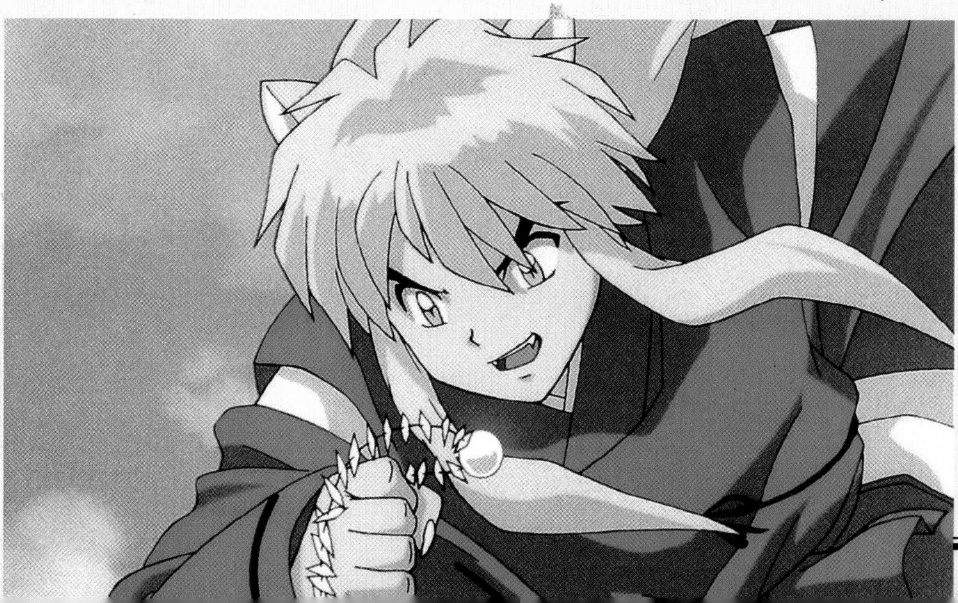

◀ This cut matches the second panel of p. 7; 17 cuts express the action in about 40 seconds.

SCROLL 1

The Accursed Youth

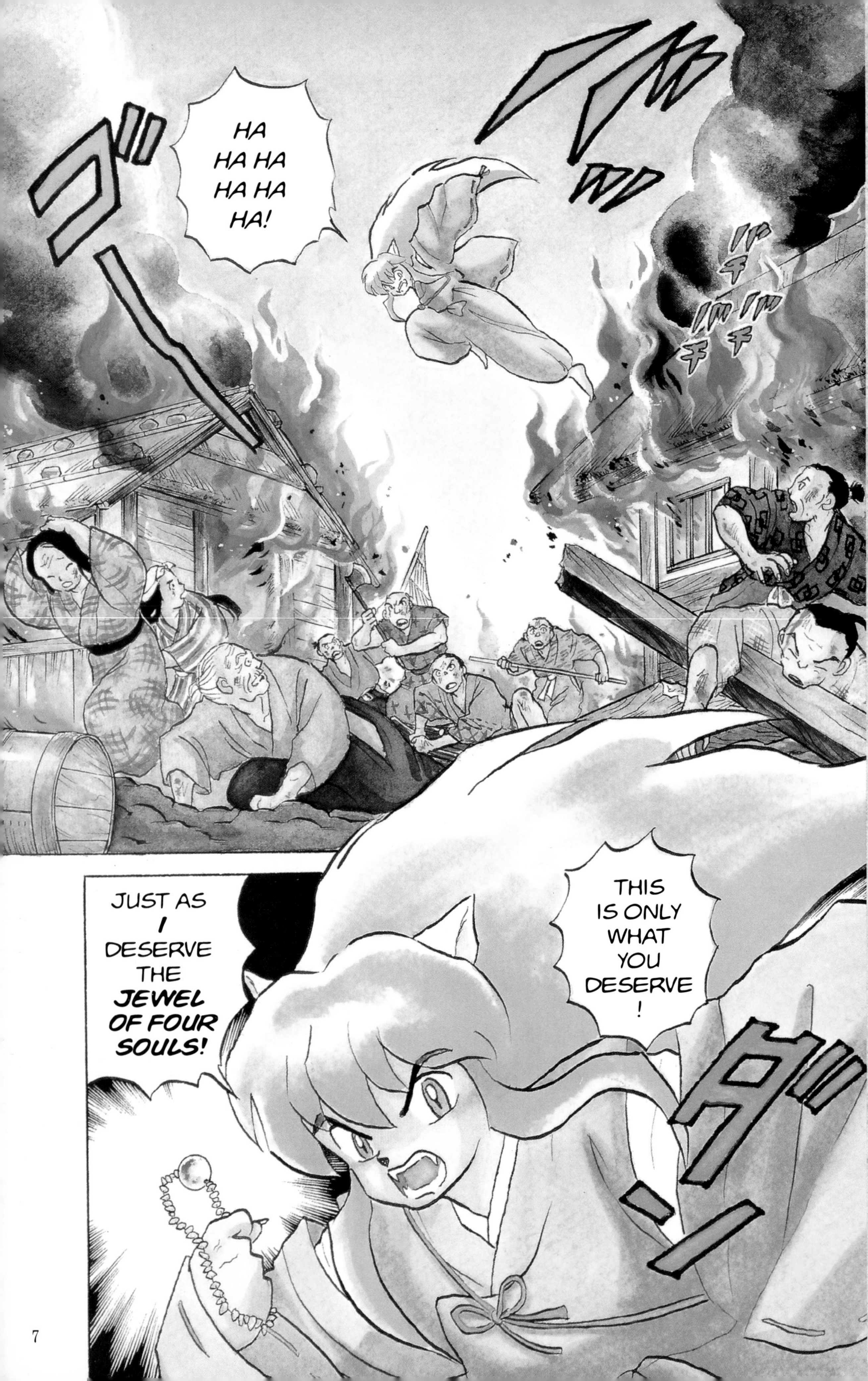

HA HA HA HA HA HA HA!
THIS IS ONLY WHAT YOU DESERVE!
JUST AS I DESERVE THE JEWEL OF FOUR SOULS!

Shonen Sunday Vol. 50, 1996
and Comic Vol. 1

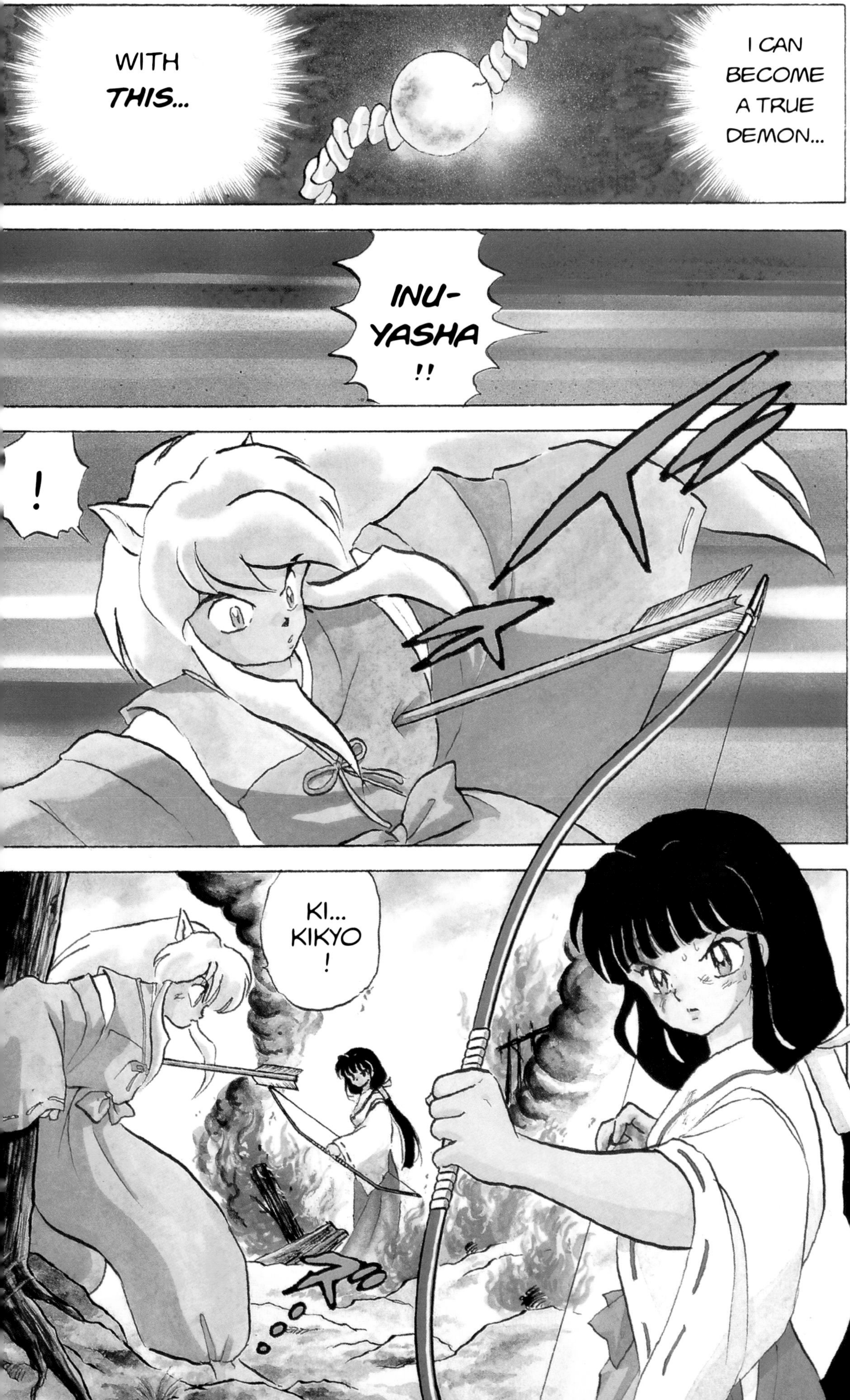
WITH THIS...
I CAN BECOME A TRUE DEMON...
INU-YASHA!!
!
KI... KIKYO!

COMPARING COMICS AND ANIMATION

Positional relationships provide immediacy

In comics, once the situation of the main characters is established, readers use their imagination to build the feeling of being present. In animation it's impossible to create those feelings without including some explanation. So the tension of the scene must be built by clearly indicating the changing of the characters and their situations.

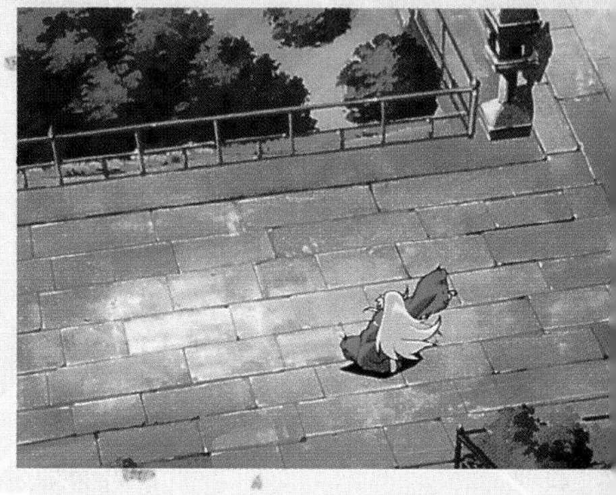

▶ Inuyasha lands after flying to grab the Jewel. The speech in the first frame of p. 8 was given in the previous cut.

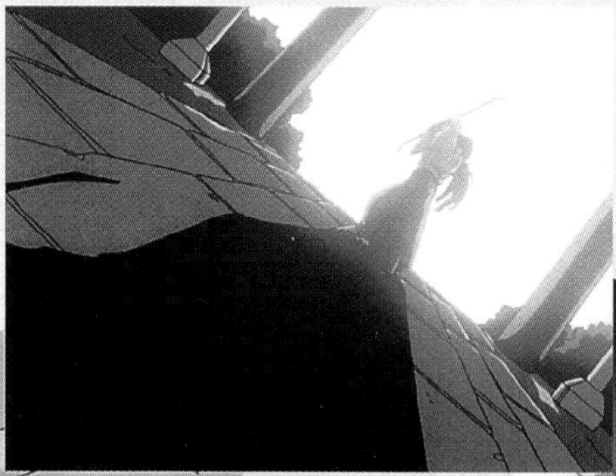

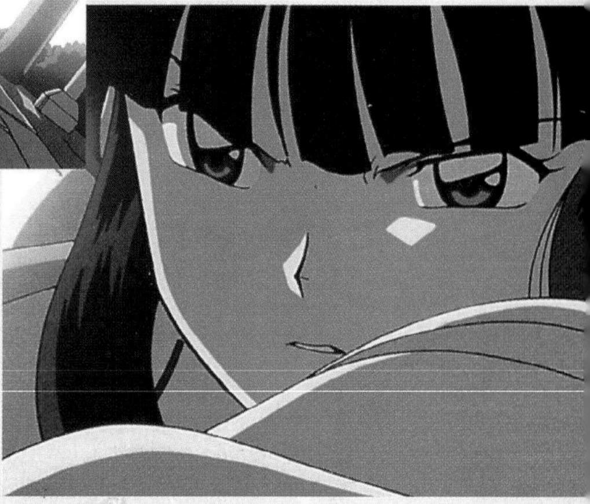

▼ The cut of Kikyo pulling an arrow is drawn for the background animation, and the cut of Inuyasha being shot in slow motion creates contrast.

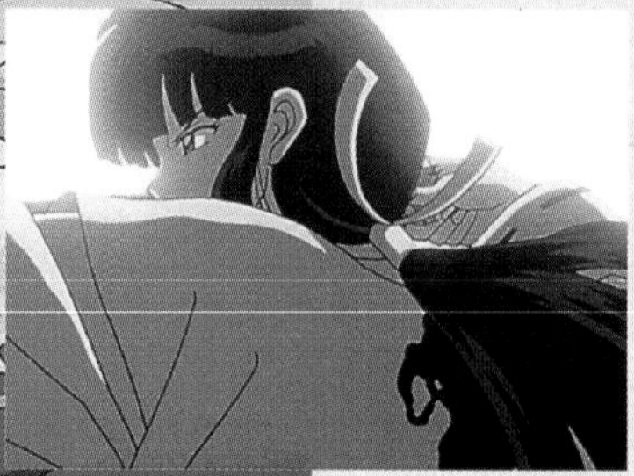

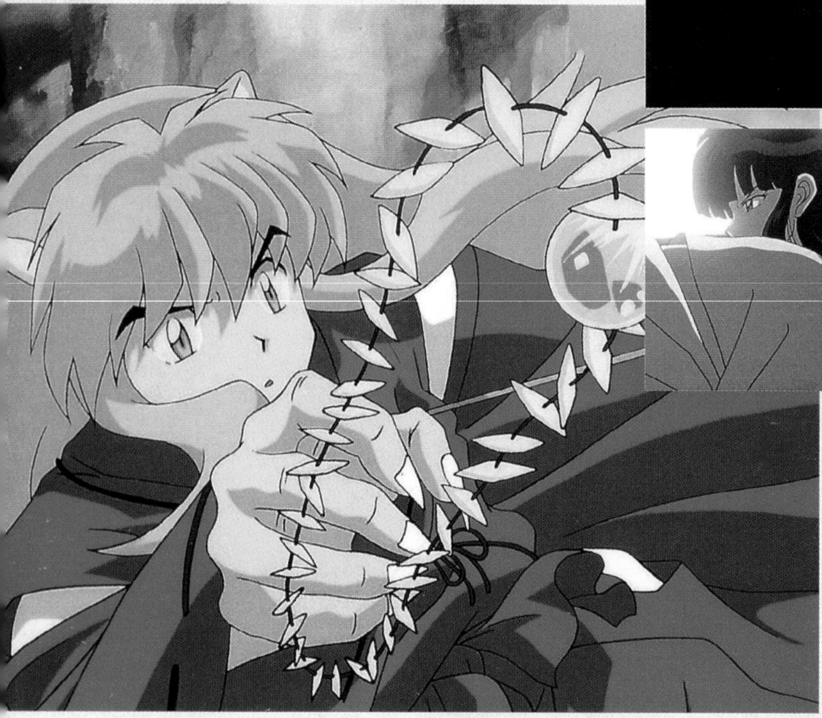

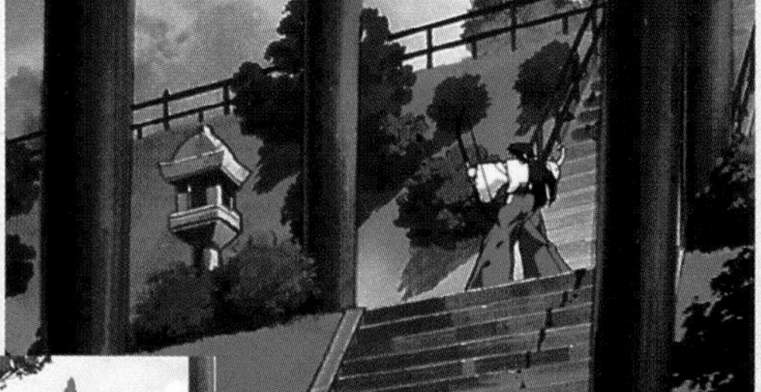

▼ ▶ The viewpoint pans slowly from Kikyo to Inuyasha. This is where the positional relationship between them is finally clarified, building the tension of conflict.

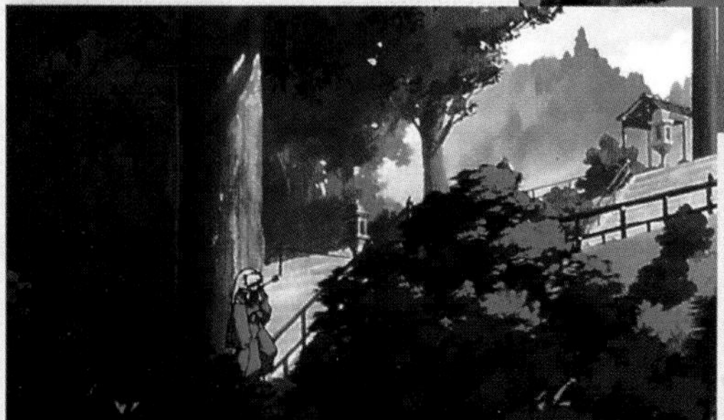

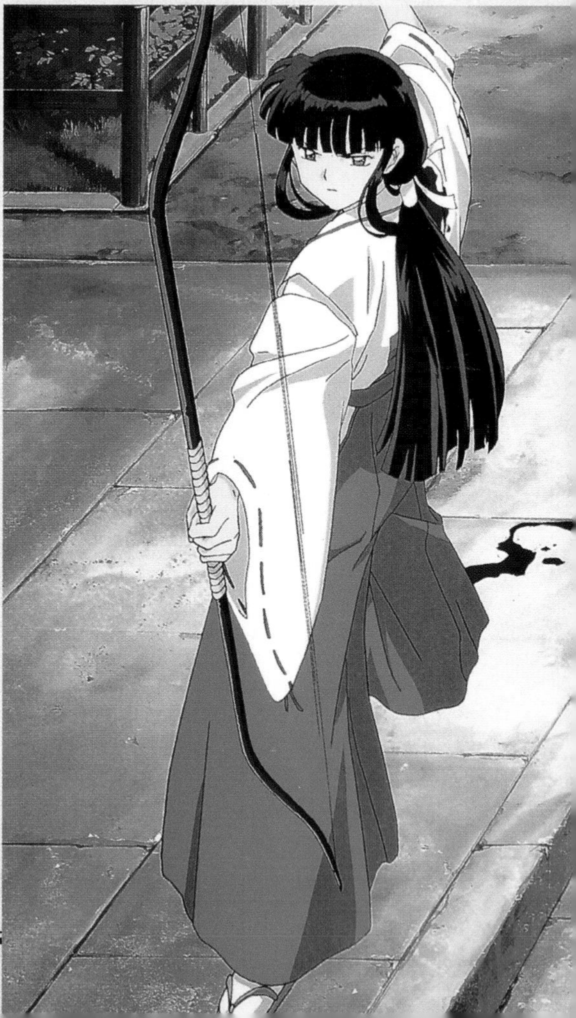

▶ With the thrum of the bow heard after a pause, the shot pans up to show Kikyo's full stature. The pace gradually slows.

COMPARING COMIC AND ANIMATION

Adding and replacing scenes

As we've seen up to now, animation is not the faithful tracing of the original pages. It is made with necessary additions of scenes, changes in view angle and the like. When a certain component needs emphasis, something special is done to make it stand out. This is done by intentionally changing the sequence of scenes or adding scenes for more information. This technique is applied in the scene of Kikyo's death.

▲ This scene matches the speech in the first frame of p. 11. In the comic this is drawn from Inuyasha's point of view, while the animation provides a neutral viewpoint.

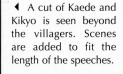

▶ This scene replaces Kikyo's speech beginning in the third frame of the comic (p. 11).

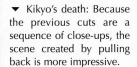

◀ A cut of Kaede and Kikyo is seen beyond the villagers. Scenes are added to fit the length of the speeches.

◀ The growing trail of blood behind Kikyo indicates that she is wounded.

▲ This scene, which corresponds to the fifth panel of p. 11, was changed to a bird's-eye view.

▼ Kikyo's death: Because the previous cuts are a sequence of close-ups, the scene created by pulling back is more impressive.

▶ While scenes are drawn from a neutral point of view in the comic, here in the animation the camera takes Kaede's then Kikyo's viewpoints. These two bust shots are designed to give the following scenes more impact.

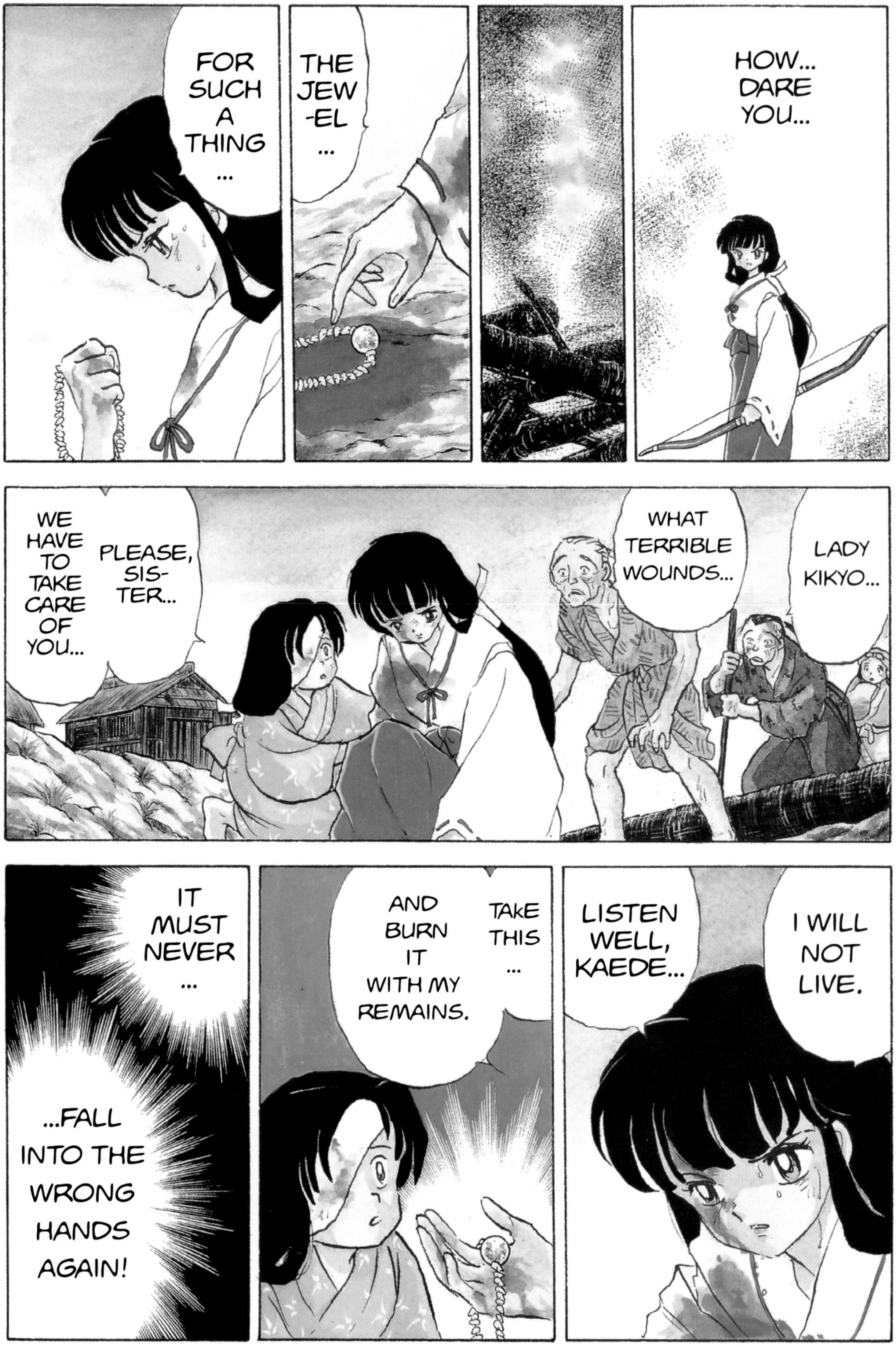
HOW... DARE YOU...
THE JEW-EL ...
FOR SUCH A THING ...
LADY KIKYO...
WHAT TERRIBLE WOUNDS...
PLEASE, SISTER...
WE HAVE TO TAKE CARE OF YOU...
I WILL NOT LIVE.
LISTEN WELL, KAEDE...
TAKE THIS ...
AND BURN IT WITH MY REMAINS.
IT MUST NEVER ...
...FALL INTO THE WRONG HANDS AGAIN!

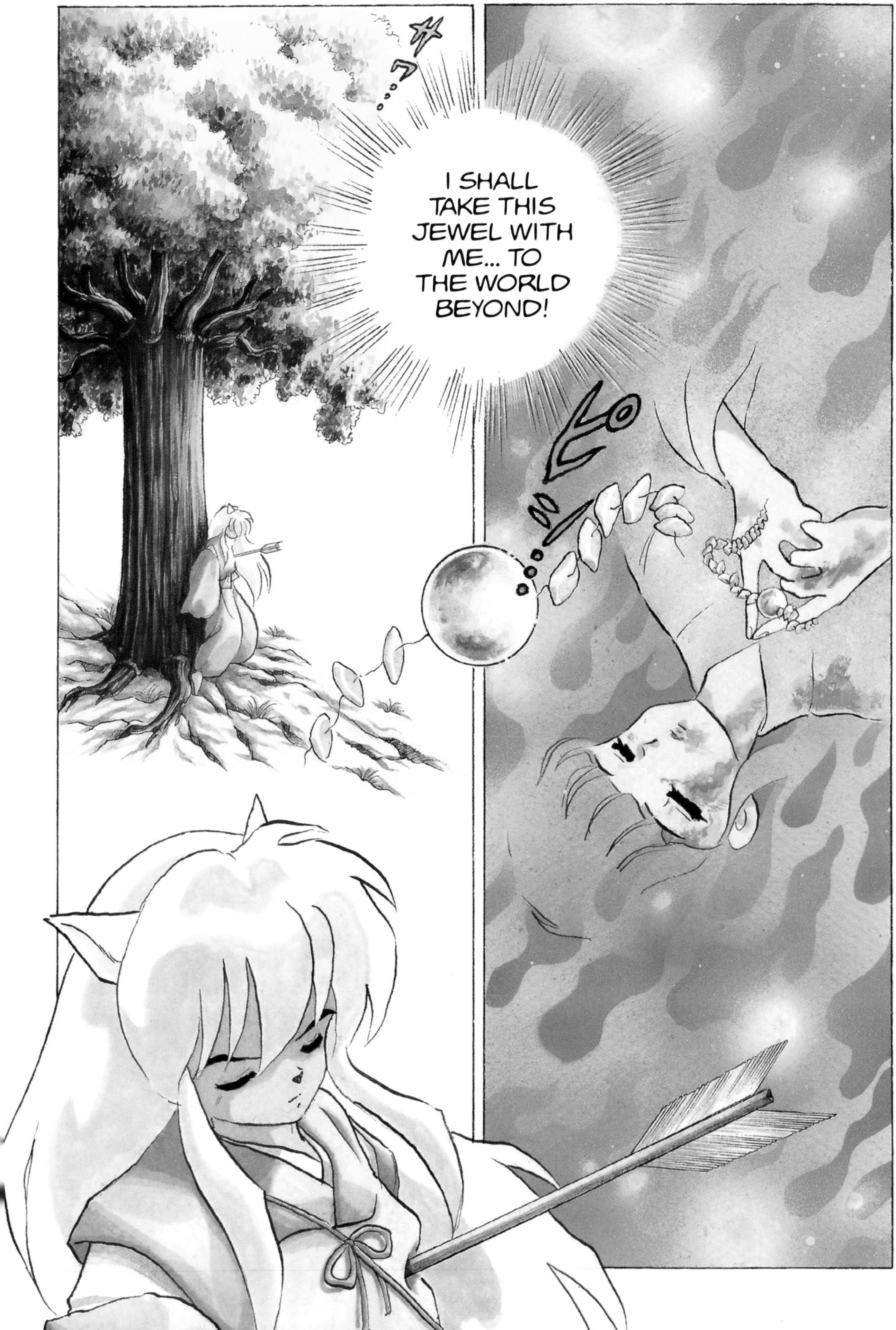
I SHALL TAKE THIS JEWEL WITH ME... TO THE WORLD BEYOND!

COMPARING COMIC AND ANIMATION

Manipulating images

In comics the reader can look at the entire page as a collage of different sized pictures. Animation, on the other hand, tells the story by overlaying short visual images along the time line. The basic approach seems the same, but the worlds of still and moving pictures are different modes of expression. In the comic the scene of Kikyo's cremation and the enchanted Inuyasha are presented in relation to the Jewel, which is the focus of interest. The animation focuses on the cremation scene. This is designed to reproduce the imagery intended in the original.

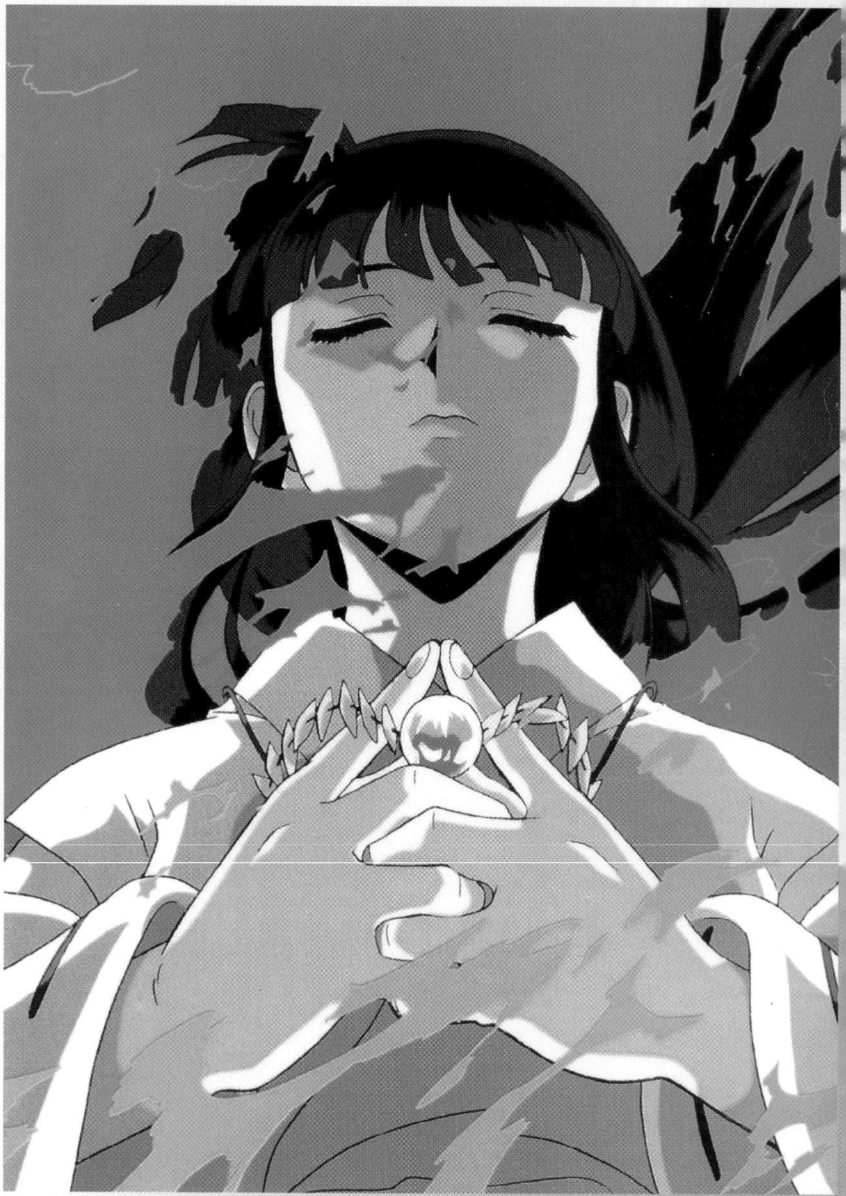

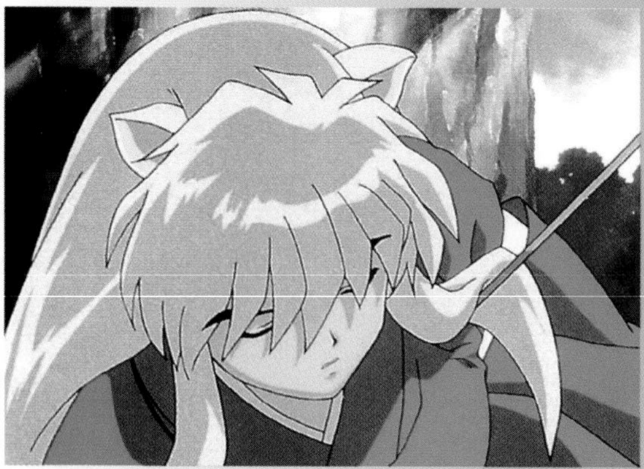

▲ In the comic, the enchanted, sleeping Inuyasha is drawn as a sequel to the shot of Inuyasha on p. 10. Here too is intentional scene switching.

▲ In the blazing fire, Kikyo frames in. When the viewpoint moves like this, a large cell, like a photograph, is used.

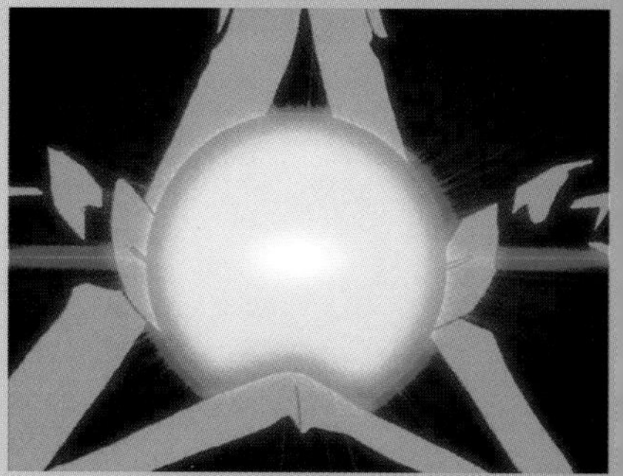

▶ From the close-up of the Jewel the viewpoint pulls away, gradually making Kikyo disappear into the fire. The fire in the background and the gleam of the Jewel are synthesized digitally.

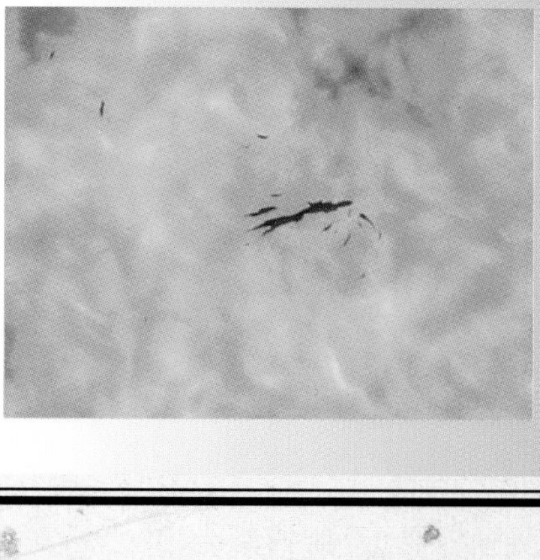

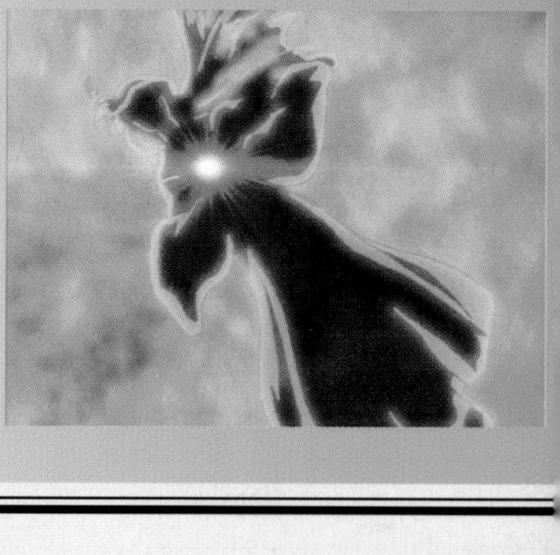

A visual effect special to animation is transparent light, which is often used to make objects look shiny. To create this effect, the cells are photographed, the film is rewound and secondary exposures of light are made using masks as needed for specific effects.

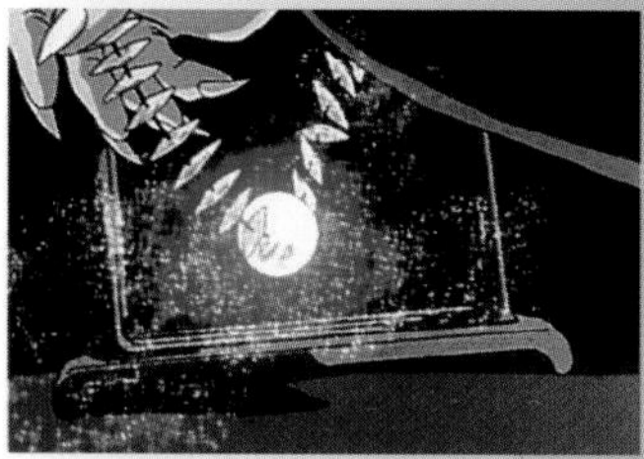

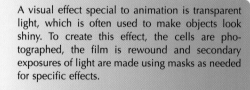

◀ ▼ An example is the gleam of the Jewel in the cut where Inuyasha steals it. By changing the shape of the mask, traces of Inuyasha's claws are expressed. ▼ These are just a few of the many possibilities offered by light effects.

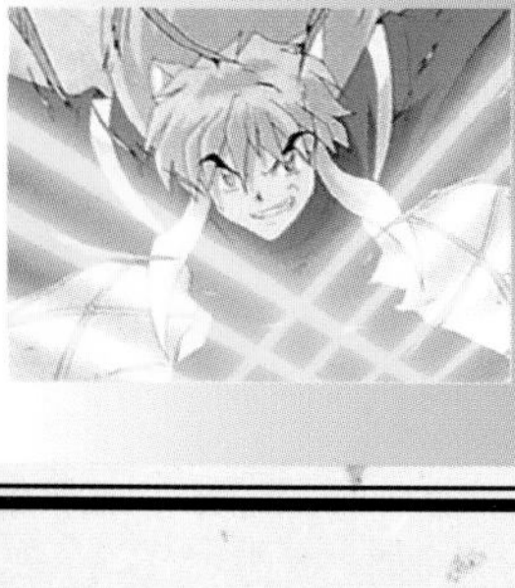

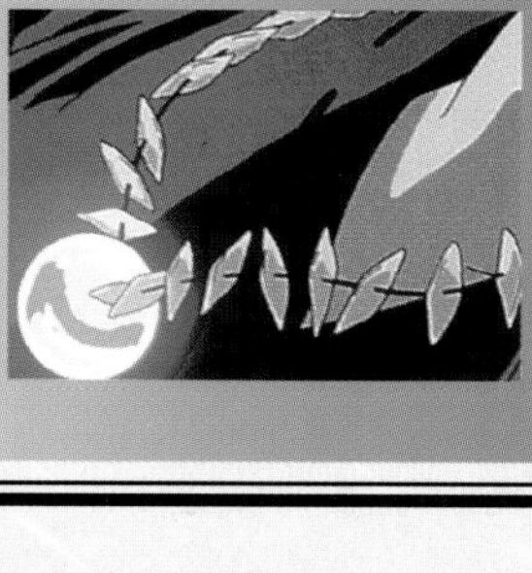

COMPARING COMIC AND ANIMATION

Controlling speed

In comics, overlaying or omitting frames controls speed. In animation adding or subtracting pictures from the basic 24 frames per second does this. The slow motion often seen in movies can be used in animation as well. The difference is that in animation the speed can be freely manipulated to match a specific scene by changing the number of pictures. In animation, view angle, cuts and speed are all easily controlled.

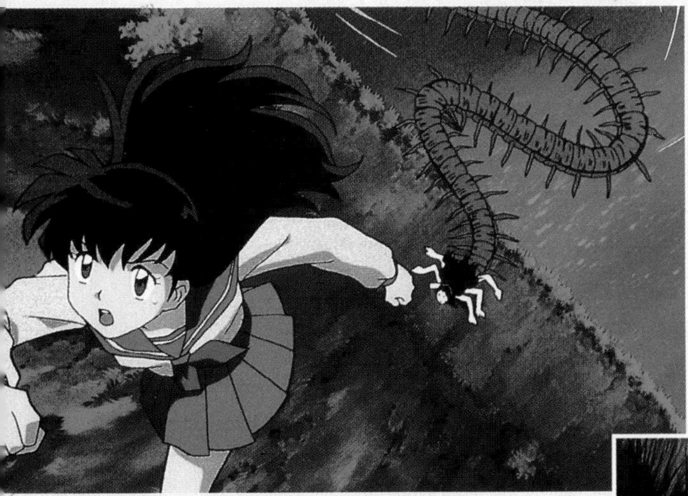

▲ This cut corresponds to the first frame of p. 15.

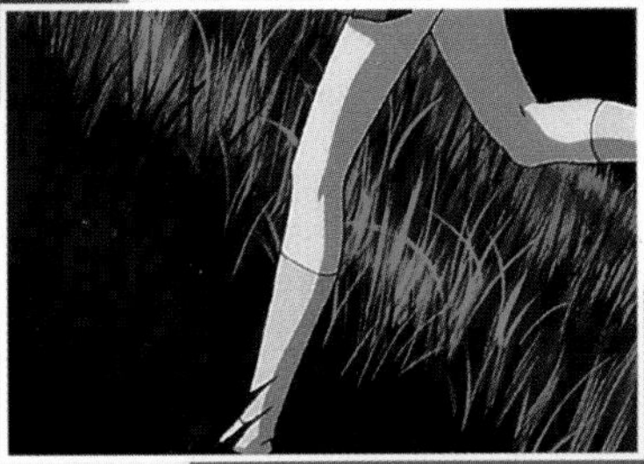

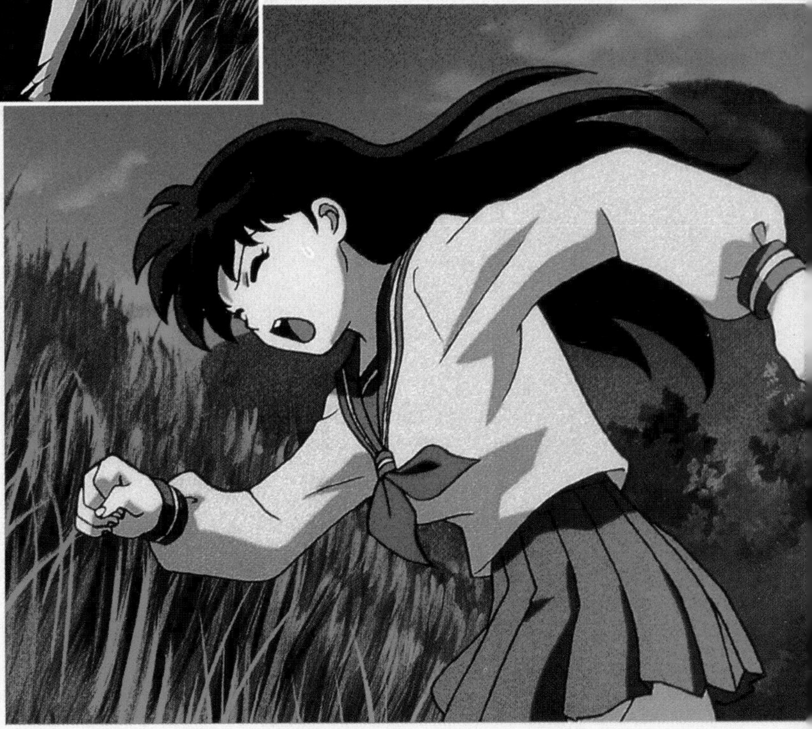

▲ The camera pans up from Kagome's legs, running. The scene is shot at regular speed.

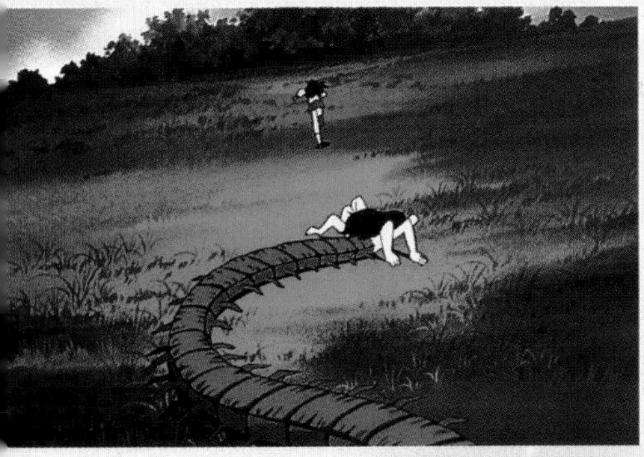

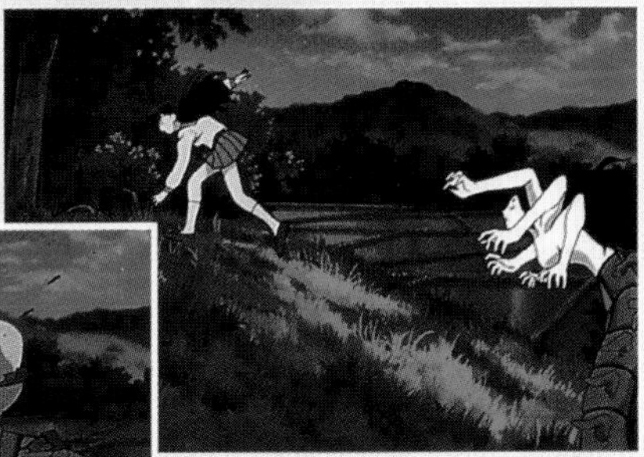

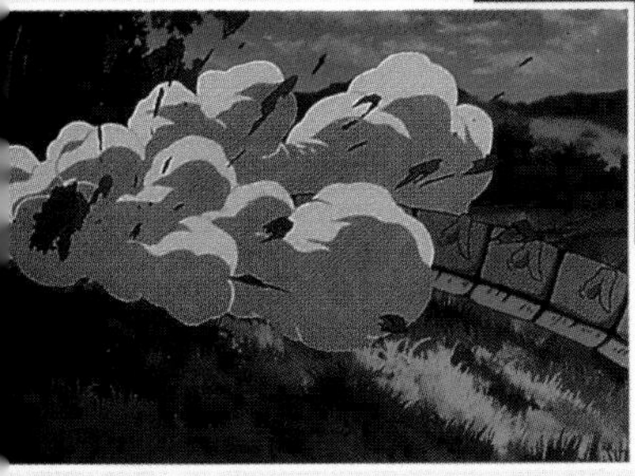

▲ This scene corresponds to the third frame of p. 15. Adding a scene here establishes Kagome's situation, being blown forward by Mistress Centipede.

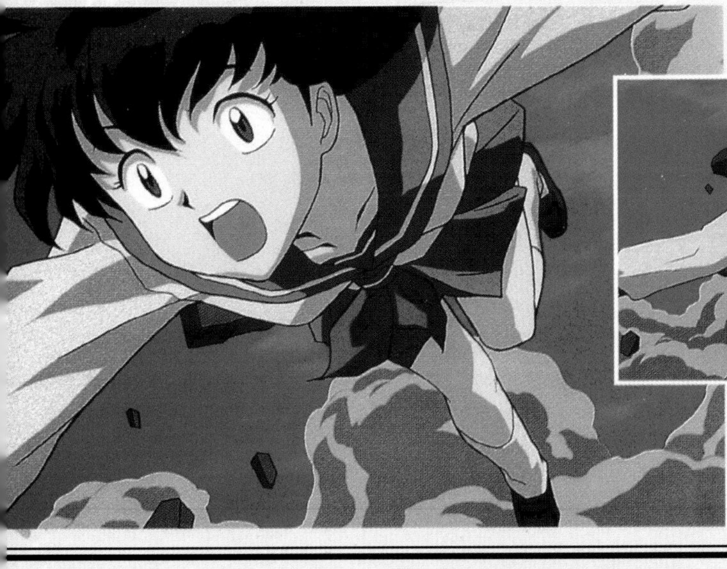

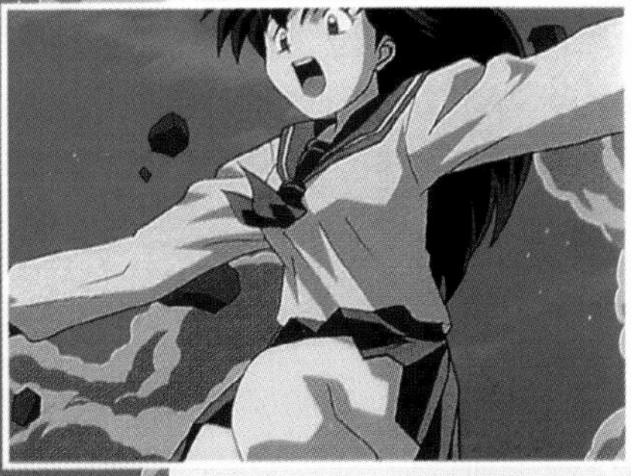

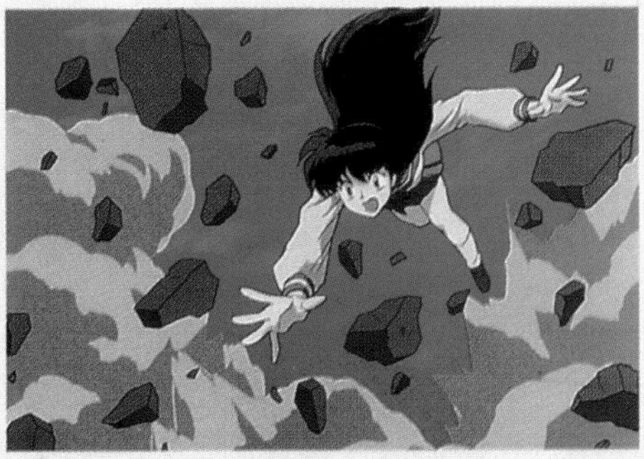

▲ Kagome is blown forward by the demon. Slow motion is used to express Kagome in the air. Kagome's slowed time sense while in mid-air is expressed by controlling the speed.

SCROLL 2

Inuyasha Resurrected

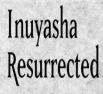

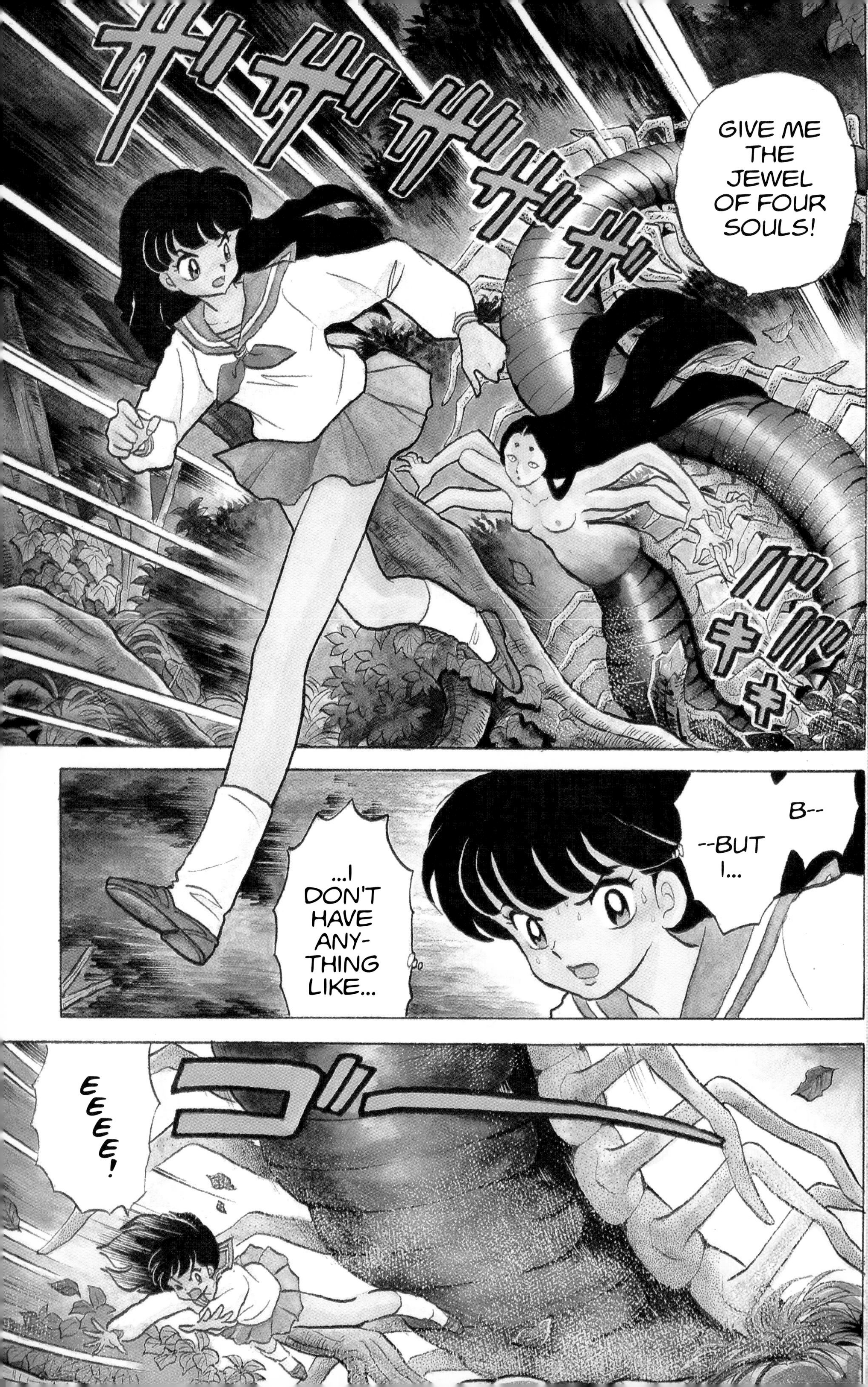
GIVE ME THE JEWEL OF FOUR SOULS!
B--
--BUT I...
...I DON'T HAVE ANYTHING LIKE...
EEEE!

Shonen Sunday Vol. 51, 1996 and Comic Vol. 1

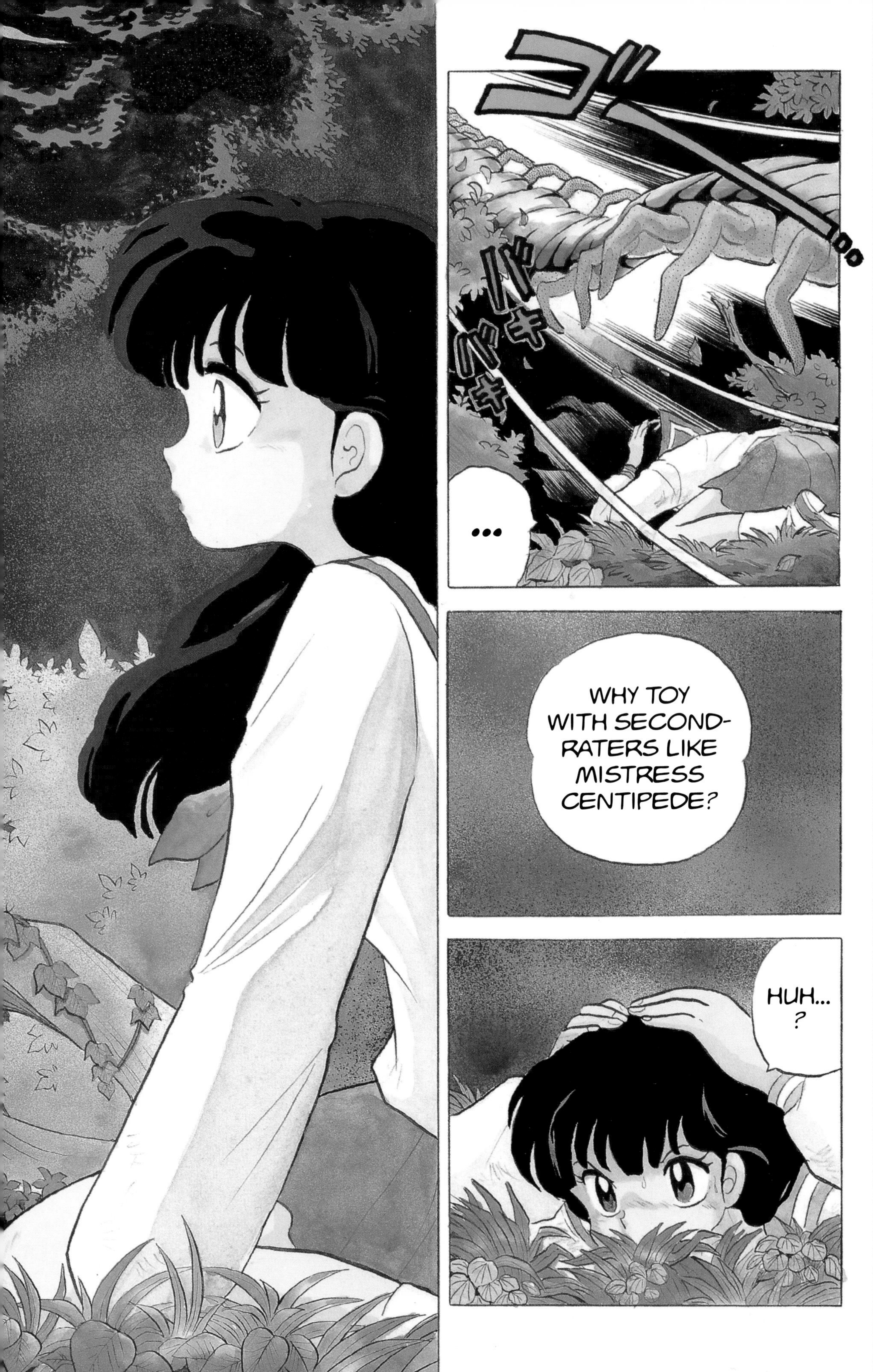
ゴ
バキバキ
...
WHY TOY WITH SECOND-RATERS LIKE MISTRESS CENTIPEDE?
HUH... ?

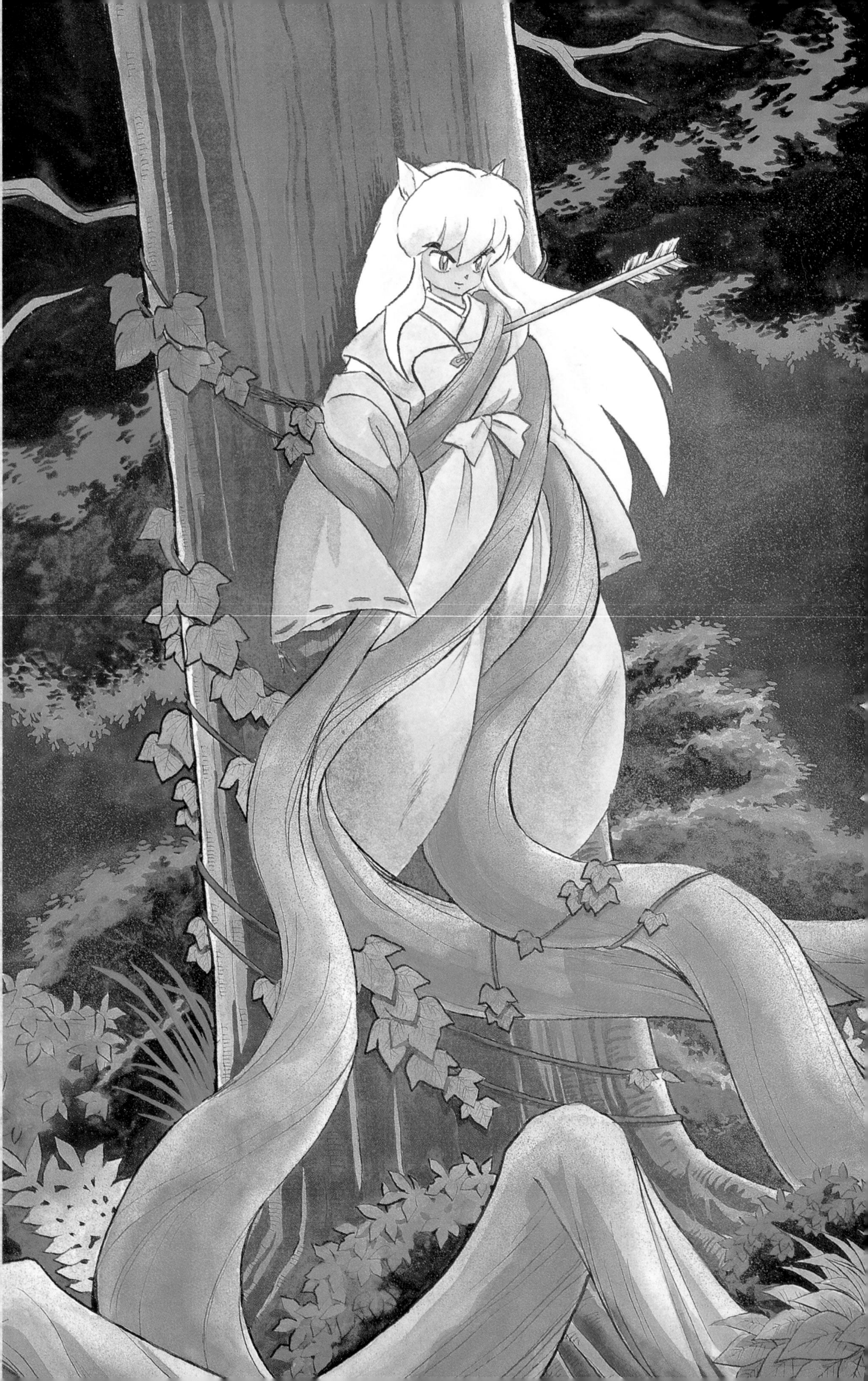

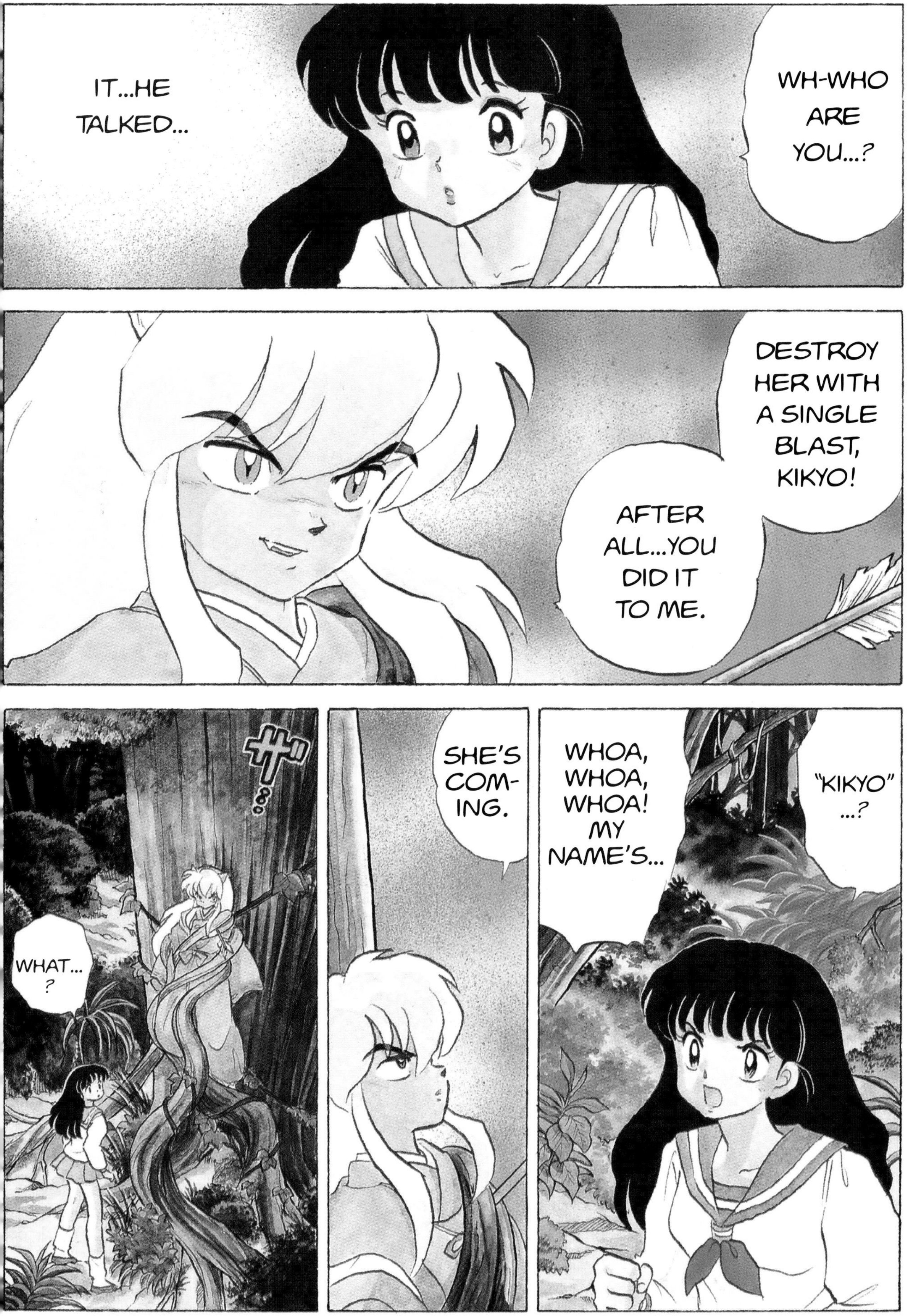
WH-WHO ARE YOU...?
IT...HE TALKED...
DESTROY HER WITH A SINGLE BLAST, KIKYO!
AFTER ALL...YOU DID IT TO ME.
"KIKYO" ...?
WHOA, WHOA, WHOA! MY NAME'S...
SHE'S COM-ING.
ザッ
WHAT... ?

COMPARING COMICS AND ANIMATION

Controlling darkness

The attack by Mistress Centipede happens at night. If a scene takes place in the village, there must be light, like a torch. In animation the light sources and locations of shadow are first determined. In the forest that Kagome escapes into, there is no light but the moon and stars. To express these natural lights in animation, the shadows are made deeper. It's also interesting to note that this scene is made intentionally gentle to contrast with the previous fast-moving chase with the centipede demon.

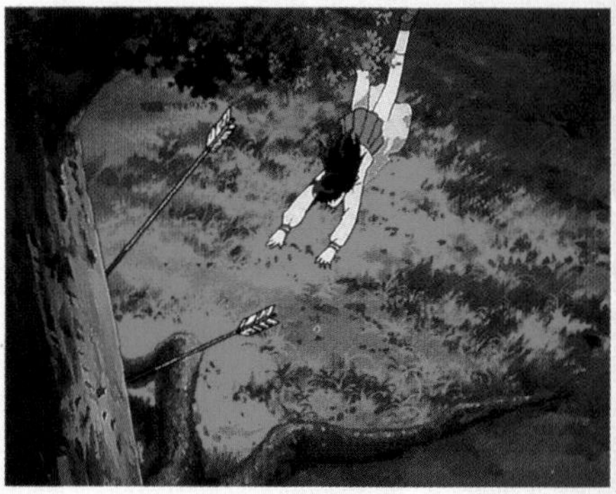

▸ Cut of Kagome landing. The cut is short, but clearly shows the positional relationship between Kagome and the tree.

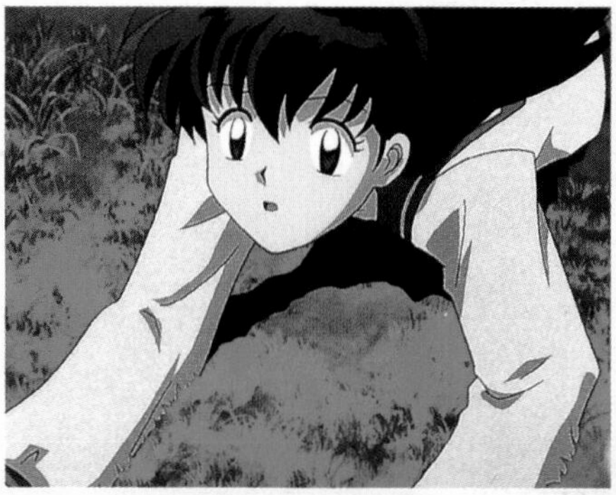

◂ In a longer cut, the action slows. The background (the ground) is in muted tones because it's night.

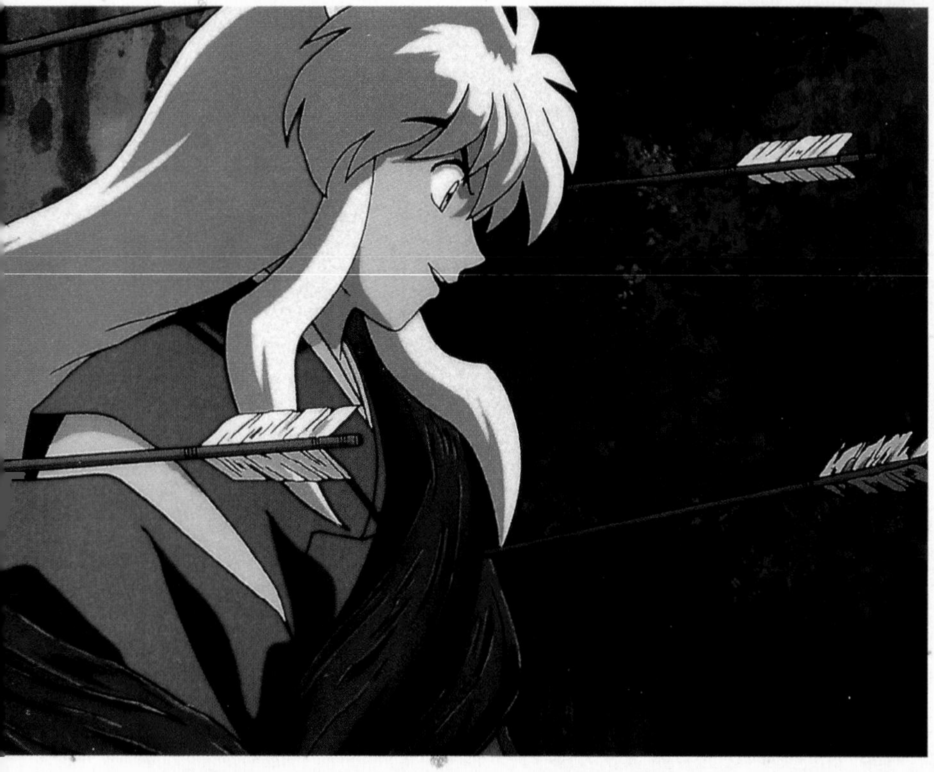

▲ This cut corresponds with the second frame of p. 18. This clarifies Inuyasha's situation by pulling farther back than in the comic. The shadows are darker than in the daytime scene.

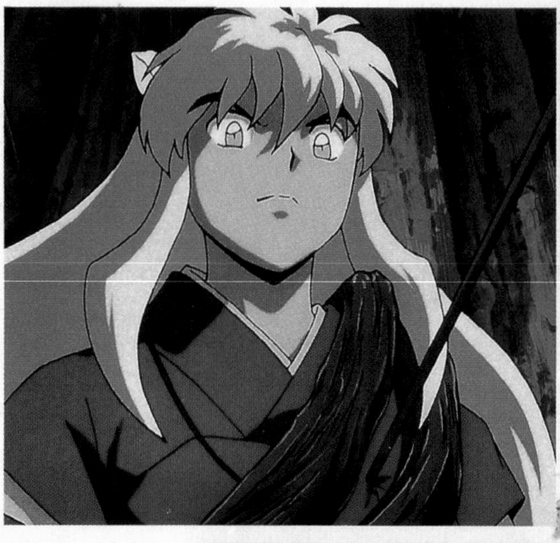

▲ Inuyasha seen from Kagome's viewpoint. This corresponds with the two-page spread of p. 16-17.

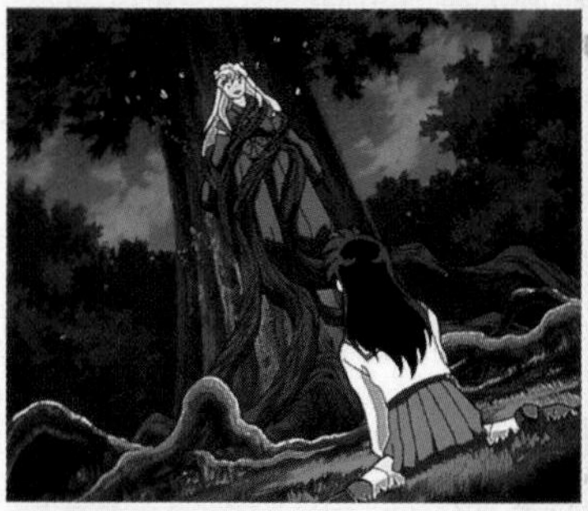

▸ Without requiring comparison to the daytime forest, a dark forest is created.

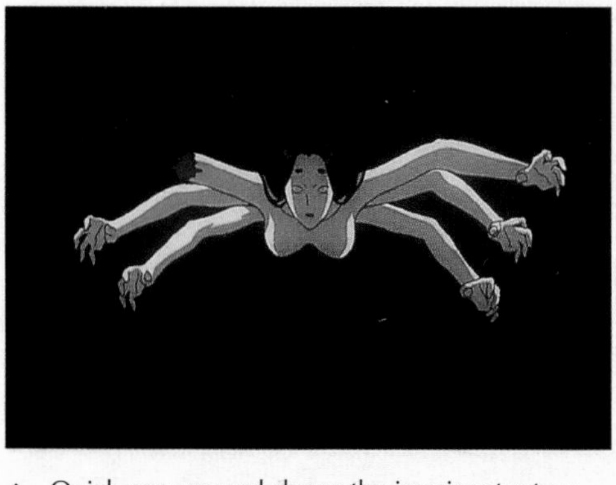

▲ Quick pan upward shows the imminent return of Mistress Centipede. This is designed to make the following still layout more dynamic.

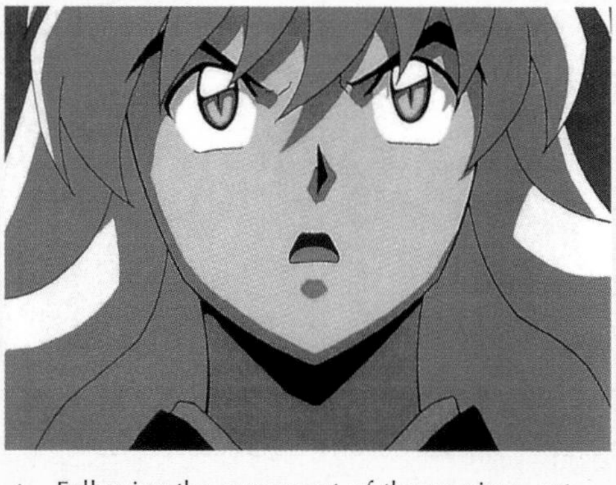

▲ Following the movement of the previous cut, the viewpoint quickly zooms to Inuyasha's face. The slow pace of the previous scene gradually builds speed toward the next.

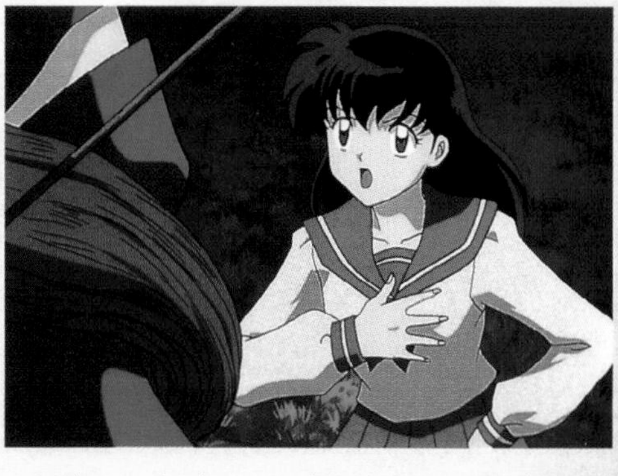

▲ The comic does not show Kagome standing up; in the animation Kagome finally stands up here. The shot pans in sync with Kagome's action.

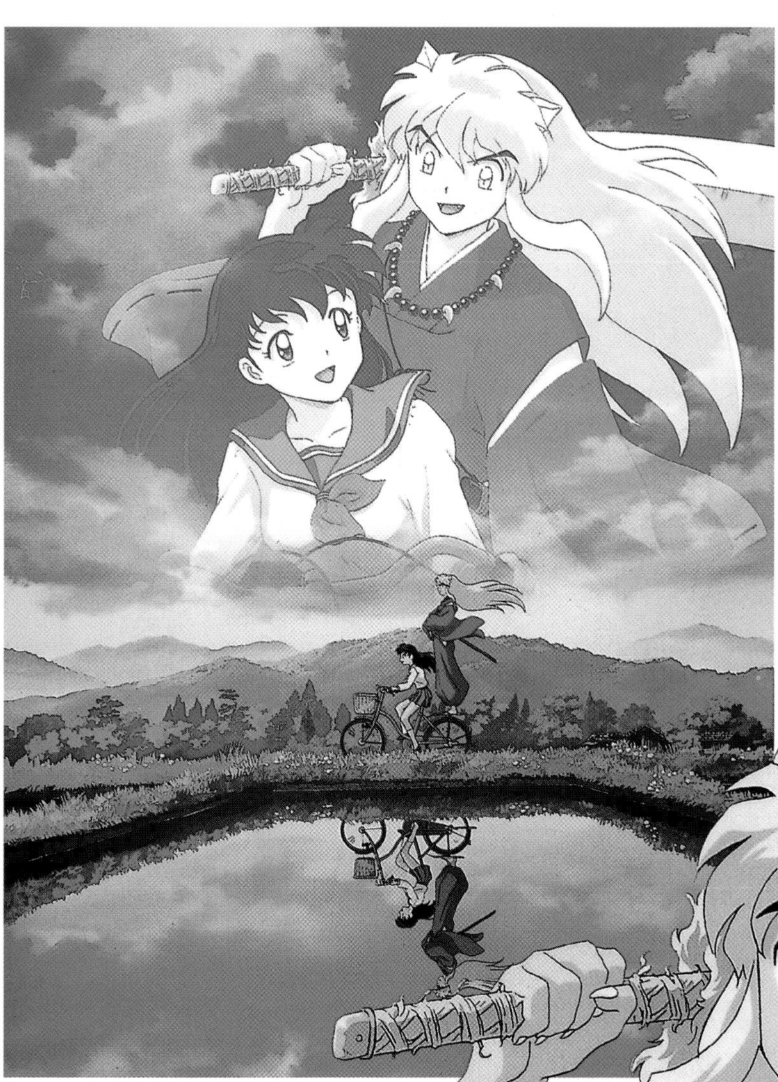

◀ Yomiuri Telecasting Corp. promotion poster

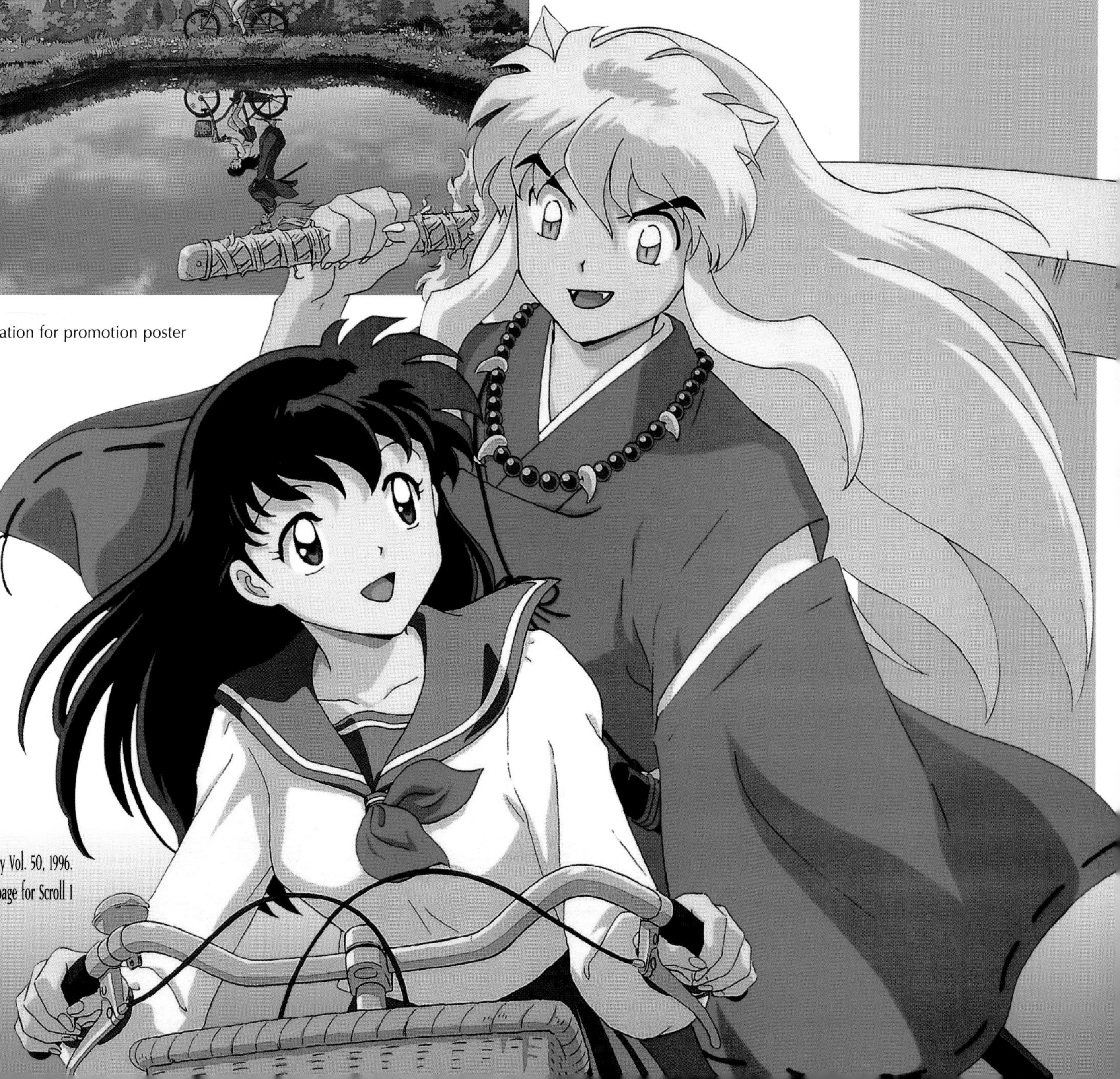

▶ Illustration for promotion poster

Shonen Sunday Vol. 50, 1996.
Fold-out page for Scroll 1

INUYASHA: ORIGINAL ILLUSTRATION COLLECTION I

Here we've collected all the color illustrations published in Shonen Sunday, from Vol. 52 in 1996 to Vol. 47 in 2000. We hope you'll enjoy these superb illustrations and the stunning world of Inuyasha in color.

SCROLL 3

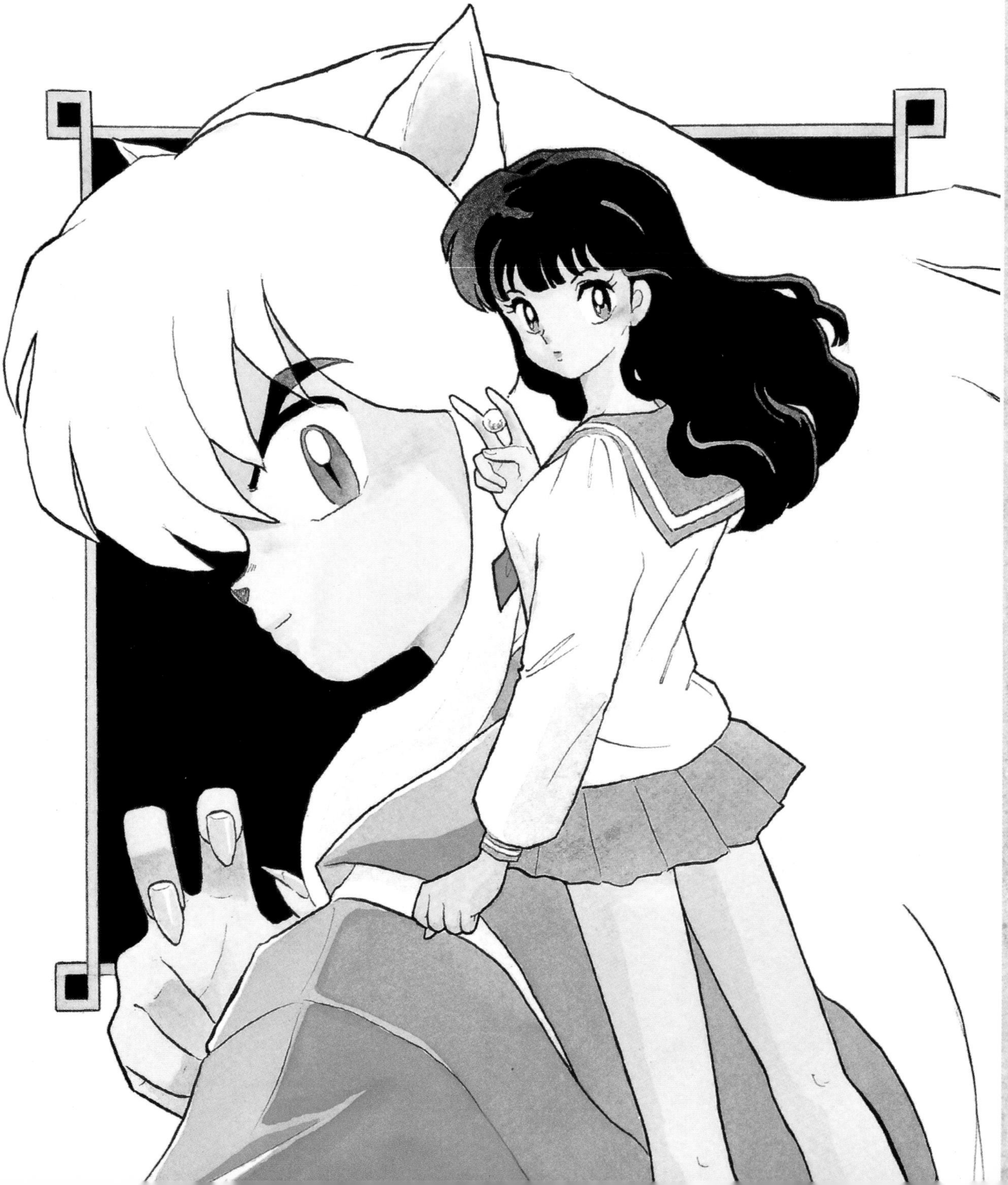

A NEW FOE (TAMA WO NERAUMONO = PURSUERS OF THE JEWEL)

Shonen Sunday Vol. 52, 1996, and Comic Vol. 1

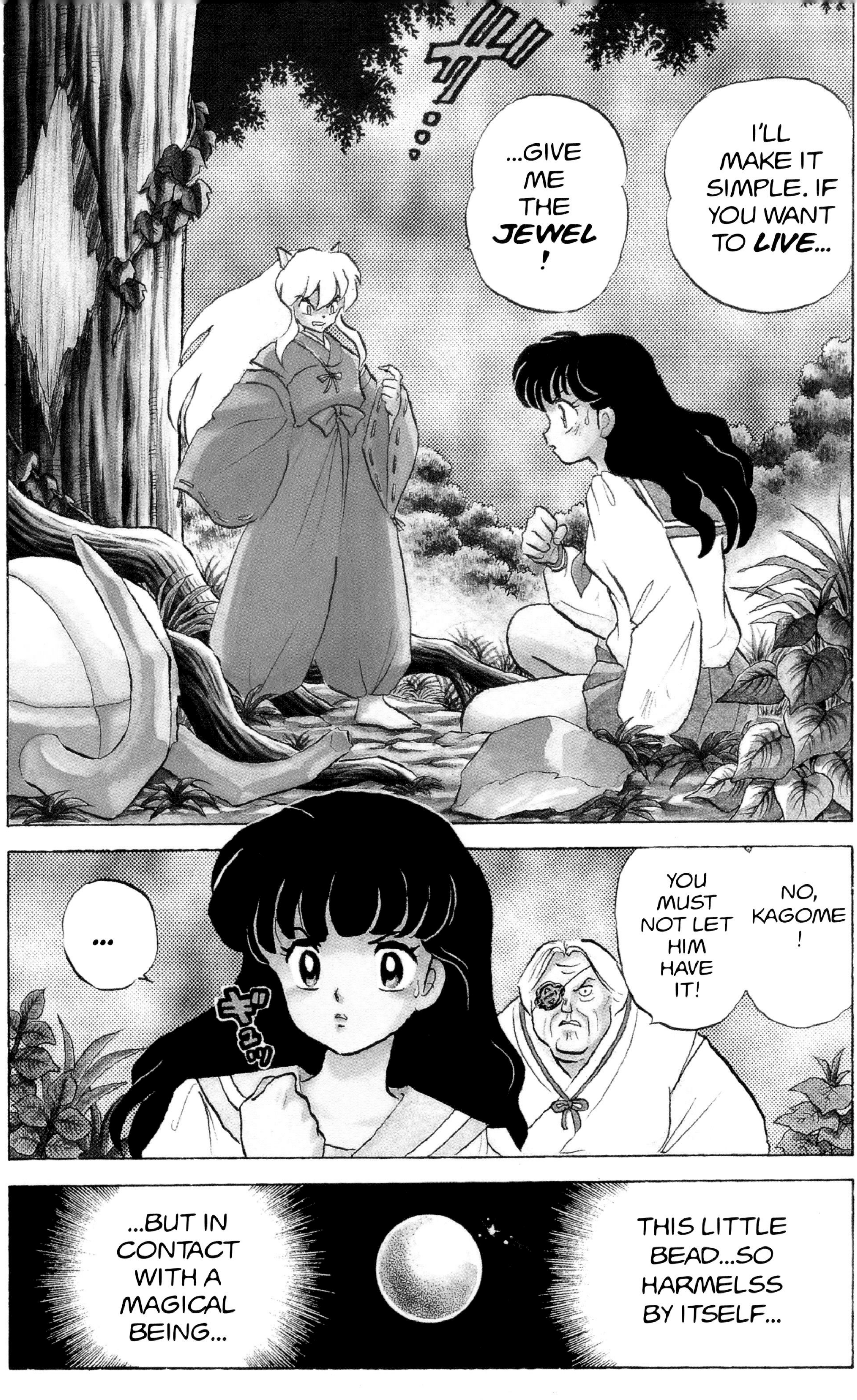
I'LL MAKE IT SIMPLE. IF YOU WANT TO LIVE...
...GIVE ME THE JEWEL!
NO, KAGOME!
YOU MUST NOT LET HIM HAVE IT!
...
THIS LITTLE BEAD...SO HARMELSS BY ITSELF...
...BUT IN CONTACT WITH A MAGICAL BEING...

PRAYER BEADS (NENJU)

Kaede prepares a string of beads to control Inuyasha. It keeps Inuyasha from killing Kagome for the Shikon Jewel. Inuyasha can't remove the beads on his own. Kagome's subduing command of "Sit" triggers the power of the necklace, which she thinks up on the spur of the moment.

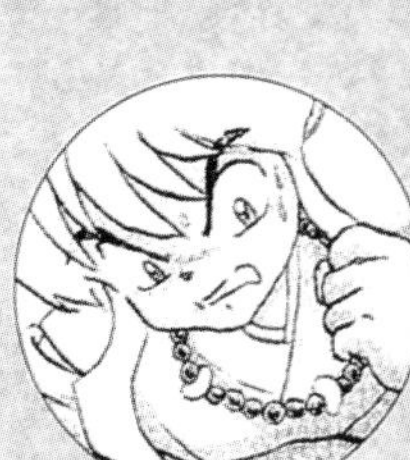

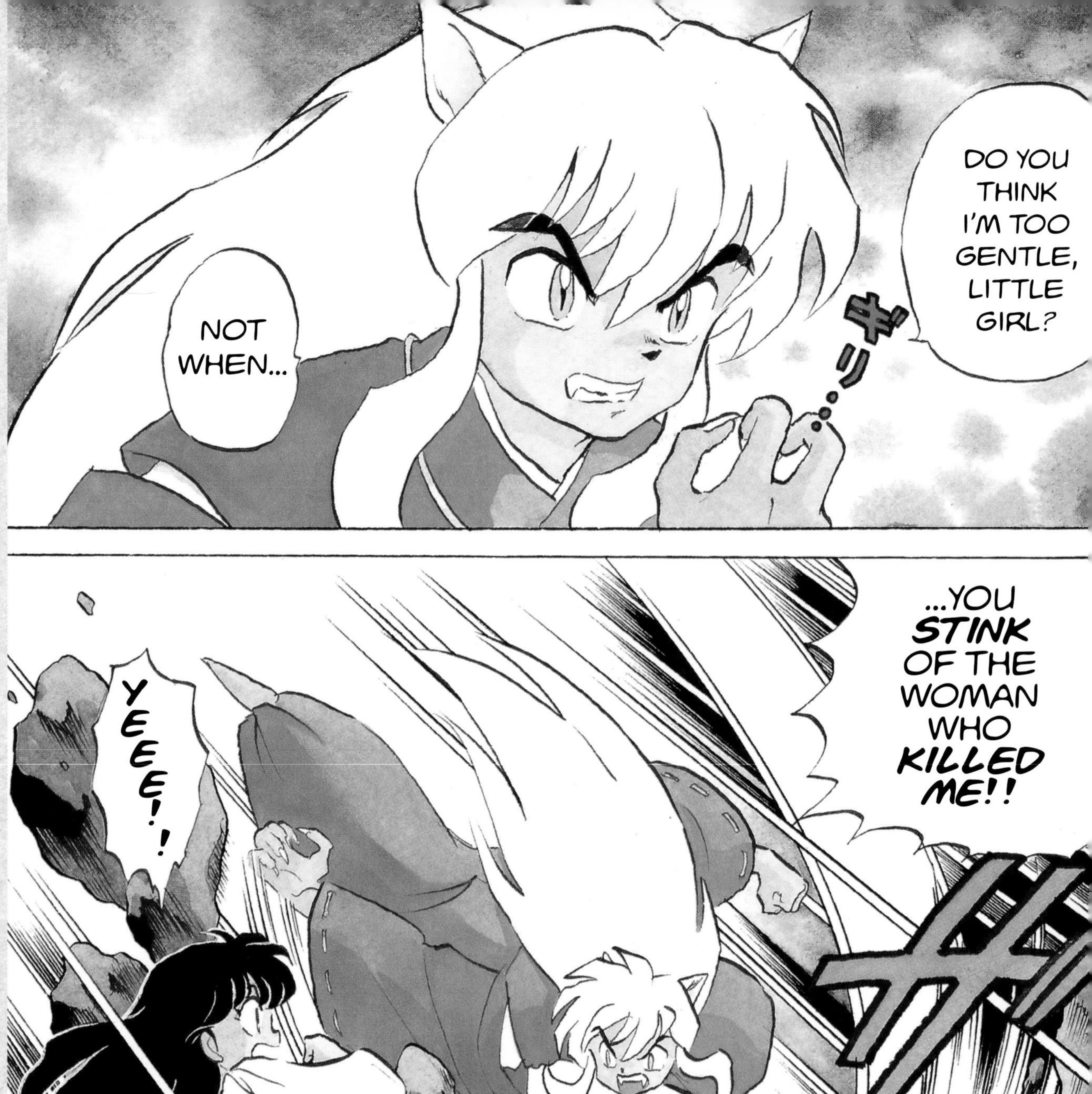
DO YOU THINK I'M TOO GENTLE, LITTLE GIRL?
ギリ…
NOT WHEN...
...YOU STINK OF THE WOMAN WHO KILLED ME!!
YEEE!!
AAAGH!
バラバラ

CARRION CROW

This demon lives on human prey. Sensing the presence of the Jewel for the first time in 50 years, it appears in Inuyasha's village. It can inhabit a corpse and manipulate it. It takes control of the leader of a gang of rogue samurai to kidnap Kagome. The demon swallows the Jewel and gains monstrous power, but is killed by Kagome's arrow. The arrow hits the Jewel and smashes it into scattering shards.

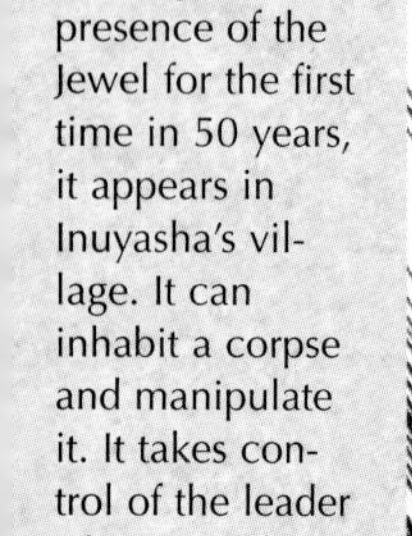

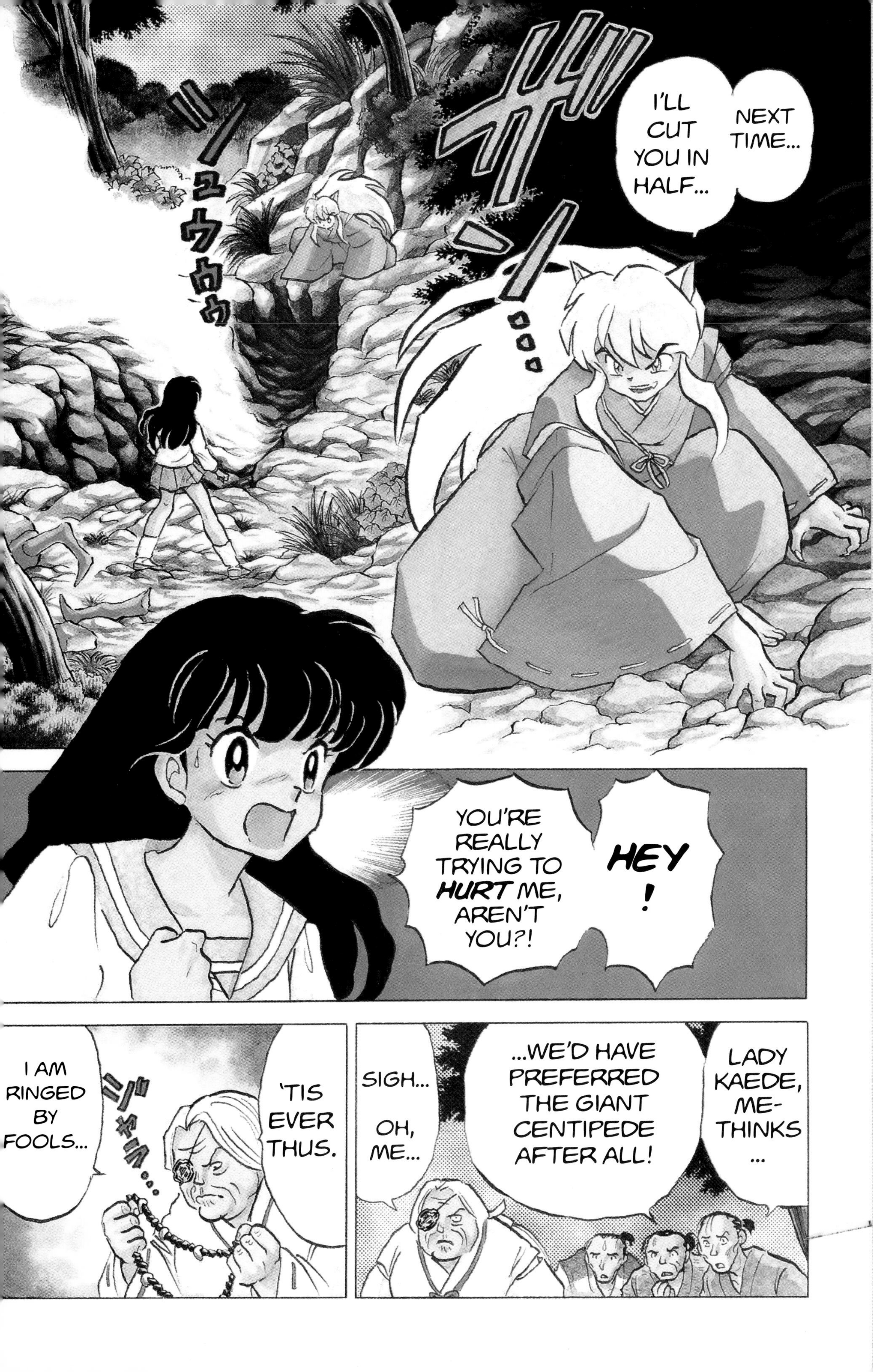
NEXT TIME...
I'LL CUT YOU IN HALF...
HEY!
YOU'RE REALLY TRYING TO HURT ME, AREN'T YOU?!
LADY KAEDE, ME-THINKS...
...WE'D HAVE PREFERRED THE GIANT CENTIPEDE AFTER ALL!
SIGH... OH, ME...
'TIS EVER THUS.
I AM RINGED BY FOOLS...

ROGUE SAMURAI (NOBUSHI)

At the command of their leader they kidnap Kagome. Because the Carrion Crow is not very good at manipulating corpses, its sword misses Kagome and instead kills two of them. When Inuyasha realizes the true nature of their leader, they are paralyzed with fear. After this many warriors appear in the story, but, like those manipulated by the Carrion Crow, they often fall victim to merciless demons.

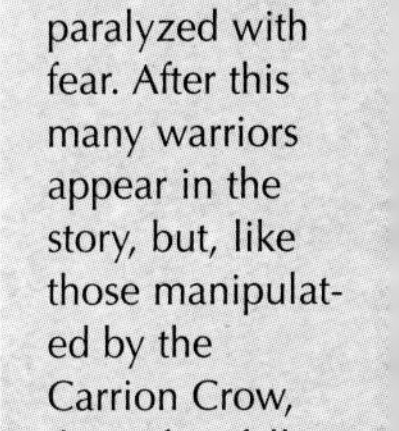

SCROLL 6

YURA OF THE DEMON HAIR

Shonen Sunday Vol. 4, 1997, and Comic Vol. 1

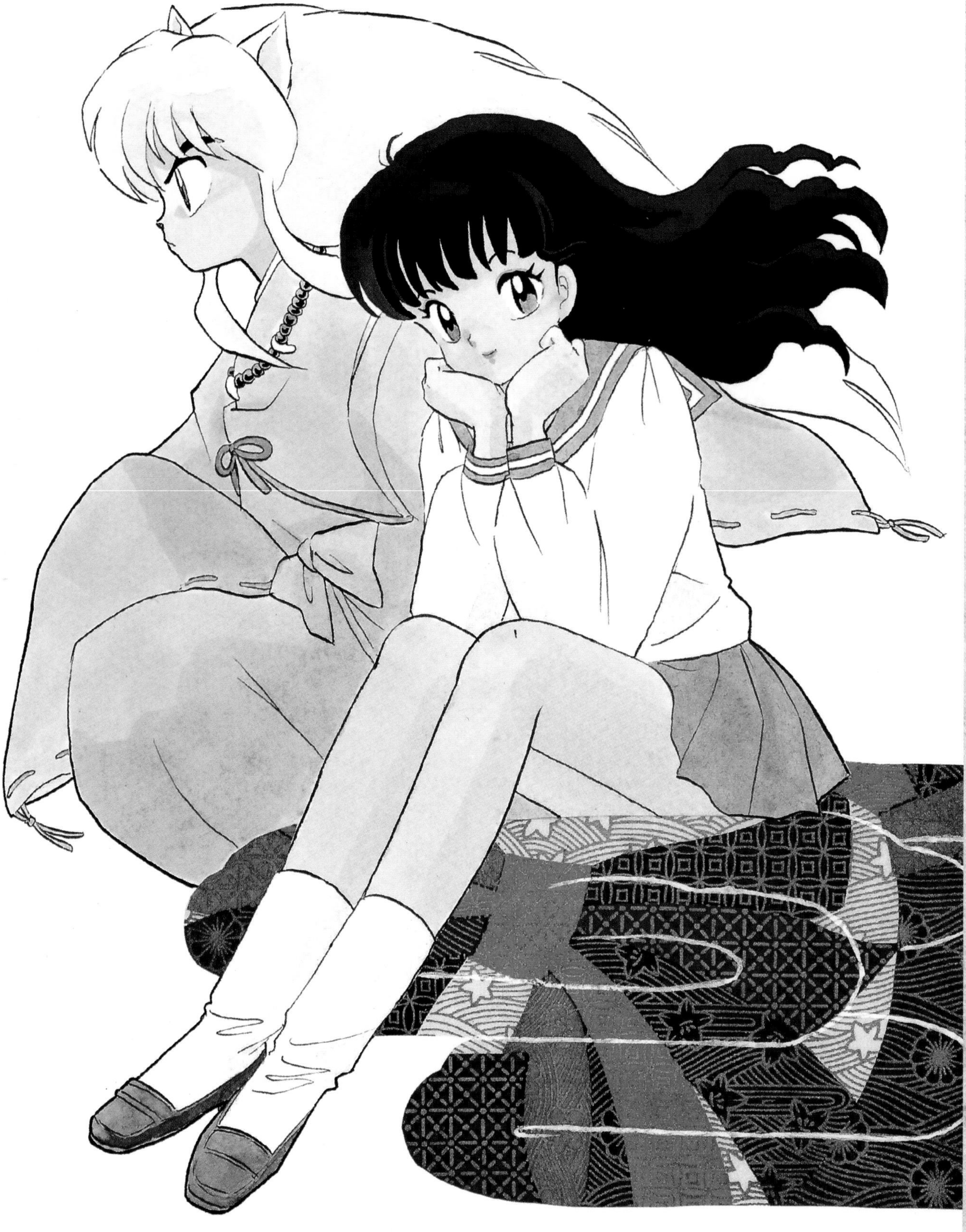

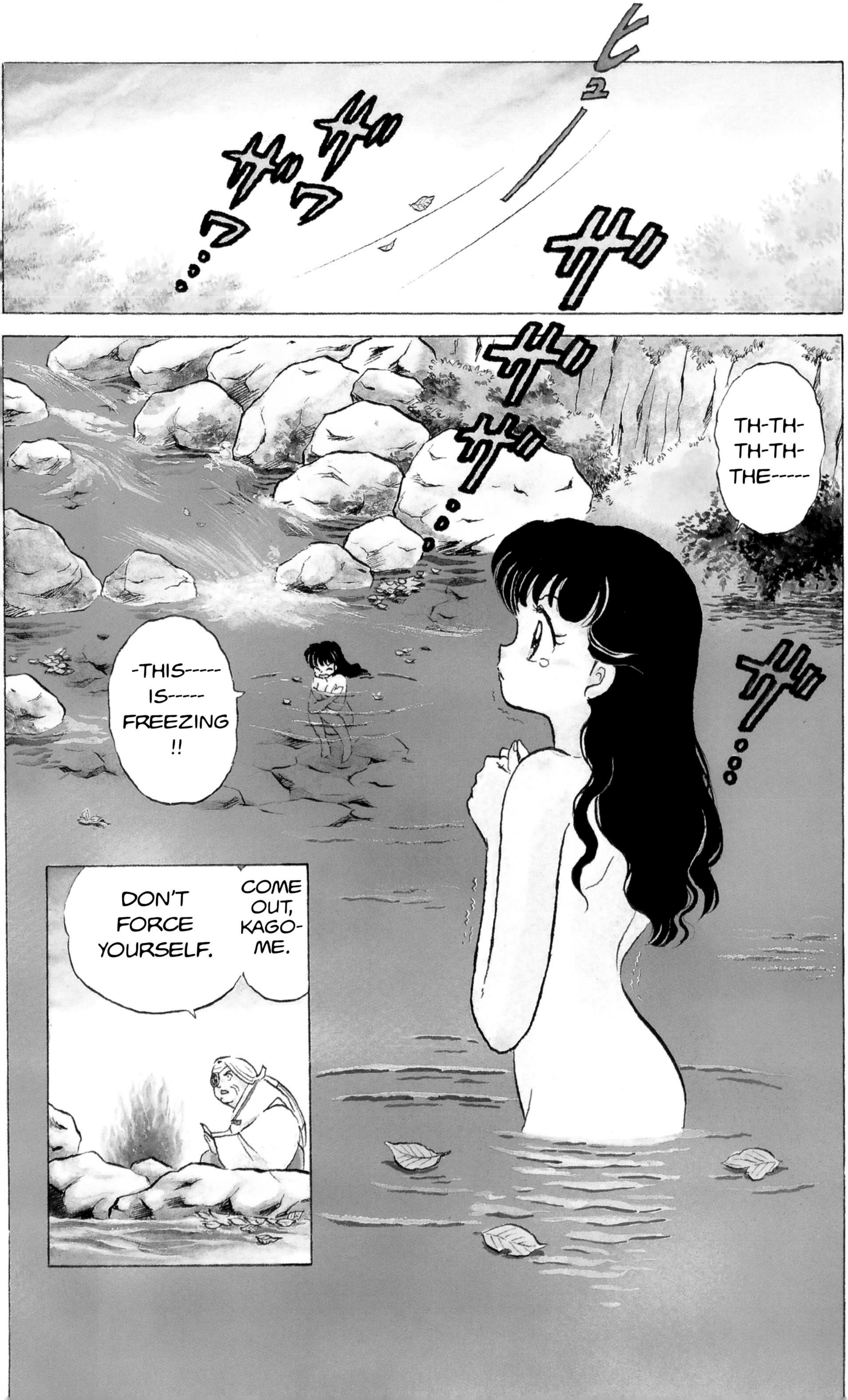
ヒュー
TH-TH-TH-TH-THE-----
-THIS----- IS----- FREEZING !!
COME OUT, KAGO-ME.
DON'T FORCE YOURSELF.

SHIKON SHARDS

The Jewel of Four Souls is a mystery. Used by a demon or villian, it makes its owner more evil; used by one with a clean soul, it purifies him or her. More often it is an evil thing that increases it's demonic power. Kagome and her friends collect 14 shards by the time they meet Sango. Then Kikyo steals them all, and then they have only the two they took from the birds of paradise.

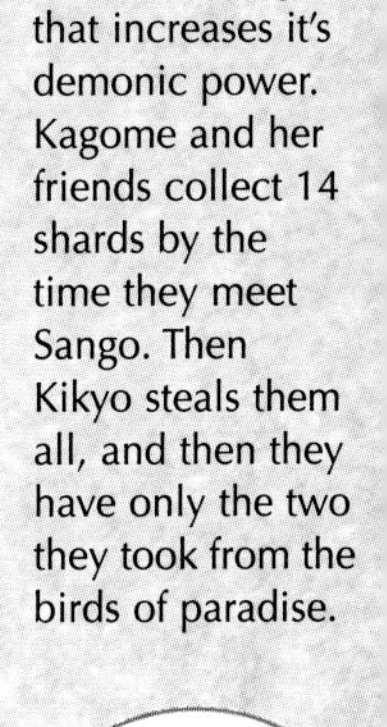

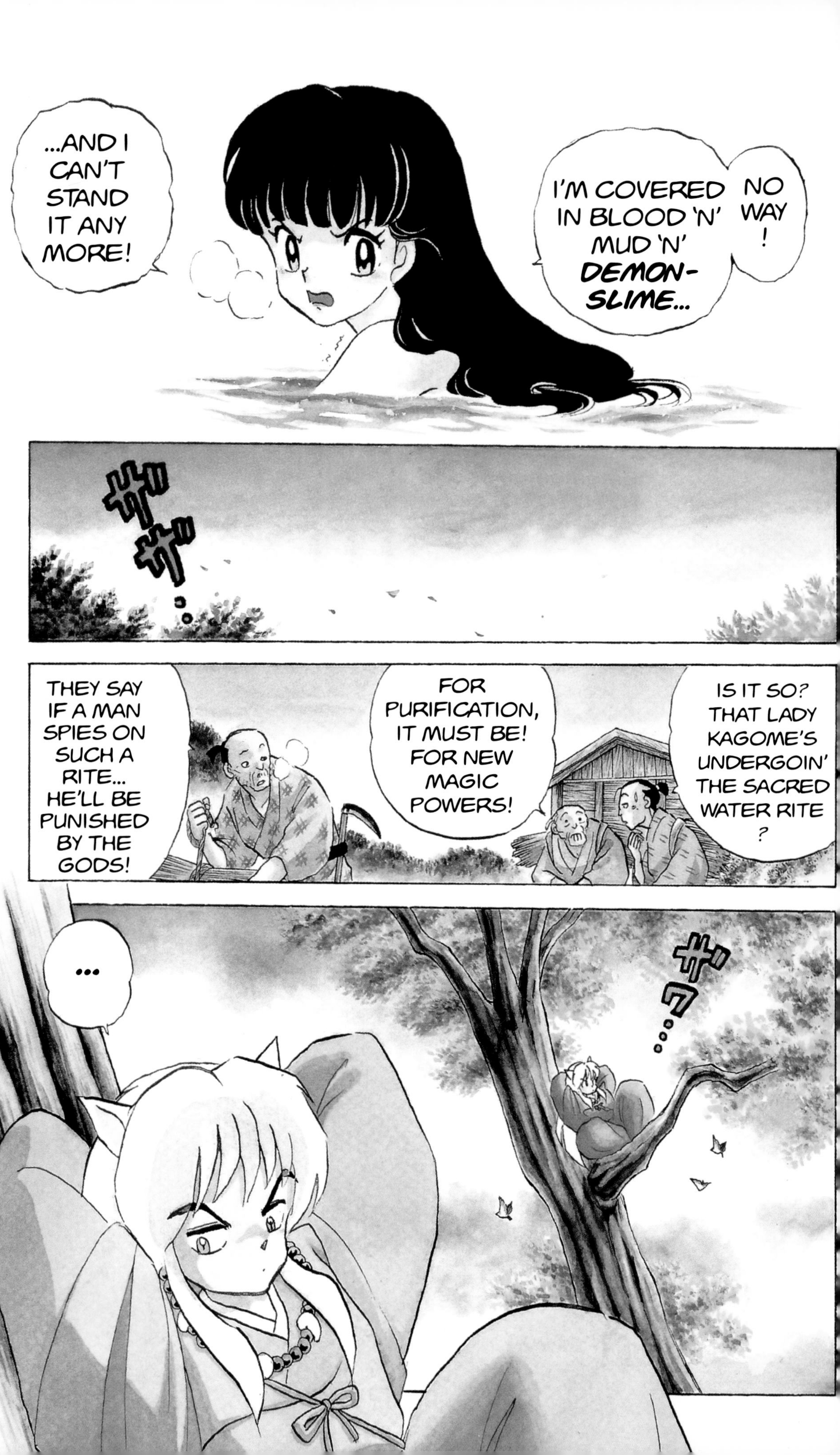
NO WAY!
I'M COVERED IN BLOOD 'N' MUD 'N' DEMON-SLIME...
...AND I CAN'T STAND IT ANY MORE!
IS IT SO? THAT LADY KAGOME'S UNDERGOIN' THE SACRED WATER RITE?
FOR PURIFICATION, IT MUST BE! FOR NEW MAGIC POWERS!
THEY SAY IF A MAN SPIES ON SUCH A RITE... HE'LL BE PUNISHED BY THE GODS!
...

SHARD CONTAINERS

The first container was a pouch, perhaps supplied by Kaede. The pouch is stained with blood after the battle with Yura, so Kagome replaces it with a small, cork-stoppered jar. In her journey back to the modern world to prepare for her exam, Kagome realizes she has brought the shards with her. So she puts them into the jar temporarily.

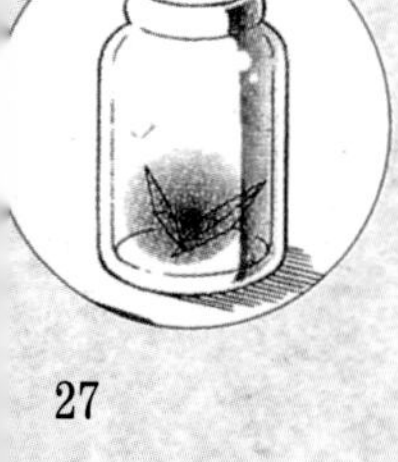

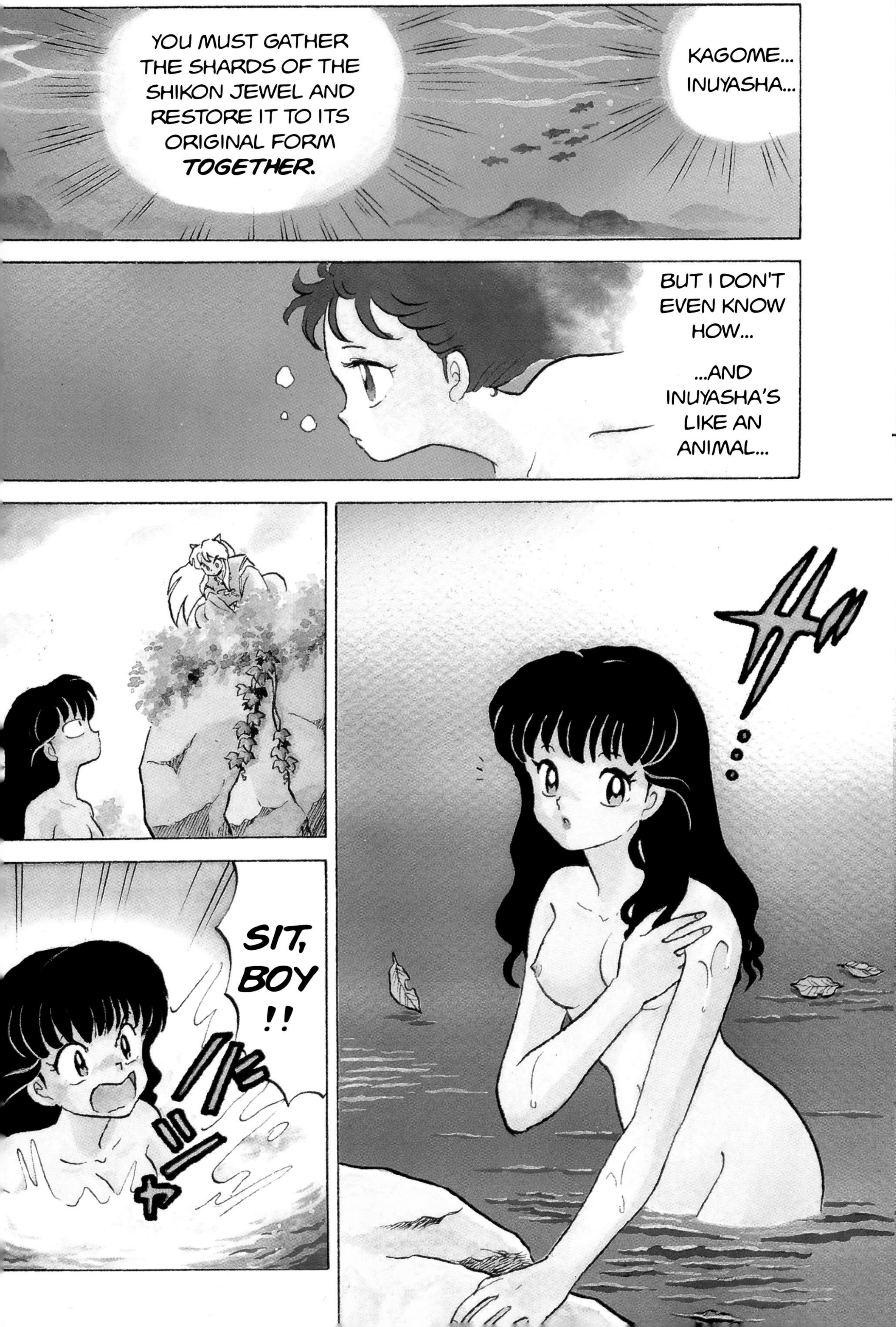
KAGOME... INUYASHA...
YOU MUST GATHER THE SHARDS OF THE SHIKON JEWEL AND RESTORE IT TO ITS ORIGINAL FORM *TOGETHER*.
BUT I DON'T EVEN KNOW HOW...
...AND INUYASHA'S LIKE AN ANIMAL...
SIT, BOY !!

SUPERNATURAL POWER

Legends of divine power come down from ancient times. In the Chinese history known in Japan as Gishi Wajin Den, third-century Queen Himiko was described as a "servant of evil who often deluded her people." The priest Kuukai, who established a temple in Koyasan, was known for his supernatural power. Kagome's power gives her arrows an evil-destroying aura and purifies the polluted shards of the Jewel.

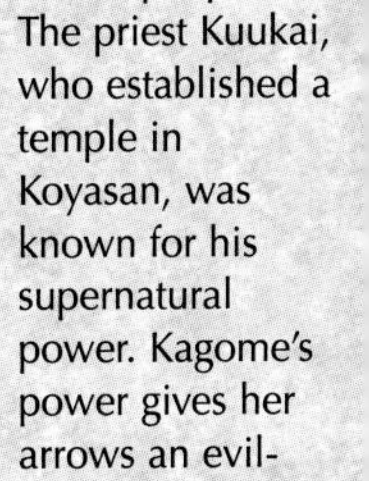

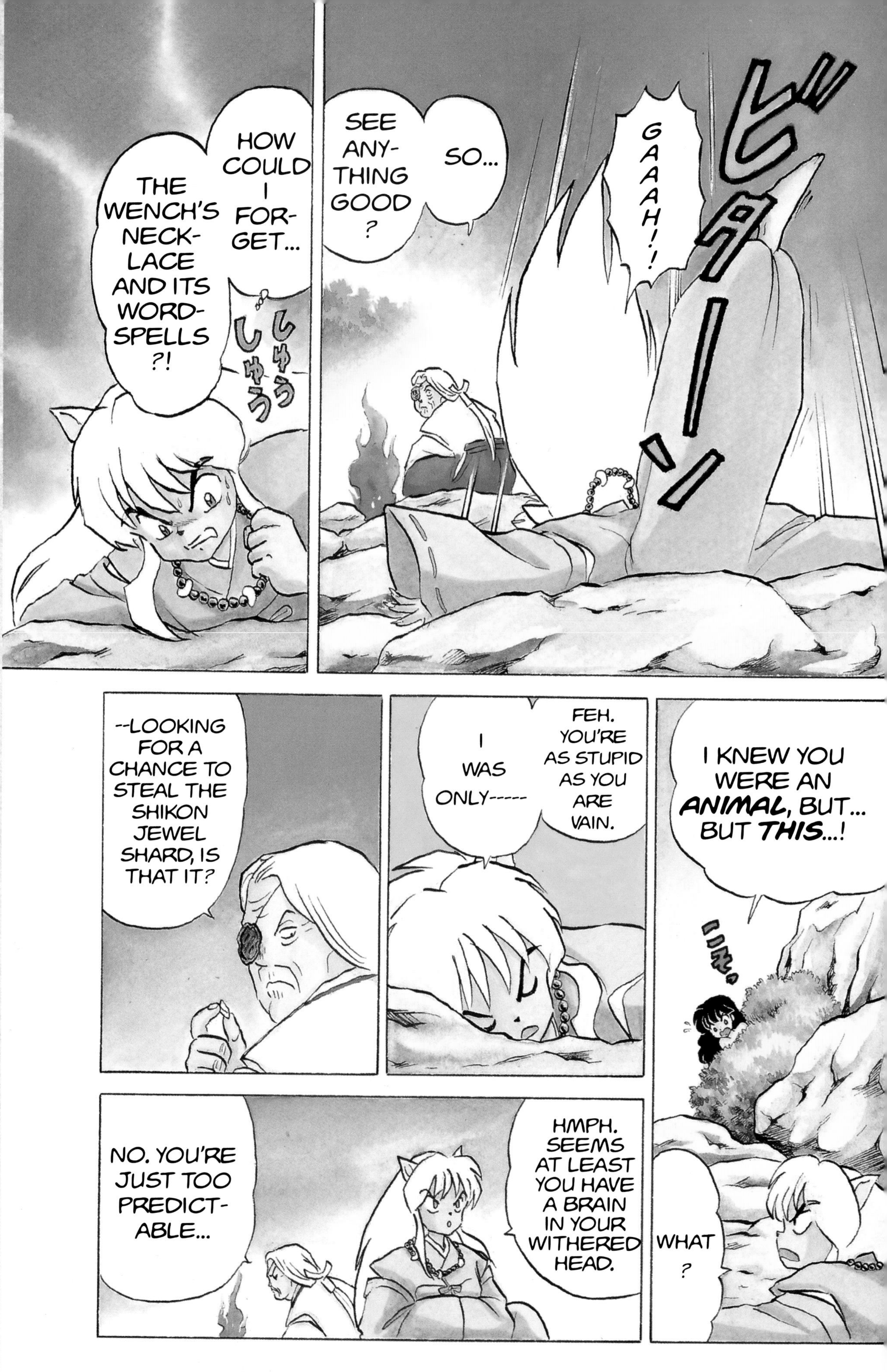
ビターン
GAAAAH!!
SO...
SEE ANYTHING GOOD?
HOW COULD I FORGET...
THE WENCH'S NECKLACE AND ITS WORD-SPELLS?!
しゅうしゅう
I KNEW YOU WERE AN ***ANIMAL***, BUT... BUT ***THIS***...!
WHAT?
FEH. YOU'RE AS STUPID AS YOU ARE VAIN.
I WAS ONLY-----
--LOOKING FOR A CHANCE TO STEAL THE SHIKON JEWEL SHARD, IS THAT IT?
HMPH. SEEMS AT LEAST YOU HAVE A BRAIN IN YOUR WITHERED HEAD.
NO. YOU'RE JUST TOO PREDICTABLE...

THE BONE-EATER'S WELL

In the Warring States period, the well that in modern times is at Higurashi Shrine was used as a dump for the corpses of demons. It was said that the corpses disappeared in a few days, and that's how the well came to be called Honekui ("bone-eating"). The well allows Kagome to travel between the modern and ancient worlds. Only Kagome and Inuyasha are able to do this.

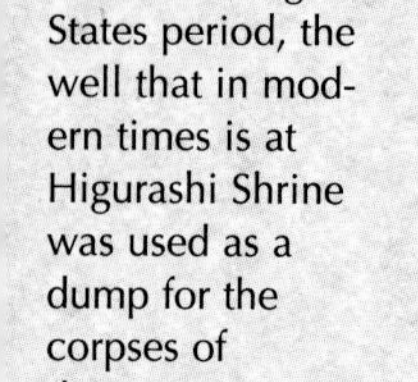

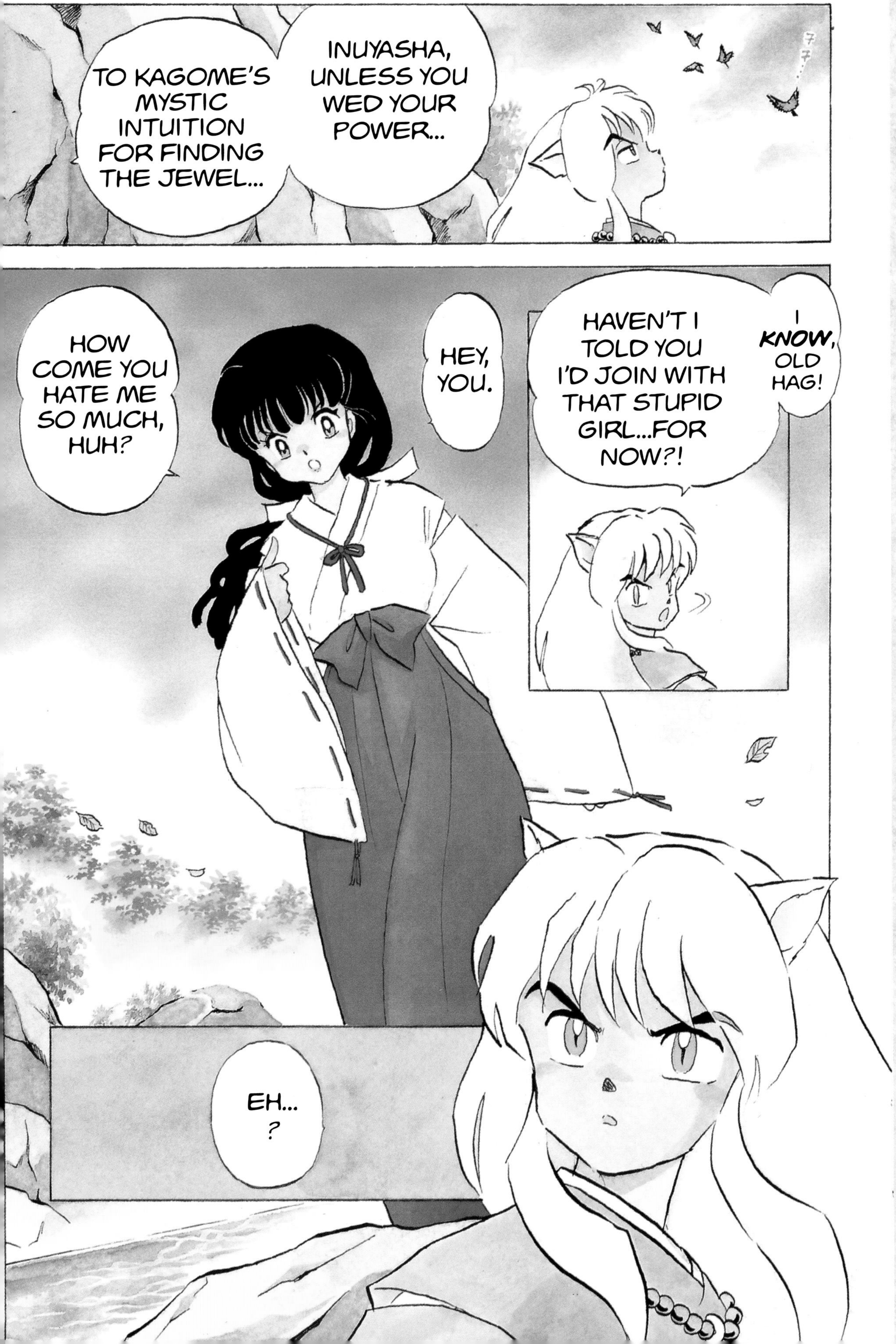
INUYASHA, UNLESS YOU WED YOUR POWER...
TO KAGOME'S MYSTIC INTUITION FOR FINDING THE JEWEL...
I **KNOW**, OLD HAG!
HAVEN'T I TOLD YOU I'D JOIN WITH THAT STUPID GIRL...FOR NOW?!
HEY, YOU.
HOW COME YOU HATE ME SO MUCH, HUH?
EH... ?

Robe of the Fire-Rat (Hinezumi no Koromo)

The cloak Inuyasha has Kagome wear is woven from the fur of fire rats (hinezumi). It's everyday clothing for him, but is stronger than any cheap armor, according to Inuyasha. It remains intact after the attack by fire and Yura's all-slicing "hair net" (kushinokago). Fire rats never appear in the story, but judging from the cloak, which is not dyed, they have red fur.

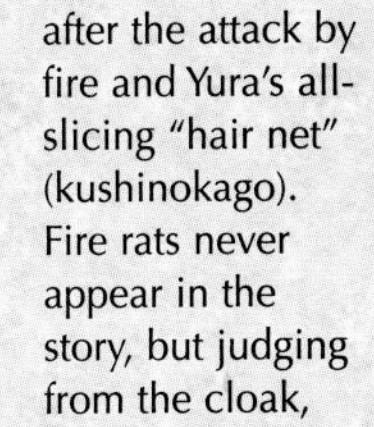

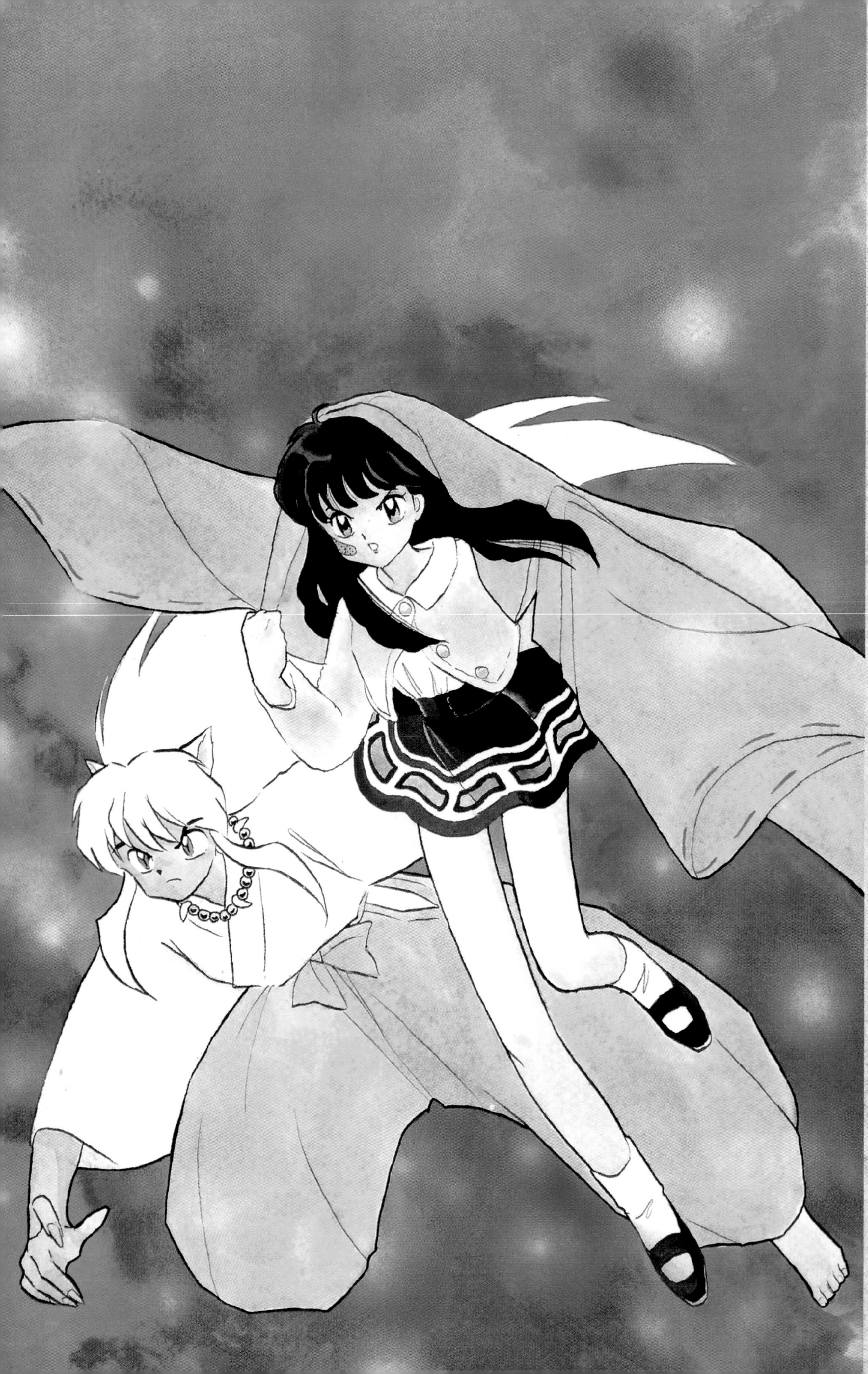

SCROLL 9

YURA'S WEB

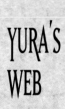

Shonen Sunday Vol. 8, 1997,
and Comic Vol. 2

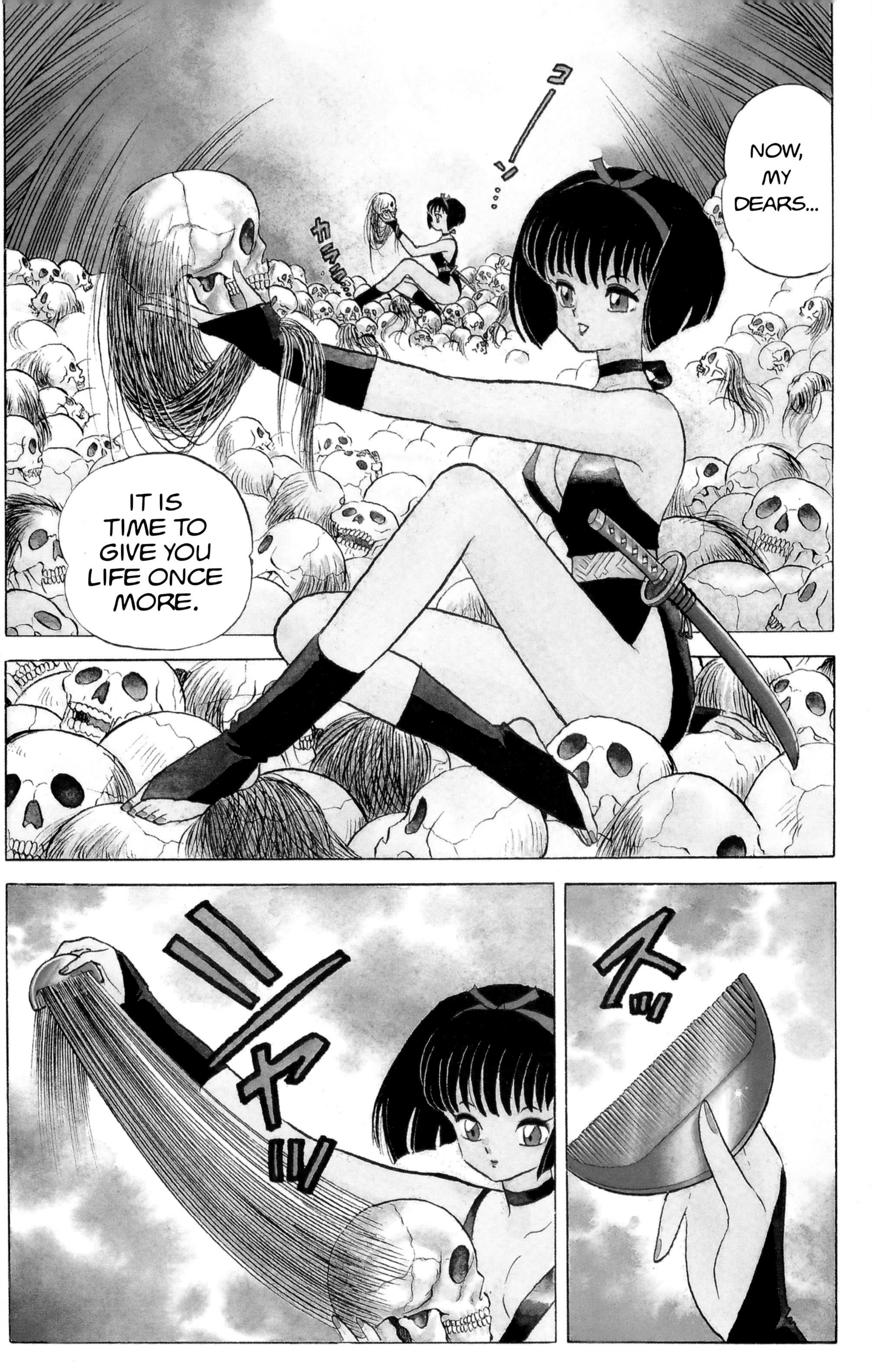
NOW, MY DEARS...
IT IS TIME TO GIVE YOU LIFE ONCE MORE.

YURA OF THE DEMON HAIR

She is the daughter of a demon, seeking Shikon shards. She can manipulate humans like puppets using the hair of the dead, and slice anything with this strong hair. She is a skilled sorceress who manipulates villagers, attacks Inuyasha and follows Inuyasha and Kagome into the modern world with her hair. She tries to kill anyone who gets between her and the shards, including Kagome and Inuyasha.

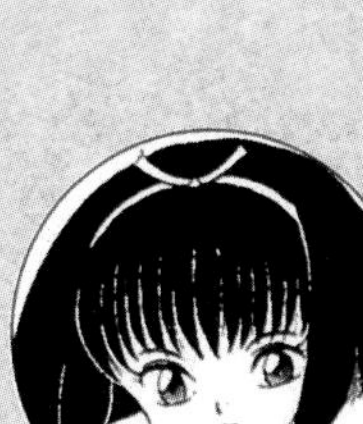

BENIGASUMI ("RED FOG")

Yura's treasured demonic sword cuts only flesh and bone, without damaging hair. It's an ideal weapon for Yura because it gives the hair-bound captive the fatal slash. Even after Yura's hand is cut off by Inuyasha's Blades of Blood, it continues to wield Red Fog (Benigasumi) and attack Inuyasha. Without Kagome's help, Inuyasha might have lost his life to Red Fog.

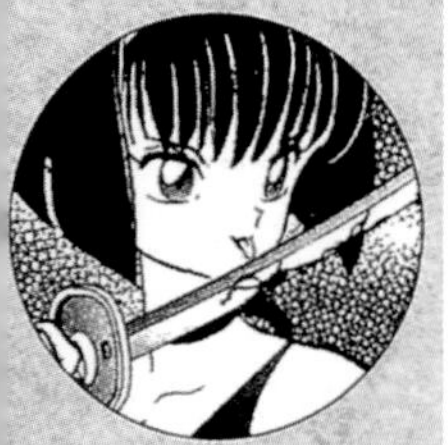

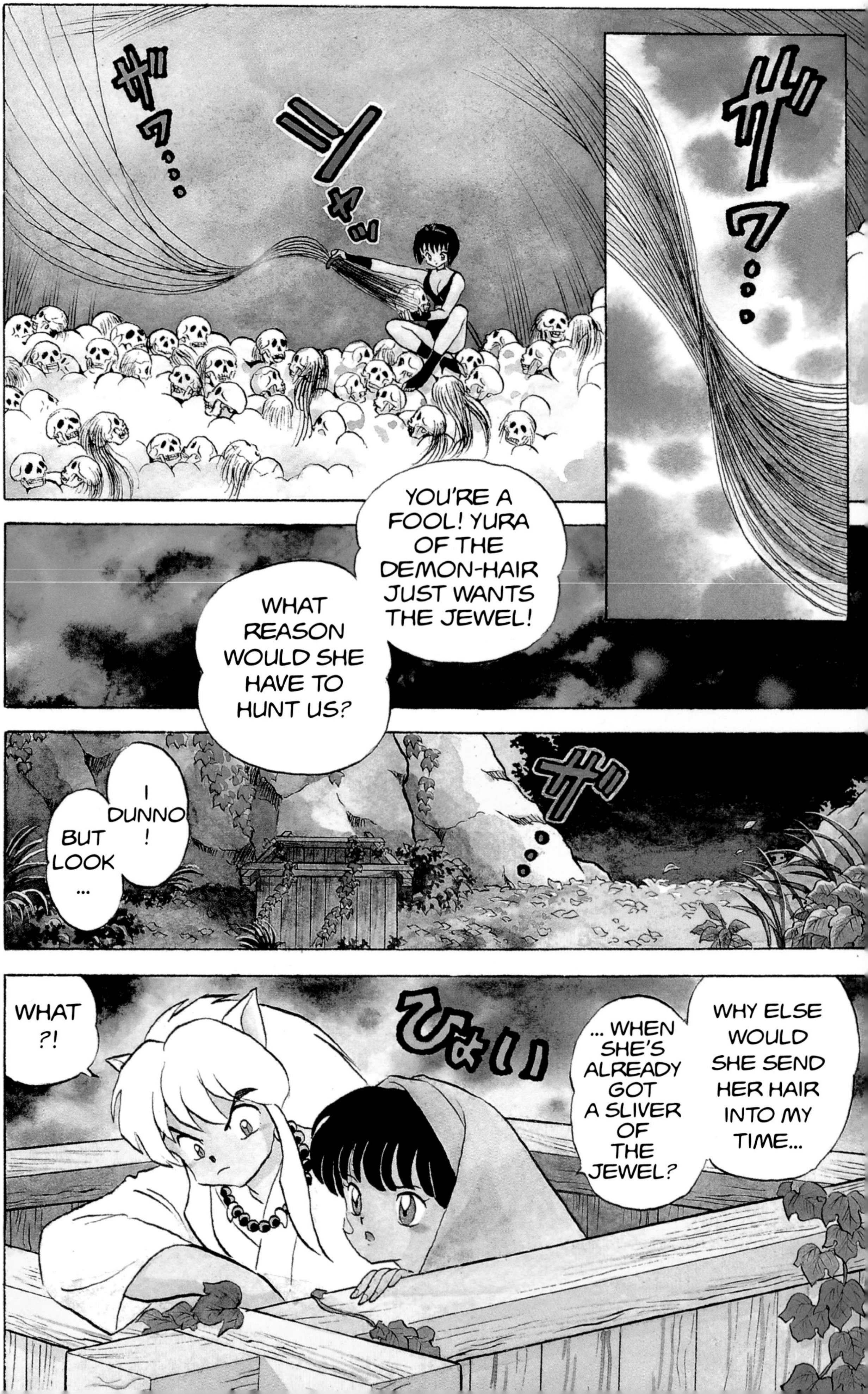
ザワ…
ザワ…
YOU'RE A FOOL! YURA OF THE DEMON-HAIR JUST WANTS THE JEWEL!
WHAT REASON WOULD SHE HAVE TO HUNT US?
I DUNNO!
BUT LOOK...
WHY ELSE WOULD SHE SEND HER HAIR INTO MY TIME...
... WHEN SHE'S ALREADY GOT A SLIVER OF THE JEWEL?
ひょい
WHAT?!

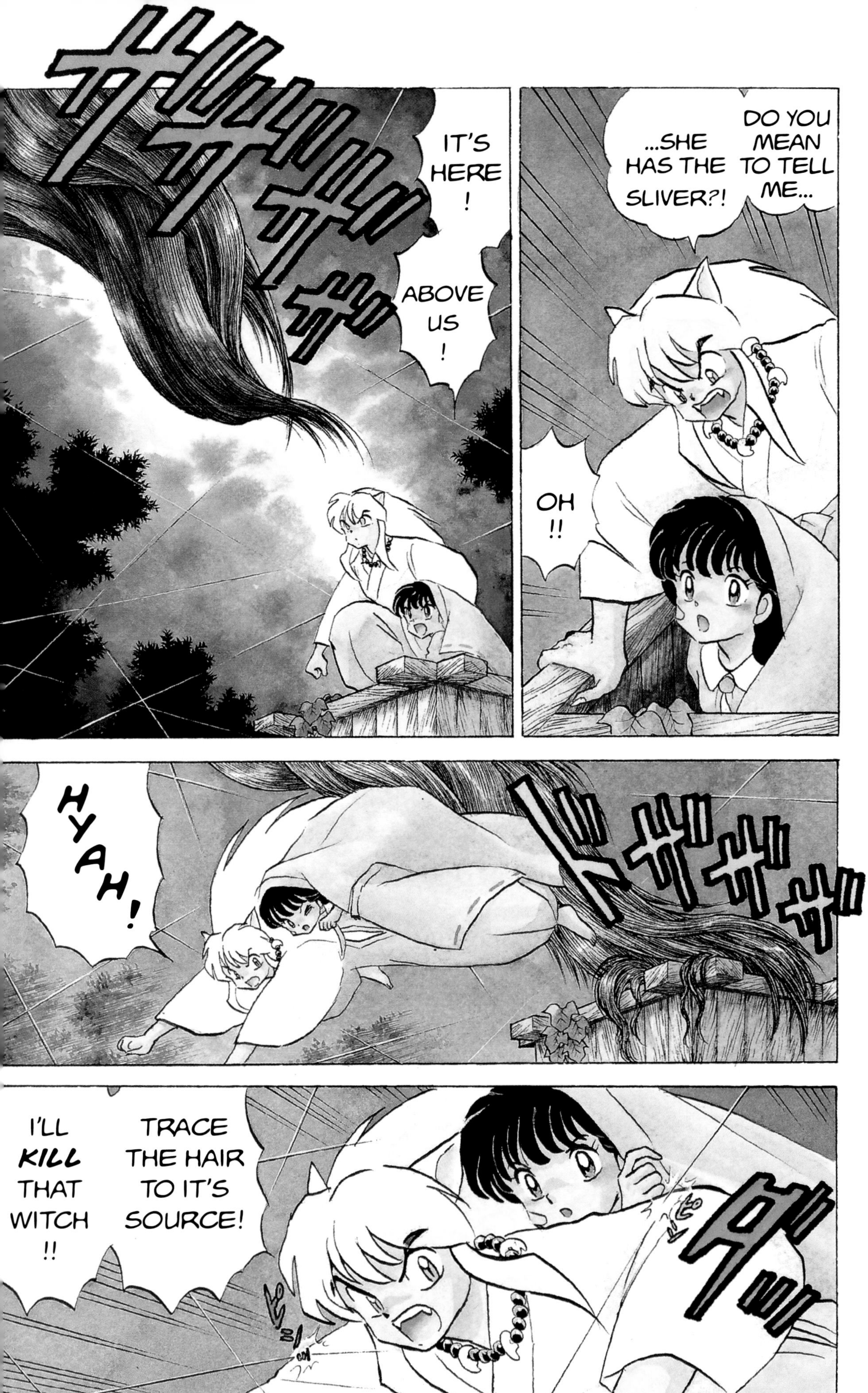
DO YOU MEAN TO TELL ME...
...SHE HAS THE SLIVER?!
OH !!
IT'S HERE !
ABOVE US !
HYAH!
TRACE THE HAIR TO IT'S SOURCE!
I'LL **KILL** THAT WITCH !!

SOUL TRANSFER (TAMAUTSUSHI)

Even after her hand is cut off and her chest gouged out, Yura is so powerful that she drives Inuyasha to his wit's end. Yura had transferred her soul into a comb inside a skull. It seems that soul transfer is only possible into an object with which one has a deep relationship.

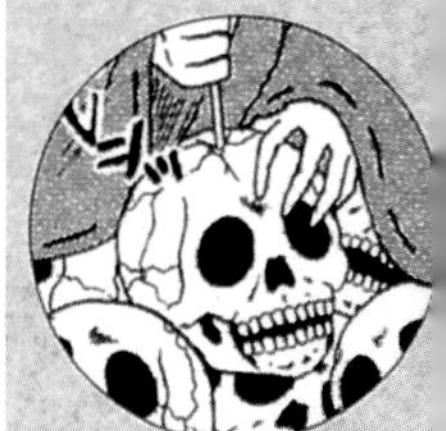

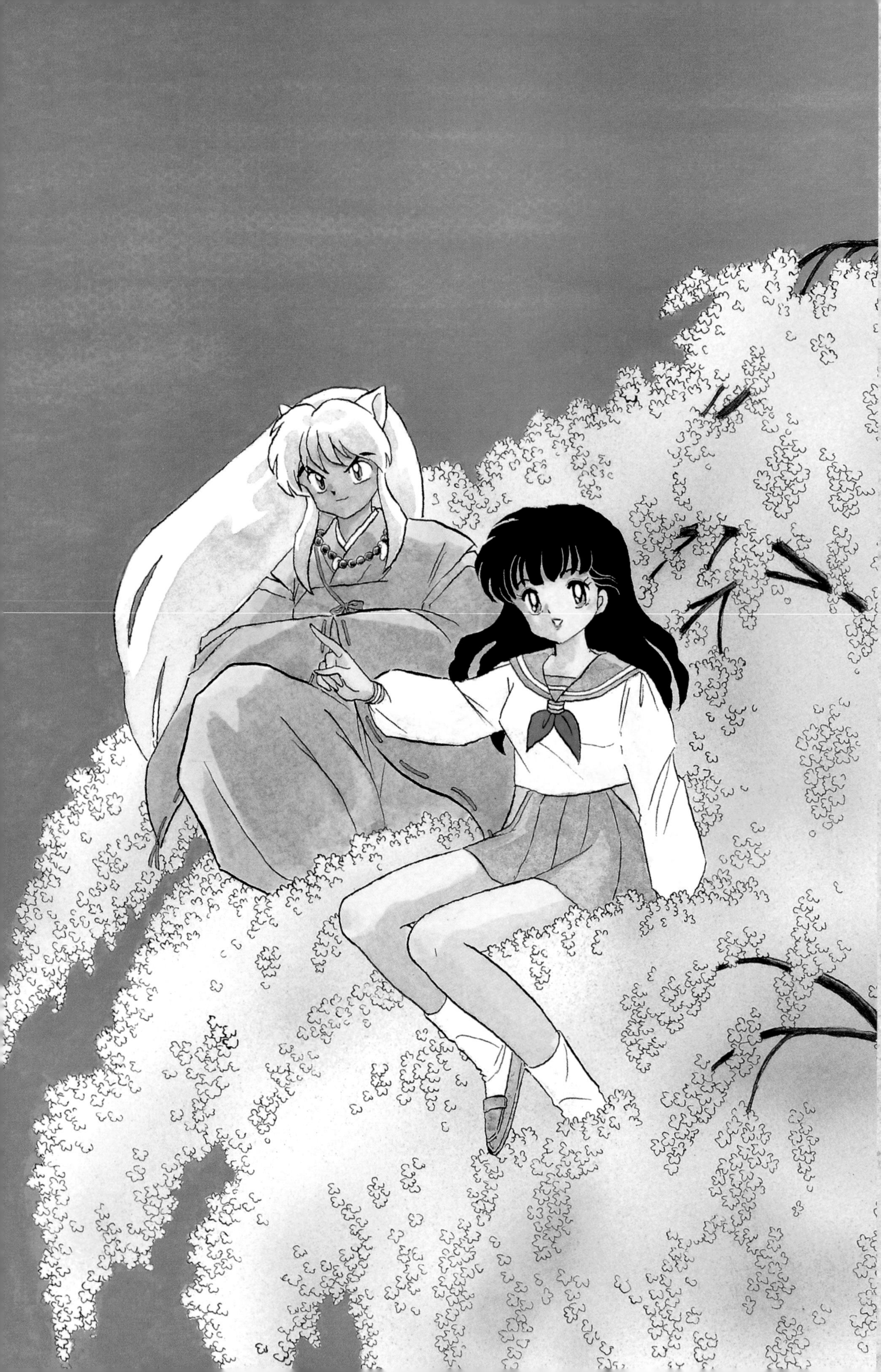

SCROLL 19

THE DARK CASTLE

Shonen Sunday Vol. 18, 1997
and Comic Vol. 3

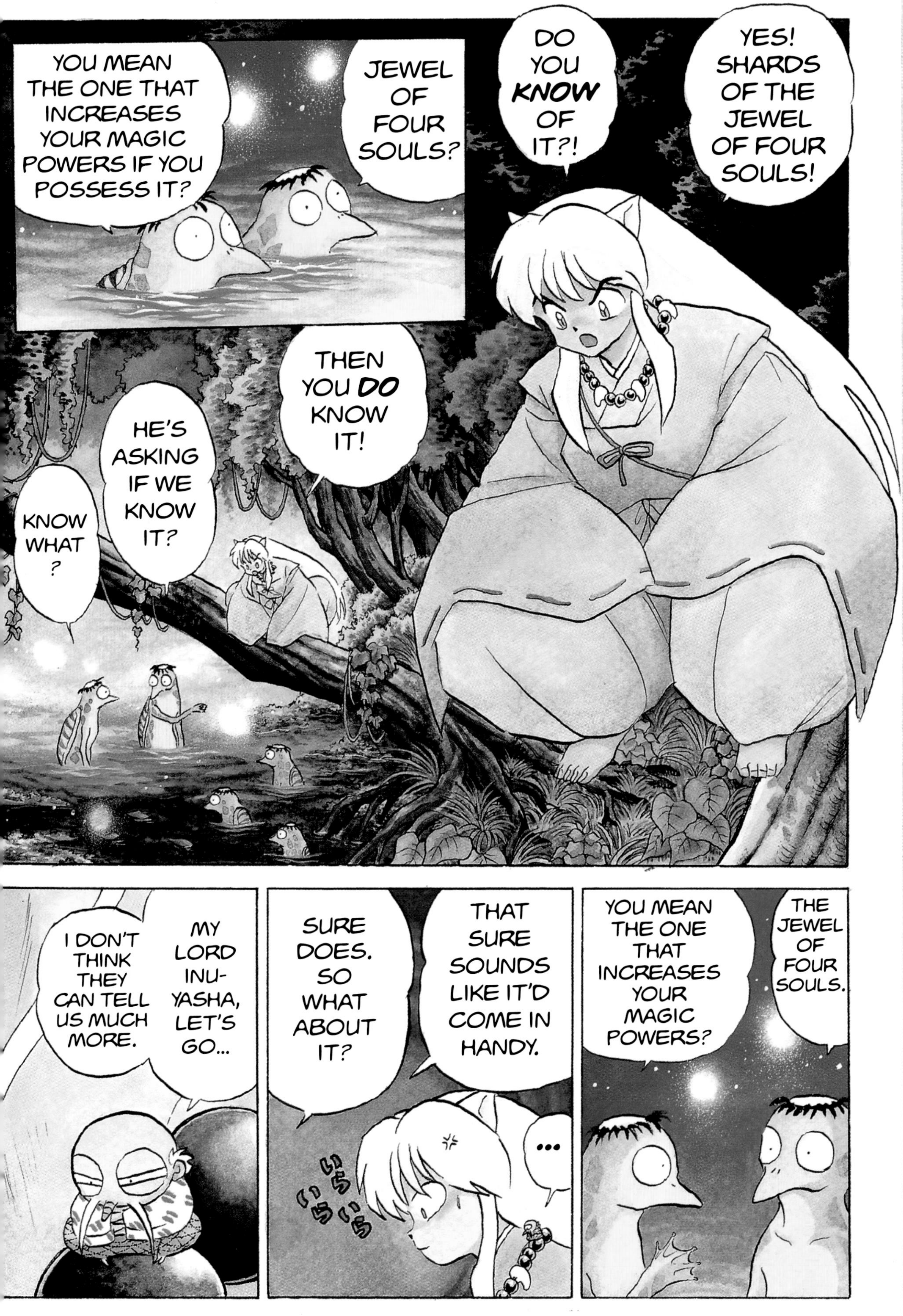
YES! SHARDS OF THE JEWEL OF FOUR SOULS!
DO YOU **KNOW** OF IT?!
JEWEL OF FOUR SOULS?
YOU MEAN THE ONE THAT INCREASES YOUR MAGIC POWERS IF YOU POSSESS IT?
THEN YOU **DO** KNOW IT!
HE'S ASKING IF WE KNOW IT?
KNOW WHAT?
THE JEWEL OF FOUR SOULS.
YOU MEAN THE ONE THAT INCREASES YOUR MAGIC POWERS?
THAT SURE SOUNDS LIKE IT'D COME IN HANDY.
SURE DOES. SO WHAT ABOUT IT?
...
MY LORD INU-YASHA, LET'S GO...
I DON'T THINK THEY CAN TELL US MUCH MORE.

Hiyoshimaru

A monkey servant of Nobunaga, who understands human language. Helping Kagome, he helps fight the Frog Demon. He is faithful, looking for food for his master (although he finds only Kagome's underwear) and the kindling needed to attack the Frog. His name has a historical parallel: Toyotomi Hideyoshi, called Hiyoshimaru in childhood, served the shogun Oda Nobunaga.

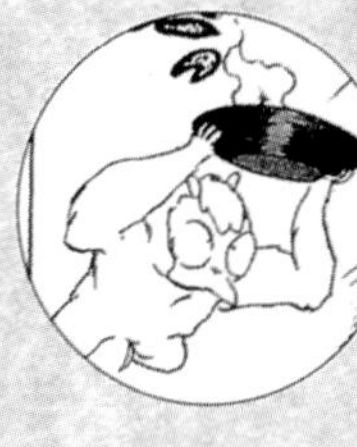

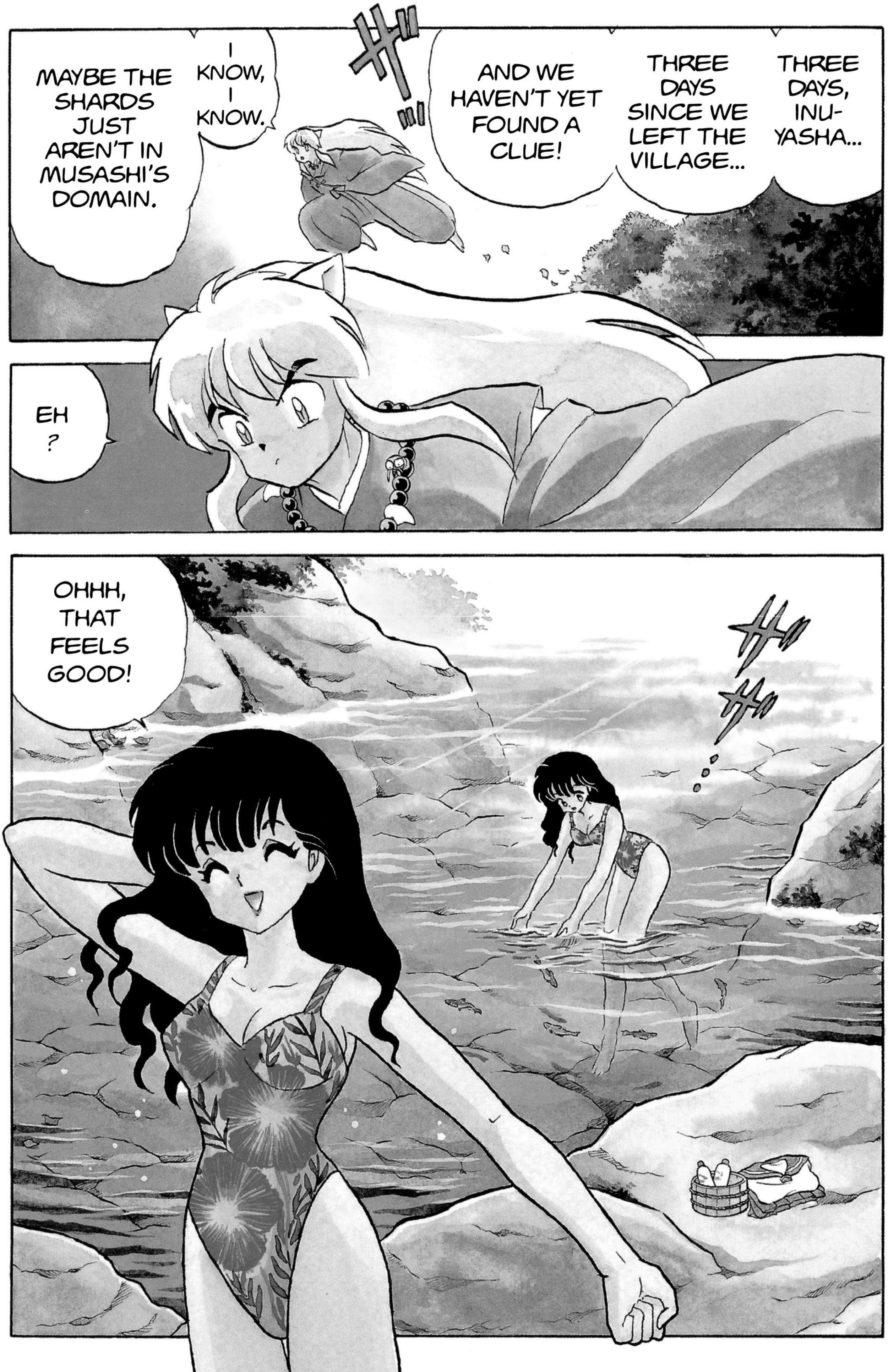
THREE DAYS, INU-YASHA...
THREE DAYS SINCE WE LEFT THE VILLAGE...
AND WE HAVEN'T YET FOUND A CLUE!
I KNOW, I KNOW.
MAYBE THE SHARDS JUST AREN'T IN MUSASHI'S DOMAIN.
EH?
OHHH, THAT FEELS GOOD!

PRINCESS TSUYU (PRINCESS DEWDROP)

She is from the Takeda clan and married to a prince who frightens her because he changes dramatically after their marriage. He is possessed by the Frog Demon which she doesn't know. She grew up with Nobunaga in the Takeda lands. She has a hard time with married life, once only narrowly escaping an attack by the frog in an attempt to eat her soul. She is so joyful about getting her prince back that she breaks Nobunga's heart. She seems a little absent-minded.

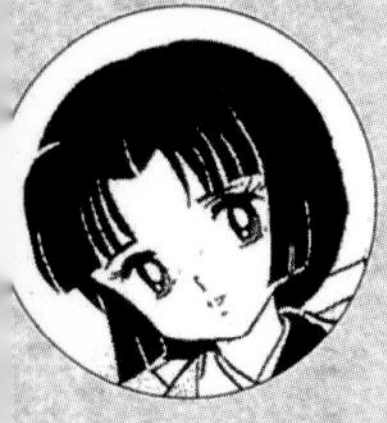

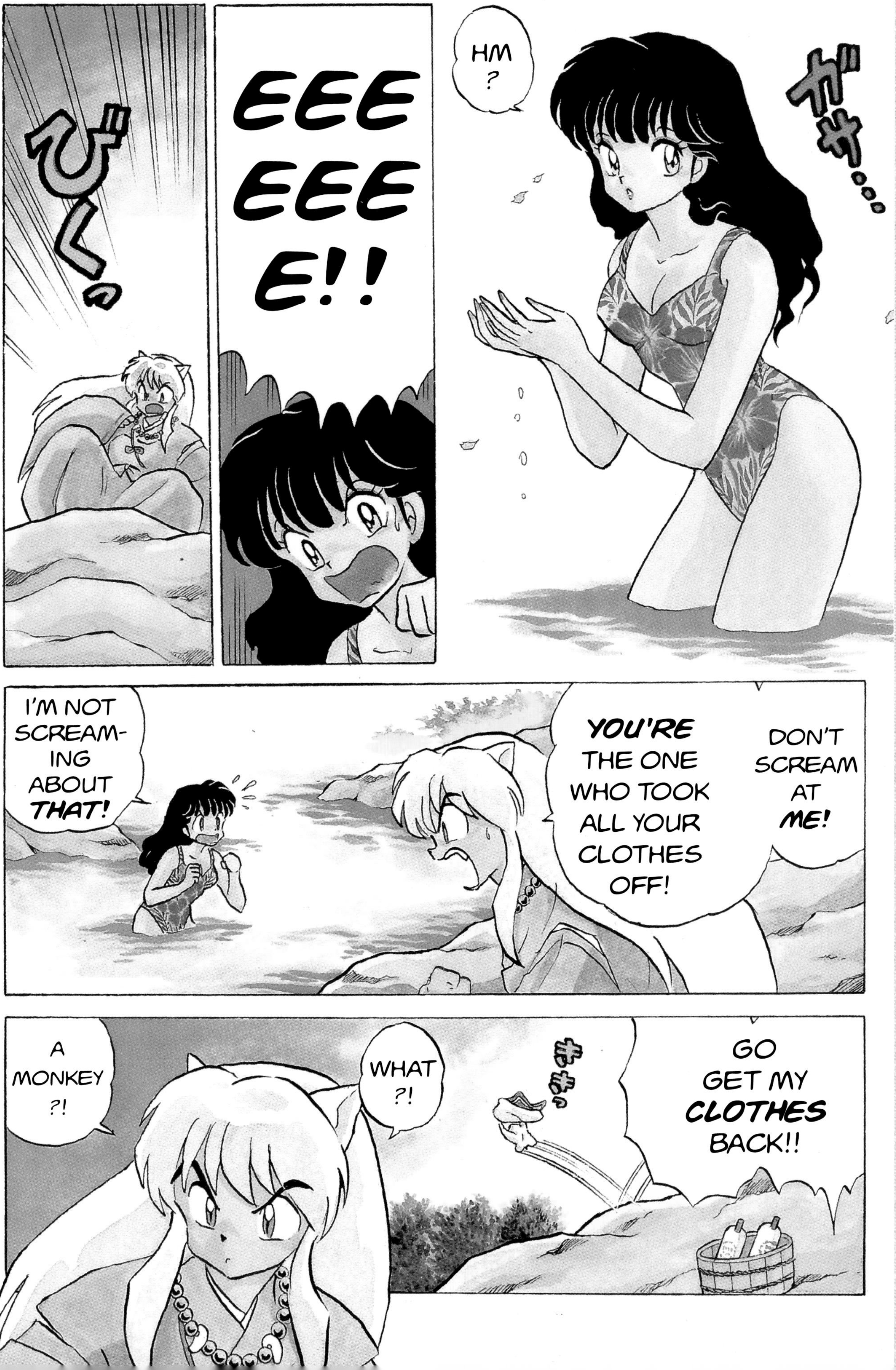
HM?
ガサ…
EEEEEEE!!
びくっ
DON'T SCREAM AT ME!
YOU'RE THE ONE WHO TOOK ALL YOUR CLOTHES OFF!
I'M NOT SCREAMING ABOUT THAT!
GO GET MY CLOTHES BACK!!
WHAT?!
A MONKEY?!

Frog Demon

This is a 300-year-old demon frog or toad. Bearing a shard of the Jewel, his demonic power grows enough to take over the body of a prince. He gathers the souls of young girls from around the country, pickles and eats them. He is killed in a coordinated attack by Kagome's hairspray and Inuyasha's sword. Because it uses its long tongue to catch its prey, the frog is traditionally thought to be a demon that sucks human souls.

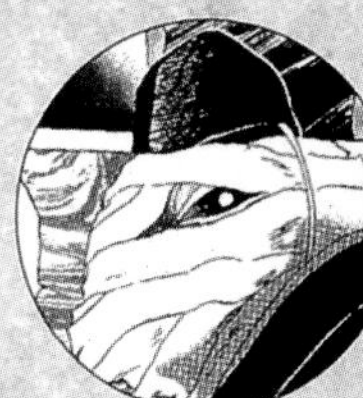

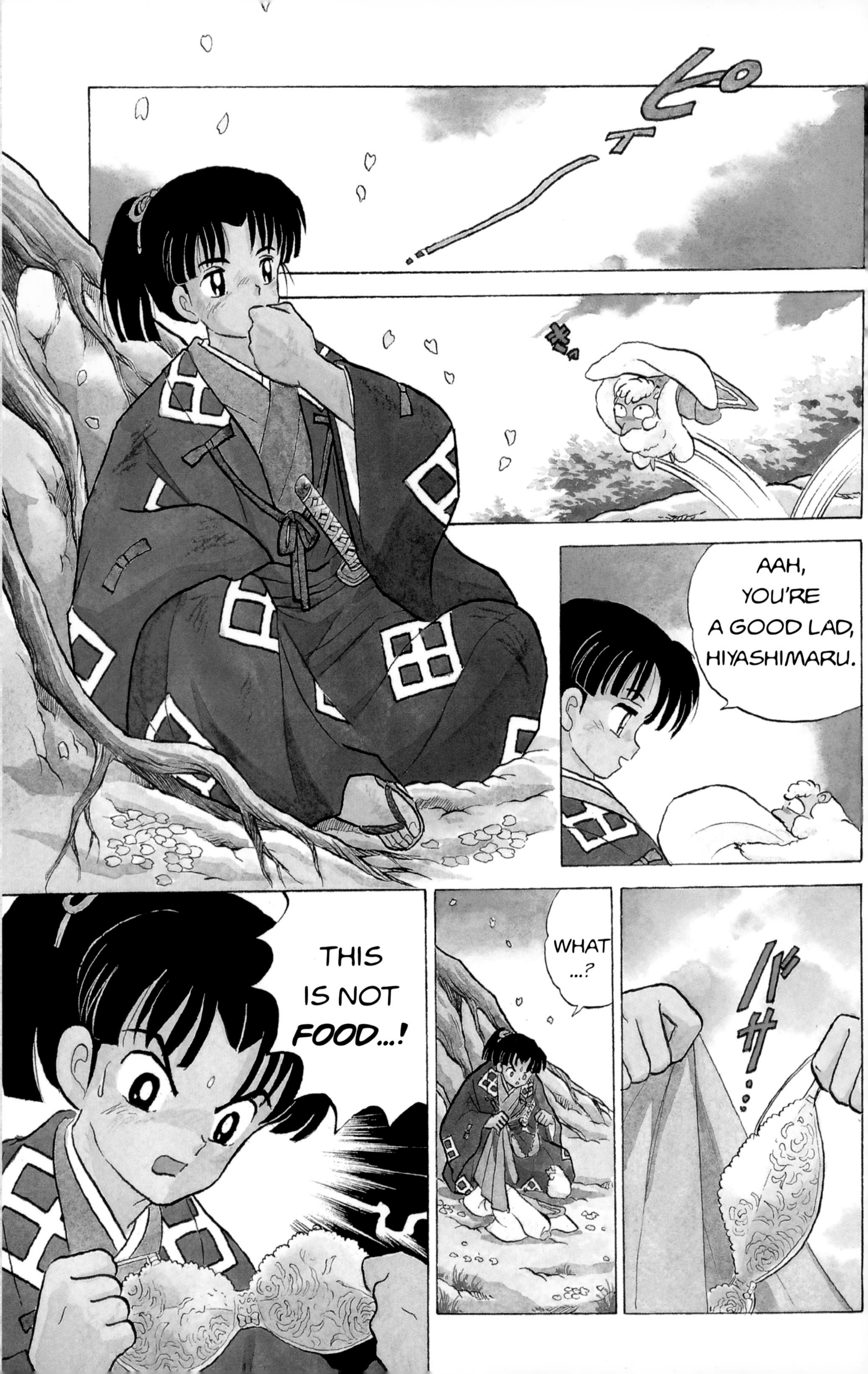
AAH, YOU'RE A GOOD LAD, HIYASHIMARU.
WHAT ...?
THIS IS NOT FOOD...!

NOBUNAGA

A warrior of the Takeda clan who happens to have the same name as the famed general, Oda Nobunaga, who rose after beating Inagawa Yoshimoto in the battle of Okehazama. He is sent by the Takadas to get Dewdrop back if her husband the prince has truly lost his mind. He is secretly in love with her and returns empty-handed after the mystery is solved. He is a man of sweet heart who hates anything that leads to some-one's death.

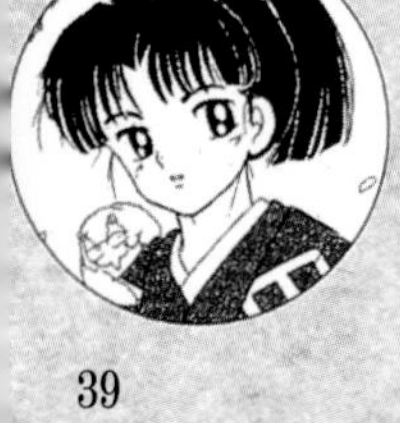

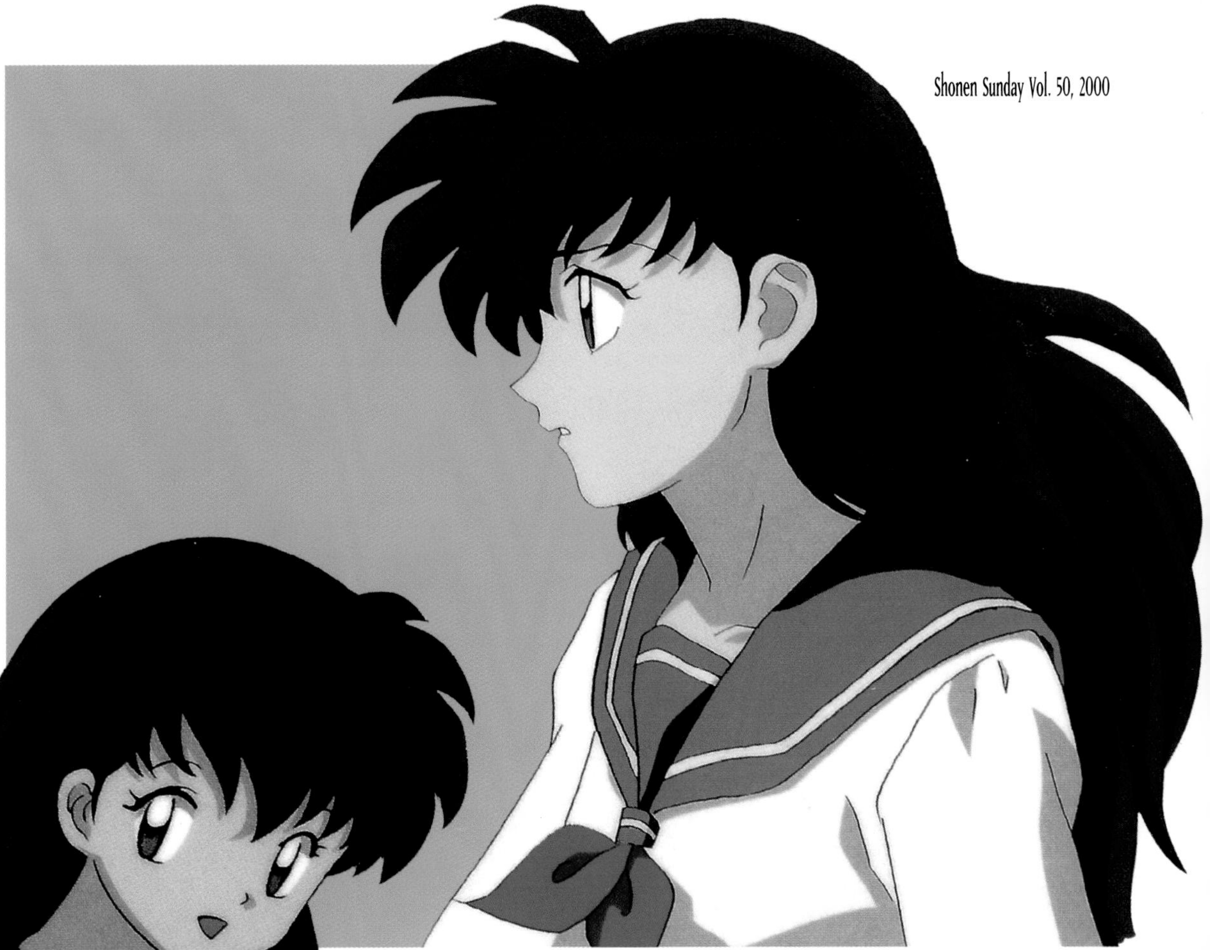

Shonen Sunday Vol. 50, 2000

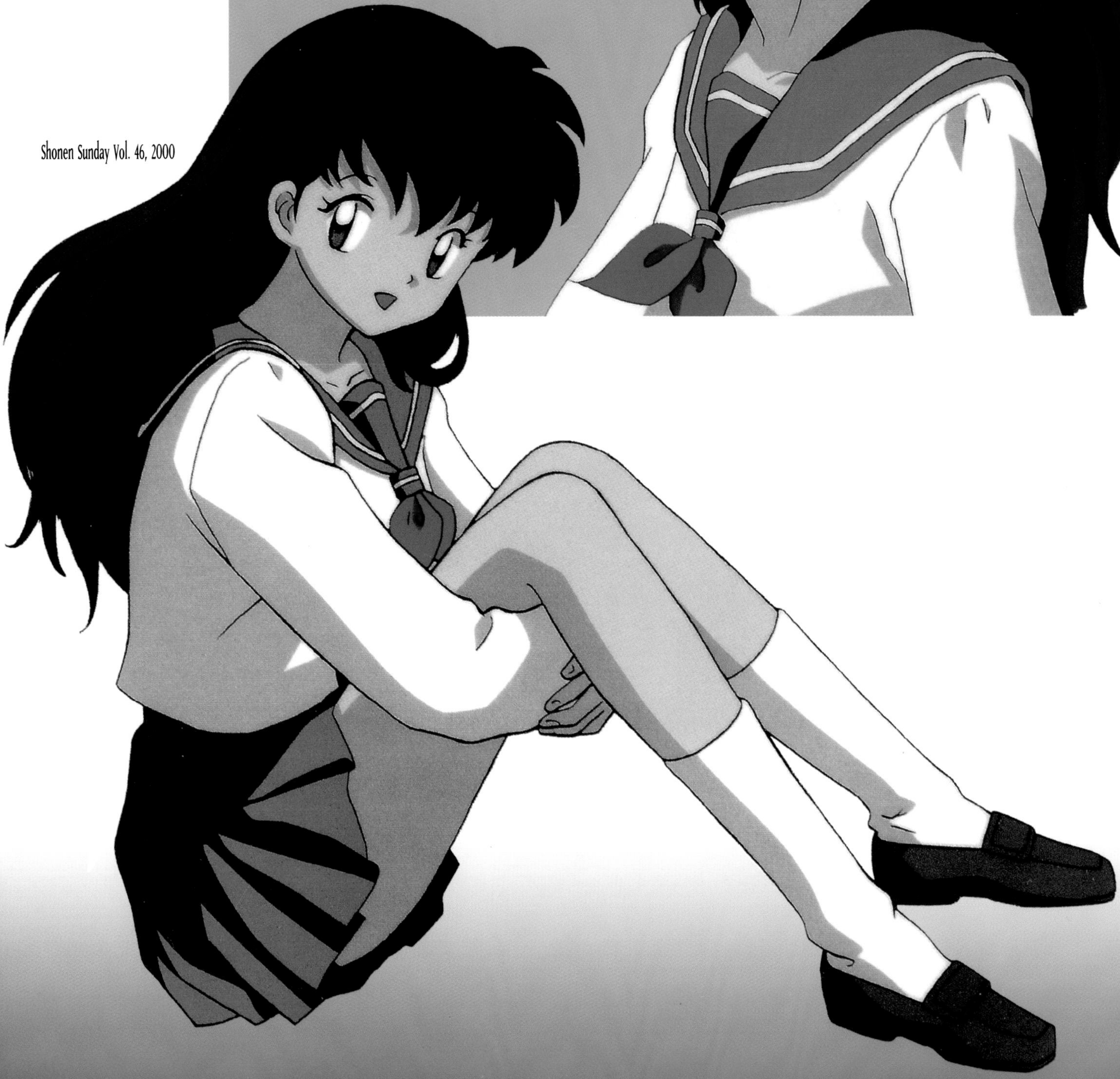

Shonen Sunday Vol. 46, 2000

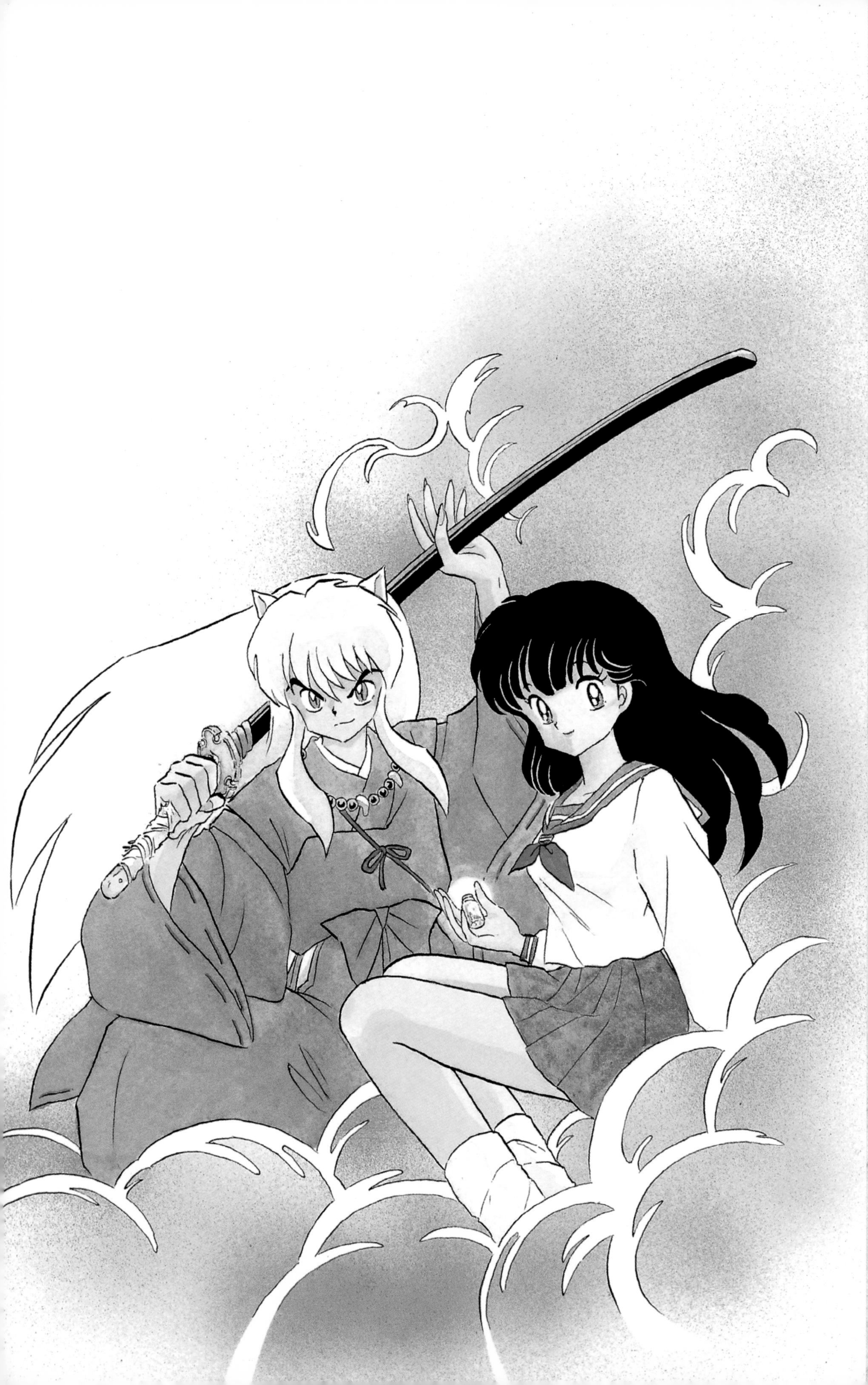

SCROLL 28

FOXFIRE

Shonen Sunday Vol. 28, 1997.
and Comic Vol. 3

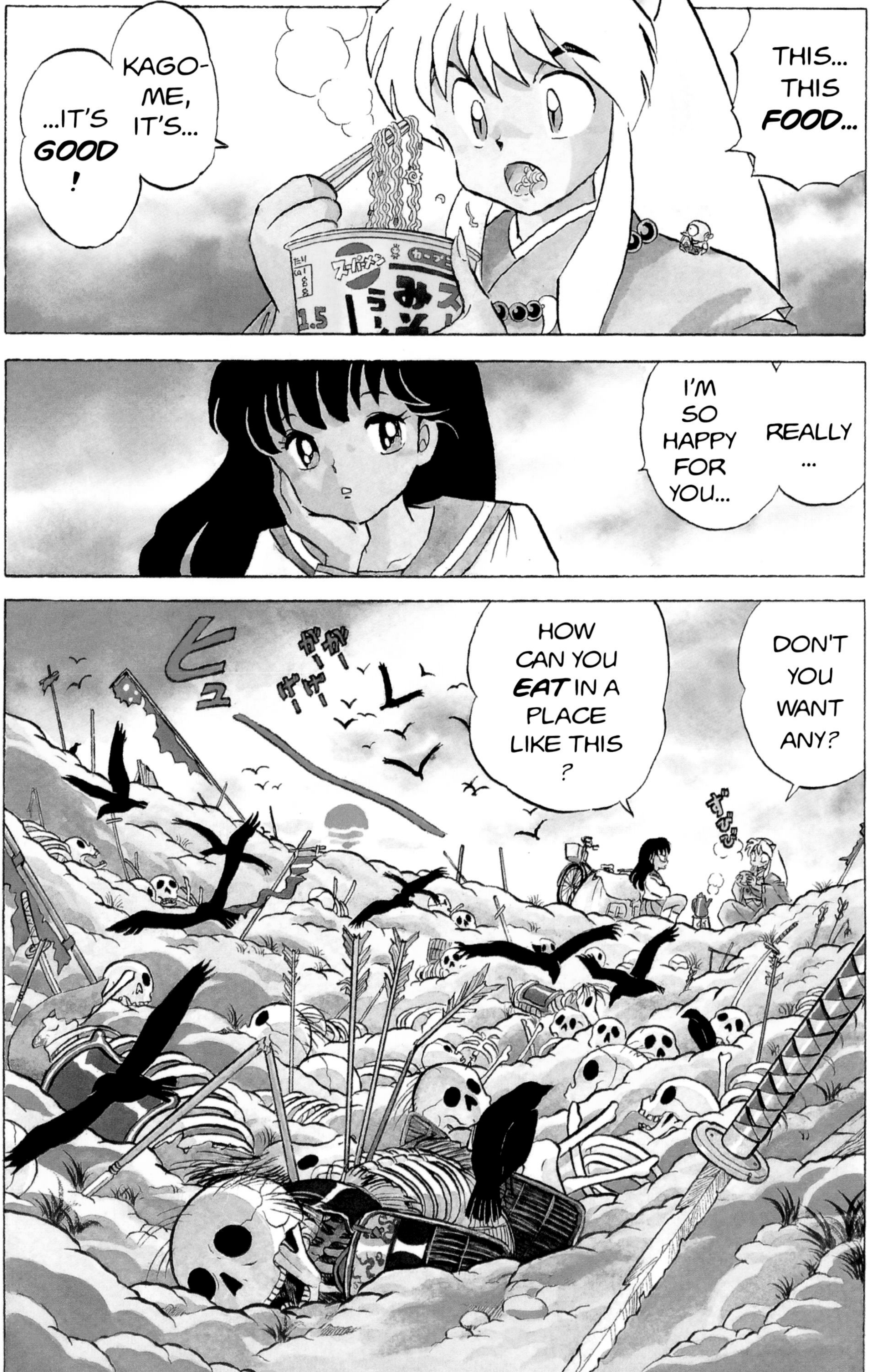
THIS... THIS FOOD...
KAGO-ME, IT'S...
...IT'S GOOD!
REALLY...
I'M SO HAPPY FOR YOU...
DON'T YOU WANT ANY?
HOW CAN YOU EAT IN A PLACE LIKE THIS?

HITEN ("FLY HEAVEN")

The elder of the Thunder brothers has three shards of the Jewel in his forehead. He was the enemy of Shippo's father. According to Myoga, he is "hopelessly violent" and enjoys nothing so much as senseless massacre. He attacks Inuyasha to steal the shards from him. He uses the powerful Thunder Pike, also known as Lightning Blade, a halberd that produces a lightning-like blast. He becomes more powerful after eating the heart of his dead brother, but dies when Tetsusaiga splits his head.

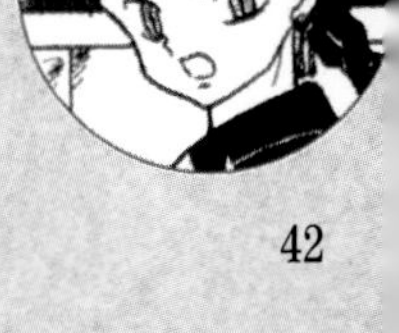

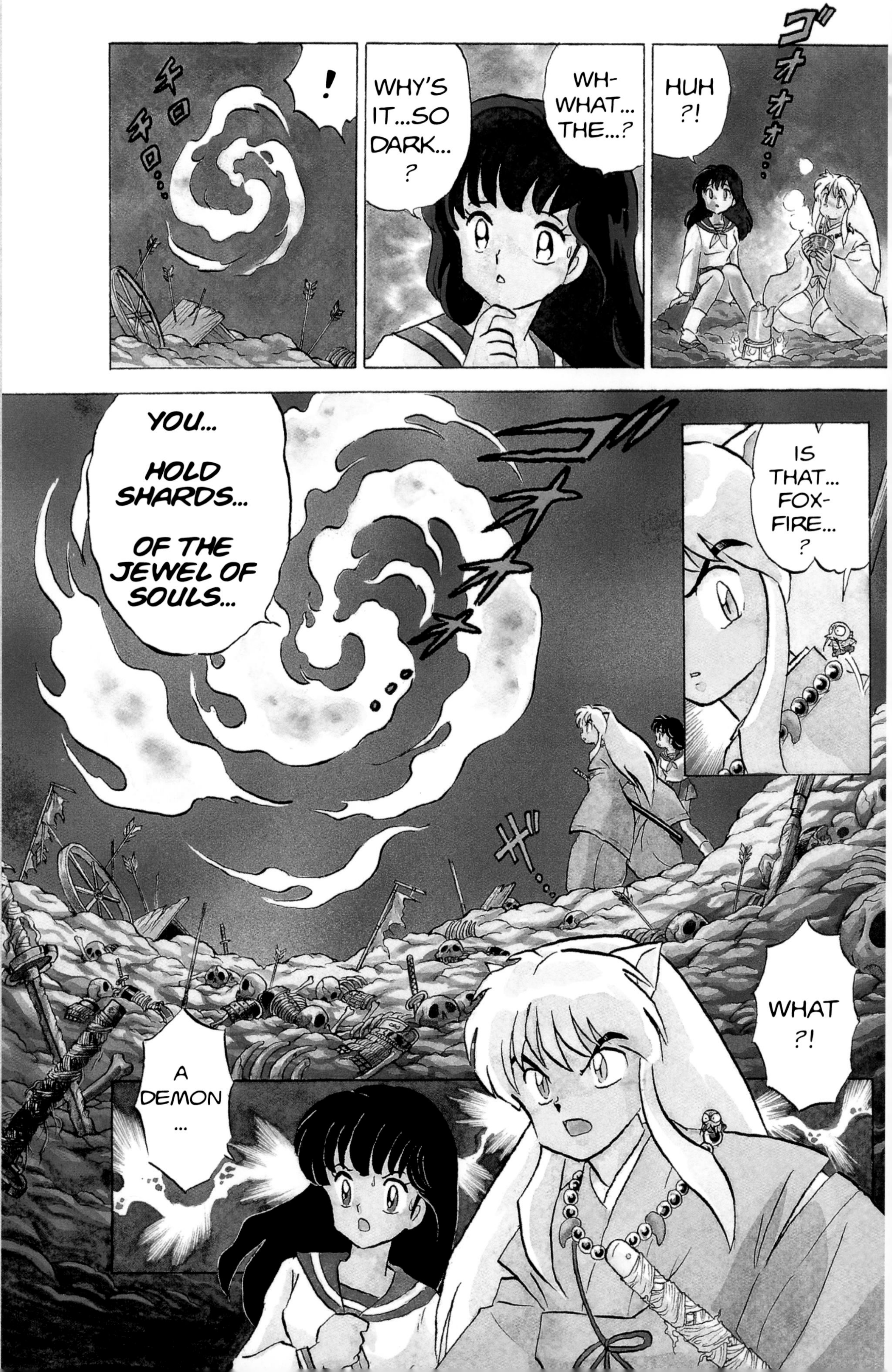
ゴオオオ…
HUH ?!
WH-WHAT... THE...?
WHY'S IT...SO DARK...?
!
チロチロ…
IS THAT... FOX-FIRE...?
YOU... HOLD SHARDS... OF THE JEWEL OF SOULS...
ザ…
WHAT ?!
A DEMON ...

MANTEN ("FULL HEAVEN")

Hiten's younger brother is gentler despite his vicious appearance. He tries to melt Kagome down to make hair restorer. He takes good care of the three hairs he has left until he loses them in an attack by Kagome and Shippo. His weapon is Raigekidan ("thunder attack bullet"), a deadly plasma that he shoots from his mouth. He nearly kills Kagome and Shippo, but is killed when Inuyasha throws Tetsusaiga.

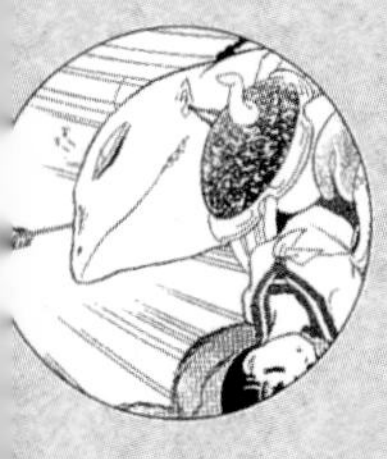

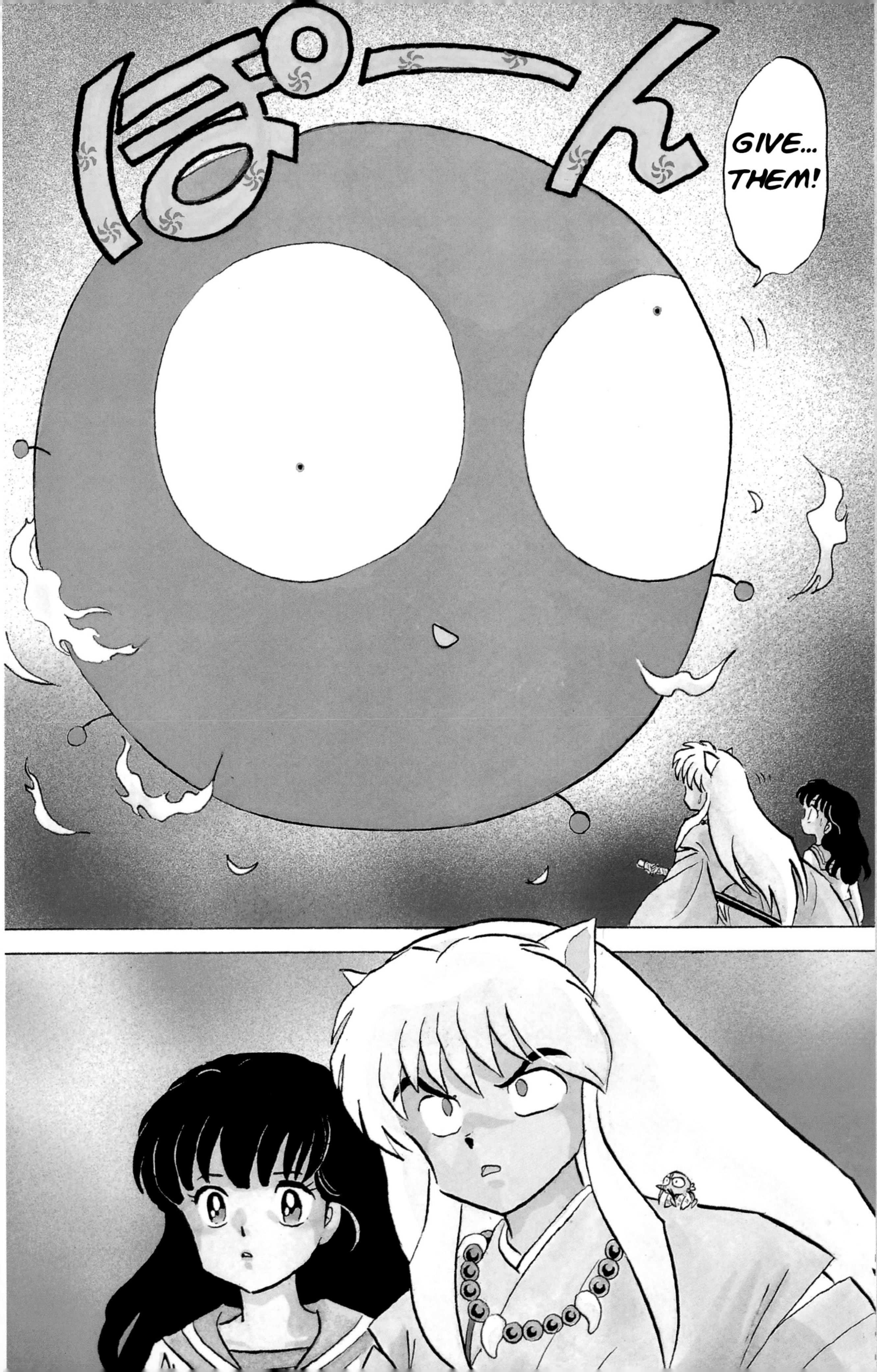
ぽーん
GIVE... THEM!

FoxFire

A mysterious fire emitted by fox-type demons. Shippo's fire is just enough to hold back the spider heads; a demon of his father's class can stop an enemy attack even when he is physically dead and exists only as a pelt. Foxfire appears in legend all over Japan except Okinawa. A line of foxfire is referred to as a vixen's wedding.

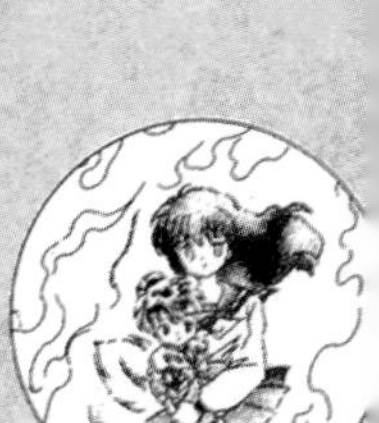

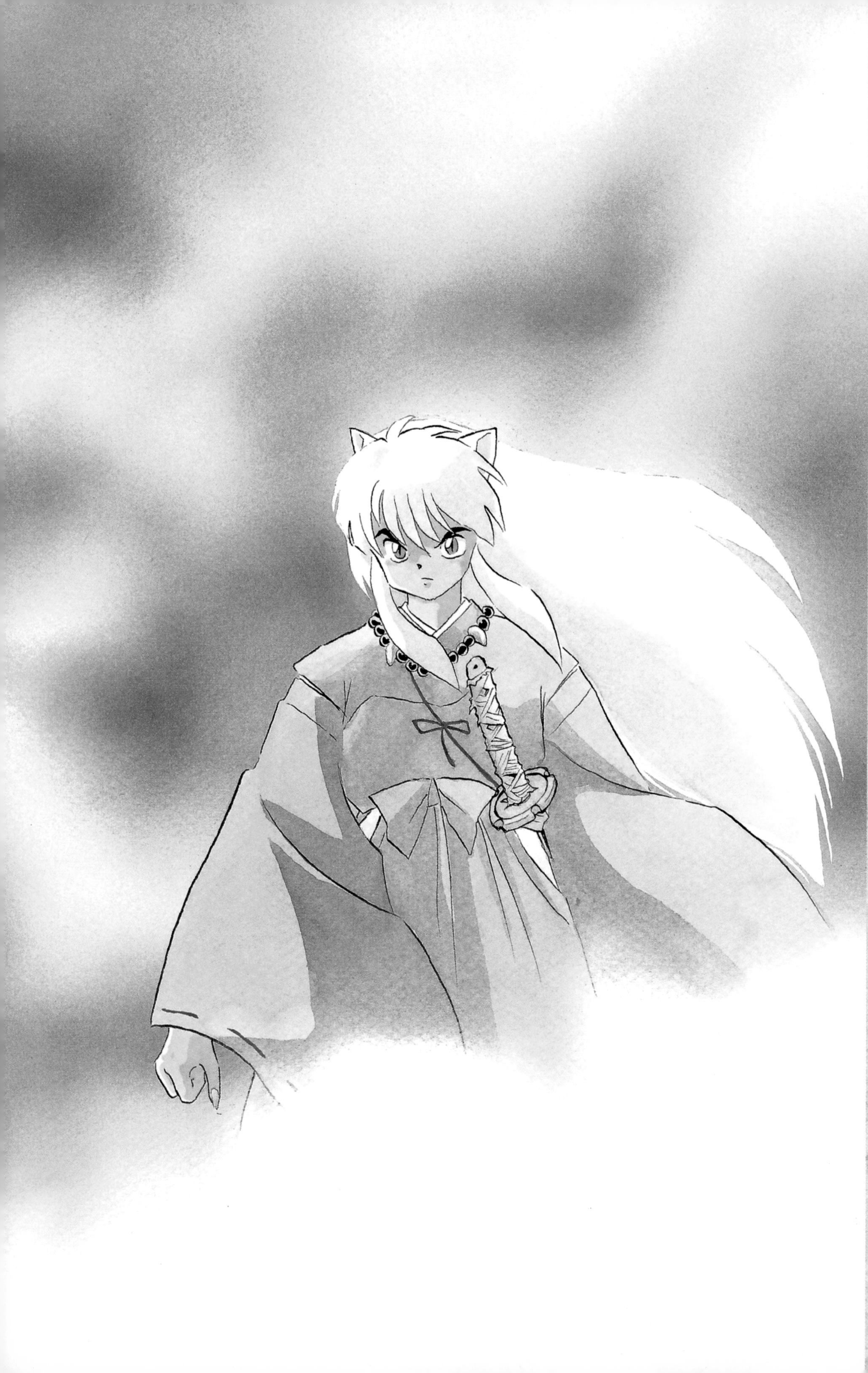

SCROLL 39

SPIDER HEAD

Shonen Sunday Vol. 40, 1997,
and Comic Vol. 5

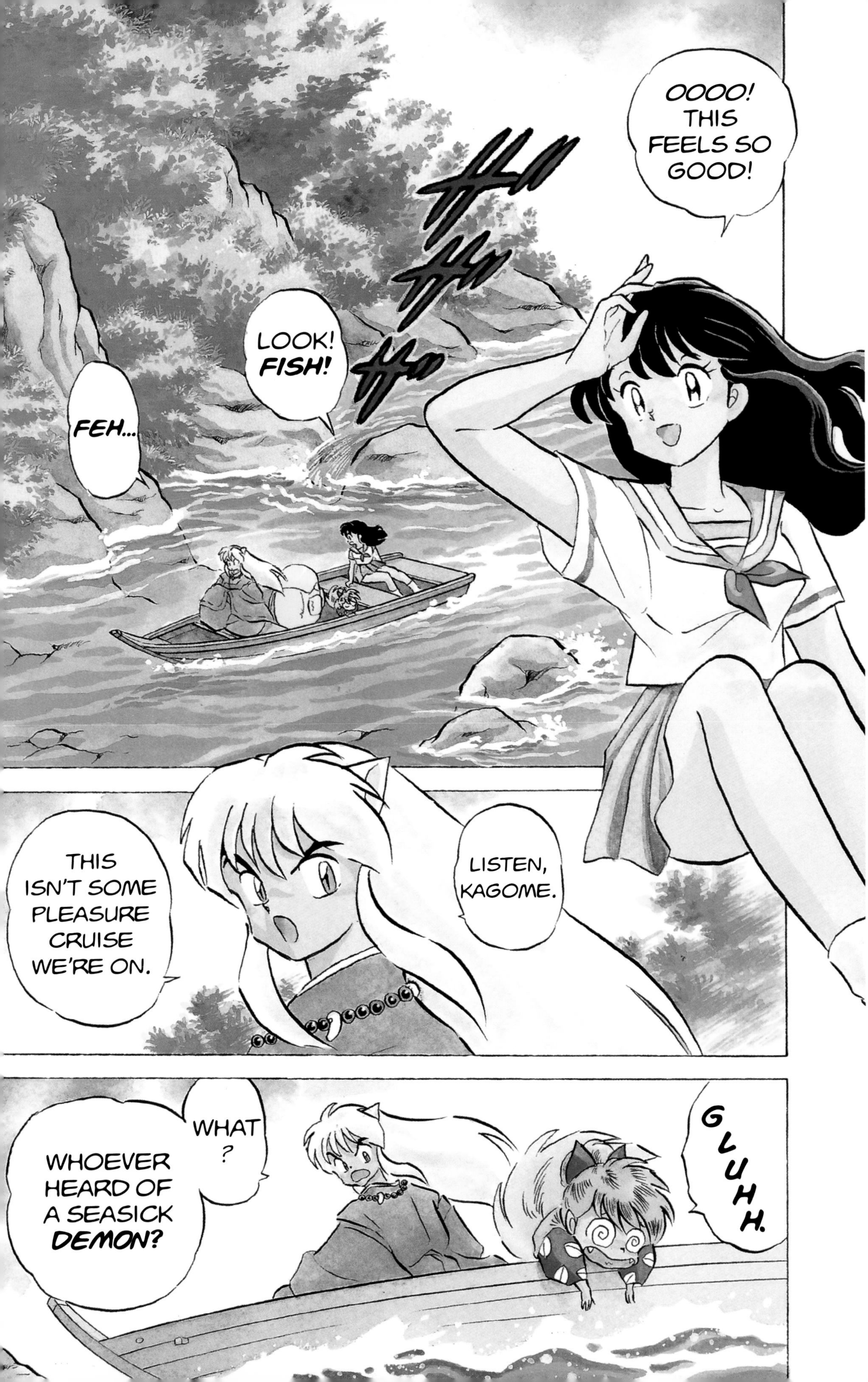
OOOO! THIS FEELS SO GOOD!
LOOK! FISH!
FEH...
LISTEN, KAGOME.
THIS ISN'T SOME PLEASURE CRUISE WE'RE ON.
GUUHH.
WHAT?
WHOEVER HEARD OF A SEASICK DEMON?

NAZUNA ("SHEPHERD'S PURSE")

A girl whose father was killed by the spider heads. Since the tragedy she has been under the care of the Buddhist priest of a mountain temple. Because demons killed her family, she hates them in general, including Inuyasha at first. Disguised as the priest, the spider heads trick her into giving up a shard of the Jewel she held. In the end she becomes the heroine, exterminating the spider heads with the help of Inuyasha.

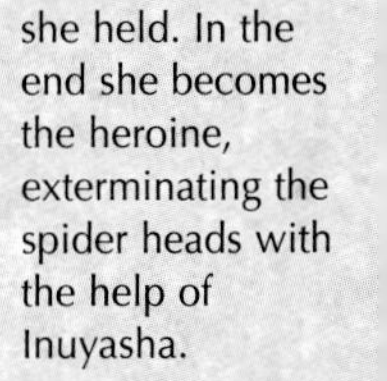

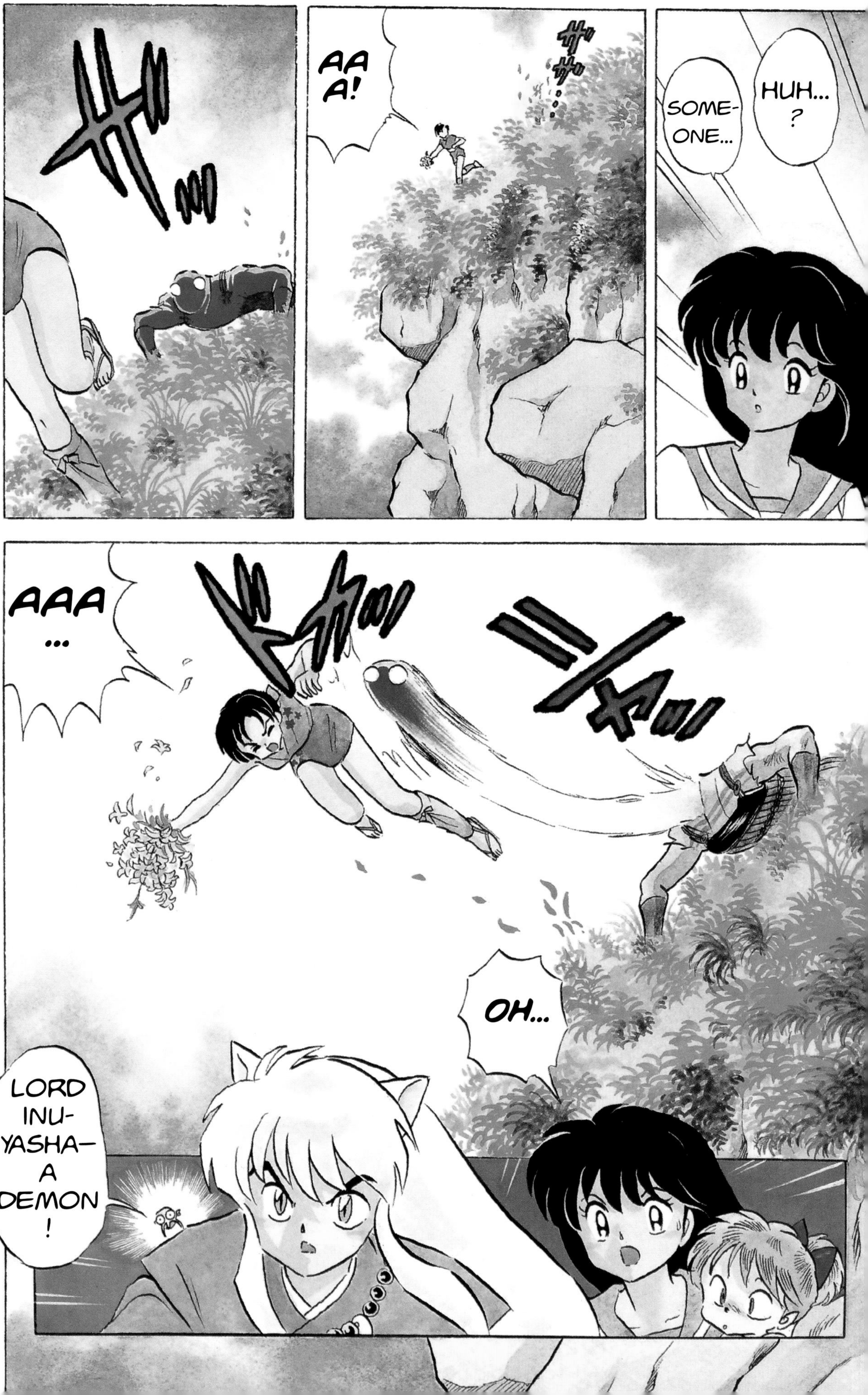
HUH...?
SOME-ONE...
AAA!
AAA...
OH...
LORD INU-YASHA—A DEMON!

SPIRIT SHIELD (AURA OR *kekkai*)

A field of demonic power, as seen when the scabbard of Tetsusaiga absorbs Hiten's lightning attack. With this power Kagome can defend herself from Sesshomaru's poison claws, so it easily stops the invasion of the spider heads. Each demon uses its aura differently. Naraku, for instance, extends his around Hitomijo castle so it will not be discovered.

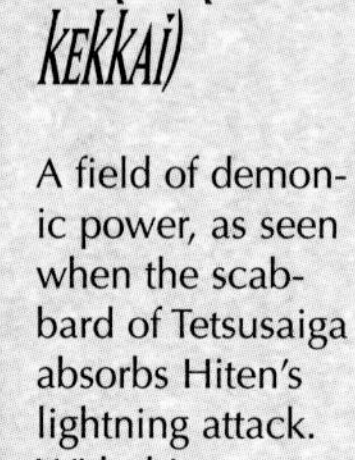

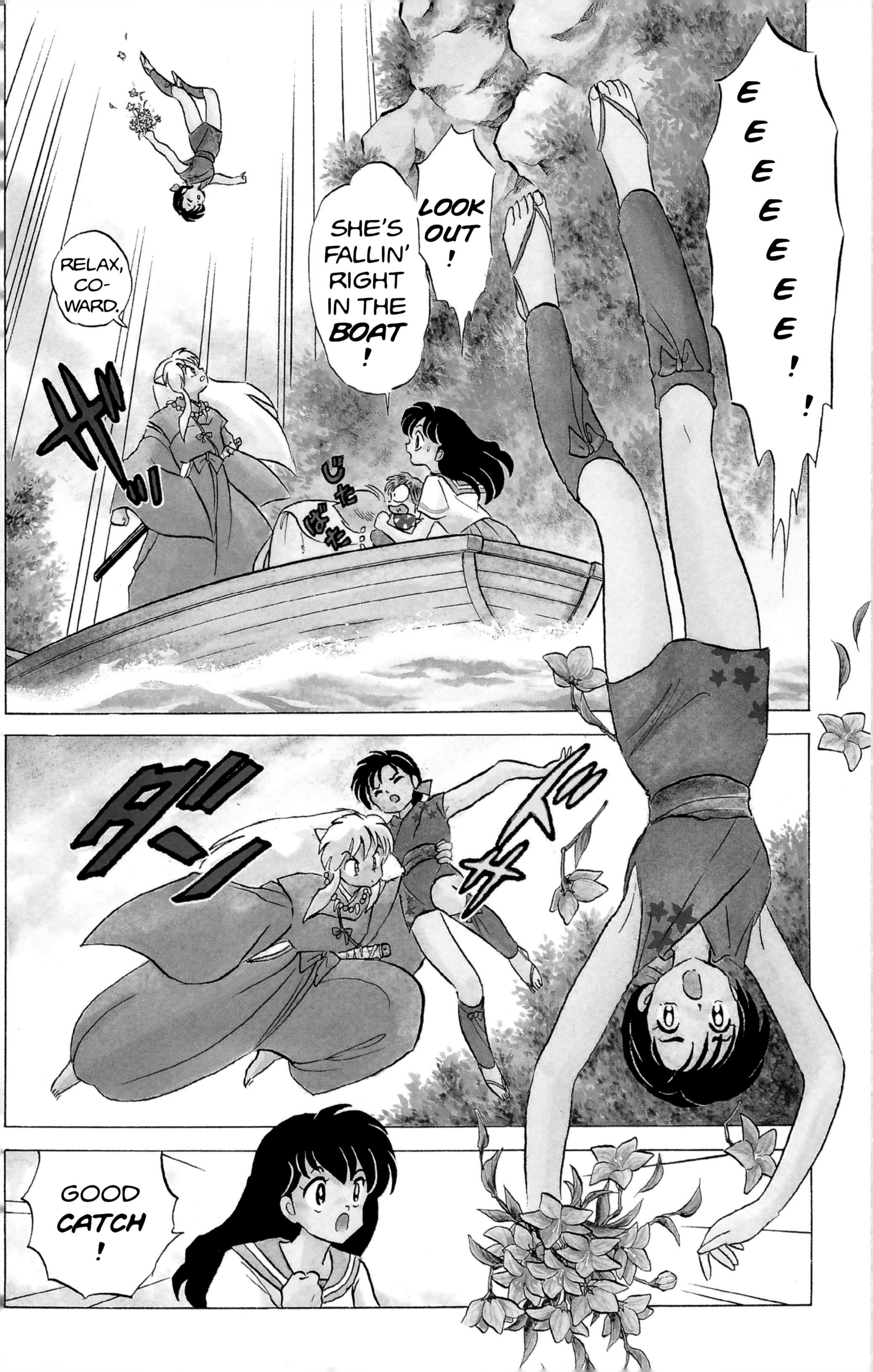
EEEEEEEEE!!
LOOK OUT!
SHE'S FALLIN' RIGHT IN THE BOAT!
RELAX, CO-WARD.
GOOD CATCH!

SPIDER HEADS

These demons live in the heads of human corpses. Their leader disguises himself as a Buddhist priest, sends soldiers out across the mountain, and waits for Inuyasha's party to be lured in by rumors of demons. Its intent, of course, is to win shards of the Jewel. It killed Nazuna's father and puts Inuyasha's party in a fix, but is killed by Tetsusaiga and more importantly by Nazuna's daredevil action.

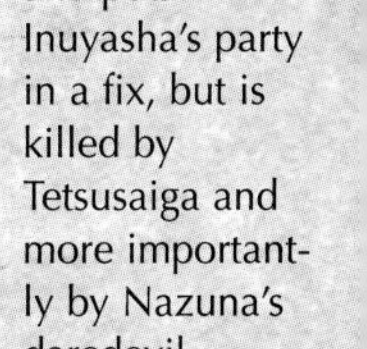

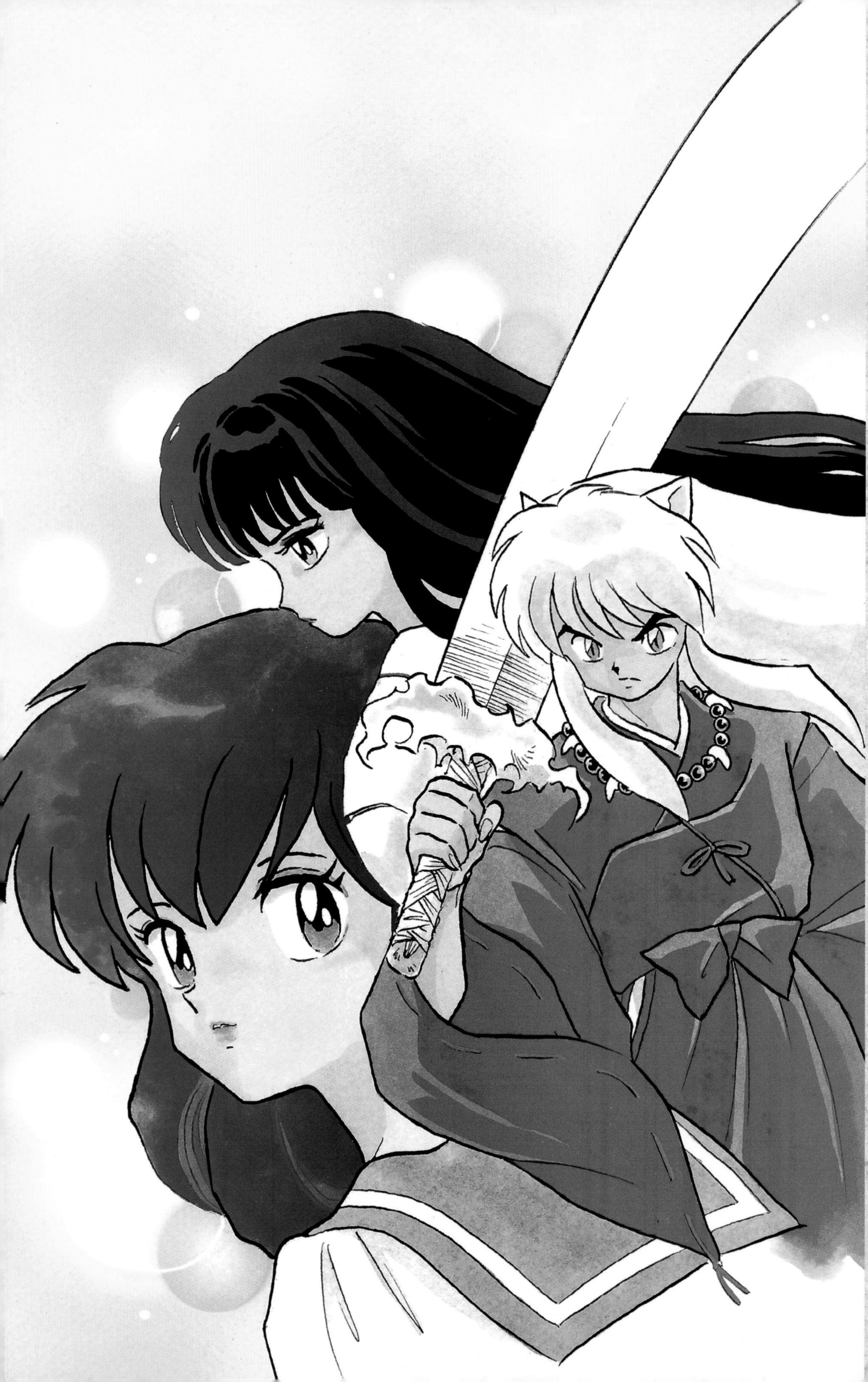

SCROLL 49

HATRED UNSPENT (ONNEN=GRUDGE)

Shonen Sunday weekly Vol. 50, 1997 and Comic Vol. 6

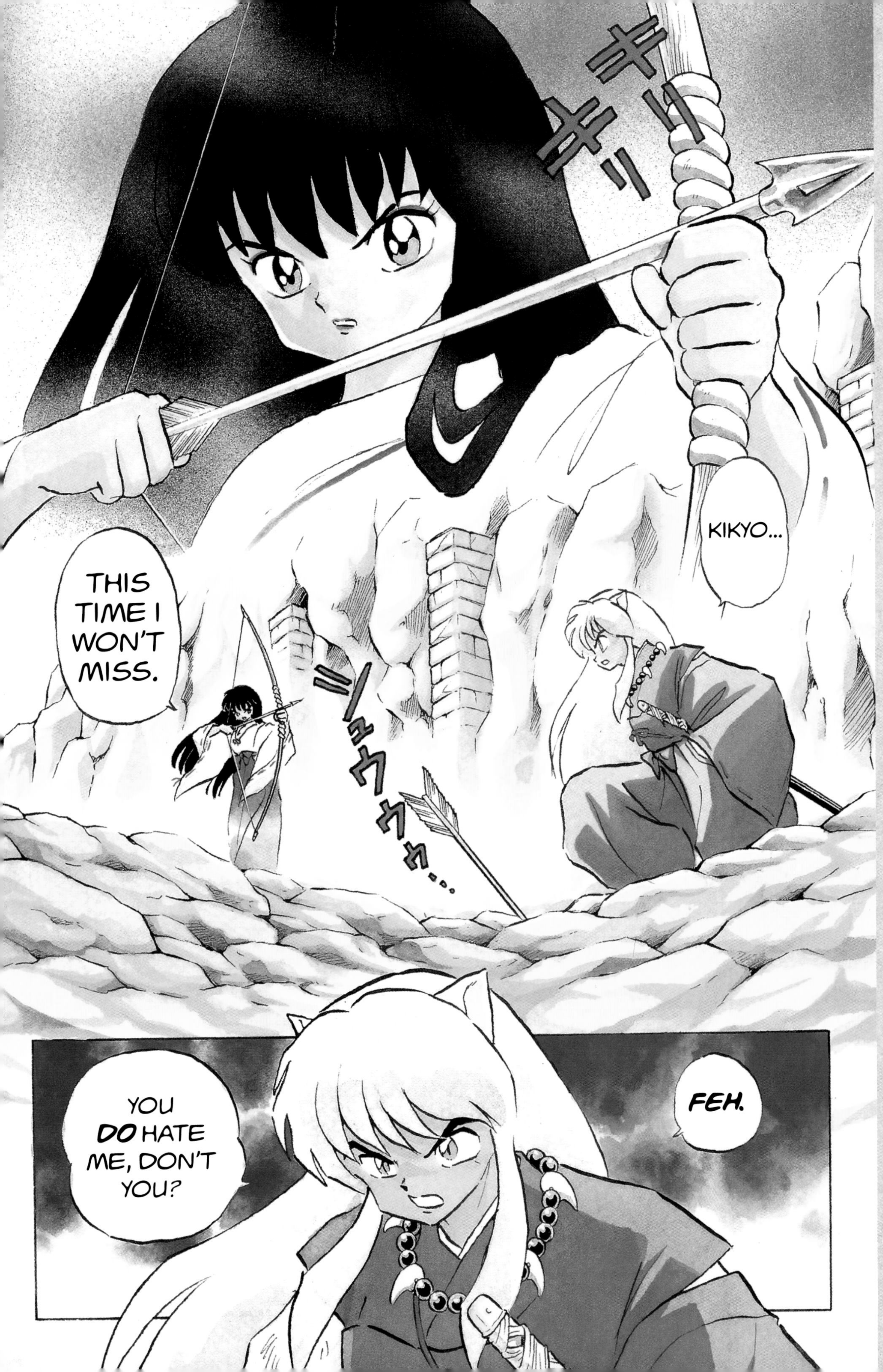
キリキリ
KIKYO...
THIS TIME I WON'T MISS.
FEH.
YOU **DO** HATE ME, DON'T YOU?

URASUE ("BLACK POTTERY")

This ogress steals the bones of Kikyo, who was among the most powerful of the priestesses. In her demon kiln, Urasue bakes a replica of Kikyo (a jinki or "human container") using Kikyo's bones and earth from her grave. She tries to bring Kikyo under her control, but is destroyed by the supernatural power of the resurrected Kikyo. Demons born of the grudges of women and bad karma are generally called kijo; when they get old, they are called onibaba ("demon hag"). ▲

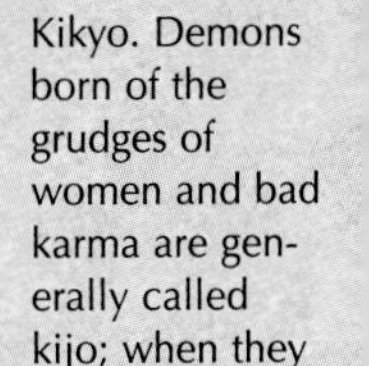

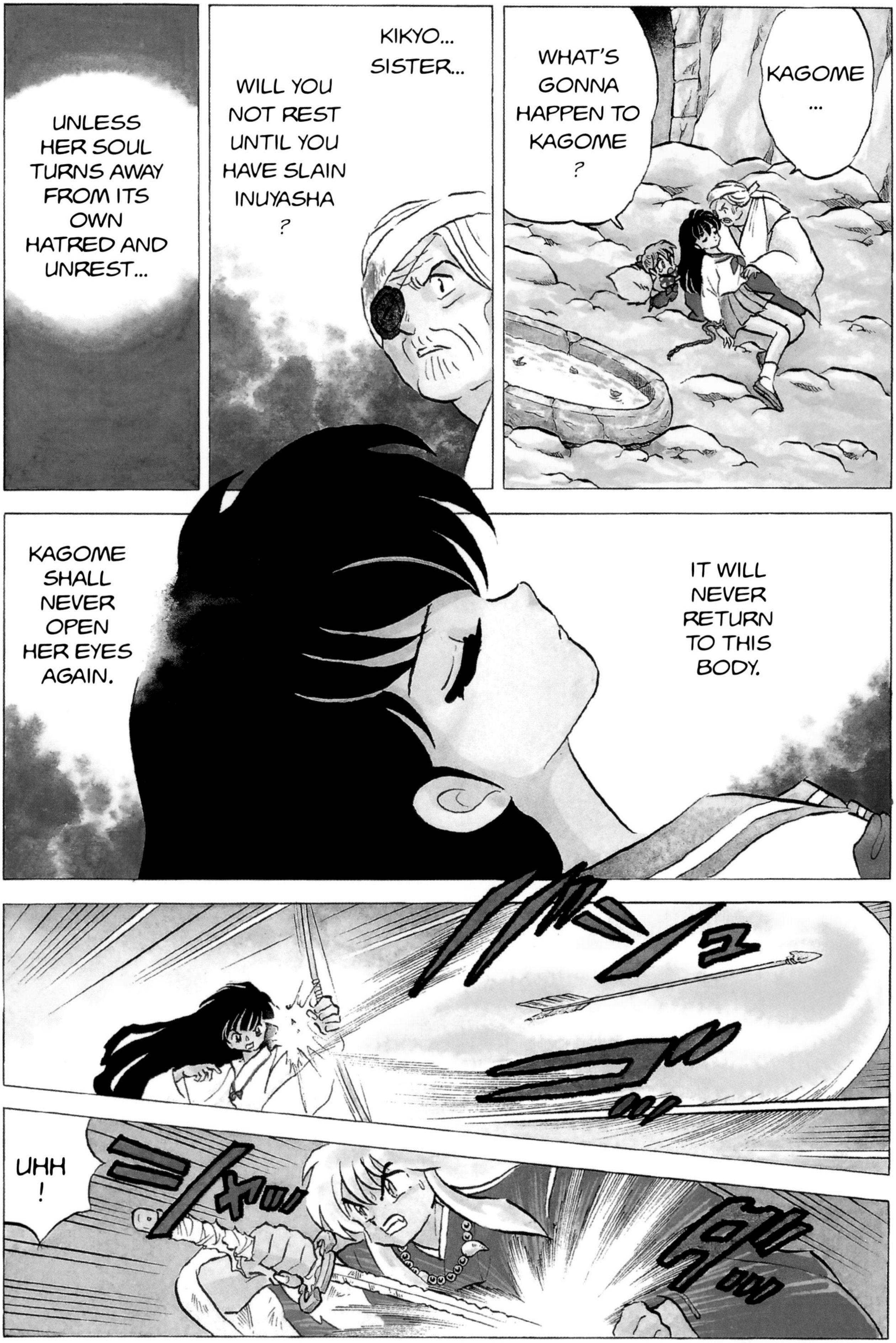
KAGOME ...
WHAT'S GONNA HAPPEN TO KAGOME ?
KIKYO... SISTER...
WILL YOU NOT REST UNTIL YOU HAVE SLAIN INUYASHA ?
UNLESS HER SOUL TURNS AWAY FROM ITS OWN HATRED AND UNREST...
IT WILL NEVER RETURN TO THIS BODY.
KAGOME SHALL NEVER OPEN HER EYES AGAIN.
UHH !

jinki ("human container")

Puppets made by Urasue from corpses and clay. Because she uses the bodies of soldiers killed in battle, her jinki tend to be defective. So she gives them various tricks and forms, like substituting a swordblade for a missing arm. The puppets, mostly guards of the demon kiln, are dangerous to humans but seem useless when facing demons like Inuyasha.

▲

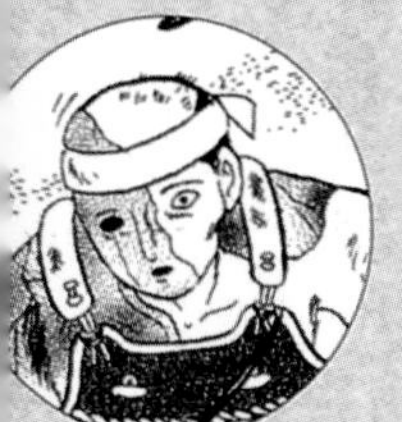

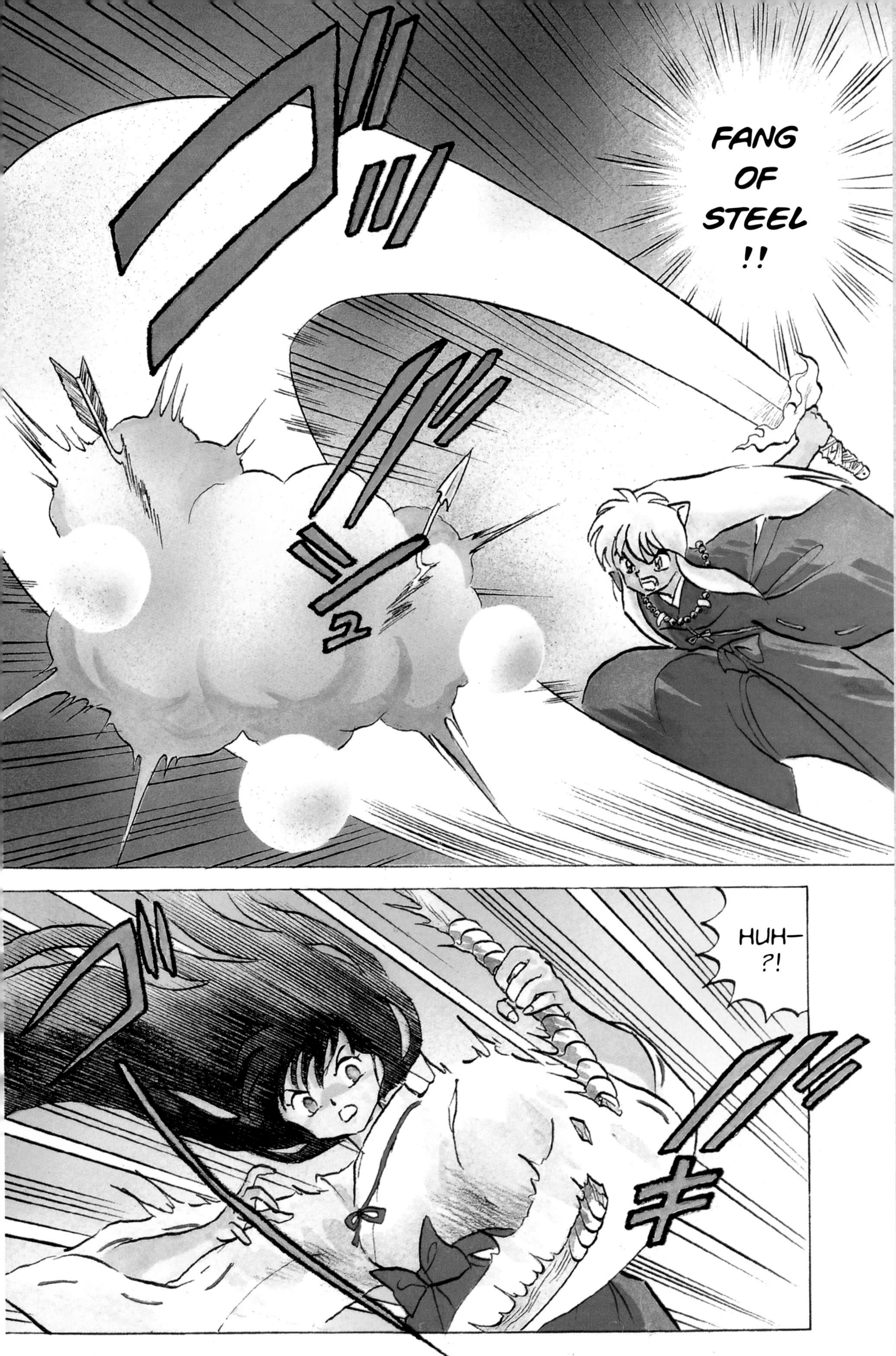
FANG OF STEEL !!
HUH— ?!

kikyo

The priestess who enchanted Inuyasha. In that battle she was fatally injured, and before her death she asked her younger sister Kaede to burn the Shikon Jewel along with her body. Fifty years later Kikyo is revived in a new body made by Urasue. To give it life, she takes the hatred from the soul of Kagome, her reincarnation. She first wants only to kill Inuyasha, but later Kikyo seems to be after something else.

▲

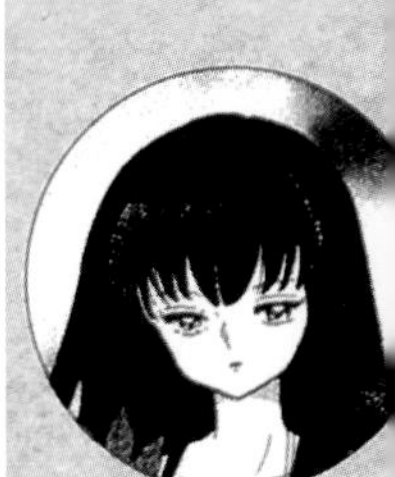

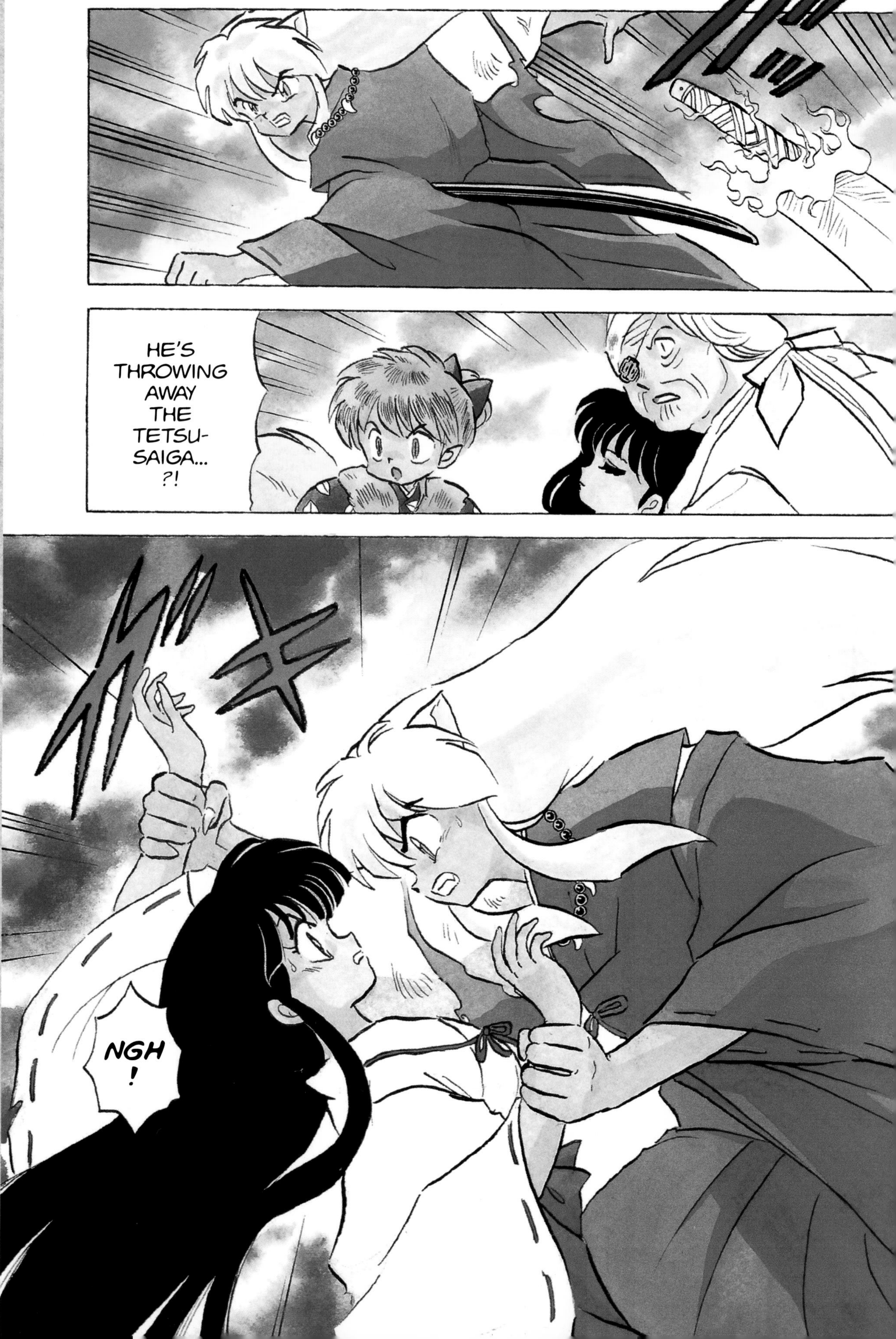
HE'S THROWING AWAY THE TETSU-SAIGA...?!
NGH!

Inuyasha and Tetsusaiga

Tetsusaiga is Inuyasha's legacy from his father and is hidden in the tomb inside Inuyasha's eye. It was a defensive weapon the demon made himself from his own fang to guard Inuyasha's mother. Because of this origin, Tetsusaiga works best when Inuyasha is defending a person. The full power of Tetsusaiga is still largely unknown.

▲

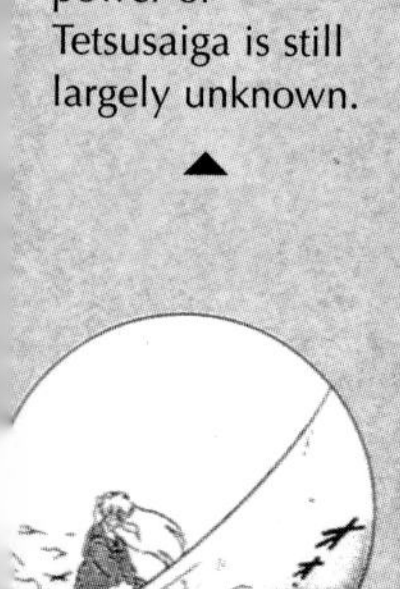

Shonen Sunday Vol. 32, 2000 poster

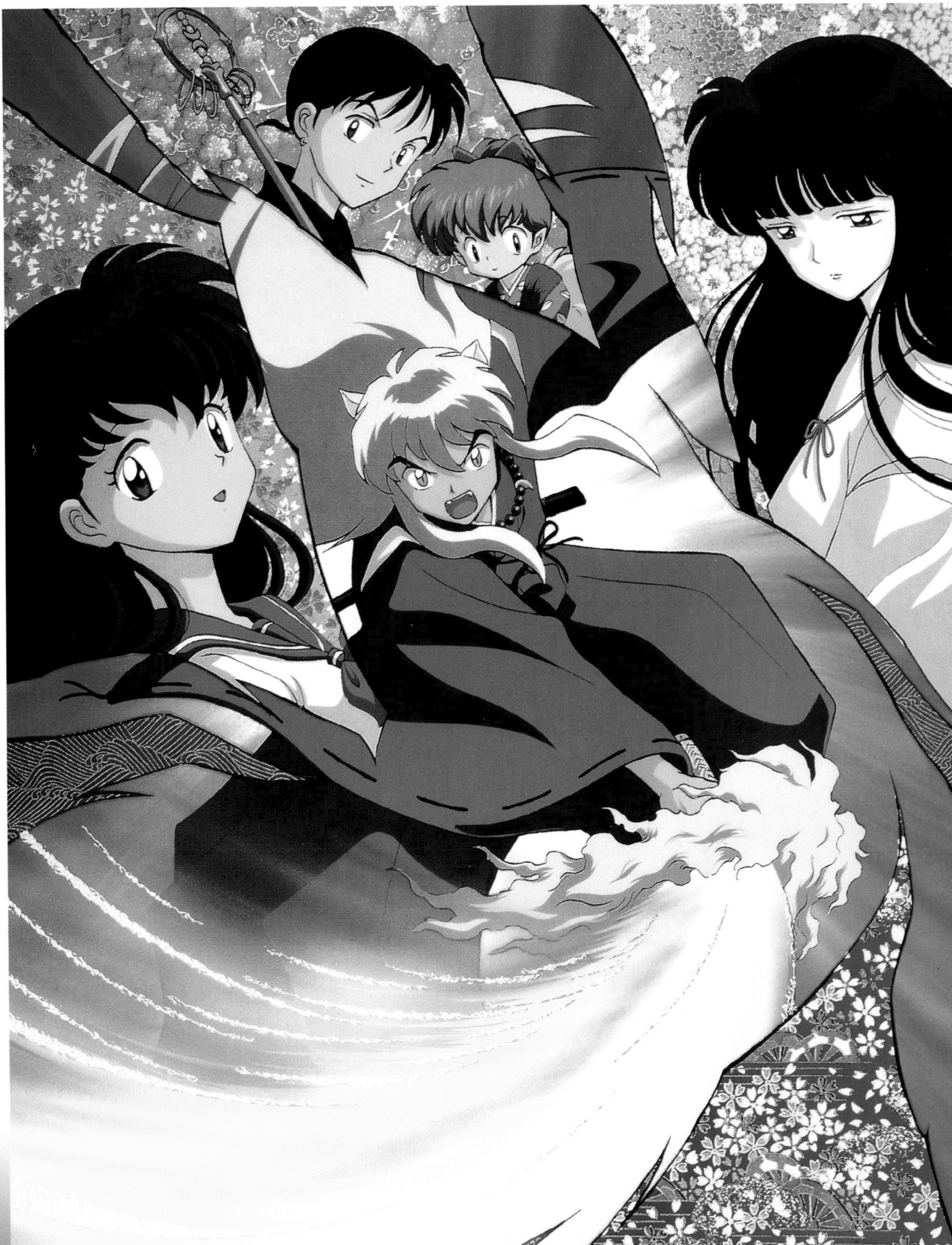

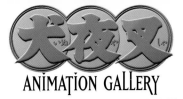

SCROLL 61
THE STING OF VICTORY

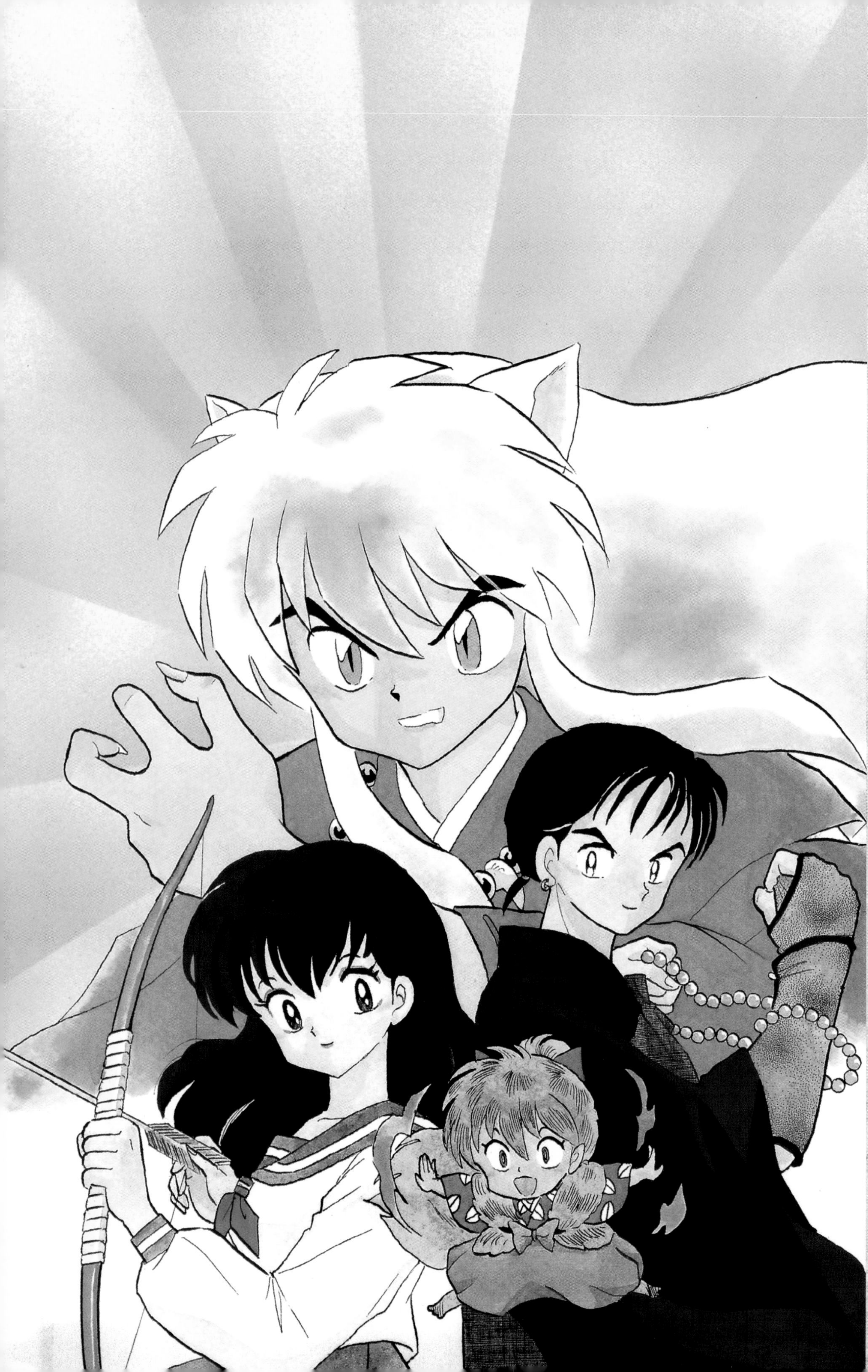

Shonen Sunday Vol. 12, 1998
and and Comic Vol. 7

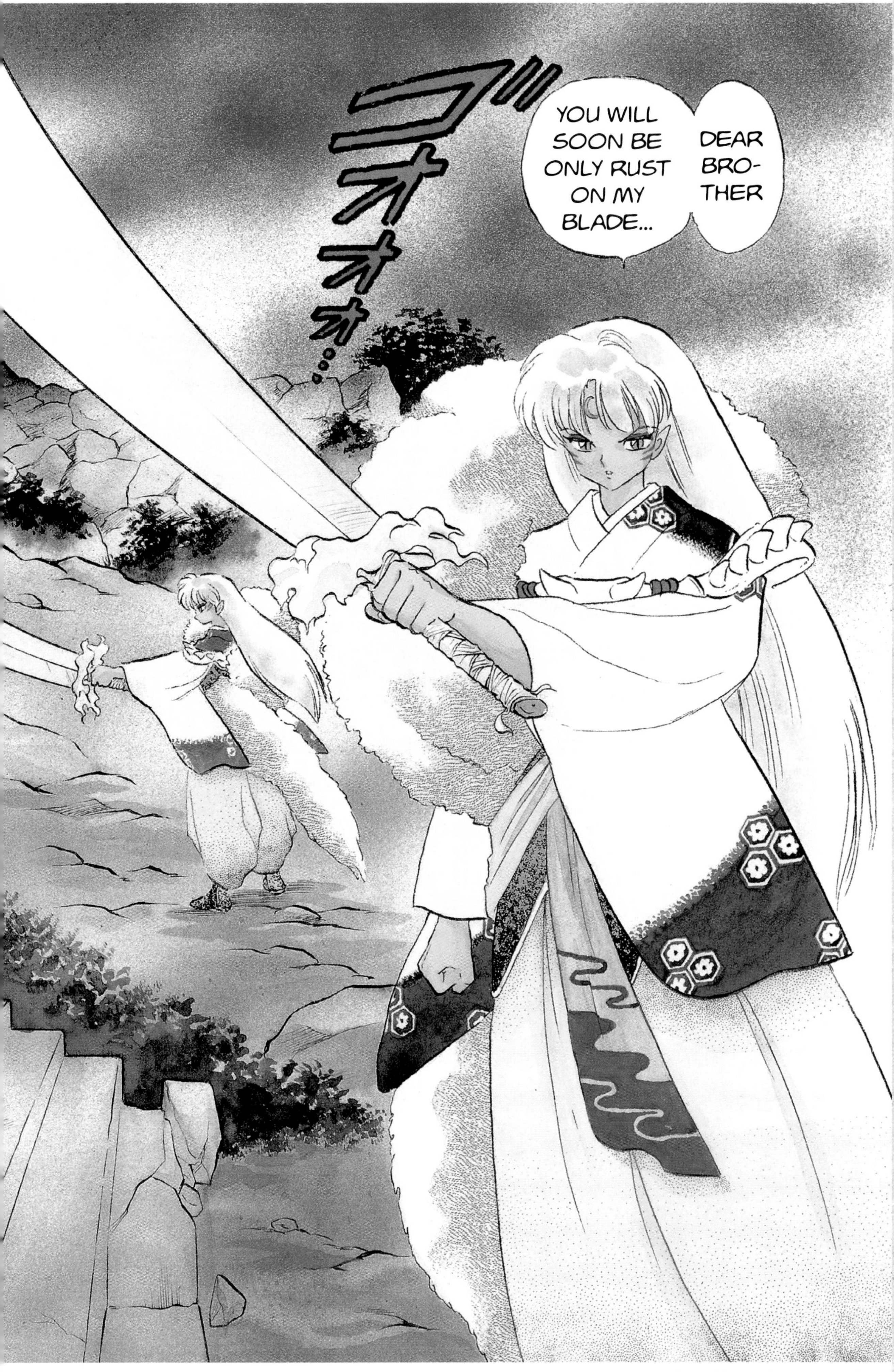
ゴオオオオ…
YOU WILL SOON BE ONLY RUST ON MY BLADE...
DEAR BRO-THER

DEMON (ONI)

This giant demon is a faithful soldier of Sesshomaru. Its only weapon seems to be physical strength. It is swallowed up by Miroku's mystic tunnel and killed. Legend says that oni — whose image was established around the Edo period — were one of two kinds: oni, which have physical substance, and mono, which are spirit entities.

▲

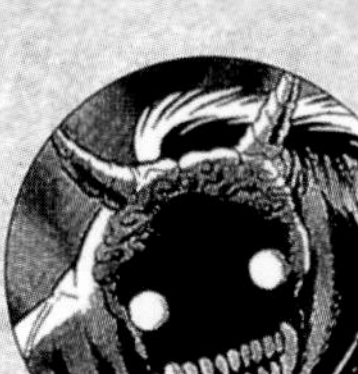

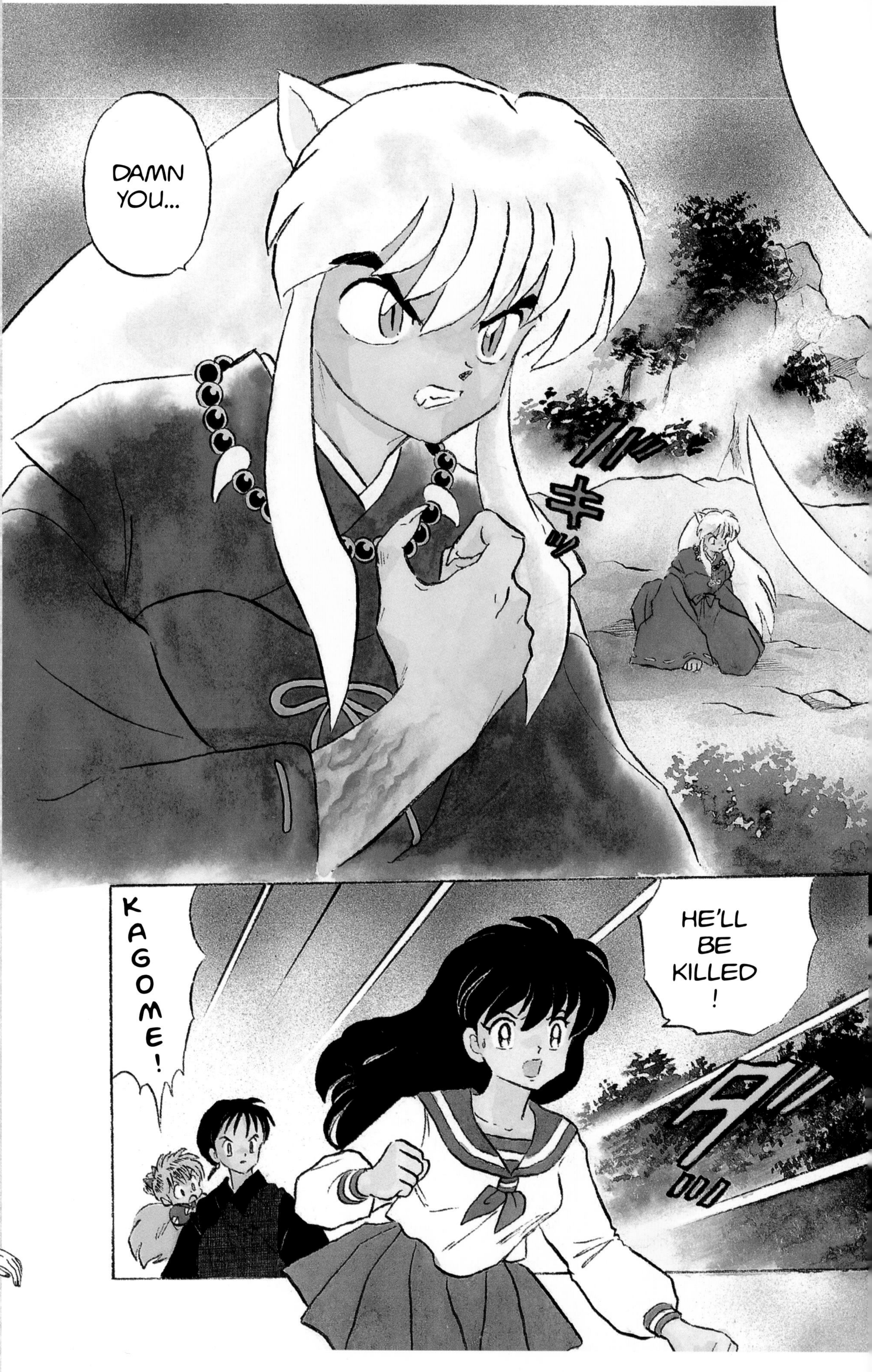
DAMN YOU...
バキッ
HE'LL BE KILLED!
KAGOME!

THE BORROWED ARM

Sesshomaru, whose right arm is cut off by Inuyasha, kills a demon, steals its arm and grafts it onto himself. Perhaps because of its demonic power, the borrowed part seems ill adapted to semi-permanent use. A human arm with a Shikon shard embedded in it seems to be most adaptable to him.

▲

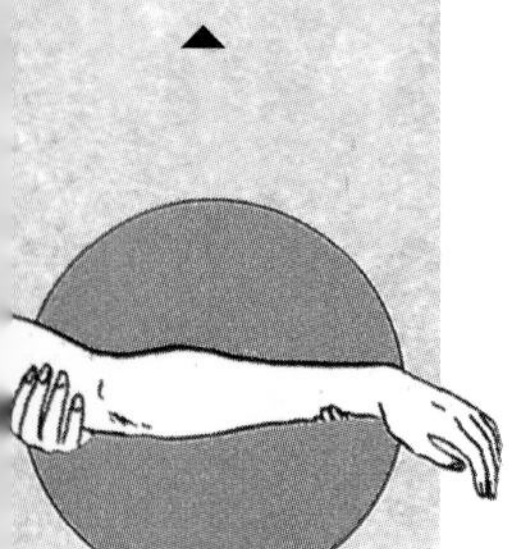

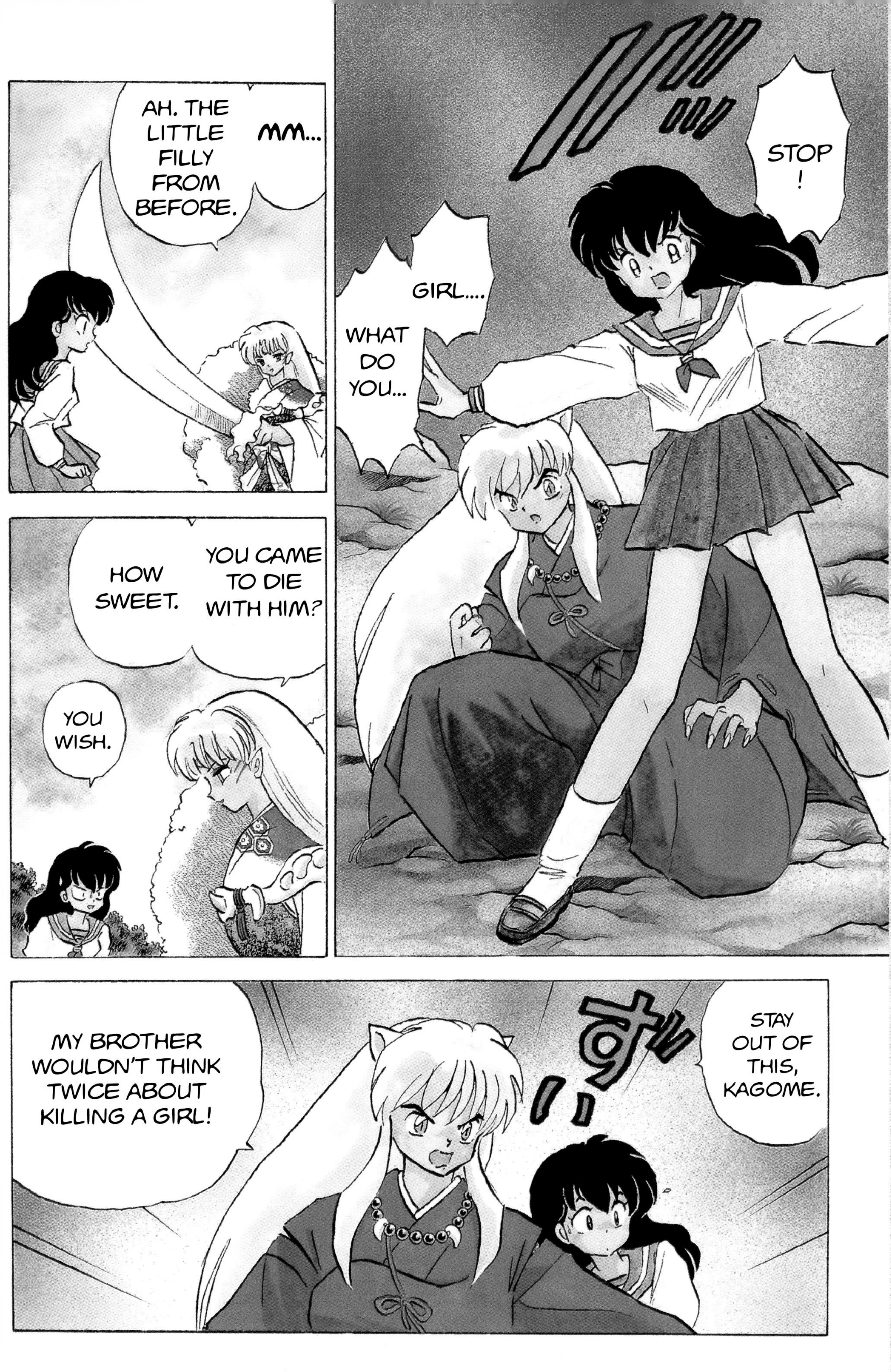
STOP!
GIRL....
WHAT DO YOU...
MM...
AH. THE LITTLE FILLY FROM BEFORE.
YOU CAME TO DIE WITH HIM?
HOW SWEET.
YOU WISH.
STAY OUT OF THIS, KAGOME.
すい
MY BROTHER WOULDN'T THINK TWICE ABOUT KILLING A GIRL!

VENOM WASPS (SAIMYOSHO)

These are the Venom Wasps, given by Naraku to Sesshomaru to counter Miroku's wind tunnel. The wasps willingly fly into the tunnel and poison Miroku's body. In addition to keeping the tunnel sealed, their mission is to watch Kagome's party and search out shards of the Jewel. For Naraku, the Venom Wasps are like intelligence operatives.

▲

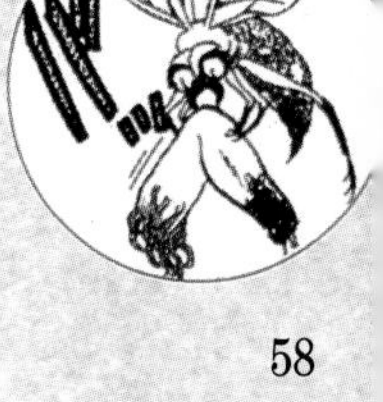

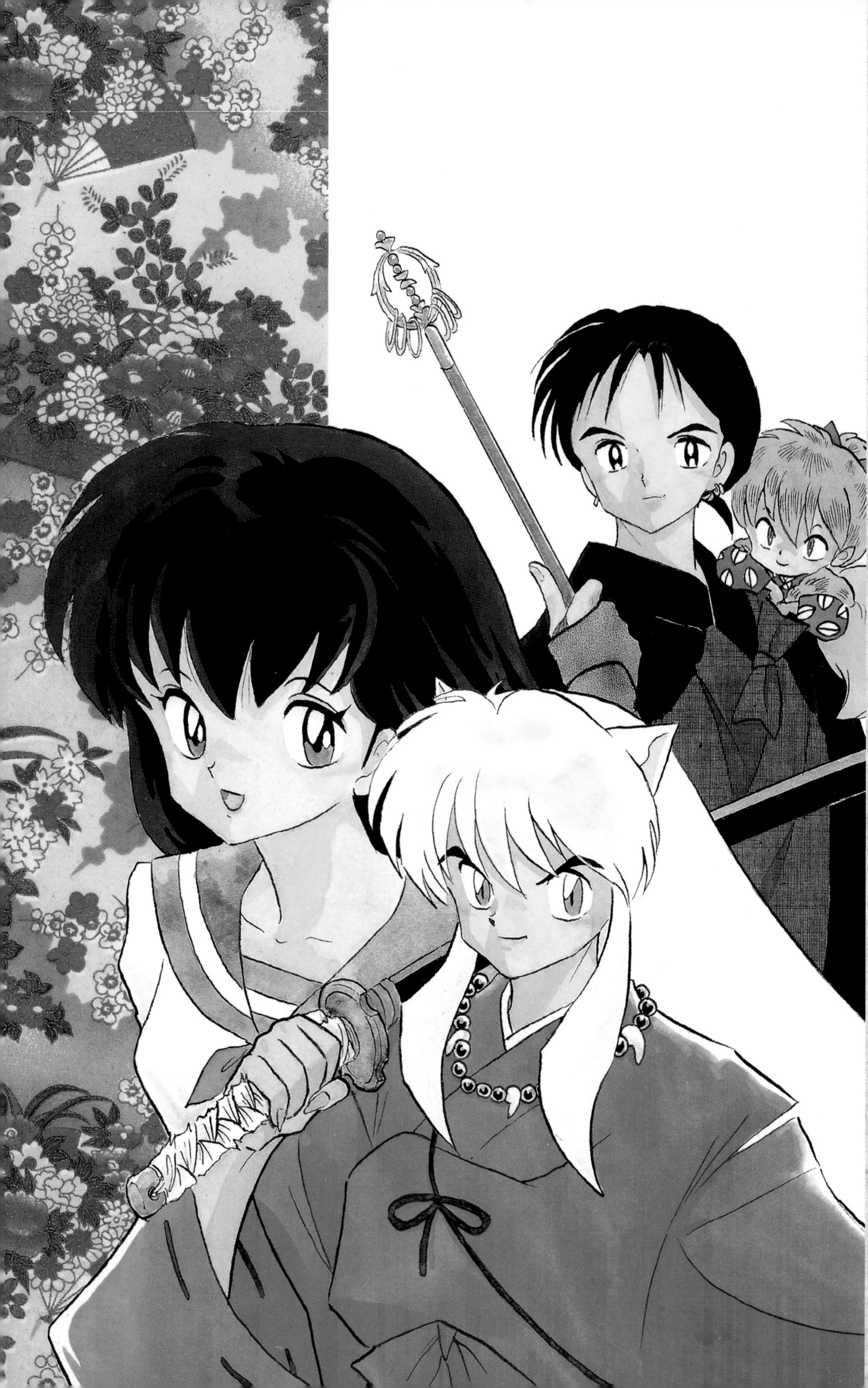

SCROLL 73

YOUNG SOULS

Shonen Sunday Vol. 25, 1998
and Comic Vol. 8

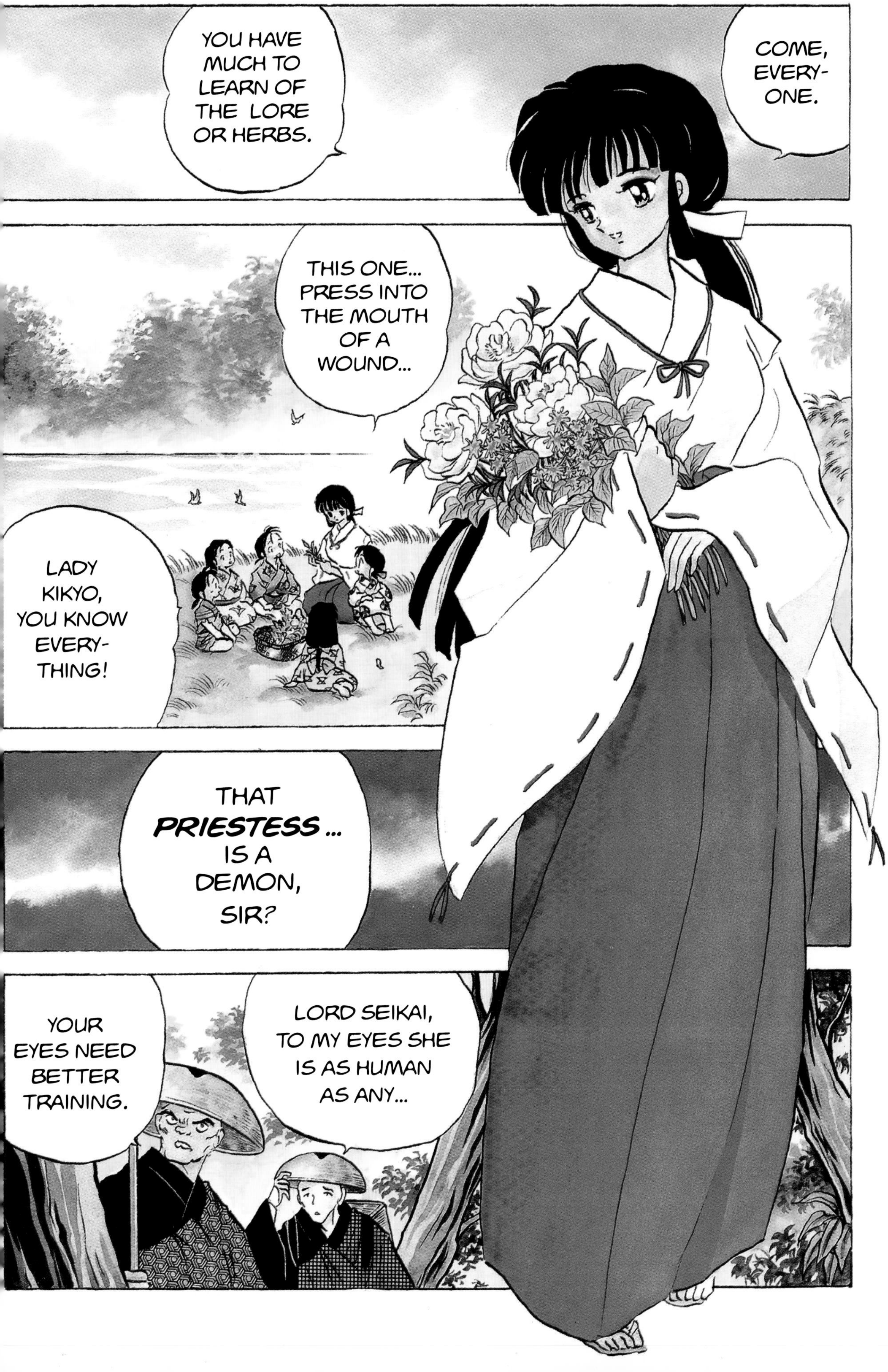
COME, EVERY-ONE.
YOU HAVE MUCH TO LEARN OF THE LORE OR HERBS.
THIS ONE... PRESS INTO THE MOUTH OF A WOUND...
LADY KIKYO, YOU KNOW EVERY-THING!
THAT PRIESTESS... IS A DEMON, SIR?
LORD SEIKAI, TO MY EYES SHE IS AS HUMAN AS ANY...
YOUR EYES NEED BETTER TRAINING.

SAYO

Kikyo finds the girl, Sayo, in the lakeside village after Kikyo falls from the cliff and is presumed dead. At first Sayo feels close to Kikyo, who is respected as a priestess, but she becomes frightened when seeing Kikyo manipulate the Soul Collectors and fight a battle of sorcery against the traveling monk, Seikai. This makes Kikyo aware that there is no place of rest for one who has died and been resurrected.

▲

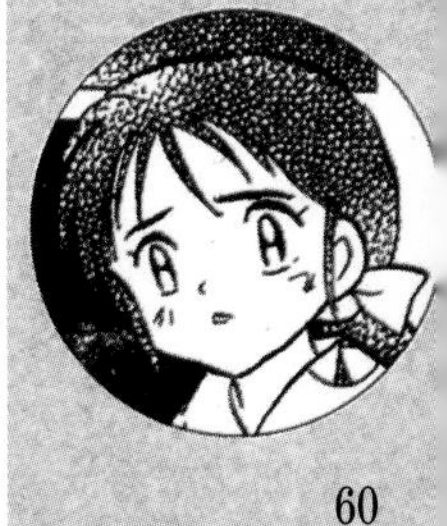

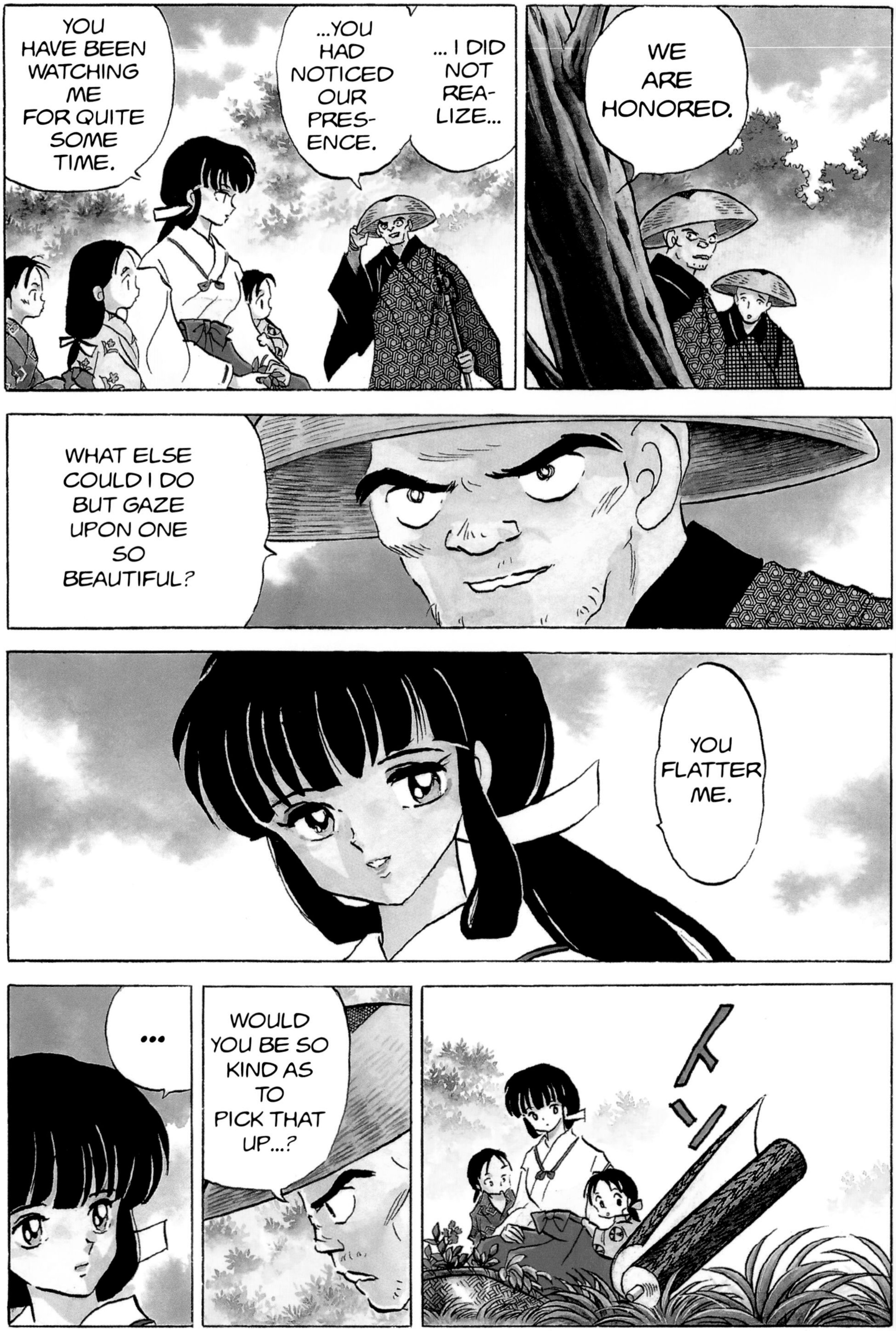
WE ARE HONORED.
... I DID NOT REA-LIZE...
...YOU HAD NOTICED OUR PRES-ENCE.
YOU HAVE BEEN WATCHING ME FOR QUITE SOME TIME.
WHAT ELSE COULD I DO BUT GAZE UPON ONE SO BEAUTIFUL?
YOU FLATTER ME.
WOULD YOU BE SO KIND AS TO PICK THAT UP...?
...

SOUL COLLECTOR OR SOUL SKIMMER (SHINIDAMACHU)

These demons carry the souls of dead girls. Without their souls these girls cannot enter heaven. Because hatred alone cannot maintain Kikyo physically, the Soul Collectors collect souls as energy for her. Because their main function is to transport souls, the demons have very little offensive capability other than to paralyze.

▲

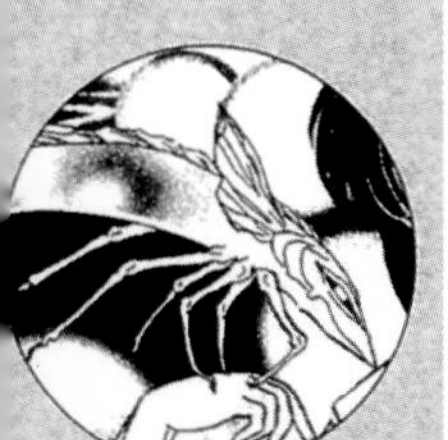

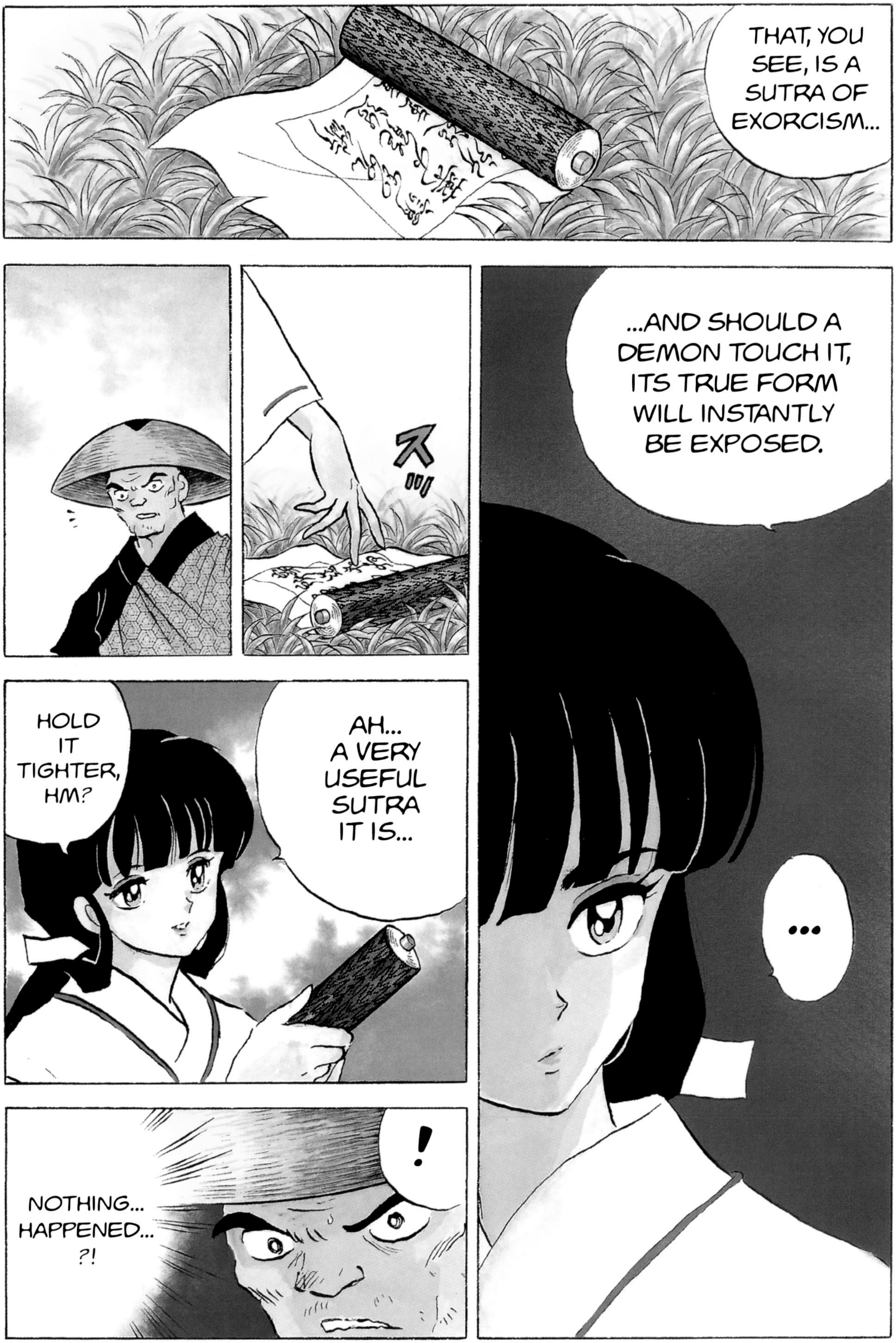
THAT, YOU SEE, IS A SUTRA OF EXORCISM...
...AND SHOULD A DEMON TOUCH IT, ITS TRUE FORM WILL INSTANTLY BE EXPOSED.
...
ス
AH... A VERY USEFUL SUTRA IT IS...
HOLD IT TIGHTER, HM?
!
NOTHING... HAPPENED...?!

SEIKAI ("CLEAR SEA")

He is a traveling Buddhist monk. Because of his dubious virtue, he is able to sense that Kikyo is dead and works to help her soul find peace. He applies kon-pakujutsu ("soul-binding technique") using a carving to conjure a dragon to subdue Kikyo, but because of her strong attachment to the world, she destroys it and he is impaled on one of its claws as it explodes. An acolyte escapes and tells Inuyasha what happened.

▲

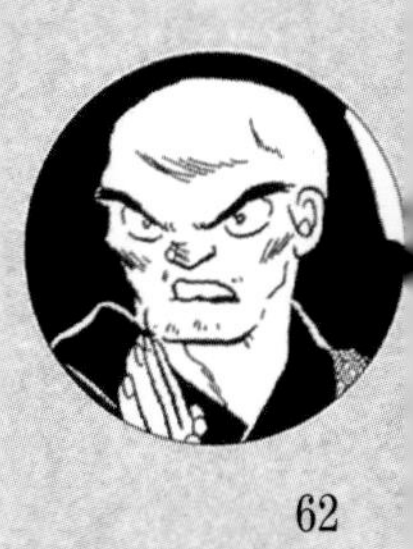

SCROLL 87

THE AMBUSH

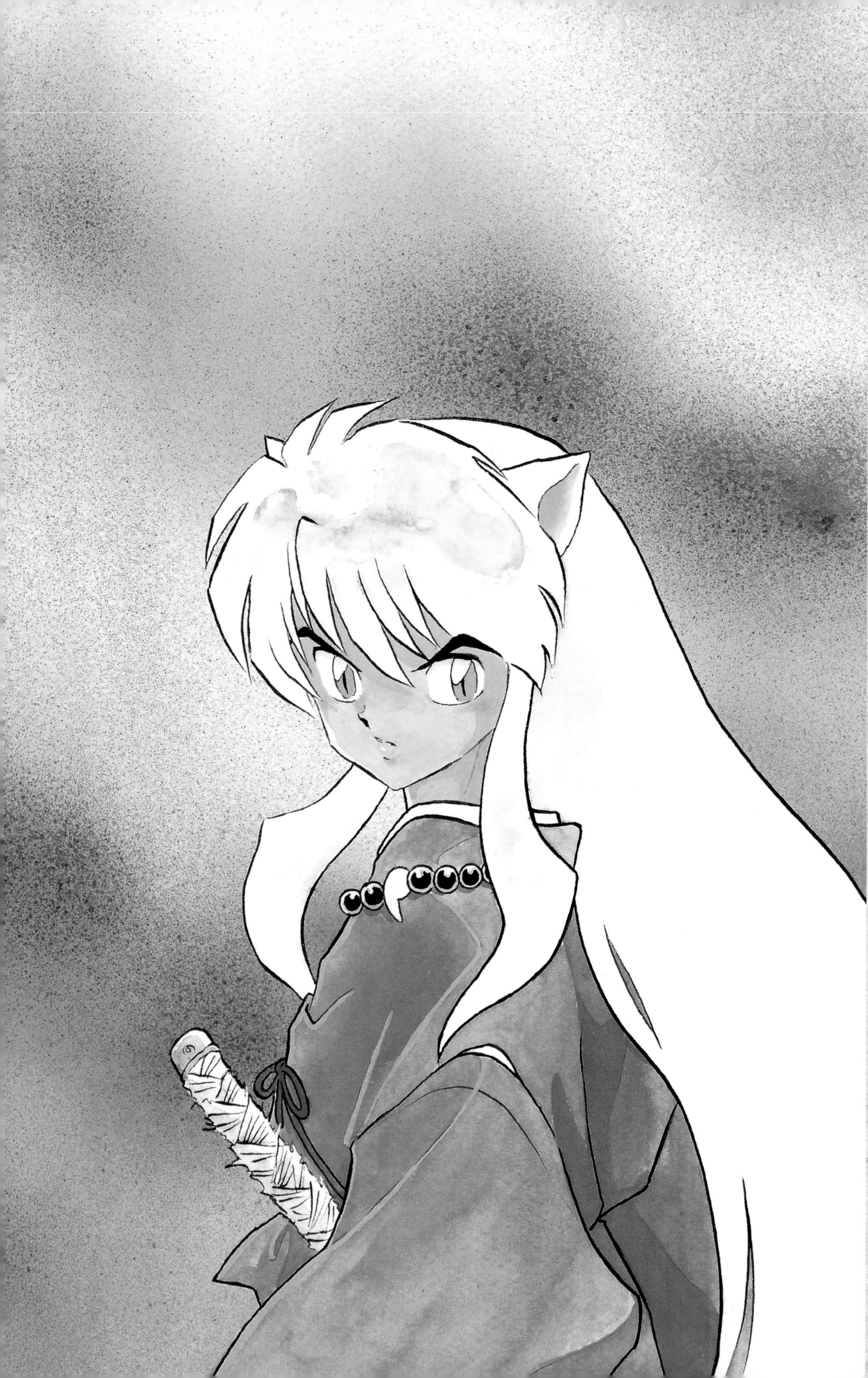

Shonen Sunday Vol. 40, 1998
and Comic Vol. 9

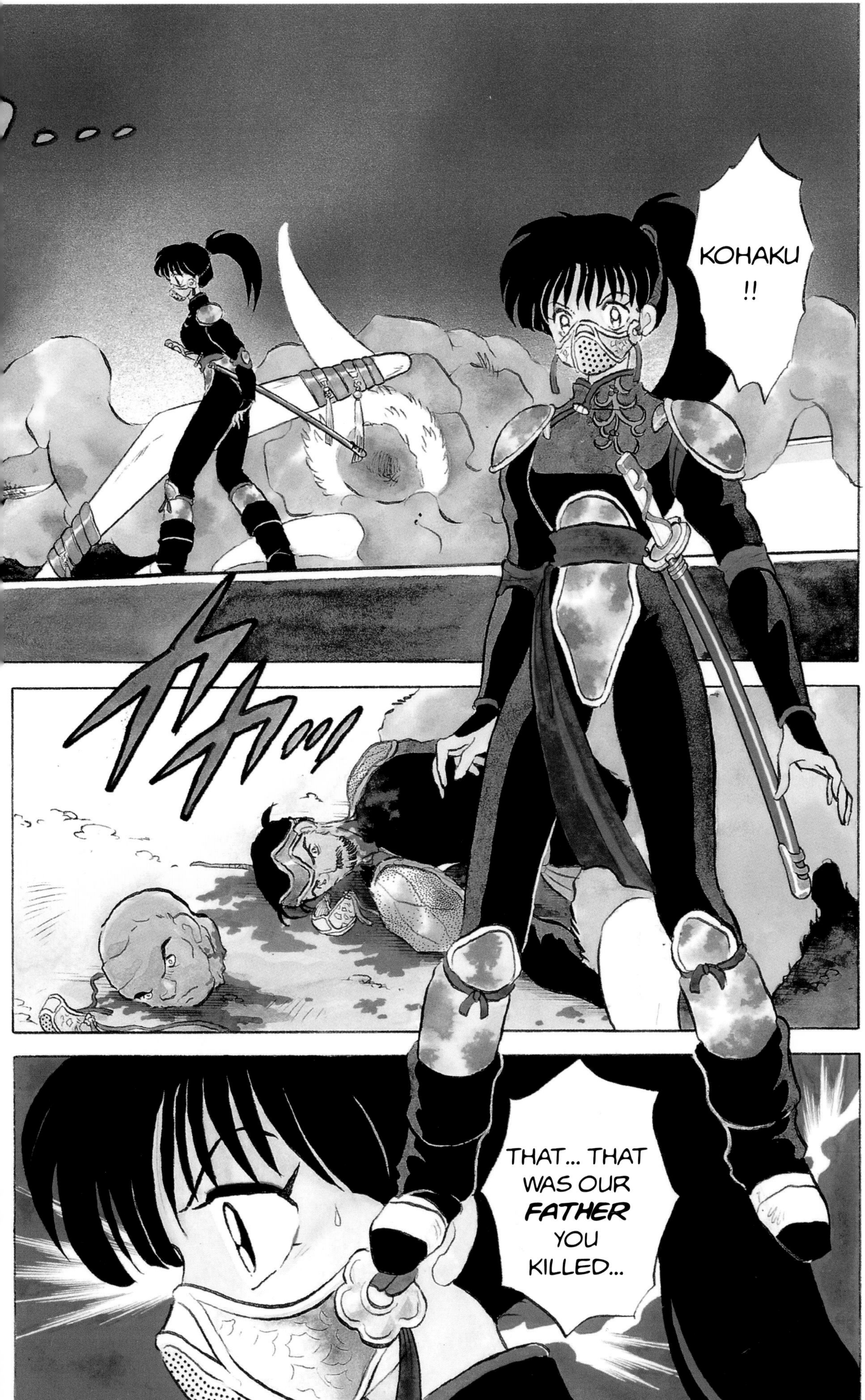
KOHAKU !!
THAT... THAT WAS OUR ***FATHER*** YOU KILLED...

TAIJIYA NO SATO ("DEMON-KILLER VILLAGE")

This village is inhabited by a clan of people who exterminate demons professionally. It was here that the Shikon Jewel came into the world. To purify the Jewel after it returned home after 400 years, the villagers gave it to Kikyo. A plot by Naraku destroys the village and all but Sango are slaughtered.

▲

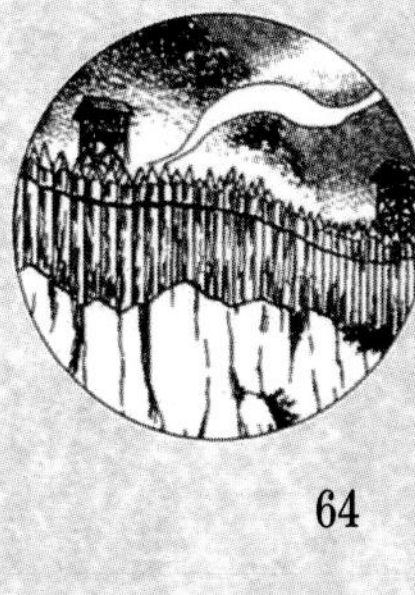

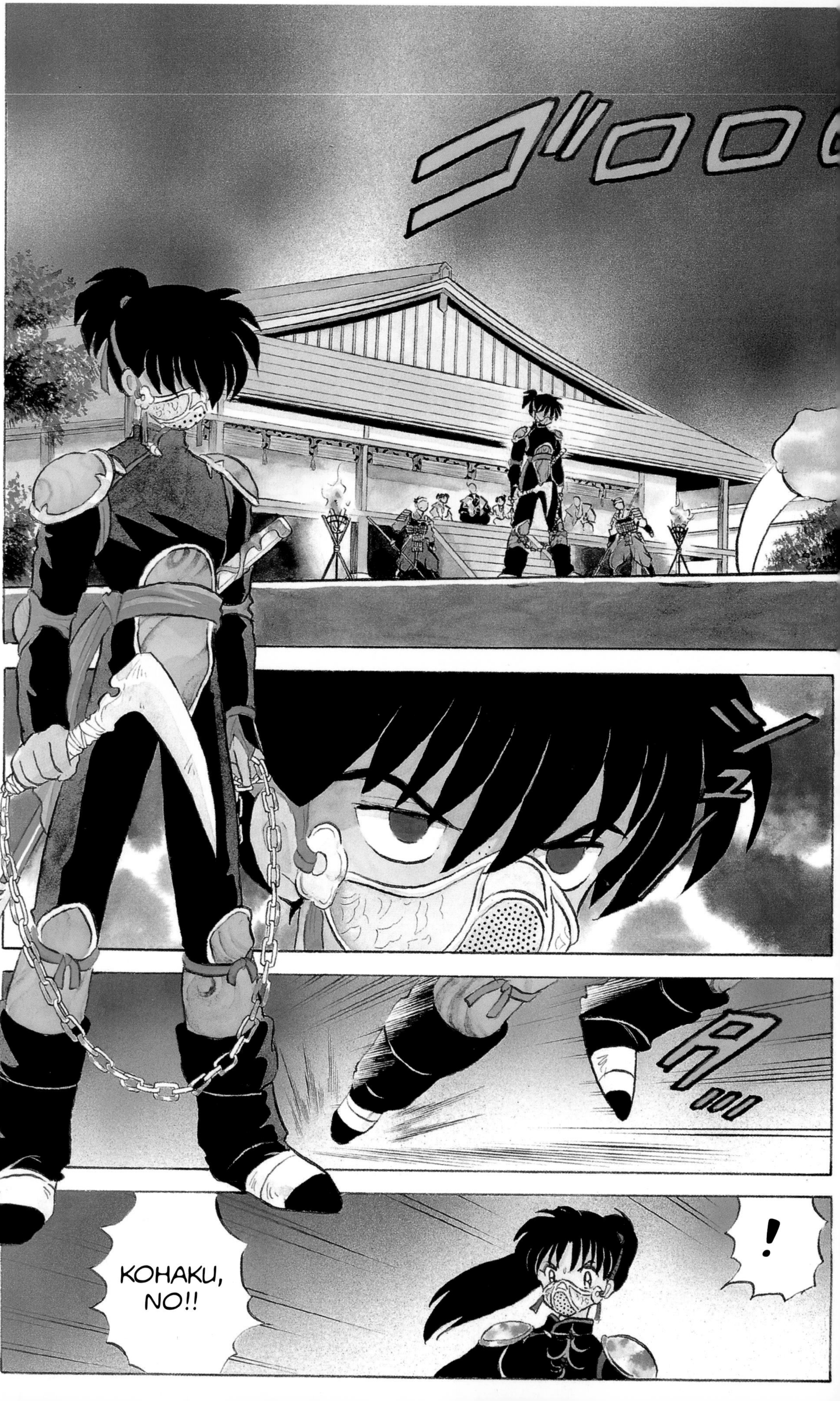
!
KOHAKU, NO!!

OGUMO ("GREAT SPIDER")

This demon attacks Hitomijo Castle in the night. It was one of the traps Naraku laid to destroy the exterminators. It was easily killed by Sango and the villagers. Ancient people believed that old spiders develop supernatural powers and become demons. Like kappa and oni, Ogumo often appear in books of ghost stories and anthropological records.

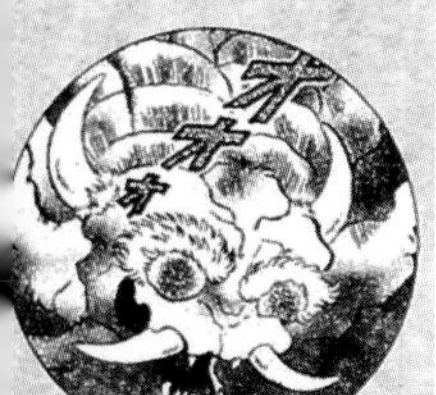

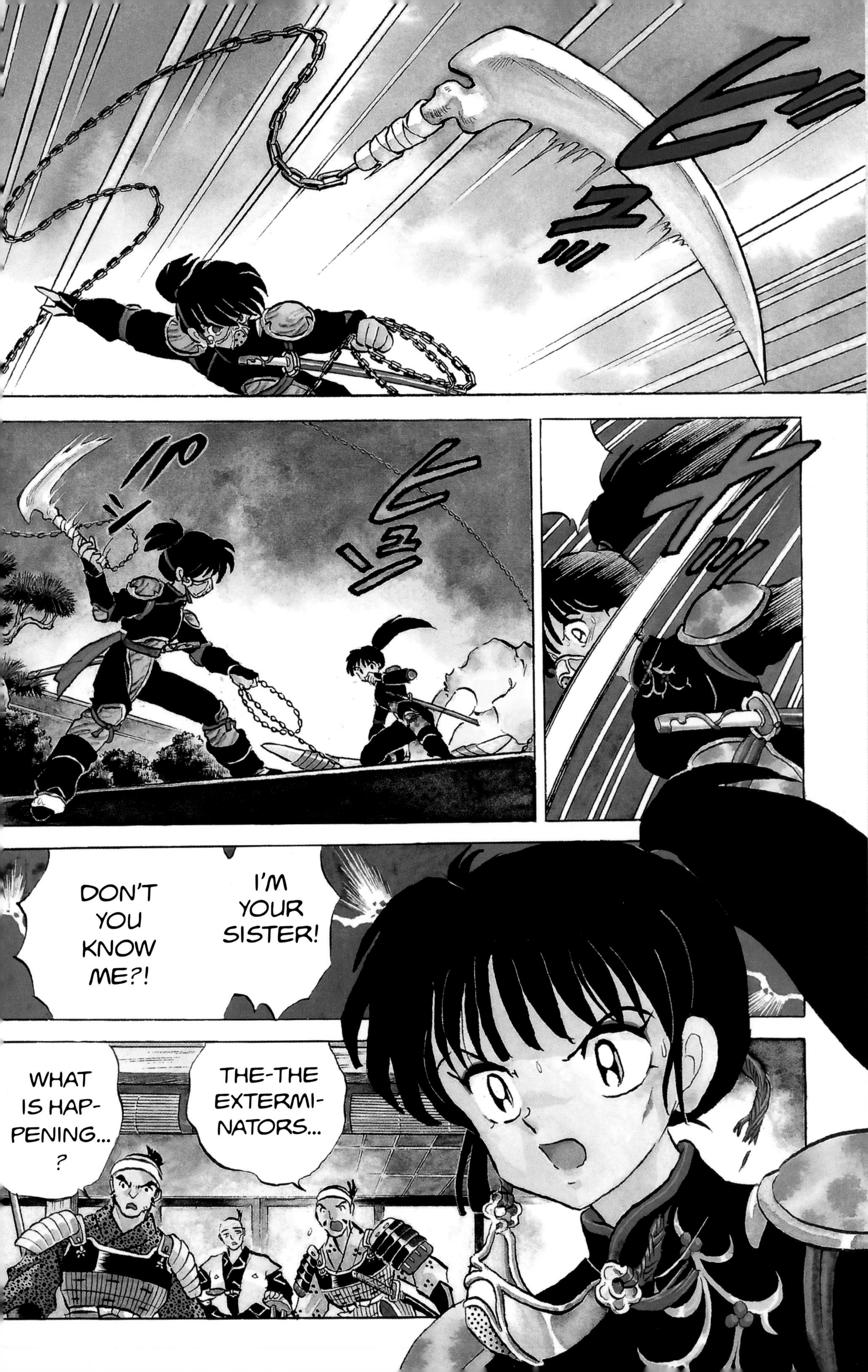
I'M YOUR SISTER!
DON'T YOU KNOW ME?!
THE-THE EXTERMI- NATORS...
WHAT IS HAP- PENING... ?

The Lord of Hitomijo

Like the Ogumo, he is a trap laid by Naraku. When Sango and the villagers were too busy to do anything other than fight the Onigumo, this demon enchants Kohaku and has him attack his sister. He gets his comeuppance for the destruction when Naraku kills him. During the commotion, Naraku succeeds in collecting a Shikon shard from the exterminator village. Using Sango to attack Inuyasha is an improvisation.

▲

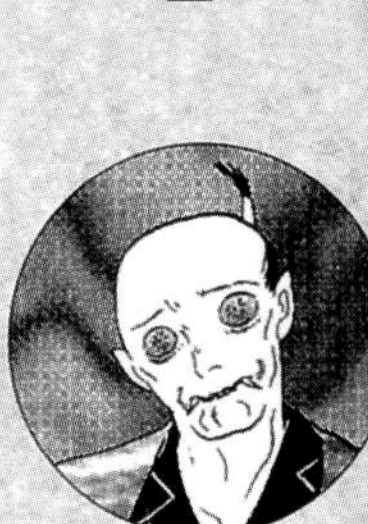

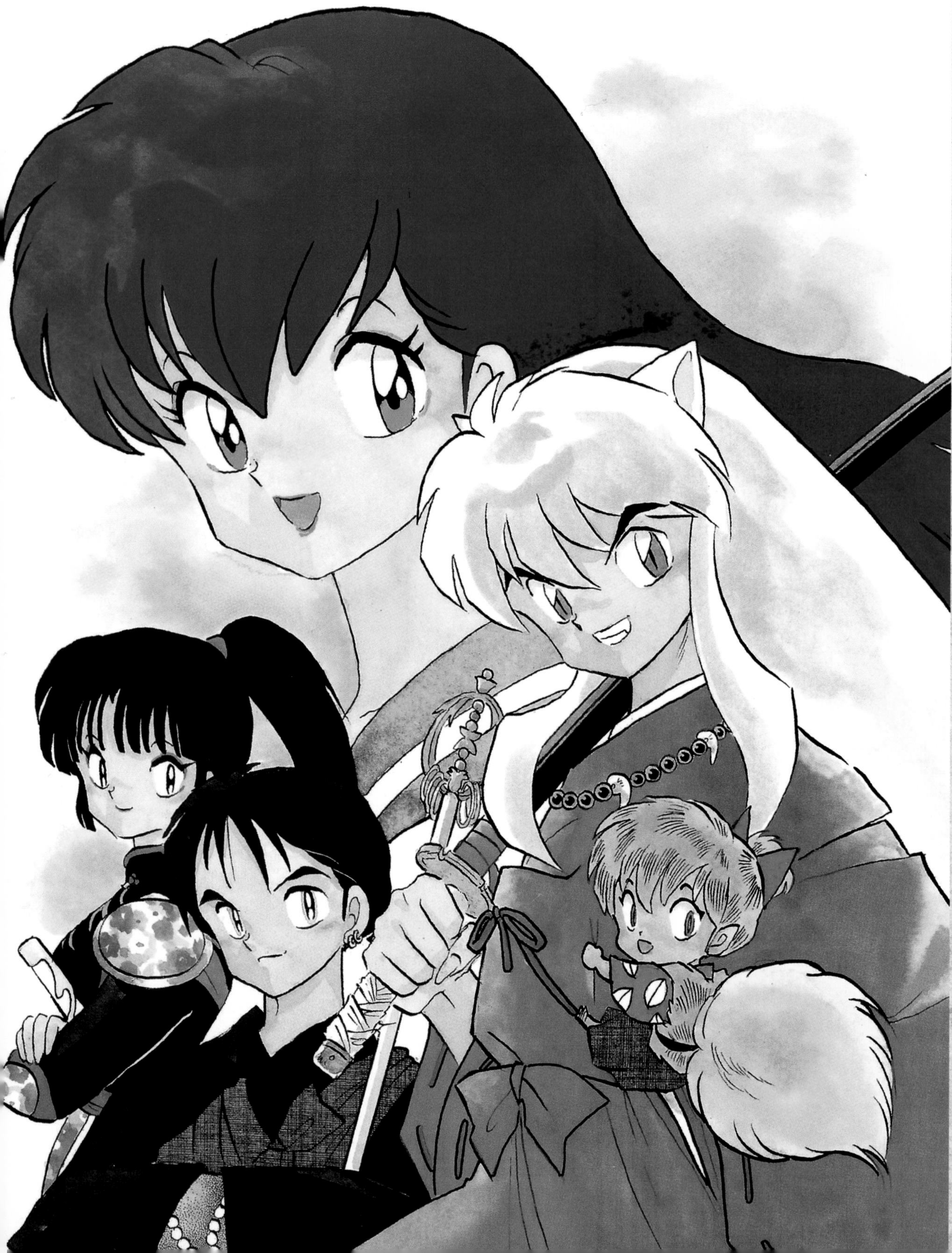

SCROLL 100

THE SLAYING OF THE SNAKE

Shonen Sunday Vol. 1, 1999
and Comic Vol. 11

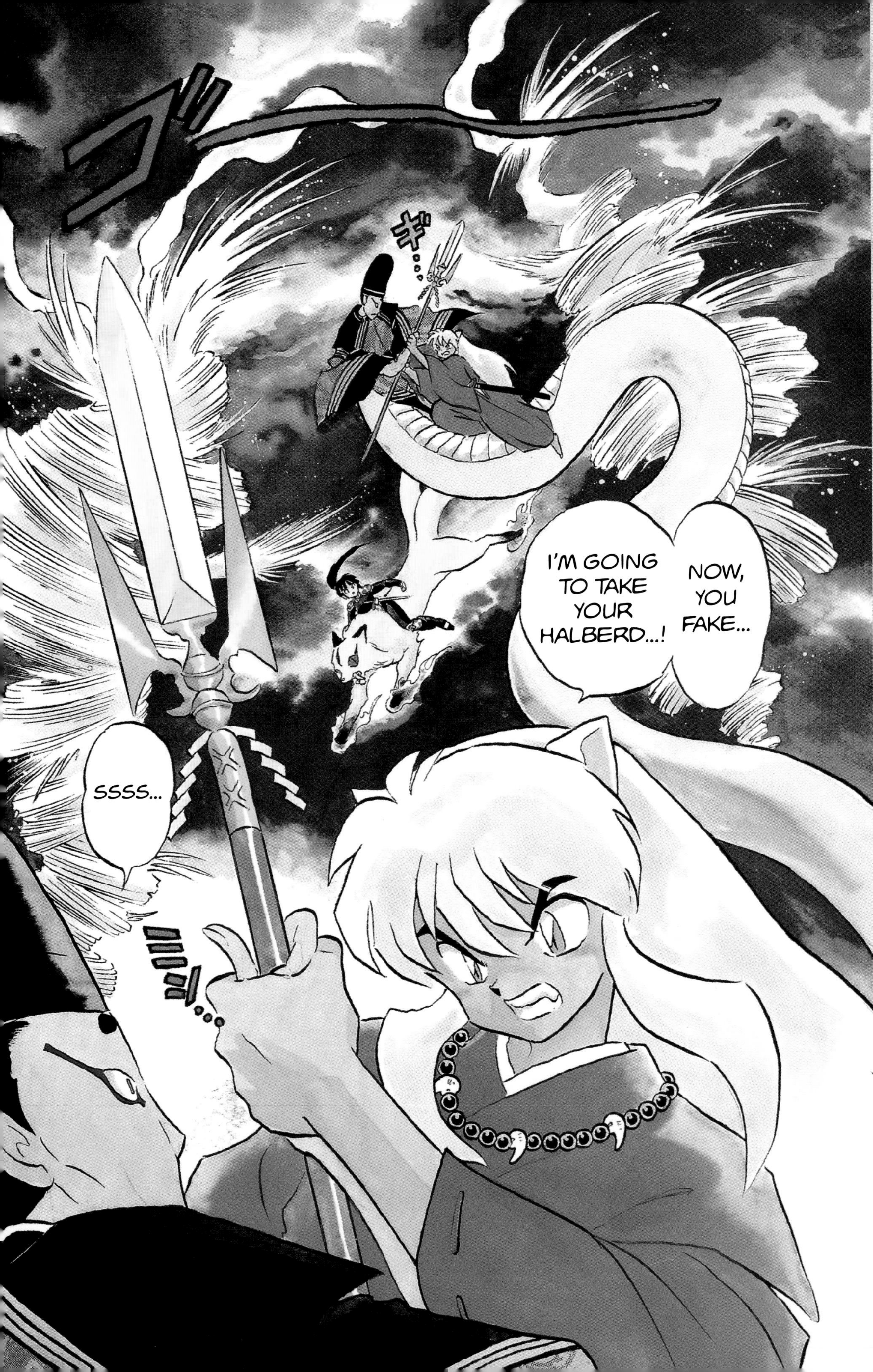
NOW, YOU FAKE...
I'M GOING TO TAKE YOUR HALBERD...!
SSSS...

NISE SUIJIN ("FALSE WATER GOD")

This is the disguise of Daija ("great snake"), who seals up the true water god, steals her sacred halberd and takes her place. He demands human offerings from the lakeside village and lives on the sacrificed children. Asked to kill the false water god by Taro-maru, the headman's son, Inuyasha gives him a fatal slash. The snake expires on being sucked into Miroku's tunnel. The halberd is returned safely to the true Suijin.

▲

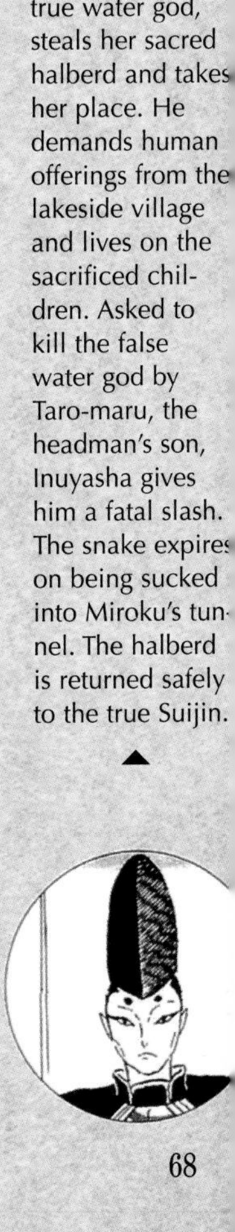

SCROLL 109

NARAKU'S CASTLE

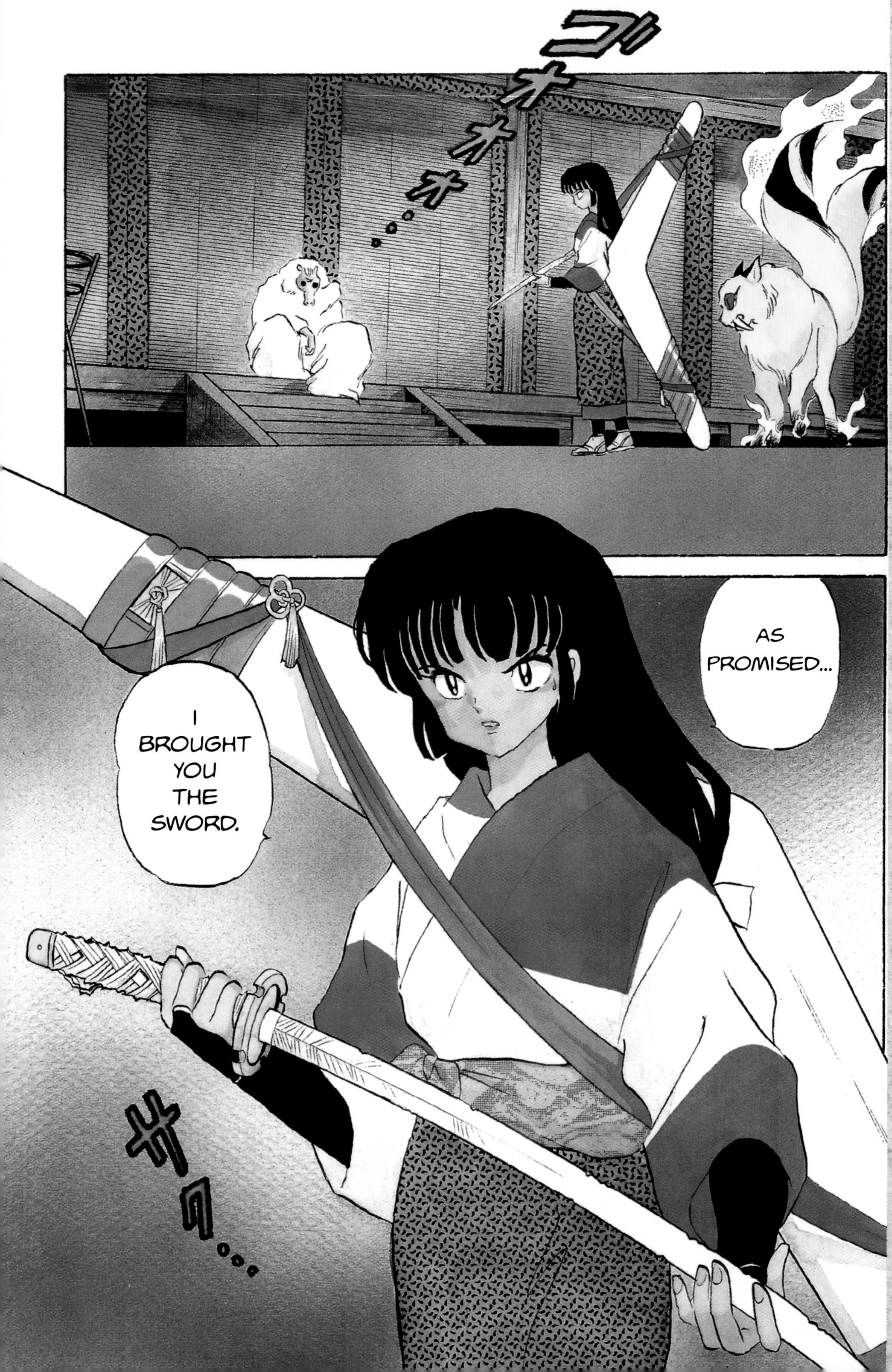
ゴオオオ…
AS PROMISED...
I BROUGHT YOU THE SWORD.
ギク…

Shonen Sunday Vol. 12, 199
and Comic Vol. 12

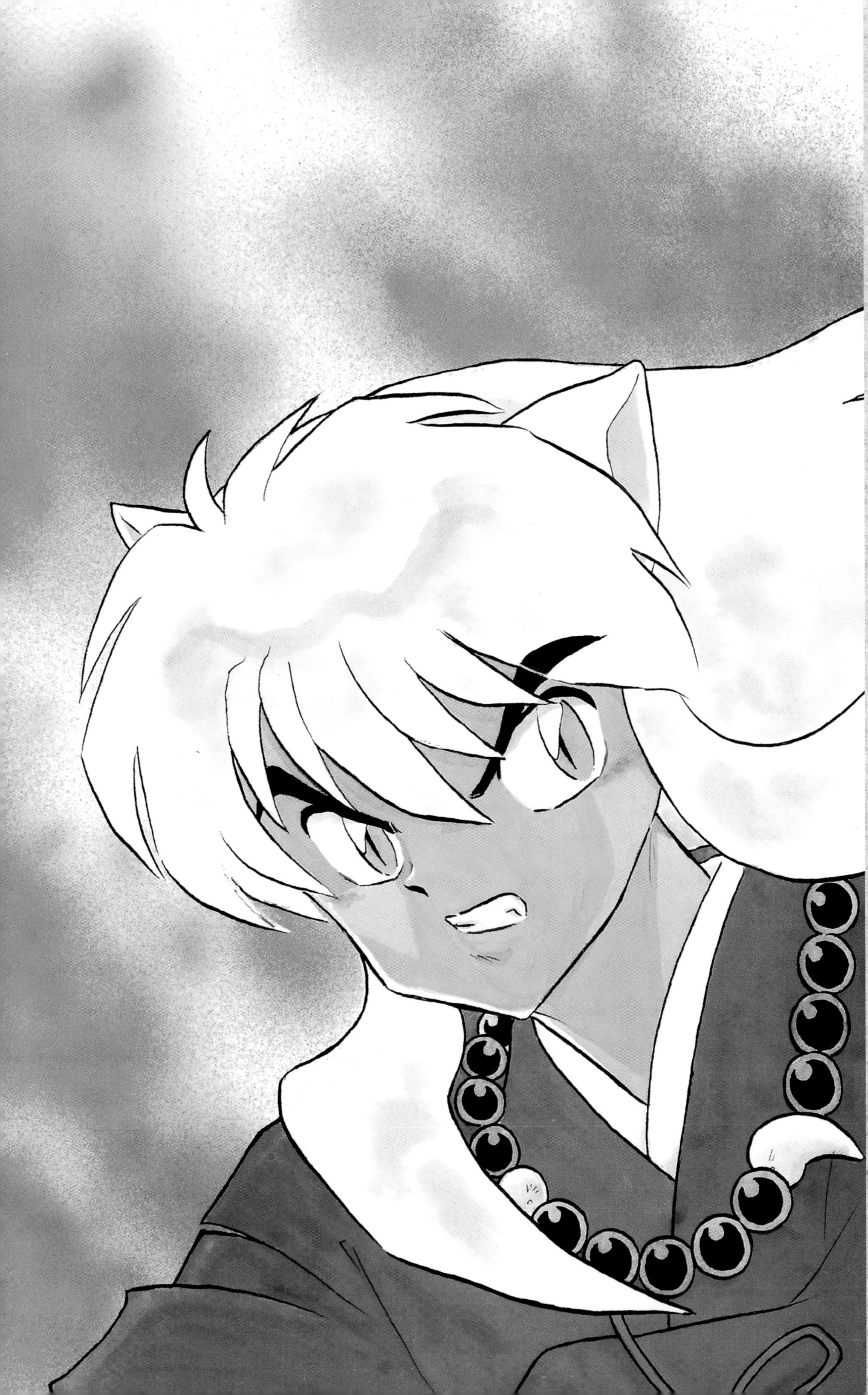

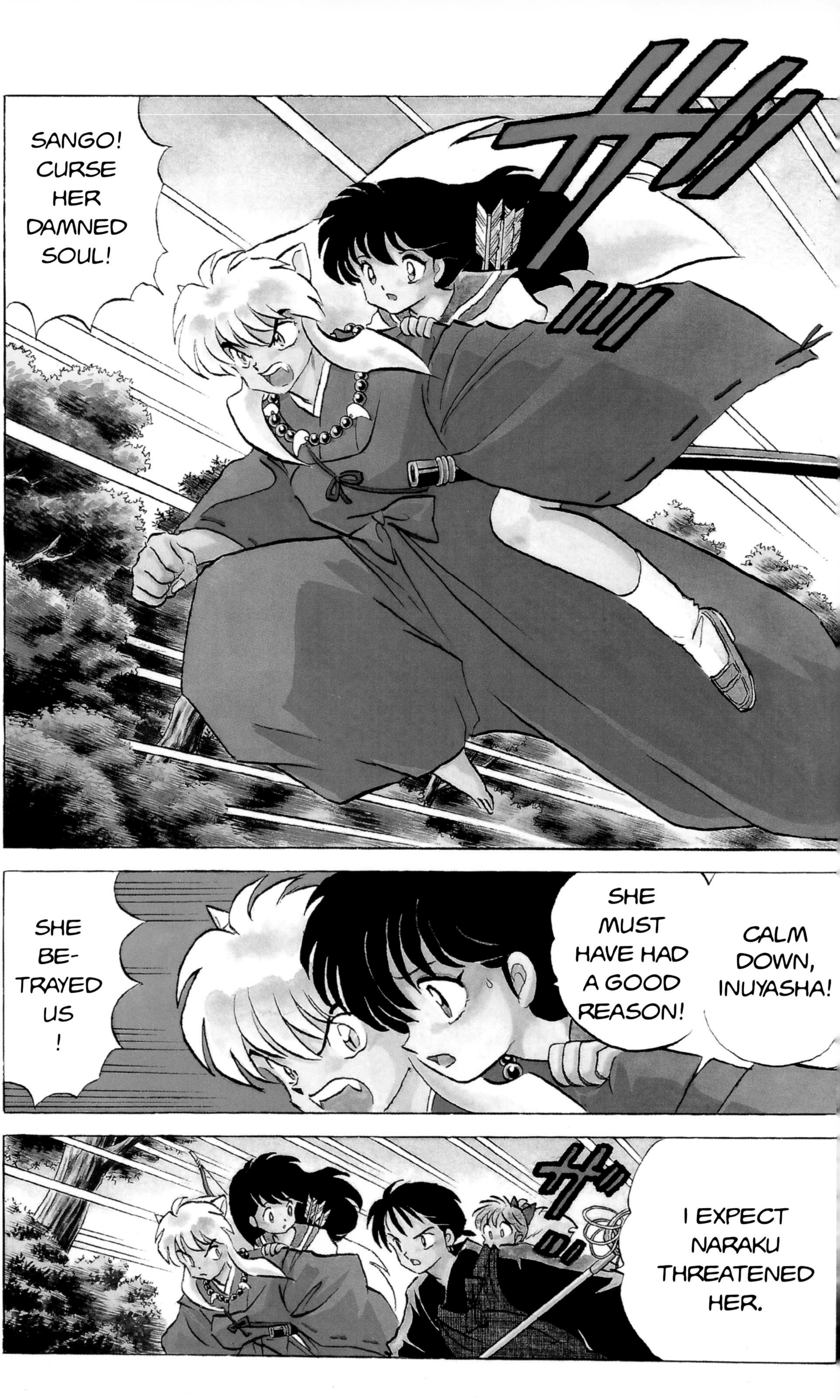
SANGO! CURSE HER DAMNED SOUL!
CALM DOWN, INUYASHA!
SHE MUST HAVE HAD A GOOD REASON!
SHE BE-TRAYED US!
I EXPECT NARAKU THREATENED HER.

WANDERING KOHAKU

Kohaku, enchanted by Naraku, kills his father and friends and is killed himself. Later Naraku revives his body with a shard of the Jewel. Naraku uses him as a hostage to force Sango to steal Tetsusaiga, then sends him to kill Kagome. To recover his memory, Kohaku must recall killing his father, but he adamantly refuses.

▲

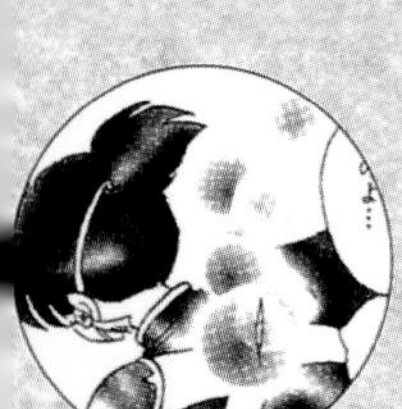

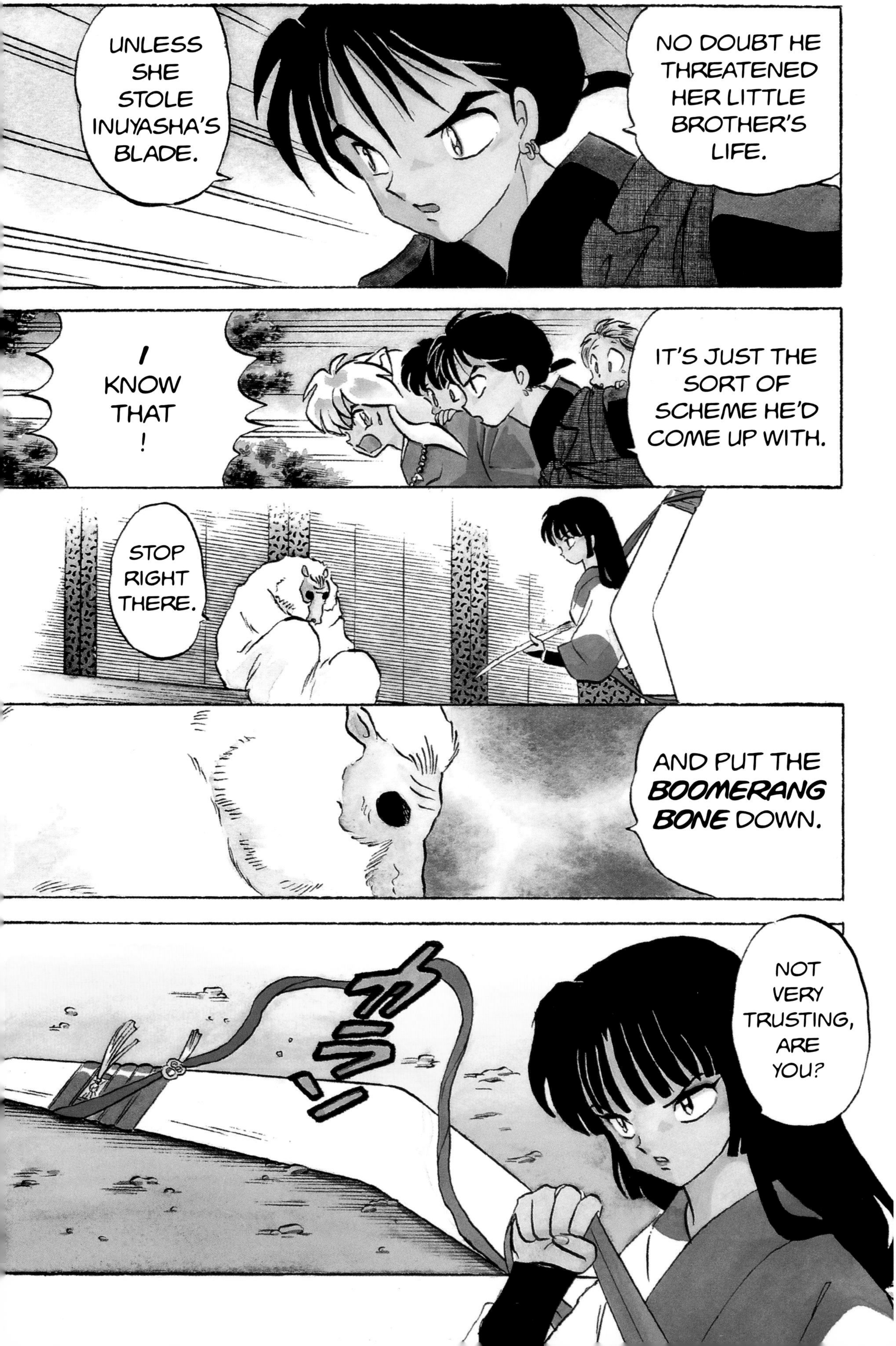
NO DOUBT HE THREATENED HER LITTLE BROTHER'S LIFE.
UNLESS SHE STOLE INUYASHA'S BLADE.
IT'S JUST THE SORT OF SCHEME HE'D COME UP WITH.
I KNOW THAT!
STOP RIGHT THERE.
AND PUT THE BOOMERANG BONE DOWN.
NOT VERY TRUSTING, ARE YOU?

GOLEMS

These are demon puppets that Naraku controls. They are made of earth and a bit of Naraku's hair wound onto a doll. Because they don't carry strong demonic auras, even Sango doesn't see their true nature. Naraku fears Kagome's arrows, so he uses golems in his place when he appears to the Inuyasha party.

▲

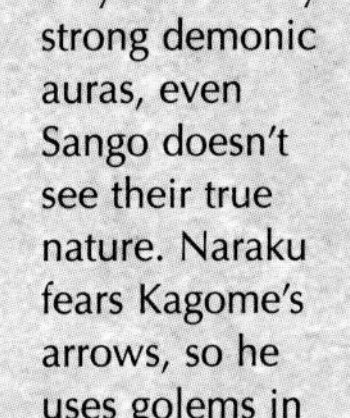

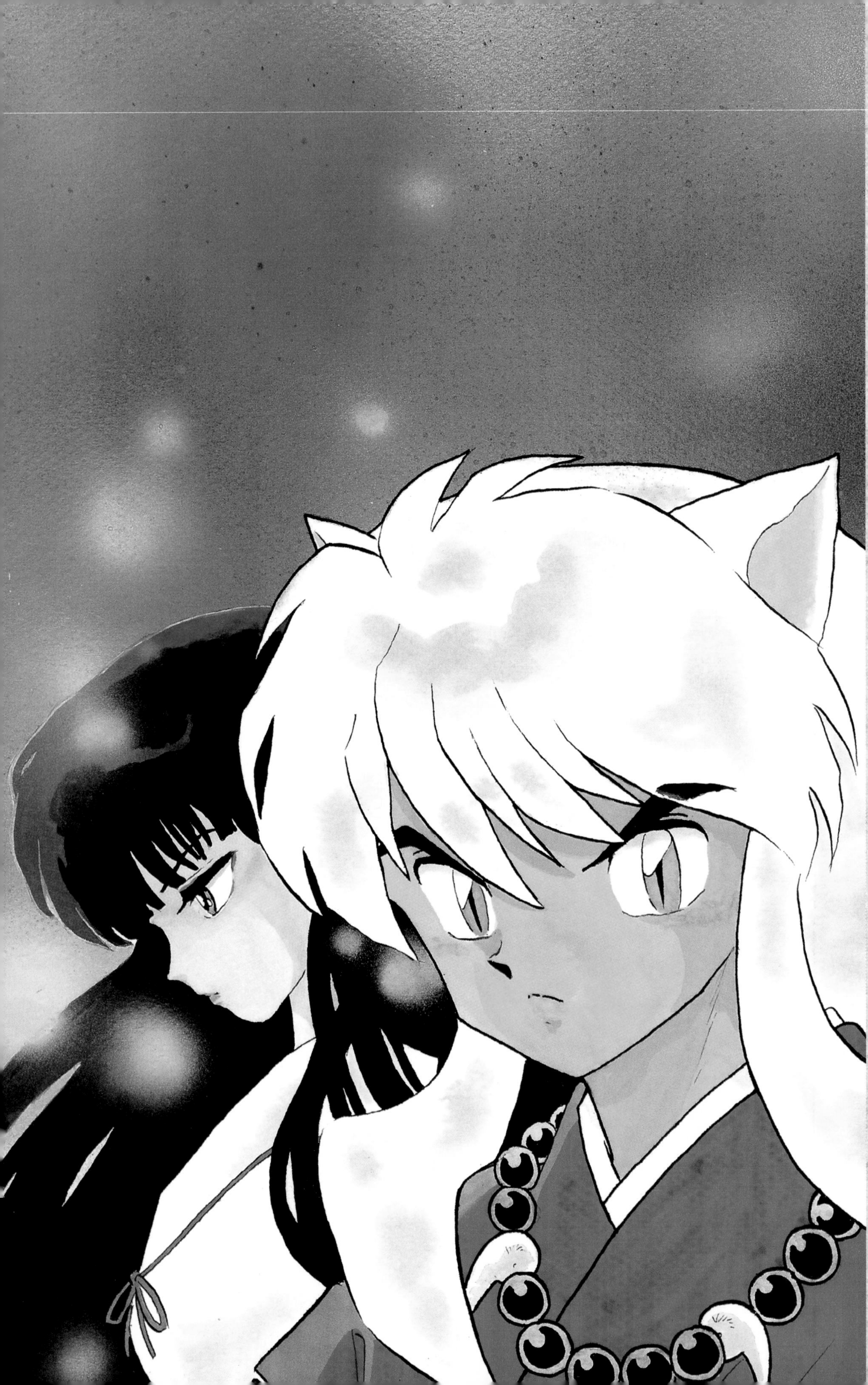

SCROLL 124

NARAKU'S IDENTITY

Shonen Sunday Vol. 28, 1999
and Comic Vol. 13

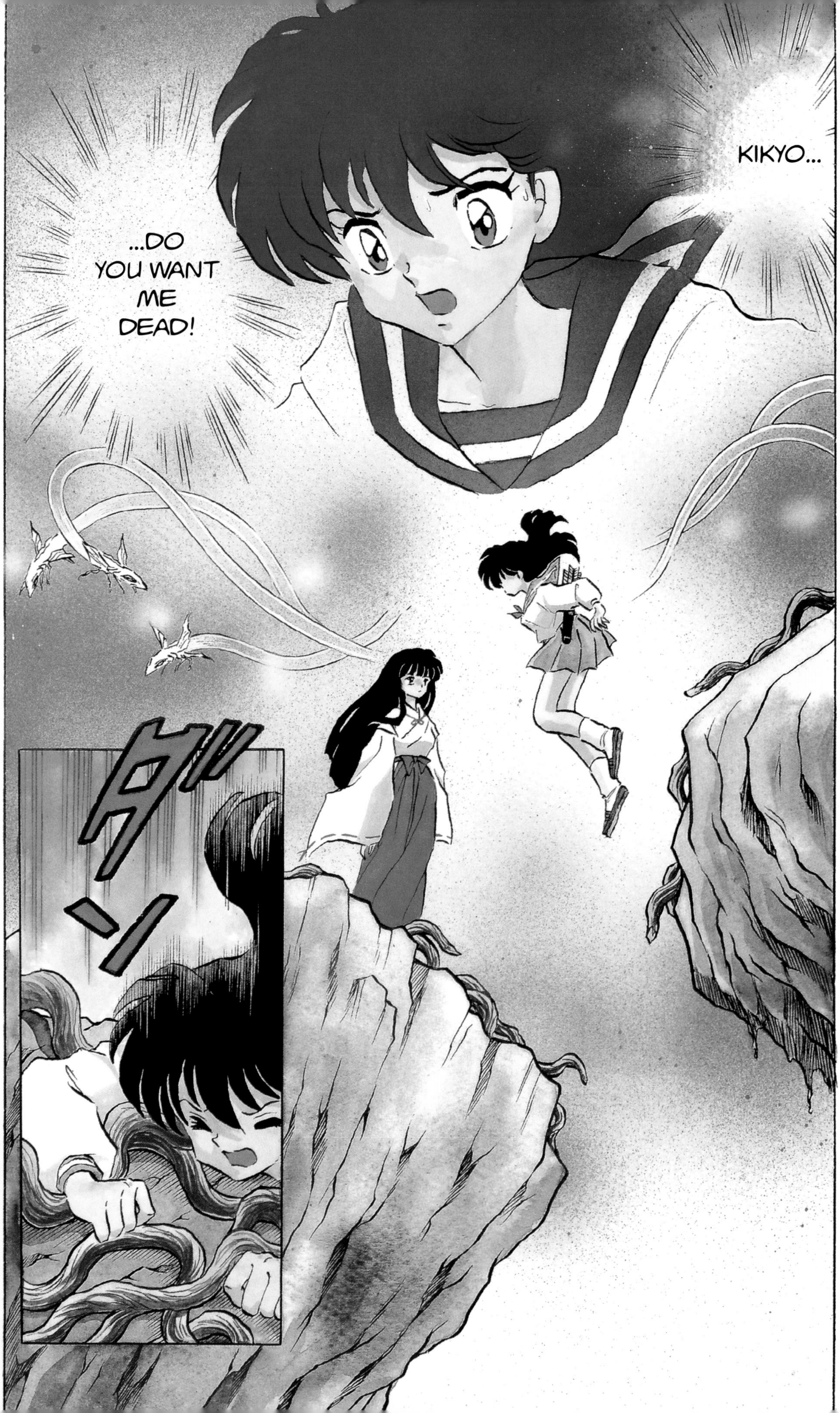
KIKYO...
...DO YOU WANT ME DEAD!

SPELL OF ILLUSORY DEATH

Naraku lays this trap for the Inuyasha group. When they touch an aura of negative human emotion, like sadness, fear or doubt, tentacles spread through the forest to trap the owners of these emotions and eat their souls. Inuyasha relives the scene of 50 years before, Miroku feels his cursed hand running amok, Sango sees Kohaku attacking her. The spell has no effect on Kagome.

▲

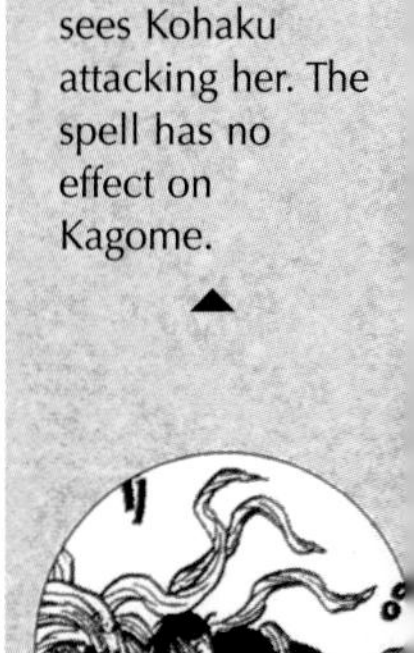

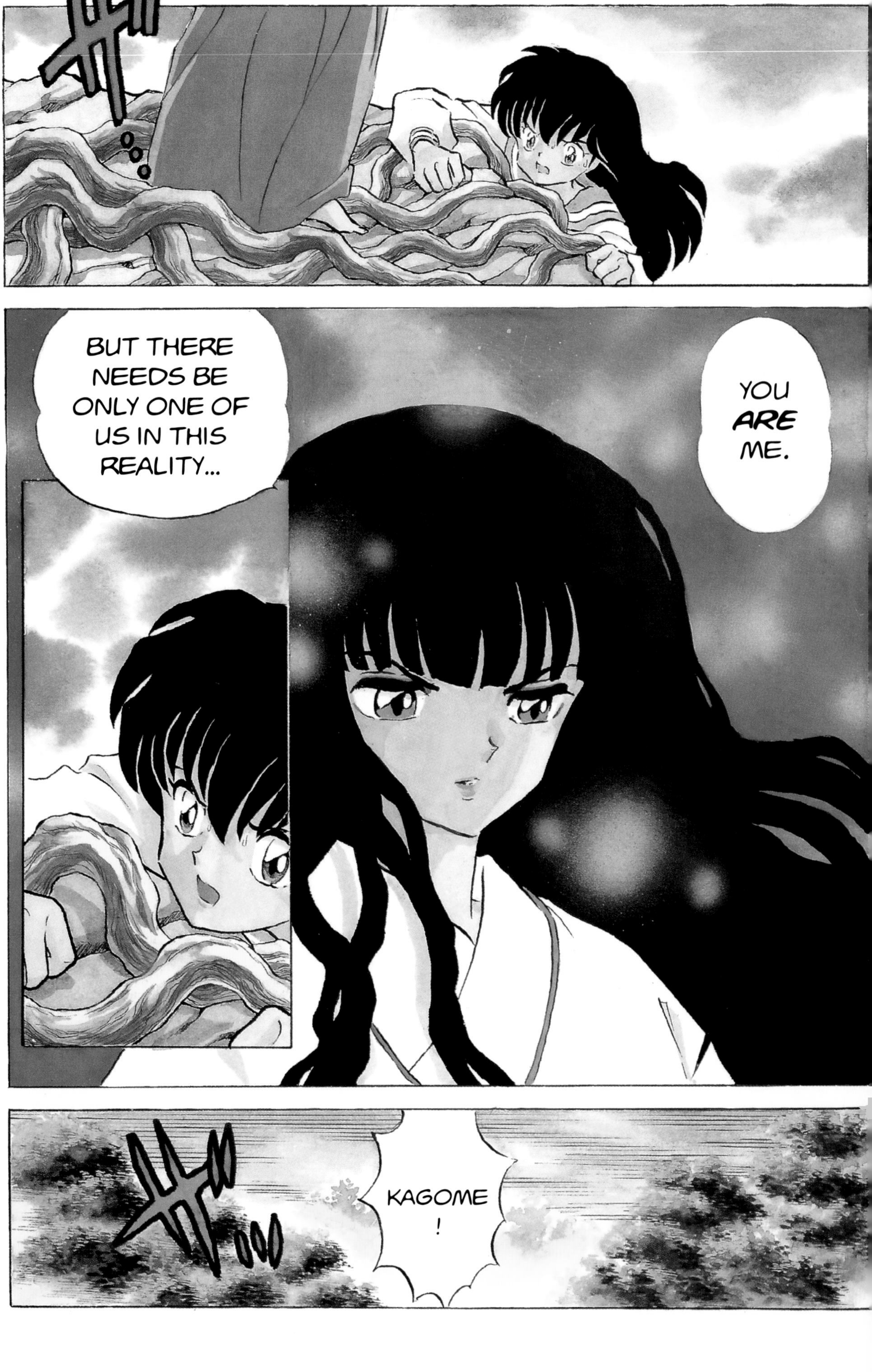
YOU ARE ME.
BUT THERE NEEDS BE ONLY ONE OF US IN THIS REALITY...
KAGOME!

Kikyo and Kagome

From the Urasue episode it's clear that Kagome is Kikyo's reincarnation, but perhaps not a simple one. Kagome revives after having her soul stolen by Kikyo, but she has too big a soul for Kanna's mirror to contain. She has enough supernatural power to eventually throw off Kikyo's binding spell. Kagome's true nature is gradually revealed.

▲

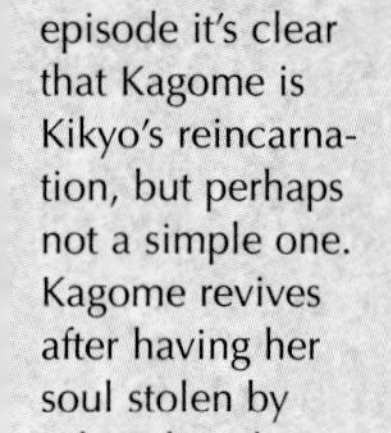

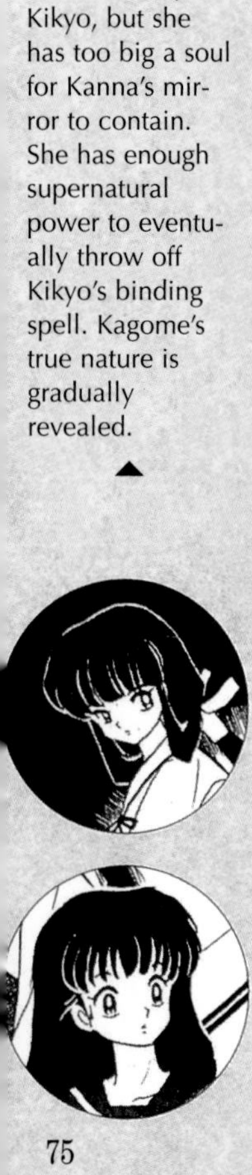

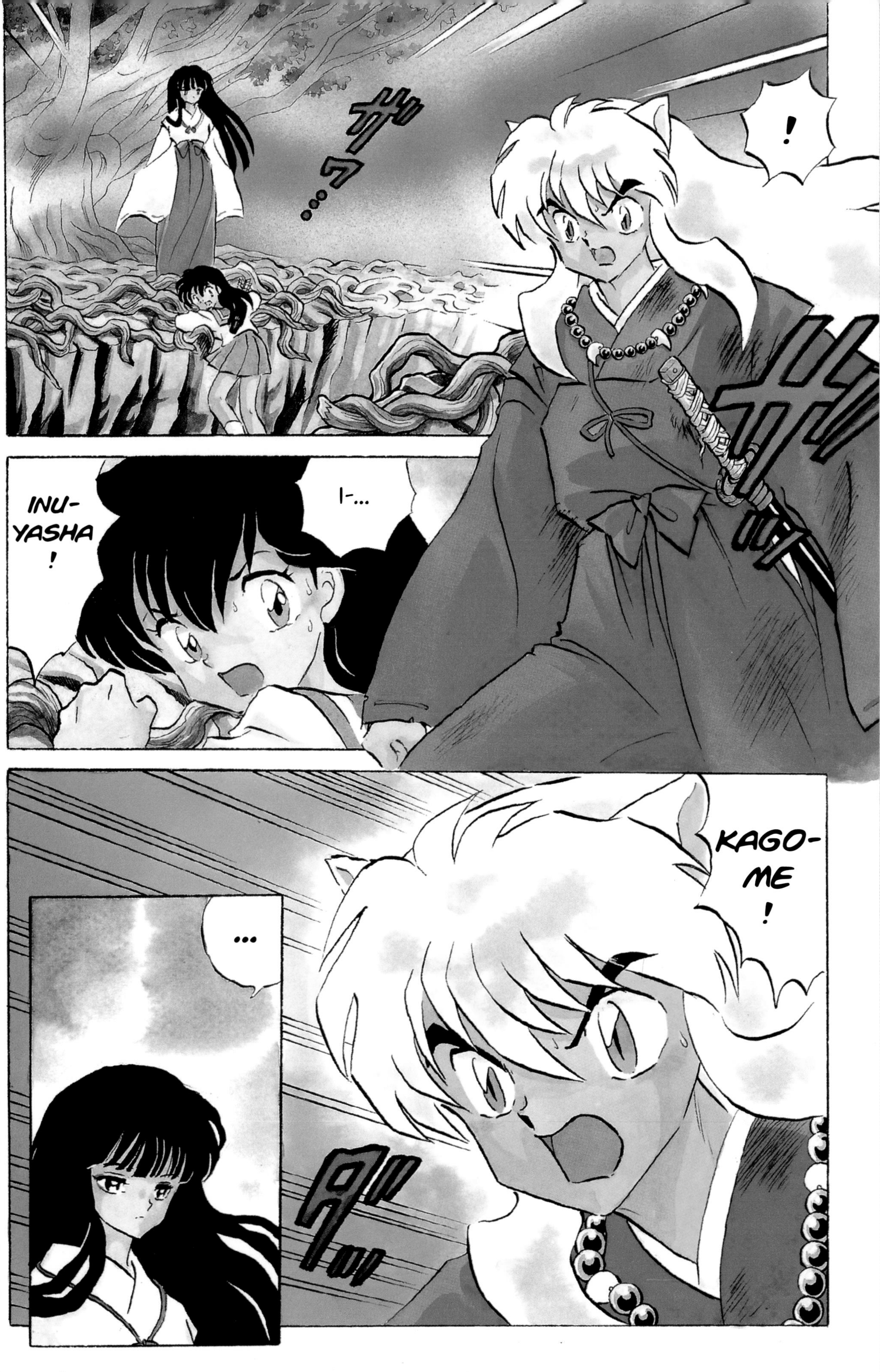

!
I-...
INU-YASHA!
KAGO-ME!
...

SHIKON SHARDS CHANGING HANDS

The Jewel of Four Souls came into Kikyo's hands from the exterminator village. It disappeared for centuries after Kikyo's death, but reappears in the modern world with Kagome. Kagome's party collects most of the shards, but the revived Kikyo steals them. As part of a plan unknown to us, Kikyo gives the shards to Naraku, who now has most of them.

▲

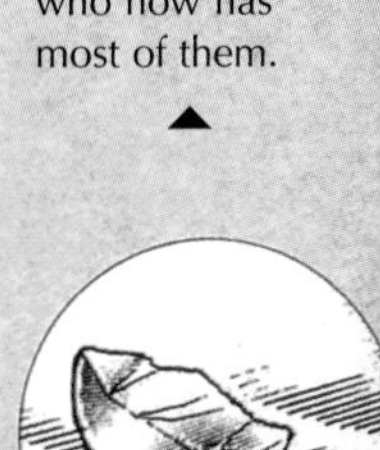

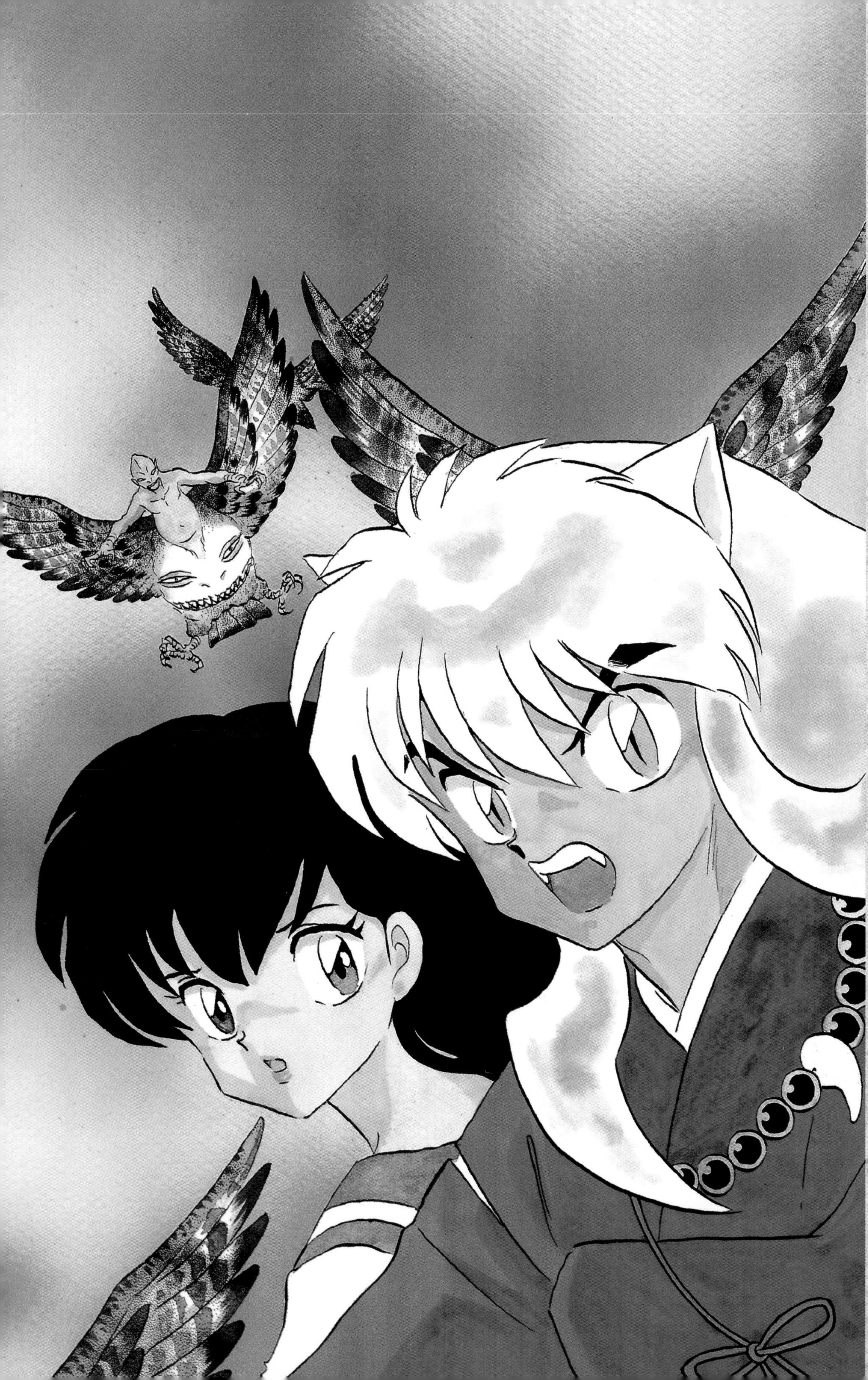

SCROLL 134

CAVE OF THE WOLVES

Shonen Sunday Vol. 39, 1999
and Comic Vol. 14

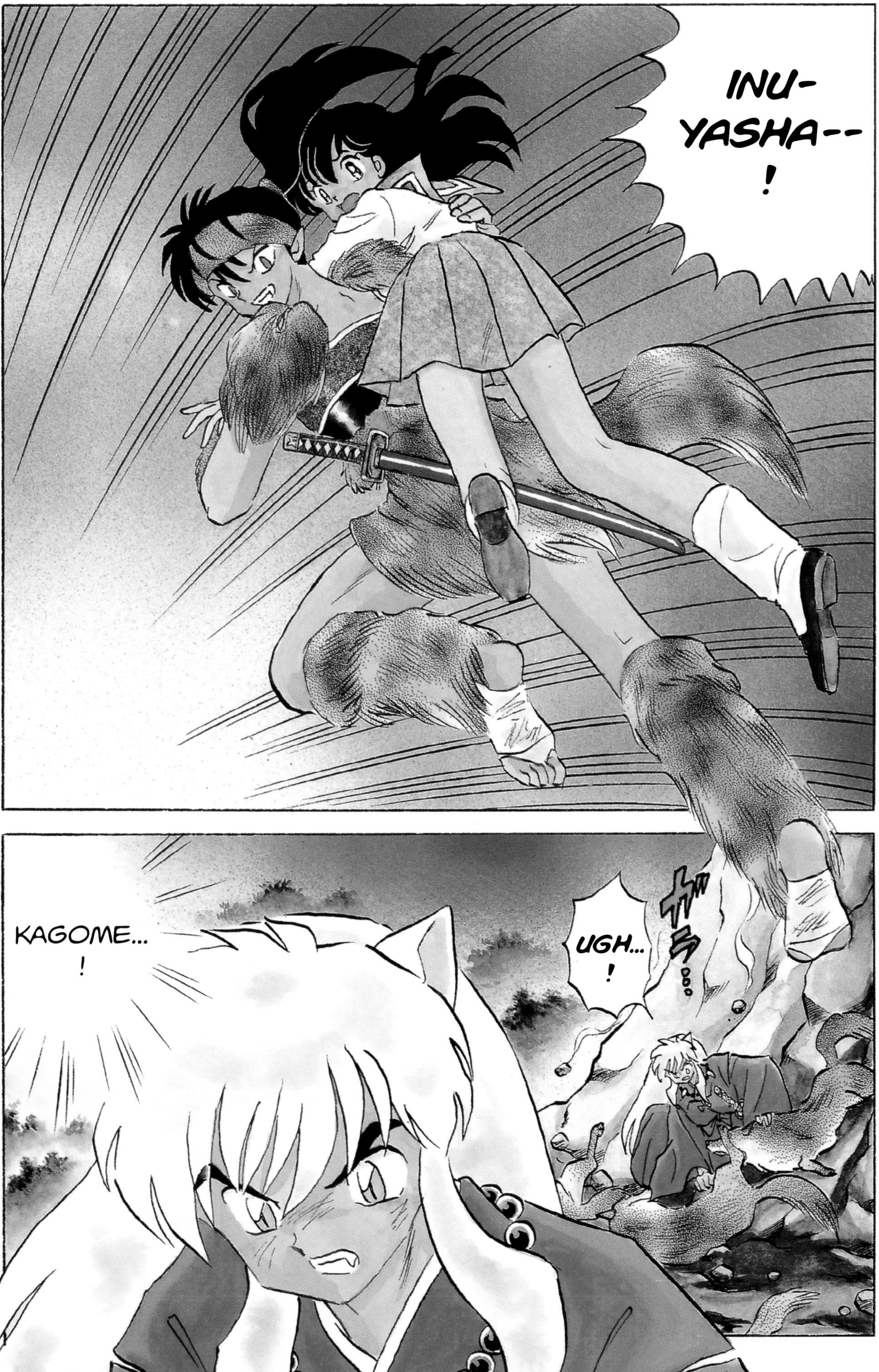
INU-YASHA--!
ガラ
UGH...!
KAGOME...!

WOLF DEMON TRIBE

This tribe of demons can manipulate man-eating wolves. Although they look like people, by nature they are as violent as wolves. They den in a cave behind a waterfall deep in the mountains. They fight the Birds of Paradise to collect shards of the Jewel. Koga, a young leader with shards embedded in his body, commands the clan's battle with the Birds of Paradise.

▲

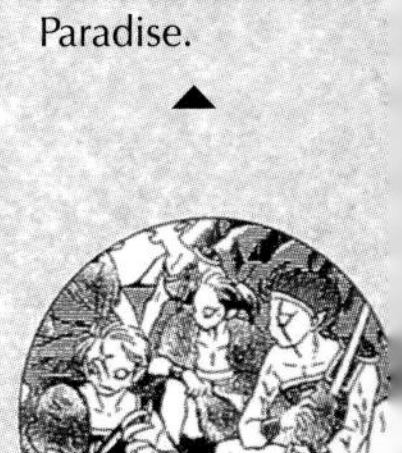

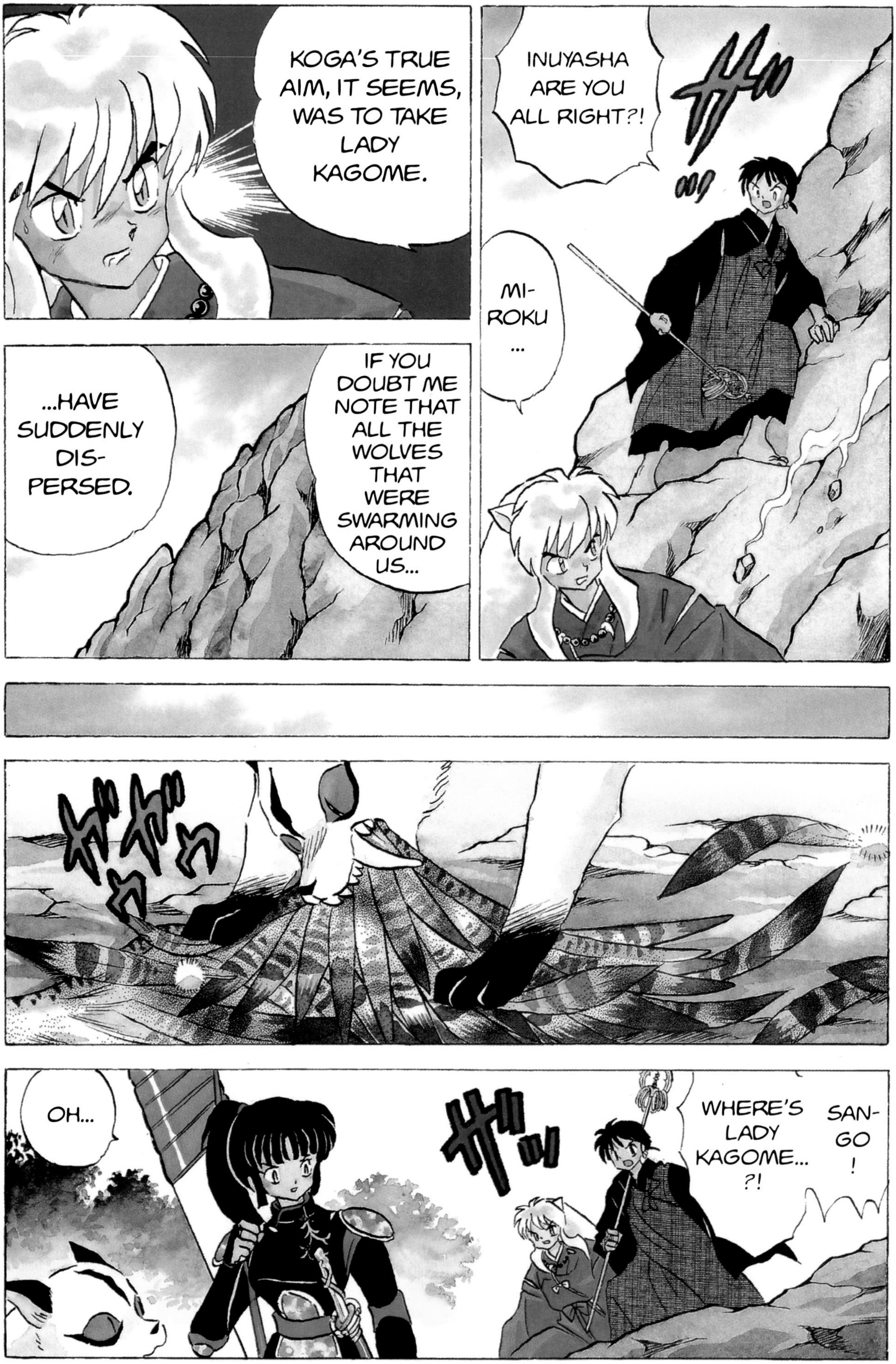
INUYASHA ARE YOU ALL RIGHT?!
MI-ROKU...
KOGA'S TRUE AIM, IT SEEMS, WAS TO TAKE LADY KAGOME.
IF YOU DOUBT ME NOTE THAT ALL THE WOLVES THAT WERE SWARMING AROUND US...
...HAVE SUDDENLY DIS-PERSED.
SAN-GO!
WHERE'S LADY KAGOME...?!
OH...

Birds of Paradise or Harpies (gokurakucho)

These are demon birds with humanlike heads and torsos who nest on a perpendicular cliff. They wage a continuing battle with the Yorozoku and prey on them. The cause, of course, is the Shikon shards. In the battle that involves Kagome, some are slashed by Tetsusaiga and others are hit by Sango's boomerang; most fall victim to Miroku's tunnel.

▲

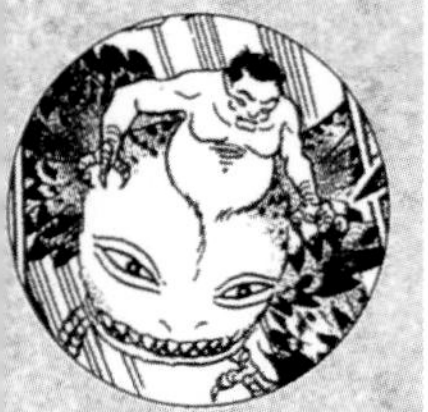

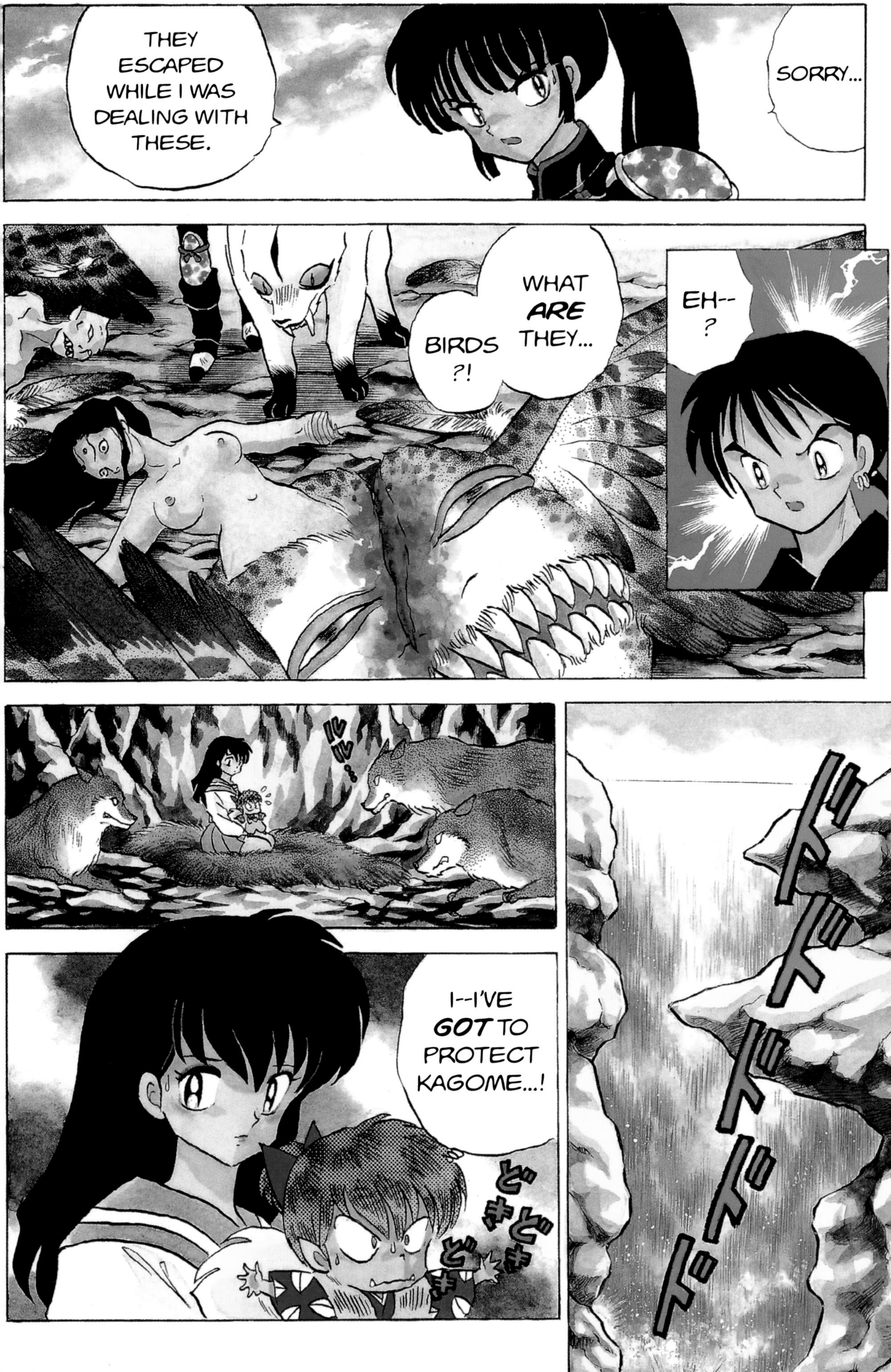
SORRY...
THEY ESCAPED WHILE I WAS DEALING WITH THESE.
EH--?
WHAT **ARE** THEY...
BIRDS?!
I--I'VE **GOT** TO PROTECT KAGOME...!
どきどき

THE BIRD OF PARADISE

Carrying the upper bodies of two brothers, the head bird is several times larger than the ordinary Bird of Paradise. He has a Shikon shard inside his huge mouth. The elder half falls to Koga's powerful arm. The younger half tries to steal the shard from Koga's arm, but Inuyasha saves the day. Tetsusaiga slashes the demon's kaze no kizu and smashes the great bird to bits.

▲

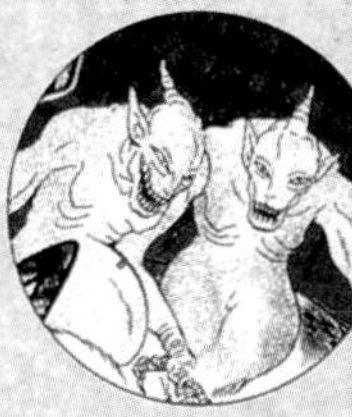

SCROLL 144
MANIPULATOR OF THE WIND

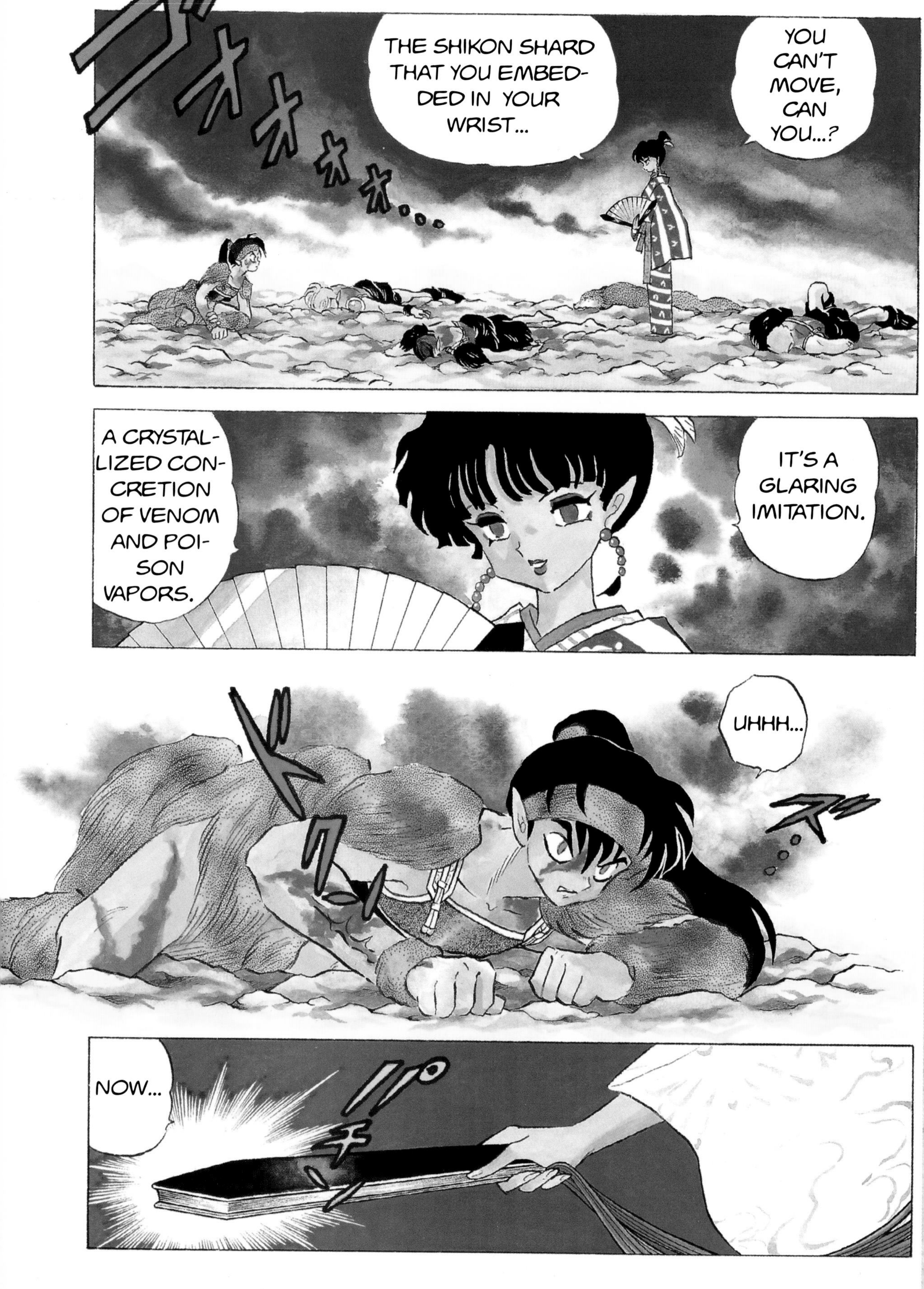
ゴオオオオ…
YOU CAN'T MOVE, CAN YOU...?
THE SHIKON SHARD THAT YOU EMBED-DED IN YOUR WRIST...
IT'S A GLARING IMITATION.
A CRYSTAL-LIZED CON-CRETION OF VENOM AND POI-SON VAPORS.
UHHH...
ズ…
ドクン
NOW...
パキ

Shonen Sunday Vol. 50, 1999, and Comic Vol. 15

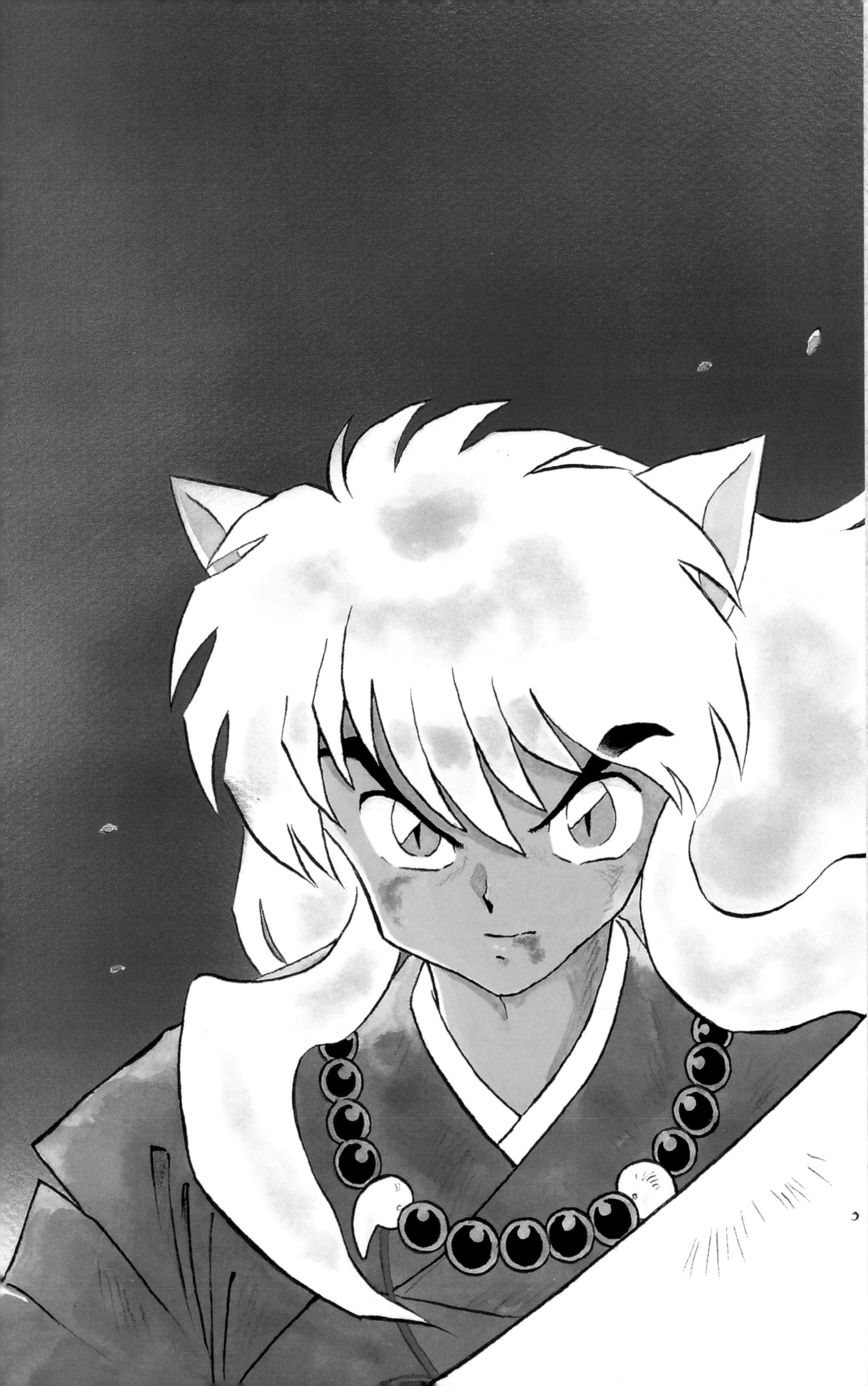

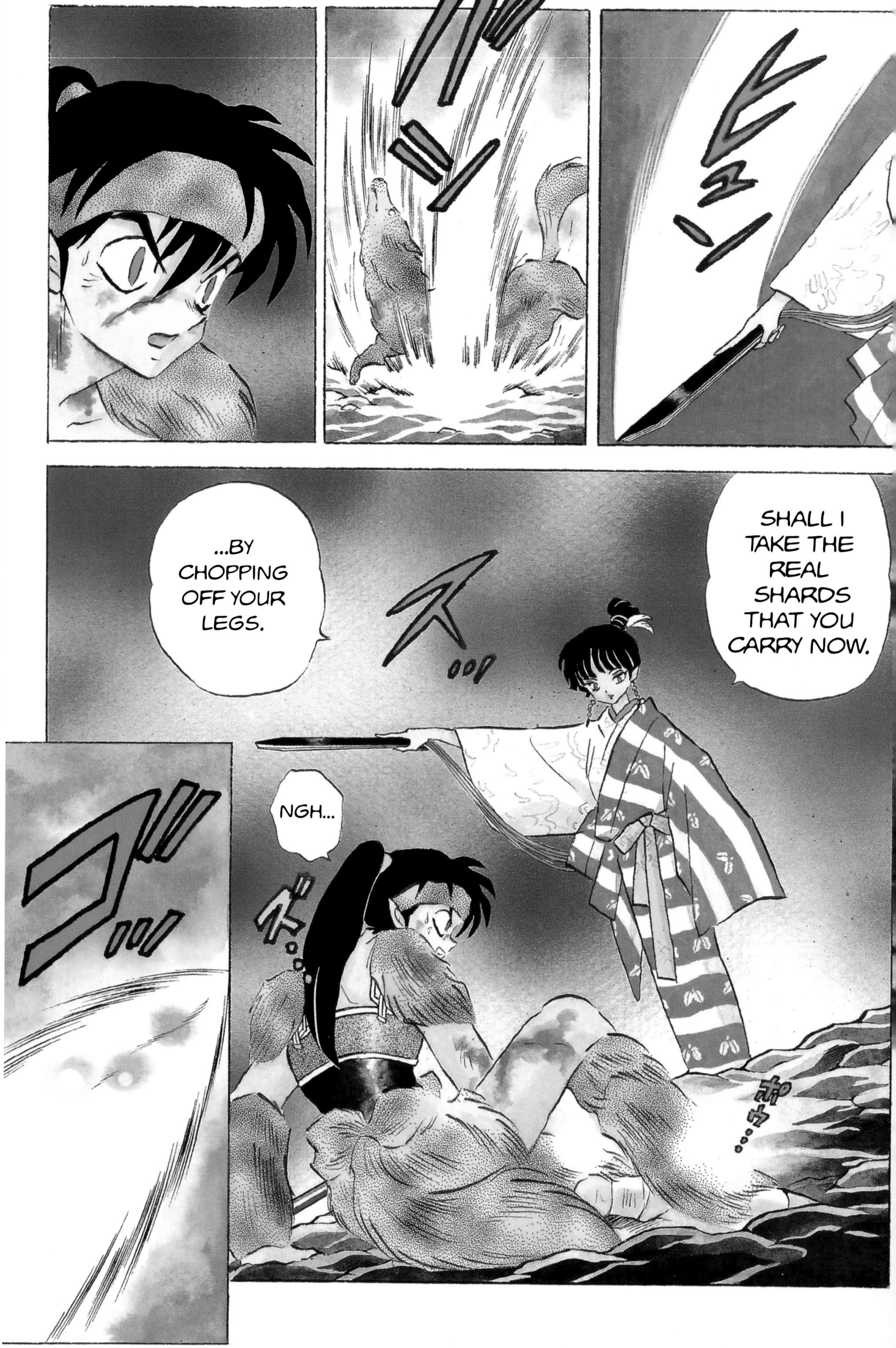
SHALL I TAKE THE REAL SHARDS THAT YOU CARRY NOW.
...BY CHOPPING OFF YOUR LEGS.
NGH...

KAGURA

A demon alter ego of Naraku, made from his own body after acquiring the Shikon shards from Kikyo. By manipulating corpses with a dance, she traps Koga and Inuyasha. She also uses sorcery, like the Fuujin no Mai ("dance of wind blades"), which with a fan can cut flesh without touching it. She dislikes Naraku, but she cannot oppose the master who controls her soul.

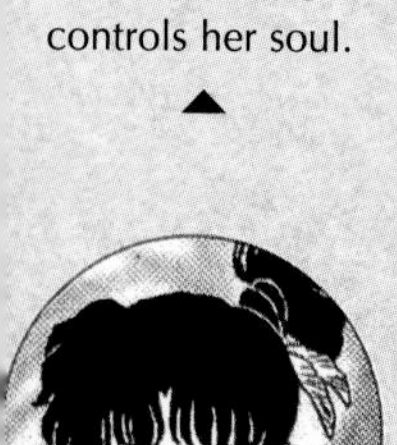

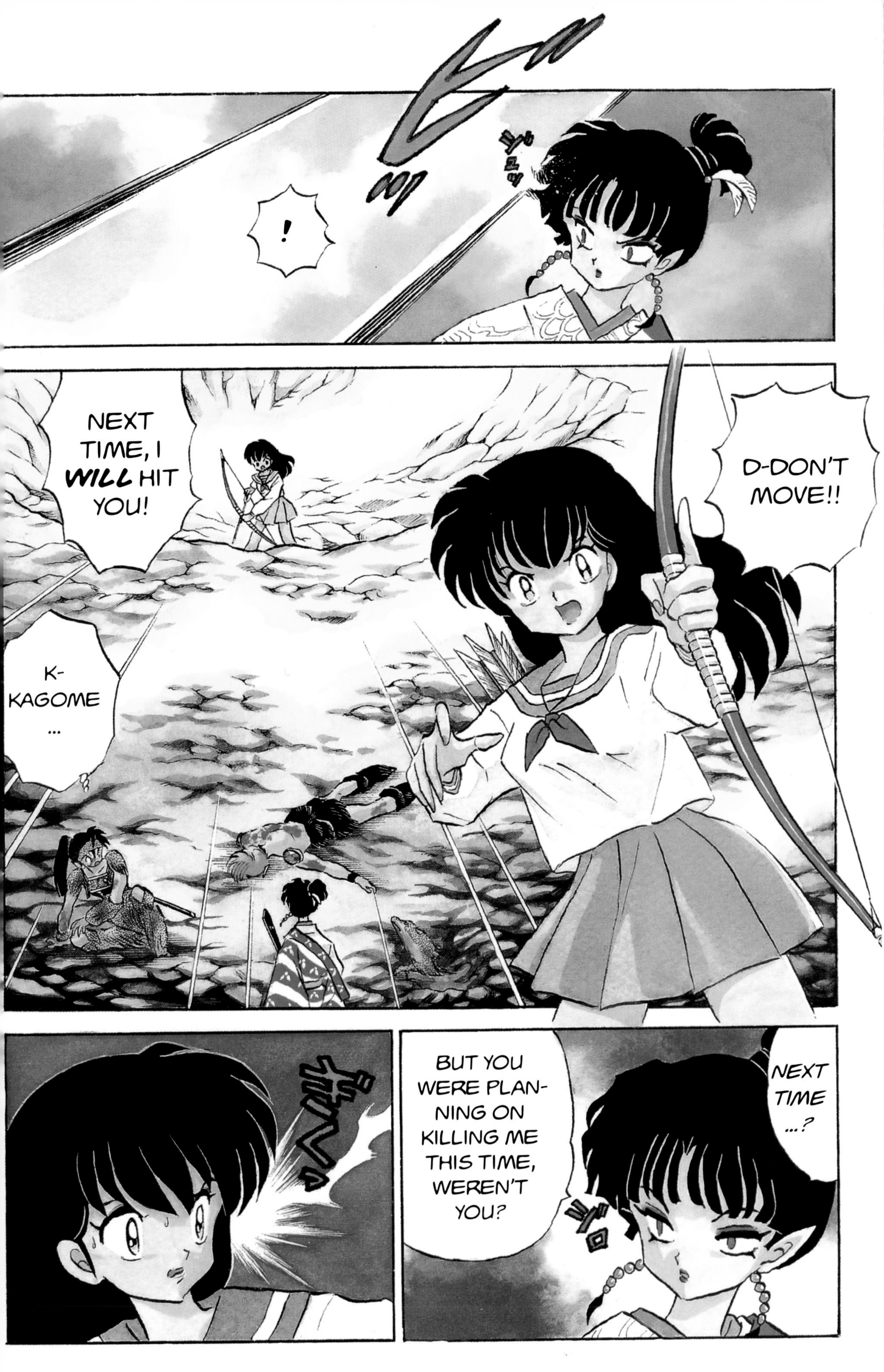
!
D-DON'T MOVE!!
NEXT TIME, I ***WILL*** HIT YOU!
K-KAGOME ...
NEXT TIME ...?
BUT YOU WERE PLANNING ON KILLING ME THIS TIME, WEREN'T YOU?

KANNA (CANNA LILY)

Like her youger sister Kagura, she is an alter ego of Naraku. While Kagura manipulates the wind, Kanna manipulates emptiness, so she carries no detectable demonic aura. She traps the souls of her opponents in a mirror and controls their psyches. She also has the power to reflect an attack back on an opponent; the exception is Kagome's arrow.

▲

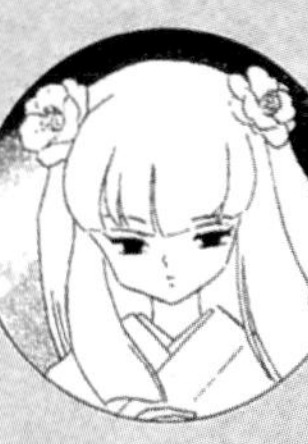

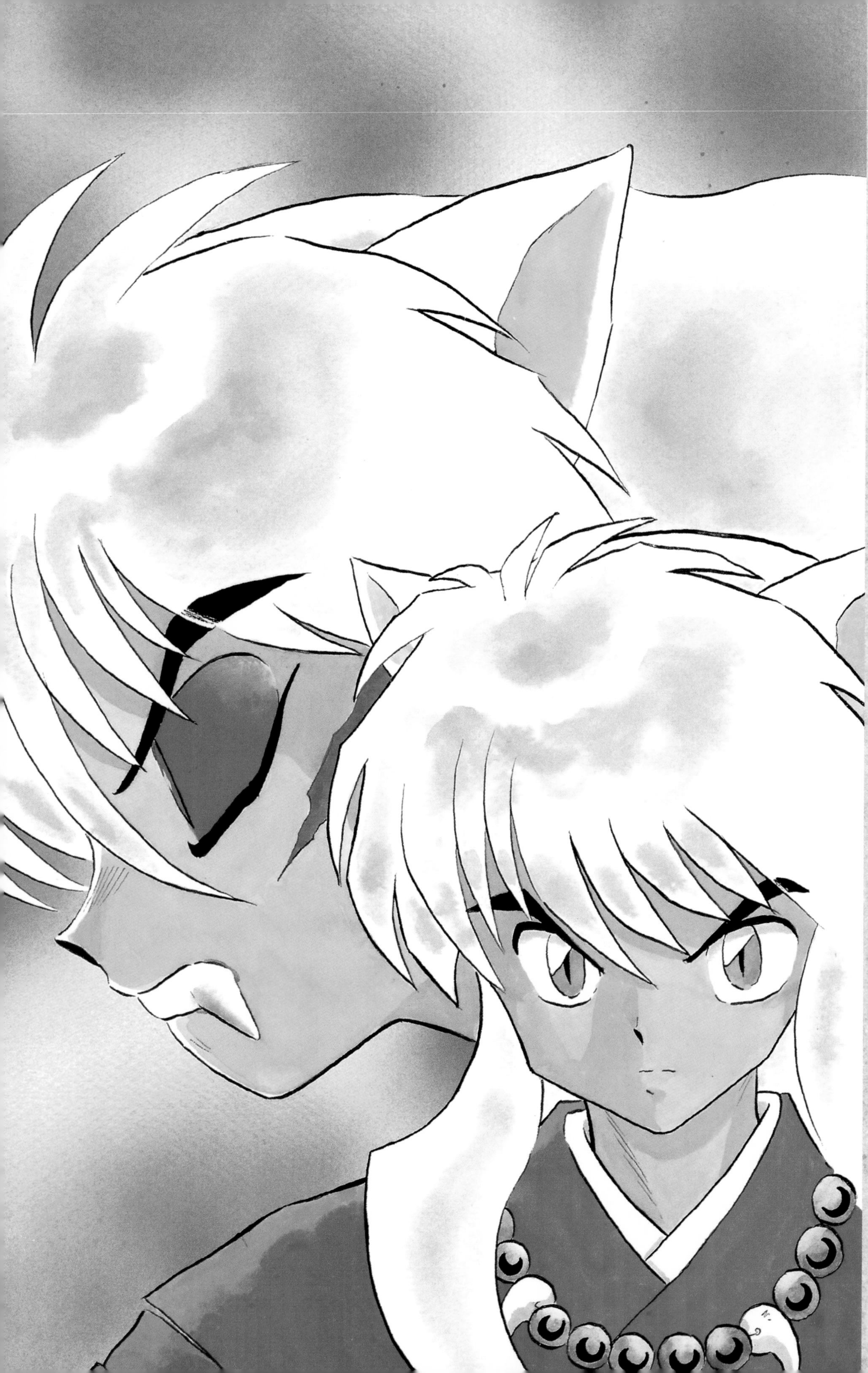

SCROLL 157

INSTINCT

Shonen Sunday Vol. 13, 2000
and Comic Vol. 16

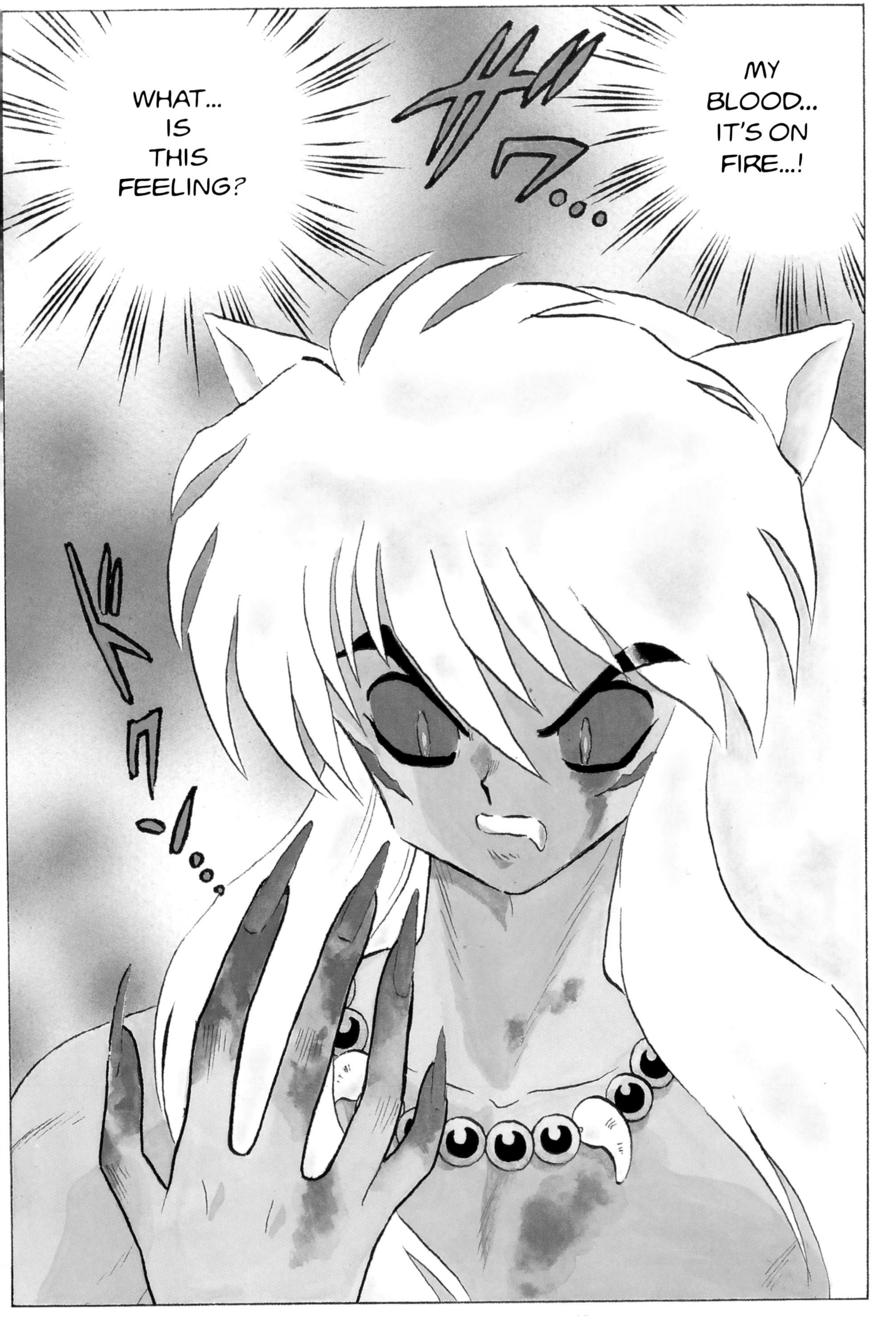
MY BLOOD... IT'S ON FIRE...!
WHAT... IS THIS FEELING?

METAMORPHOSIS

The state of half-demon Inuyasha awakening to his demon blood when his life is in danger. He experiences this for the first time when Tetsusaiga is smashed in the battle with Goshinki. Because the blood he inherits from his dog-demon father is so strong, it attacks his human heart and sends him out of control. With every metamorphosis Inuyasha loses a bit of his human heart.

▲

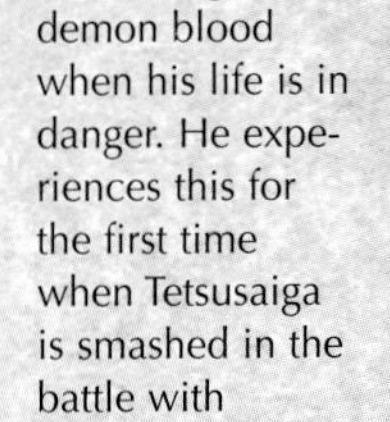

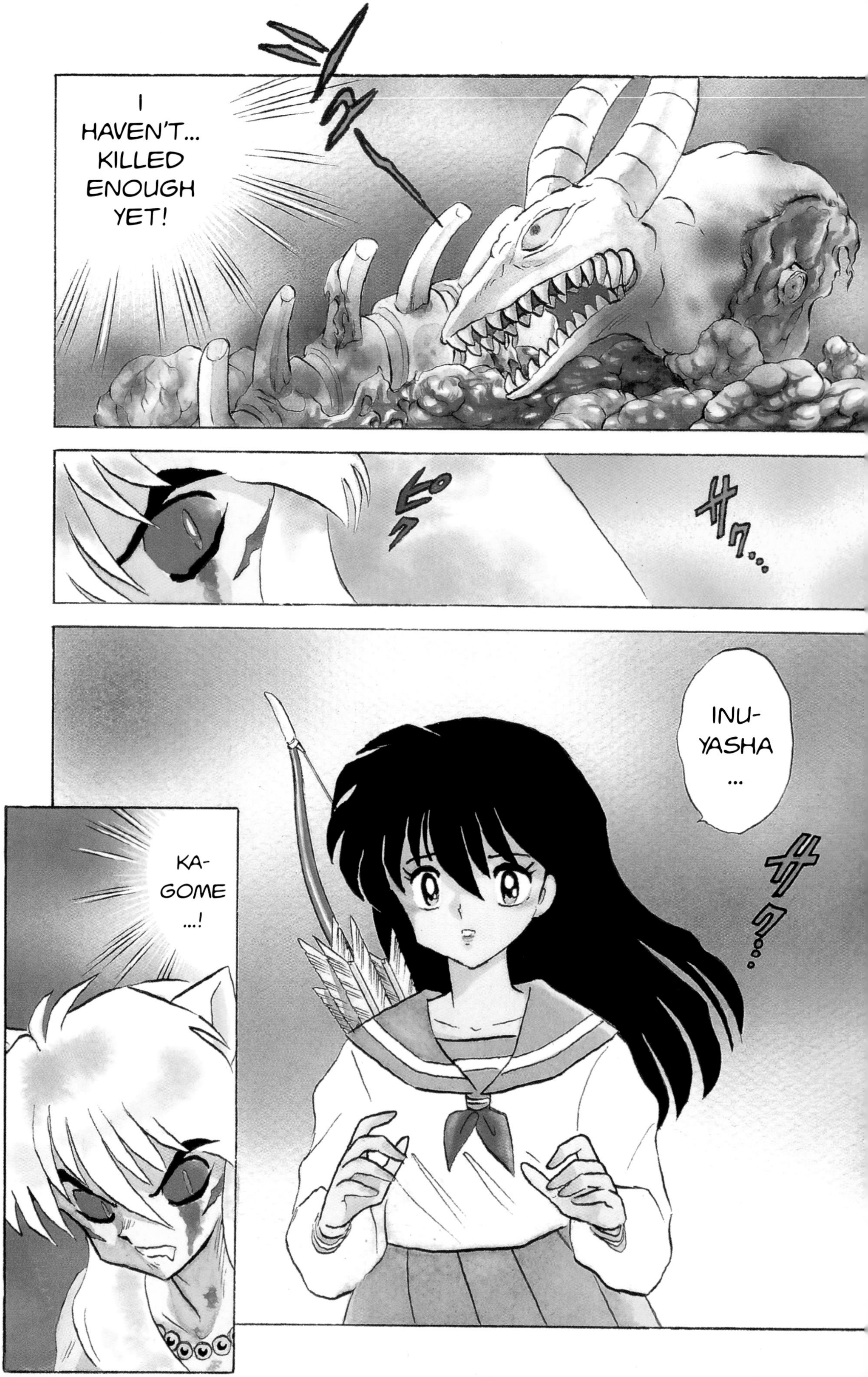
I HAVEN'T... KILLED ENOUGH YET!
INU-YASHA ...
KA-GOME ...!

GOSHINKI ("MIND-READING DEMON")

Another alter ego of Naraku and the younger brother of Kanna and Kagura. He has the ability to read an adversary's mind. He uses this skill in battle with Inuyasha, and smashes Tetsusaiga. Near to victory, he is cut to pieces by the metamorphosed Inuyasha.

▲

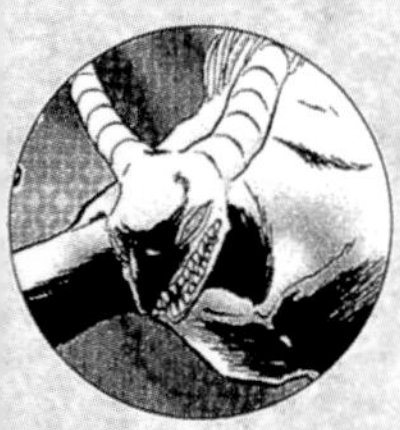

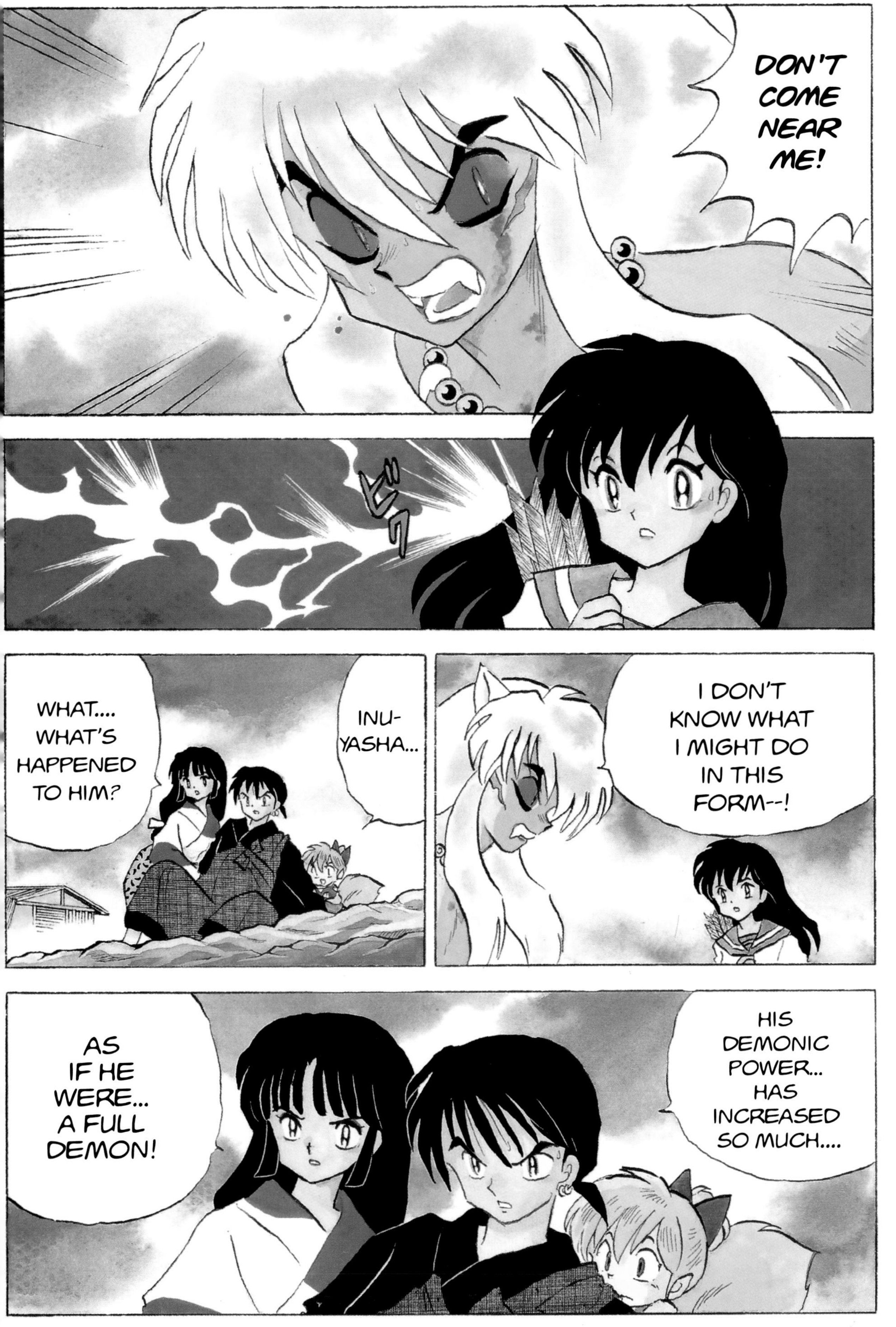
DON'T COME NEAR ME!
ビク
I DON'T KNOW WHAT I MIGHT DO IN THIS FORM--!
INU-YASHA...
WHAT.... WHAT'S HAPPENED TO HIM?
HIS DEMONIC POWER... HAS INCREASED SO MUCH....
AS IF HE WERE... A FULL DEMON!

Kaijinbo ("Ash-Blade Child")

The unworthy pupil of Totosai. Discovered making evil swords, he was banished by his master. Asked by Sesshomaru, Kaijinbo makes the treasure sword Tokijin from Goshinki's fang. He becomes obsessed by the hate of Goshinki, which is trapped in Tokijin. To temper the blade with the demonic power of hatred, he kills ten children and puts their blood and fat into it. Crossing swords with Inuyasha, he falls to Tetsusaiga.

▲

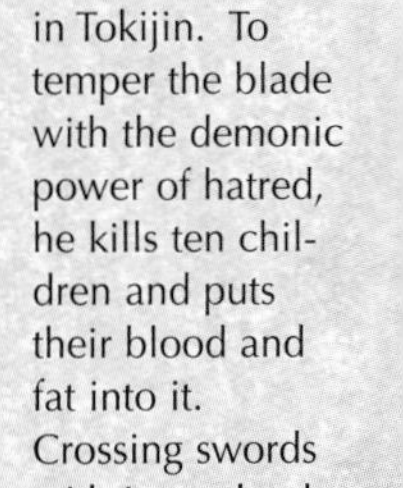

SCROLL 176
KAGOME'S MIND

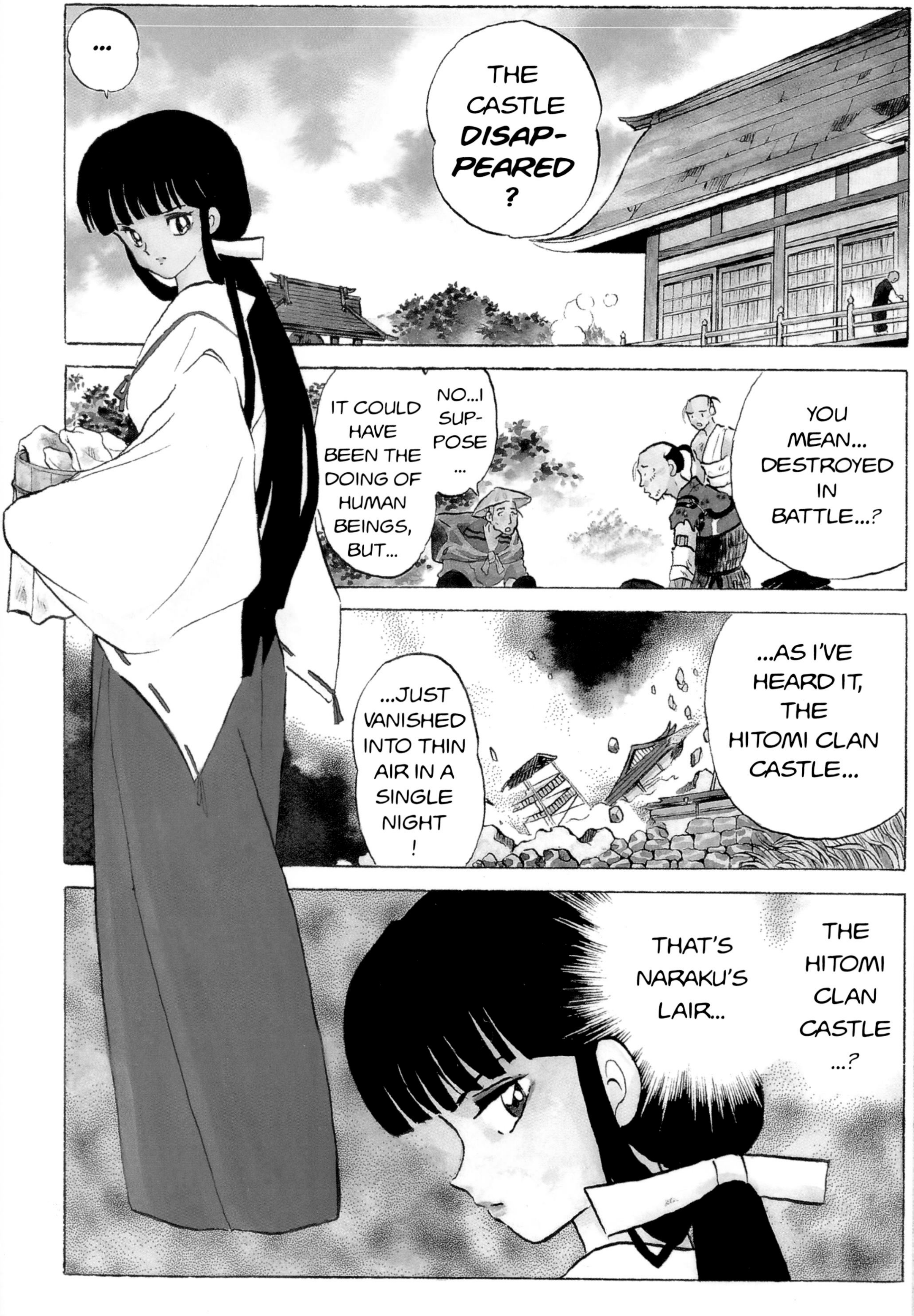
THE CASTLE DISAPPEARED?
...
YOU MEAN... DESTROYED IN BATTLE...?
NO...I SUPPOSE...
IT COULD HAVE BEEN THE DOING OF HUMAN BEINGS, BUT...
...AS I'VE HEARD IT, THE HITOMI CLAN CASTLE...
...JUST VANISHED INTO THIN AIR IN A SINGLE NIGHT!
THE HITOMI CLAN CASTLE...?
THAT'S NARAKU'S LAIR...

Shonen Sunday Vol. 33, 200
and Comic Vol. 18

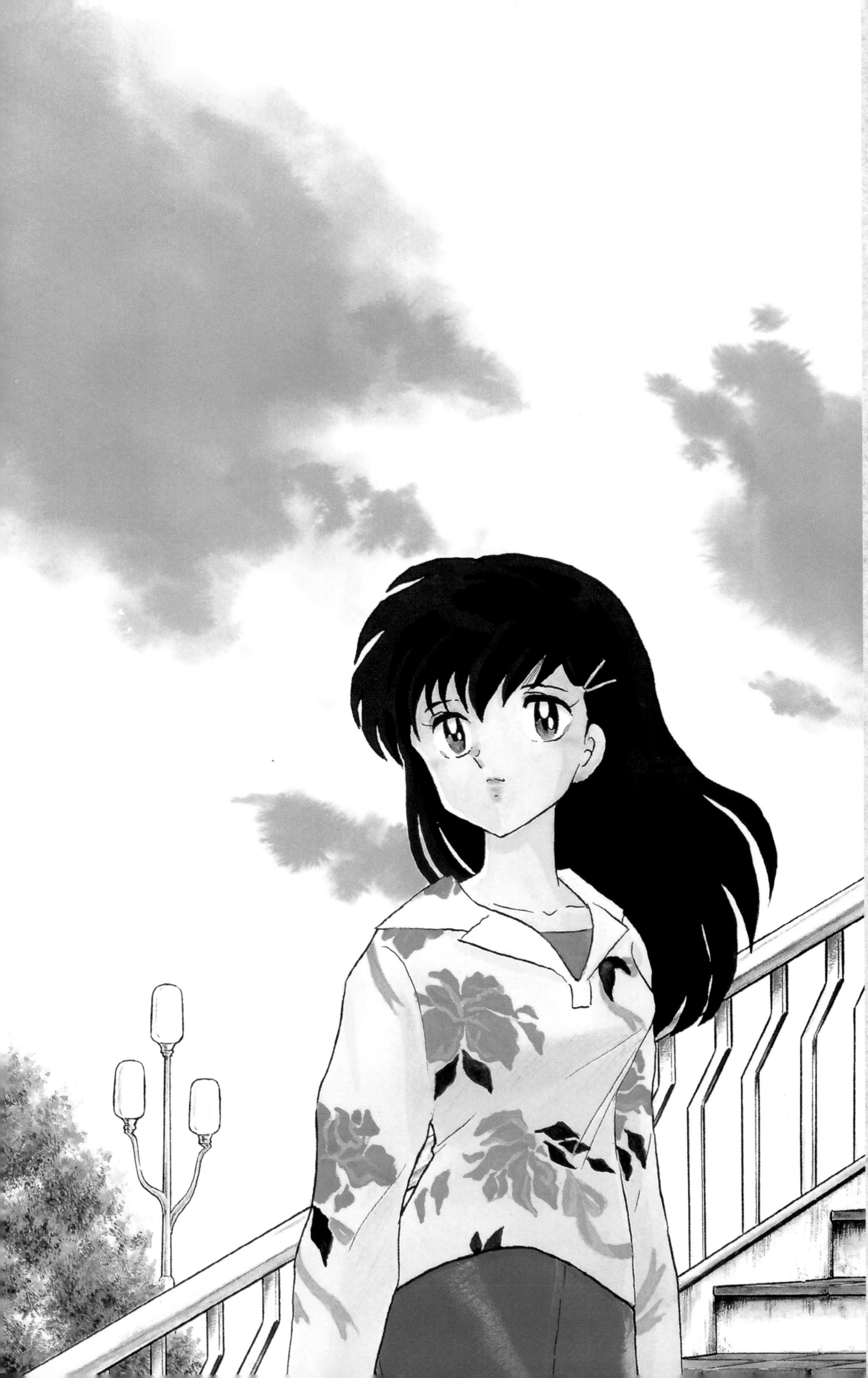

GIANT SOUL COLLECTOR (KYODAI SHINIDAMACHU)

Naraku sends the giant insect to murder Kikyo. It feeds on the souls of the dead, and tries to eat the one in Kikyo's body. Kikyo instinctively heads for home and runs into Inuyasha, who slashes the demon. It appears that Naraku is trying to dispel the yearning toward Kikyo of Onigumo, who is still a strong presence in his heart.

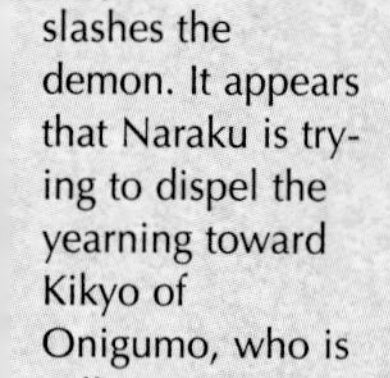

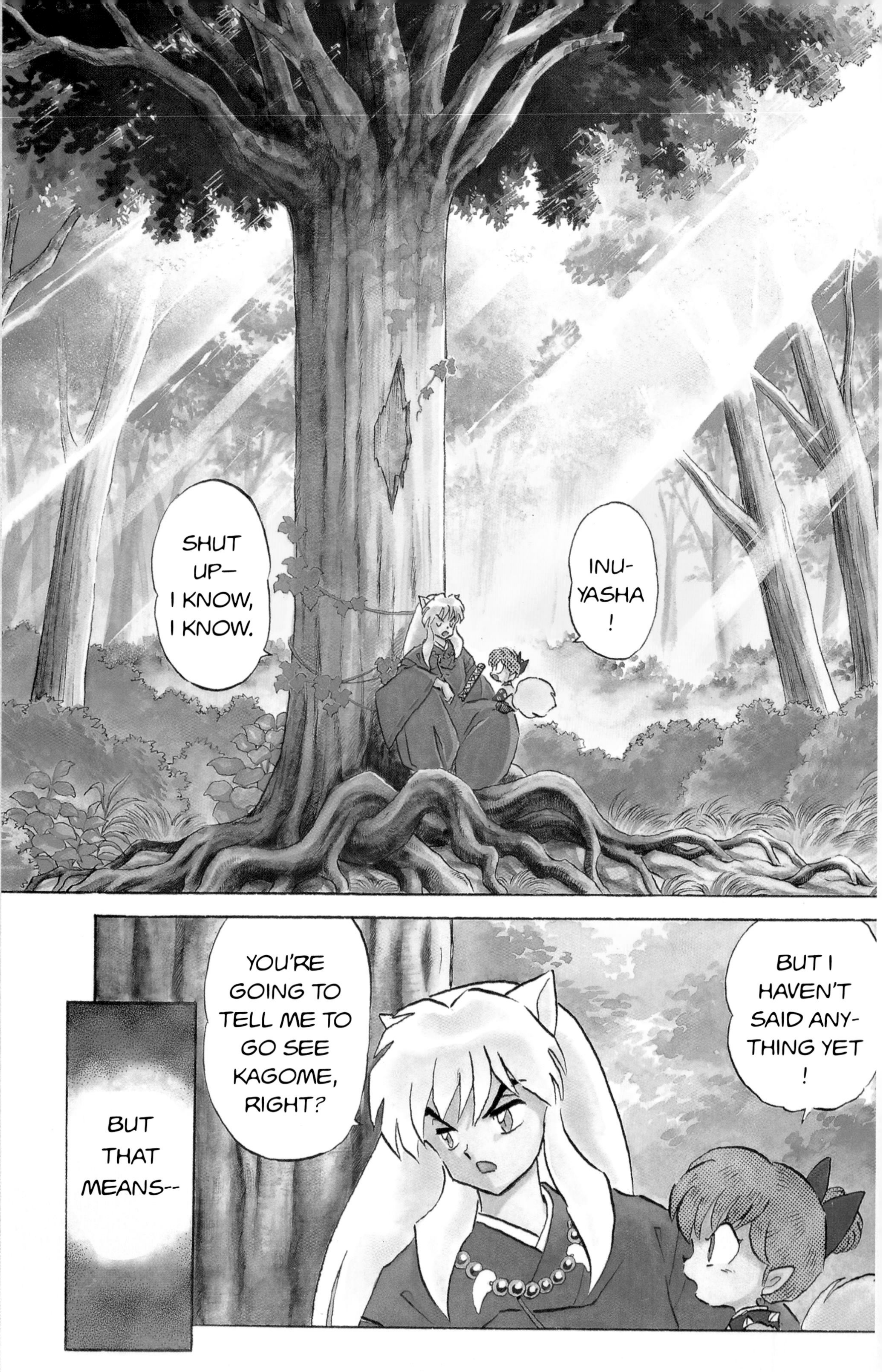
INU-YASHA!
SHUT UP— I KNOW, I KNOW.
BUT I HAVEN'T SAID ANYTHING YET!
YOU'RE GOING TO TELL ME TO GO SEE KAGOME, RIGHT?
BUT THAT MEANS--

Shonen Sunday Vol. 50, 2000

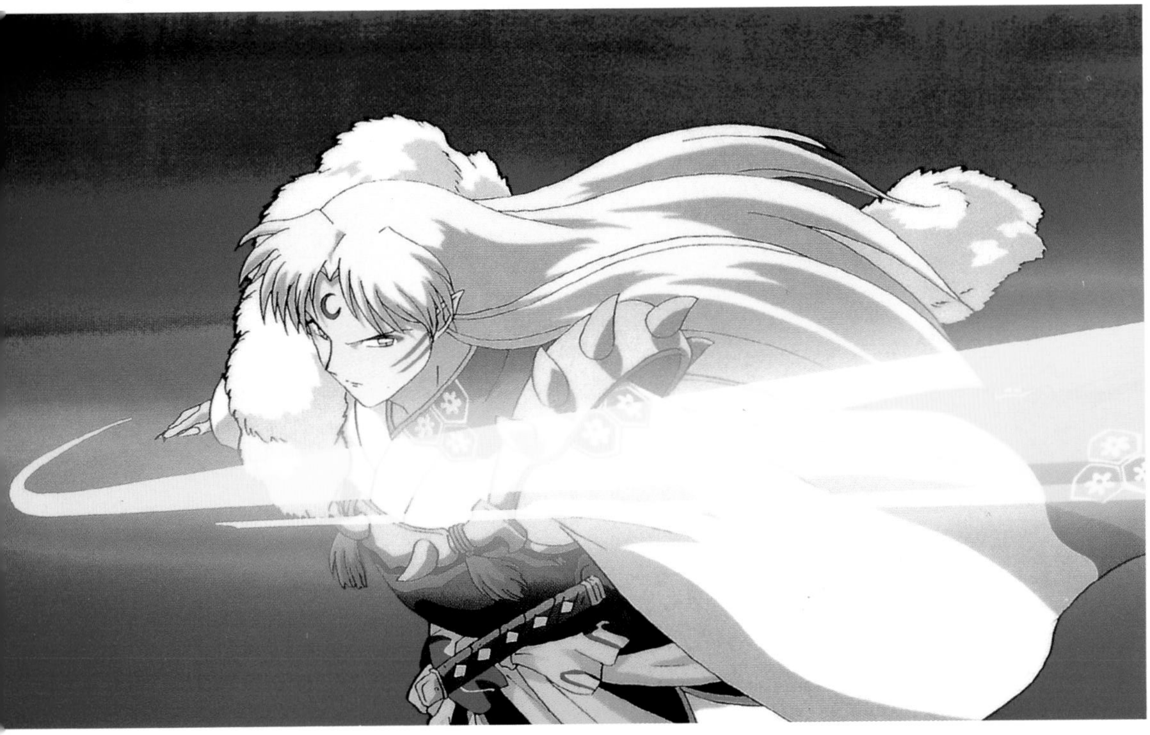

Shonen Sunday Vol. 50, 2000

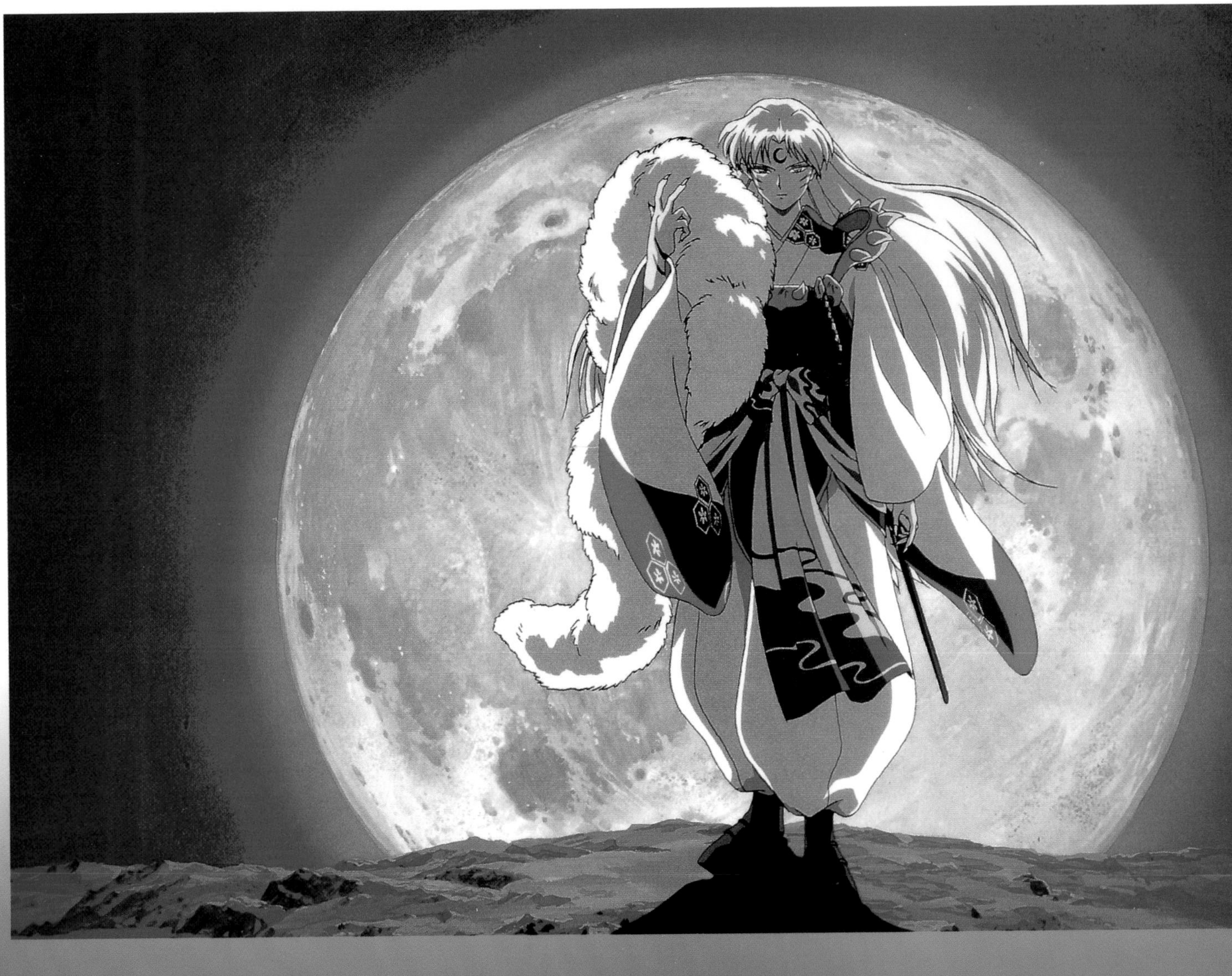

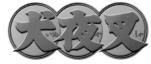

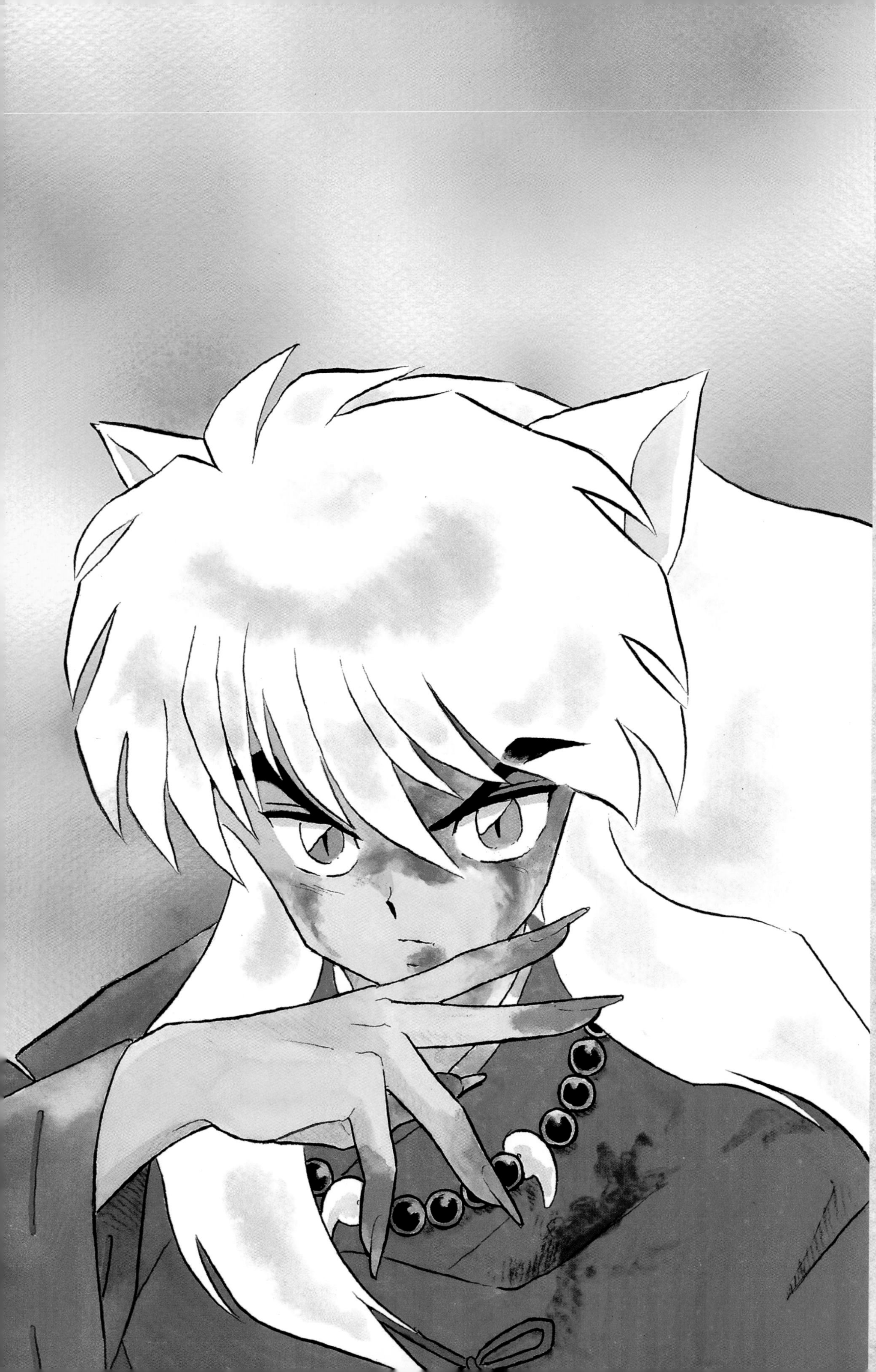

SCROLL 187

STAINED BLOOD

Shonen Sunday Vol. 45, 2000
and to appear in
Comic Vol. 19

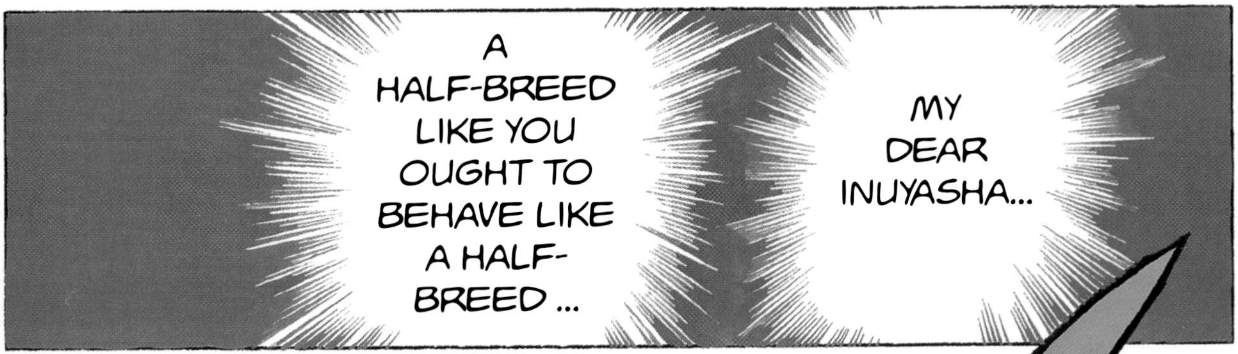
MY DEAR INUYASHA...
A HALF-BREED LIKE YOU OUGHT TO BEHAVE LIKE A HALF-BREED ...

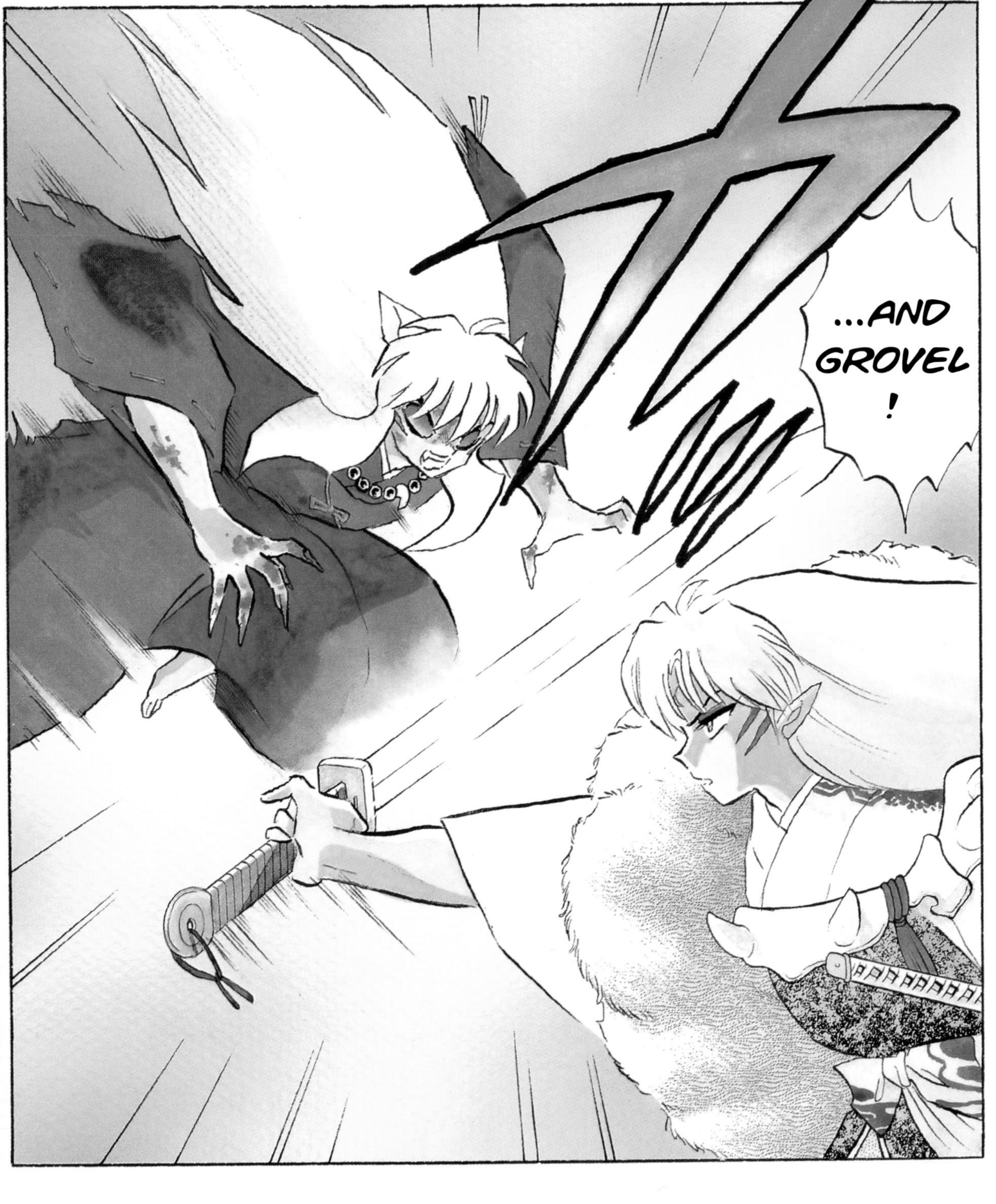
...AND GROVEL!

Tokijin ("Demon-Fighting God")

Kaijinbo carves this treasure sword from the fang of Goshinki over three full days. It contains Goshinki's hatred for Inuyasha. Possessed by this hatred, Kaijinbo goes after Inuyasha's life. Even after his head is smashed, Kaijinbo's body, still controlled by hate, continues to challenge Inuyasha. But Kaijinbo's body can't withstand Tetsusaiga. The sword is currently held by Sesshomaru.

▲

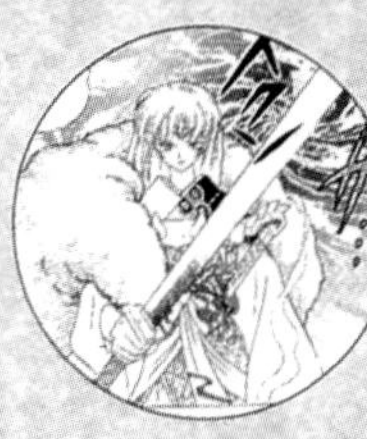

Tenseiga ("Natural Fang")

The sword given to Sesshomaru by his father. Like Tetsusaiga, it was forged by Totosai. The opposite of Tetsusaiga, which takes down the strong, Tenseiga has the power to support the lives of the weak. With a truly caring heart, one swing of Tenseiga can save 100 lives. Does Sesshomaru's rescue of the girl Rin show a change of heart? ▲

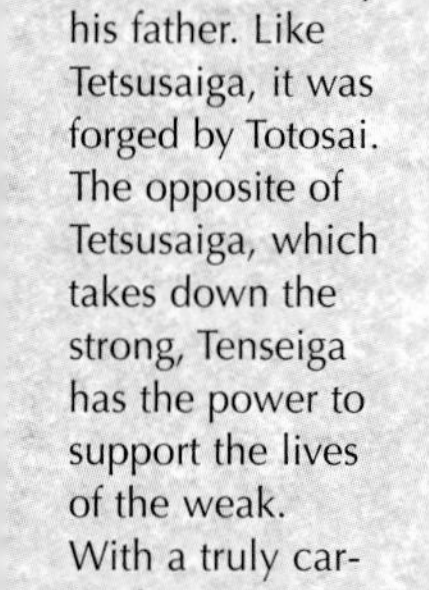

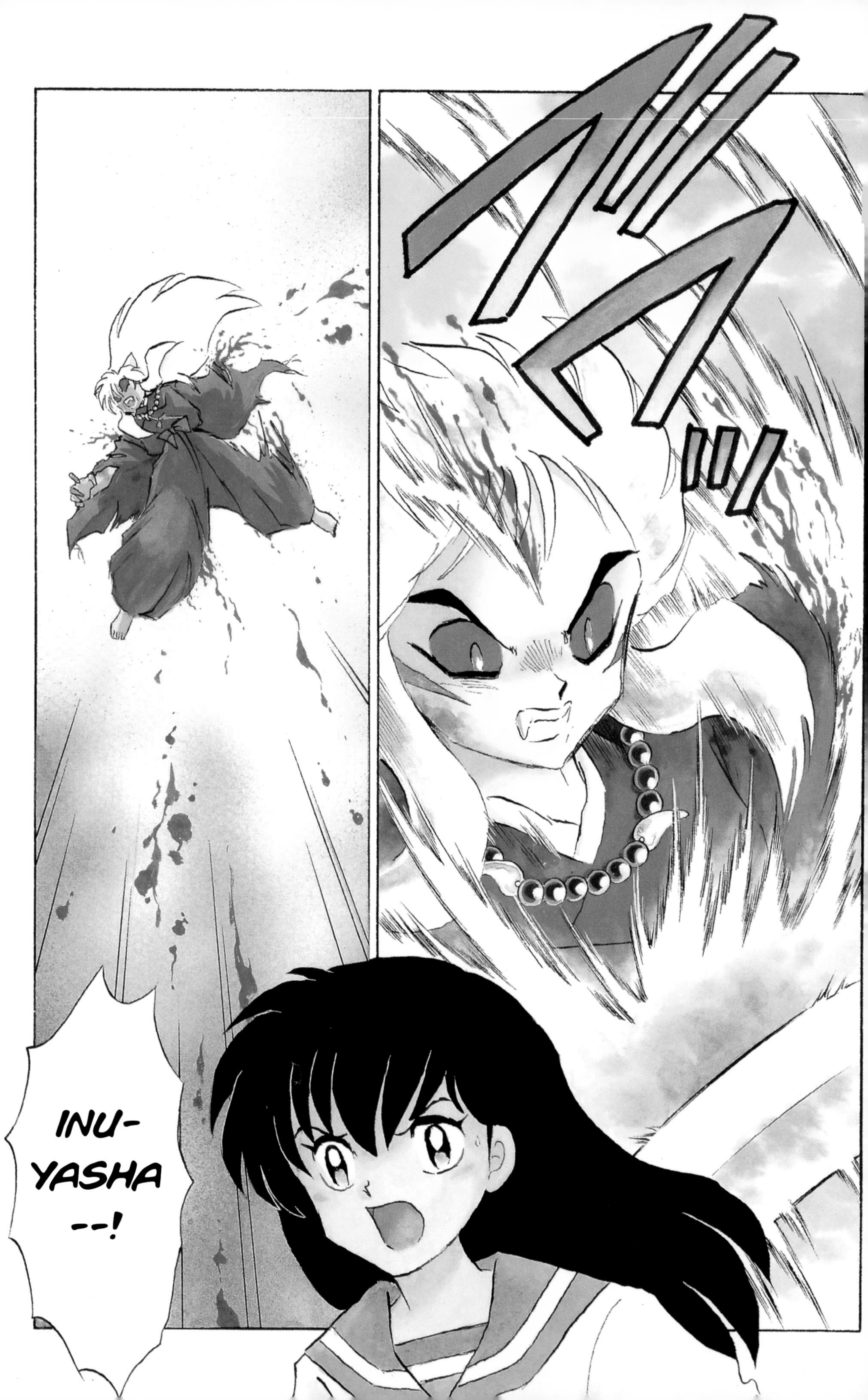
INU-YASHA --!

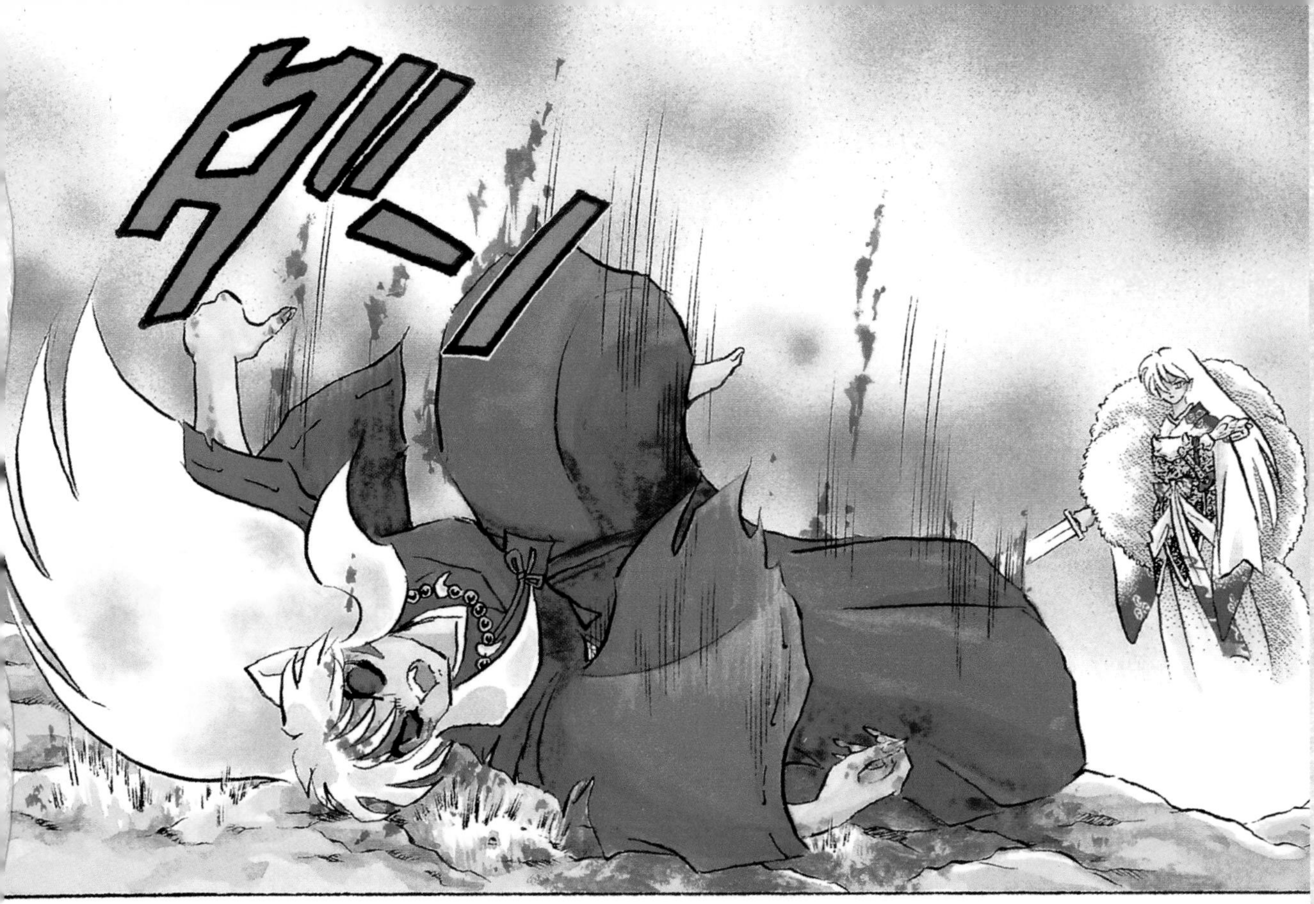

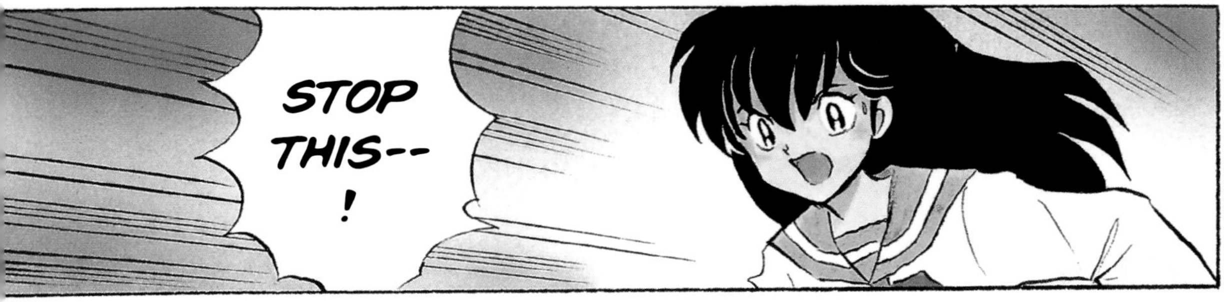
STOP THIS-- !

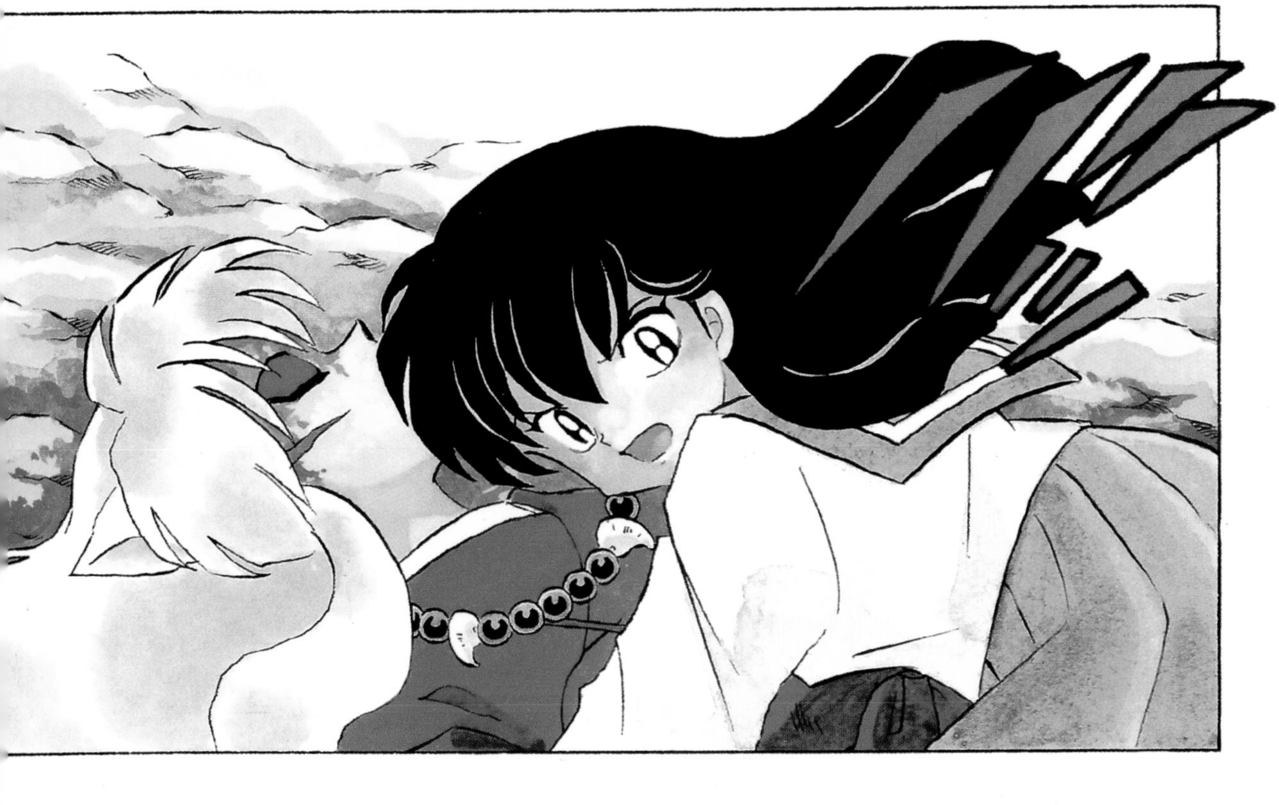

INUYASHA AND TETSUSAIGA (2)

Broken to pieces by Goshinki, Tetsusaiga is retempered by Totosai. The sword becomes heavier than before because Inuyasha's fang is used as a binder. This also shows that Inuyasha's power is still less than his father's. Because it has the power to restrain Inuyasha's metamorphosis, Tetsusaiga is now essential for Inuyasha to continue living without losing his self.

▲

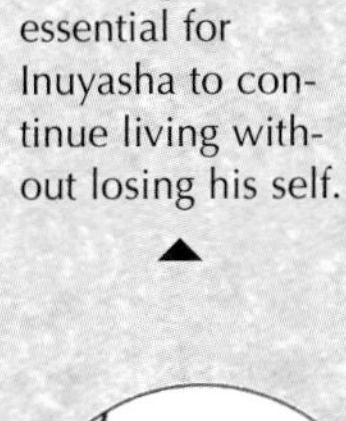

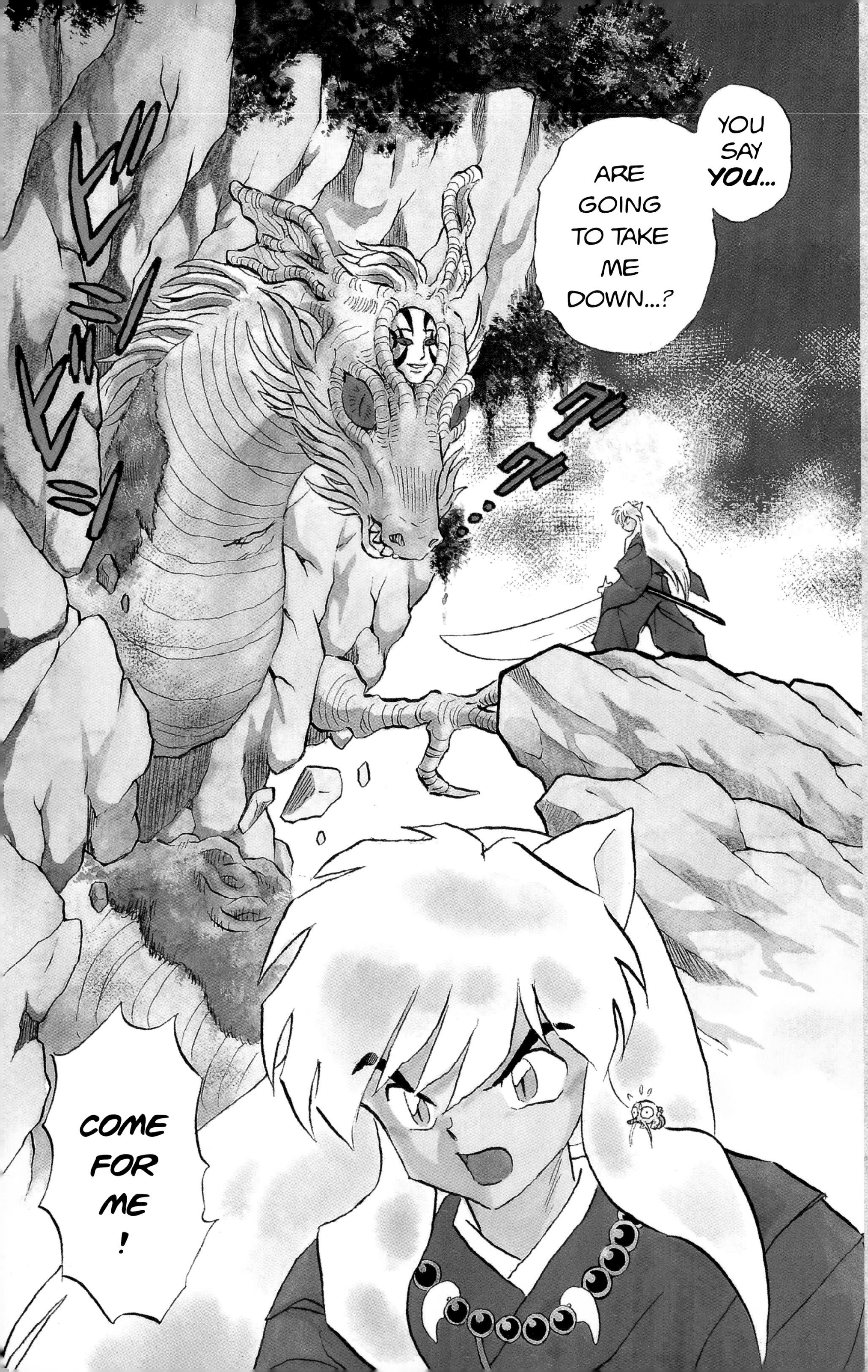
YOU SAY YOU...
ARE GOING TO TAKE ME DOWN...?
COME FOR ME!

SCROLL 189

DRAGON-BONE SPIRIT

Shonen Sunday Vol. 47, 2000 and to be included in Comic Vol. 20

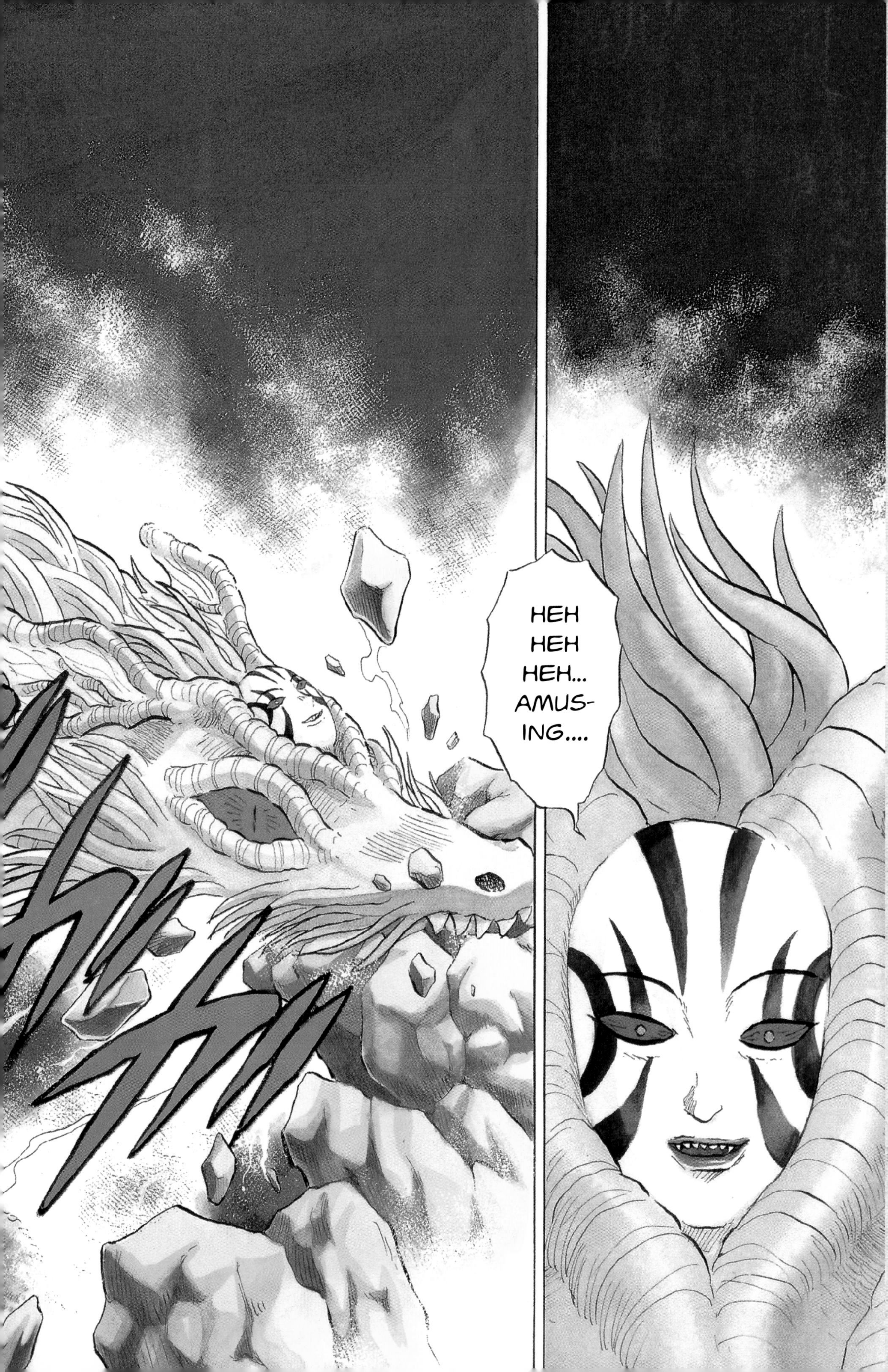
HEH HEH HEH... AMUS- ING....

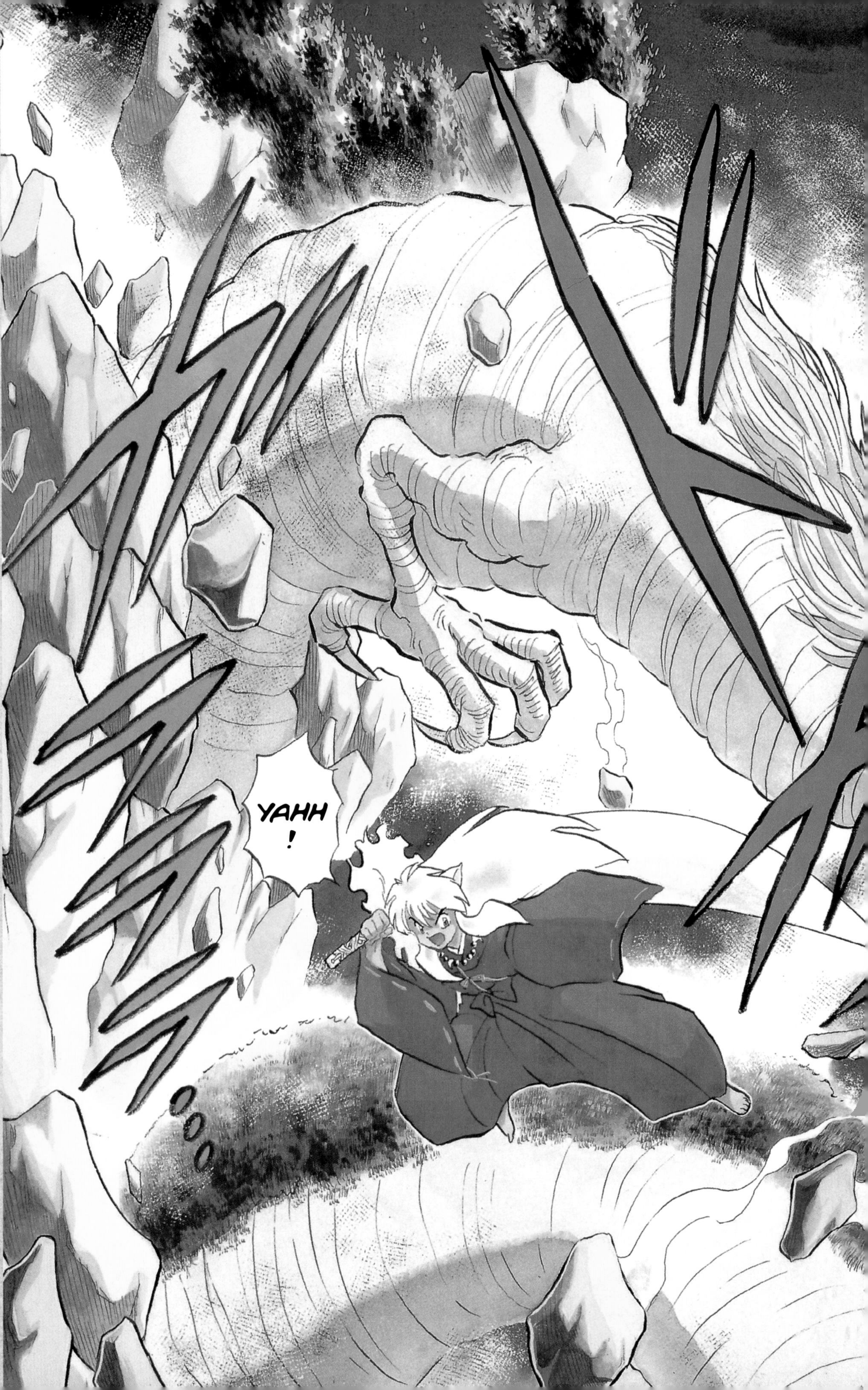
YAHH
!

RYUKOTSUSEI ("DRAGON-BONE SPIRIT")

This demon, trapped by the claws of Inuyasha's father, is freed by Naraku. To make Tetsusaiga lighter, Inuyasha goes to fight Ryukotsusei, who fatally wounded his father. Its weapon is Raigekidan ("thunder attack bullet"). It attacks Inuyasha with tremendous power, but is felled by Bakuryuha ("explosive flow destruction") from Inuyasha, now the master of Tetsusaiga.

▲

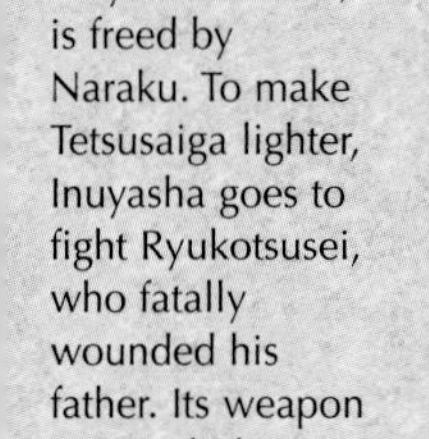

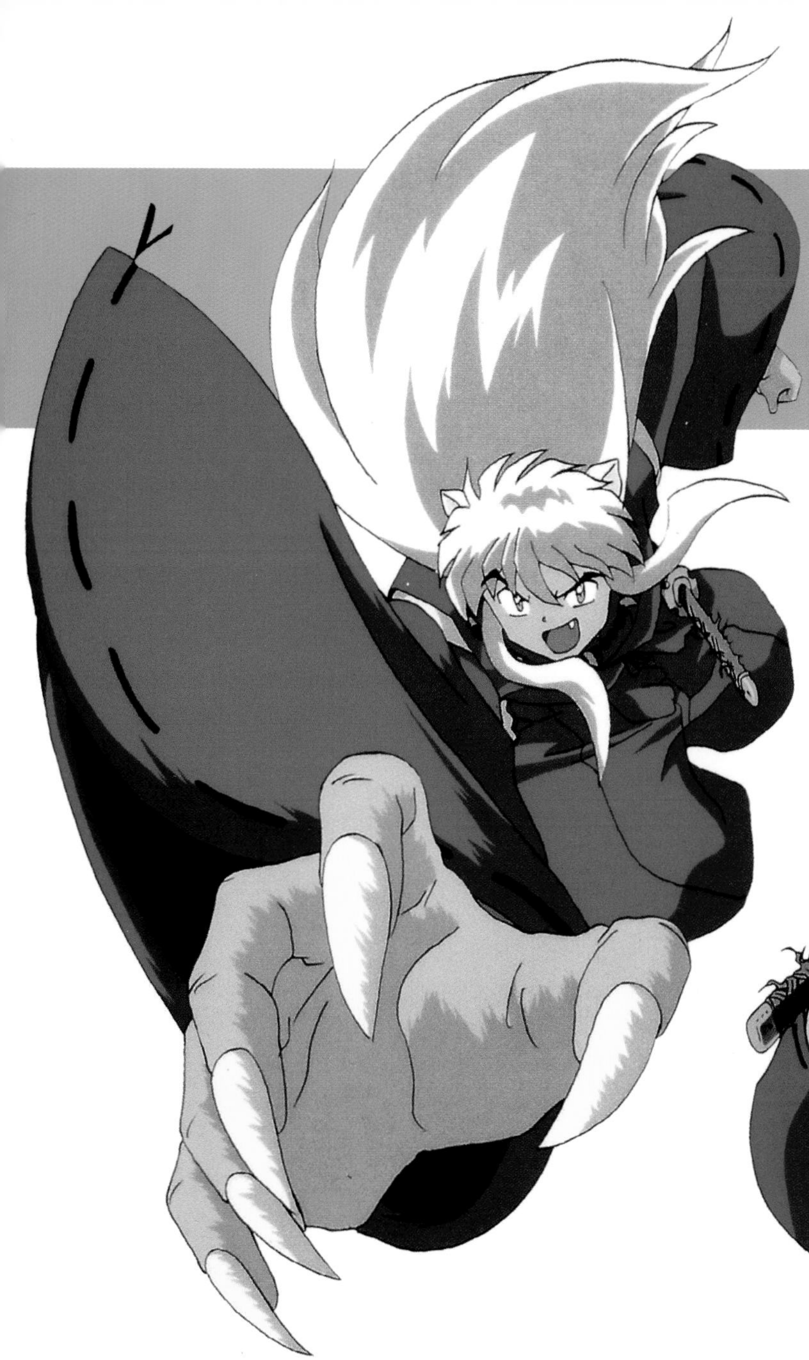

Shonen Sunday Vol. 47, 2000

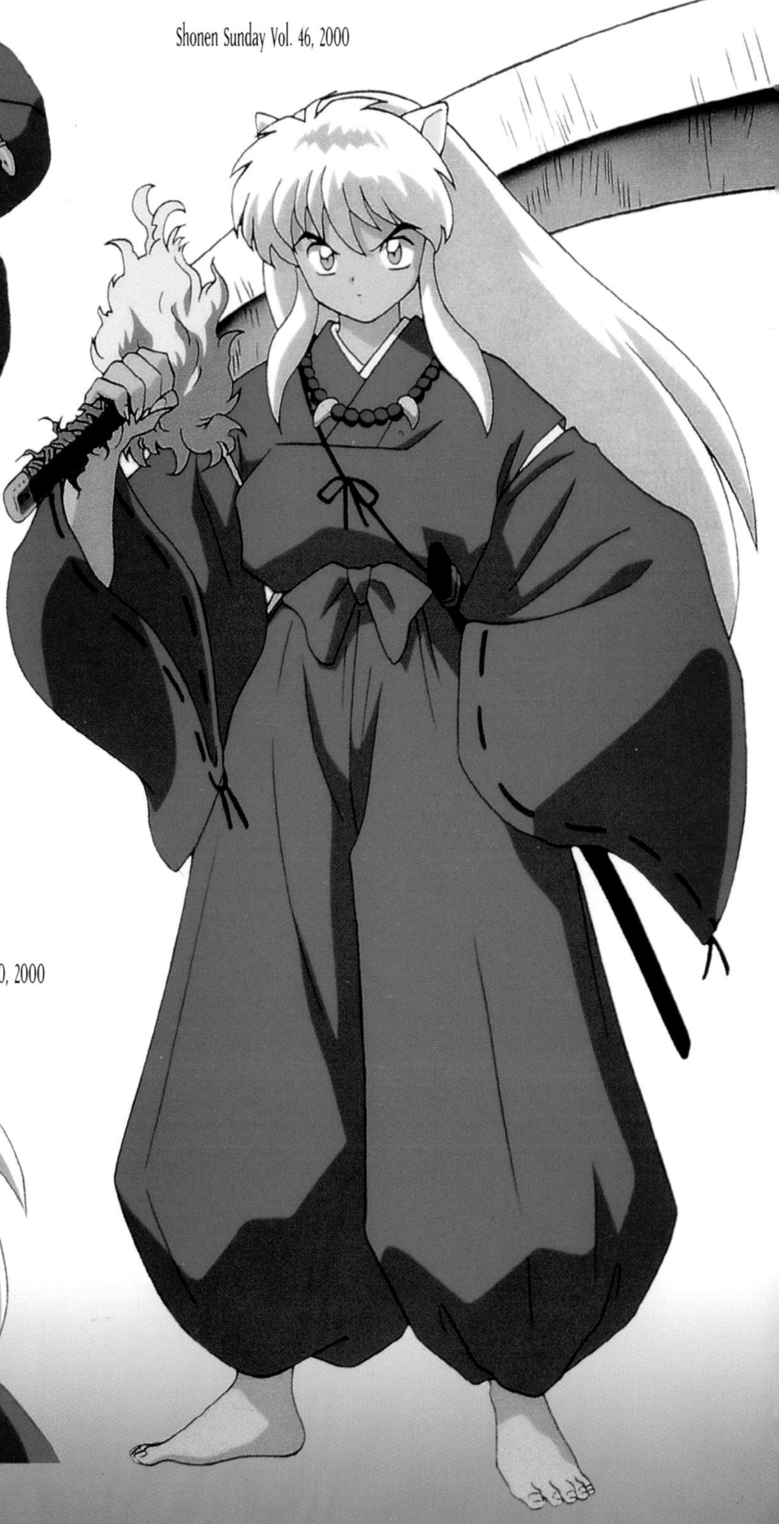

Shonen Sunday Vol. 46, 2000

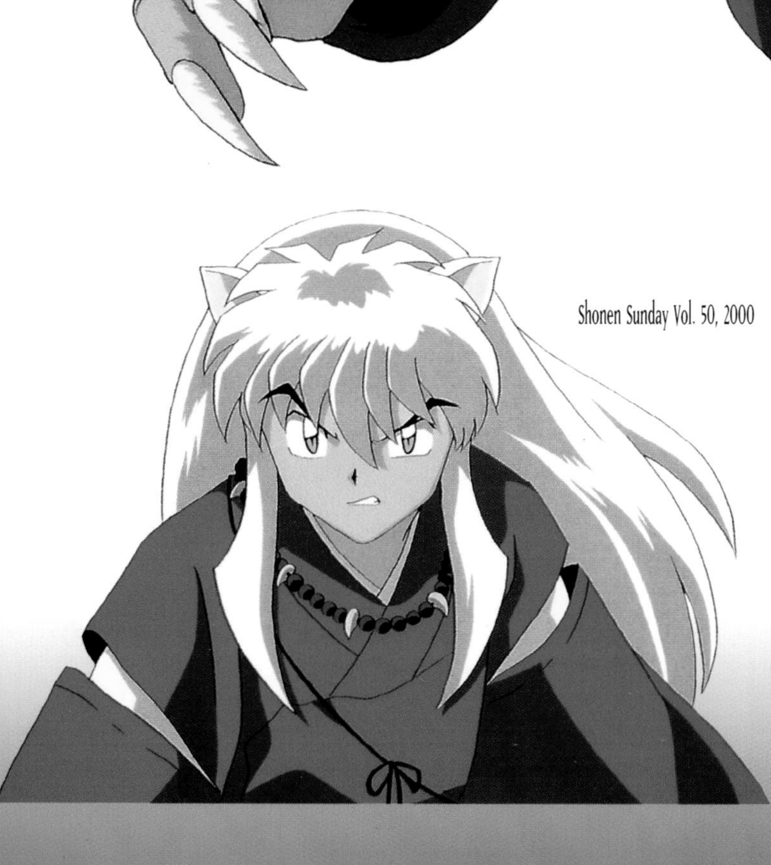

Shonen Sunday Vol. 50, 2000

Inuyasha: Original Illustration Collection II

Here we've gathered pictures that weren't seen in the comics. They include color illustrations for Shonen Sunday covers, book covers up to Vol. 18, and various other media.

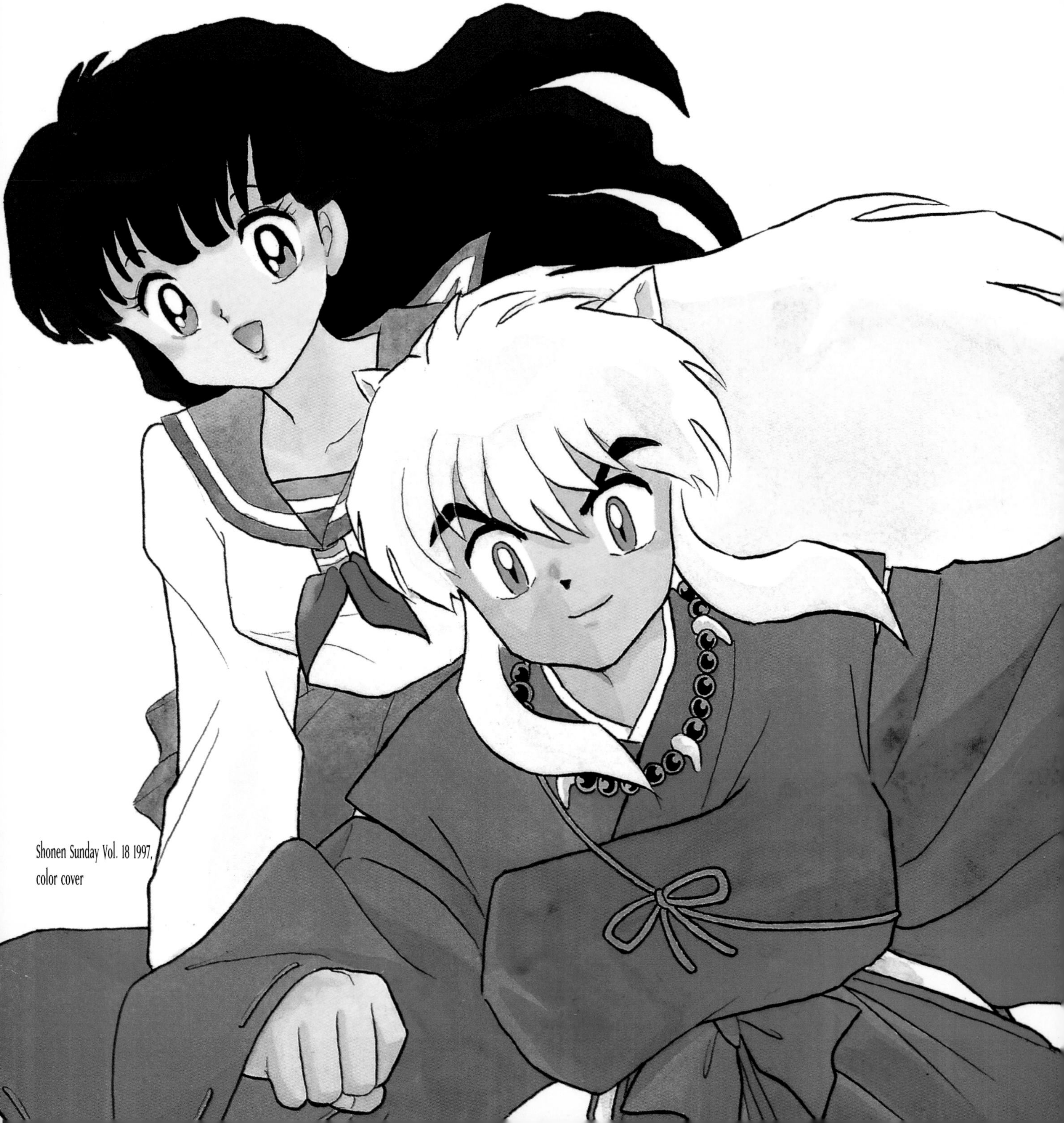

Shonen Sunday Vol. 18 1997, color cover

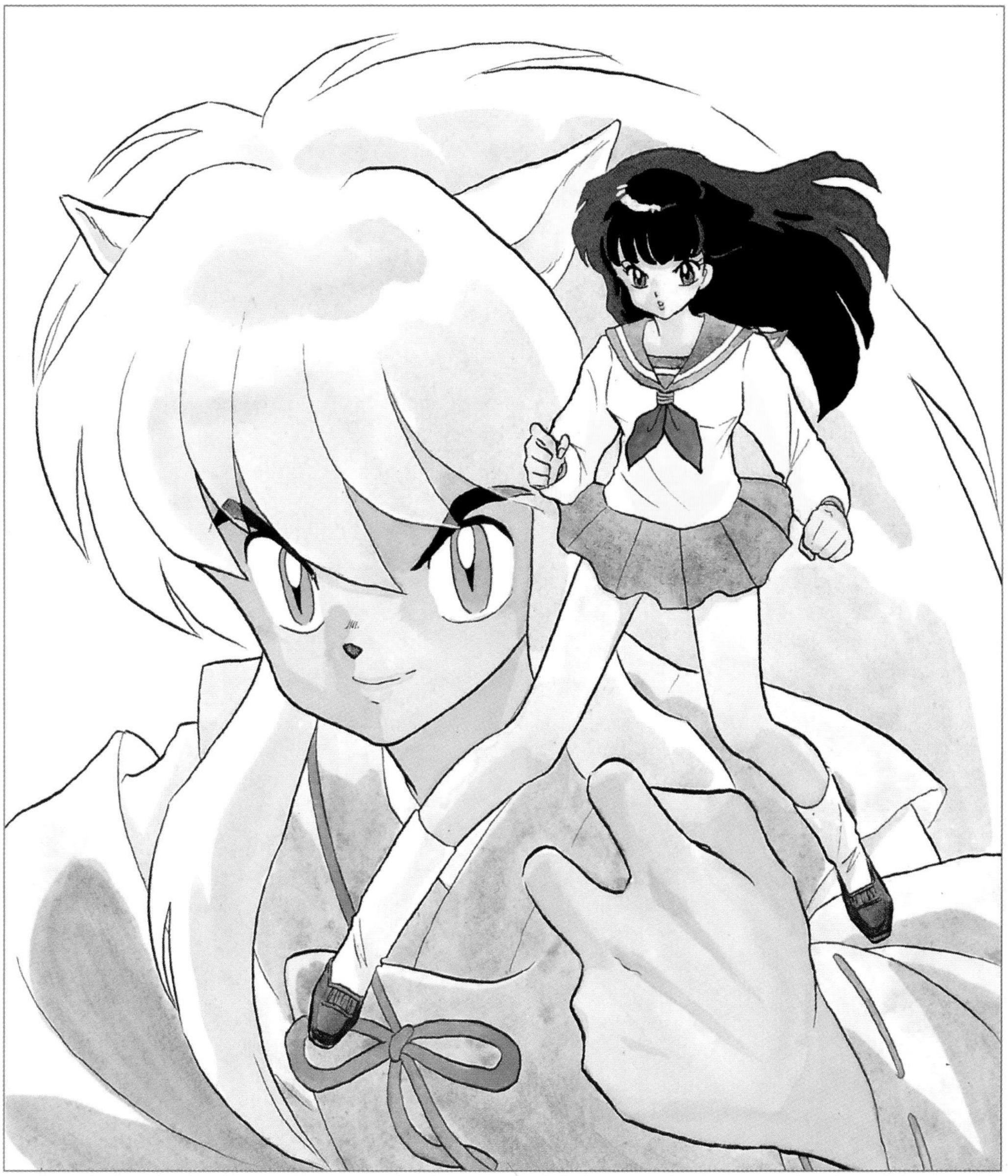

Shonen Sunday Vol. 50 1996, color cover

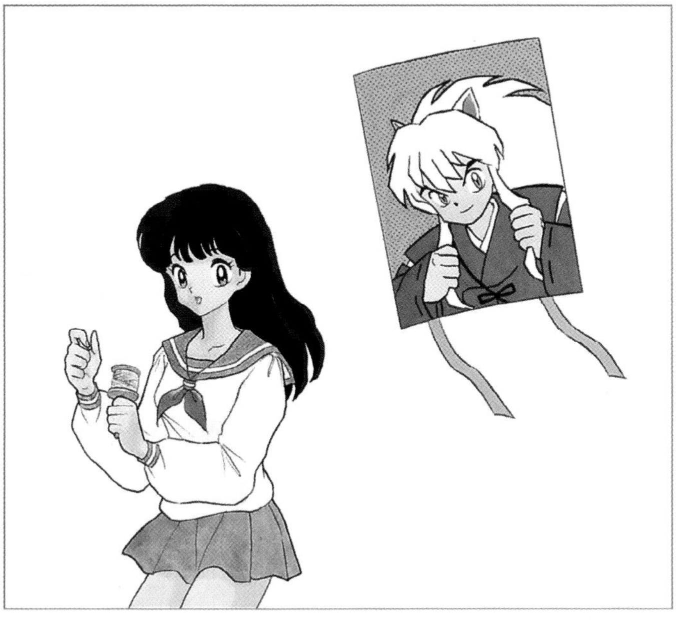

Shonen Sunday Vol. 4 1997, color cover

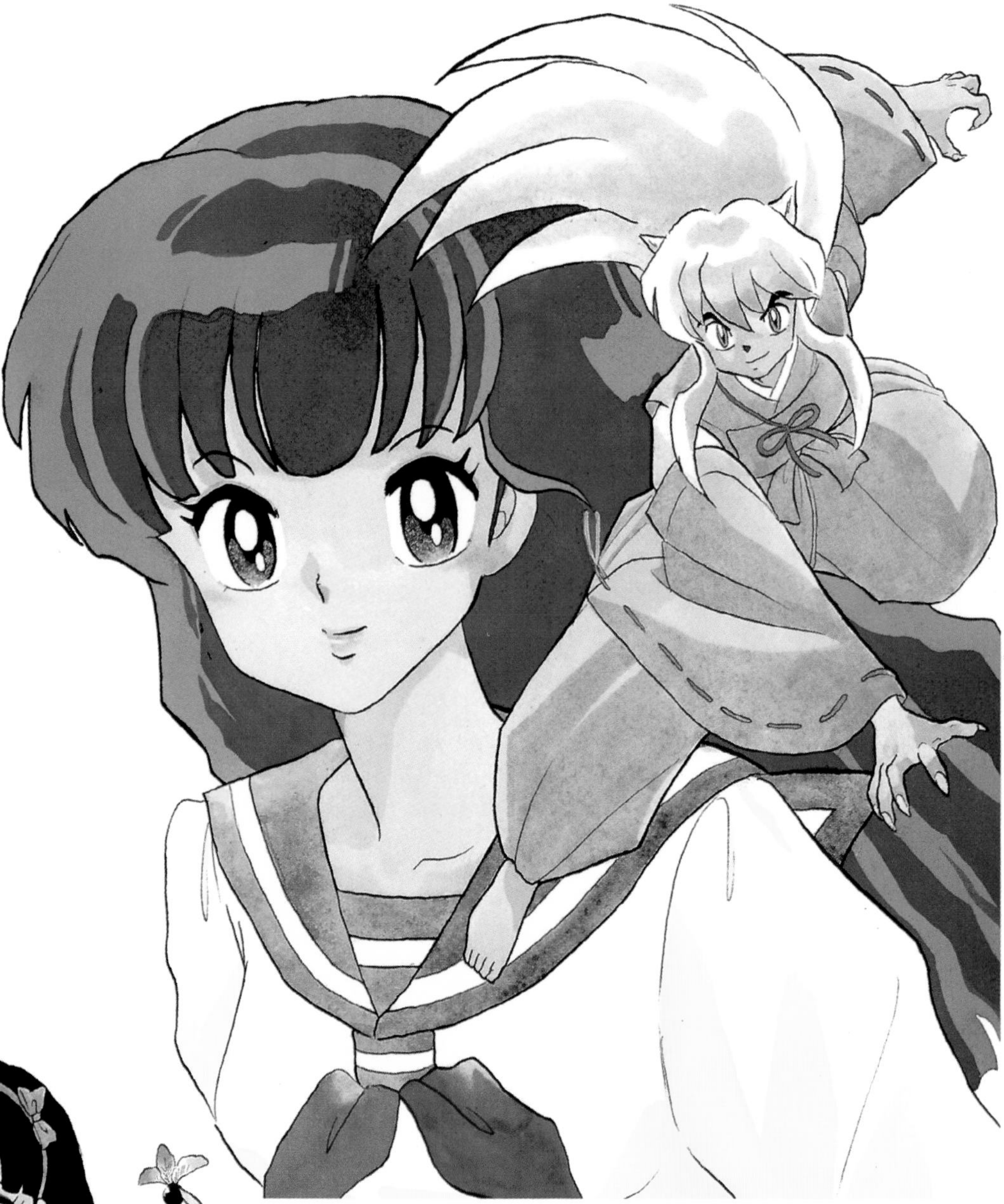

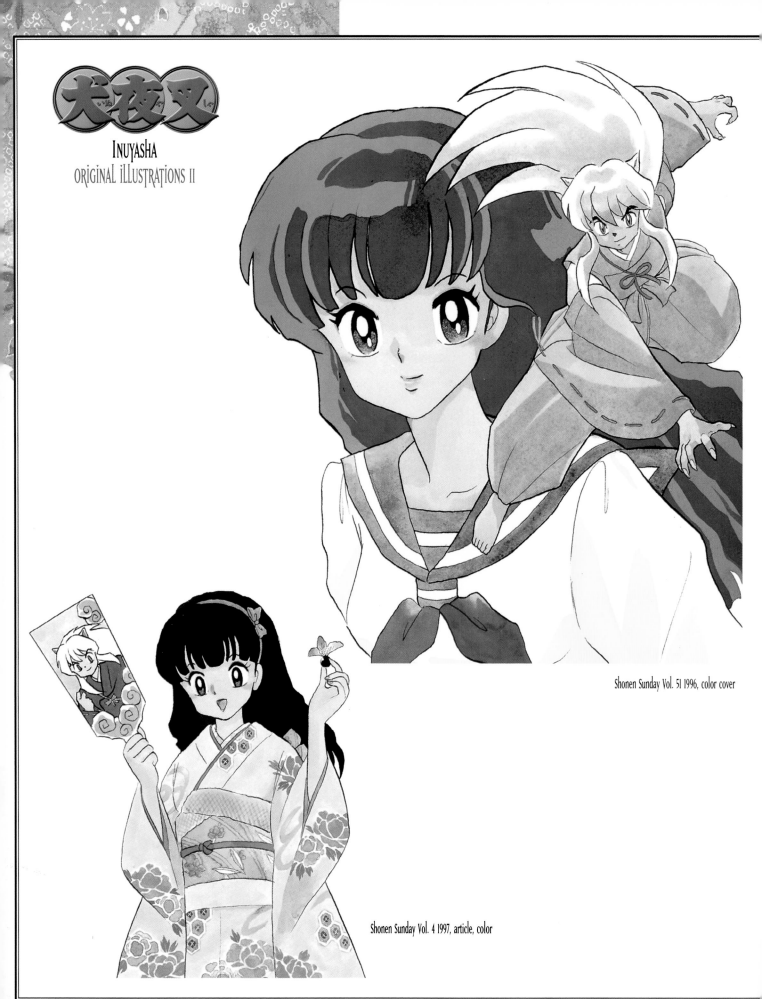

Shonen Sunday Vol. 51 1996, color cover

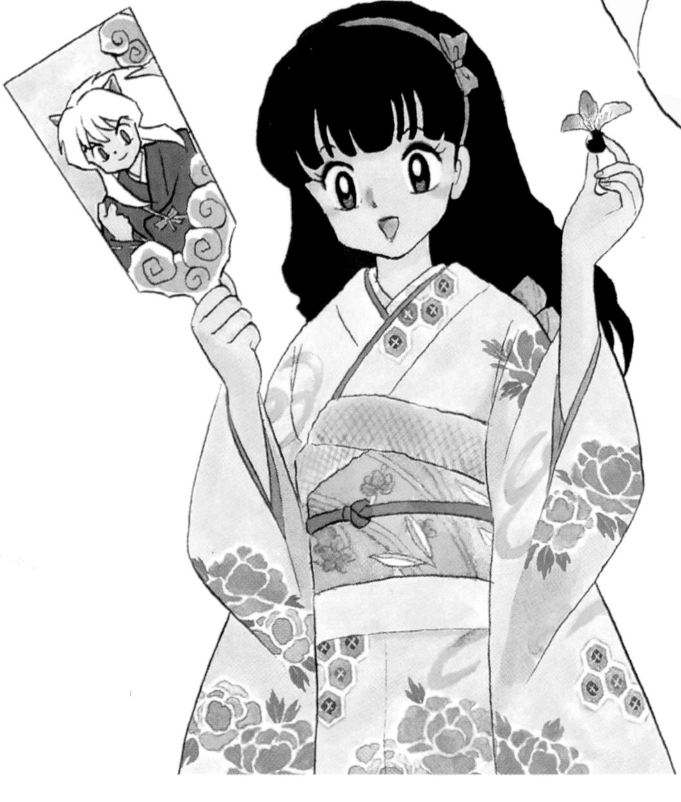

Shonen Sunday Vol. 4 1997, article, color

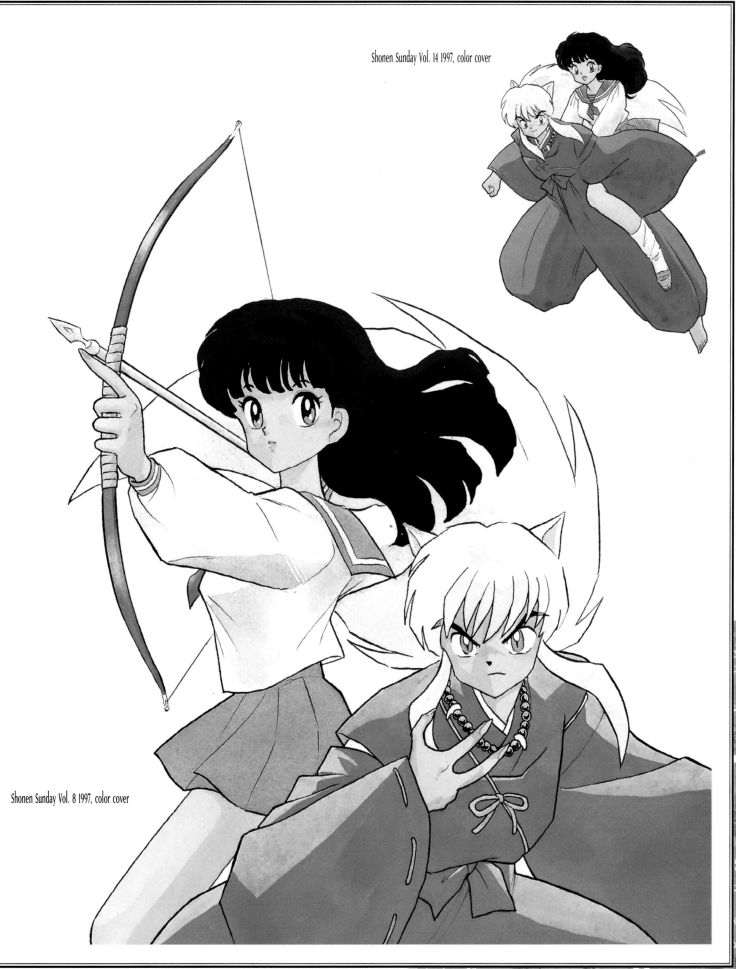

Shonen Sunday Vol. 14 1997, color cover

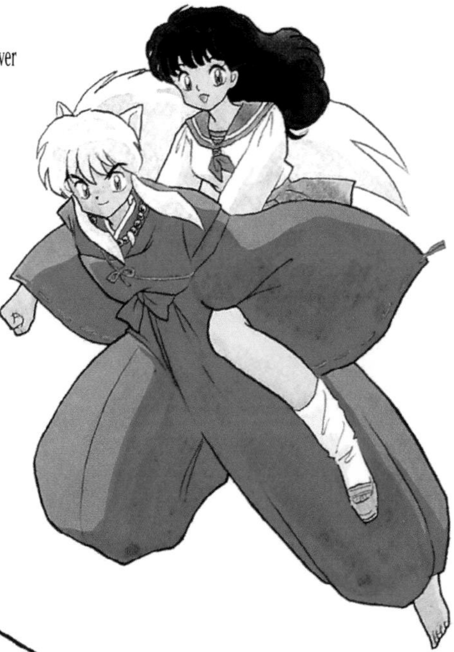

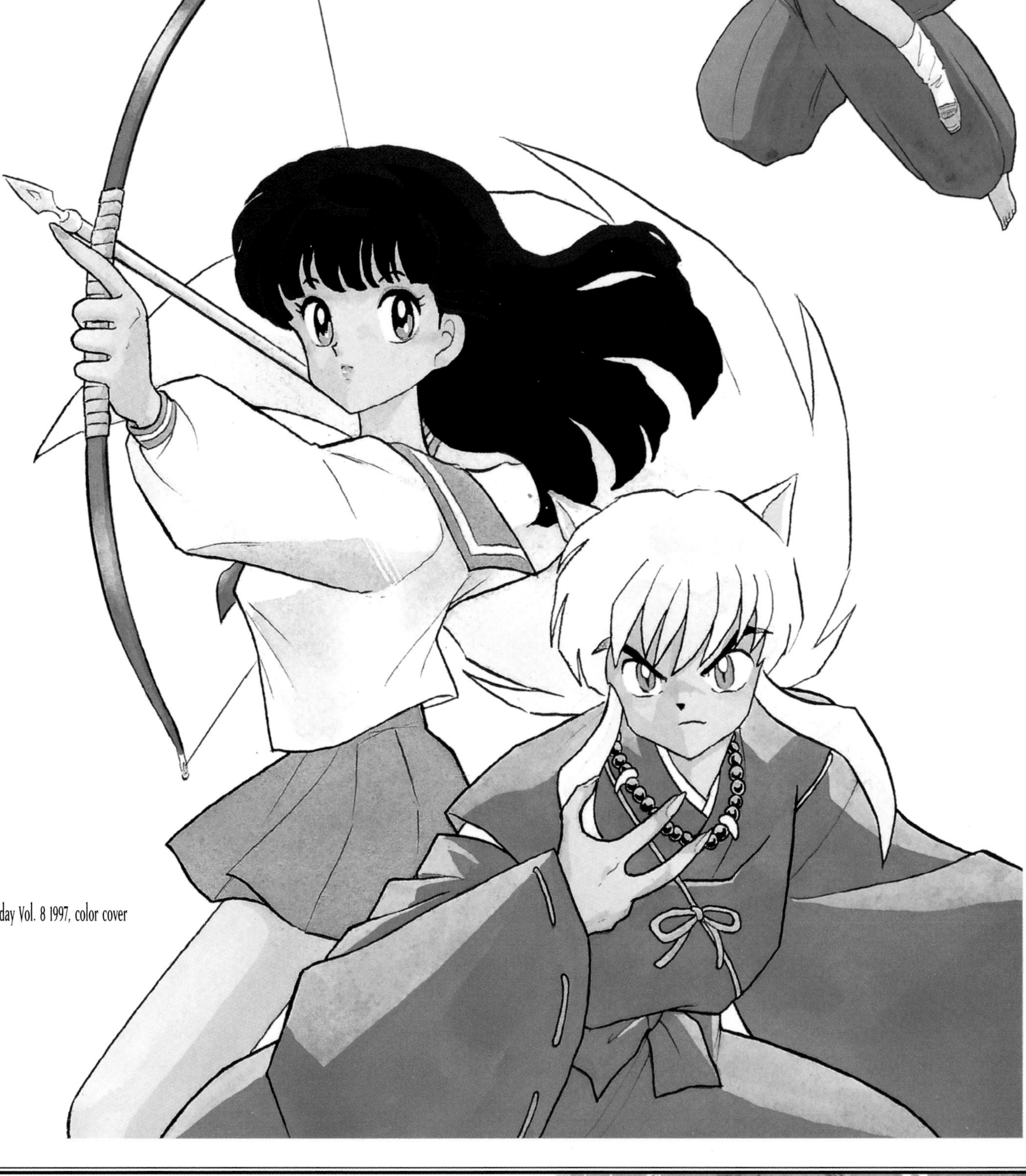

Shonen Sunday Vol. 8 1997, color cover

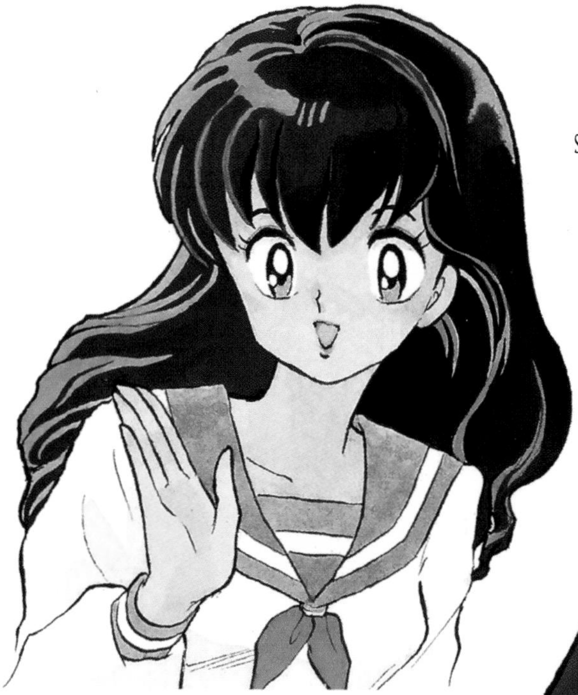

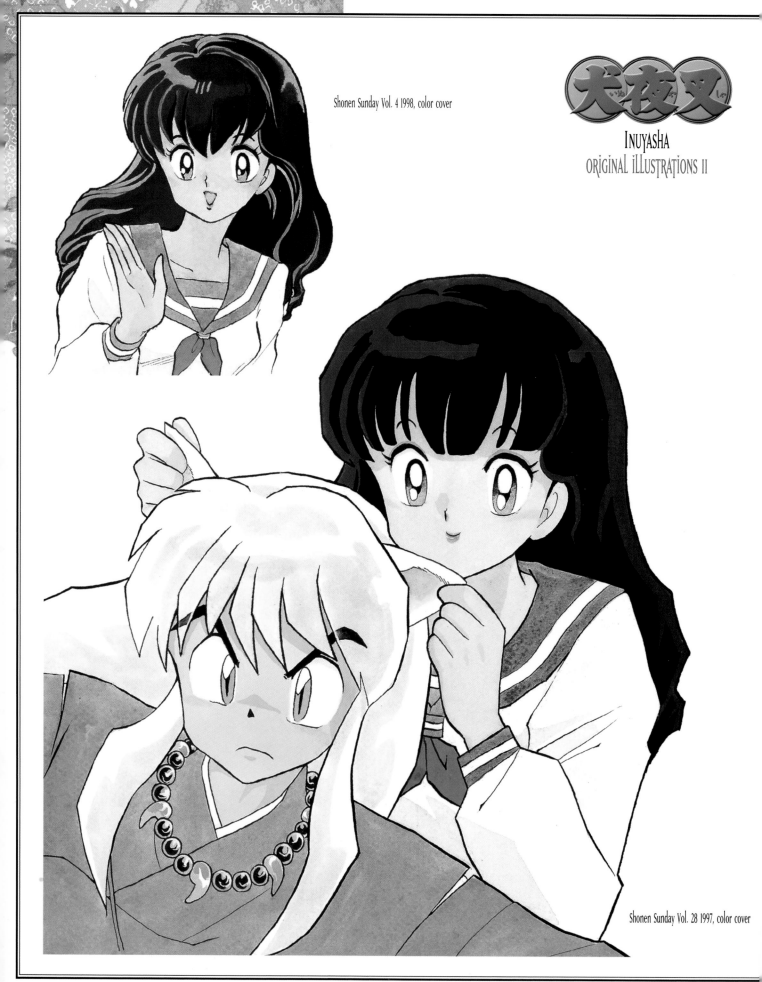

Shonen Sunday Vol. 4 1998, color cover

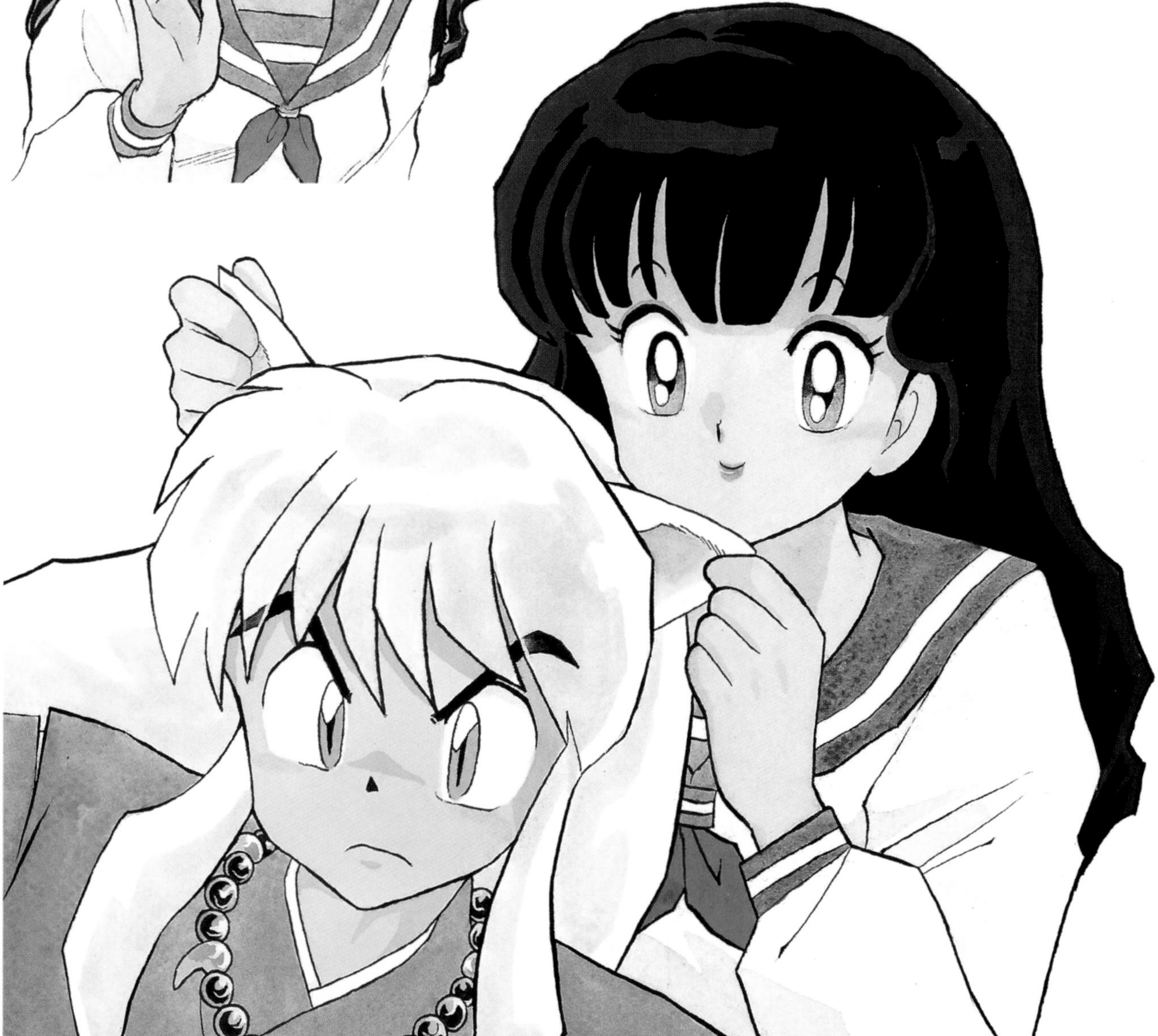

Shonen Sunday Vol. 28 1997, color cover

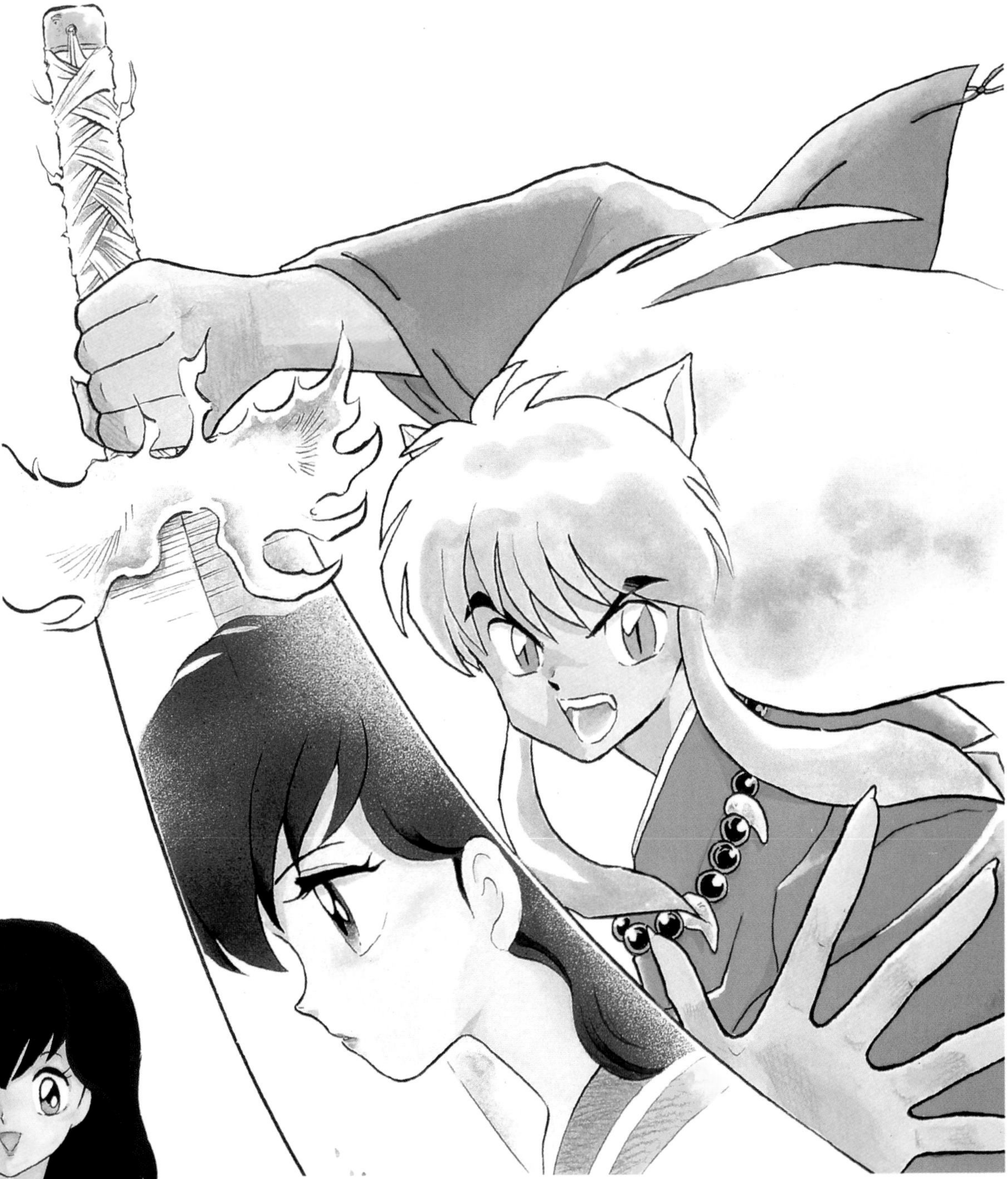

Shonen Sunday Vol. 50 1997, color cover

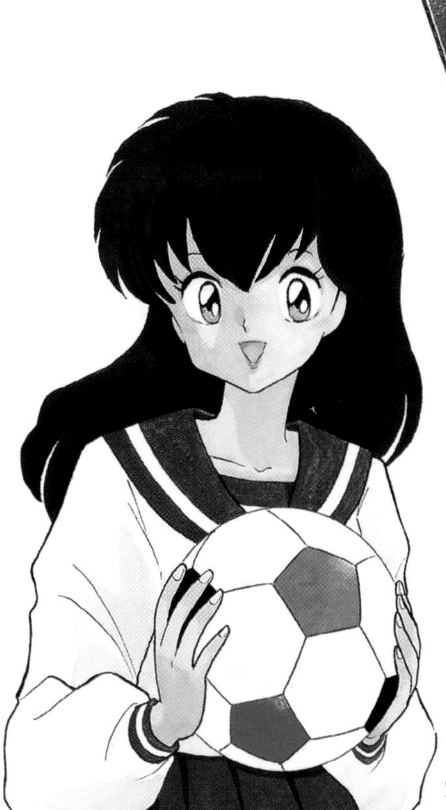

Shonen Sunday Vol. 14 1998, color cover

Shonen Sunday Vol. 25 1998, color cover

Shonen Sunday Vol. 40 1998, color cover

INUYASHA
ORIGINAL ILLUSTRATIONS II

Shonen Sunday Vol. 12 1998, color cover

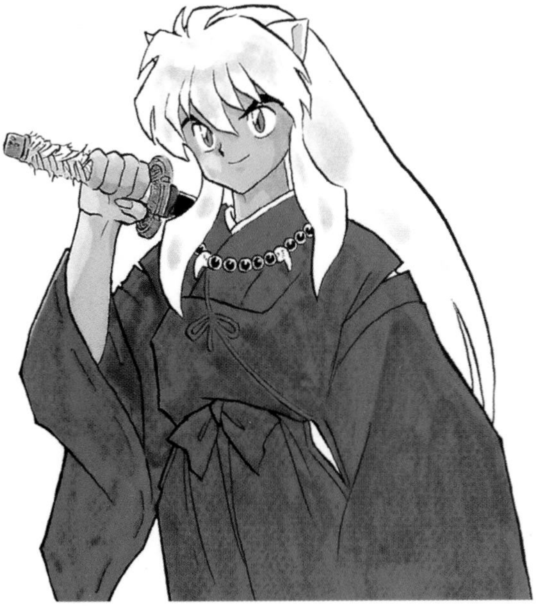

Shonen Sunday Vol. 28 1999, color cover

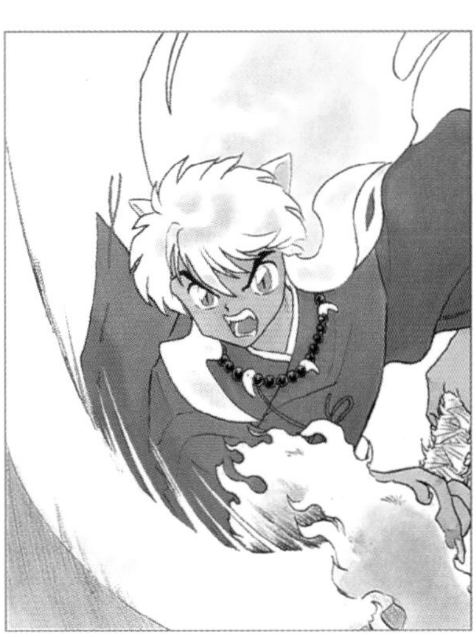

Shonen Sunday Vol. 16 1999, color cover

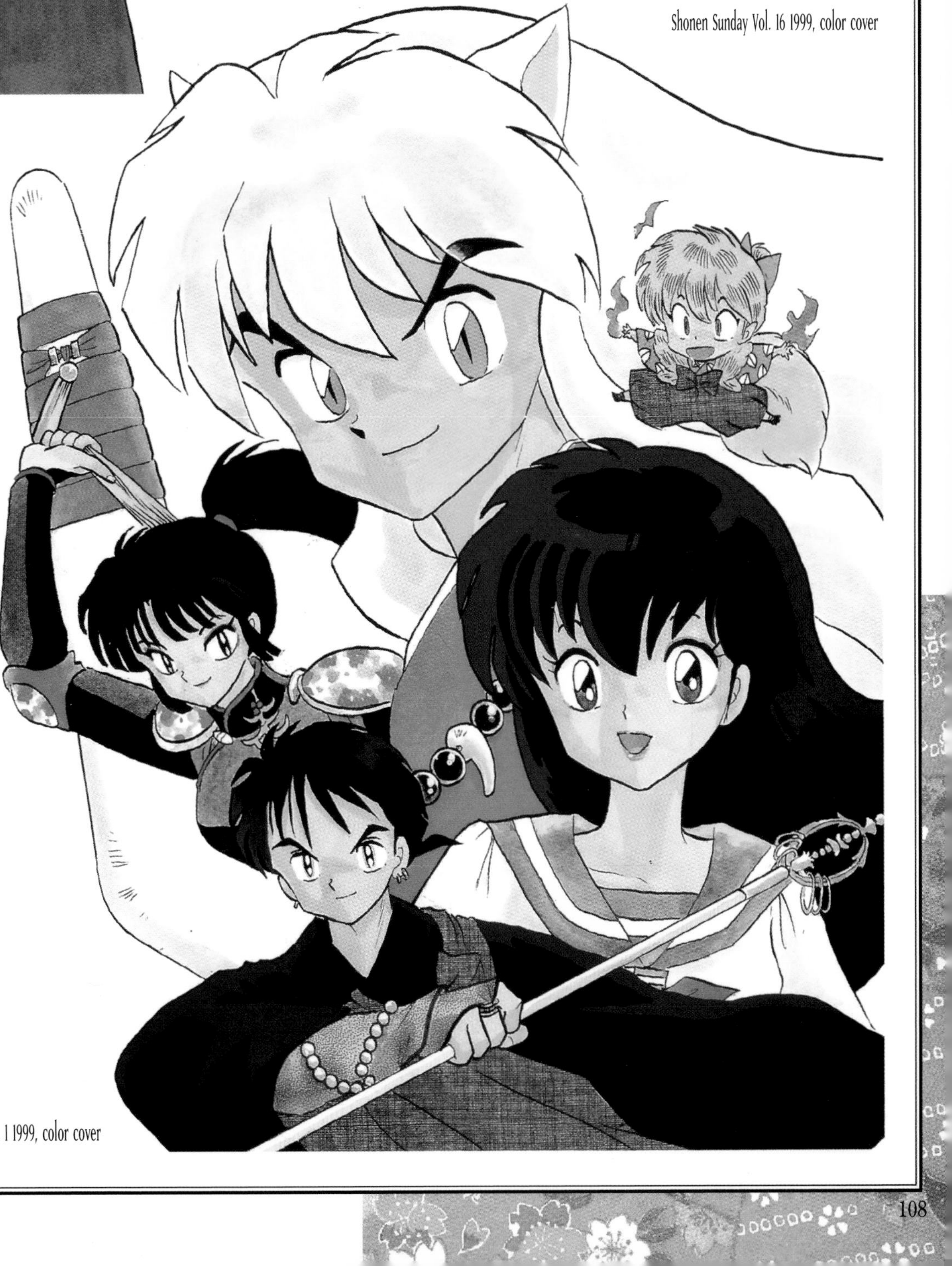

Shonen Sunday Vol. 1 1999, color cover

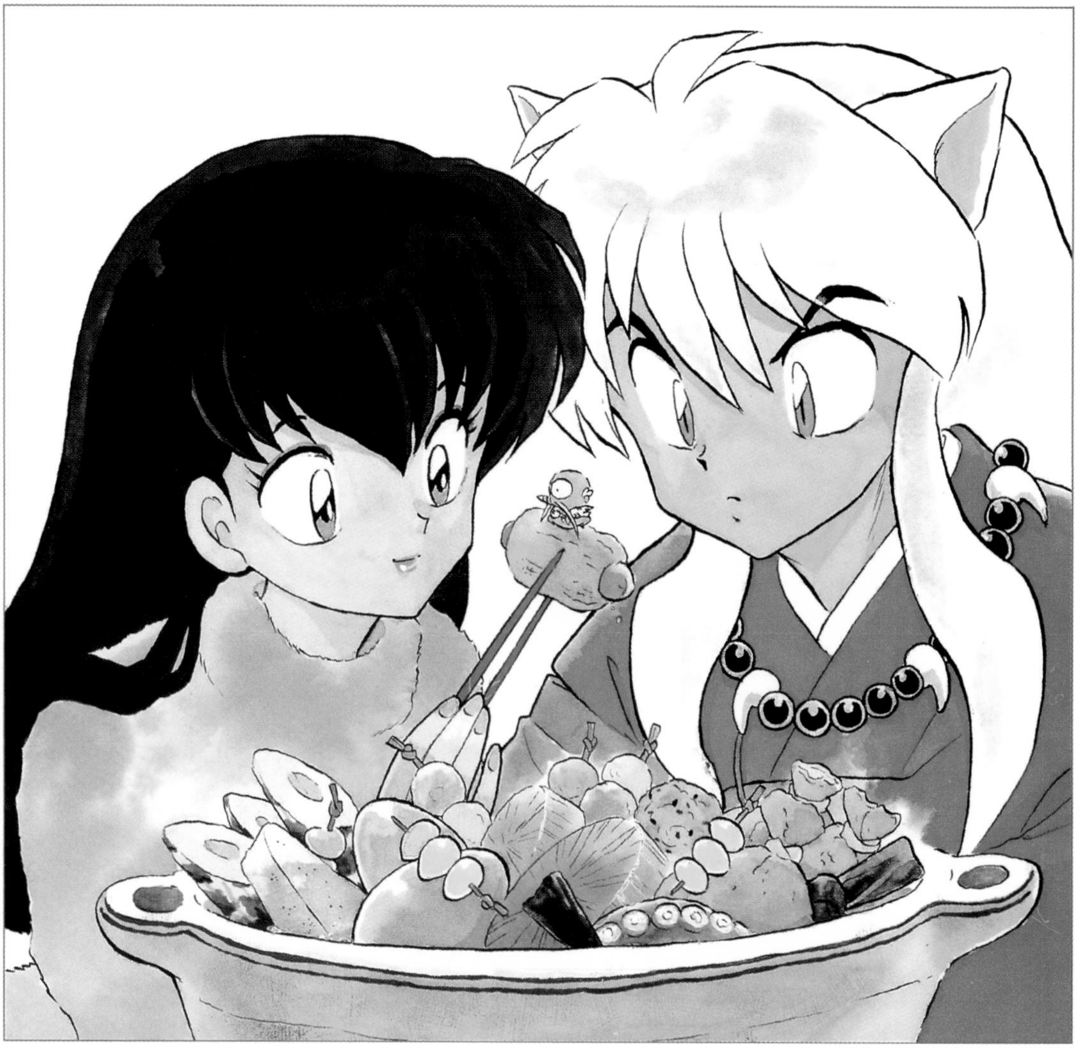

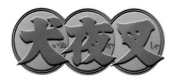

Shonen Sunday Vol. 12 1999, color cover

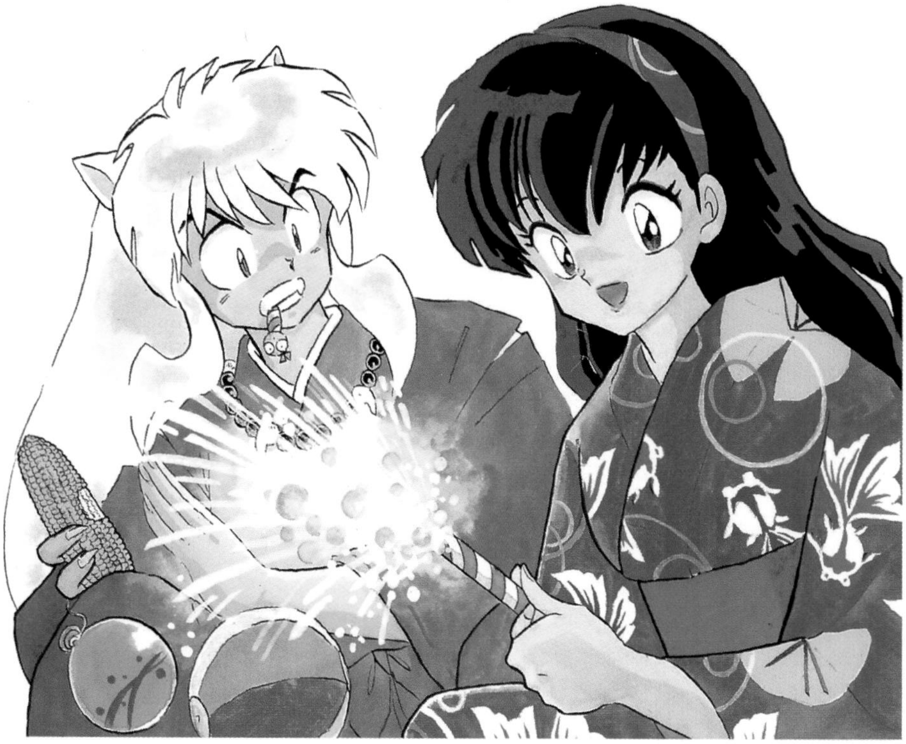

Shonen Sunday Vol. 39 1999, color cover

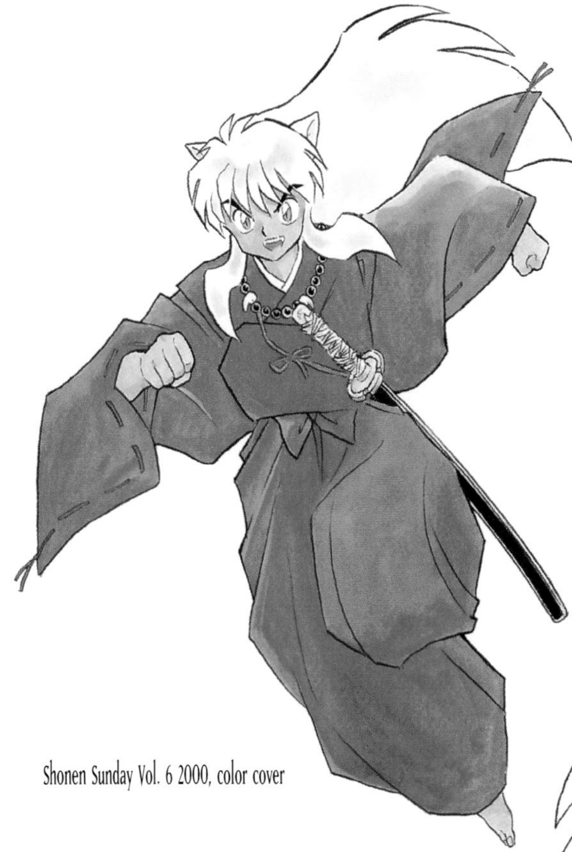

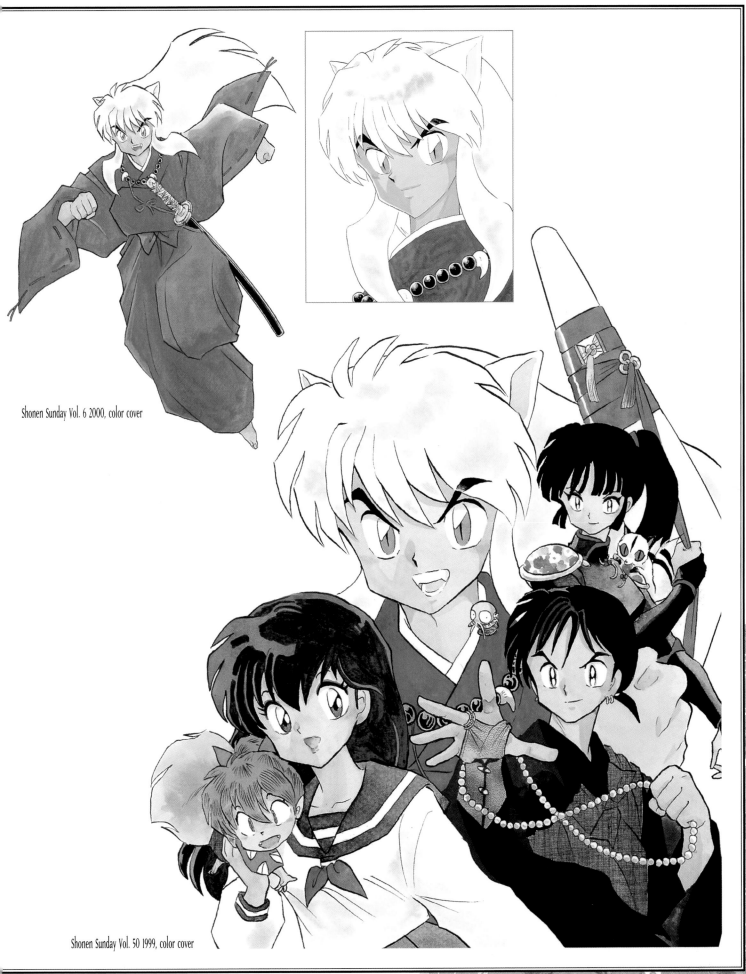

Shonen Sunday Vol. 6 2000, color cover

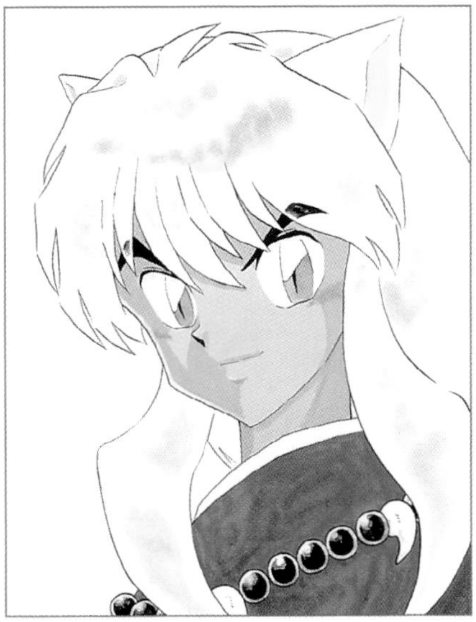

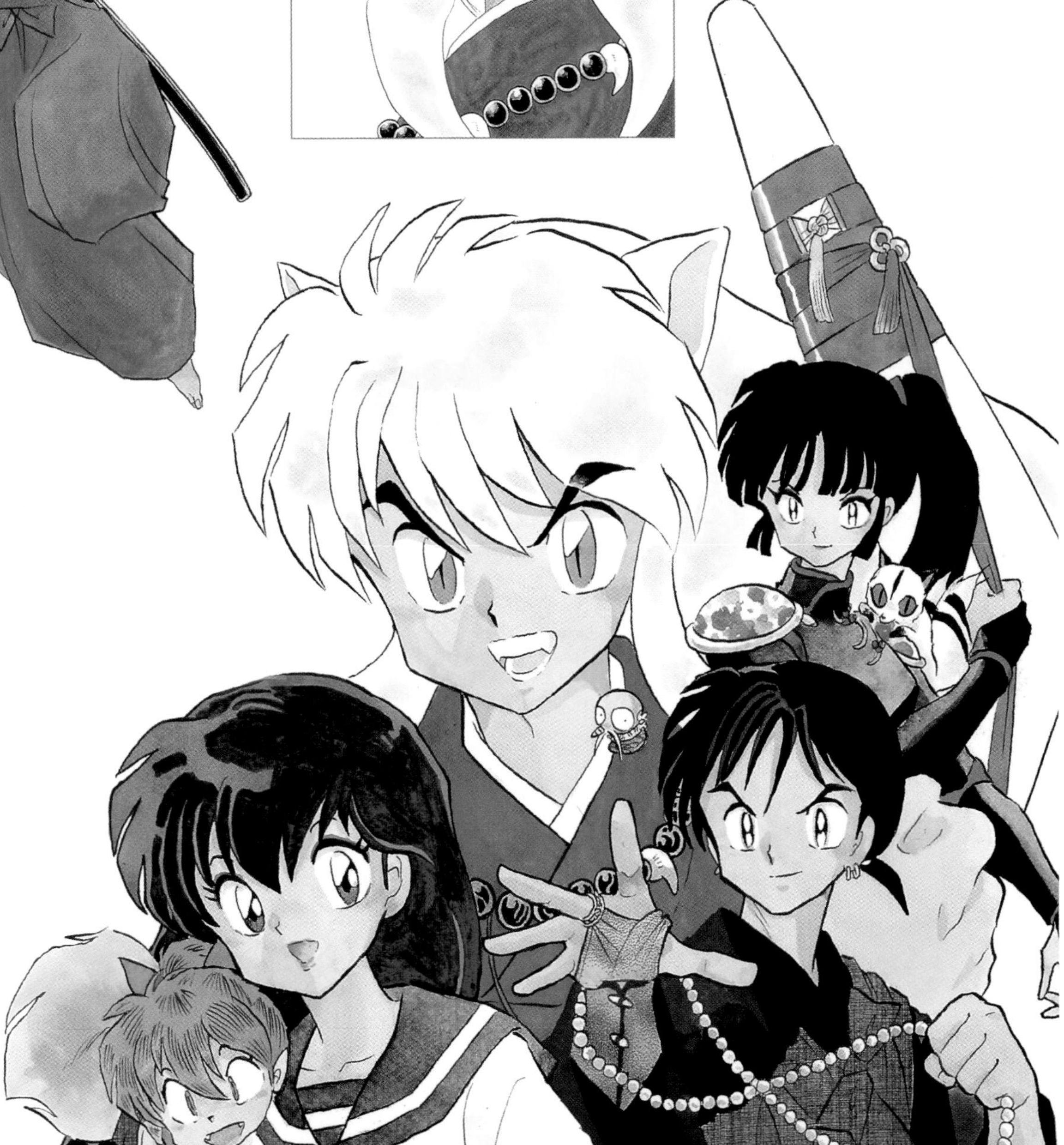

Shonen Sunday Vol. 50 1999, color cover

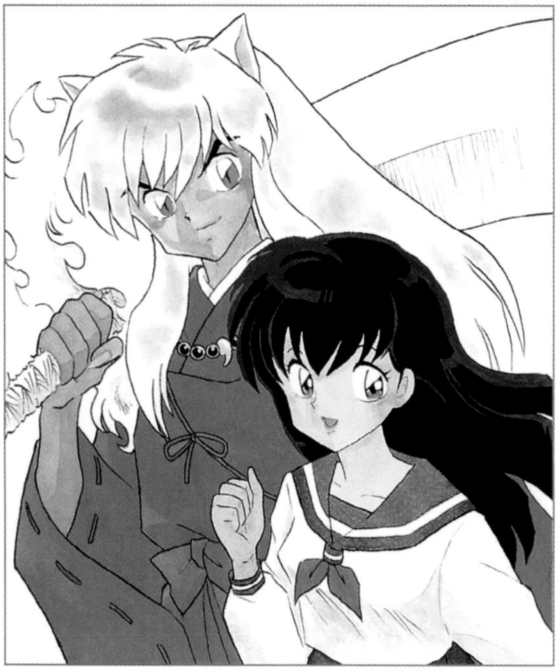

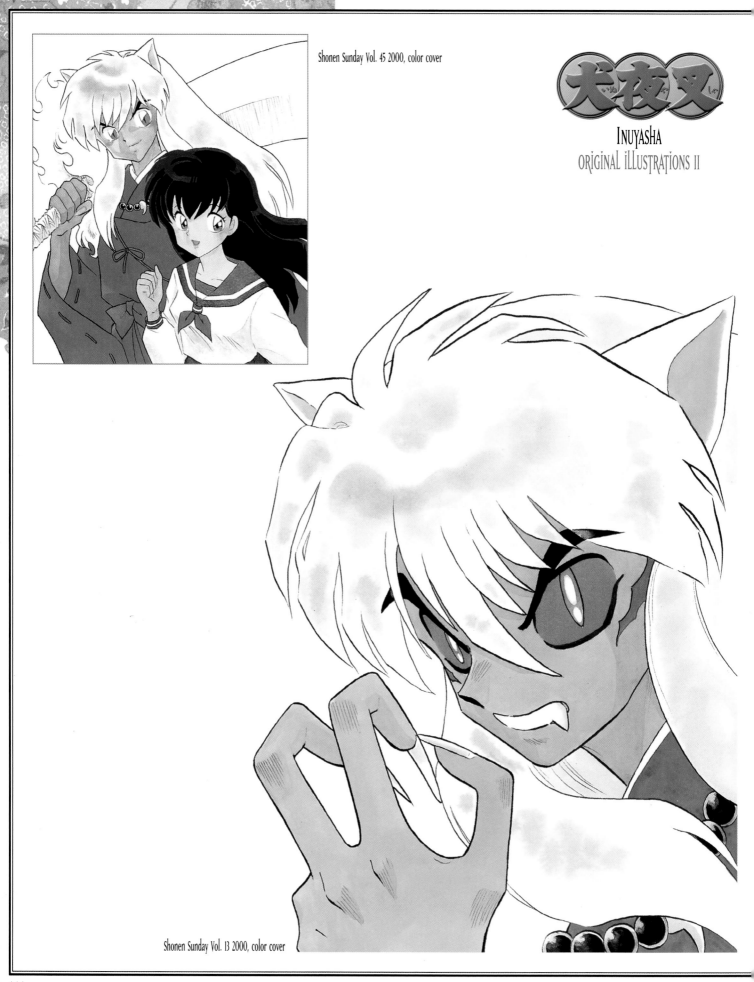

Shonen Sunday Vol. 45 2000, color cover

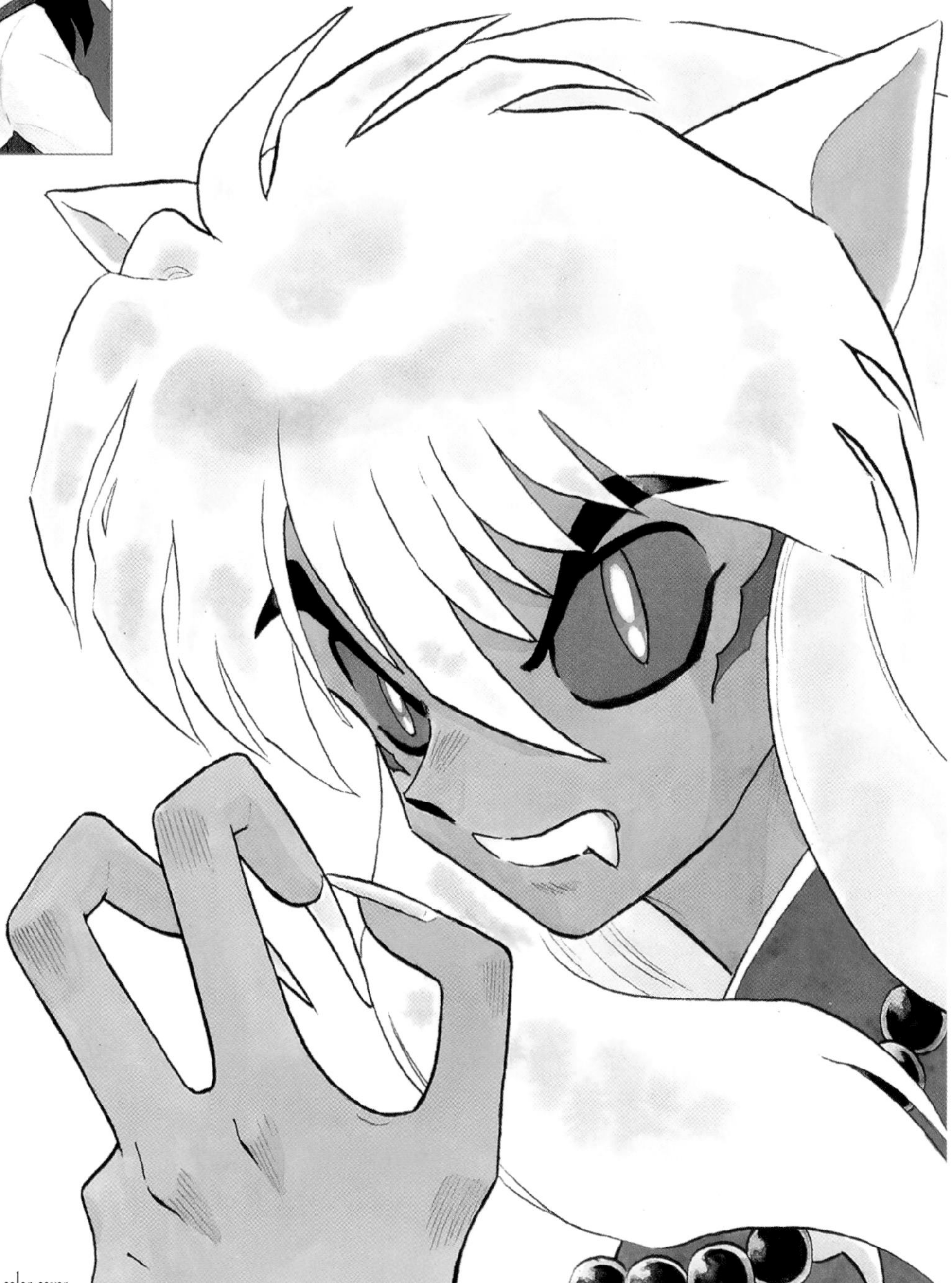

Shonen Sunday Vol. 13 2000, color cover

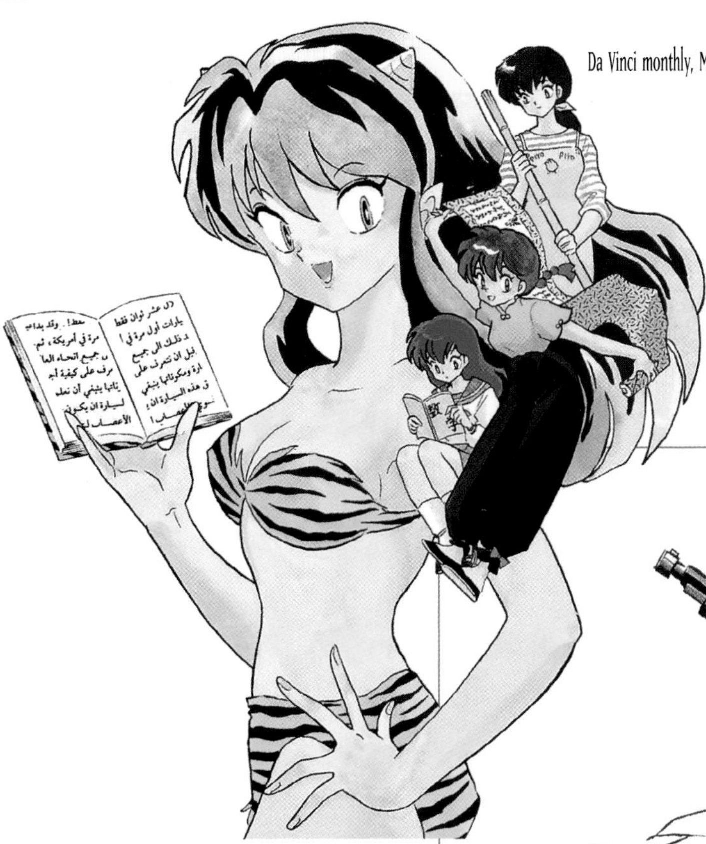

Da Vinci monthly, May 1999, color

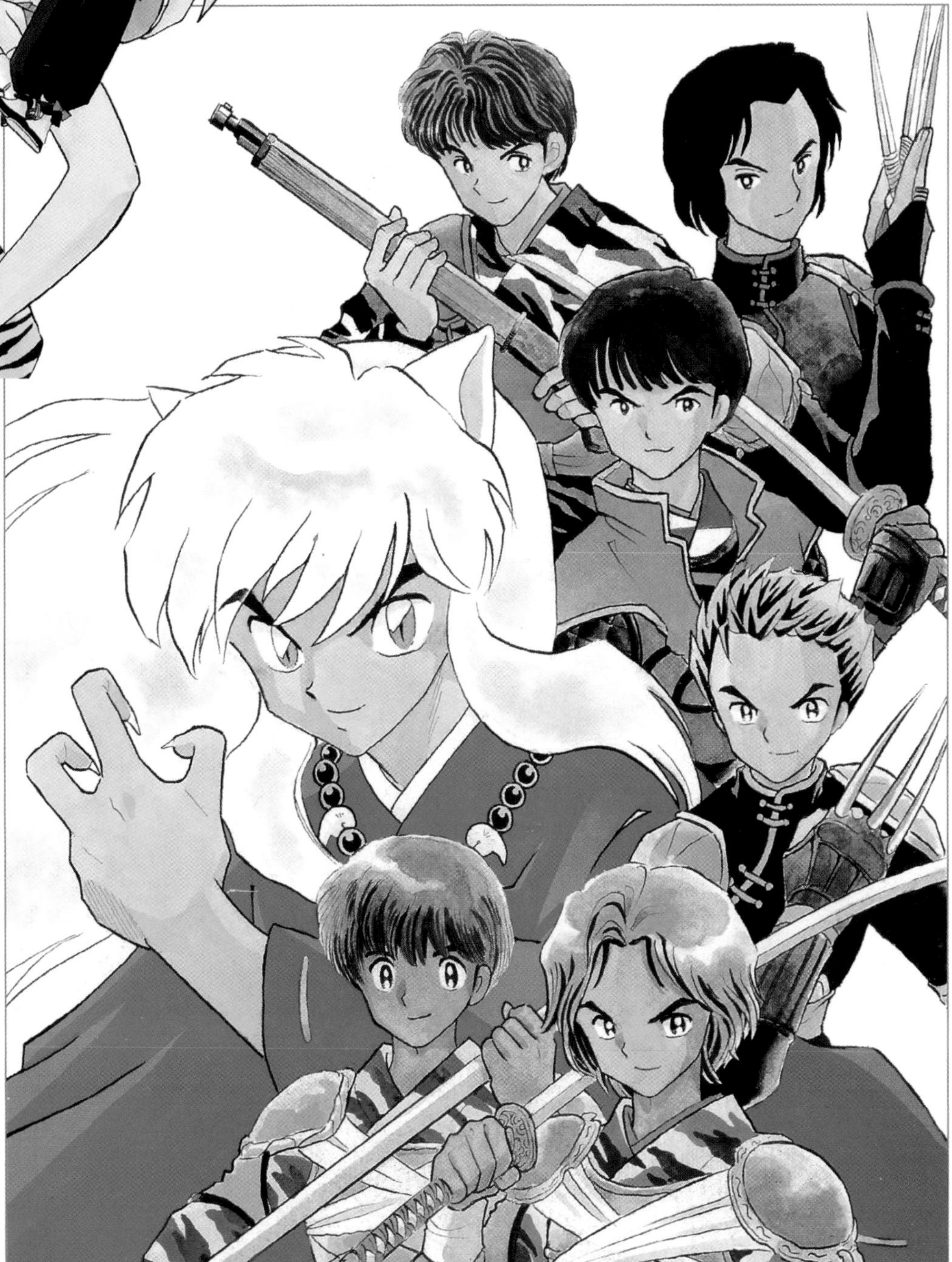

V6 "Change the World" (first CD single), gift clear file, color

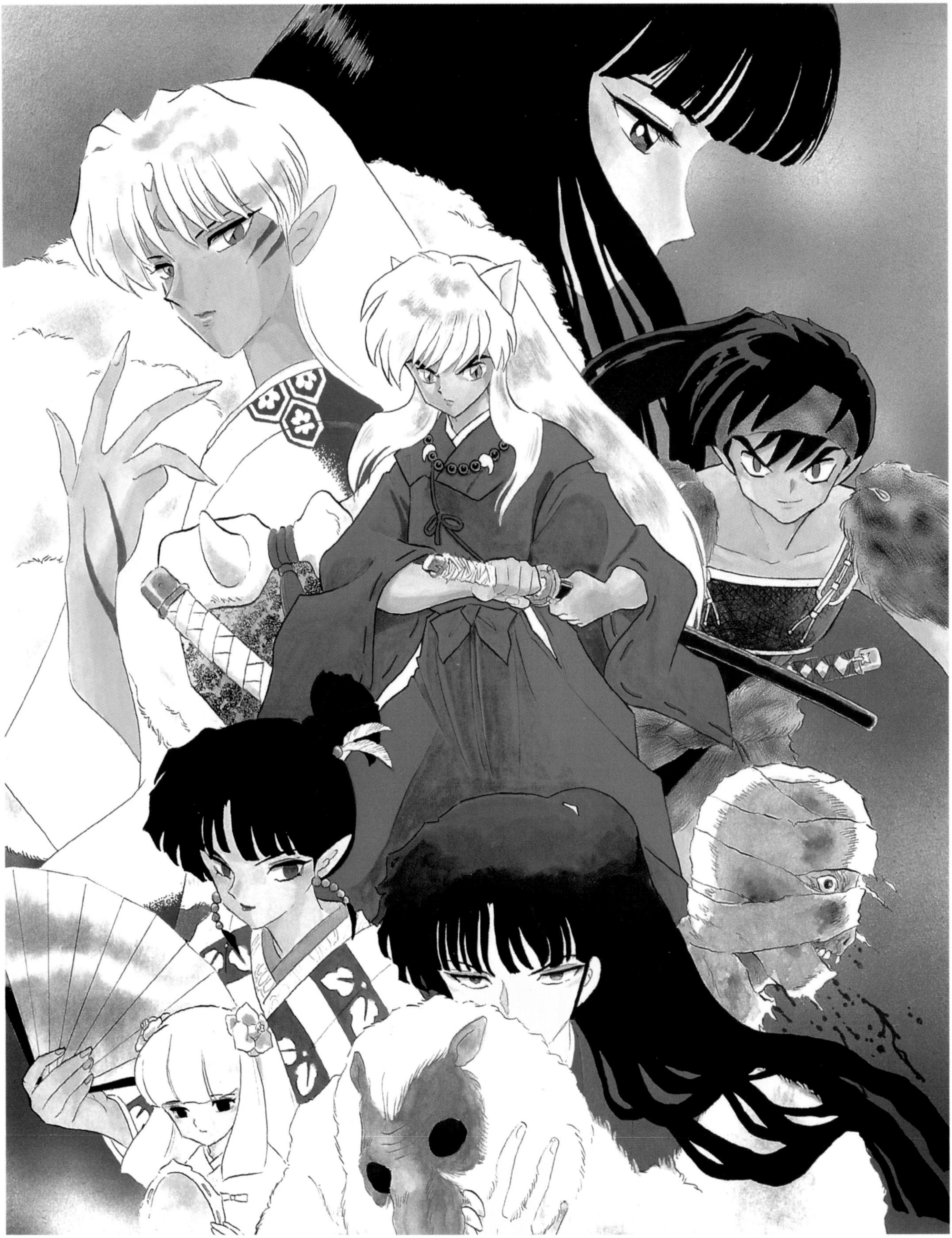

Sunday monthly GX, November 2000, fold-in poster

Comic Vol. 1 Cover Illustration

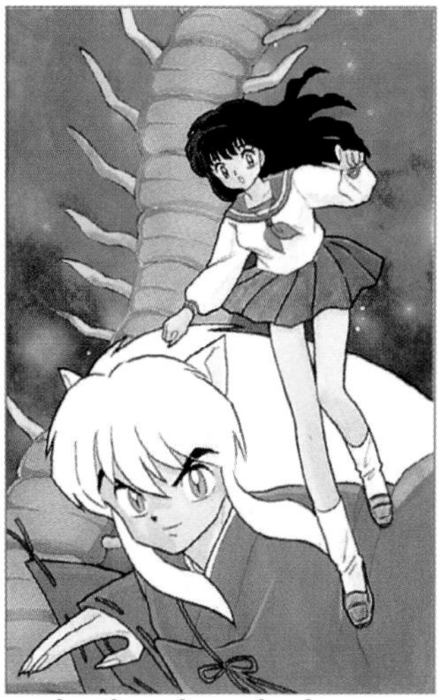

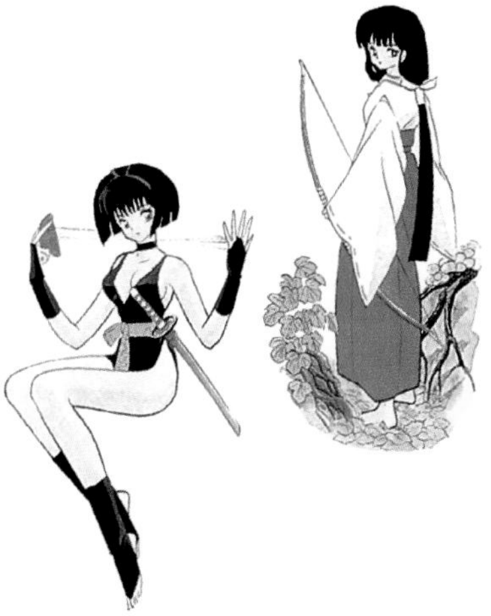

color flap/color back/color cover

Comic Vol. 2 Cover Illustration

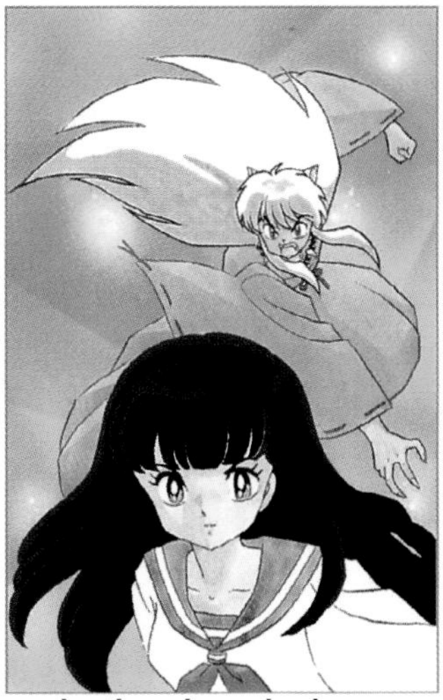

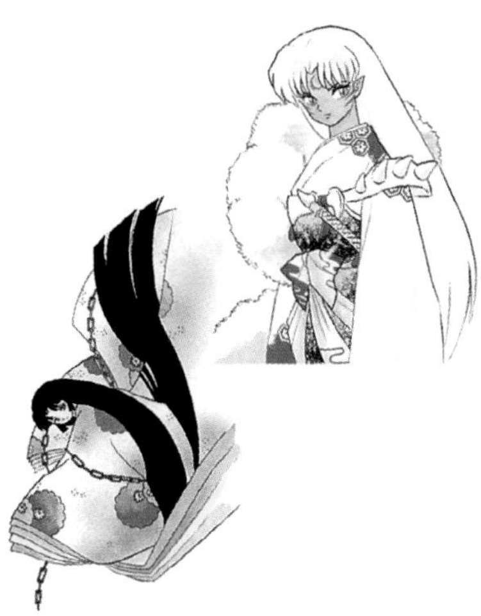

color flap/color back/color cover

Comic Vol. 3 Cover Illustration

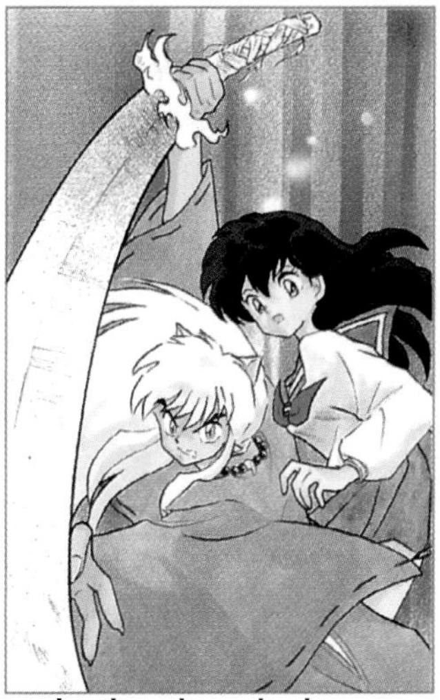

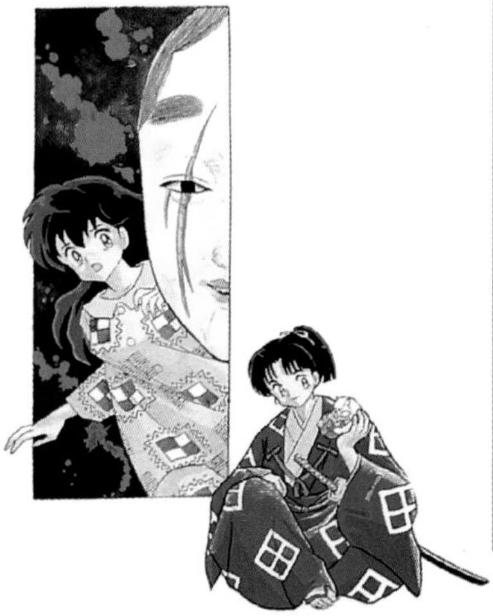

color flap/color back/color cover

Comic Vol. 4 Cover Illustration

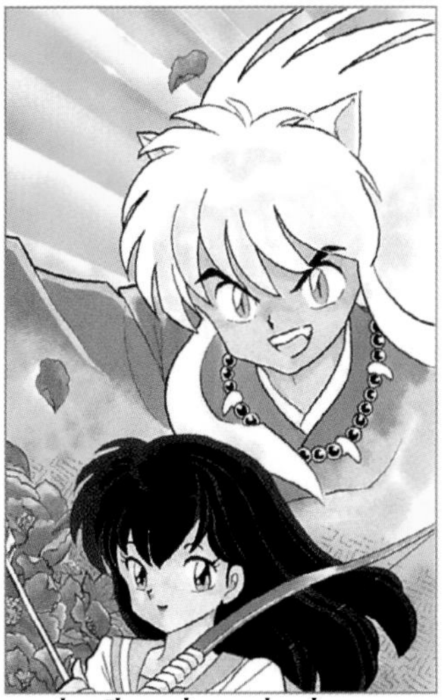

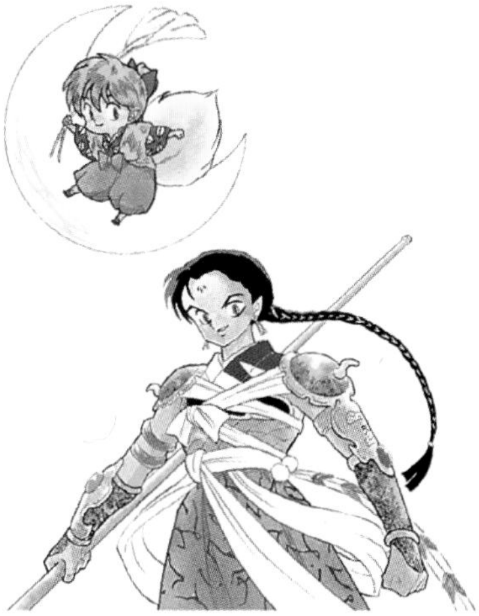

color flap/color back/color cover

Comic Vol. 5 Cover Illustration

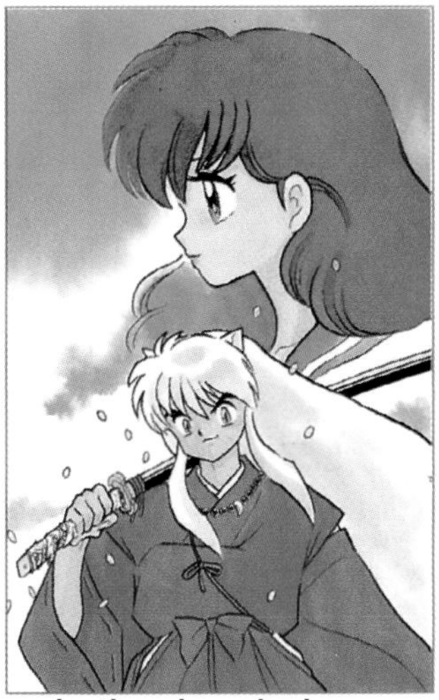

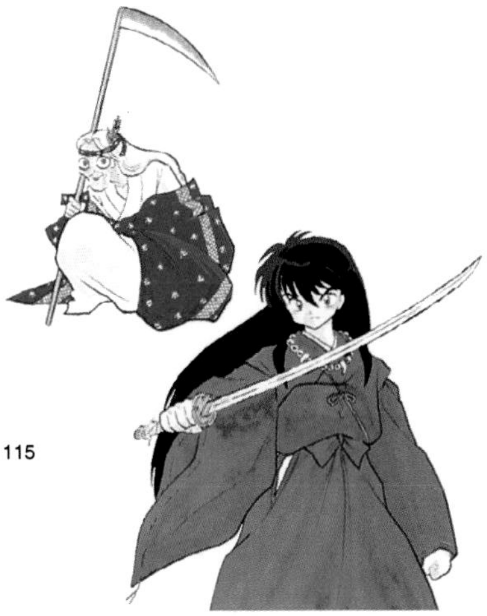

color flap/color back/color cover

Comic Vol. 6 Cover Illustration

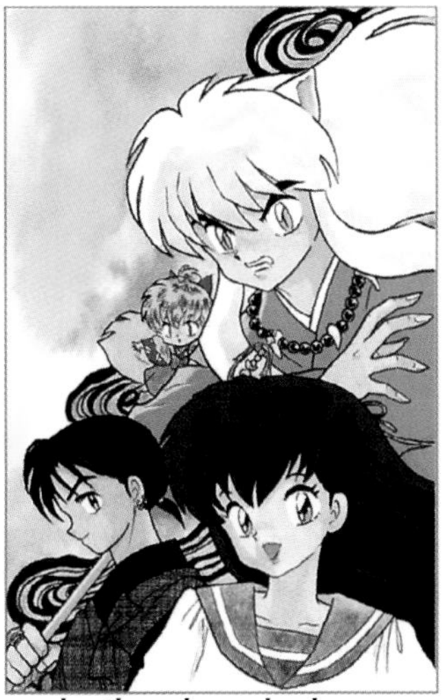

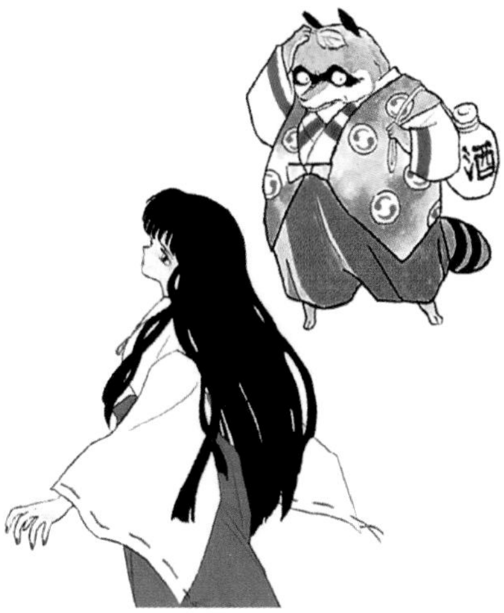
酒

color flap/color back/color cover

COMIC VOL. 7 COVER ILLUSTRATION

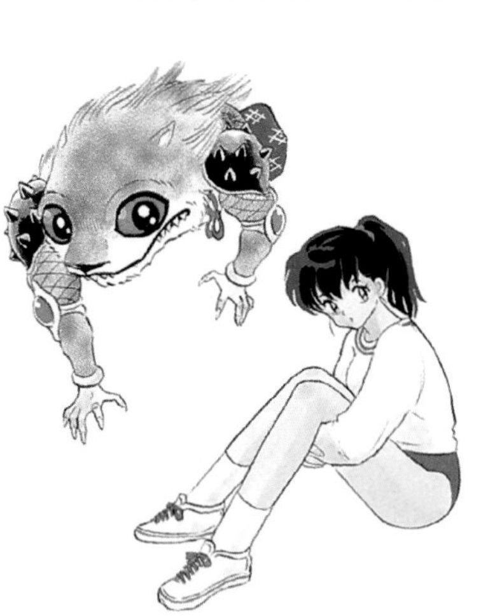

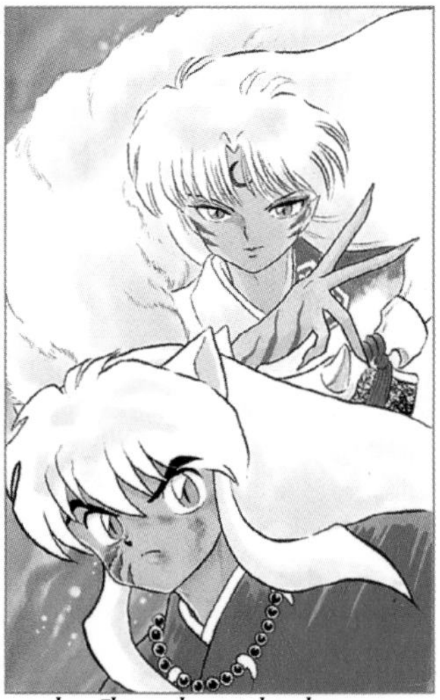

COLOR FLAP/COLOR BACK/COLOR COVER

COMIC VOL. 8 COVER ILLUSTRATION

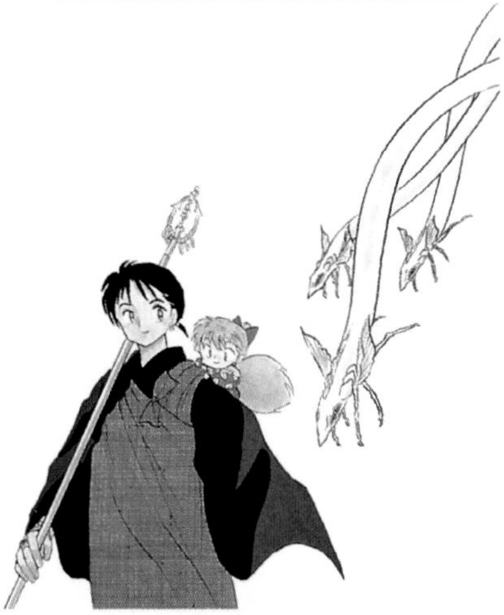

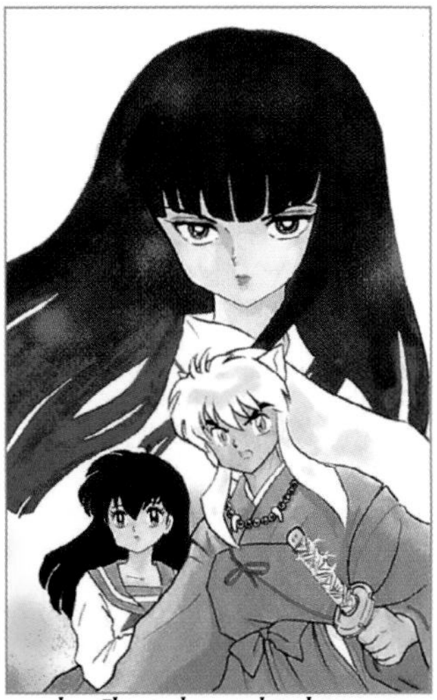

COLOR FLAP/COLOR BACK/COLOR COVER

COMIC VOL. 9 COVER ILLUSTRATION

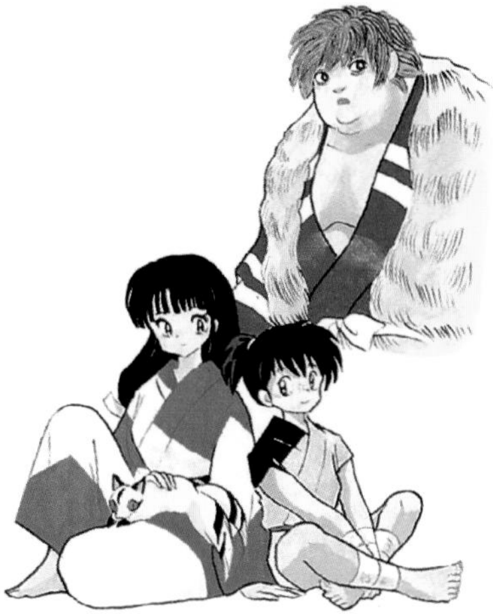

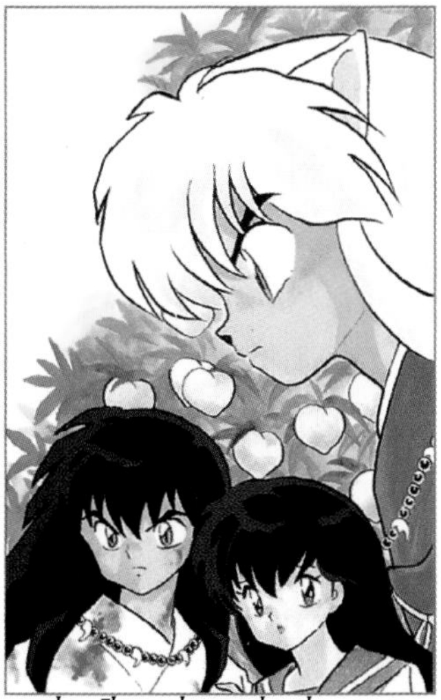

COLOR FLAP/COLOR BACK/COLOR COVER

COMIC VOL. 10 COVER ILLUSTRATION

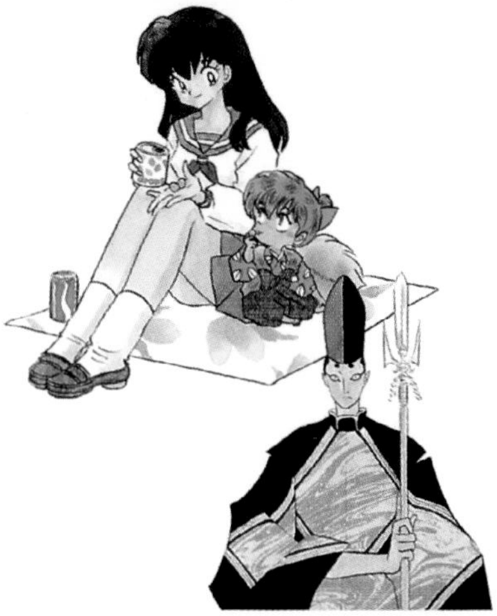

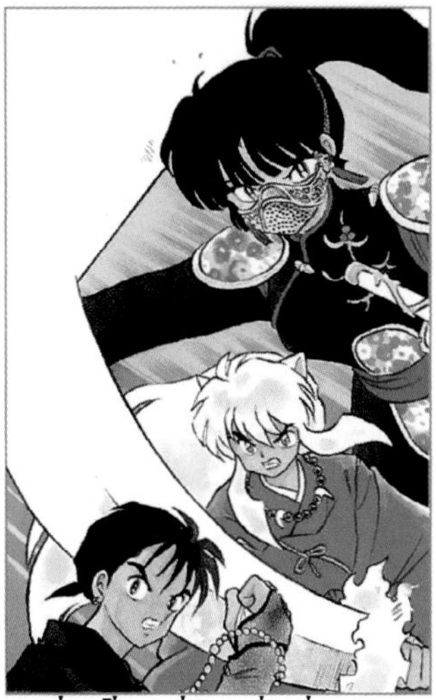

COLOR FLAP/COLOR BACK/COLOR COVER

COMIC VOL. 11 COVER ILLUSTRATION

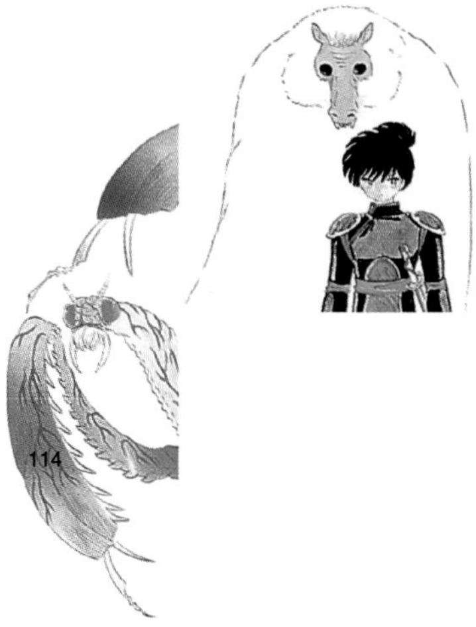

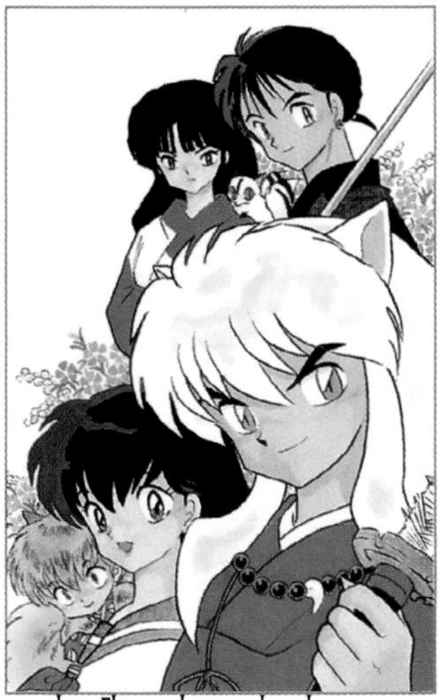

COLOR FLAP/COLOR BACK/COLOR COVER

COMIC VOL. 12 COVER ILLUSTRATION

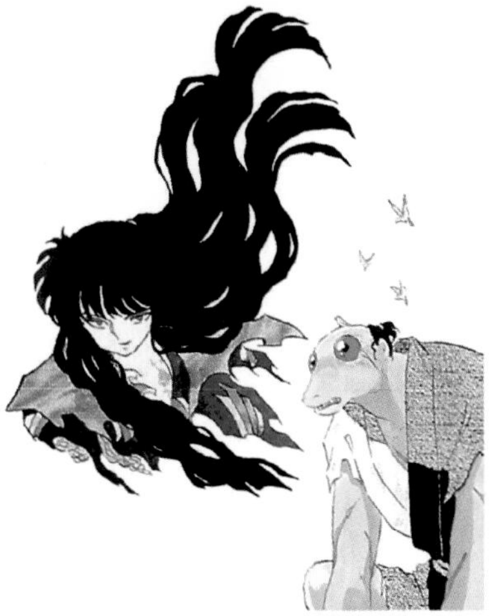

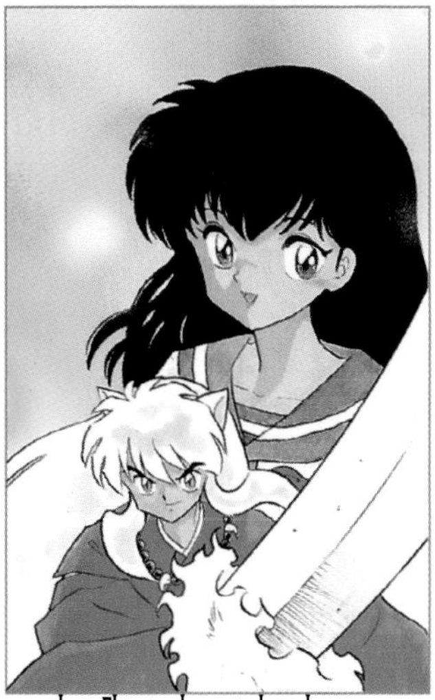

COLOR FLAP/COLOR BACK/COLOR COVER

COMIC VOL. 13 COVER ILLUSTRATION

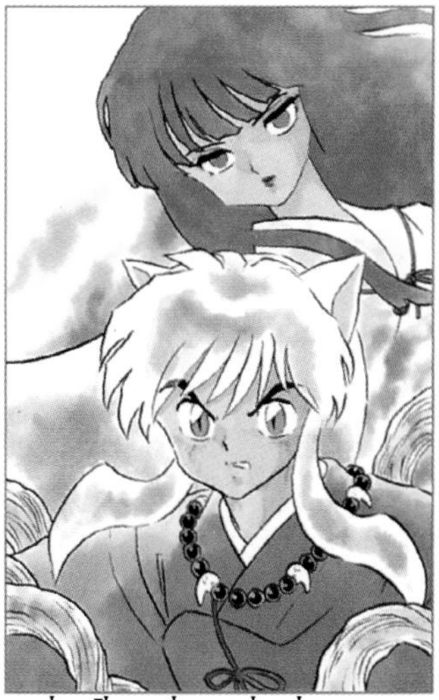

COLOR FLAP/COLOR BACK/COLOR COVER

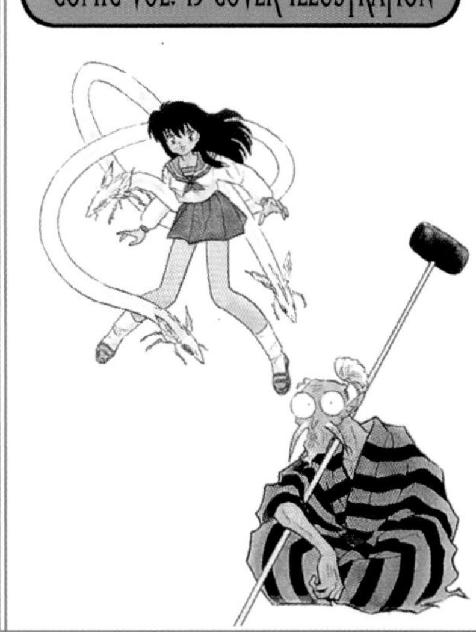

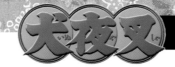

COMIC VOL. 14 COVER ILLUSTRATION

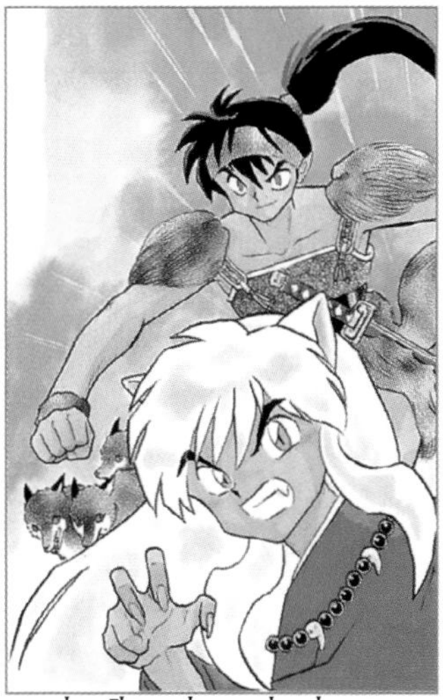

COLOR FLAP/COLOR BACK/COLOR COVER

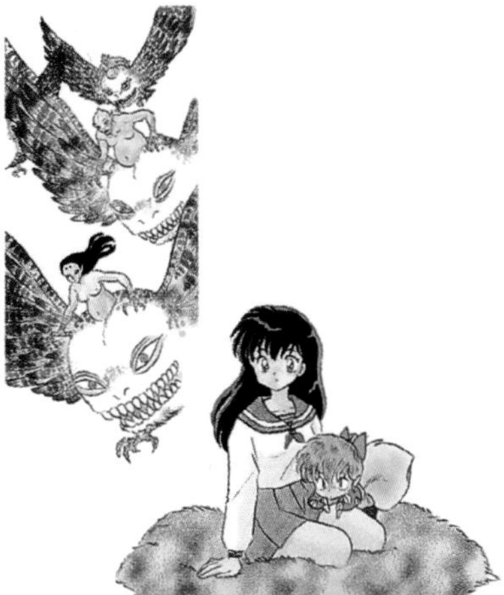

COMIC VOL. 15 COVER ILLUSTRATION

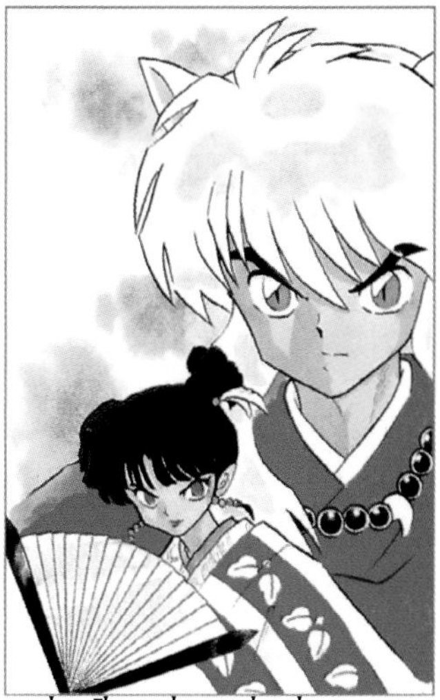

COLOR FLAP/COLOR BACK/COLOR COVER

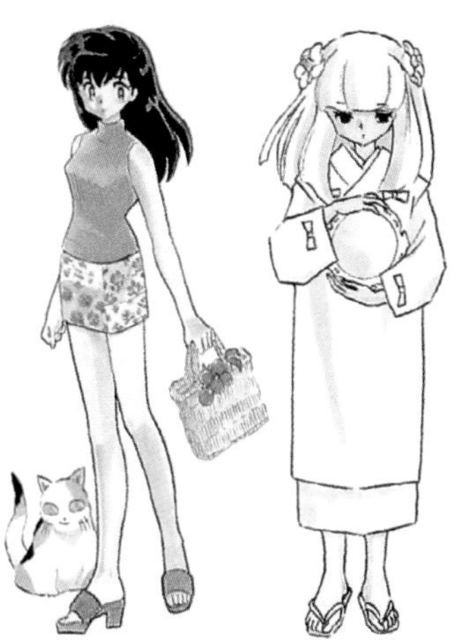

COMIC VOL. 16 COVER ILLUSTRATION

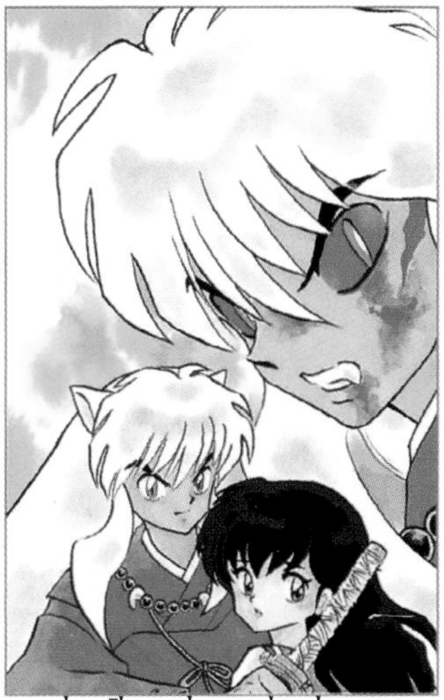

COLOR FLAP/COLOR BACK/COLOR COVER

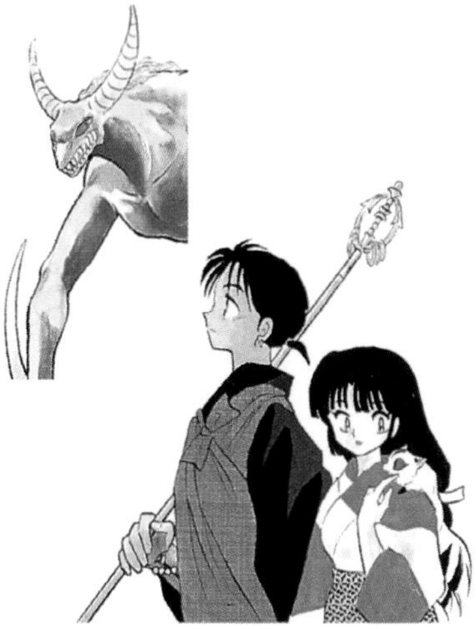

COMIC VOL. 17 COVER ILLUSTRATION

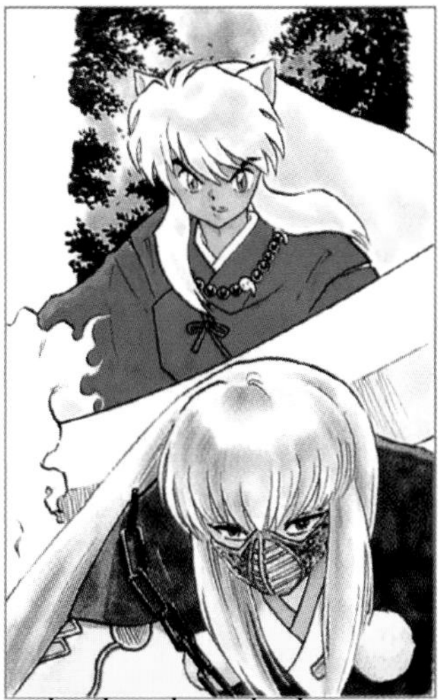

COLOR FLAP/COLOR BACK/COLOR COVER

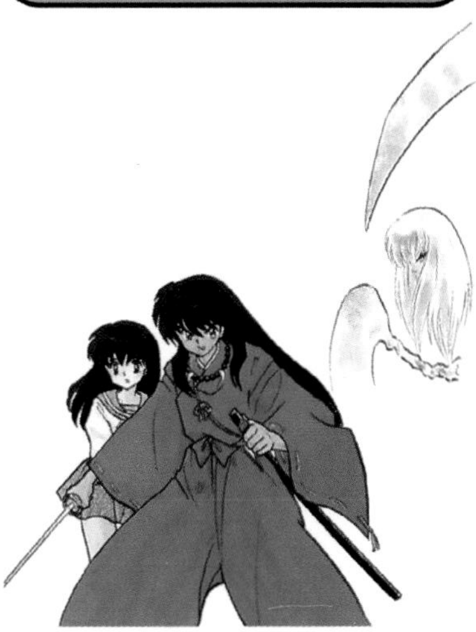

COMIC VOL. 18 COVER ILLUSTRATION

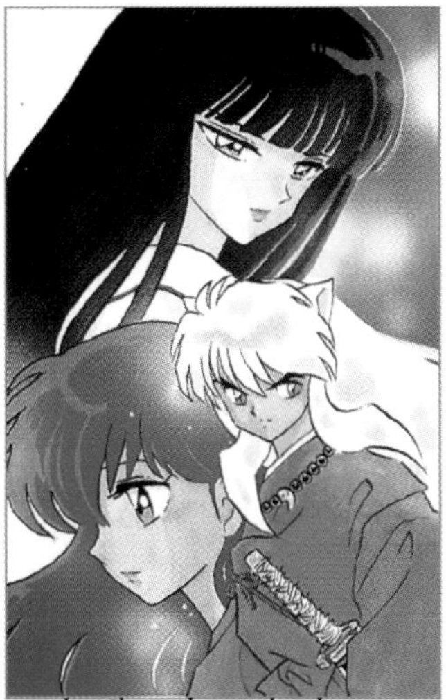

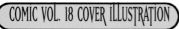

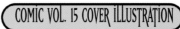

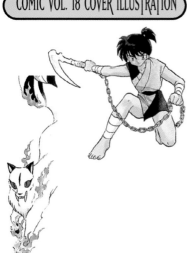

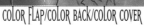

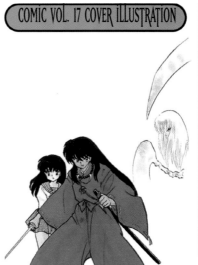

COLOR FLAP/COLOR BACK/COLOR COVER

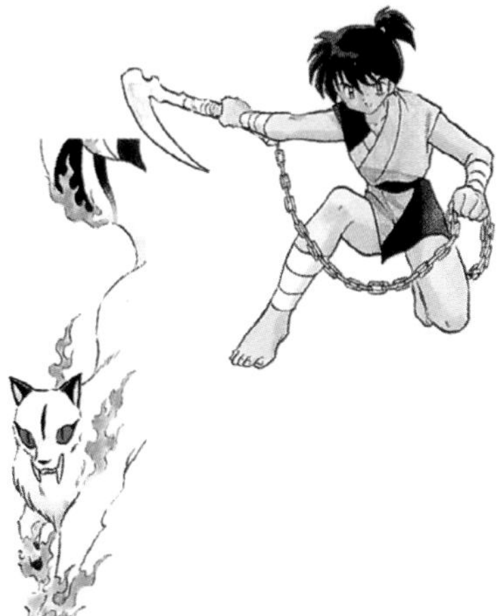

ANIMATION WORLD

- DATABASE OF ANIMATION CHARACTERS
- STORYBOARDS
- COMPLETE STUDY OF THE OPENING SEQUENCE

犬夜叉

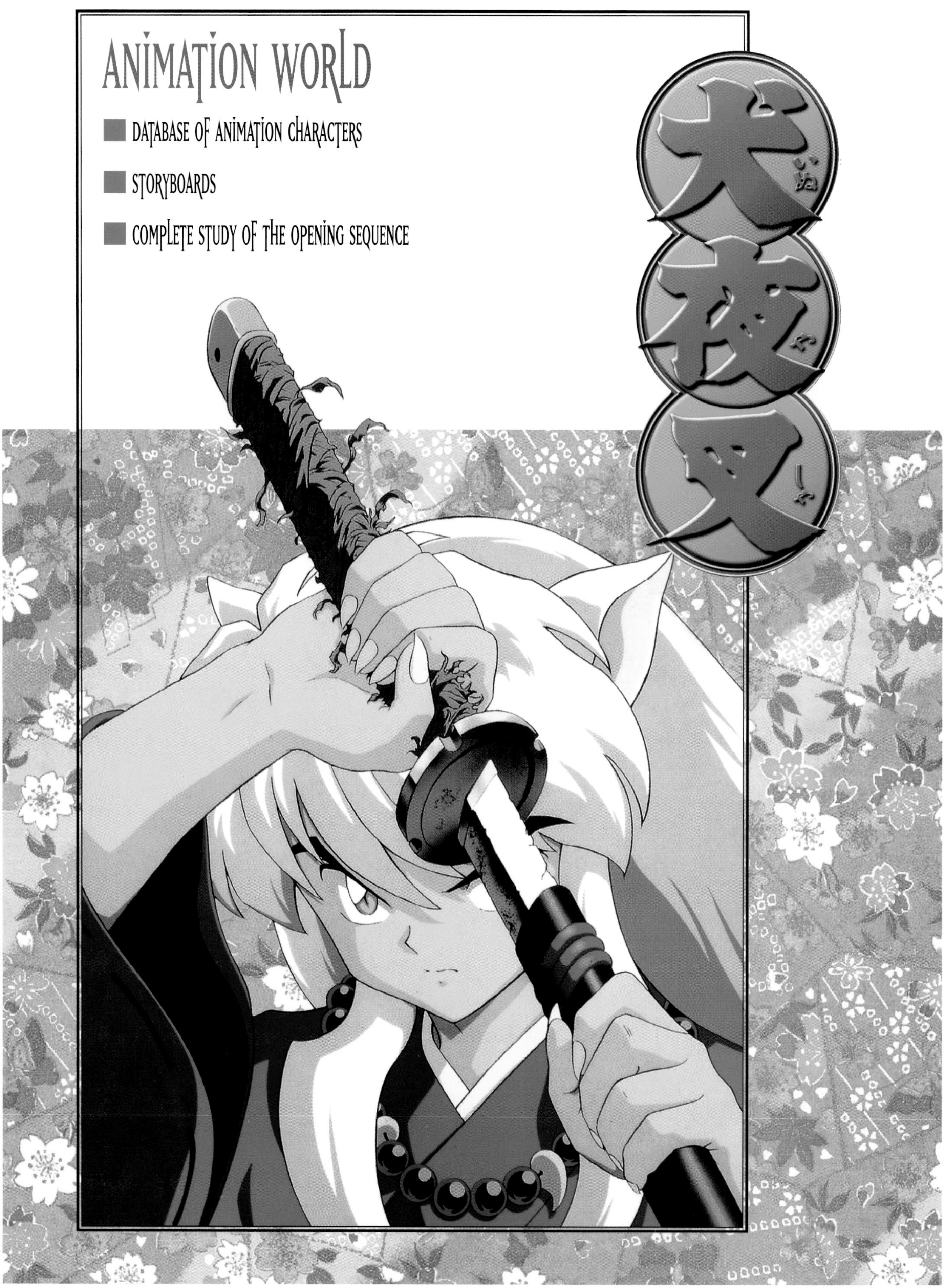

DATABASE OF "INUYASHA" ANIMATION CHARACTERS

How are the Inuyasha characters defined in animation by costumes and colors?
Let's take a look at them, with brief introductions.

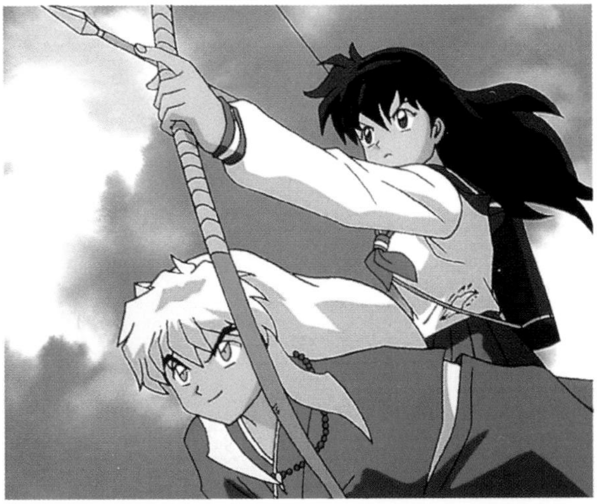

KAGOME HIGURASHI

A ninth-grader who travels through time from the modern world to a world of civil war in the Middle Ages. She gets involved in a battle for the Jewel of Four Souls. She is cheerful, active and courageous, with a strong sense of justice. She wears a sailor-collared school uniform, as in the original comic, but her loose socks are replaced with regular socks.

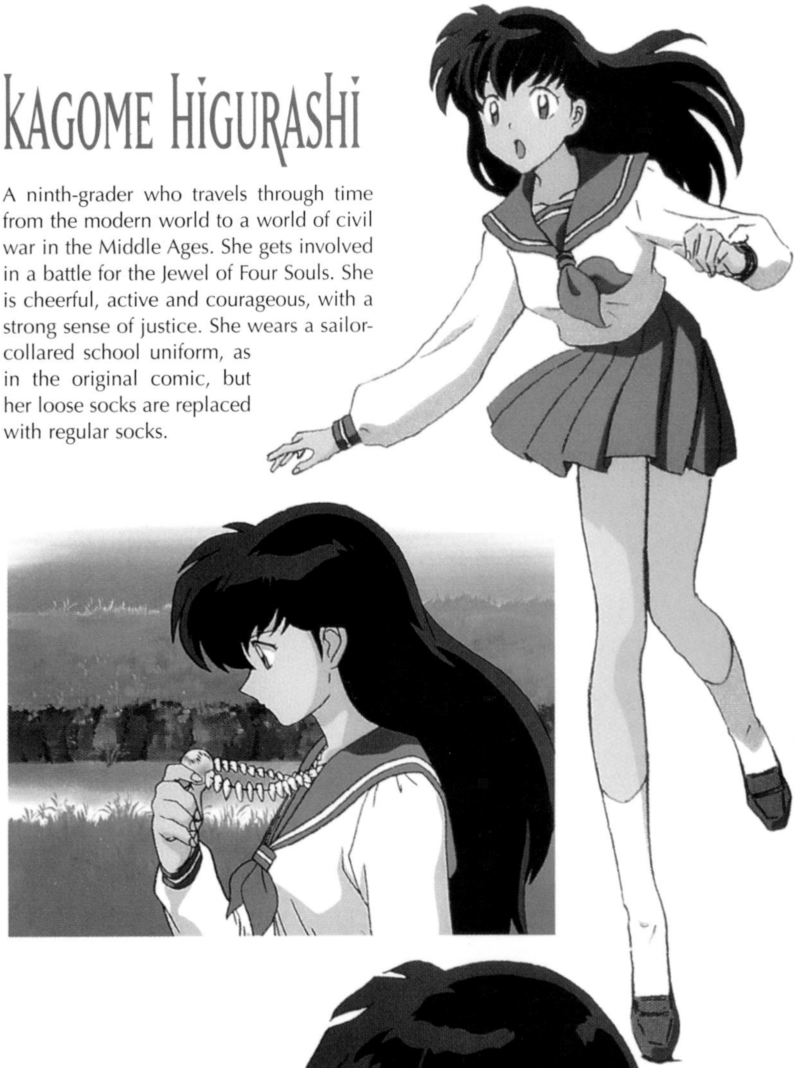

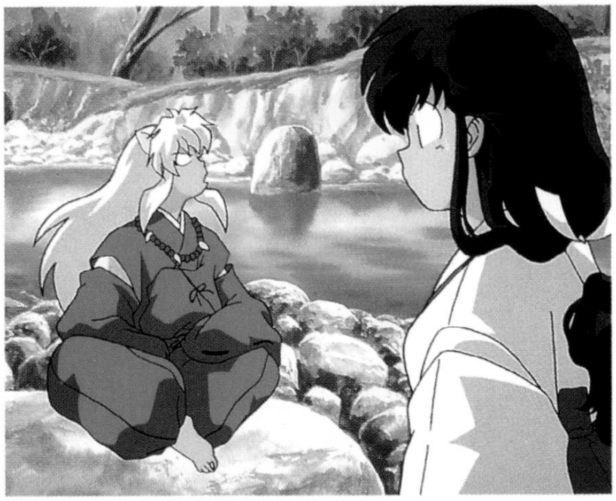

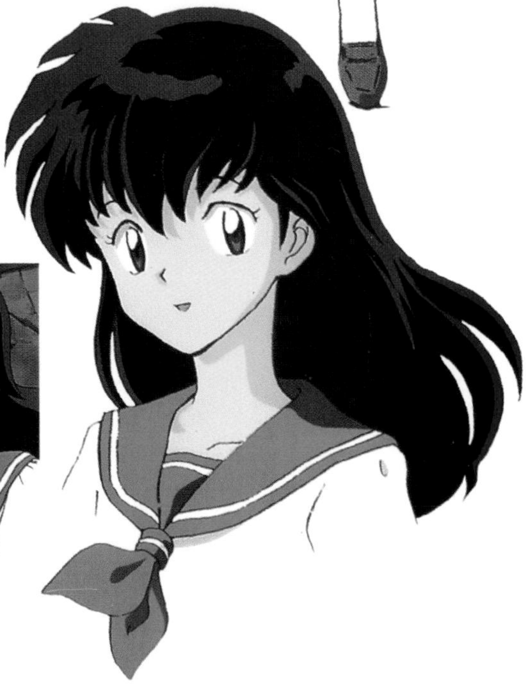

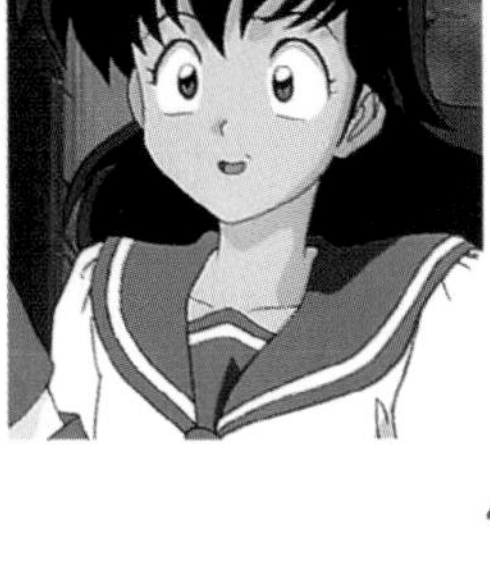

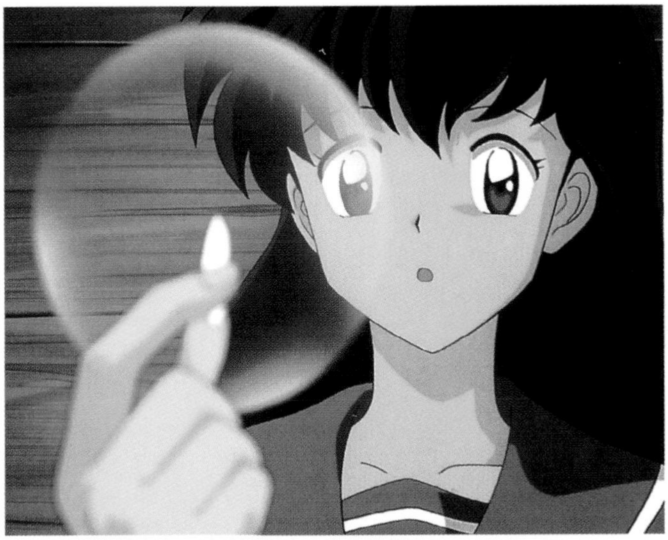

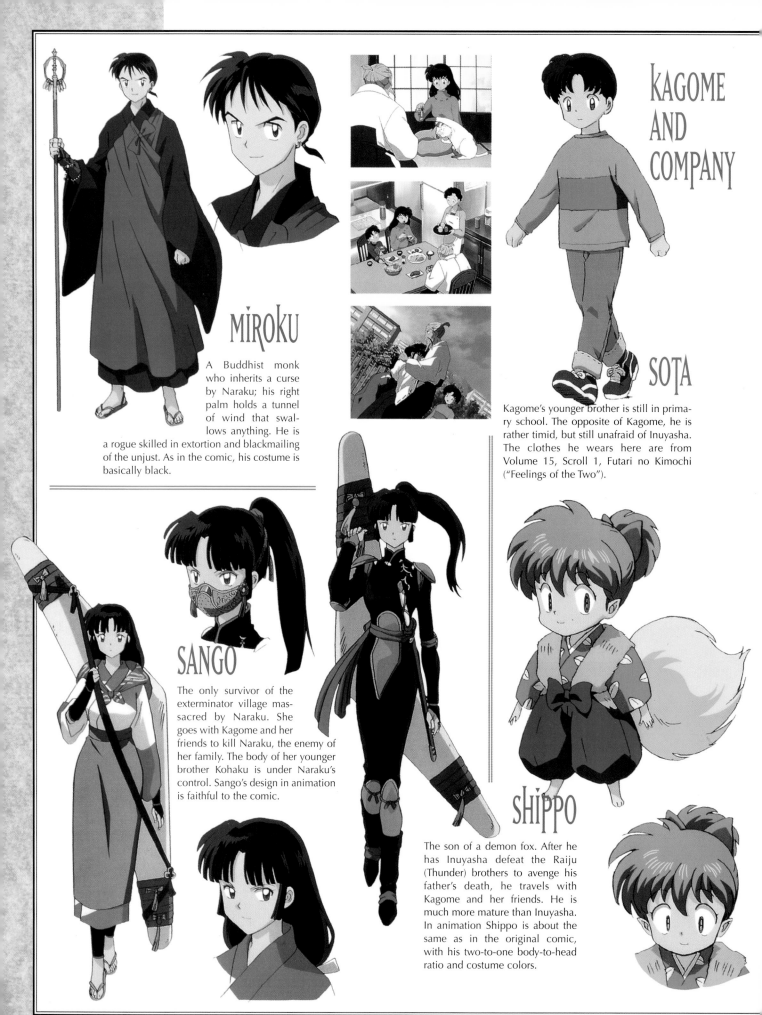

KAGOME AND COMPANY

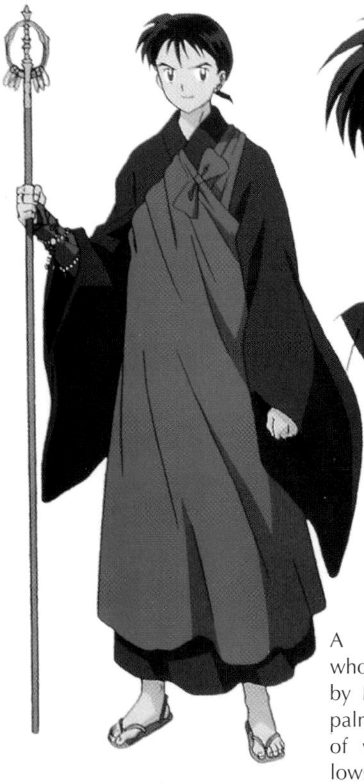

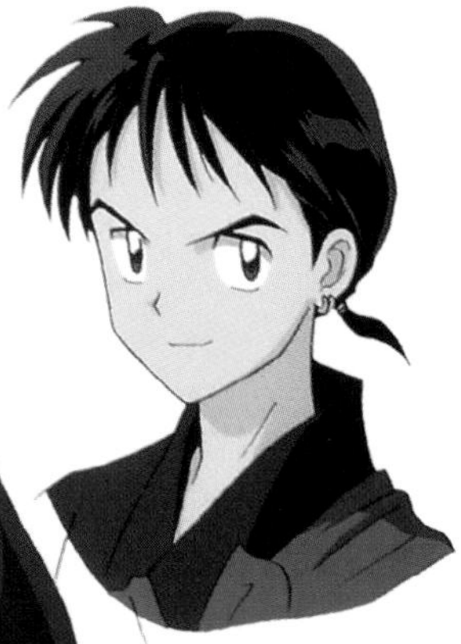

MIROKU

A Buddhist monk who inherits a curse by Naraku; his right palm holds a tunnel of wind that swallows anything. He is a rogue skilled in extortion and blackmailing of the unjust. As in the comic, his costume is basically black.

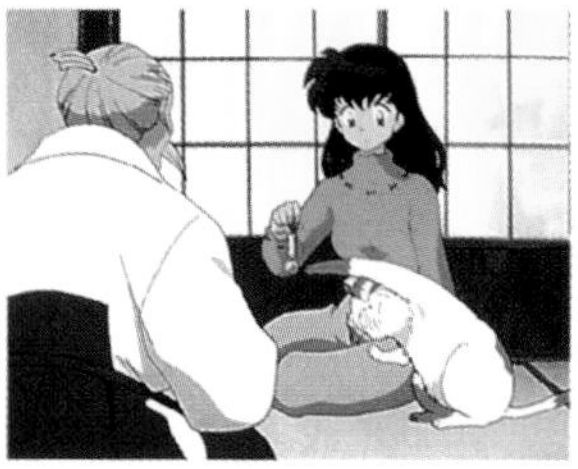

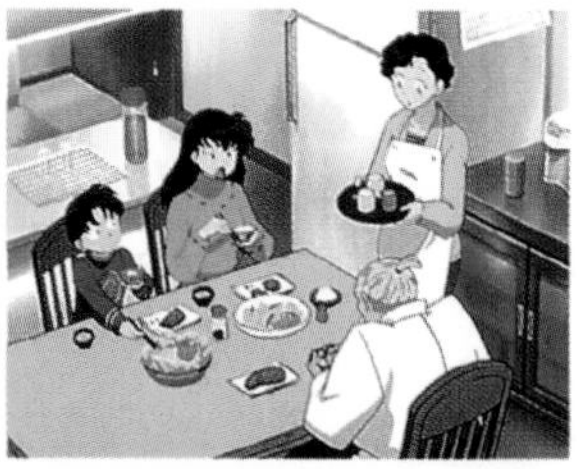

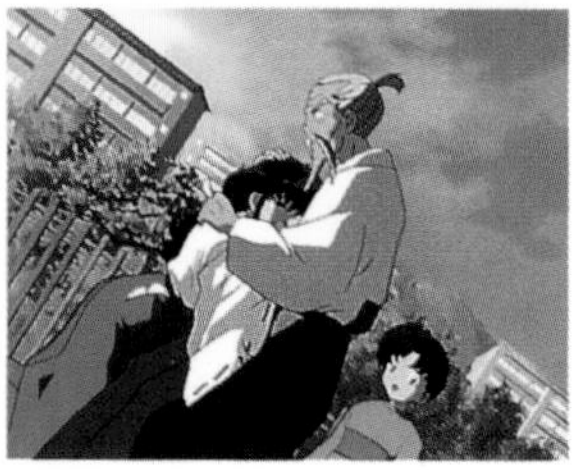

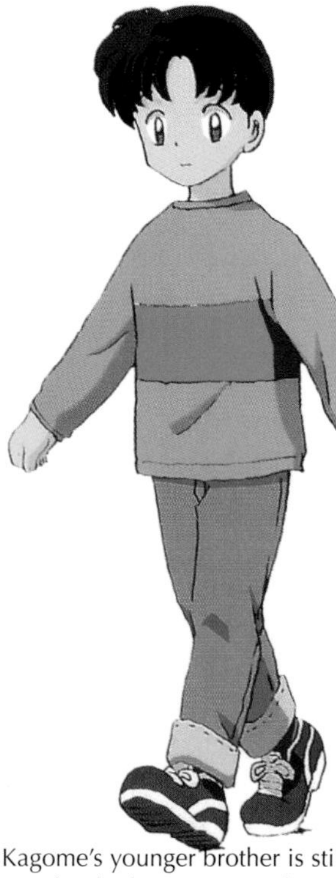

SOTA

Kagome's younger brother is still in primary school. The opposite of Kagome, he is rather timid, but still unafraid of Inuyasha. The clothes he wears here are from Volume 15, Scroll 1, Futari no Kimochi ("Feelings of the Two").

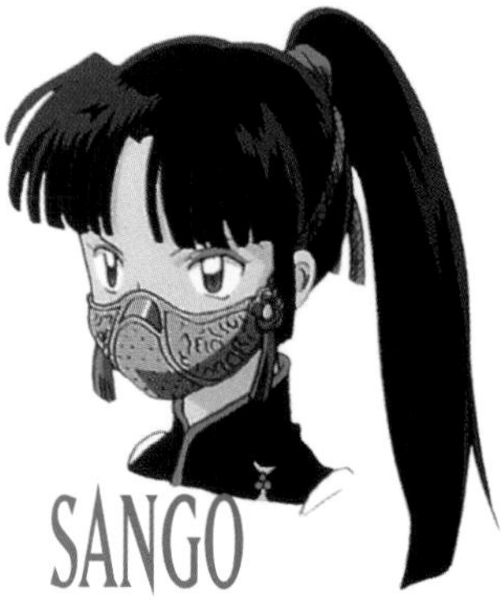

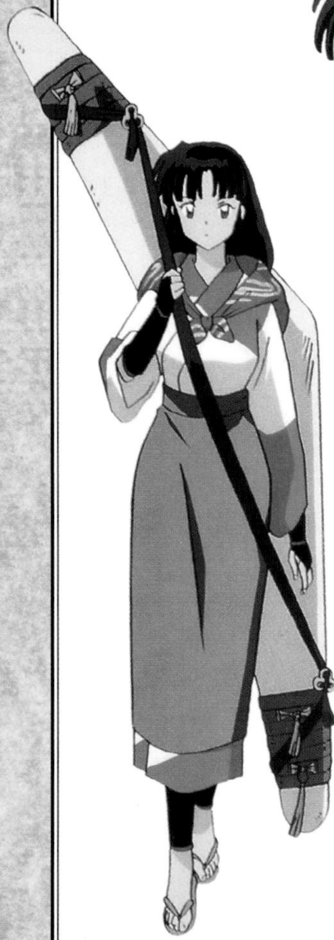

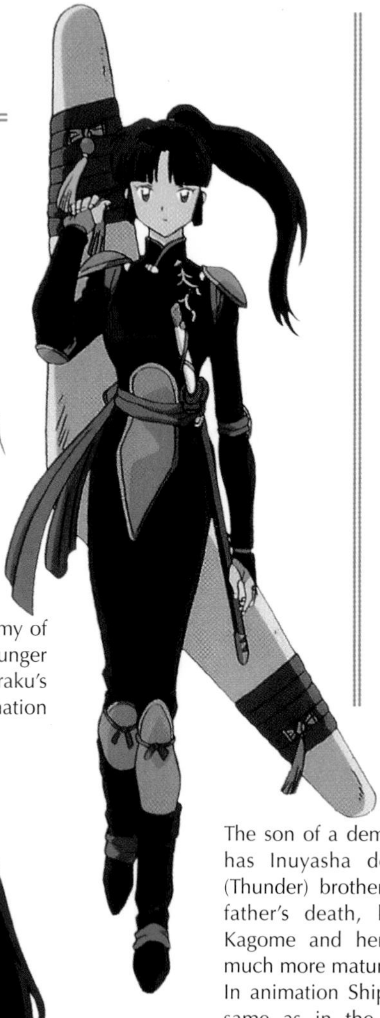

SANGO

The only survivor of the exterminator village massacred by Naraku. She goes with Kagome and her friends to kill Naraku, the enemy of her family. The body of her younger brother Kohaku is under Naraku's control. Sango's design in animation is faithful to the comic.

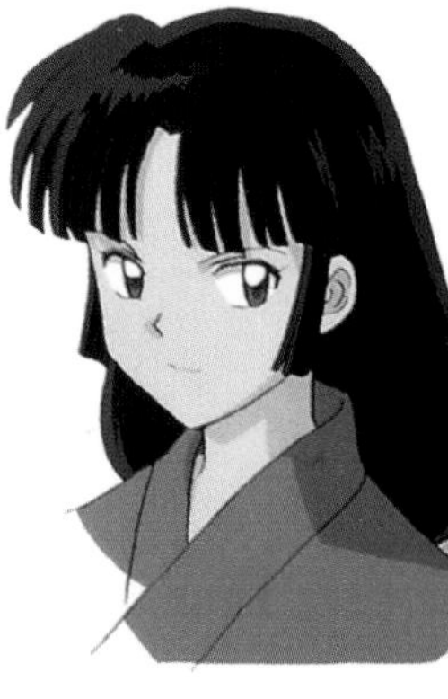

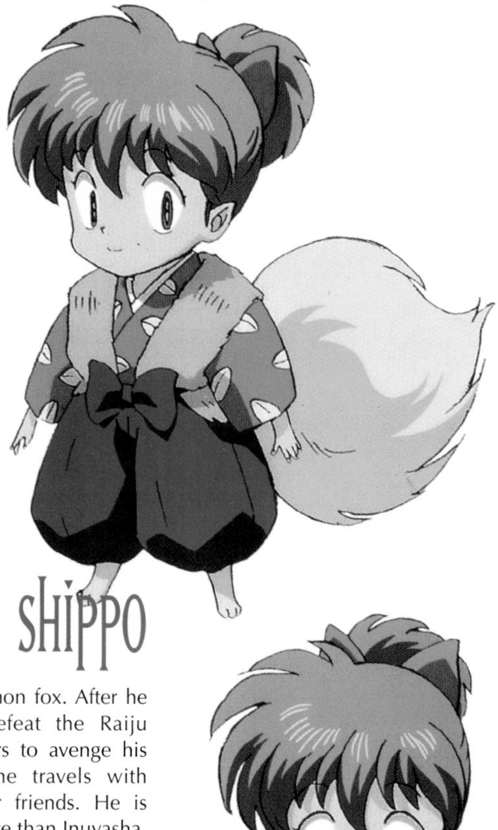

SHIPPO

The son of a demon fox. After he has Inuyasha defeat the Raiju (Thunder) brothers to avenge his father's death, he travels with Kagome and her friends. He is much more mature than Inuyasha. In animation Shippo is about the same as in the original comic, with his two-to-one body-to-head ratio and costume colors.

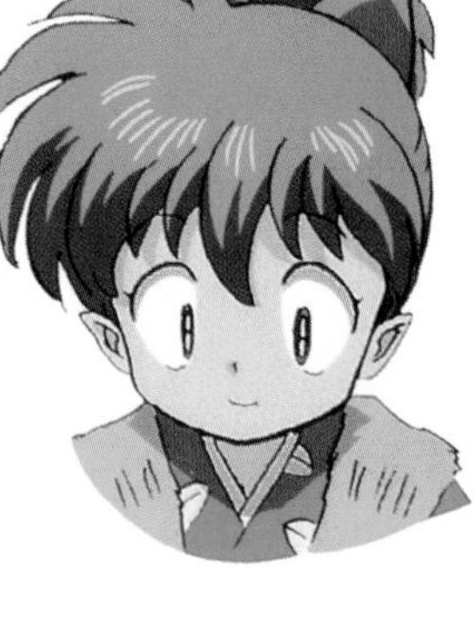

Inuyasha and the Demons

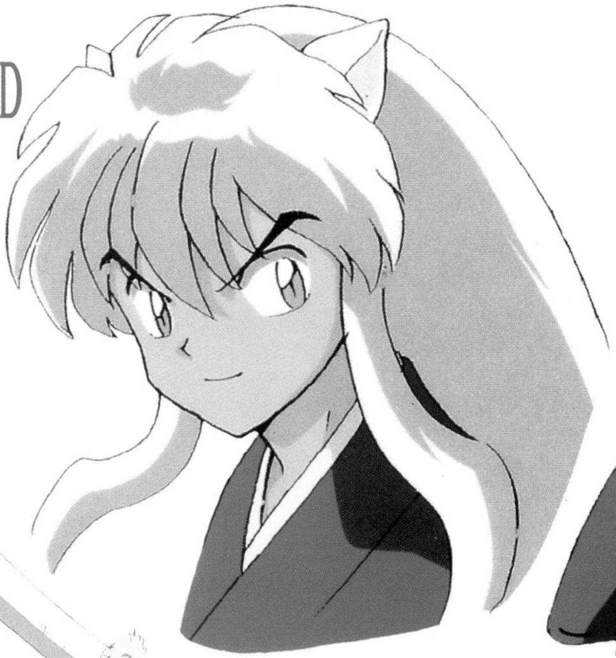

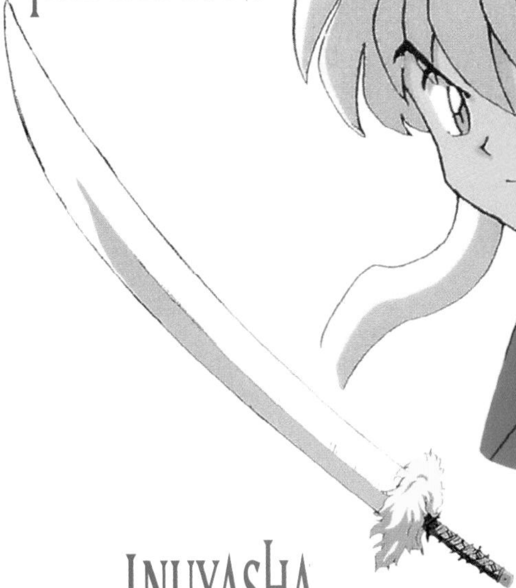

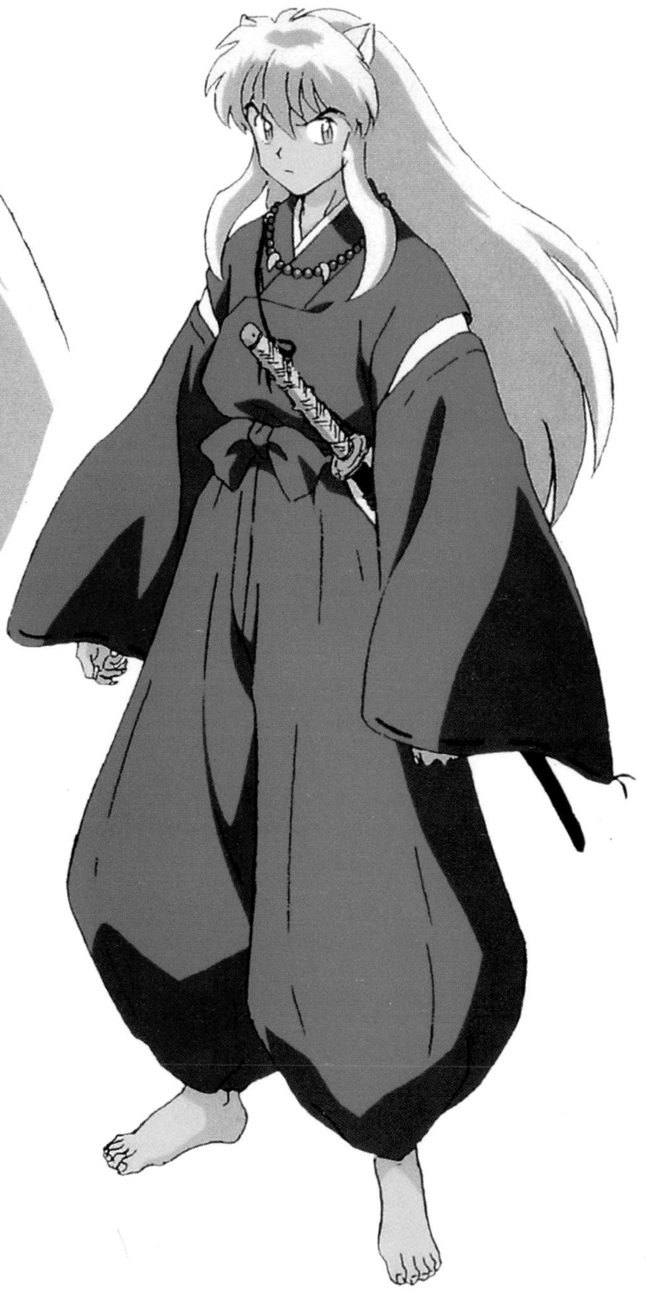

Inuyasha

A half-demon, on the road with Kagome in search of shards of the Shikon Jewel. He is stubborn and unyielding, and has a hard time expressing his feelings. Inuyasha's costume is derived from the kariginu, the festive robes of a shrine priest. In animation his costume is a darker red.

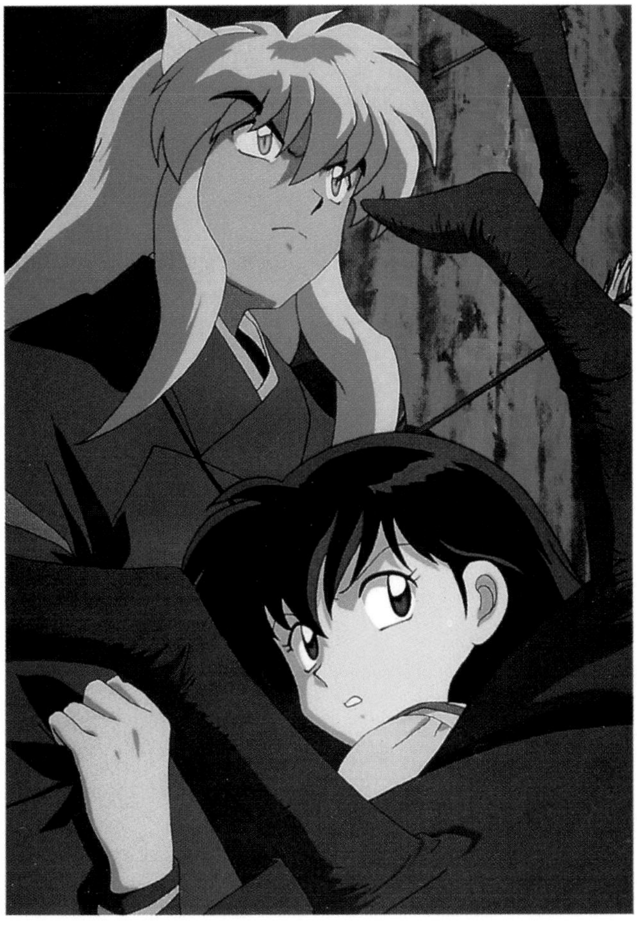

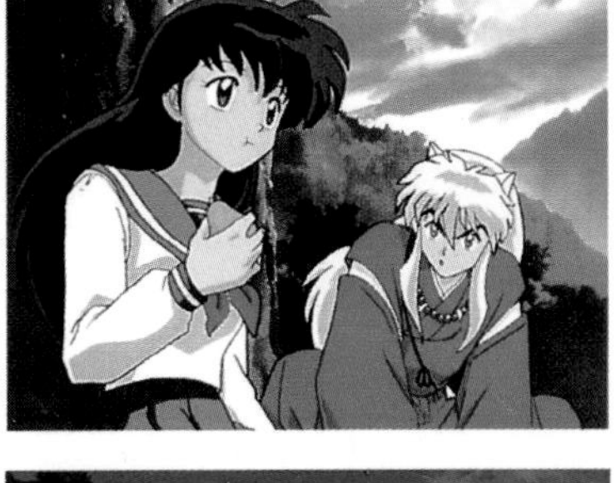

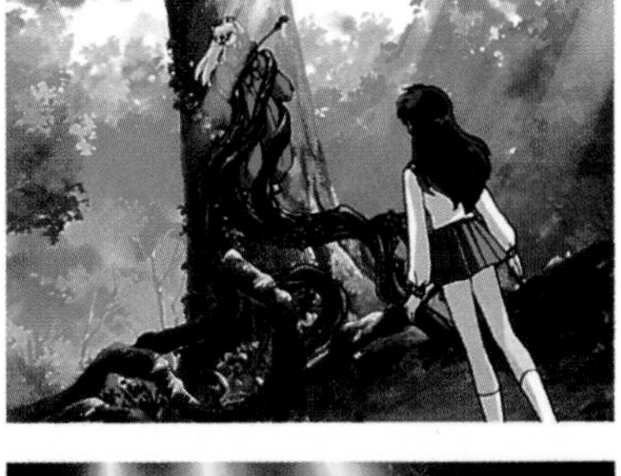

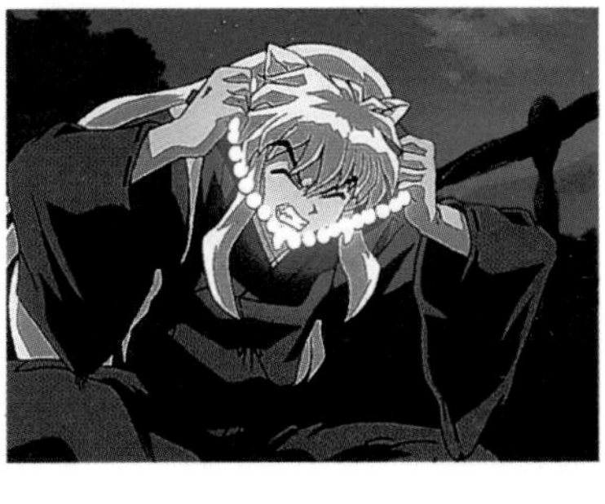

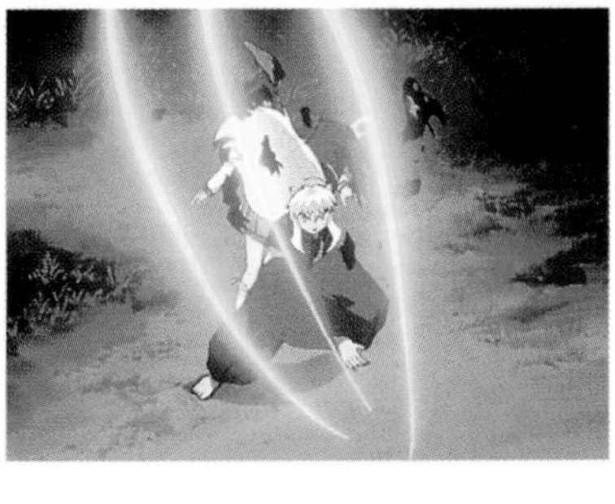

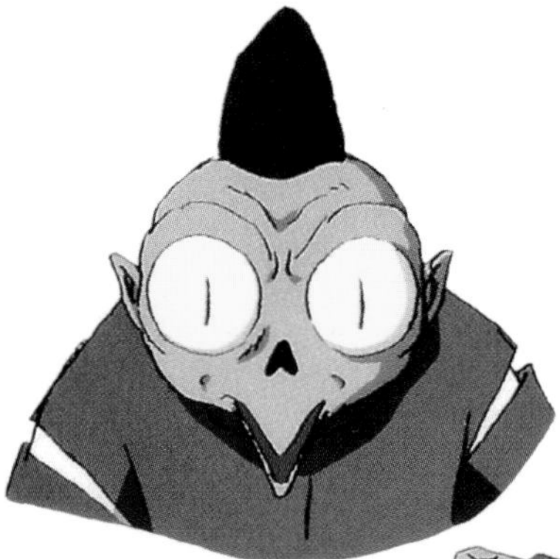

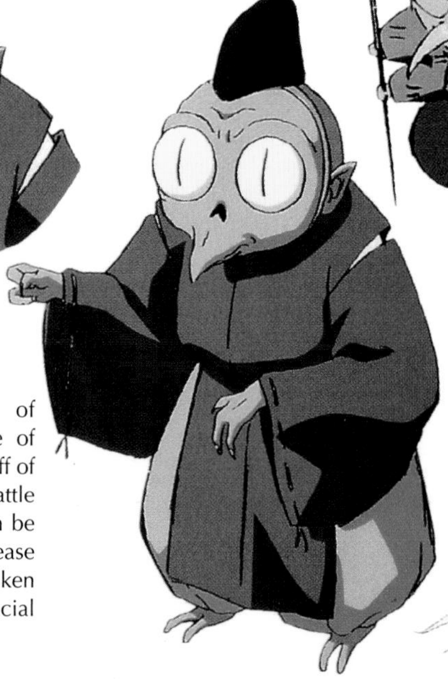

JAKEN

The demon companion of Sesshomaru seeks the grave of Inuyasha's father using his staff of two heads, a jintojo. His battle skills are so poor that he can be easily kicked by Kagome. To ease production, in animation Jaken does not have his original facial spots.

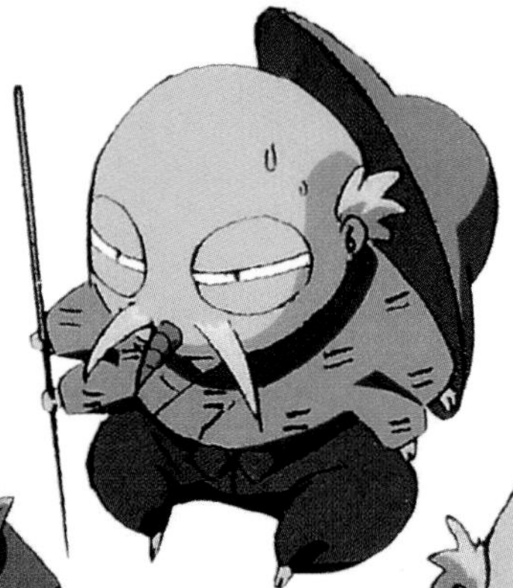

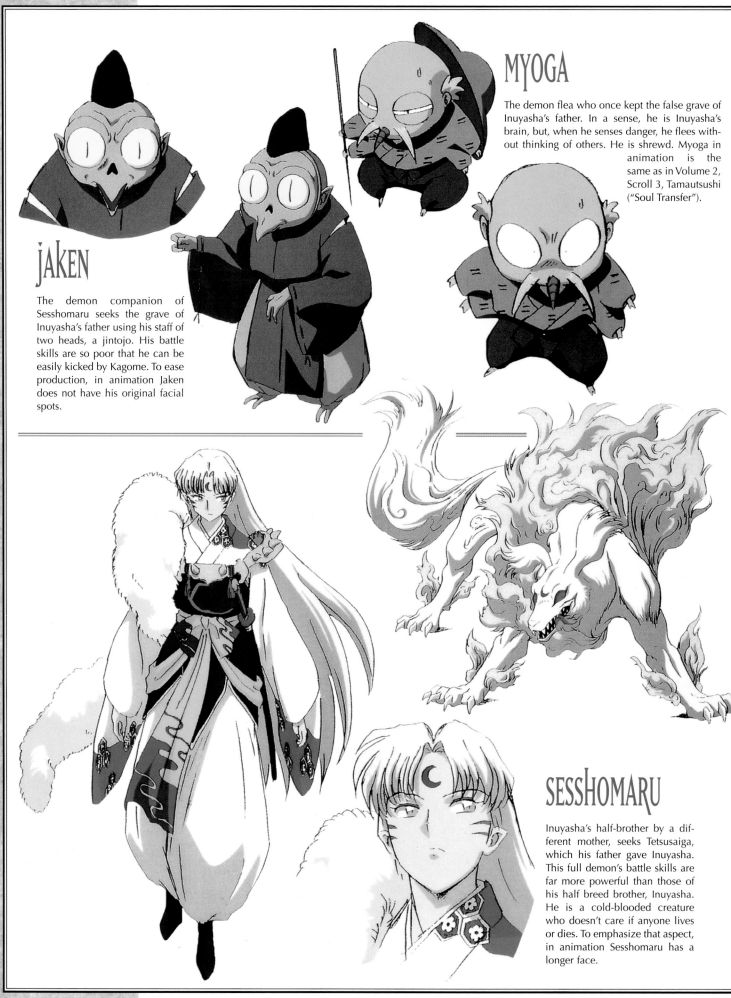

MYOGA

The demon flea who once kept the false grave of Inuyasha's father. In a sense, he is Inuyasha's brain, but, when he senses danger, he flees without thinking of others. He is shrewd. Myoga in animation is the same as in Volume 2, Scroll 3, Tamautsushi ("Soul Transfer").

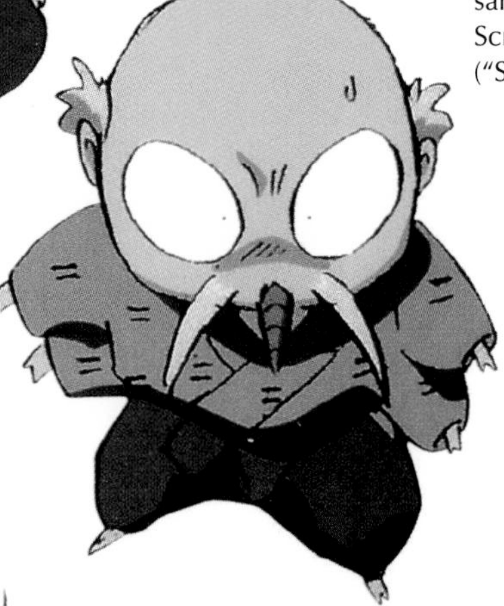

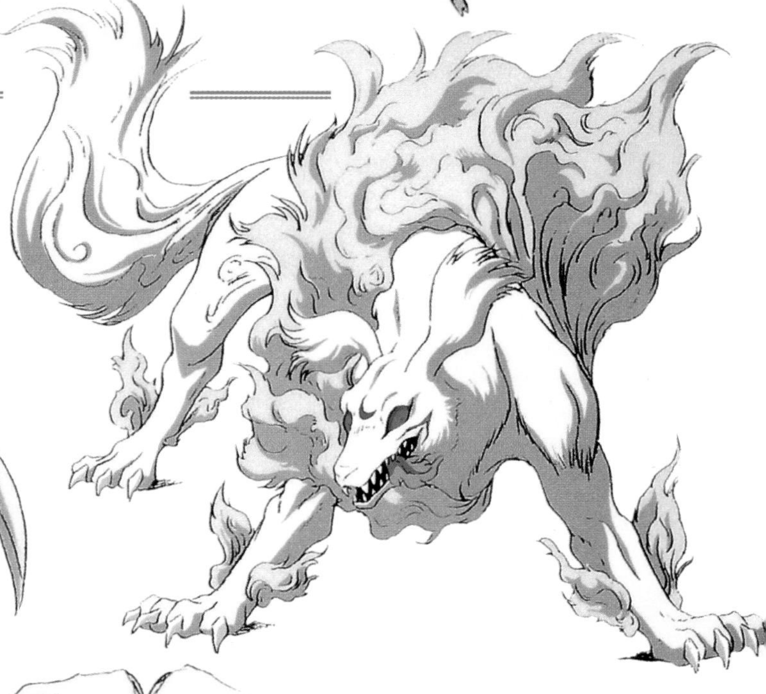

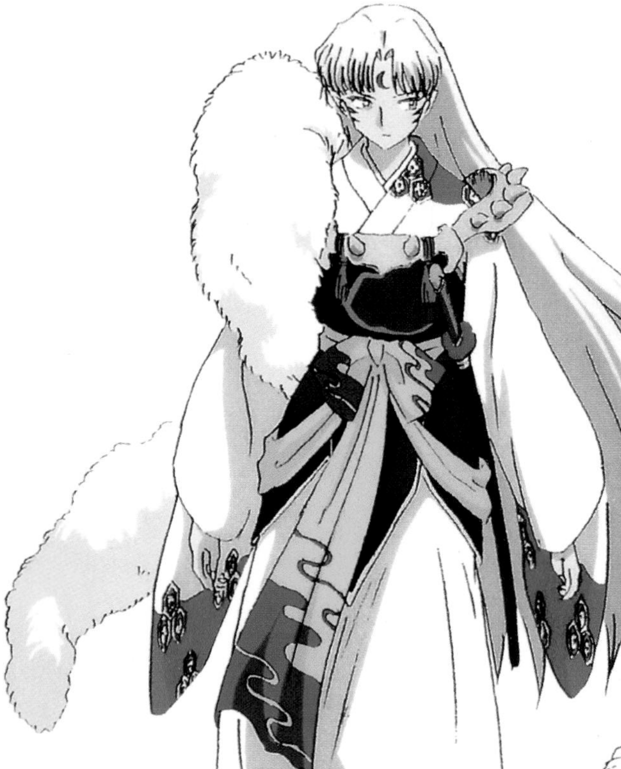

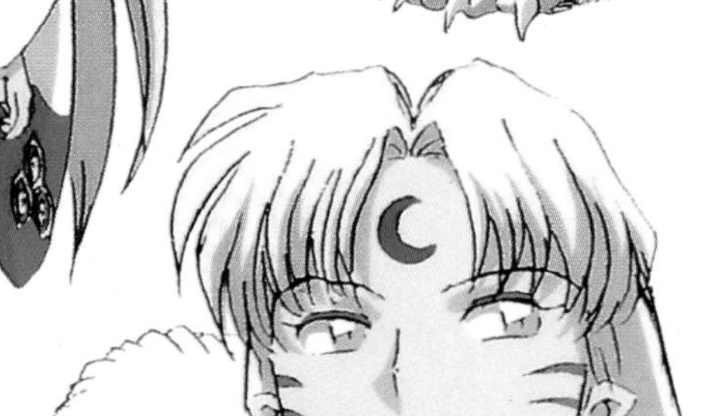

SESSHOMARU

Inuyasha's half-brother by a different mother, seeks Tetsusaiga, which his father gave Inuyasha. This full demon's battle skills are far more powerful than those of his half breed brother, Inuyasha. He is a cold-blooded creature who doesn't care if anyone lives or dies. To emphasize that aspect, in animation Sesshomaru has a longer face.

kikyo, kaede and others

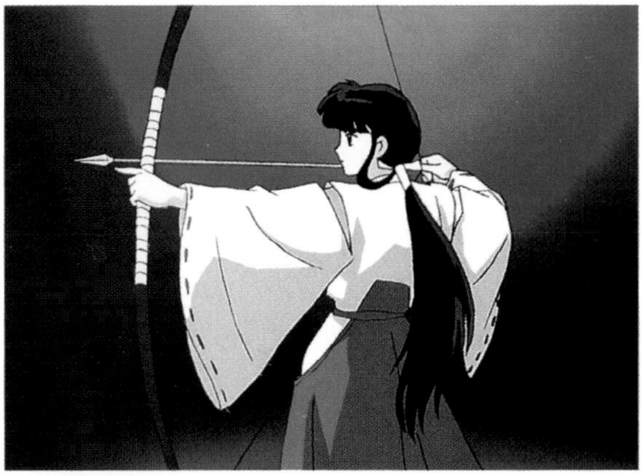

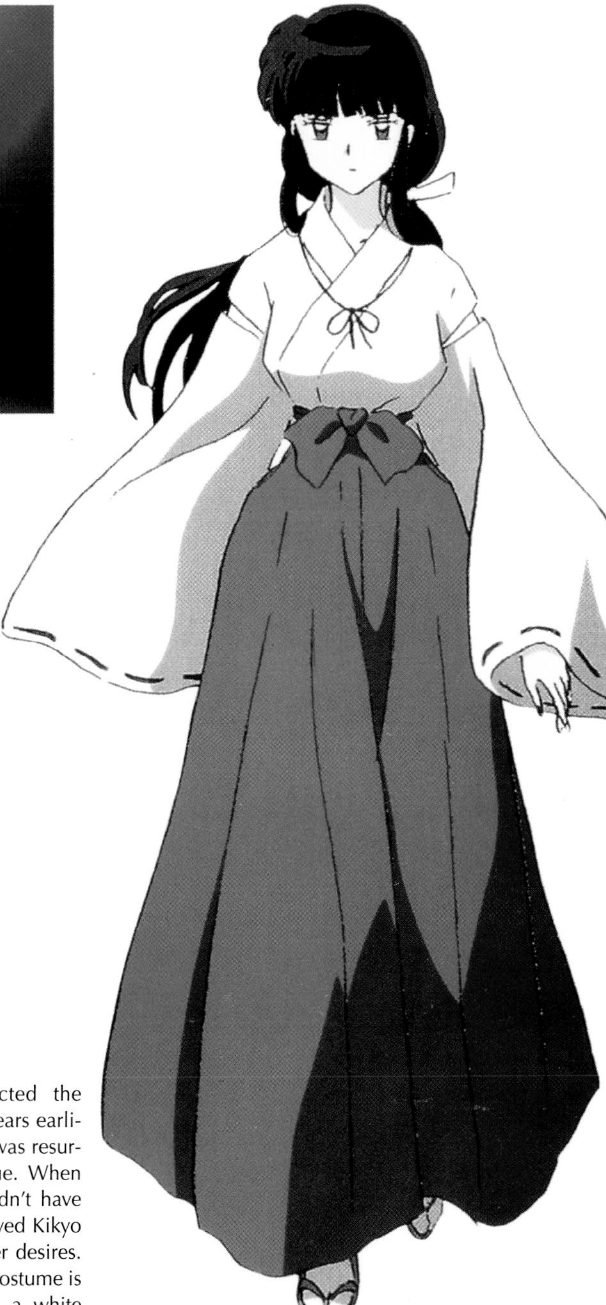

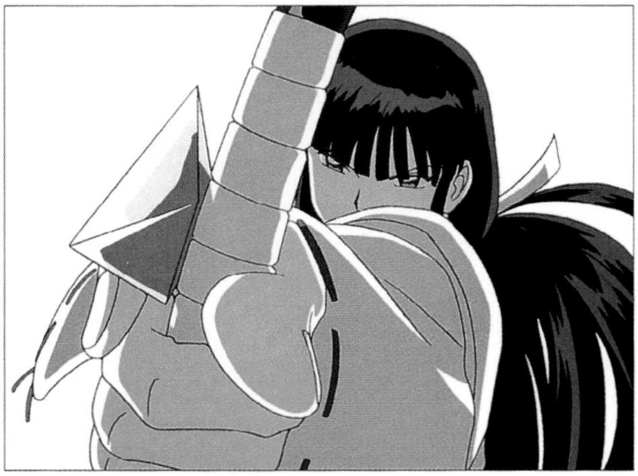

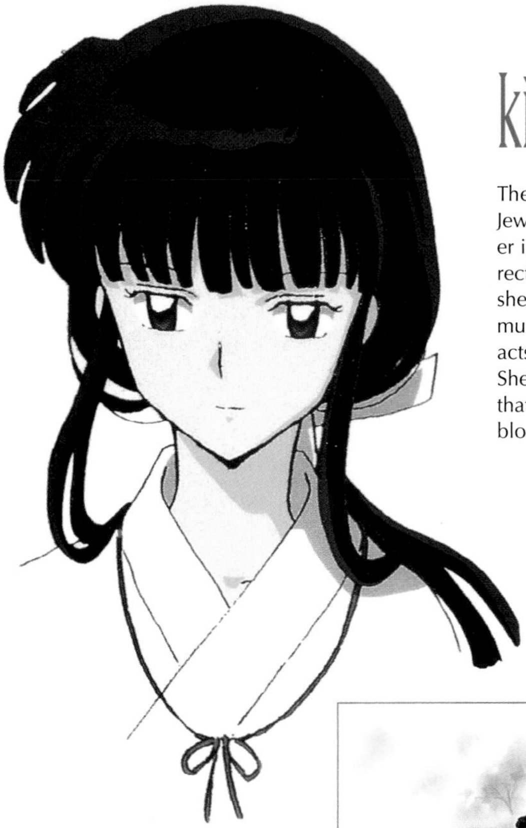

kikyo

The priestess who protected the Jewel. She lost her life 50 years earlier in a plot by Naraku, but was resurrected by the ogress Urasue. When she was a priestess, she didn't have much freedom, but the revived Kikyo acts more freely to fulfill her desires. She is a master archer. Her costume is that of a Shinto priestesss, a white blouse and a pair of red hakama.

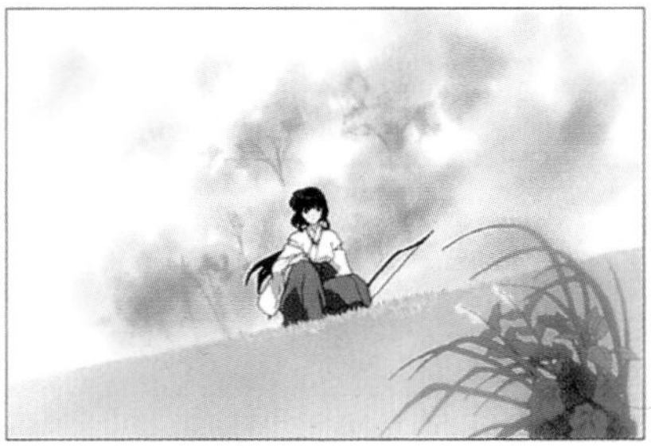

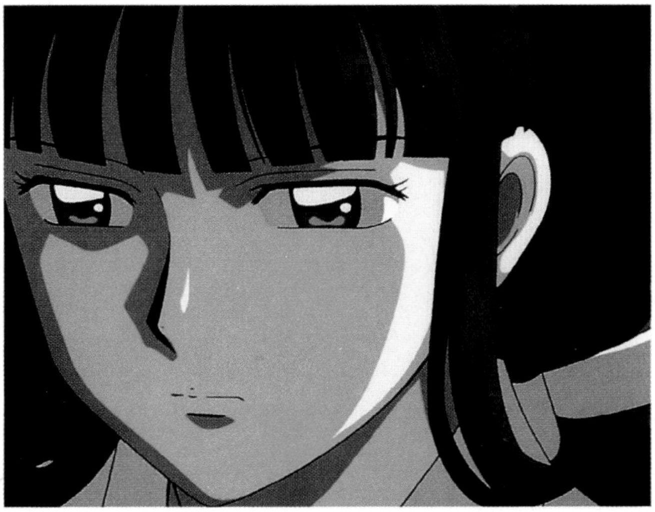

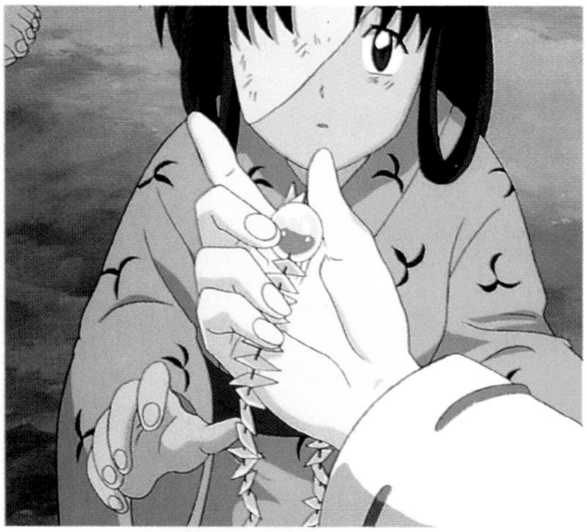

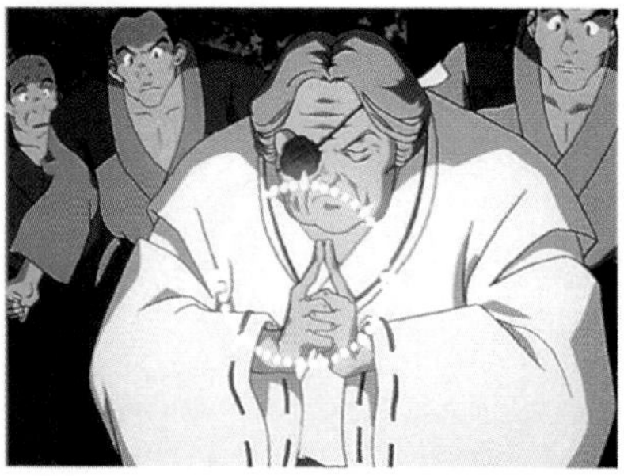

Kaede

Kikyo's younger sister and the priestess who protects the village adjacent to Inuyasha's forest. She is the first to realize that Kagome is Kikyo reincarnated. She lost her right eye in a battle 50 years earlier. Shinto priestesses were once masters of festivals who used sorcery as well.

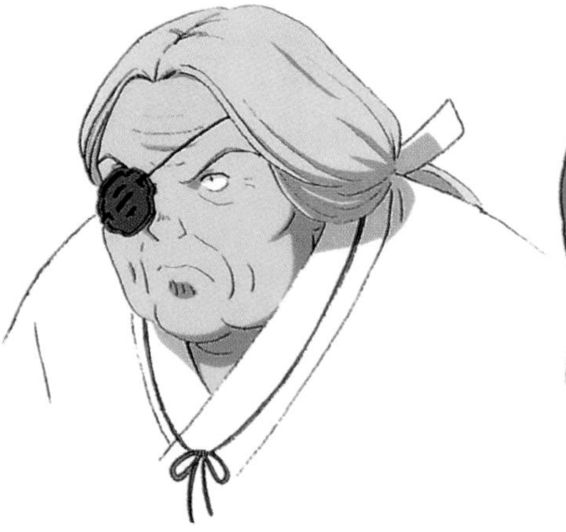

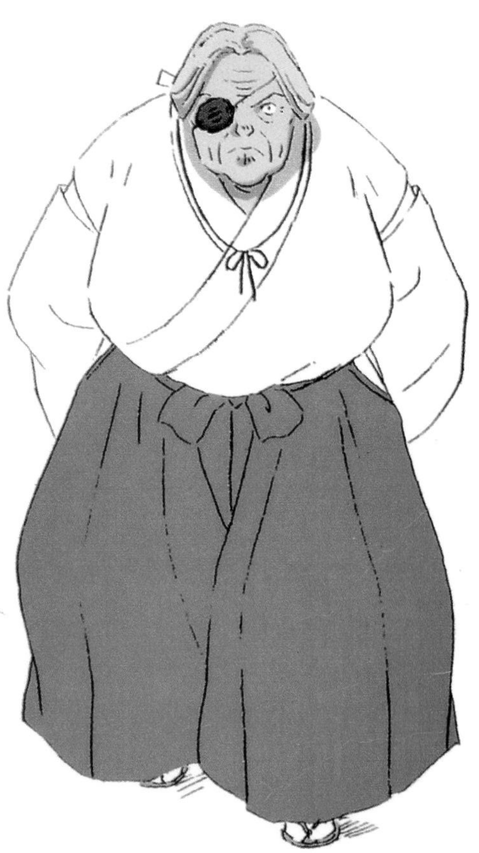

Crow Demon

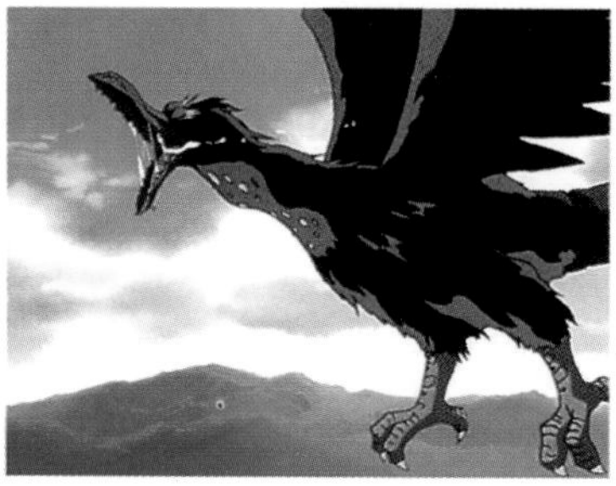

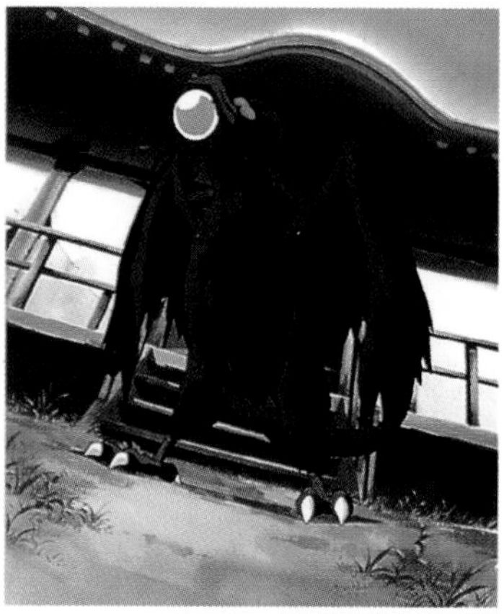

Yura of the Demon Hair

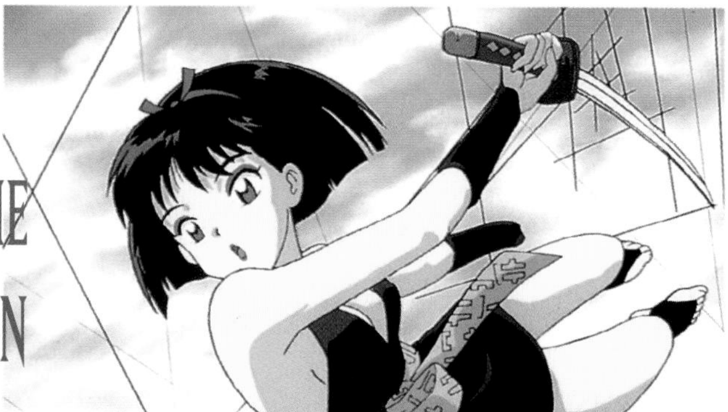

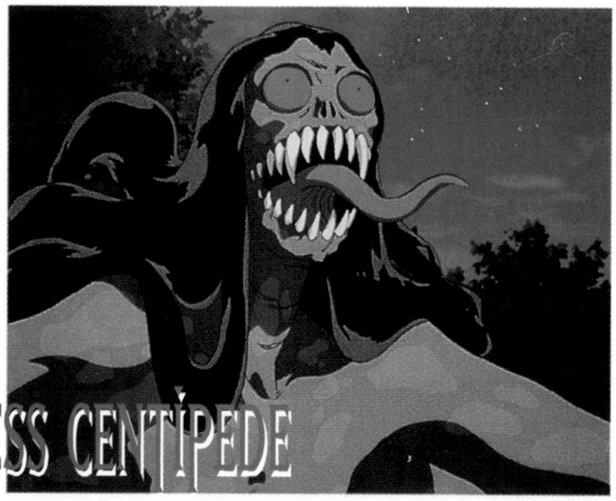

Mistress Centipede

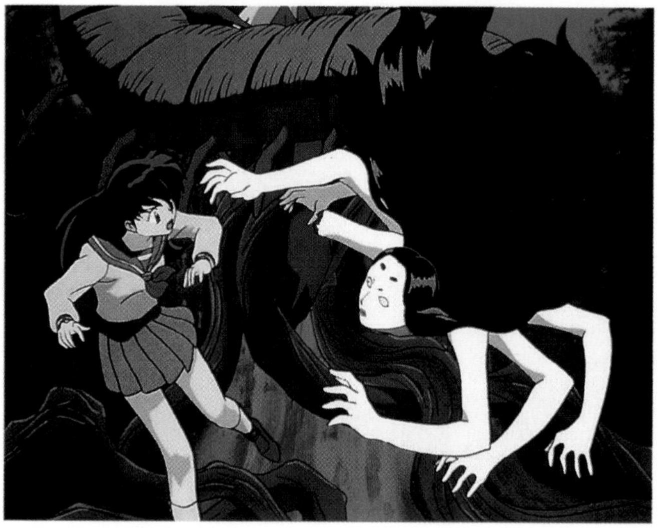

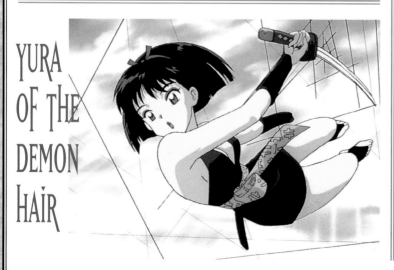

INUYASHA STORYBOARDS

These Storyboards are color drawings of the major scenes in Inuyasha, carefully defined to provide a basis for the animated world.

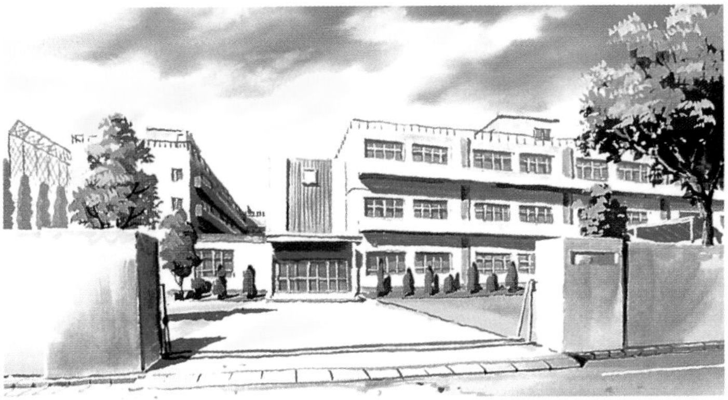

▲ KAGOME'S MIDDLE SCHOOL.

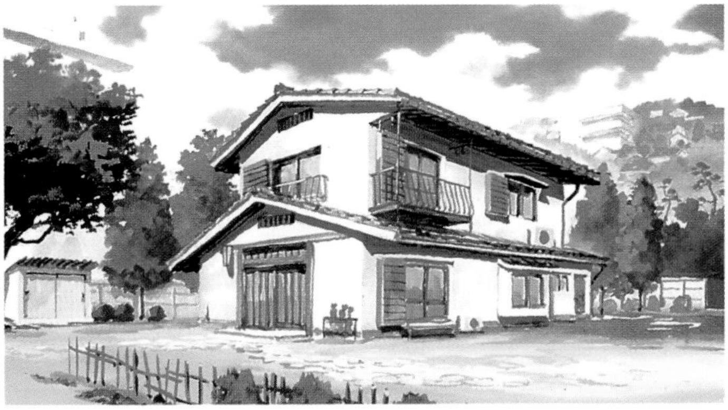

▲ VIEW OF KAGOME'S HOUSE (ON THE PREMISES OF HIGURASHI SHRINE).

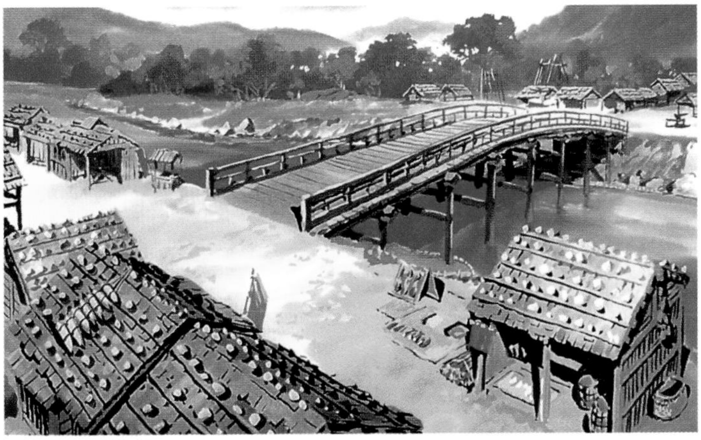

▲ THE INN DISTRICT ON THE MAIN STREET (SCROLL 2).

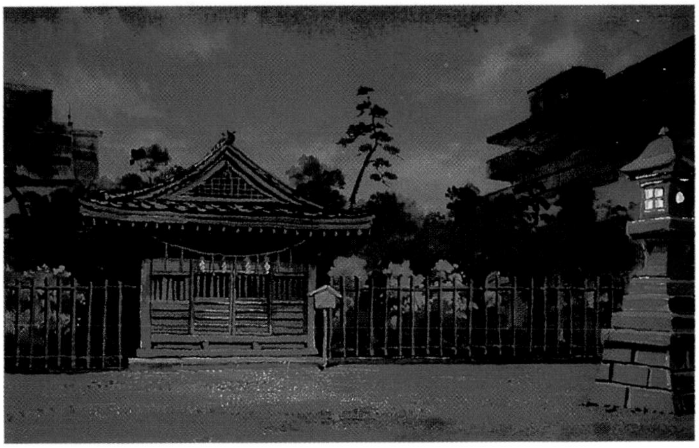

▲ SHRINE WITH A WELL (INSIDE THE HIGURASHI SHRINE TODAY).

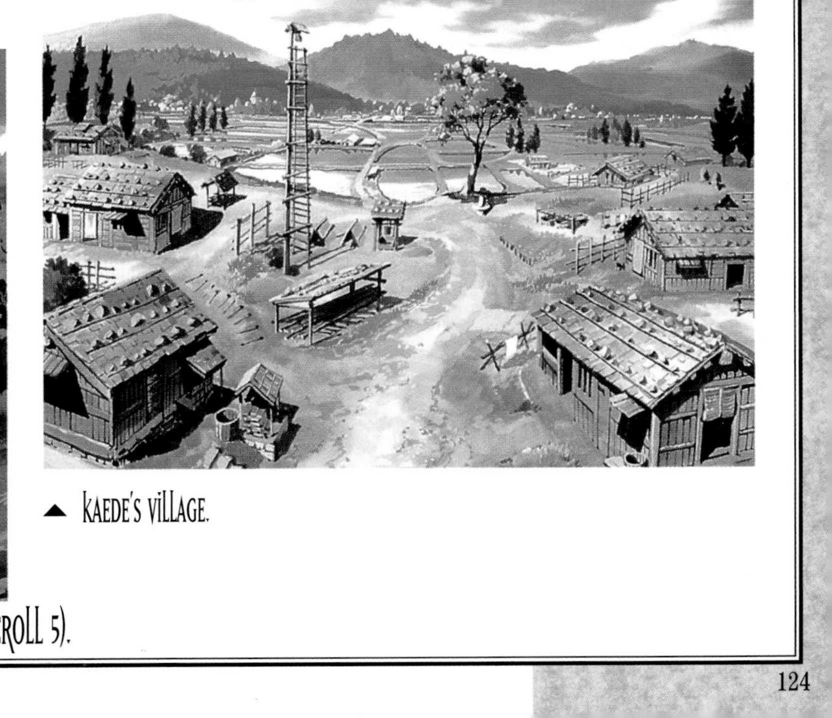

▲ KAEDE'S VILLAGE.

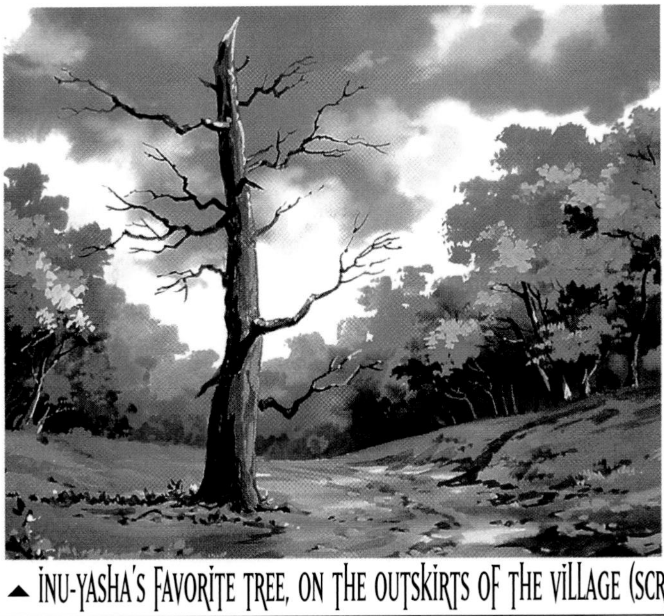

▲ INU-YASHA'S FAVORITE TREE, ON THE OUTSKIRTS OF THE VILLAGE (SCROLL 5).

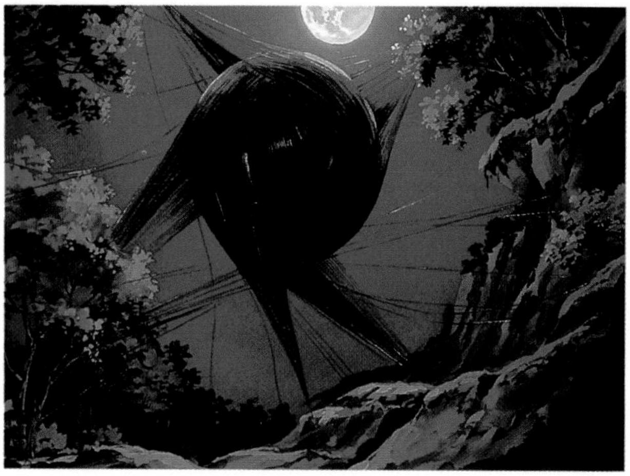

▲ OUTSIDE VIEW OF YURA'S NEST (SCROLL 4).

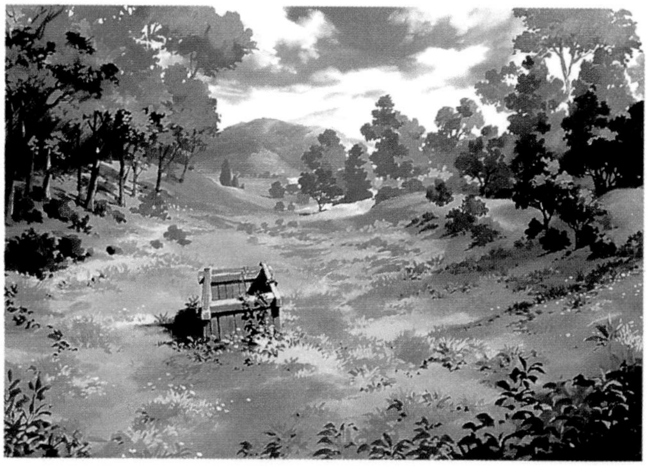

▲ THE BONE-EATER'S WELL (IN ANCIENT TIMES).

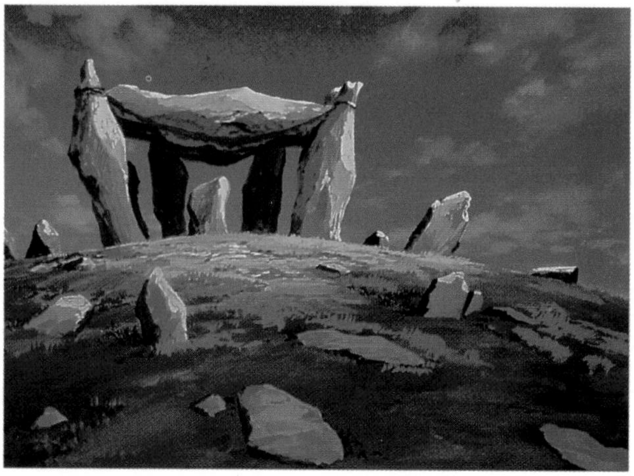

▲ THE FALSE GRAVE OF INUYASHA'S FATHER (SCROLL 5).

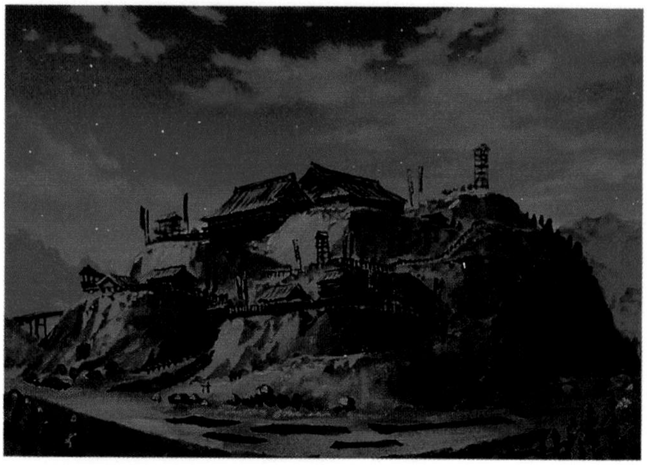

▲ OVERALL VIEW OF THE MOUNTAIN CASTLE (SCROLL 8).

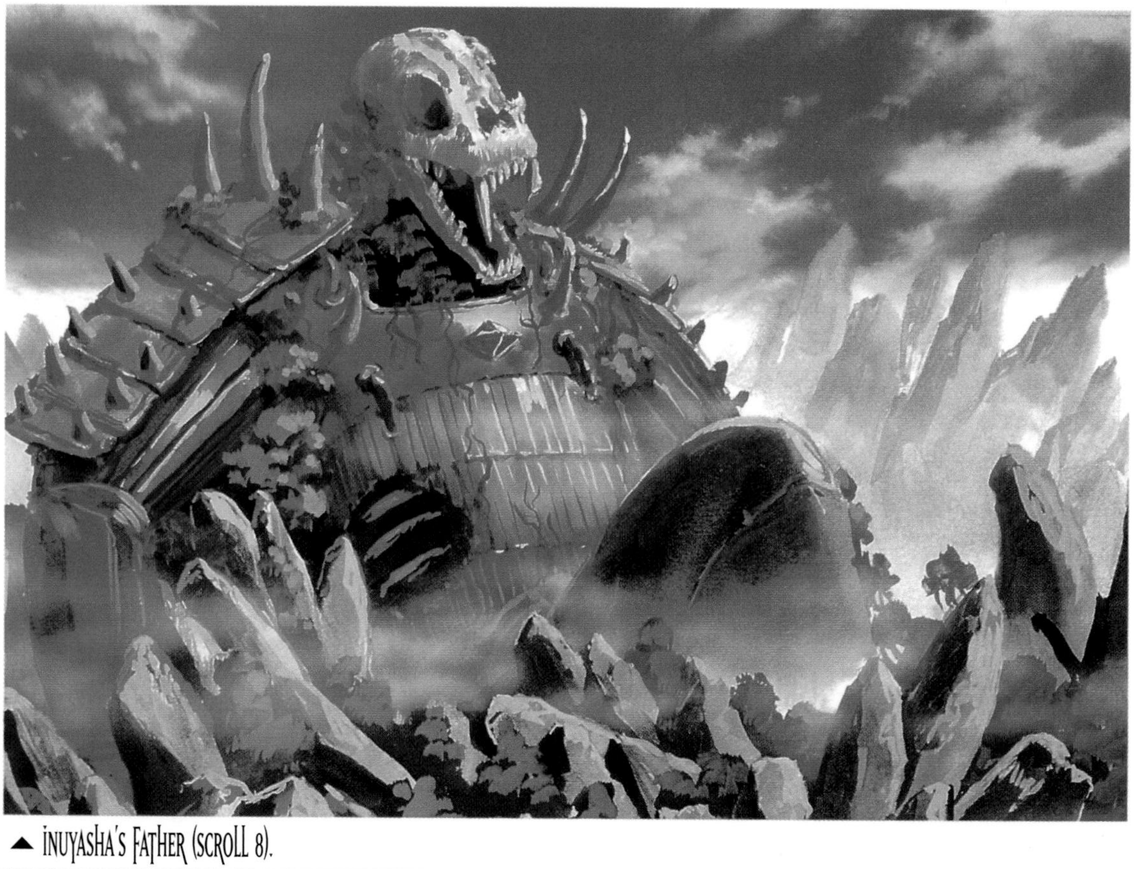

▲ INUYASHA'S FATHER (SCROLL 8).

COMPLETE STUDY OF THE OPENING SEQUENCE

The opening sequence of "Inuyasha" can be roughly divided into five parts. Here's a complete analysis.

Subtitles in frames 1-8 give the basic setup of the story. Each character in "Inuyasha" has properties that need explaining. The opening gives partial explanations, mostly about Kagome. It was originally planned that each scene showing a specific character in an action would have subtitles explaining something about him or her. Here, the relationship between Kagome and the Bone-Eater's Well is clearly presented. The theme song is "Change the World," sung by V6.

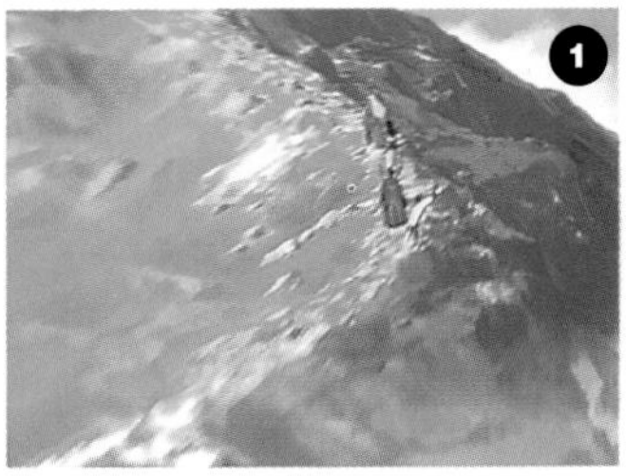
1

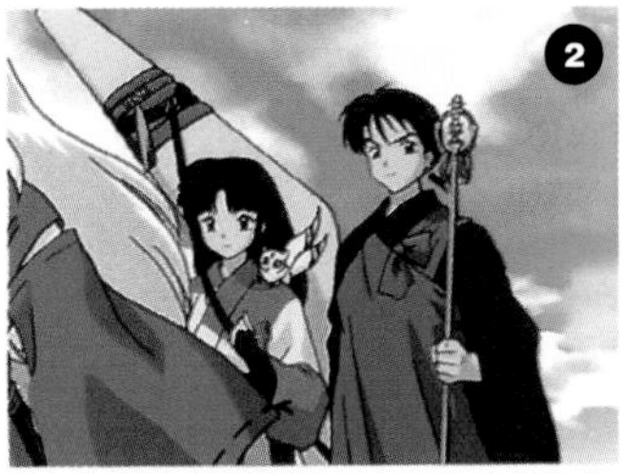
2

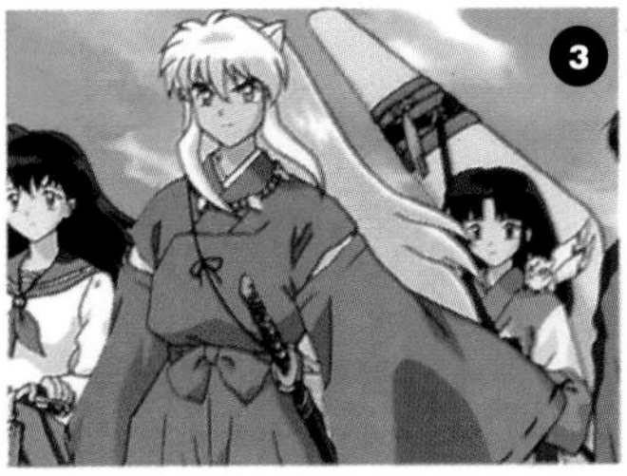
3

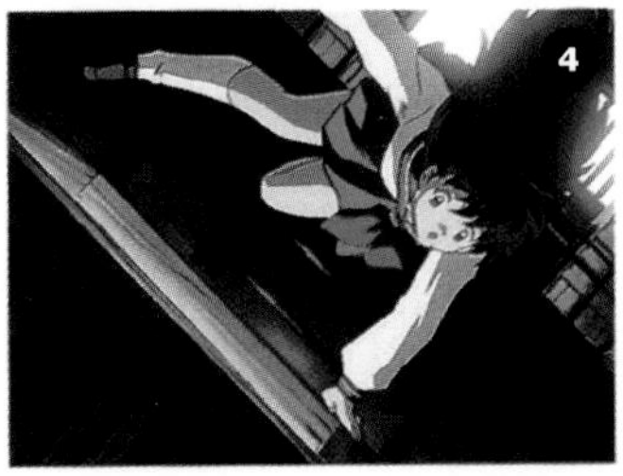
4

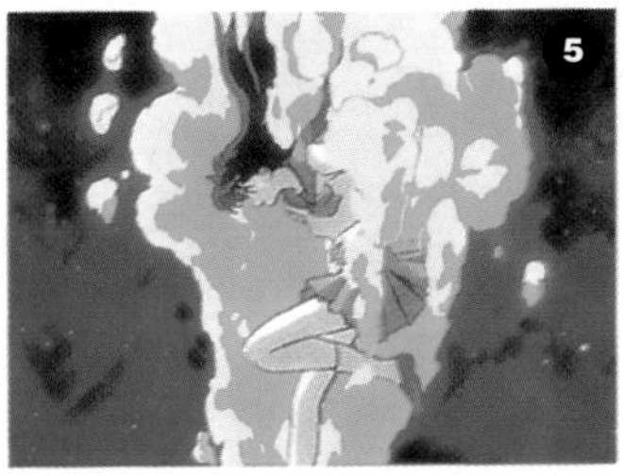
5

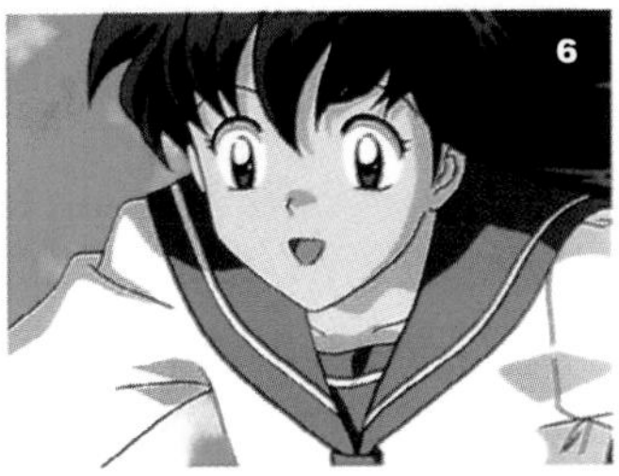
6

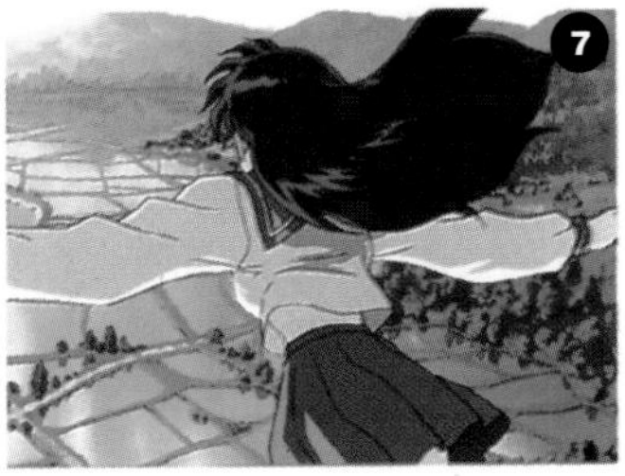
7

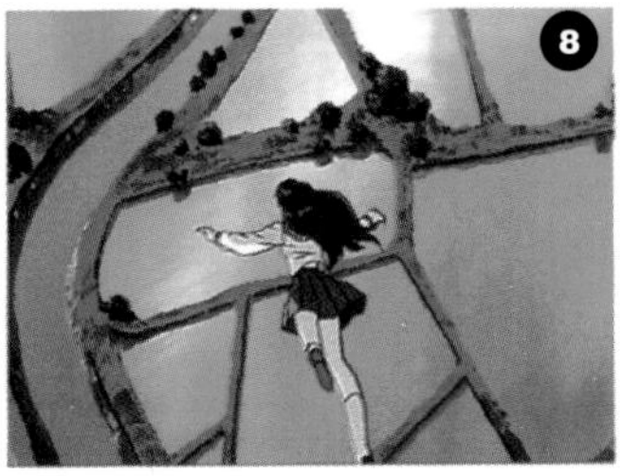
8

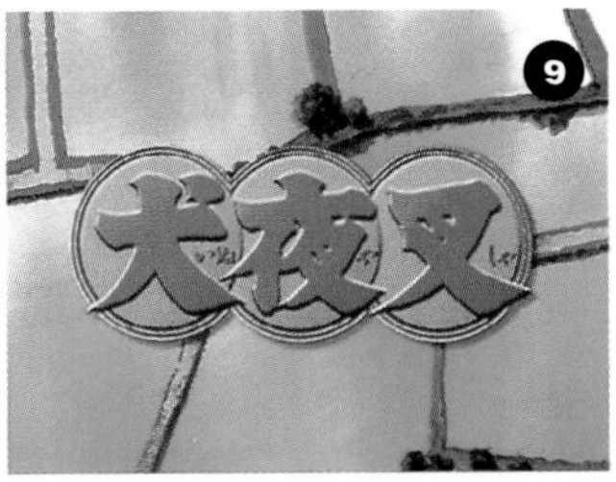
9
犬夜叉

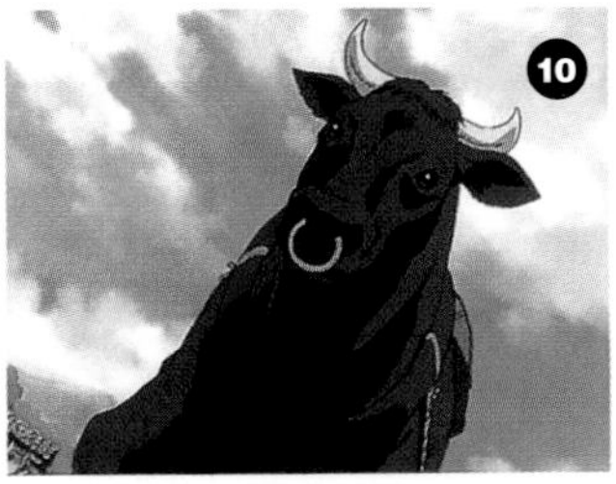
10

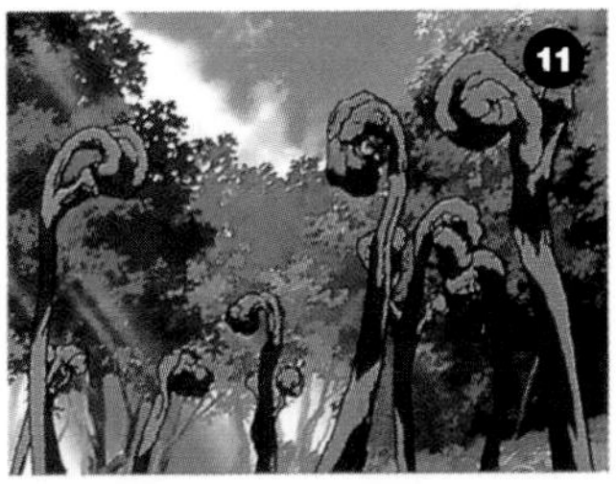
11

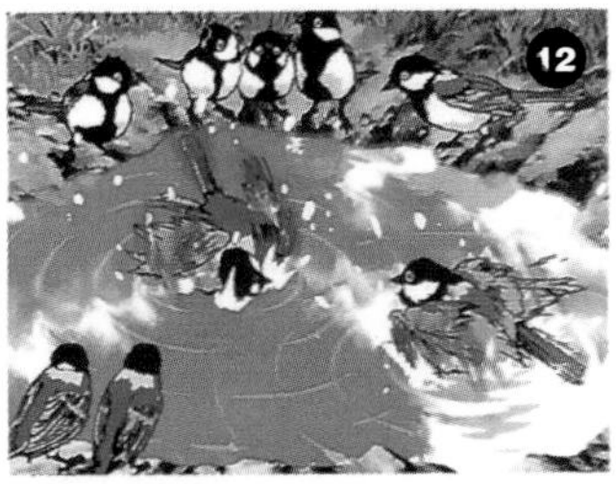
12

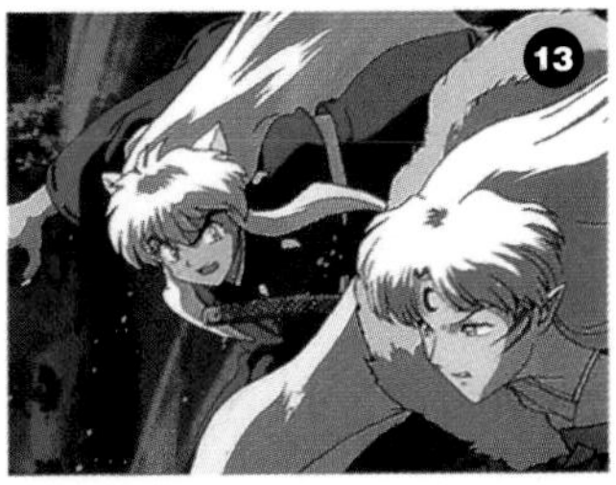
13

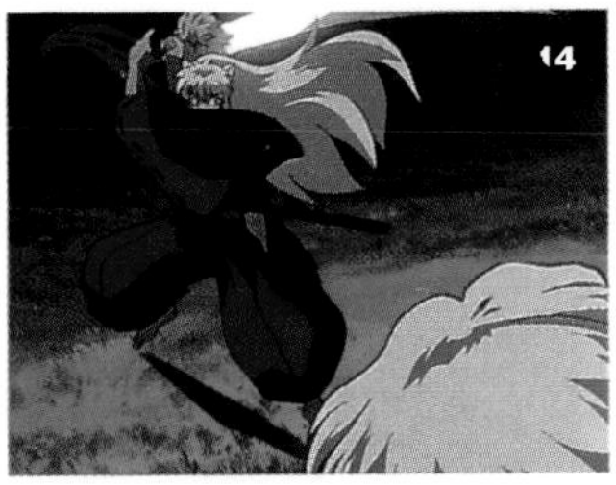
14

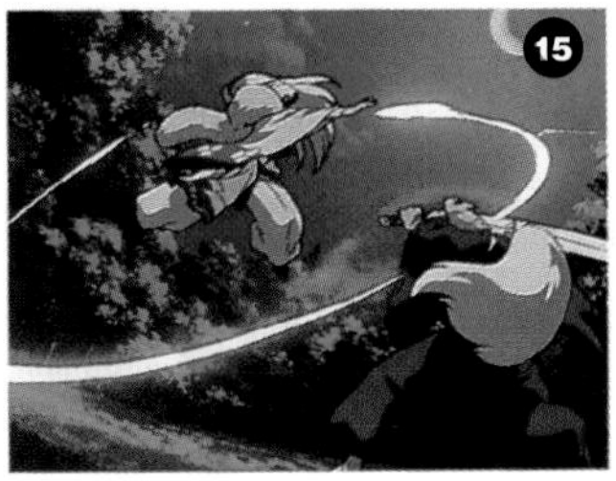
15

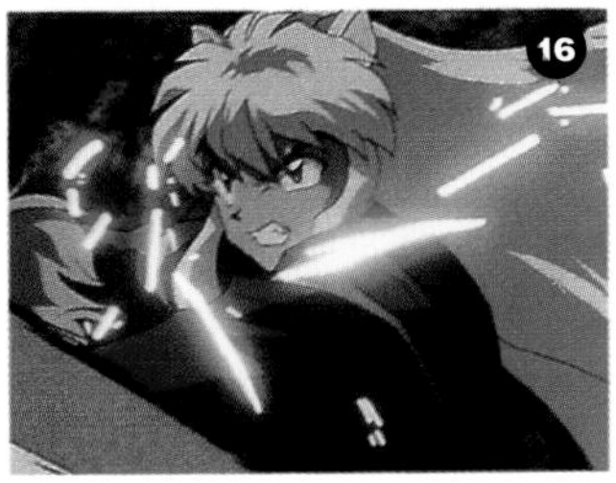
16

Frame 9 shows the title over a scene from ancient times. Frames 10-12 quickly interject pastoral scenes from those times. Frames 13-16 are overlaid one after another to show the intense battle between Inuyasha and Sesshomaru. In Frame 15, Sesshomaru cracks a whip. Frame 16 shows sparkles from the whip as they touch Tetsusaiga's aura. By overlaying several cuts in a few seconds, the sequence shows the adversarial relationship between the two half-brothers.

Frames 17-22 introduce Kagome's friends, Miroku, Sango and Shippo. Frames 17 and 18 are a single cut. From the bust shot of Miroku, who is about to lift the seal off his wind tunnel, and Sango, who is about to employ her boomerang, the camera pans down to reveal Shippo in changed form. Frame 20 shows the effects of Miroku's tunnel, and Frame 21 shows how devastating Sango's boomerang can be.

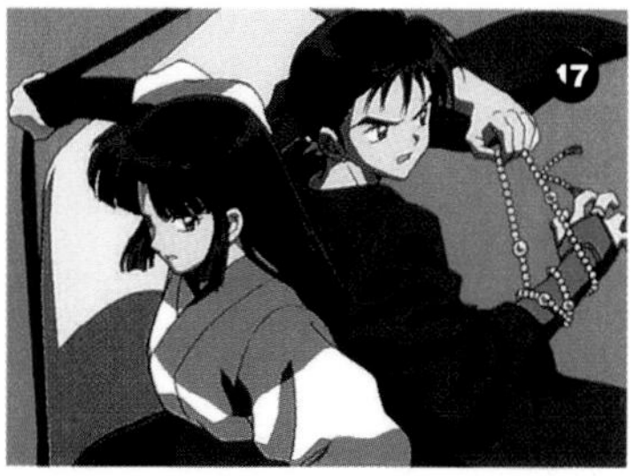
17
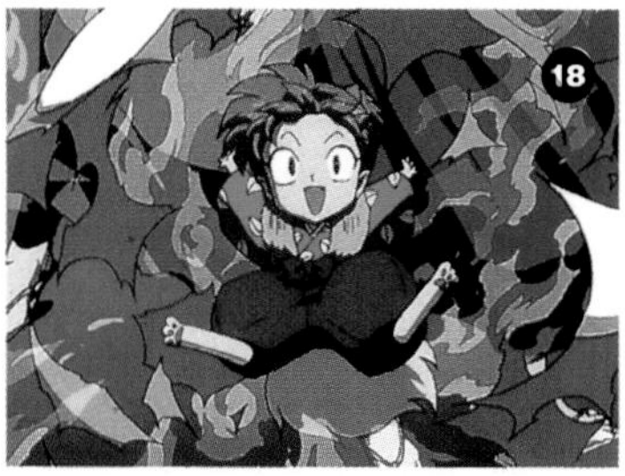
18
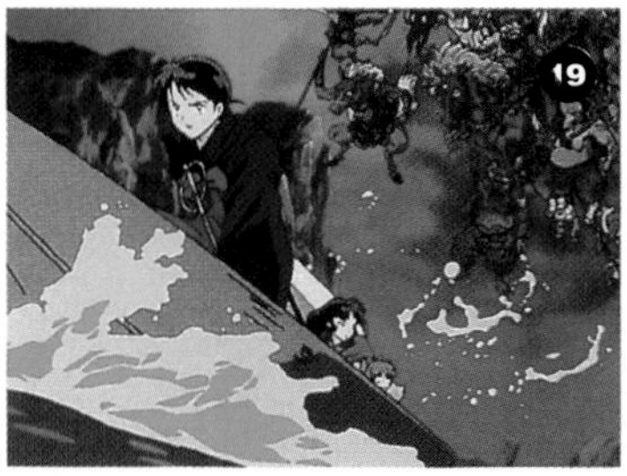
19
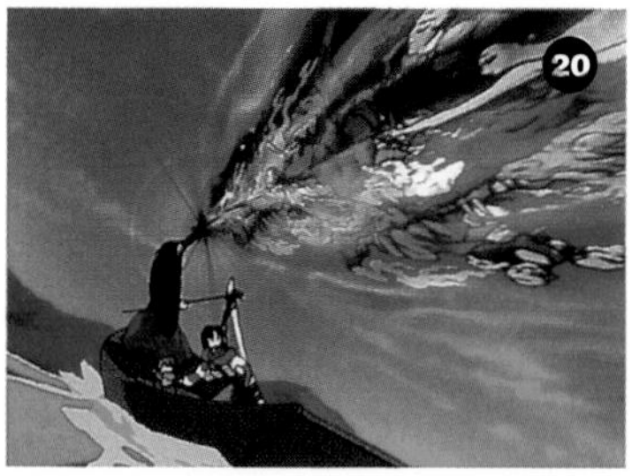
20
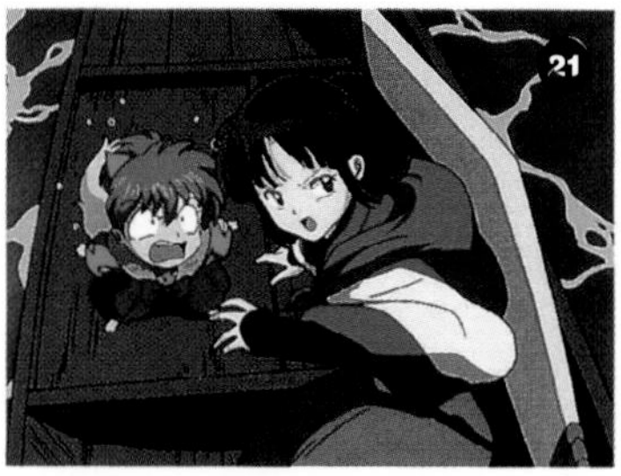
21
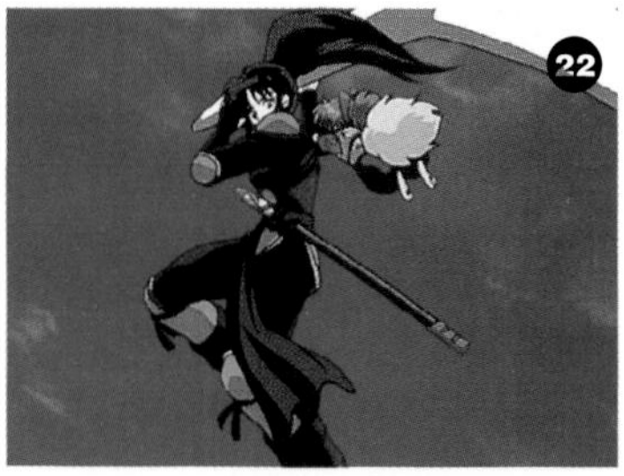
22

Frames 23-28 imply the relationship between Kagome, Kikyo and Inuyasha using mood. Kikyo is very important to the story, as her presence lays heavy on Inuyasha, and Kagome is her reincarnation. On the other hand, after Scroll 1 Kikyo does not appear for a while. So the opening must have a scene about Kikyo. Frames 27 and 28 show Inuyasha in agony over the misunderstanding with Kikyo.

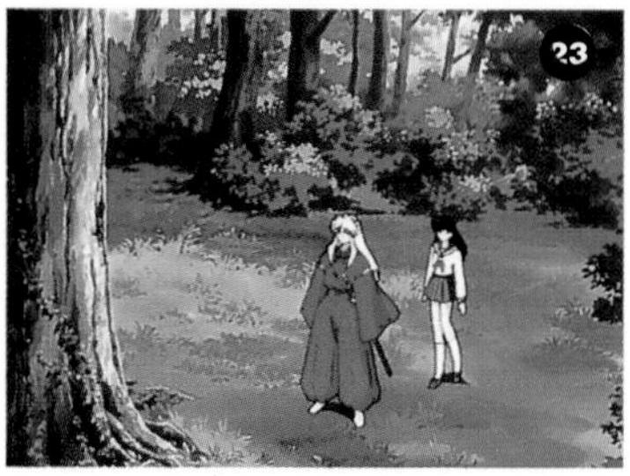
23
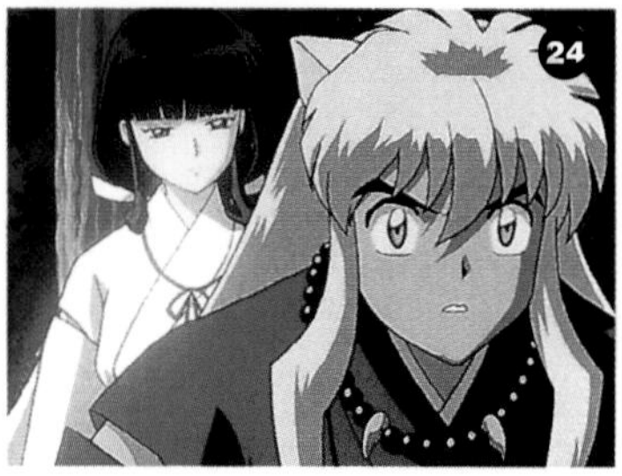
24
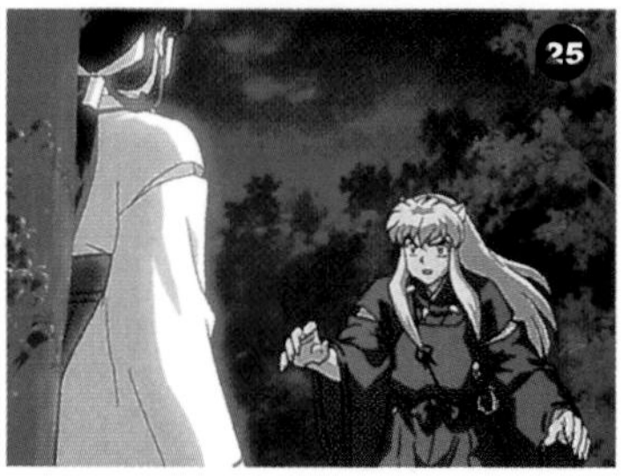
25
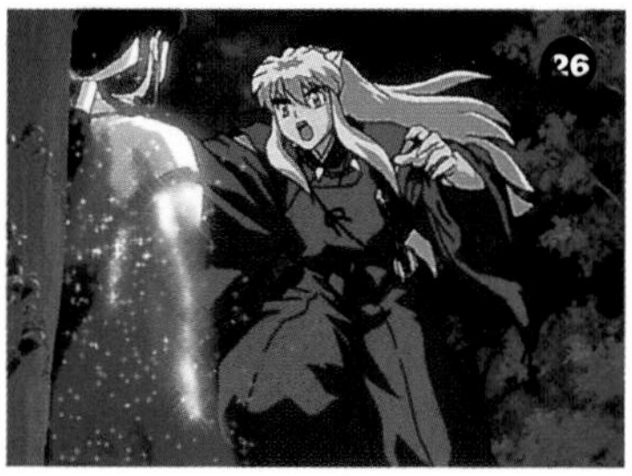
26
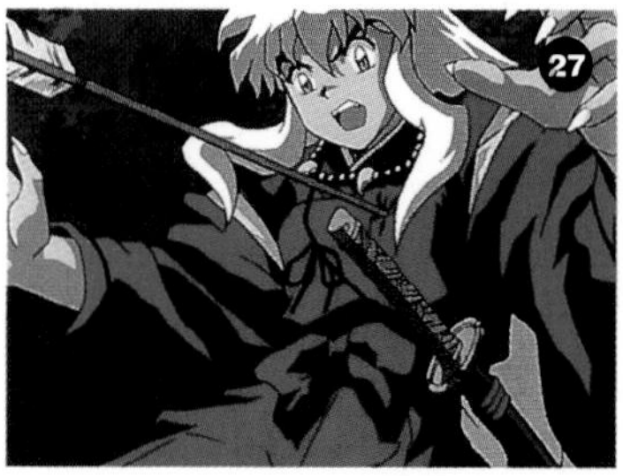
27
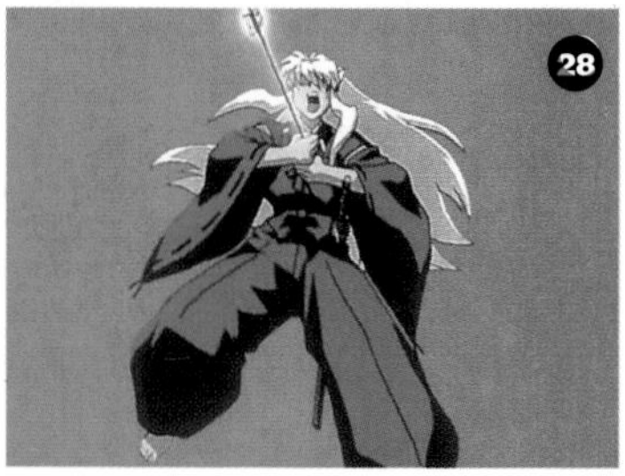
28

Following the previous part, Frames 29-34 show a lonely Inuyasha. Then Kagome and her friends appear. Kagome smiles at the lonely, agonizing Inuyasha, and Inuyasha smiles back slightly. This sequence superbly establishes the relationship between Kagome and Inuyasha.

A more action-packed opening was planned at first, but it became gentler with Kikyo's presence and less action.

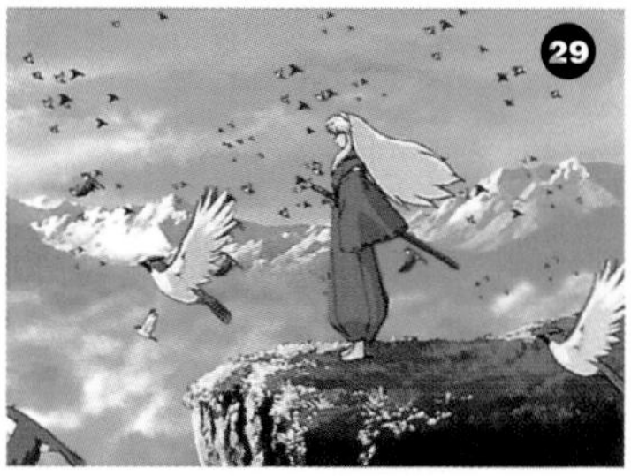
29
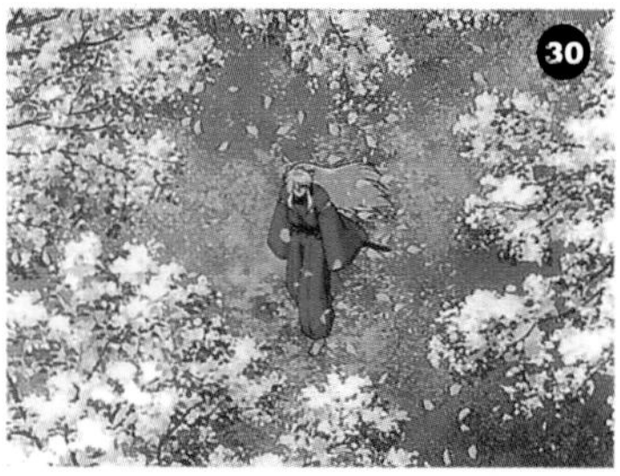
30
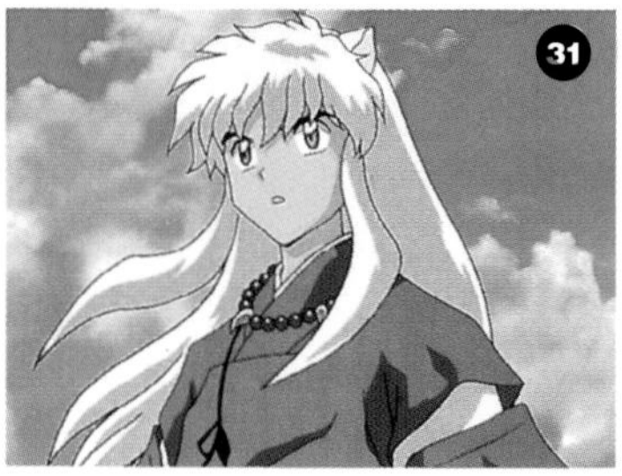
31
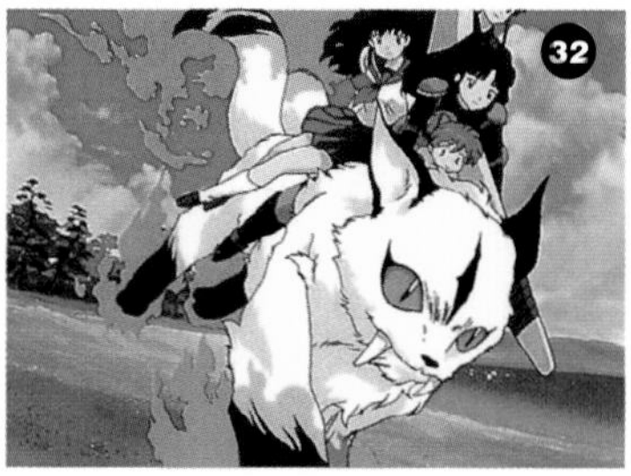
32
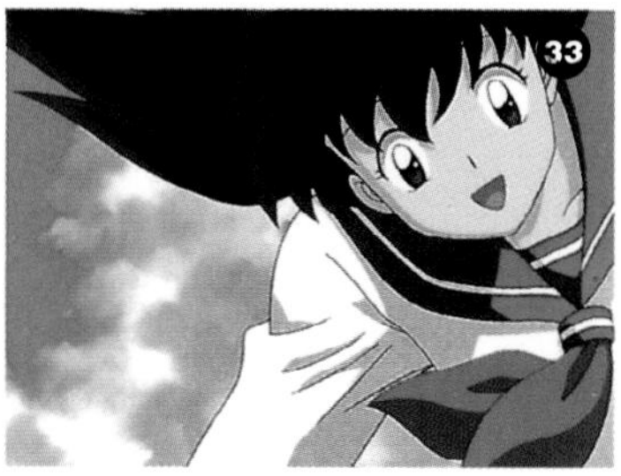
33
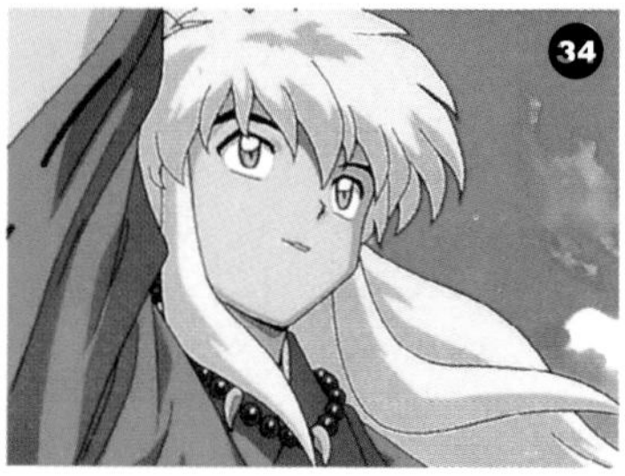
34

"INUYASHA" CLOSING SEQUENCE

THE ANIMATION CLOSER HAS A FEMININE FLAIR, FOCUSING ON THE THREE WOMEN, KAGOME, KIKYO AND SANGO.

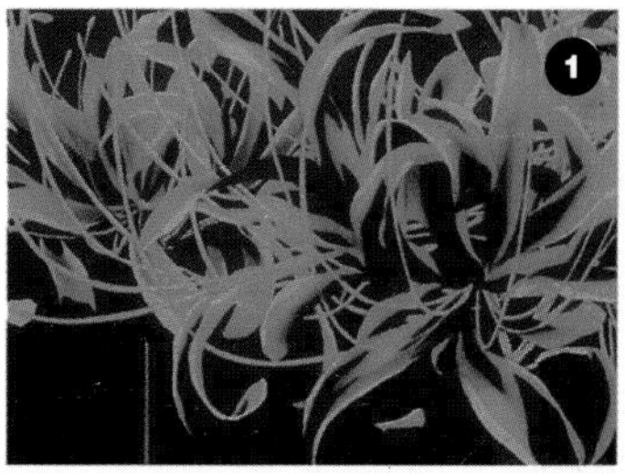
1
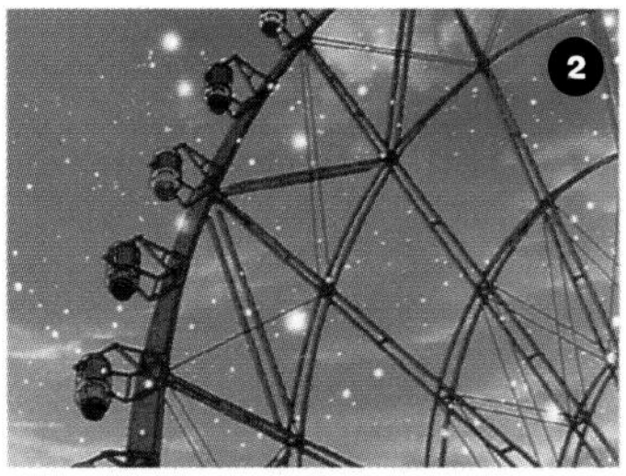
2
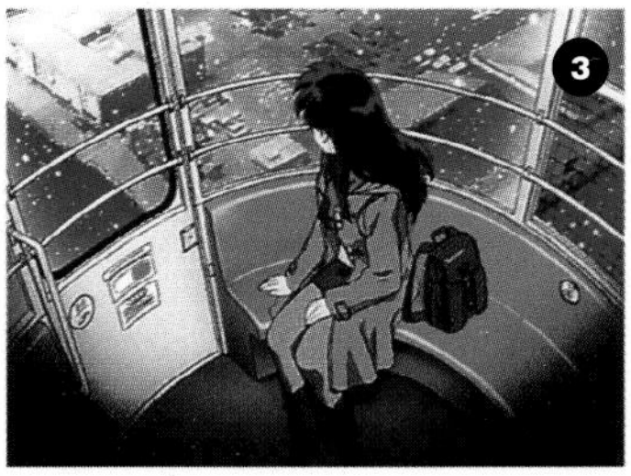
3
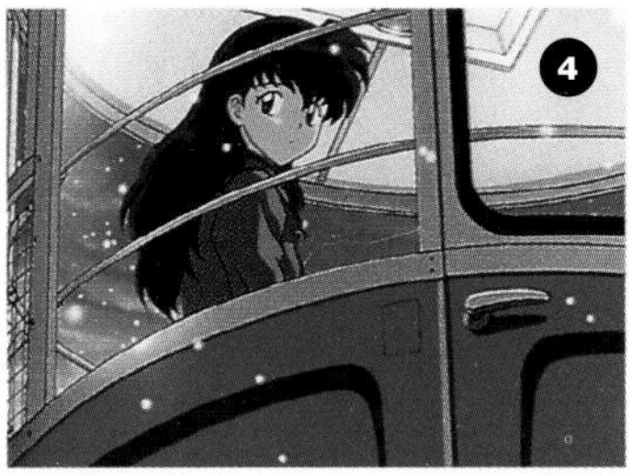
4
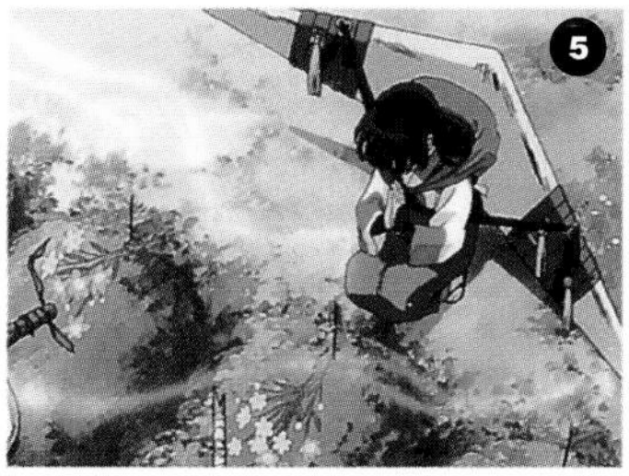
5
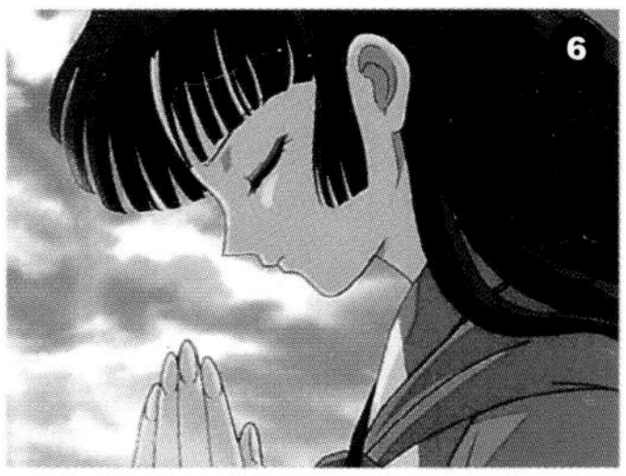
6
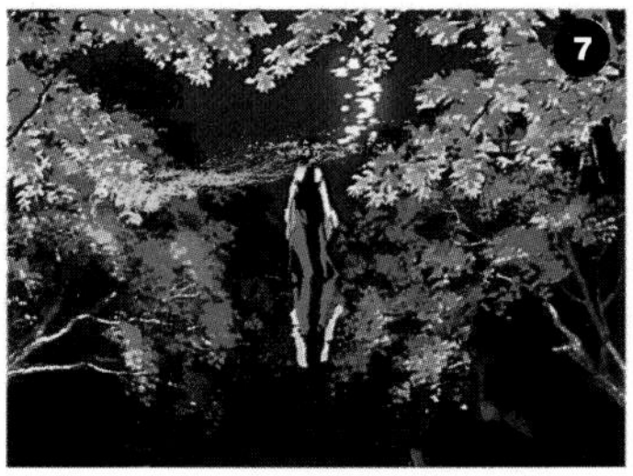
7
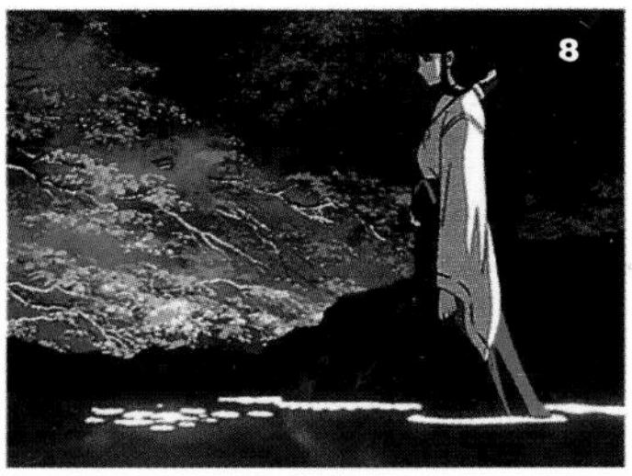
8
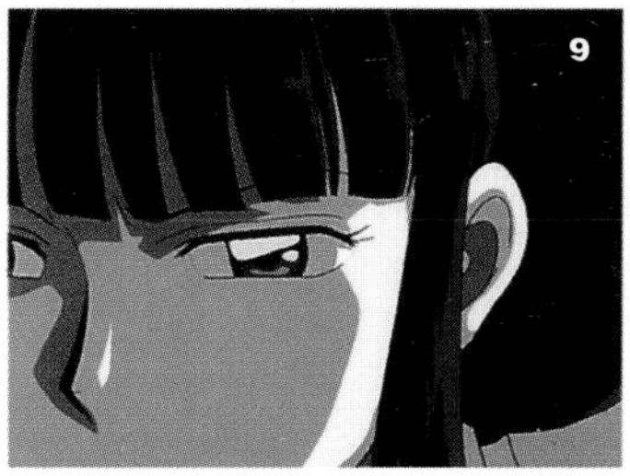
9
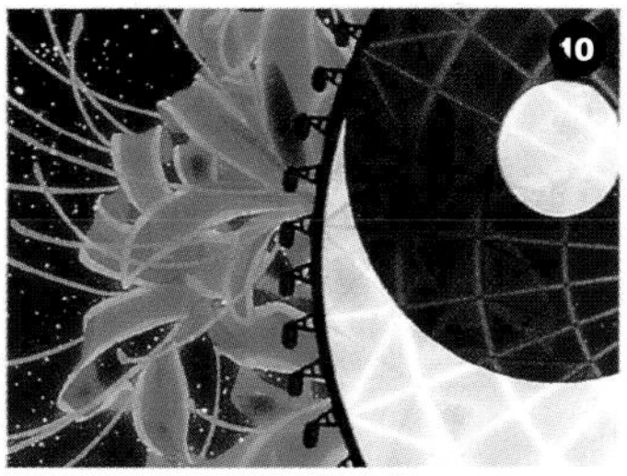
10
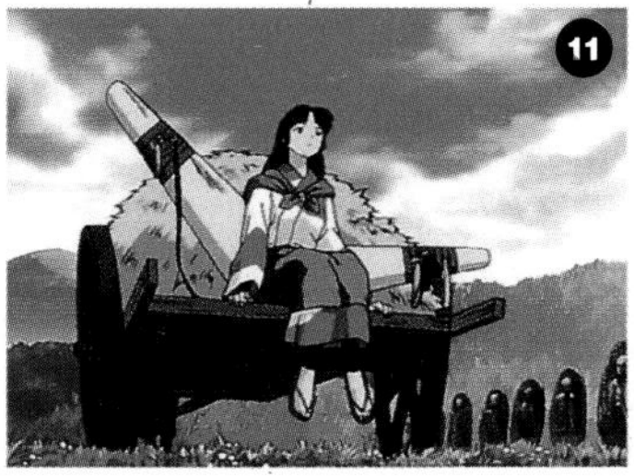
11
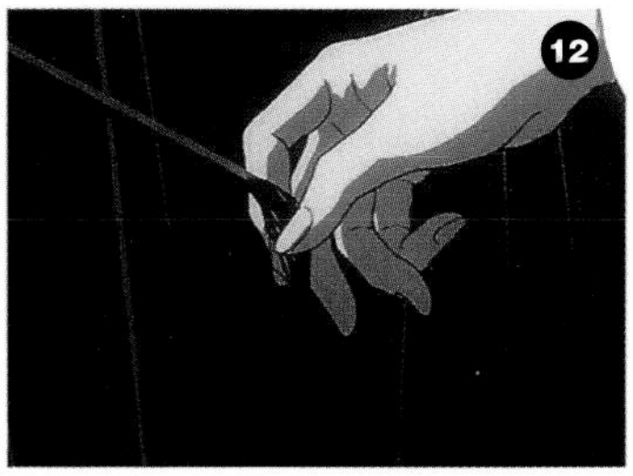
12
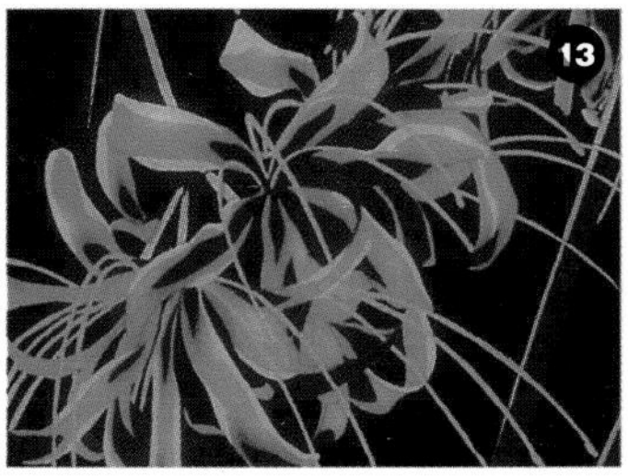
13
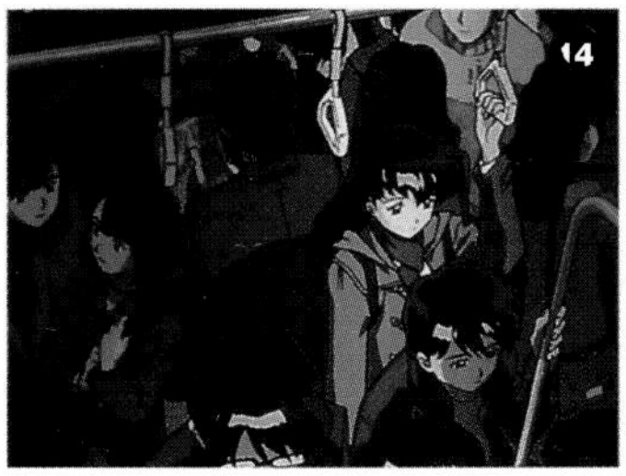
14
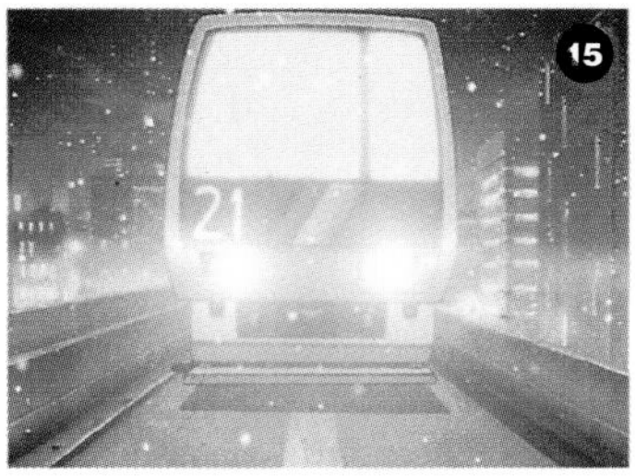
15
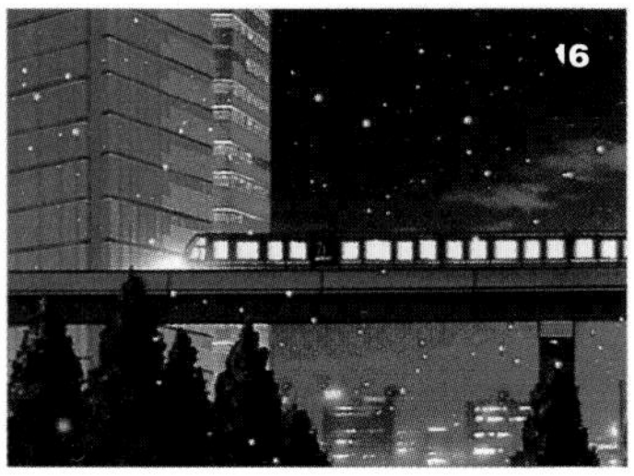
16
21

THE ENDING THEME SONG IS "MY WILL," SUNG BY DREAM, AN ALL GIRL TRIO. THIS IS PROBABLY WHY THE ANIMATION FOCUSES ON KAGOME, KIKYO AND SANGO. FRAME 10, WHICH OVERLAYS AN IMAGE OF A CLUSTER-AMARYLLIS (KIKYO'S DESIRE) AND AN IMAGE OF THE TAO (SANGO'S DESIRE), IS WONDERFUL. DIRECTOR MASASHI IKEDA DREW THE OPENING AND CLOSING SEQUENCES.

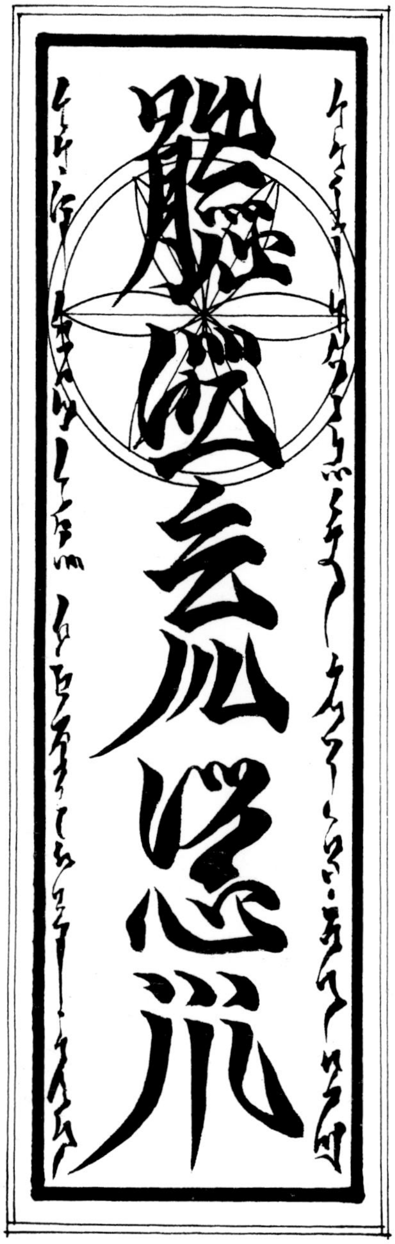

INUYASHA REFERENCE MATERIALS

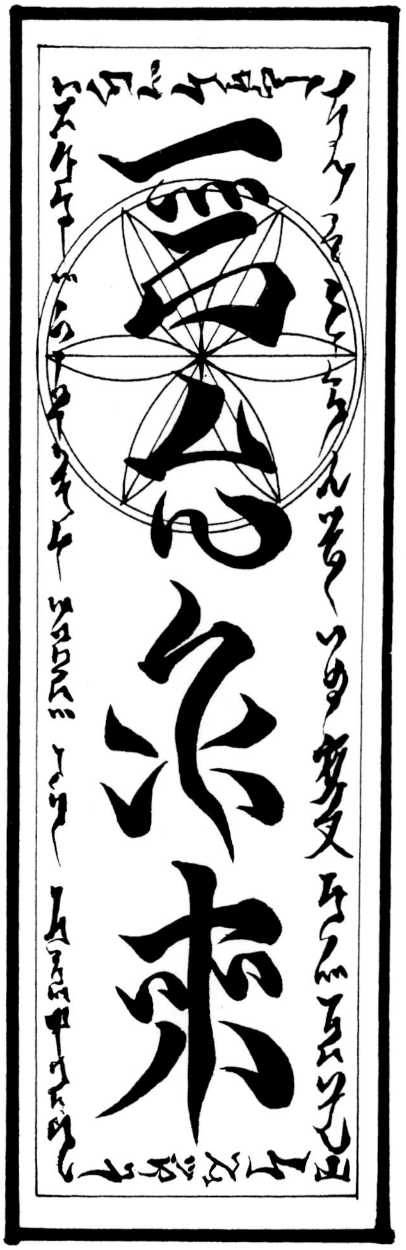

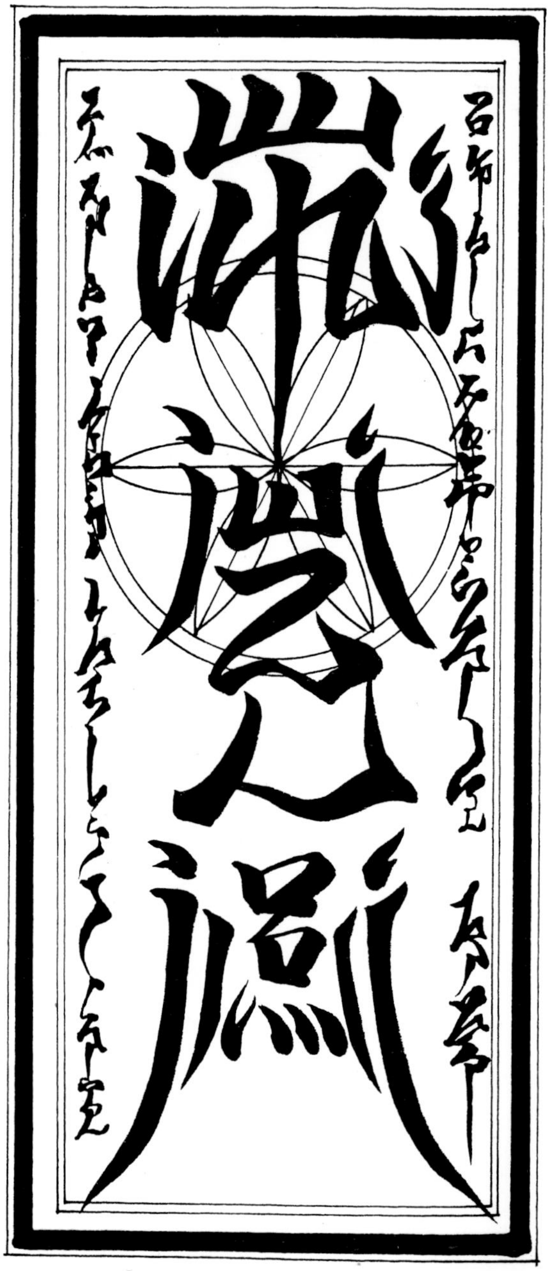

- INUYASHA SCROLL 1: RECORDING REPORT
- A FANTASY FROM A TIME OF WAR: RUMIKO TAKAHASHI TALKS WITH THE VOICE ACTORS
- STAFF INTERVIEWS
- ANIMATION SETUP MATERIALS
- INUYASHA GLOSSARY

For pages 130-138 read page on the right, then the left. Read the left column, then right.

INUYASHA RECORDING REPORT

SCROLL 1

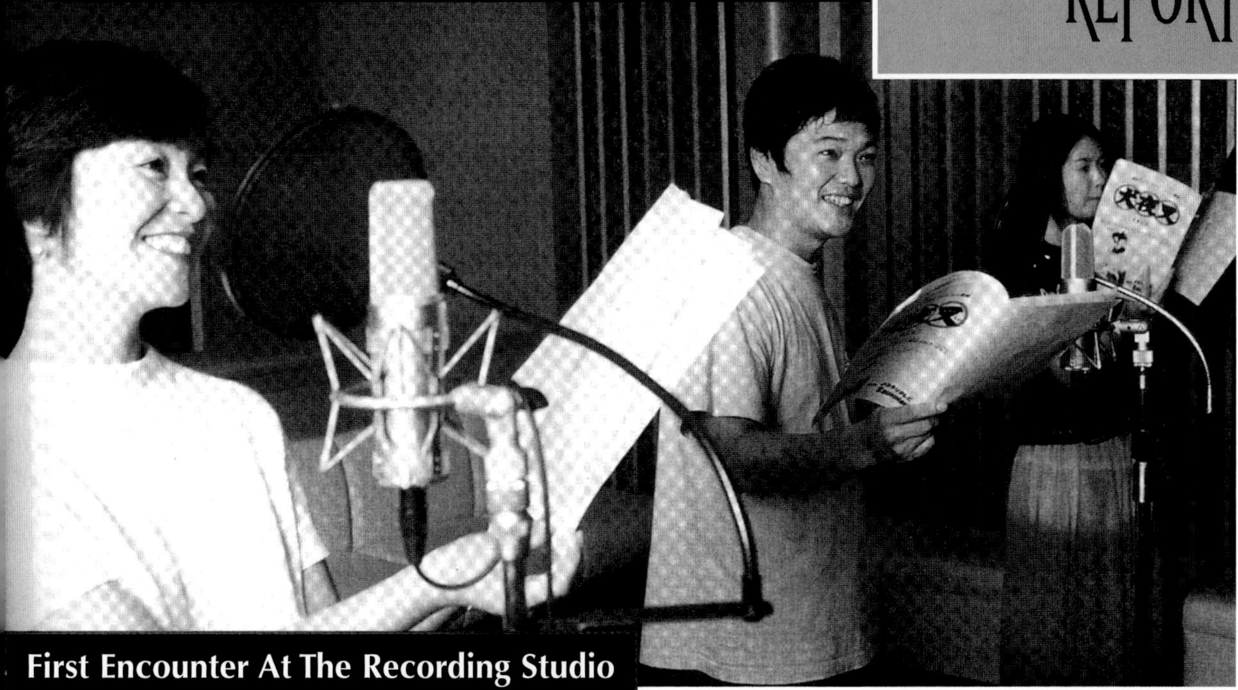

First Encounter At The Recording Studio

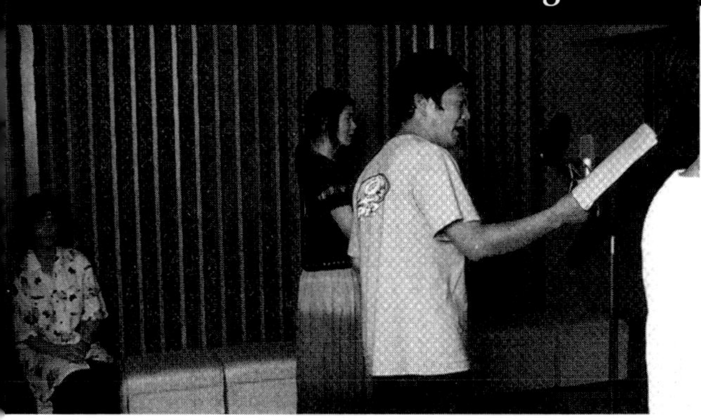

Behind the voice actors performing with smiles, there is the presence of Ms. Takahashi!

RUMIKO TAKAHASHI WITNESSES HER FIRST RECORDING SESSION!

Rumiko Takahashi witnessed the first recording of the television animation of Inuyasha, the exciting moment when the animation came to life. Despite having many hit animations as well as comics to her credit, this was Ms. Takahashi's first experience at a studio recording session. How did she like it?

It was late August, about two months before the animation series would be launched, when a memorable recording of Scroll 1 of Inuyasha was made. Because it was the first episode, every crew member and voice actor coming into the studio was a little tense. When the people were assembled, the producer gave a pep talk: "Let's do a good job together." To avoid putting unnecessary pressure on them, the voice actors were not told that Takahashi was there. It was arranged that she would enter the studio after the recording began.

And so it began! Rather than all the voice actors going immediately to their mikes, they watched the video first to learn the timing of each character. Since it was the first episode, it was also the first time they saw Inuyasha and the other characters in motion. Some cried out in excitement because of the beautiful animation! Kappei Yamaguchi, playing the leading role, Inuyasha, watched the monitor with shining, passionate eyes. Then ...

The actors finally stood before their mikes. There was plenty of time before the final take. First came rehearsal. There was no doubt that the voices coming through the mikes were those of Inuyasha and Kagome. The voices were perfectly in sync with the characters' motions on the monitor. This was the exciting first appearance of the walking and talking Inuyasha! The director and crew watched the performances with grave faces. They discussed their opinions, concerns and needed changes, and told each actor. The actors explored their characters and coordinated the timing of the dialogue. From the control

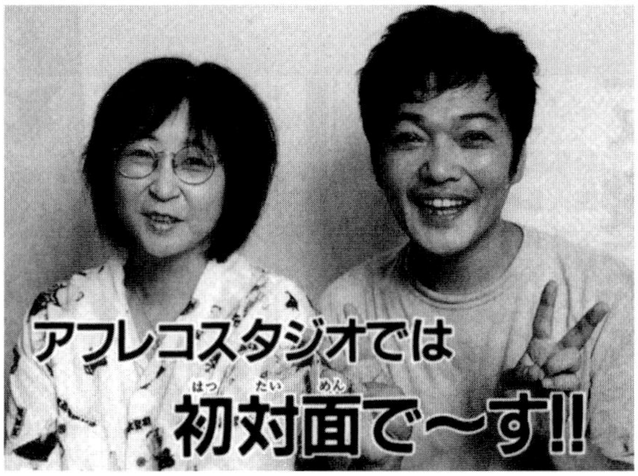
アフレコスタジオでは
初対面で～す!!

Kappei Yamaguchi, who also played Ranma in "Ranma 1/2," has known Ms. Takahashi for a long time and often sees her here and there. But this was the first time for them to be together at the recording studio.

アフレコ本番!!
調整室から熱い視線をそそぐ高橋先生!!

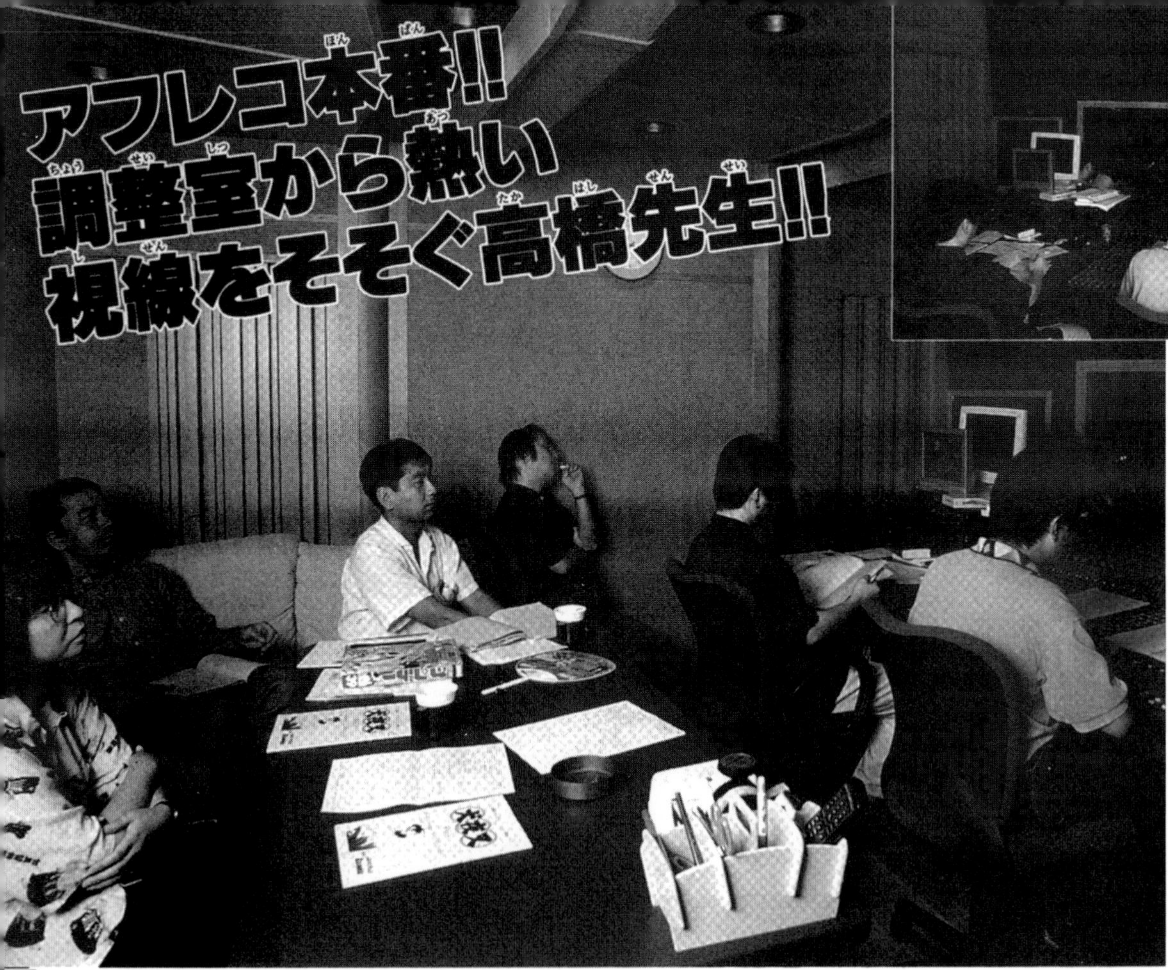

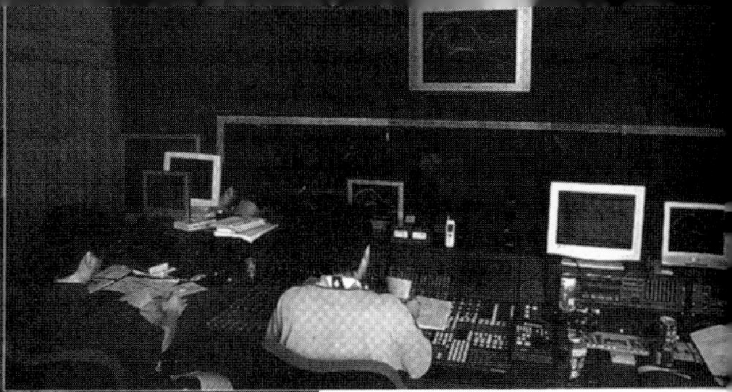

No one is allowed to enter the studio during the take, but it is okay during tests. The smiling actors were skillfully hiding their tension. Ms. Takahashi was satisfied, feeling the close teamwork of the actors right in front of her.

Here's a view of the control room seen from where Ms. Takahashi was seated. There are several monitors in the room so everyone can see easily. In the studio beyond the soundproof glass, the actors were deeply involved in their performances.

The take! Ms. Takahashi watches with enthusiasm from the control room.

room, the director would ask the actors to change something, and they would satisfy him; everyone was so professional! As the rehearsal went on, the voices of Inuyasha and Kagome were refined and developed to their very best.

In the control room, one woman watched the session with a curious expression. Rumiko Takahashi had sneaked into the studio without being noticed by the actors. This was her first visit to a studio during a session. "There were probably many opportunities before, but no one ever invited me," she said. She appeared intrigued by everything she saw. Between tests she asked questions. During tests she was riveted by the performances. She seemed to deeply enjoy the session.

Then came a minor slip-up. Ms. Takahashi was supposed to greet the actors after the final take of the first half, but due to a miscommunication, she did it just before the final take. At the sudden appearance of Ms. Takahashi, Satsuki Yukino, a longtime fan of Takahashi's "Urusei Yatsura" and "Ranma 1/2," got a little panicky. But since she is a professional, she did a perfect job on the final take.

"I was totally beside myself and don't remember anything I did," said Yukino later. She is like the courageous Kagome. The recording was finished, taking about five hours for both halves. After enjoying the recording so much, we asked Ms. Takahashi what she thought of it.

"It was my first time seeing a recording. I'd learned how TV animation is made, and it was kind of late to do this, but I was very impressed and excited about it. I had a great time. Above all, I'm happy to have such terrific voice actors. As I expected, Kappei Yamaguchi proved to be exactly the right man for Inuyasha. I'm so glad to have the all-star cast that I wanted so much. Surprisingly, I had some difficulty imagining Kagome's voice at first. On hearing Satsuki Yukino, I was convinced. I said to myself, "Hmmmm ... Now I know how Kagome sounds!"

In person Ms. Yukino looks like a pretty girl of good breeding, but her acting was much more energetic than I imagined. Noriko Hidaka, who played Kikyo, also did Akane in "Ranma 1/2." Kikyo is the opposite of Akane in personality, but her restrained acting was wonderful. I am so happy to be able to see the hard work of the voice actors and staff. I can't wait to see it on TV!"

You already know the on-air result. Ms. Takahashi was completely satisfied with it.

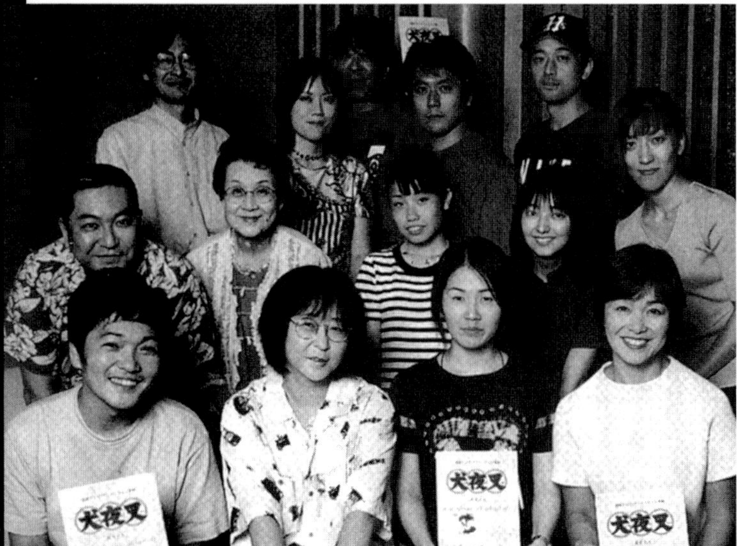

犬夜叉

Commemorative shot with all the voice actors!

Front row, from left: Kappei Yamaguchi, Ms. Takahashi, Satsuki Yukino, Noriko Hidaka, Toshihiko Nakajima, Hisako Kyoda, Mika Ito, Akiko Nakagawa, Asako Dodo, Tomoshisa Aso, Shirei Igarashi, Kazunari Tanaka, Tadahisa Seizen and Ginzo Matsuo.

A Fantasy From a Time of War: Rumiko Takahashi Talks with the Leading Voice Actors

To commemorate a great start for the animation of Inuyasha, we have a very special interview, a round-table discussion with the four stars of the program: author, Rumiko Takahashi, Kappei Yamaguchi (the voice of Inuyasha), Satsuki Yukino (Kagome) and Noriko Hidaka (Kikyo). Their passionate discussion of the Inuyasha project was a dream come true for us. We know you won't want to miss a word of it, so here's the complete transcript!

- TAKAHASHI: Thank you so much for the opening party for the animation last week!
- YAMAGUCHI: Thank YOU! We had a lot of fun.
- YUKINO: My ears are still ringing from Kappei-san singing "Change the World" (laughs)!
- YAMAGUCHI: Did that really happen?
- HIDAKA: It sure did (laughs)! There were too many people around last week for a good chat, let's take some time and really talk today.
- TAKAHASHI: Episode 3 will go on the air at seven, so we should finish up by then. I set my VCR to record it just in case, though.

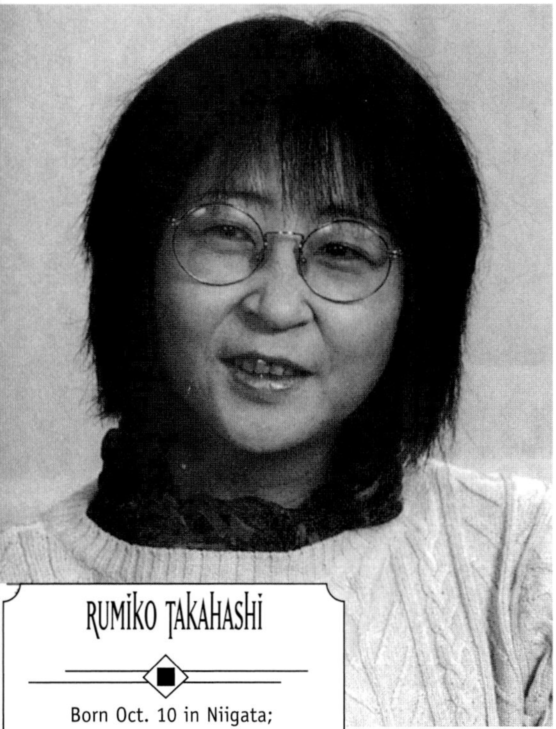

RUMIKO TAKAHASHI

Born Oct. 10 in Niigata; blood type A

She made her professional debut with "Kattena Yatsura" ("Selfish Guys") in Shonen Sunday while a student at Japan Women's University. That same year she started the "Urusei Yatsura" series, then "Ranma 1/2" and "Inuyasha." All her stories have been made into animations.

Terrific Results For Animation Project

Exclusive Background Info

- YAMAGUCHI: Let's start with Takahashi-sensei. Just among ourselves, now. You watched the first two episodes on TV. I'd like you to feel free to be completely honest and tell us what you thought of our performances.
- TAKAHASHI: Everything was so well done, including your acting, which I was totally blown away by. Episode 1 was very special. I came to the studio recording and watched the whole process come together. When it was done, I was so impressed with the results that I said, "It's just too good to be true!" Kappei-san's Inuyasha was the best, of course.
- YAMAGUCHI: Such direct praise from you makes me feel a little shy. Well ... I don't know what to say!
- TAKAHASHI: I've been thinking about it, and I just can't think of anyone who could do Inuyasha better, Kappei-san.

Takahashi: *"My only specific request related to the animation was the voice actor who would play Inuyasha."*

- HIDAKA: That's got to put Kappei on Cloud Nine!
- YUKINO: We better hurry up and bring him down (laughs)!
- TAKAHASHI: I liked Yukino-san as Kagome, too. I was utterly convinced; I thought, "Now I know how she sounds!" And you have such a cute scream!
- YUKINO: I've got to make that scream cuter!
- TAKAHASHI: Don't push it too much, it sounded fine to me. And Kikyo, I'd been looking forward to that performance since the day they picked Hidaka-san! How would you do? Kikyo doesn't show up often in the story, but she has a huge presence. Hidaka-san's Kikyo, just like in the comic, makes me feel that she's right there at my side, making me feel good.
- YAMAGUCHI: I know what you mean — she's always there!
- HIDAKA: Take a picture in the studio and you'll probably see me in it, even when I'm not there.

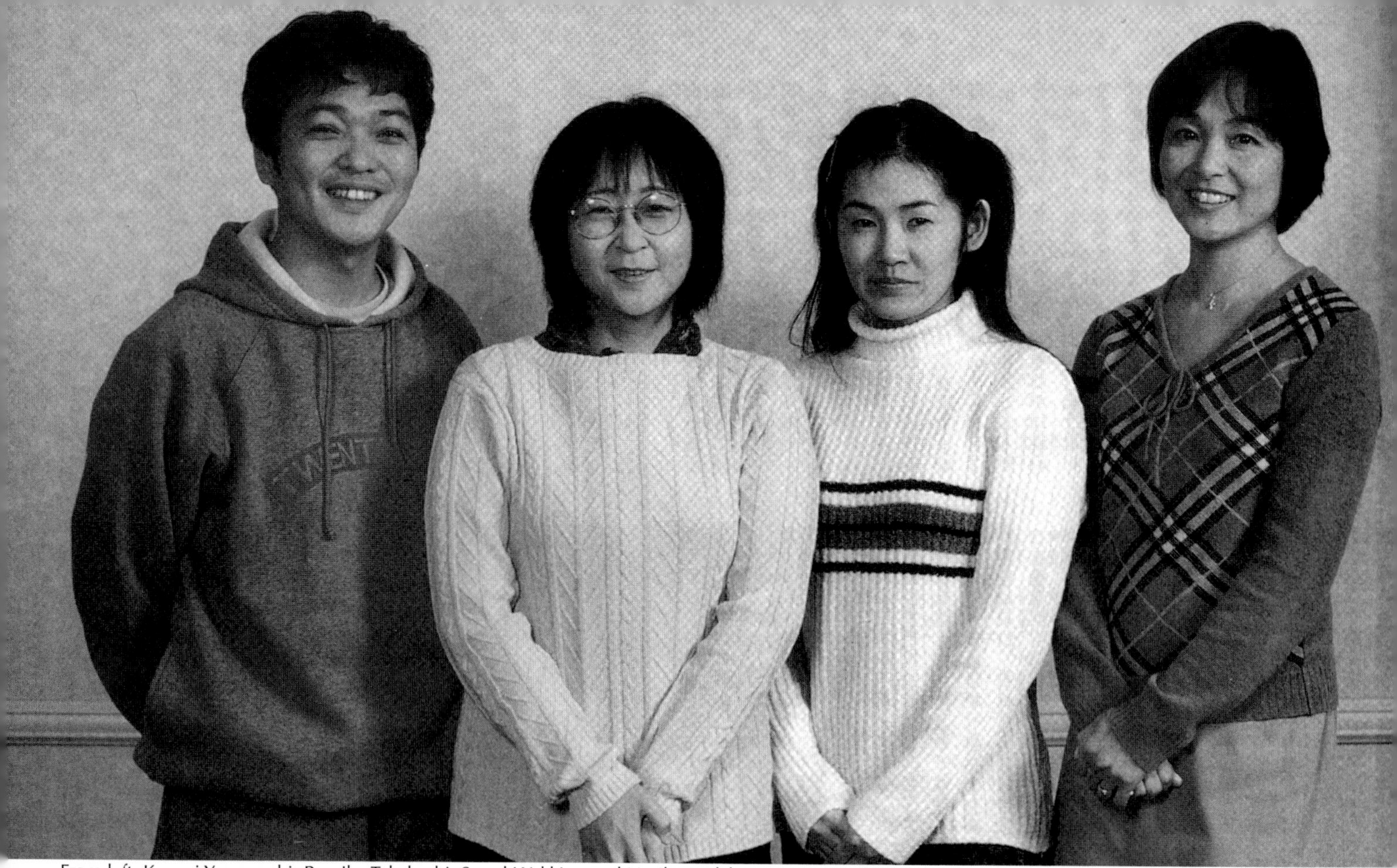
TWENT
From left: Kappei Yamaguchi, Rumiko Takahashi, Satsuki Yukkino and Noriko Hidaka

- YUKINO: No kidding, really! Even when Hidaka-san isn't in the studio, it's like your aura is still there, I swear.

- YAMAGUCHI: Yeah, it's like you're watching us from somewhere.

- HIDAKA: I'm probably peeking through the crack in the door (laughs)! You know, I was real tense and nervous when I gave my first line: "Inuyasha!" Kikyo is so conflicted about Inuyasha and so tense, I really wondered how it'd sound coming out of my throat. I had no idea. I worried that it might be exactly like Akane's "Ranma!" My heart was pounding! But an entirely different voice came out, I was so relieved! It felt good, and I knew, "this is it" (laughs)!

- TAKAHASHI: I knew Hidaka-san was doing it, but if I hadn't known that ahead of time I couldn't have told you who was in the role.

A Surprise Hit

- YAMAGUCHI: I've been hearing from a lot of people since the show went on the air, from TV people to my neighbors (laughs). I've found out that a lot more people are watching "Inuyasha" than I expected.

- HIDAKA: I went to a gig at a different studio, and people were talking about "Inuyasha" all the time, not the show they were working on (laughs)! "Noriko-san, I'll play Shippo. And he'll probably play Hojo."

- TAKAHASHI: Will Kumiko Watanabe do Shippo? I'm looking forward to hearing that. I wonder what sort of voice she'll use. I saw her at the opening party last week, but I didn't have the guts to ask her to do a little Shippo right there (laughs)!

- YAMAGUCHI: We had Miroku and Koga at the party, too. I'd tell the readers who they are, but it's still supposed to be secret, sorry!

- TAKAHASHI: Indeed. I can't wait to hear that person do Miroku (laughs)!

- HIDAKA: He couldn't come to the party, but Ken'ichi Ogata, who's doing Myoga, told me he's looking forward to the sessions very much. Everyone who got parts are really excited and waiting anxiously for their sessions. That's so cool!

- YAMAGUCHI: For myself, when I got the part, I was so blown away that I couldn't believe it really happened, and I couldn't feel anything, even joy. When I got back to my house, it all gradually dawned on me and I suddenly just went, "Yesss!"

- TAKAHASHI: From a long time ago, since the very beginning, I thought long and hard about Inuyasha's voice. I couldn't think of anyone but Kappei-san. In the early production meetings the staff asked me if I had any requests. There was only one: "Please have Kappei-san do Inuyasha."

- YAMAGUCHI: That's wonderful, I'm so grateful! It's a lot of responsibility.

- TAKAHASHI: Honestly, I want you to play it the way you feel it. I told them then that I take it for granted that the animation would be very different from the original story. I firmly believe that everything will be better if all the voice actors are completely comfortable with how they're doing their parts.

- YUKINO: I've been a fan of Ms. Takahashi's work since I was a little kid, and it was so strange to be playing what I'd been reading. I went to the audition for Kagome thinking, "I HAVE to get this part!" It came true, and I got it. After that the pressure, gradually built up. I asked myself, "Am I really Kagome? Me? Are you sure?" It got really heavy.

- TAKAHASHI: Don't worry, you're perfect for it!

- HIDAKA: That's so funny. I go to an audition absolutely resolved that I'll get the part, then after the audition I'm sure I was terrible, then I do get the part and I'm ecstatic, then I realize I really have to do it and the pressure makes me all nervous again. This emotional roller coaster seems to be the same for everybody.

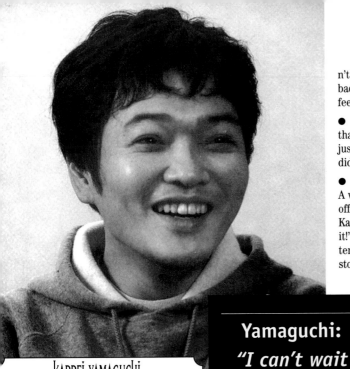

KAPPEI YAMAGUCHI
(voice of Inuyasha)

Born May 23 in Fukuoka;
blood type B

Major roles for Yamaguchi include Ranma Saotome in "Ranma 1/2," Shin'ichi Kudo and the Kaito Kid in "Meitantei Conan" ("Master Detective Conan"), Tonbo in "Majo no Takkyubin" ("Witch's Parcel"), Bugs in "Loony Toons Bugs Bunny," and Usopp in "One Piece."

Yamaguchi: *"I can't wait for the Master to hear my Inuyasha!"*

- YAMAGUCHI:: For me the hardest time was between getting the part and recording Episode 1. But that's when it's most exciting, too, huh?
- HIDAKA: I was going to the audition for Kagome, but I knew nothing about her, so I went to a bookstore, picked up the comic, took a look at her and was shocked to find a 15-year-old girl!
- YAMAGUCHI: Younger than Akane ....
- HIDAKA: No, no, (laughs) that's not what I mean! For the past few years I've been looking for more adult characters. So at 15, Kagome didn't look very good in that way. Anyway I kept reading, drawn in by the story. I didn't pay much attention to the characters at all and I finished the whole thing. It was great. But, well, that's not what I should have done, right?
- YAMAGUCHI: That happens, I can relate.
- HIDAKA: Then I went back to the story and rediscovered Kagome as an attractive character, typical of Ms. Takahashi's heroines. Looking at her as an actress, I wanted to play her. But, personally, I was still so attached to my favorite character, Akane in "Ranma 1/2." Anyway I went to the audition and read my lines, feeling a strange sense of deja vu. I didn't know whether that was good or bad, and I went home with mixed feelings about the whole thing.
- YAMAGUCHI: I don't catch that you were feeling that way. I just kept going on about myself, didn't I? I apologize.
- HIDAKA: Thank you (laughs)! A while later, as I expected, I was offered "another" character, not Kagome. I said to myself, "I knew it!" I thought that "other" character would be Yura, so I reread the story over and over thinking about her (everyone bursts into laughter)!
- HIDAKA: Then they told me I got Kikyo, and I thought that made a lot of sense. Now I was elated, playing the wonderful past life of Kagome. (laughs) This time ,I read the story focusing on Kikyo. Honestly, she's a tough one, not like any other character I've done, but I could see some challenge in her. To get to Kikyo, I had to wander around through several characters (laughs).
- YAMAGUCHI: Now I understand the long history behind that first line (laughs)!

Recording Excitement
Fun And Professionalism In The Studio

- TAKAHASHI: Watching Hidaka-san working in the studio, I only thought of your professionalism. I never imagined such a history behind it (laughs).
- YUKINO: But Ms. Takahashi, was that really your first time in a recording session?
- TAKAHASHI: Yes, indeed. The first since I was born (laughs). Everything was new, and it was quite a show. Listening to you chat during the break, I was seeing you totally as ordinary fans, saying, "this person plays this character, that person plays that ...."
- YAMAGUCHI: During the session, before they introduced you, I looked back and saw Ms. Takahashi there. That made doing my part more fun.
- YUKINO: I was too involved to look around.
- YAMAGUCHI: 'Fun' might not be the right word. I was told that Ms. Takahashi recommended me for the role, so I wanted you to hear me as soon as possible; naturally I'd decided I had to live up to your confidence and turn in the best possible performance.
- Takahashi: I didn't realize that. It was a little weird dropping in so casually, as if I'd come to play or have a bite. It was clear that you were all having so much fun with your parts.
- YAMAGUCHI: In addition to every "Inuyasha" actor having a good time, there's a really good balance among us, from very young people to very experienced actors. It's particularly great to have Hisako Kyoda there doing Kaede.
- YUKINO: She is such a great actress!
- YAMAGUCHI: She gives us little comments about our acting, saying things like, "that inflection was a little odd," or "something's not quite right about that." This alone is so precious. Once she began commenting to me, I felt her watching me constantly. This makes rehearsal really fun, but builds up a lot of pressure for the final take.
- TAKAHASHI: In that way, "Inuyasha" is blessed.

Yukino: *"Sometimes Kappei-san calls me Akane!"*

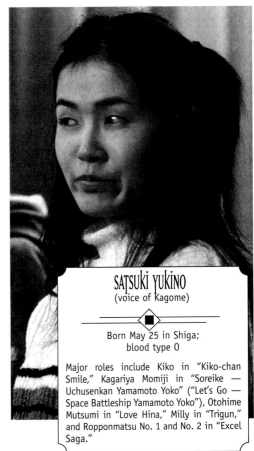

SATSUKI YUKINO
(voice of Kagome)

Born May 25 in Shiga;
blood type O

Major roles include Kiko in "Kiko-chan Smile," Kagariya Momiji in "Soreike — Uchusenkan Yamamoto Yoko" ("Let's Go — Space Battleship Yamamoto Yoko"), Otohime Mutsumi in "Love Hina," Milly in "Trigun," and Ropponmatsu No. 1 and No. 2 in "Excel Saga."

- Yukino: Kyoda-san and the experienced actors are great, but look at you, Kappei-san.
- Yamaguchi: (surprised) What?
- Yukino: You're terrible, Kappei-san, always calling me Akane!
- Yamaguchi: I got a good chewing out for that the other day.

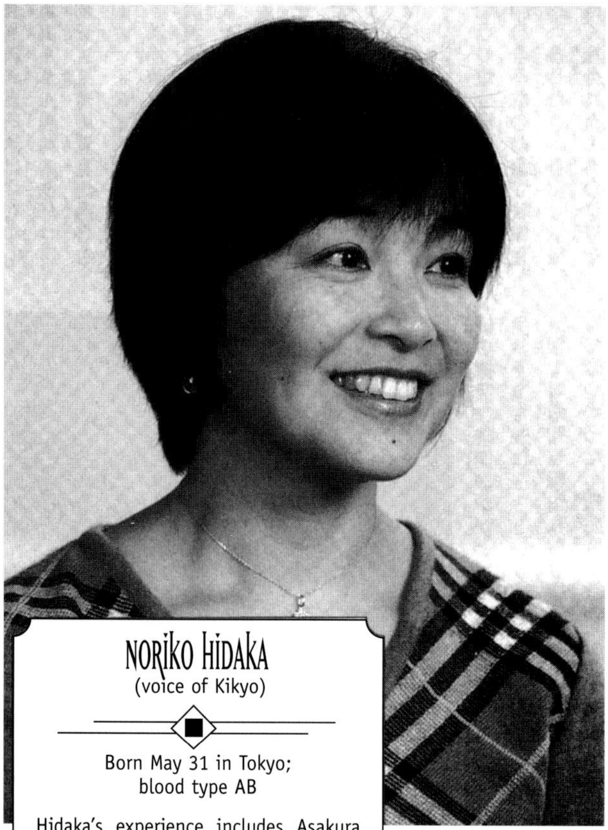

NORIKO HIDAKA
(voice of Kikyo)

Born May 31 in Tokyo;
blood type AB

Hidaka's experience includes Asakura Minami in "Touch," Tendo Akane in "Ranma 1/2," Satsuki in "Tonari no Totoro" ("My Neighbor Totoro"), Endo Kazumi in "Aoki Densetsu Shuto" ("Blue Legend Shoot"), Shiine in "Akazukin Chacha" ("Red-Hood Chacha"), and Ceena in "ZOIDS."

- Yukino: I let it go twice, but the third time? I thought I shouldn't be so sweet to you!
- Yamaguchi: She sounded just like Kagome in the first episode telling me, "You know, I'm not Akane, I'm Kagome! Kah, Goh, Meh! Right?"
- Hidaka: It's the same three syllables (laughs).

Pronunciation Questions
What Are The Origins?

- Yamaguchi: Anyway ... Ms. Takahashi, I sometimes wondered how I should pronounce certain names, like Kikyo and Shikon no Tama.
- Hidaka: Everybody was doing it their own way, so we talked about it a lot in the studio.
- Yamaguchi: All my readings turned out to be wrong.
- Yukino: I still say 'Kikyo' wrong once in a while. I did it last week, too.
- Yamaguchi: The guest actors wonder, too. They often whisper to me, "Hey, how do you say this?"
- Hidaka: We need an Inuyasha Dialect Dictionary so everyone will be clear.
- Takahashi: I had some ideas about pronunciation when I thought of these names. Because I created so many characters, I ran out of normal names, so I got some names you don't ordinarily hear spoken.

Hidaka: *"I auditioned for Kagome and didn't make it, then thought I'd make a good Yura."*

- Yamaguchi: 'Inuyasha' is also a rare name.
- Takahashi: He's both a dog (inu) and a forest spirit (yasha). There you have it, Inuyasha (laughs).
- Yukino: Kappei gets mad when I call him 'inu,' even though it's in the script.
- Yamaguchi: Don't call me "inu." I don't know why, but I hate being called a dog.
- Takahashi: (laughs) Come to think of it, I did a lot of thinking before deciding on Kagome. I wrote down everything that came to mind. Kagome sounded cute. I like names that end with 'me,' so, for no particular reason, I chose Kagome (laughs).
- Hidaka: How did you come up with Kikyo?
- Takahashi: The language of flowers was the key. I happened to see a balloonflower (kikyo) on TV, and its meaning was introduced: "unchanging love." I said, "That's it!"

Inuyasha, Kikyo and Kagome:
You ain't seen nothin' yet!

- Yamaguchi: I have to say it's so much fun doing Inuyasha. At this moment, the character's focus is on the Jewel rather than Kagome. So what I play is joy, anger, joy, anger, joy, anger.... The director warned me not to be so argumentative all the time. I love Inuyasha that way, he's a stress reliever (laughs).
- Yukino: You may be having fun, but when Inuyasha calls me 'stupid woman' over and over, I'm offended (laughs)! I feel like he's getting a little sweeter lately, though.
- Yamaguchi: Is he? I worry that after Kikyo appears, I won't know how to switch my feelings between Kagome and Kikyo. Don't you think that'll be difficult, Ms. Takahashi?
- Takahashi: Don't worry. I avoided situations where the three of them would be together talking. Inuyasha always likes the girl he is with the best.
- Yamaguchi: Uh-huh (laughs)! Shame, shame, bad Inuyasha!
- Takahashi: I think he's all right that way (laughs). There might be a problem if the three of them were together.
- Yamaguchi: I still can't believe I'm doing Inuyasha. I feel so blessed, it might be better that I have a little difficulty with the character (laughs). The thought of Inuyasha always makes me happy. I know I'll fully enjoy this character. I'll think about the hard stuff later.
- Hidaka: It's hard to really understand Inuyasha's emotions, but Kikyo's are mysterious, too. I feel I have to read the original story more and work harder. My mission is to keep frightening everyone as much as I can, both as a character and in the studio.
- Takahashi: We can't wait, can we? The revived Kikyo just explodes to life. She makes the scenes with all her screaming and such. She has so much hatred, but enormous love as well. I wonder what sort of voice she'll have....
- Hidaka: Because she has so much love, her hatred is deep, right? Her only reason to come back from death is that 'unchanging love.'
- Yukino: Without thinking too hard about it, I hope to directly express my feelings as I identify with Kagome. I've got experienced colleagues to watch me, so I can't go too far wrong with that approach. My ideal is to relax and play it without trying too hard.
- Takahashi: A job is well done when it's done at ease. I'll watch you on TV every week. Good luck everyone!
- Yamaguchi: Please come back to more sessions!
- Yukino: Our regular crew is expanding.
- Hidaka: Please come back when Kikyo appears (laughs).
- Takahashi: I will, but only if I don't get in your way (laughs)!

DIRECTOR MASASHI IKEDA:

"THE REUNION BETWEEN INUYASHA AND KIKYO IS A CRUCIAL POINT IN THE EARLY PART OF THE STORY."

Q: What impression did you get when you first read the story?

A: In the comic I saw the marriage of two elements: a love comedy typical of Rumiko Takahashi, and a darker aspect. The two are indispensable elements of "Inuyasha." I also thought of this as the complete expression of Rumiko Takahashi.

Before starting the animation project, many were concerned about how we would recreate for TV dark elements like the death matches between demons and people falling victim to evil. I decided to bring out the drama and themes of those dark aspects by concentrating on Ms. Takahashi's intentions rather than simply translating them technically from the page to the screen.

Kikyo has a dark world within her, and I frequently felt that her position was very important to the story.

In a sense Inuyasha is the hero and Kagome is the accidental heroine. Kikyo is a challenging character because she's so scary that she made me wonder whether I could go that far. She's the one I got most involved with in developing the story, sharing her journey and her agony.

I learned about Ms. Takahashi's vision from the producers. For instance, she said, "I want to express Kikyo's passion. Once she goes through death and comes back, her spirit and soul, which were shaped by the restrictions of the role of the priestess and doing what's right, were set free. Now she can wander wherever her emotions take her. That's what I want to communicate." I've been putting a lot of time into exploring Kikyo, because at this moment I have no idea where the character is heading.

I really agonized over that first scene with Sesshomaru. Then I got through that and I found myself hitting a wall again over Kikyo. When we finally finished reviving Kikyo,

I had to deal with Sesshomaru again. I stumbled at the climax to every volume. There are many cases where early character definitions and hints make so much sense later. So I often have to check out the latest chapters and coordinate where I am with them. "Inuyasha" is a tough piece of work that doesn't let us get away with a patchwork approach to solving problems.

The episode where Urasue brings Kikyo back from the dead nearly sank my boat. This was the reunion of Inuyasha and Kikyo. It's a crucial episode in the early story. Directing it was really hard, because I had to calculate Kikyo's every expression and move and recheck over and over again to be sure they were convincing.

Q: Tell us about another climactic moment. Sesshomaru, maybe?

A: Inuyasha is a half-demon, the child of a demon and a human. This gives the story some really interesting elements, like Inuyasha's inferiority complex toward Sesshomaru and the sibling rivalry over Tetsusaiga. I think these can be presented clearly in a soap-opera-like drama, and I think that's where we'll be heading with Inuyasha.

I thought the first major climax of the animation is the period between Inuyasha's encounter with Kagome and the emergence of Sesshomaru. I've been thinking a lot about this.

Q: Will the animation develop in the same way as the original story?

A: In the beginning I was asked if I could make the more popular characters appear sooner than in the comic. But the original is so tightly structured, I don't want to force that kind of change. Before characters like Shippo, Miroku and Sango appear, we can keep the story interesting enough with just Inuyasha and Kagome. I've never thought we can make the animation better by changing the structure.

Staff Interviews

It's just one man's opinion, but in turning Rumiko Takahashi's original work into animation, I feel strongly that we must not betray the fans; I have to be as dedicated a fan of the work as they are. My ideal is to have everyone involved in the production work in close identification with the author. We have to aim for that.

Q: Anything else before we close?

A: The series will air once a week. There are both advantages and disadvantages to that. I want some room for the staff to grow with the series. I think that's what a TV series should be, and that's how we were trained.

PROFILE:
Born in 1961 in Kanagawa Prefecture. After graduating from Tokyo University of Art and Design, he worked making illustrated sketches for "Doraemon" and other animated series. He got more involved in direction, worked for the animation company Animaruya, then began freelancing. He directed the animation "Gundam Wing."

CHARACTER DESIGNER YOSHIHITO HISHINUMA

CHARACTER CHANGES FROM COMICS TO ANIMATION

Staff Interviews

Q: What gets your special attention as you redesign characters for animation?

A: Director Ikeda's first request to me was a tough one: to make "pictures that are exactly like those in the comics, but are beautiful in animation too." What I could do to meet this request was to maintain the attractive features of the originals. I could draw pretty much as I pleased, but the results would no longer be the Takahashi characters, but mine.

For the animation I changed the physical proportions of the characters a little, from a 1:6 head-to-body ratio to 1:6.5 or 1:7, for instance. This way the characters don't seem so heavy and look real. In the original, hair tends to be bulky and the faces relatively smaller. This is different from characters I've designed before in terms of balance.

Q: What other requests did the director make?

A: At the meeting, he said, "I've learned that you struggle with designing pretty girls, Hishinuma-san" (laughs). My drawings must have shown my wandering thoughts about creating Kagome.

Q: Which character was the most difficult?

A: Kagome, of course. It was a struggle to retain her original balance and distinctive facial expressions. Also, speaking more technically, the pattern on Sesshomaru's kimono was a big hassle.

I think that subtle balance is the life of Takahashi's drawings. I still haven't done enough to reproduce that.

In "V Gundam," which I worked on last year, it was easy to ask questions of character designer Akira Tanaka, because he was working in the same studio. With "Inuyasha" I don't have Ms. Takahashi in the studio.

Inuyasha's ears, for instance, were a problem. Like a dog's ears, they're on top of his head. So when they asked me what to do with the part of his head where human ears ordinarily would be, I wound up telling them to just hide that part under hair (laughs).

I wonder about the structure of traditional Japanese costumes. I've only seldom drawn them, and they drape differently from regular clothes. One difficult thing in production is that a kimono doesn't look good without some sort of pattern. But it's hard to simplify the pattern so it stays manageable in a TV series. In comics, you only have to put in screen tone. In animation, we can process that sort of thing digitally, but it takes a lot of work.

There are characters that discourage me from drawing them like the original. Urasue, for instance (laughs). It's more fun to draw demons that don't look like humans.

Q: Kikyo is a difficult one, isn't she?

A: Inuyasha, Kikyo and Kagome are the most important characters in the story. The Kikyo character has a subtlety that can be hard to handle. She looks like Kagome and is Kagome's past life, but I intentionally gave them different physical appearances. When I read the original, it didn't feel right to have them look just alike.

The character setup is the springboard for the character, and it grows on its own. I want the draftsmen to draw the characters while looking at the original comics, not my setup (laughs).

Q: Is there a last thought you'd like to share with our readers?

A: When working on mecha animation, like Gundam, I've had mecha directors. "Inuyasha" has no mecha elements, so I have to direct the whole thing by myself. To that extent my workload is a lot heavier than ever. Of course, there are a lot of people who can supervise the mecha and the characters at the same time on their own, and that's impressive. I'd like to maintain quality so the characters don't lose their original nuances.

PROFILE:
Born in 1964 in Hokkaido. He was involved in the animation production of "Yawara," "Hao Taikei Ryu Night," "Shin Kidosenki Gundam W," and "V Gundam." He designs characters for "Inuyasha."

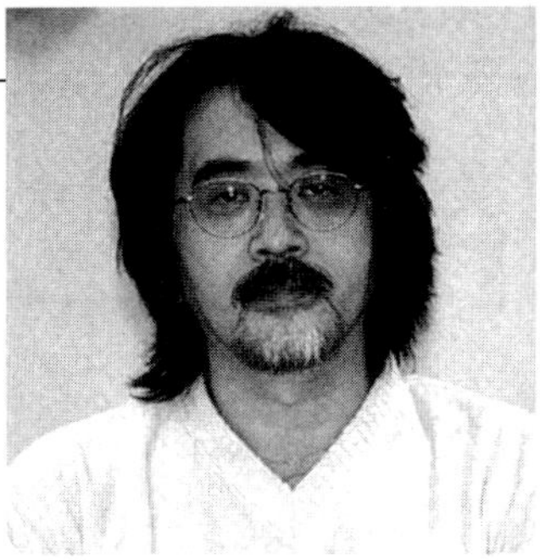

ART DIRECTOR SHIGEMI IKEDA

"THE ART DIRECTOR'S MAIN

Q: Did the project start smoothly?

A: After "V Gundam," which is in the masterpiece category, I was able to switch very comfortably to "Inuyasha." The nature of our work doesn't change much even when the world of the specific animation is radically different.

Q: Do you mean your work is not much affected when the the title changes?

A: Exactly. We have just as much research to do. So when we get a plan for a new title, we have to read and study.

Q: You make an early start.

A: There's a lot to be done before the character setup and storyboards are done. We have to get an early start on the background research and find out, for instance, the structure of the house from the period of the story. It's like location-hunting for a film shoot. For "Inuyasha" we went to Takayama in the Hida region to look at old structures. We try to pinpoint the time in history, and get to know the lifestyles of the people in that period, for minute details like the shapes of pots and pans and flooring materials.

Q: Are sketches and storyboards done after your research?

A: This is the blueprint stage, like the design in a theater production. Once the outlines are drawn, we decide on colors. Then we think about the specific season and other effects. We're like stage carpenters.

The director told us to "make it a clean job." He wants it "clean and serene." "You know, it's the Takahashi world," he said. Some people approach this work with the original comic as "just a good ingredient" for animation. I disagree entirely, and so does the director. He says, "Because this is based on the original, what matters is whether we can communicate the original atmosphere without betraying the people who are familiar with it." So we pay special attention to how we express the positive qualities of the original in animation.

Q: Tell us about your progress. Where are you?

A: Now we're working on Kikyo's first appearance. Isn't she wonderful? She's so human.

Q: How did the original make your work easier or harder?

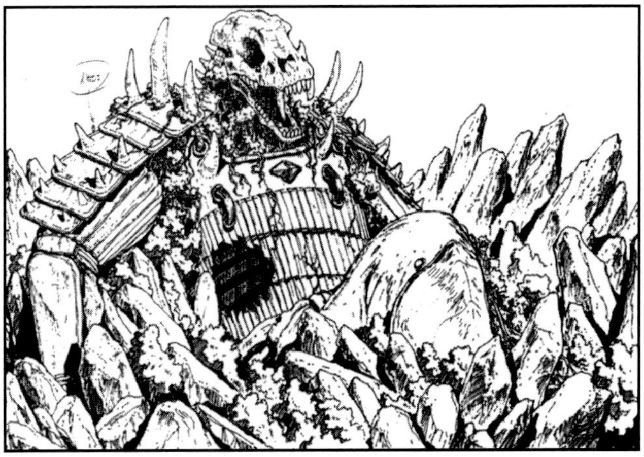

A: I really appreciate the reference materials the author provided. There was one strange room in the original, but our research confirmed that such a room really could have existed.

The comic and the animation flow differently. In the animation we have to show the viewer what the comic didn't show. We have to create all this from scratch. That's a lot of work, hard work, too.

My work is like archaeology. It's interesting to look at the original and find its consistencies. Based on the fragments of information that the comic gives me, I have to imagine the complete structure of the house, the shrine, etc. It's fascinating brain work. From the entrance to Kagome's house, we imagine her living room.

In the context of the modern story, Higurashi Shrine looks more the way a shrine should look. We spot key ideas in the original, like the particular ways people visit the shrine, and the priest's family living behind the shrine, then assemble the complete picture. That's really interesting. We find ways to include all the original elements in the animation without deviating from them.

At one point we thought it'd be cool to make the bones of Inuyasha's father look like a dinosaur's, and we did it without telling anyone. Then someone checked it and made us change it so the bones look more like the original.

We really get into the scenes that imply a specific time.

Q: What do you mean?

A: So far we have scenes like inside a mountain or a solitary castle on a mountain. They're not tied to specific time periods, and that makes our work harder. We look forward to expressing more period-specific elements.

PROFILE:
Born in 1953 in Tokyo. After working for ??Ad Cosmo, Group Tack and Studio Uni,?? he established Atelier Musa. He was an art director for "Seisenshi Bandain," "Jusenki Erugaimu," "Garasaki," and "V Gundam."

ANIMATION SETUP MATERIALS

COMPARISON OF THE MAIN CHARACTERS

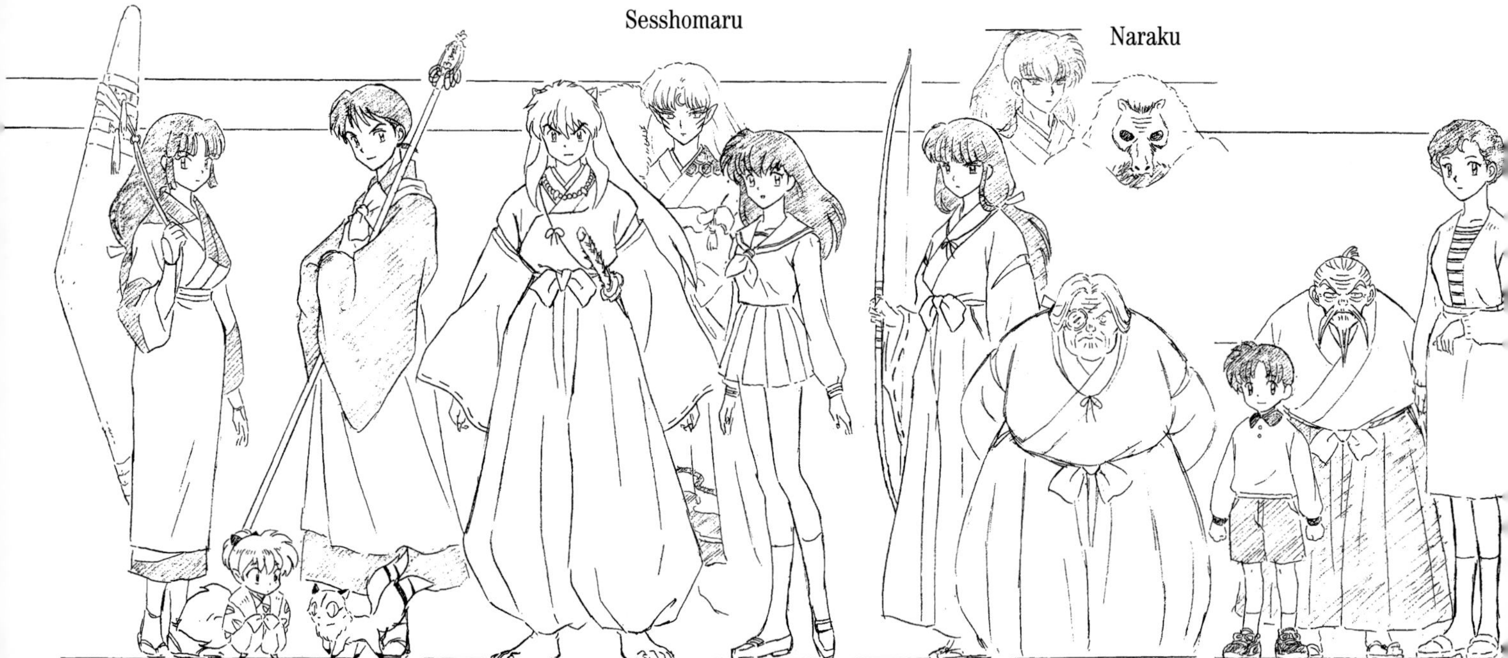
Sesshomaru
Naraku
Sango
Shippo
Kirara
Miroku
Inuyasha
Kagome
Kikyo
Kaede
Sota
Grampa
Mo

INUYASHA

Half demon, half human, Inuyasha seeks the Shikon jewel, the jewel of Four Souls, because it will give him full power as a demon. Impatient and self-centered, he was in love with Kikyo, a priestess of the jewel.

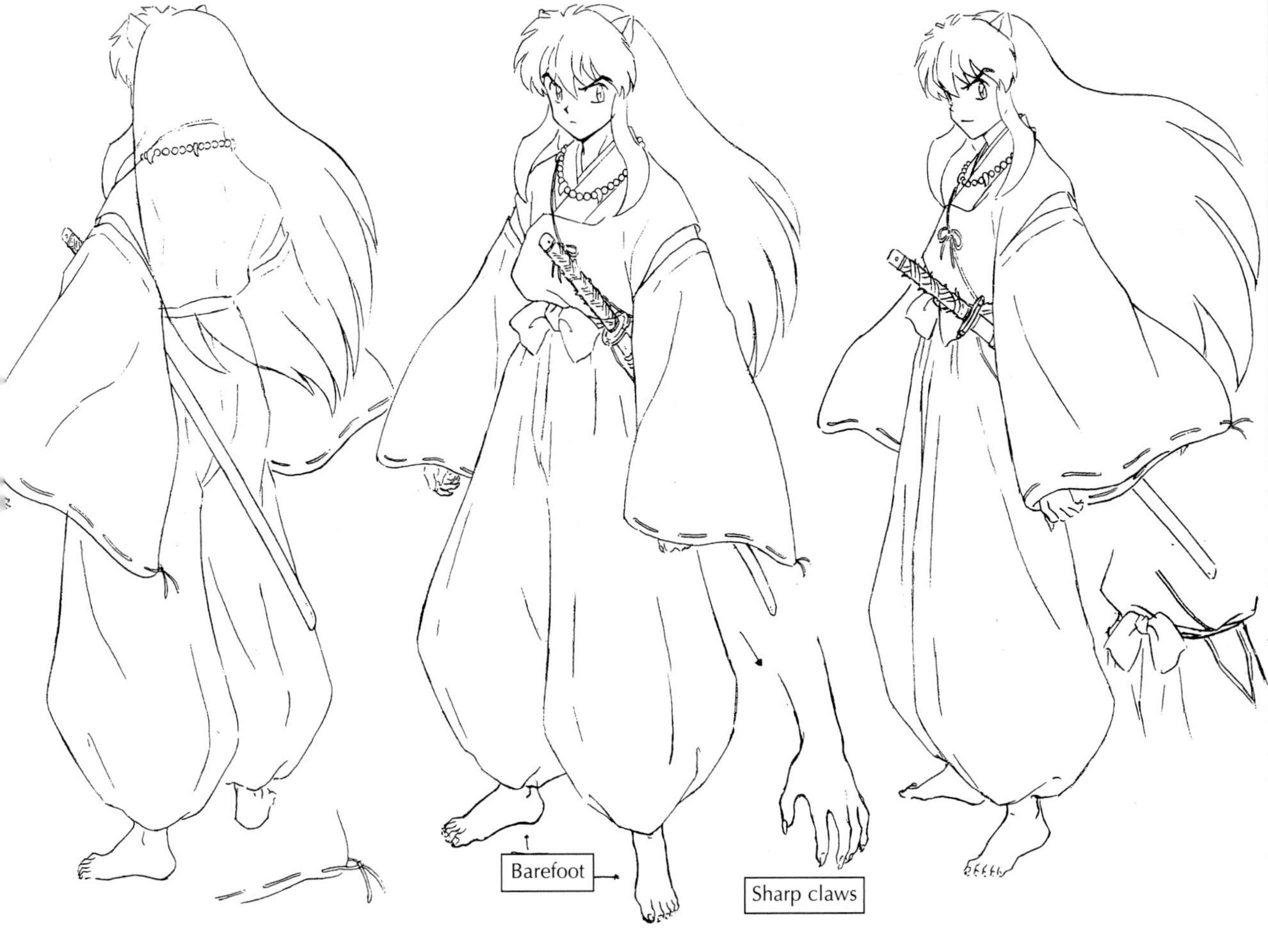

Barefoot
Sharp claws

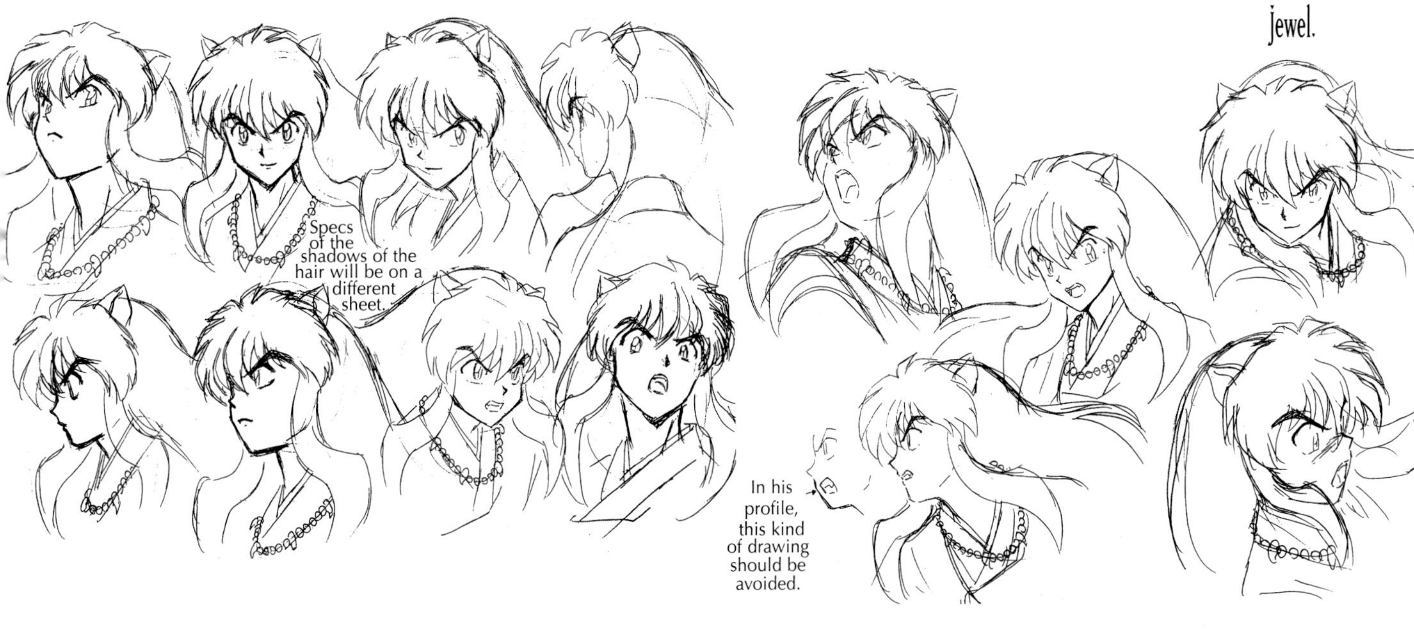

Specs of the shadows of the hair will be on a different sheet.
In his profile, this kind of drawing should be avoided.

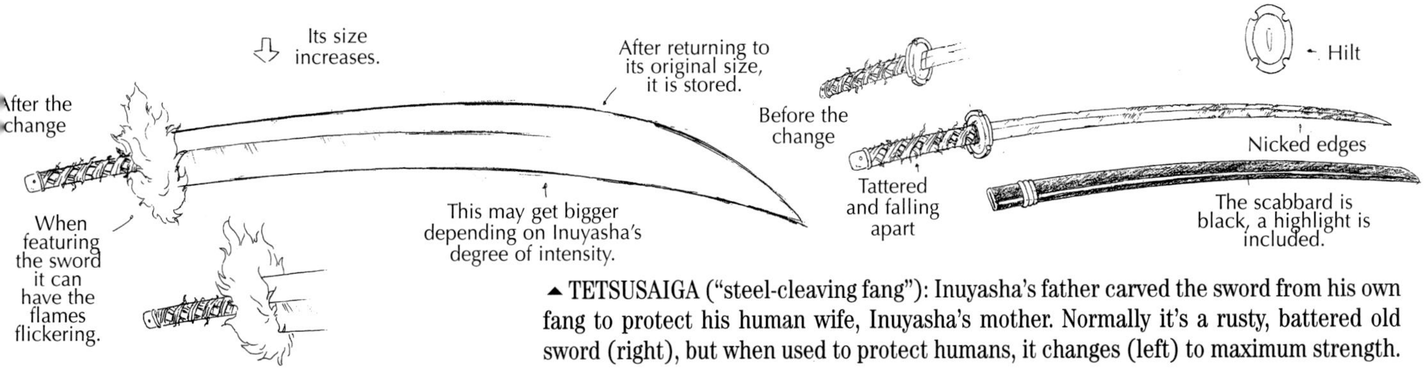

Its size increases.
After returning to its original size, it is stored.
After the change
When featuring the sword it can have the flames flickering.
This may get bigger depending on Inuyasha's degree of intensity.
Before the change
Tattered and falling apart
Hilt
Nicked edges
The scabbard is black, a highlight is included.

▲ TETSUSAIGA ("steel-cleaving fang"): Inuyasha's father carved the sword from his own fang to protect his human wife, Inuyasha's mother. Normally it's a rusty, battered old sword (right), but when used to protect humans, it changes (left) to maximum strength.

ANIMATION SETUP MATERIALS

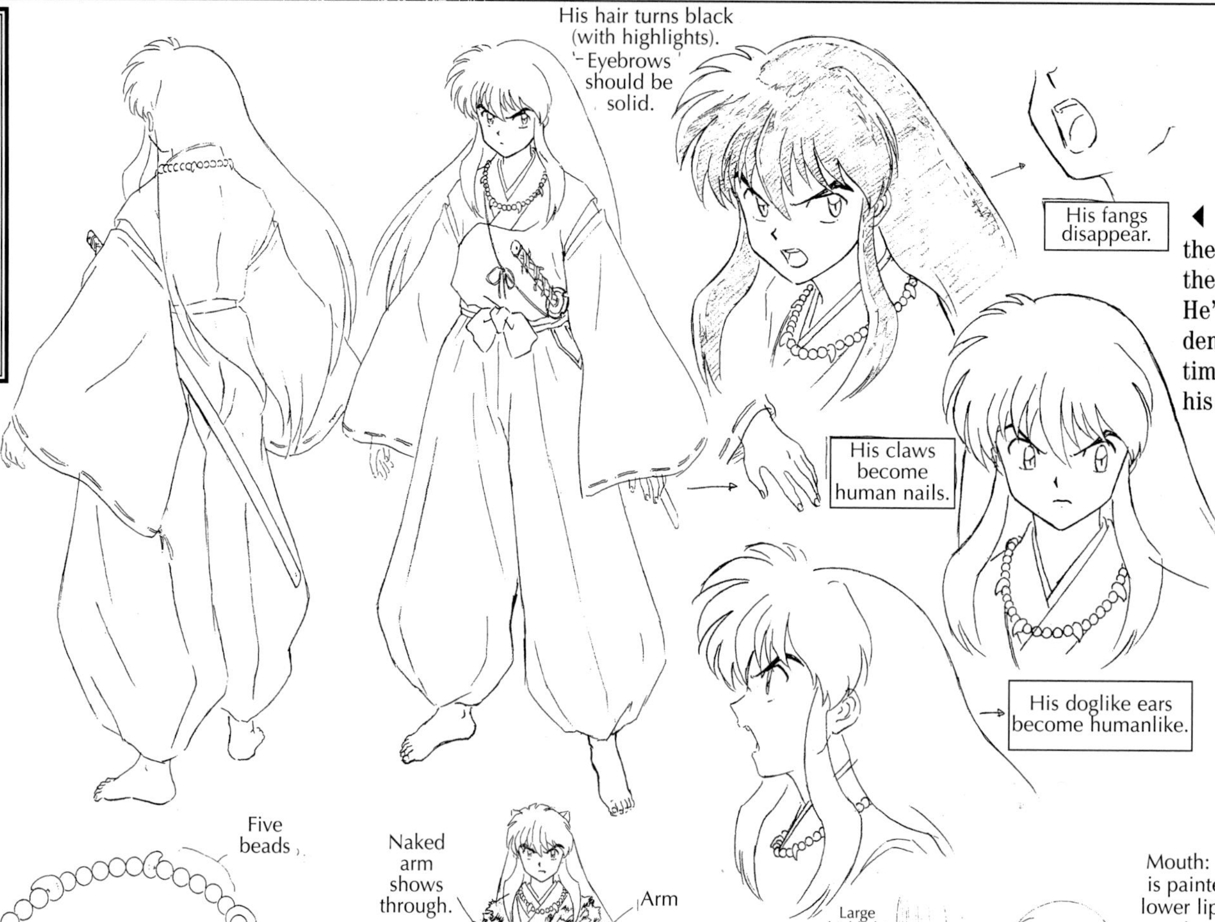

His hair turns black (with highlights). Eyebrows should be solid.
His fangs disappear.
His claws become human nails.
His doglike ears become humanlike.

◀ Inuyasha on the first day of the new moon. He's only half demon so sometimes he loses his power. On nights of the new moon his power falls to that of an ordinary human.

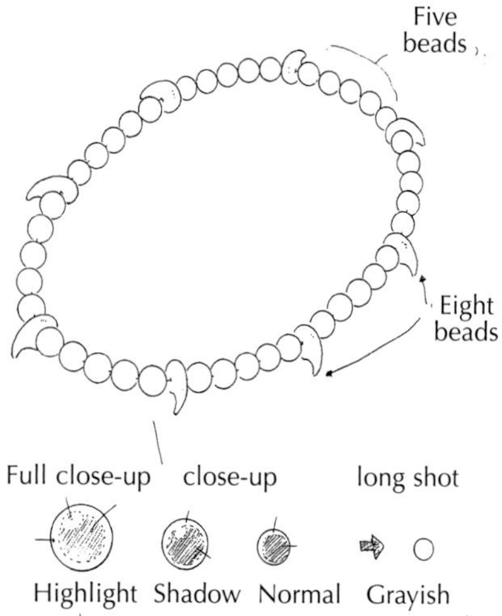

Five beads
Eight beads
Full close-up
close-up
long shot
Highlight
Shadow
Normal
Grayish

▲ PRAYER-BEADS: The subduing word "sit" activates them.

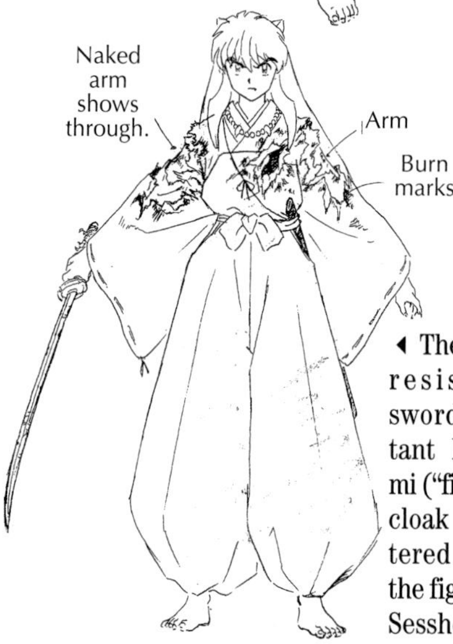

Naked arm shows through.
Arm
Burn marks

◀ The fire-resistant, sword-resistant hinezumi ("fire-rat") cloak is tattered after the fight with Sesshomaru.

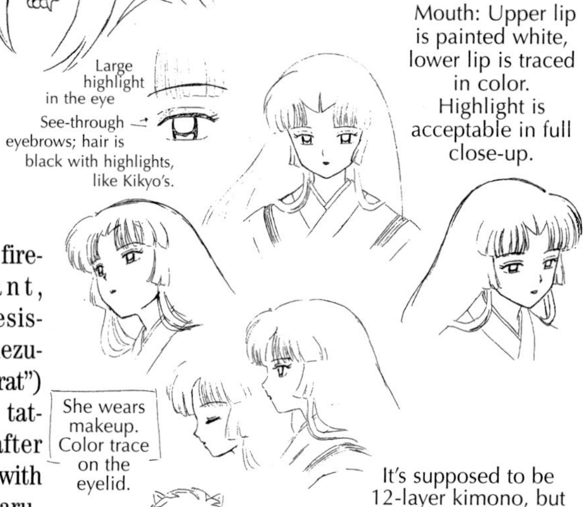

Large highlight in the eye
See-through eyebrows; hair is black with highlights, like Kikyo's.
Mouth: Upper lip is painted white, lower lip is traced in color. Highlight is acceptable in full close-up.
She wears makeup. Color trace on the eyelid.

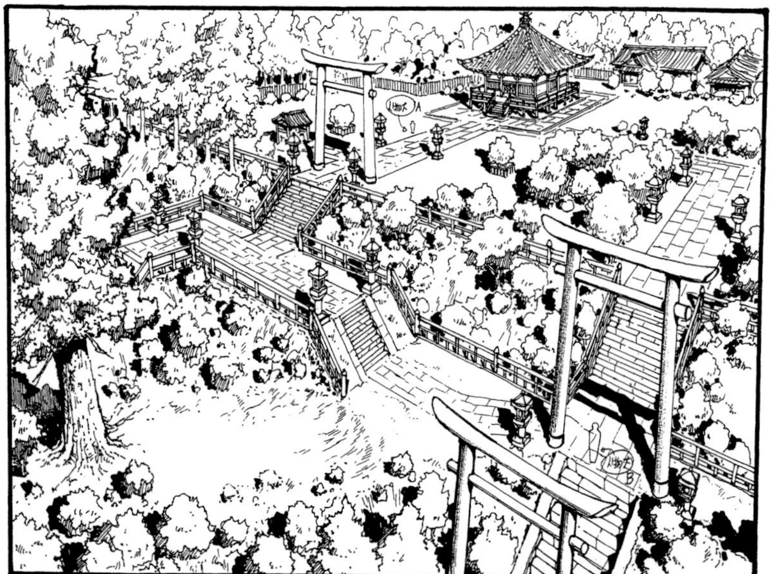

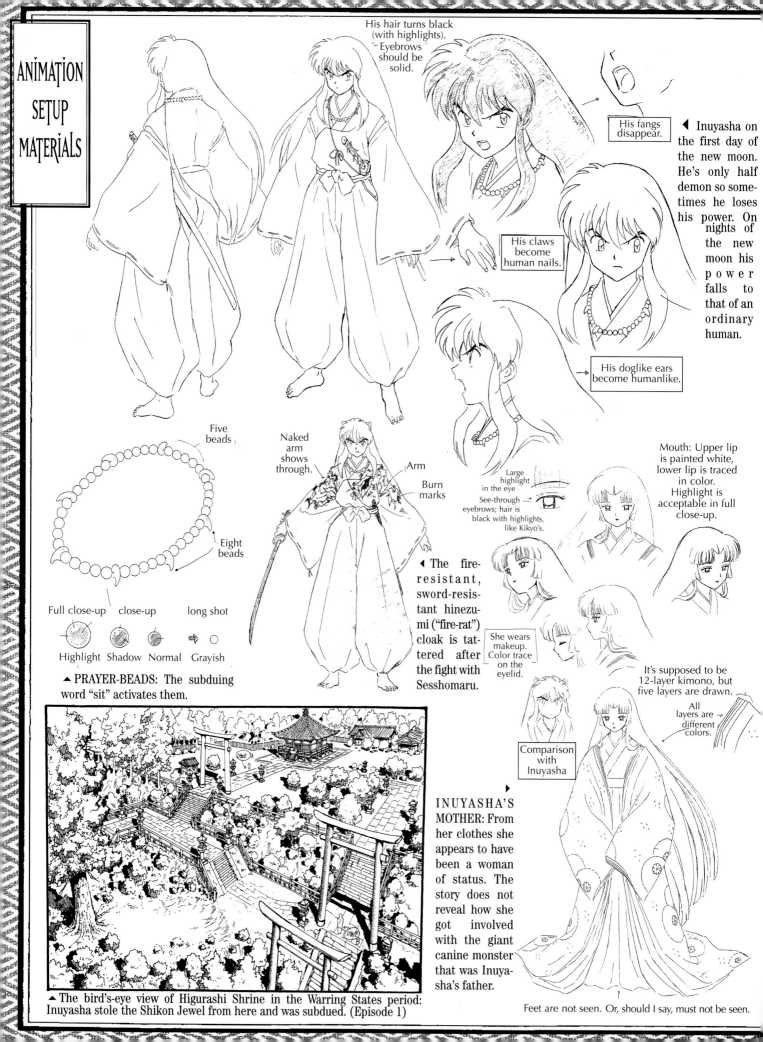

▲ The bird's-eye view of Higurashi Shrine in the Warring States period: Inuyasha stole the Shikon Jewel from here and was subdued. (Episode 1)

▶ INUYASHA'S MOTHER: From her clothes she appears to have been a woman of status. The story does not reveal how she got involved with the giant canine monster that was Inuyasha's father.

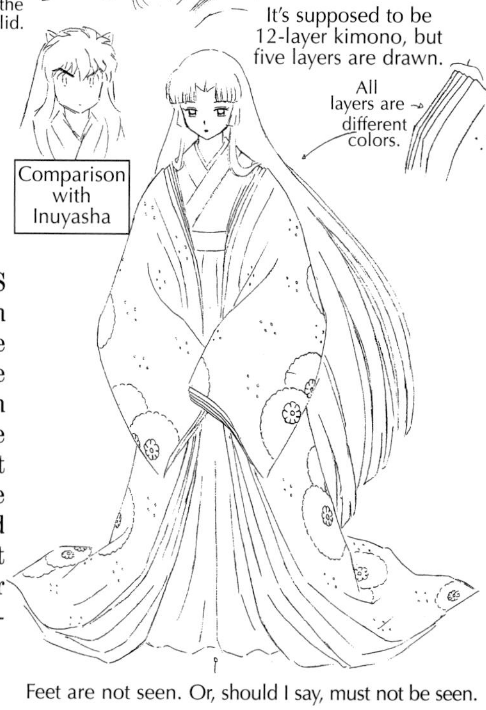

It's supposed to be 12-layer kimono, but five layers are drawn.
All layers are different colors.
Comparison with Inuyasha
Feet are not seen. Or, should I say, must not be seen.

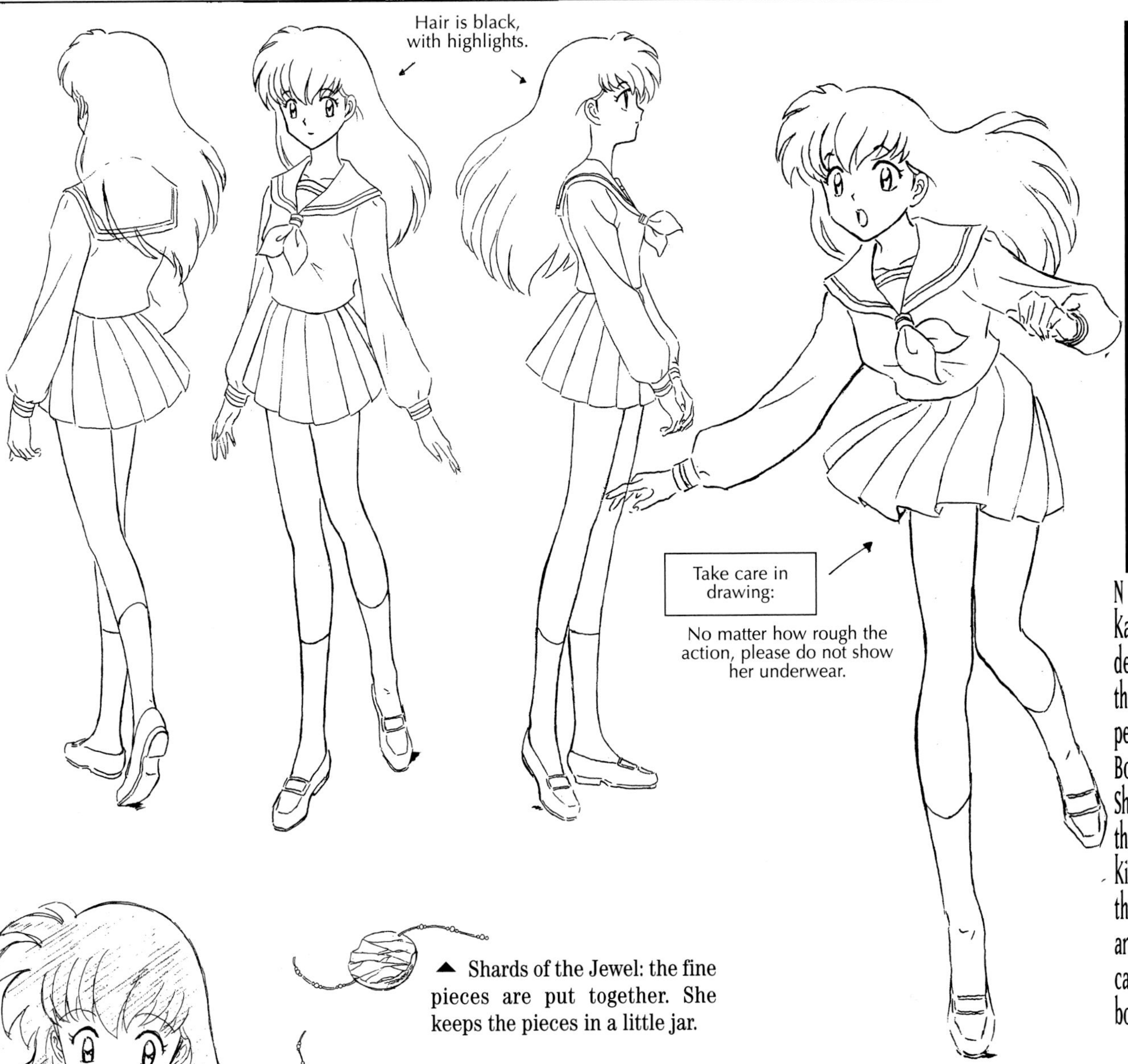

Hair is black, with highlights.
Take care in drawing:
No matter how rough the action, please do not show her underwear.

HIGURASHI KAGOME

Ninth-grader Kagome was suddenly drawn into the Warring States period through the Bone-Eater's Well. She is thought to be the reincarnation of Kikyo because of their resemblance and since the jewel came out of her body.

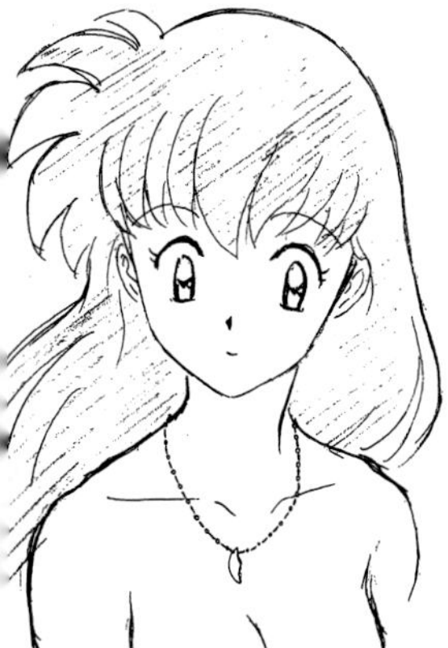

Compare (reference)

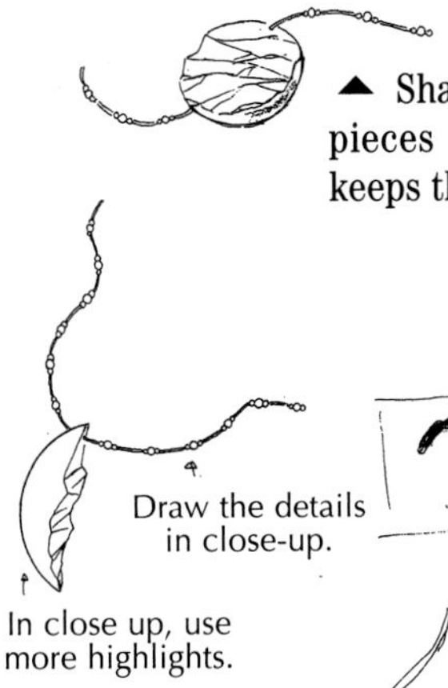

Draw the details in close-up.
In close up, use more highlights.

▲ Shards of the Jewel: the fine pieces are put together. She keeps the pieces in a little jar.

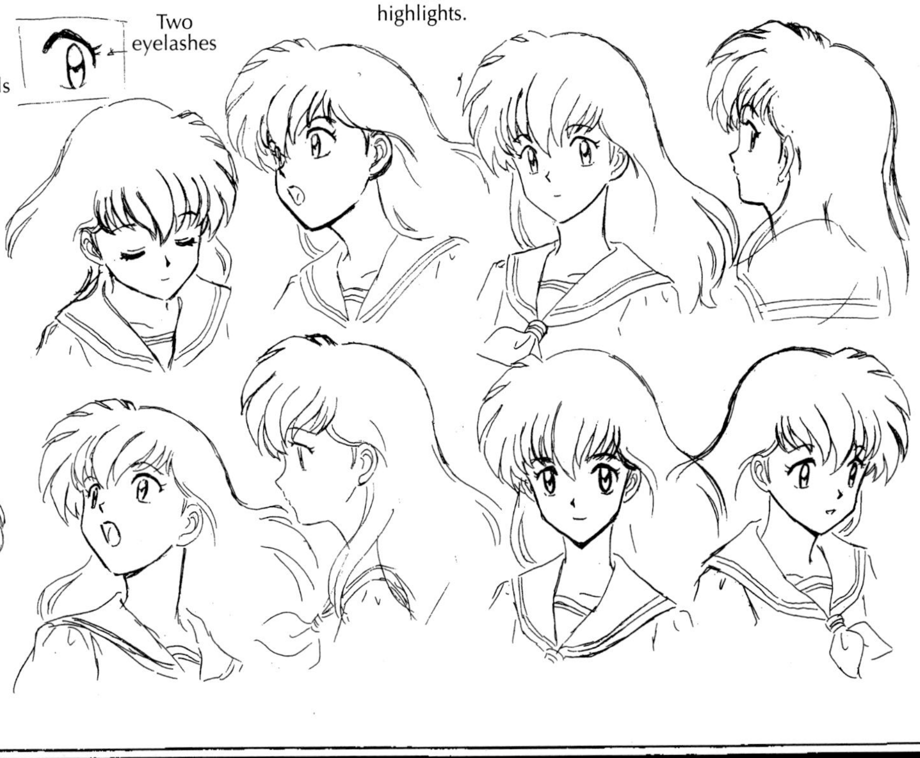

Two eyelashes
Hair is black, with highlights.

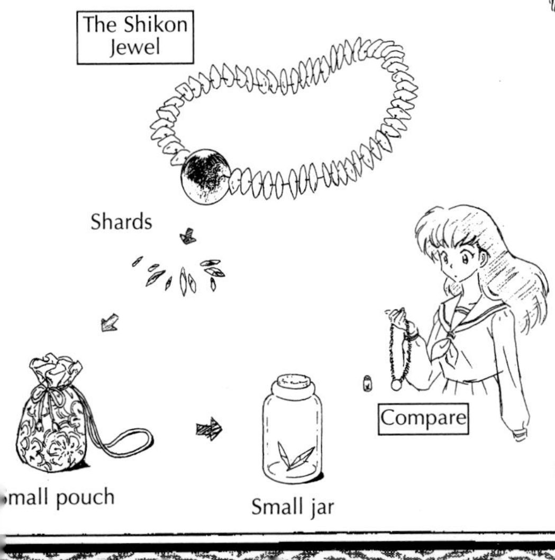

The Shikon Jewel
Shards
Compare
Small pouch
Small jar

ANIMATION SETUP MATERIALS

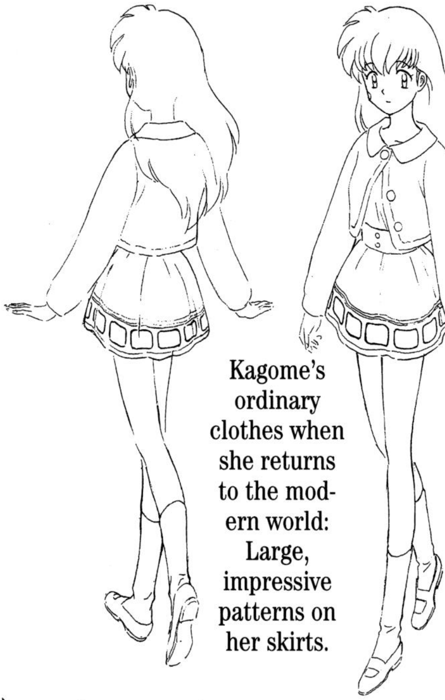

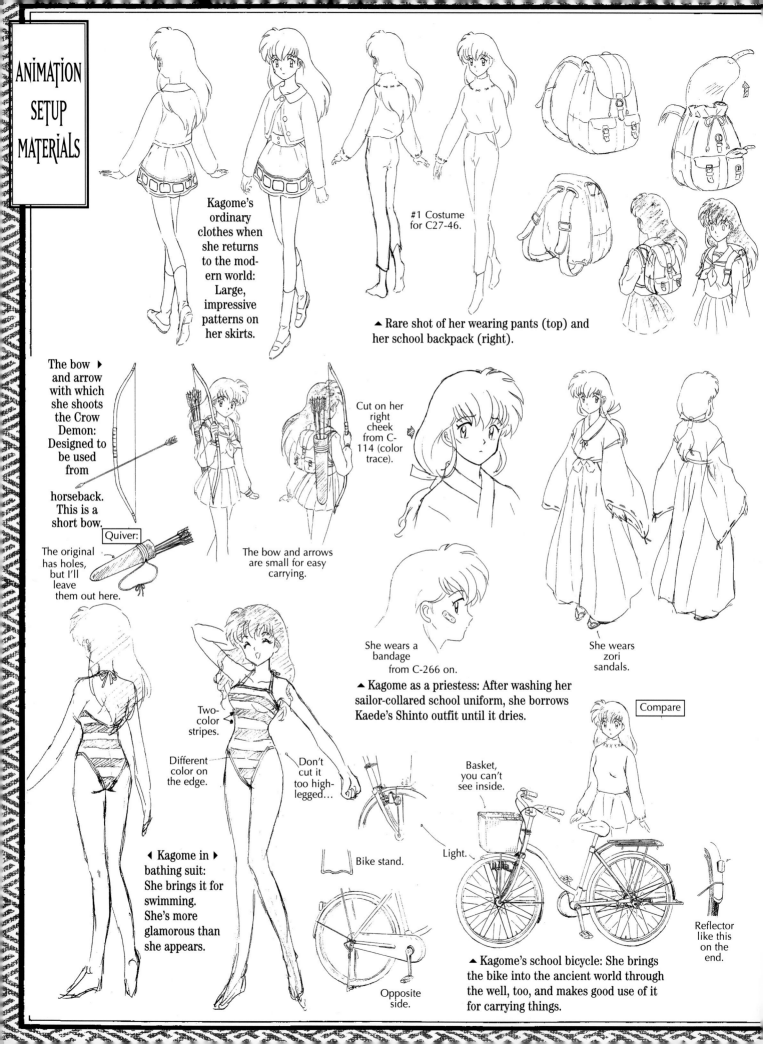

Kagome's ordinary clothes when she returns to the modern world: Large, impressive patterns on her skirts.

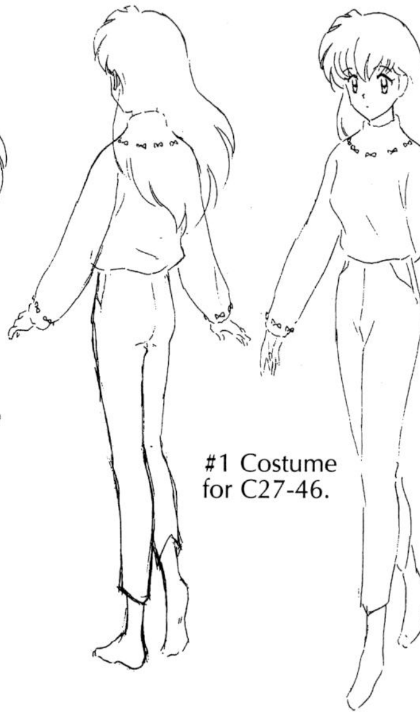
#1 Costume for C27-46.

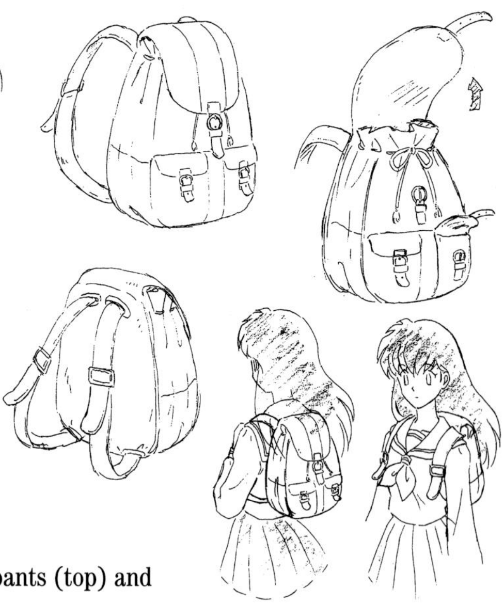

▲ Rare shot of her wearing pants (top) and her school backpack (right).

The bow ▶ and arrow with which she shoots the Crow Demon: Designed to be used from horseback. This is a short bow.

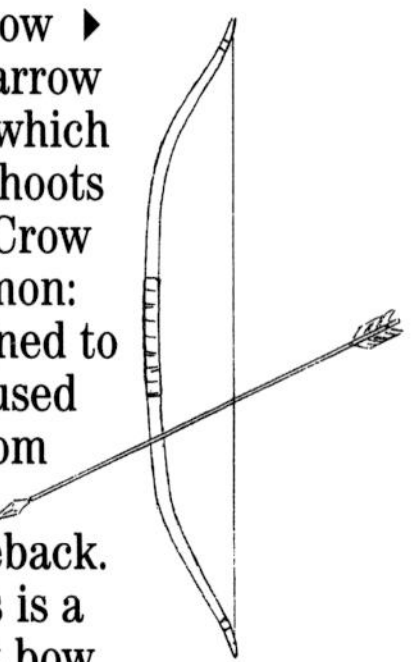

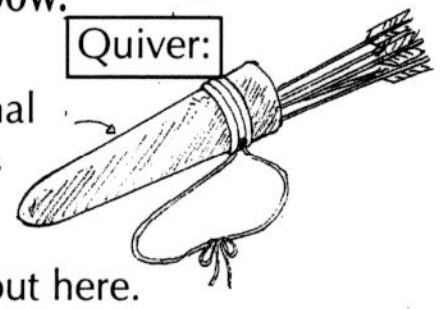
Quiver:
The original has holes, but I'll leave them out here.

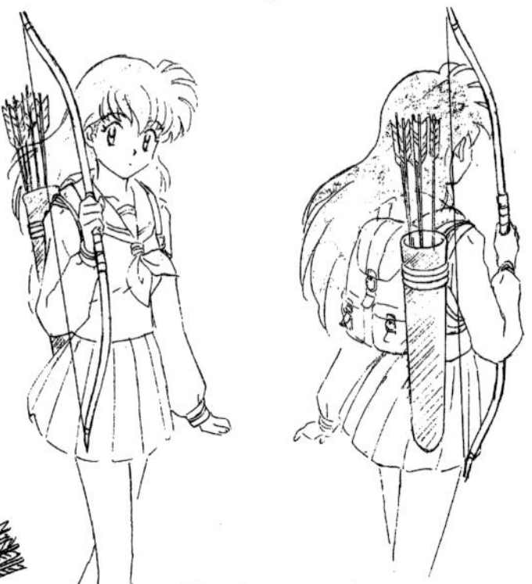

The bow and arrows are small for easy carrying.

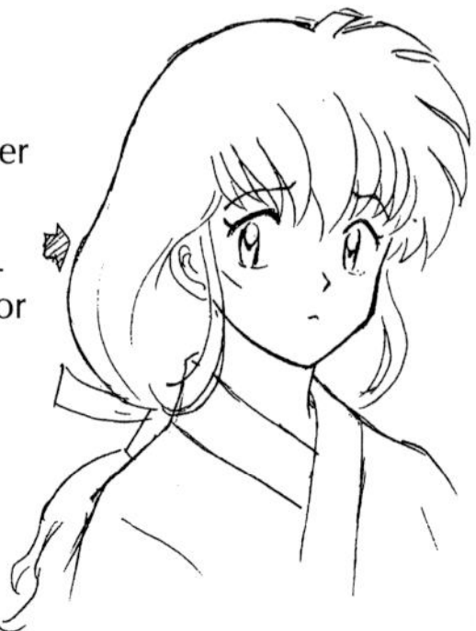
Cut on her right cheek from C-114 (color trace).

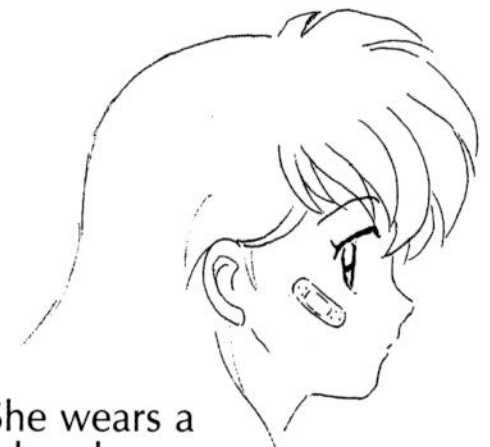
She wears a bandage from C-266 on.

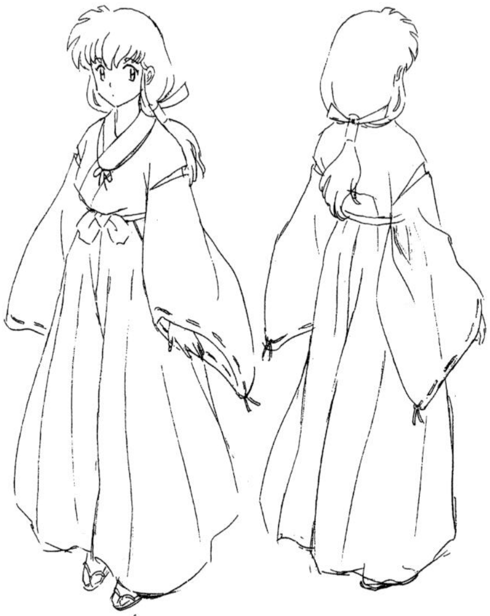
She wears zori sandals.

▲ Kagome as a priestess: After washing her sailor-collared school uniform, she borrows Kaede's Shinto outfit until it dries.

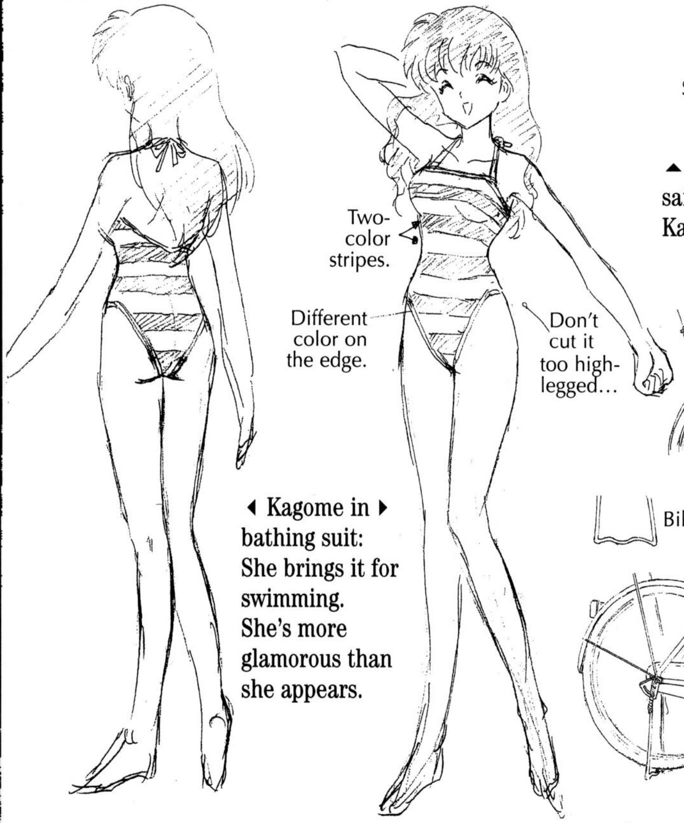
Two-color stripes.
Different color on the edge.
Don't cut it too high-legged…

◀ Kagome in ▶ bathing suit: She brings it for swimming. She's more glamorous than she appears.

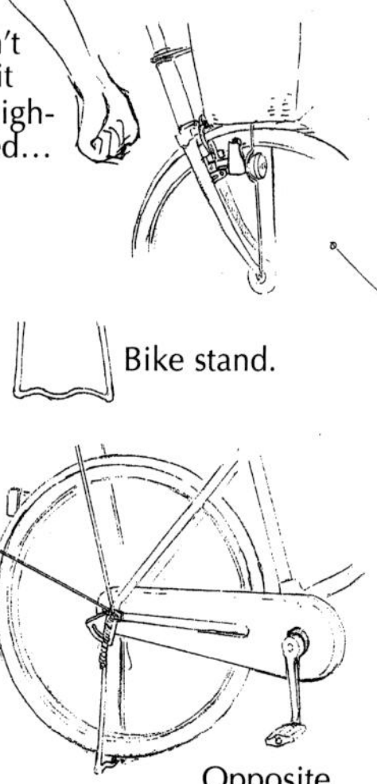
Bike stand.
Opposite side.

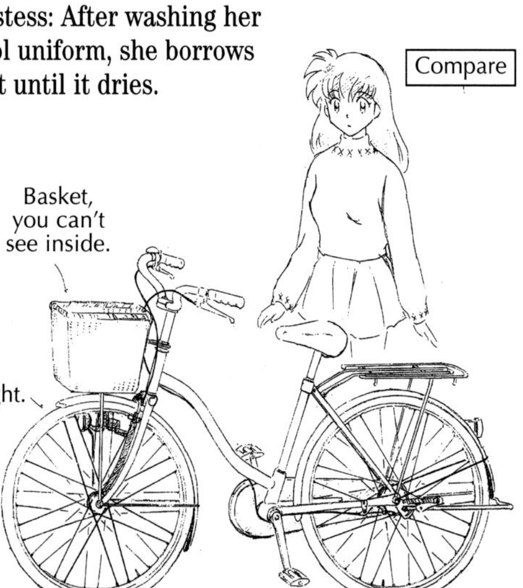
Compare
Basket, you can't see inside.
Light.

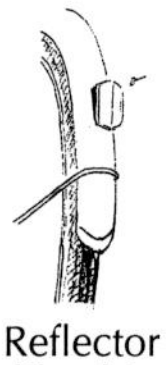
Reflector like this on the end.

▲ Kagome's school bicycle: She brings the bike into the ancient world through the well, too, and makes good use of it for carrying things.

kikyo

The priestess who subdued Inuyasha and died 50 years before the time of Kagome. She was the guardian of the jewel. Kaede is her younger sister. Kikyo is revived at the hand of the ogress, Urasue, but her heart is filled with revenge.

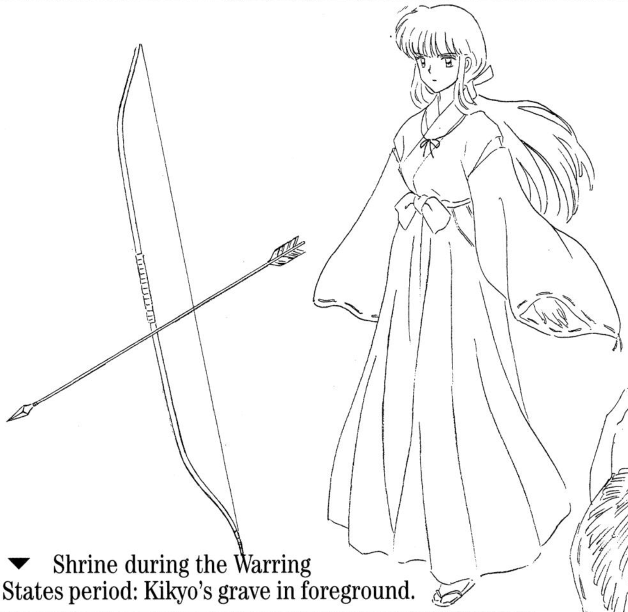

◀ The left compares Kikyo and a bow set. She is a master archer and has the power to subdue even Inuyasha.

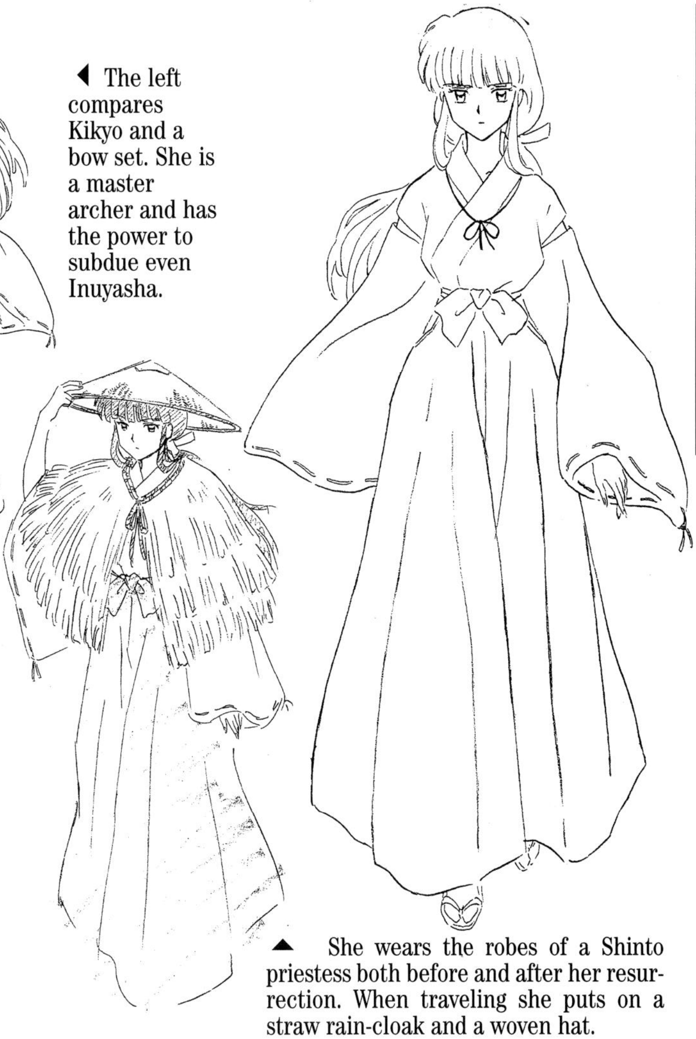

▲ She wears the robes of a Shinto priestess both before and after her resurrection. When traveling she puts on a straw rain-cloak and a woven hat.

▼ Shrine during the Warring States period: Kikyo's grave in foreground.

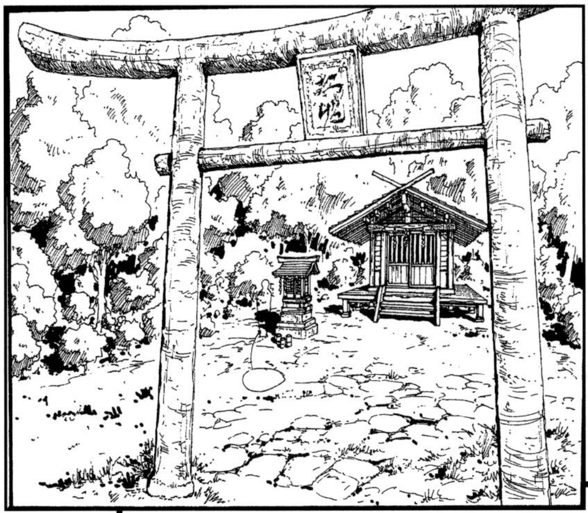

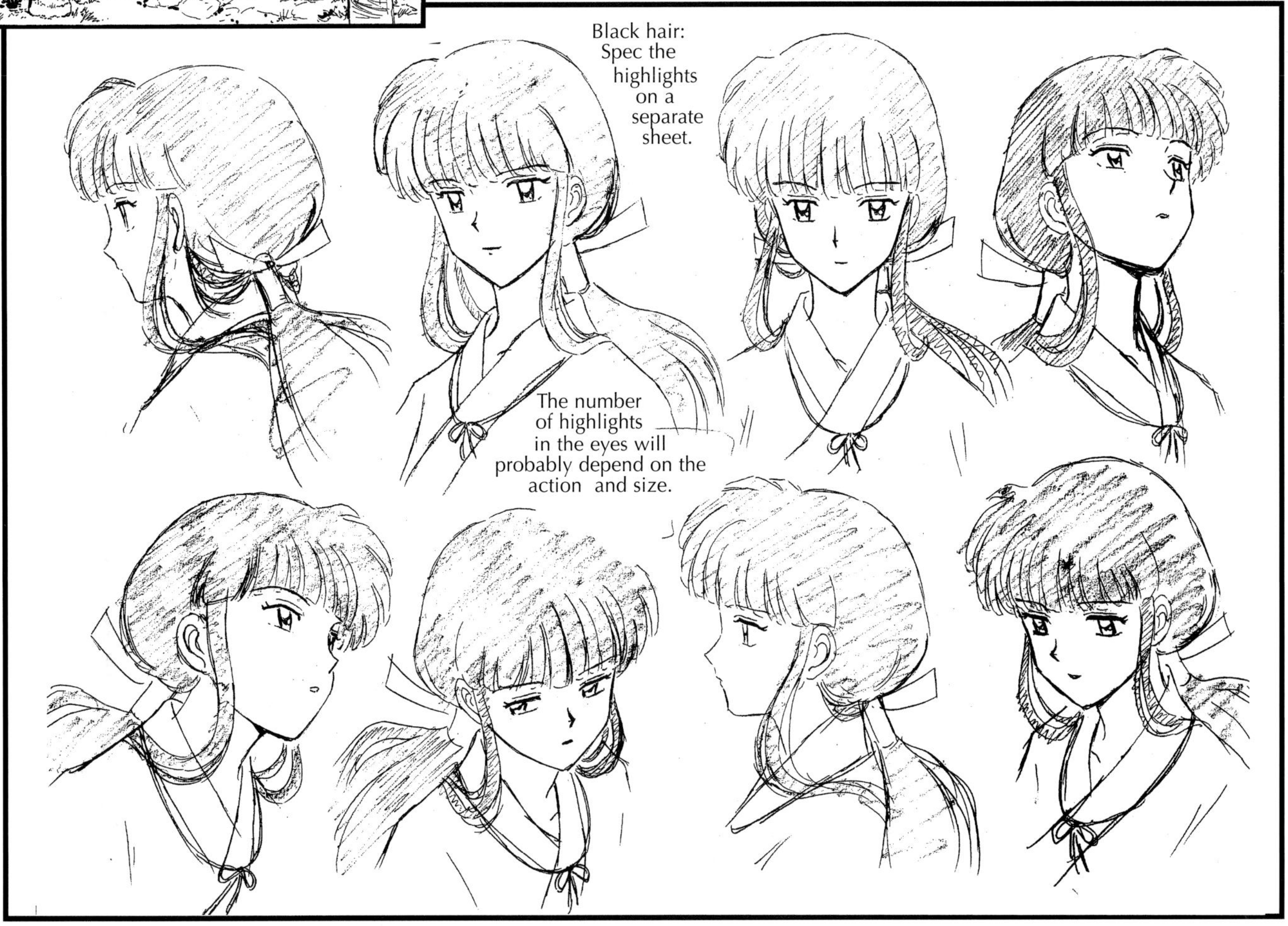
Black hair: Spec the highlights on a separate sheet.
The number of highlights in the eyes will probably depend on the action and size.

ANIMATION SETUP MATERIALS

KAEDE

Kikyo's younger sister is the priestess and protector of the village in Kikyo's place, living near the shrine. She is a strong ally to Kagome and Inuyasha in their quest for the jewel. Like her sister she is an archer, but her supernatural power is much less than Kikyo's.

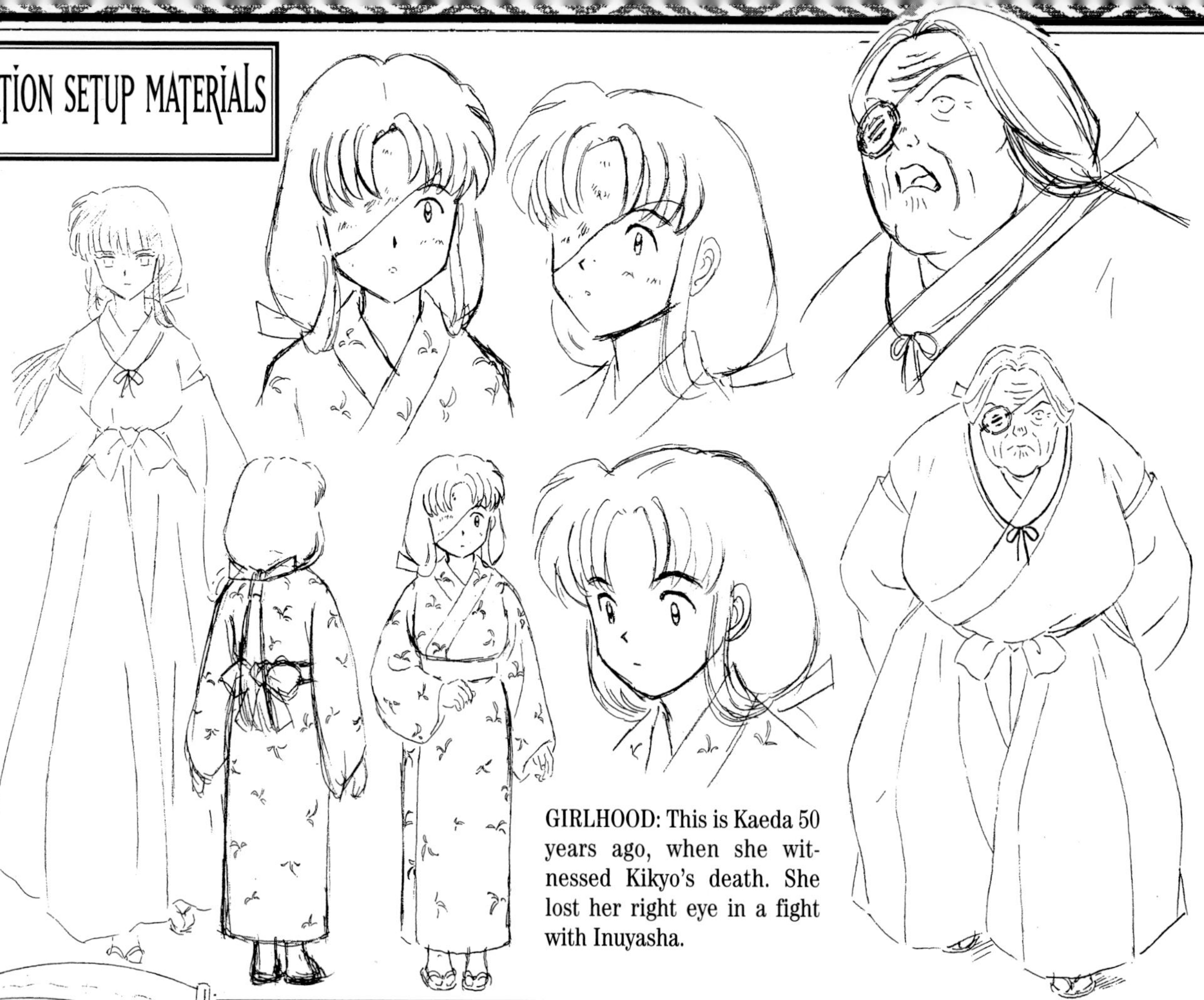

GIRLHOOD: This is Kaeda 50 years ago, when she witnessed Kikyo's death. She lost her right eye in a fight with Inuyasha.

URASUE

She gives the soul of the deceased Kikyo a false body to use. The new body is fired like ceramic in a kiln called Onigama. She specializes in firing "spiritual ceramics."

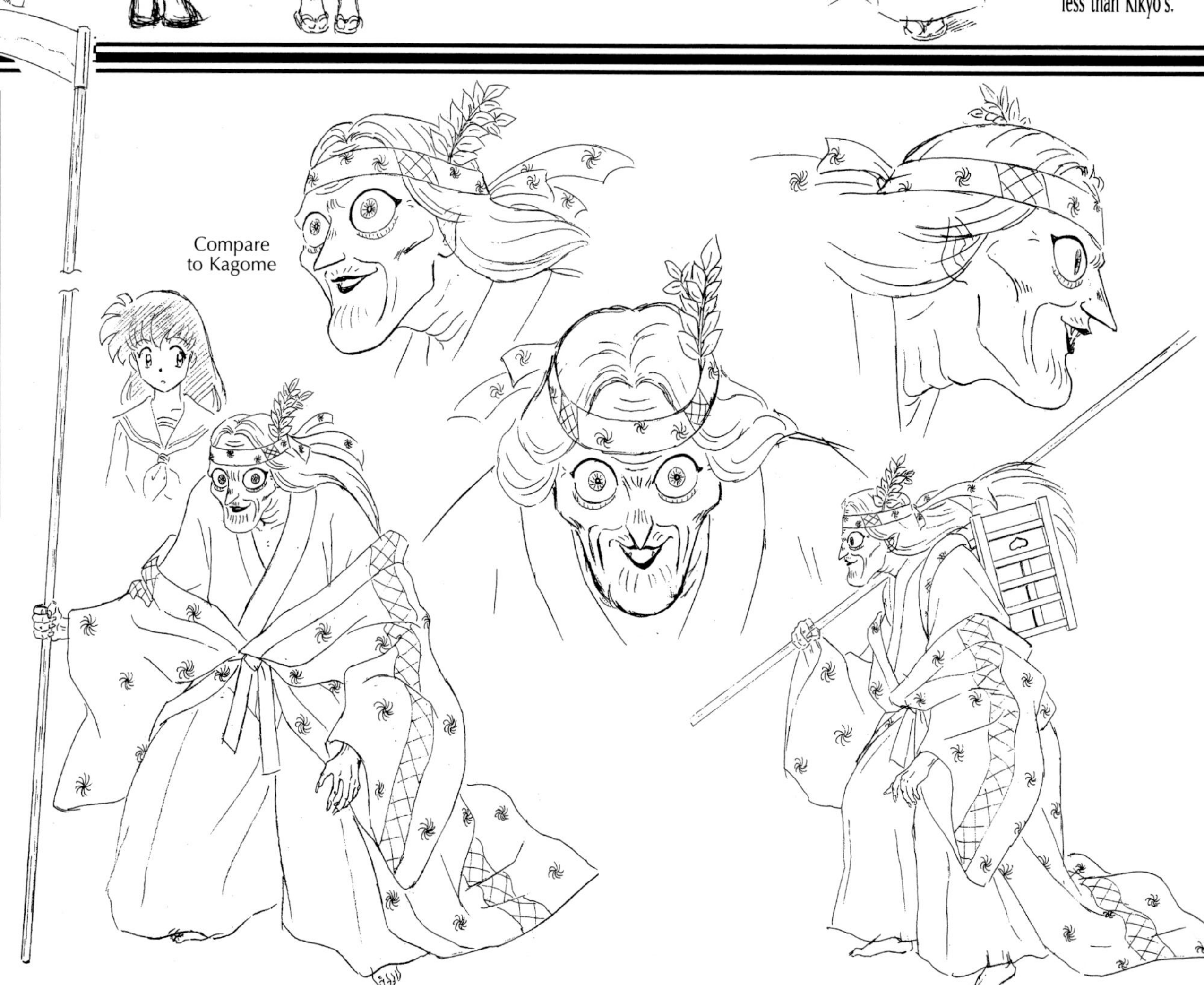
Compare to Kagome

MIROKU

A roving Buddhist monk, a ladies' man and very skilled in the magical arts. A curse by Naraku created a void in his right hand. The Kazaana ("wind tunnel") is an entrance to another dimension. Unless he breaks the curse, the void will eventually swallow him up.

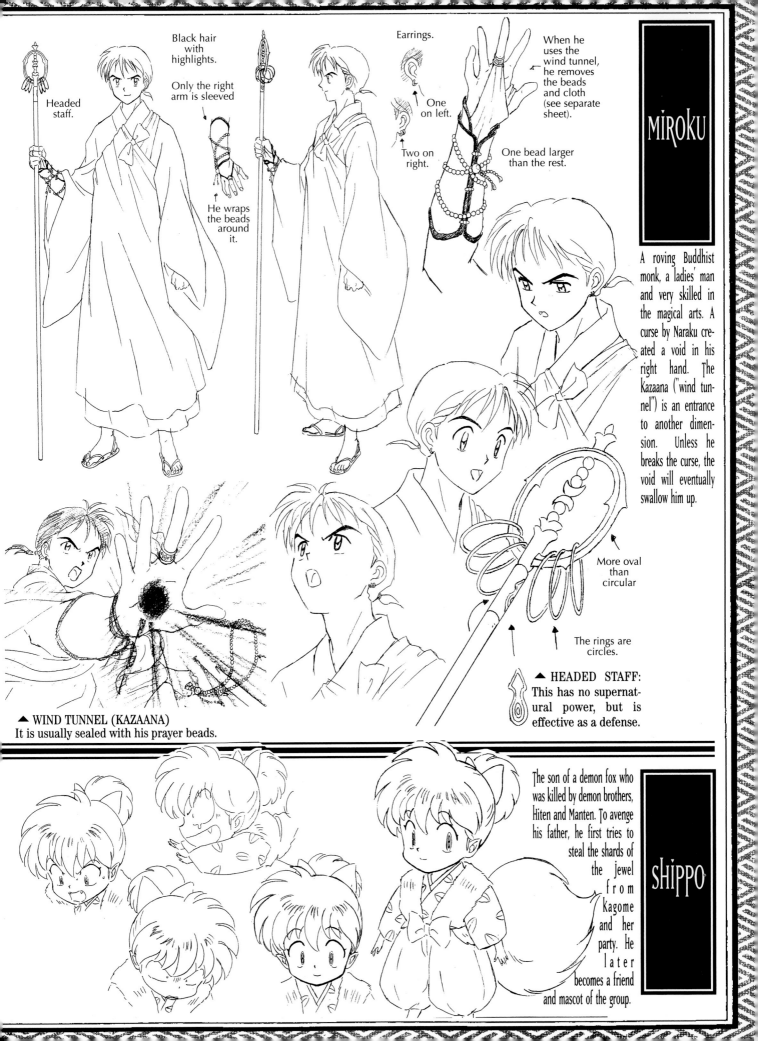

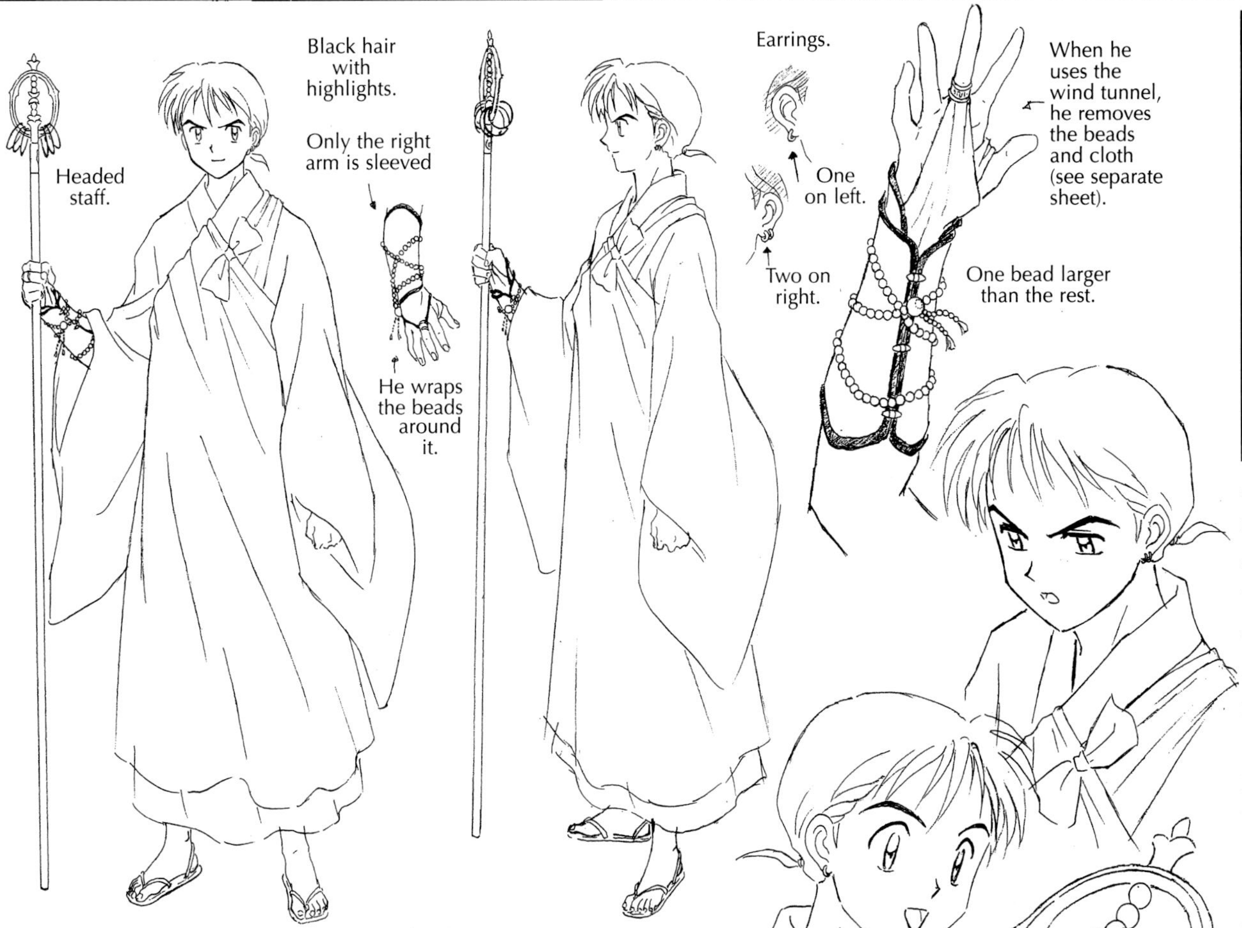
Headed staff.
Black hair with highlights.
Only the right arm is sleeved
He wraps the beads around it.
Earrings.
One on left.
Two on right.
When he uses the wind tunnel, he removes the beads and cloth (see separate sheet).
One bead larger than the rest.

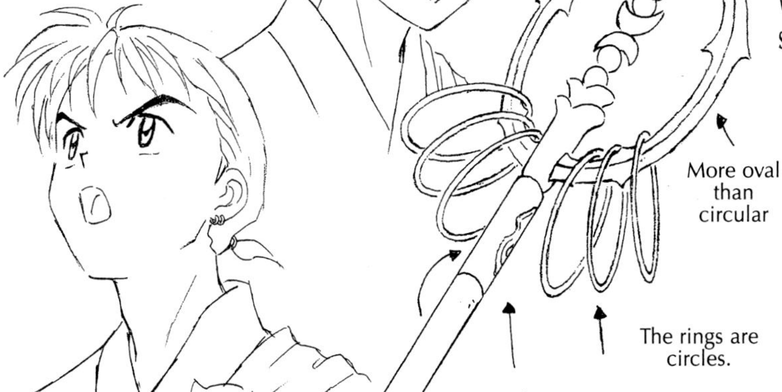
More oval than circular
The rings are circles.

▲ HEADED STAFF: This has no supernatural power, but is effective as a defense.

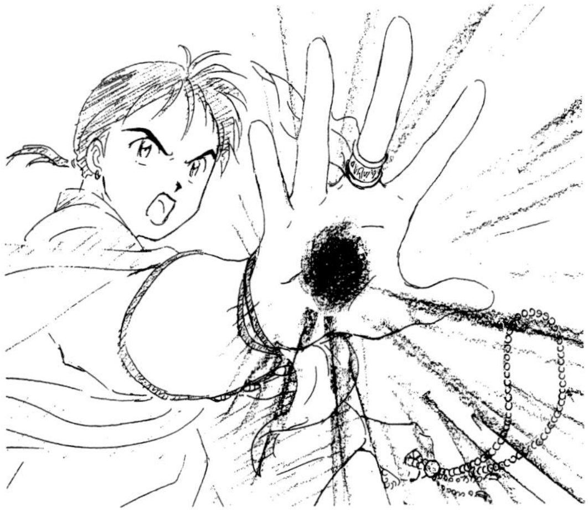

▲ WIND TUNNEL (KAZAANA)
It is usually sealed with his prayer beads.

SHIPPO

The son of a demon fox who was killed by demon brothers, Hiten and Manten. To avenge his father, he first tries to steal the shards of the jewel from Kagome and her party. He later becomes a friend and mascot of the group.

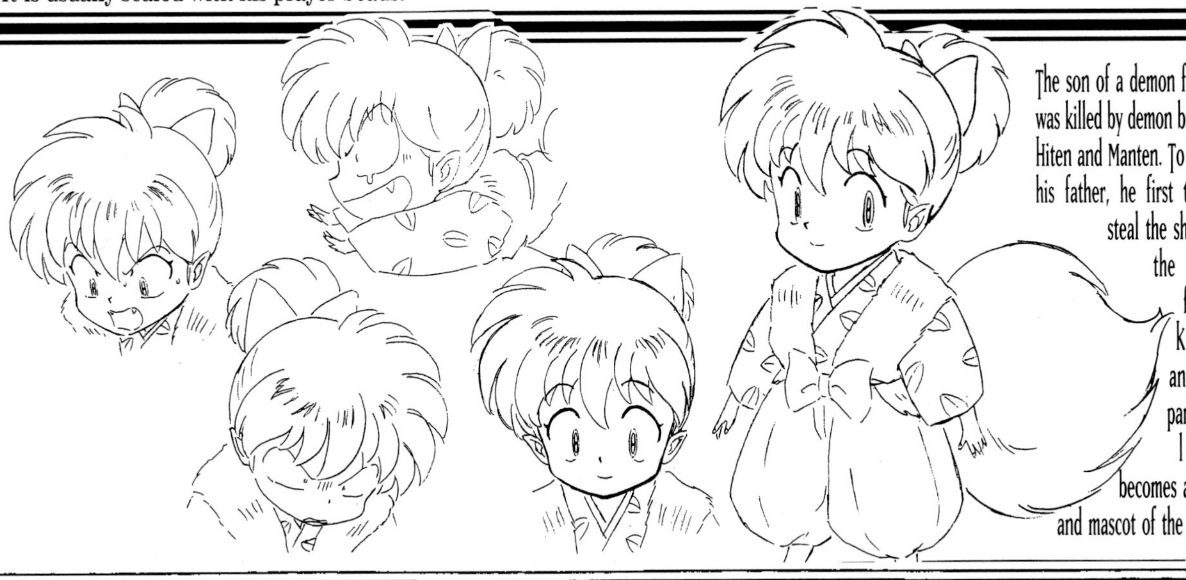

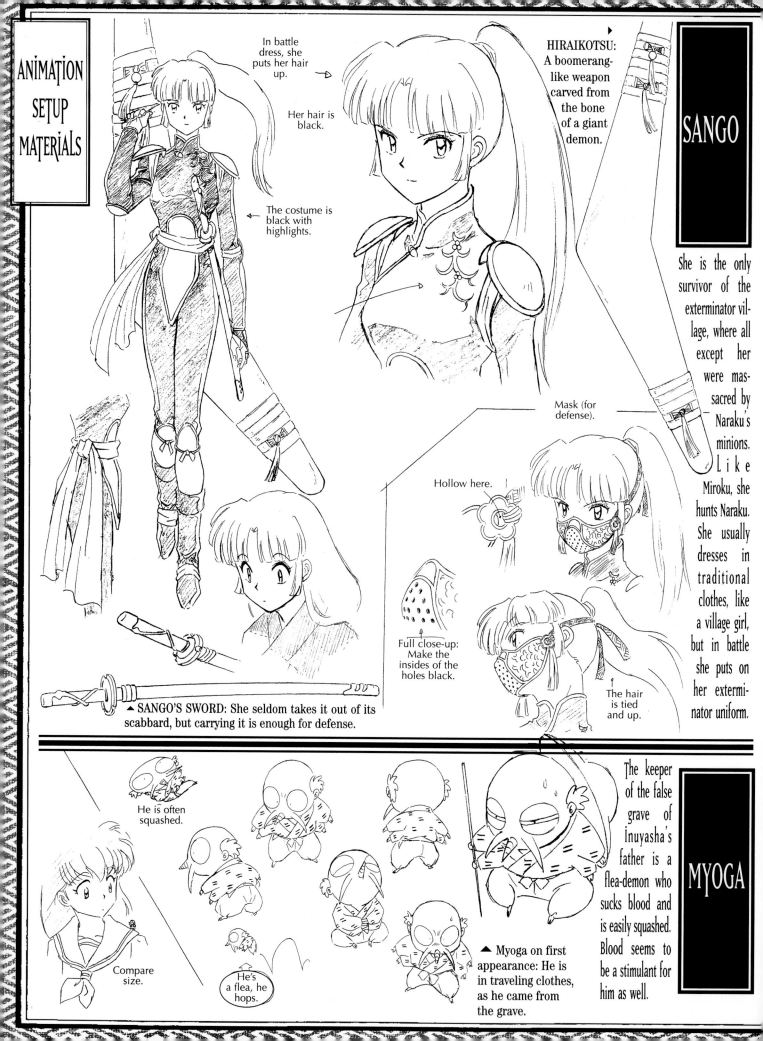

ANIMATION SETUP MATERIALS

SANGO

She is the only survivor of the exterminator village, where all except her were massacred by Naraku's minions. Like Miroku, she hunts Naraku. She usually dresses in traditional clothes, like a village girl, but in battle she puts on her exterminator uniform.

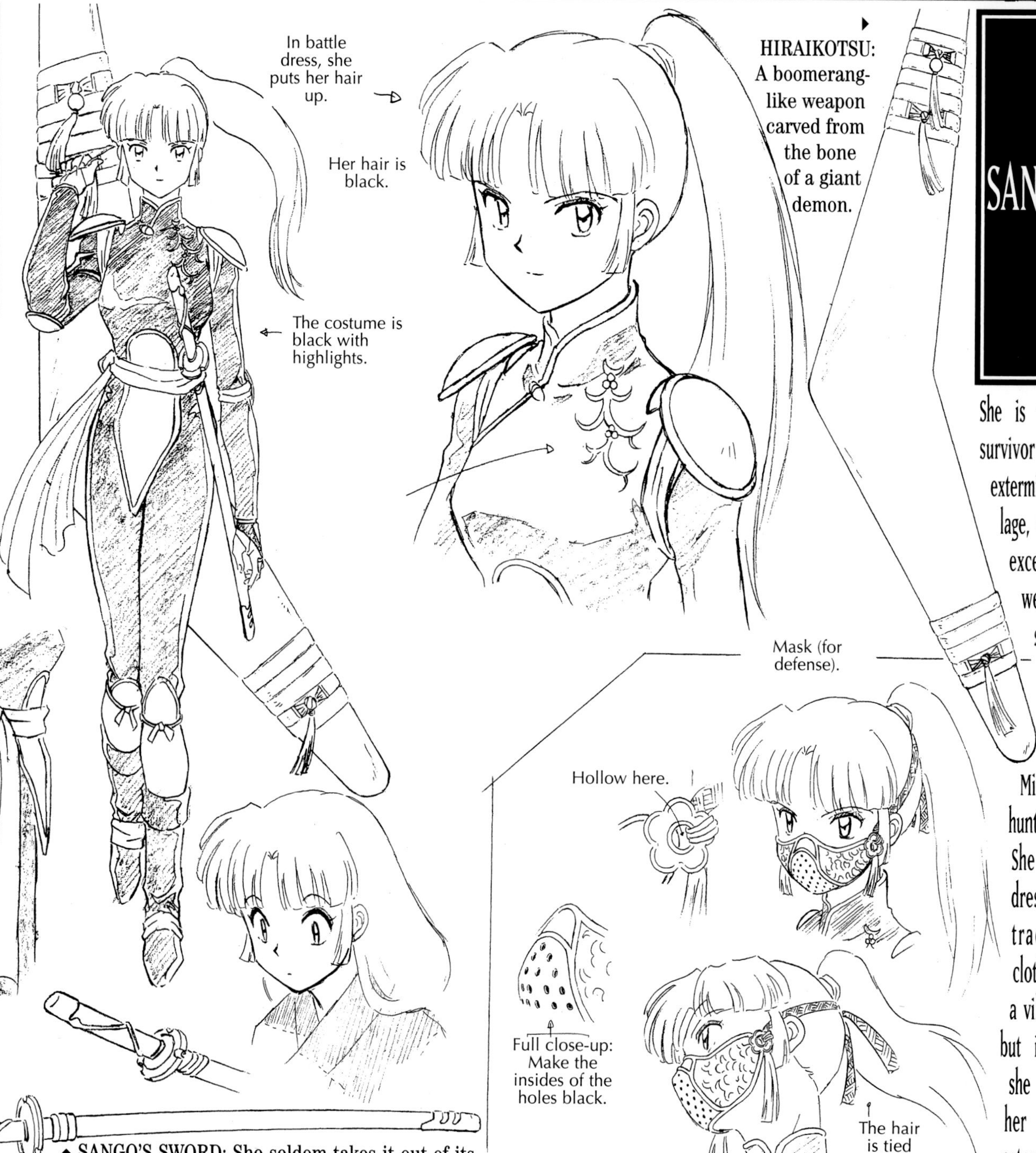

In battle dress, she puts her hair up.
Her hair is black.
The costume is black with highlights.
HIRAIKOTSU: A boomerang-like weapon carved from the bone of a giant demon.
Mask (for defense).
Hollow here.
Full close-up: Make the insides of the holes black.
The hair is tied and up.

▲ SANGO'S SWORD: She seldom takes it out of its scabbard, but carrying it is enough for defense.

MYOGA

The keeper of the false grave of Inuyasha's father is a flea-demon who sucks blood and is easily squashed. Blood seems to be a stimulant for him as well.

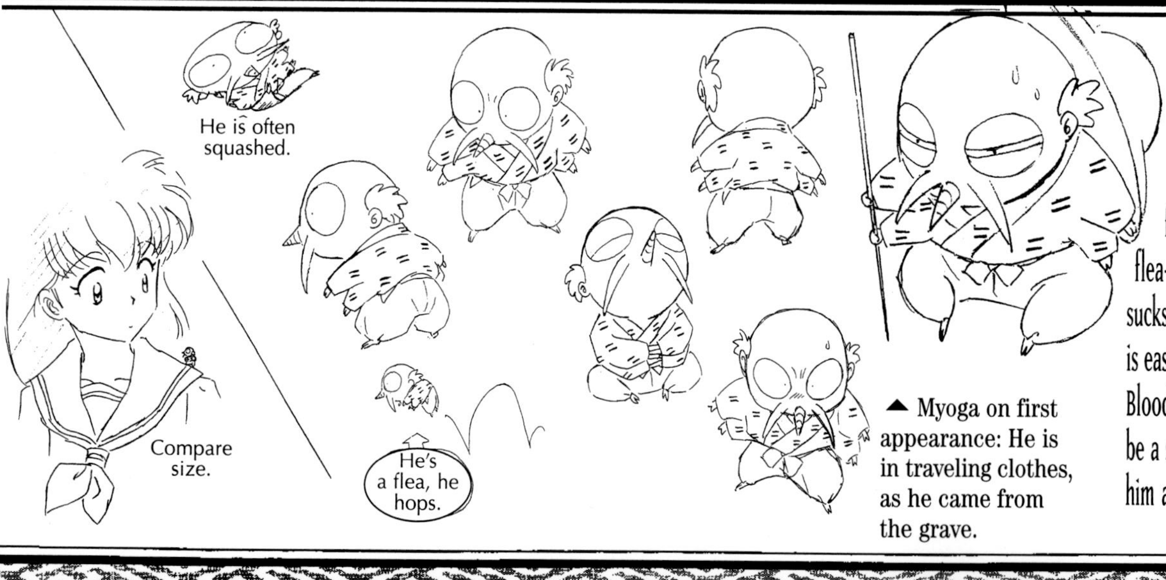

He is often squashed.
Compare size.
He's a flea, he hops.

▲ Myoga on first appearance: He is in traveling clothes, as he came from the grave.

KAGOME'S FAMILY

Kagome's family belongs to the old established Higurashi Shrine. It's an ordinary family who are kind enough to make excuses for Kagome's absence (in her time travels to the past), saying that she's in the hospital with one illness or another.

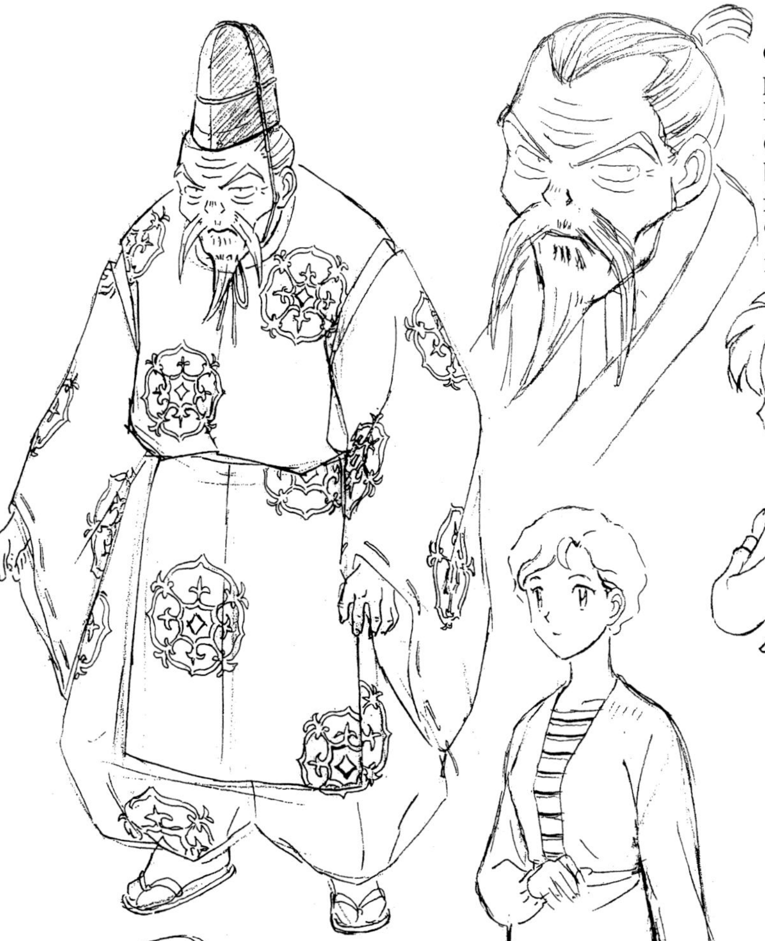

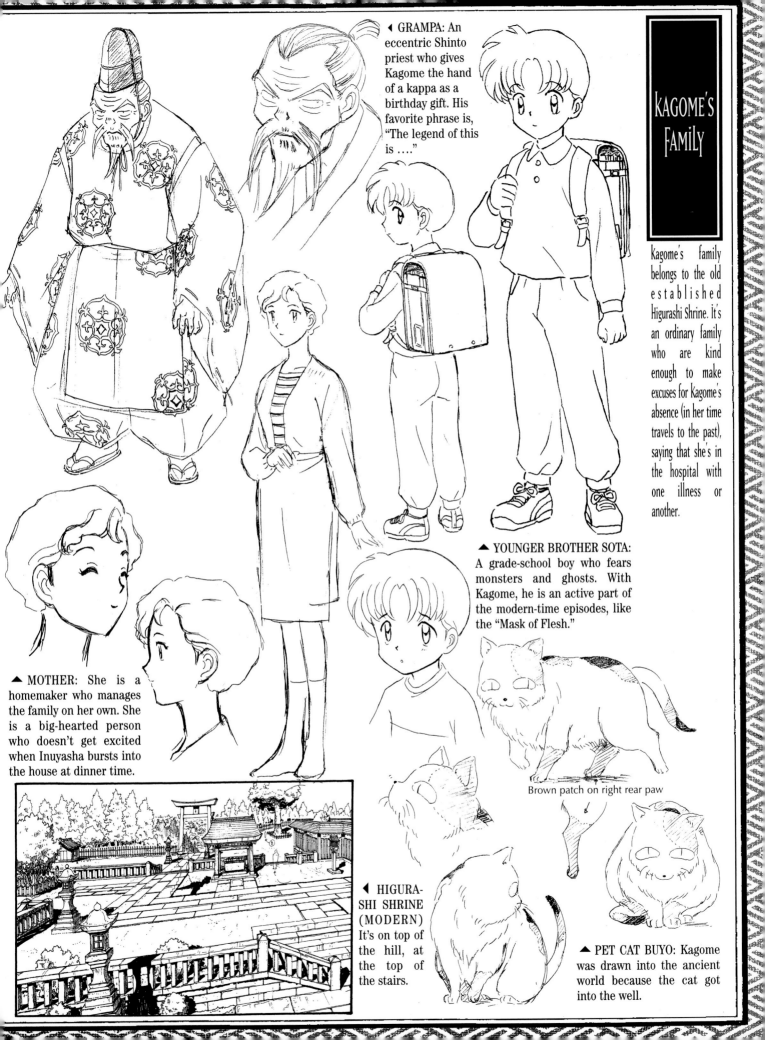

◀ GRAMPA: An eccentric Shinto priest who gives Kagome the hand of a kappa as a birthday gift. His favorite phrase is, "The legend of this is …."

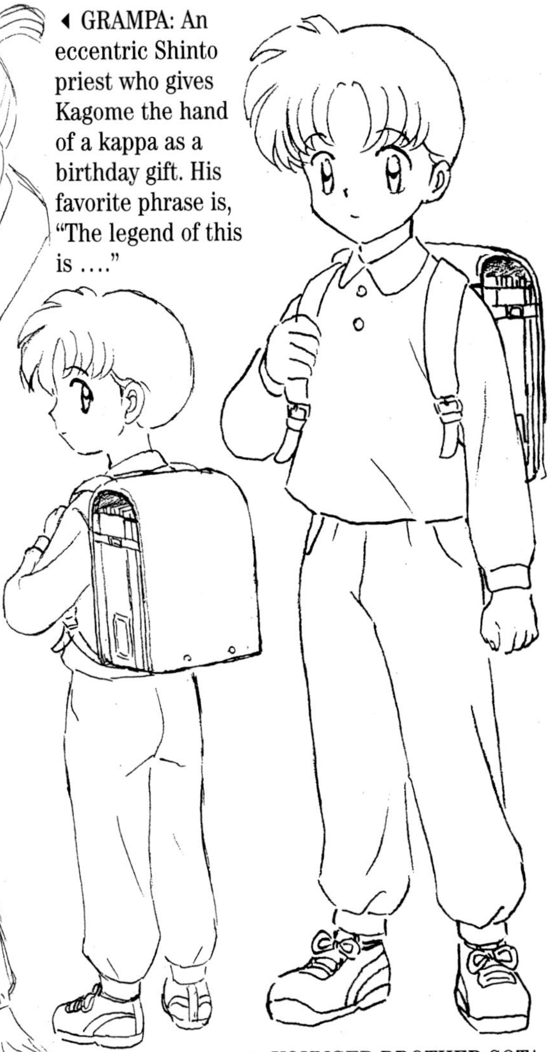

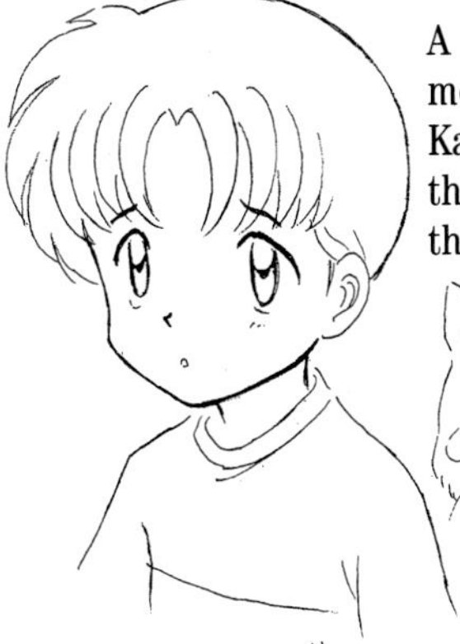

▲ YOUNGER BROTHER SOTA: A grade-school boy who fears monsters and ghosts. With Kagome, he is an active part of the modern-time episodes, like the "Mask of Flesh."

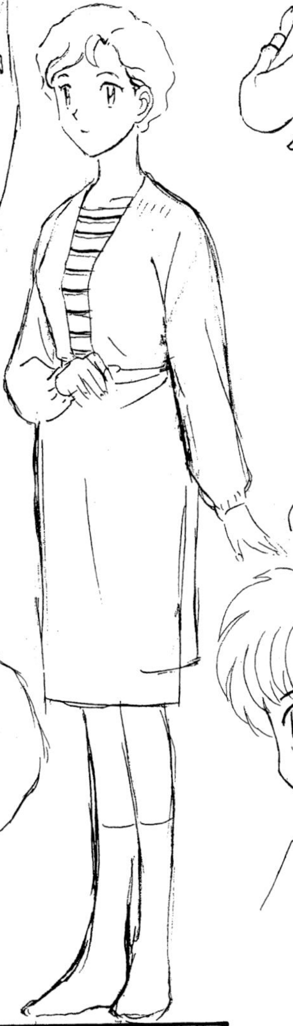

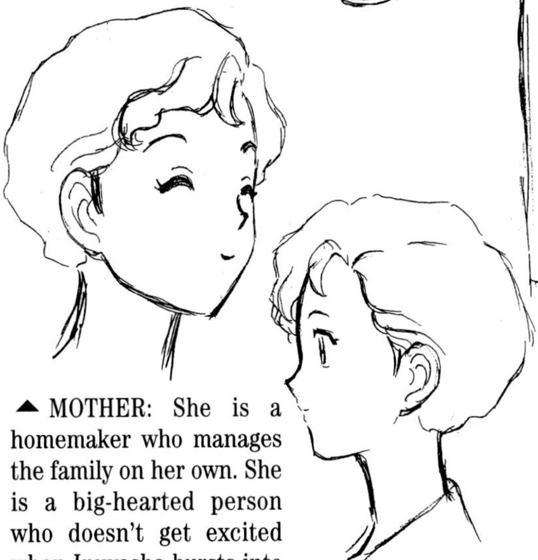

▲ MOTHER: She is a homemaker who manages the family on her own. She is a big-hearted person who doesn't get excited when Inuyasha bursts into the house at dinner time.

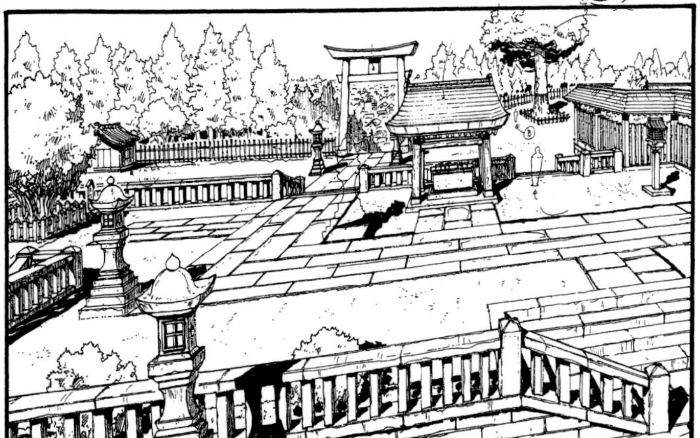

◀ HIGURASHI SHRINE (MODERN) It's on top of the hill, at the top of the stairs.

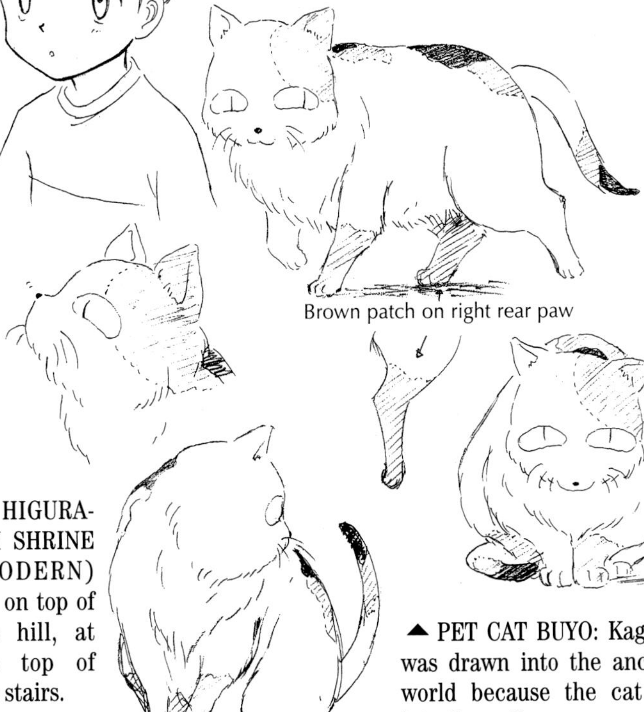
Brown patch on right rear paw

▲ PET CAT BUYO: Kagome was drawn into the ancient world because the cat got into the well.

ANIMATION SETUP MATERIALS

CLASSMATES

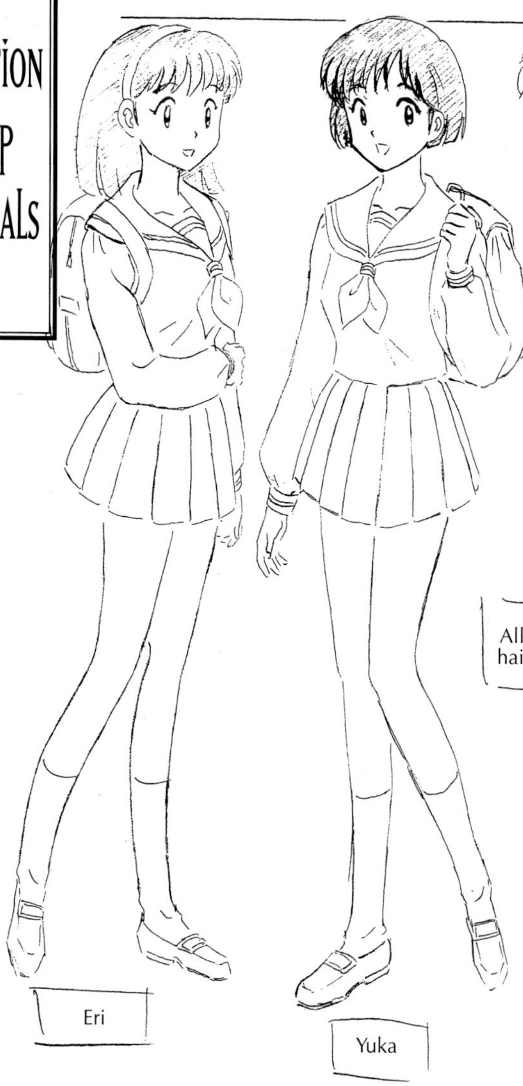

Eri
Yuka
All three have black hair with highlights.

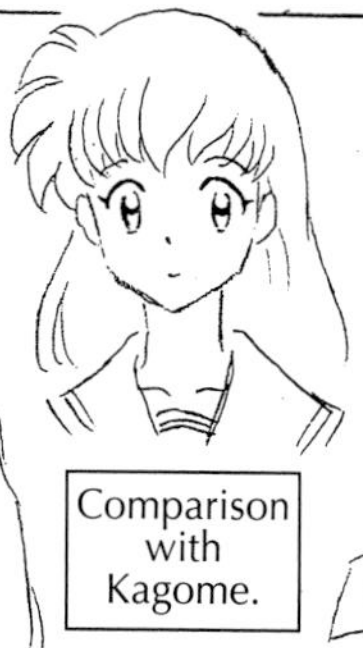

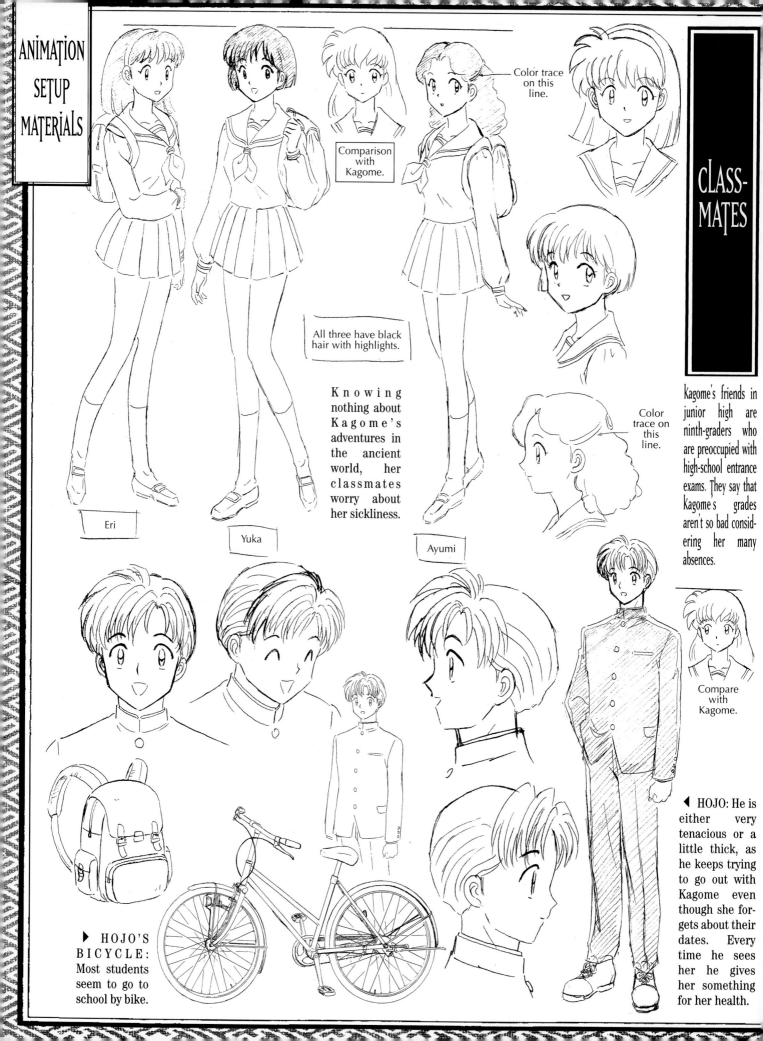

Comparison with Kagome.

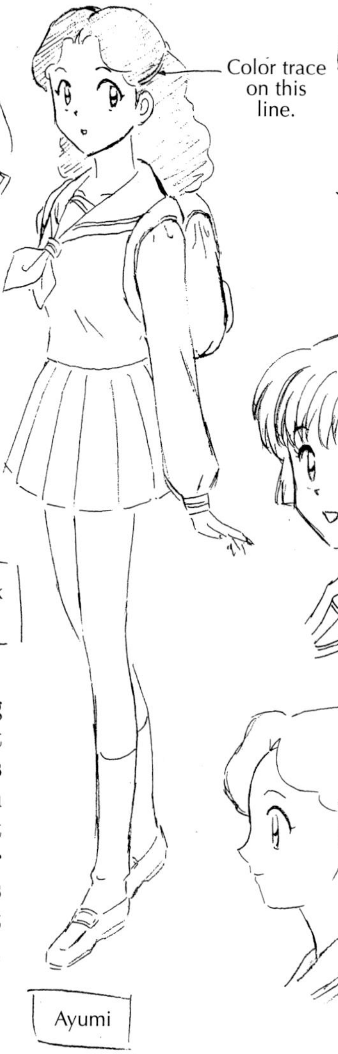

Color trace on this line.
Ayumi

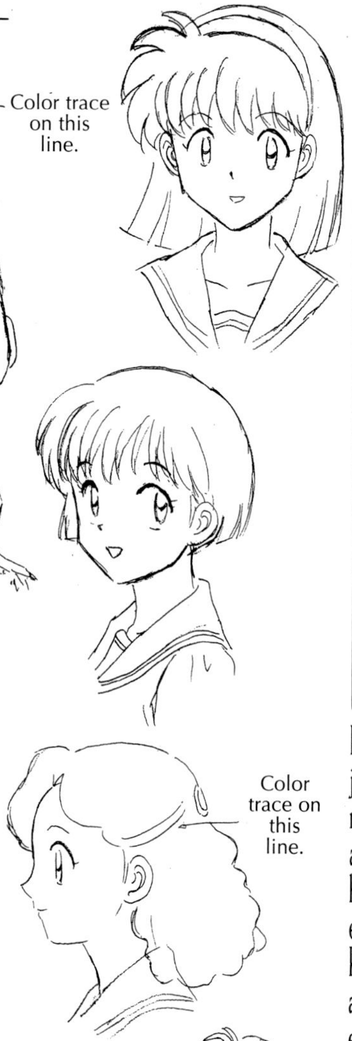

Color trace on this line.

Knowing nothing about Kagome's adventures in the ancient world, her classmates worry about her sickliness.

Kagome's friends in junior high are ninth-graders who are preoccupied with high-school entrance exams. They say that Kagome's grades aren't so bad considering her many absences.

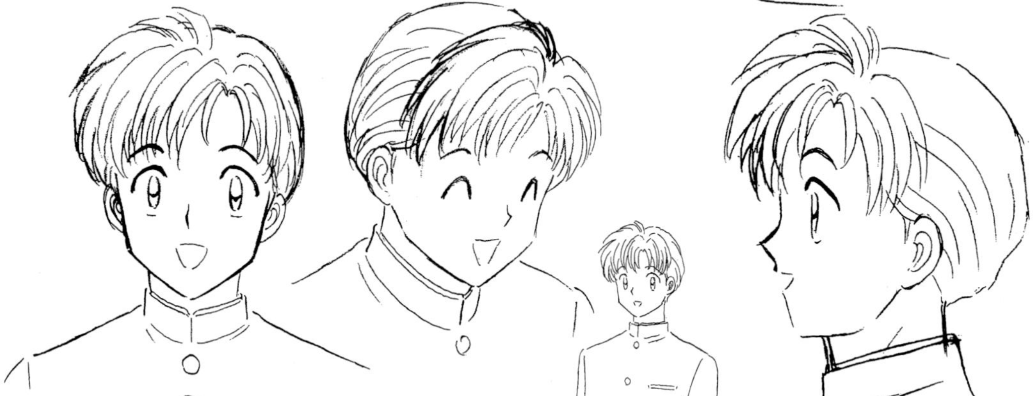

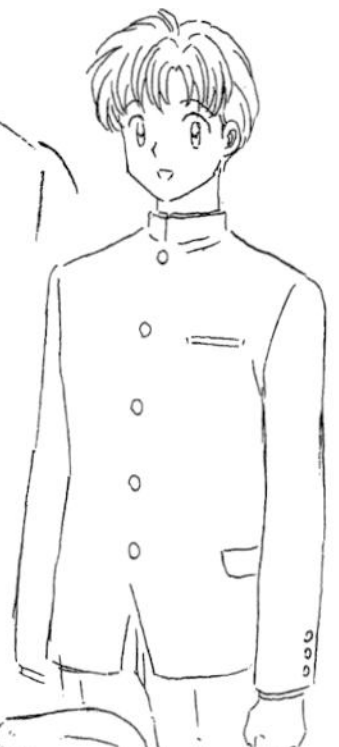

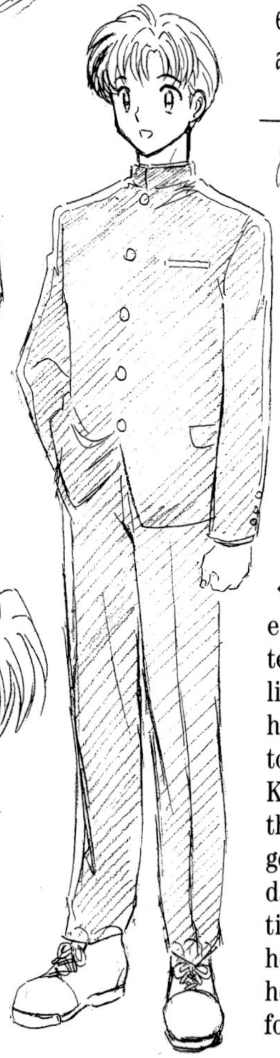

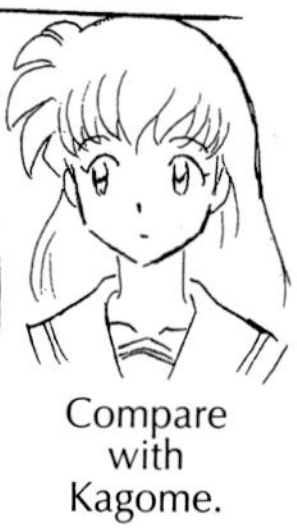

Compare with Kagome.

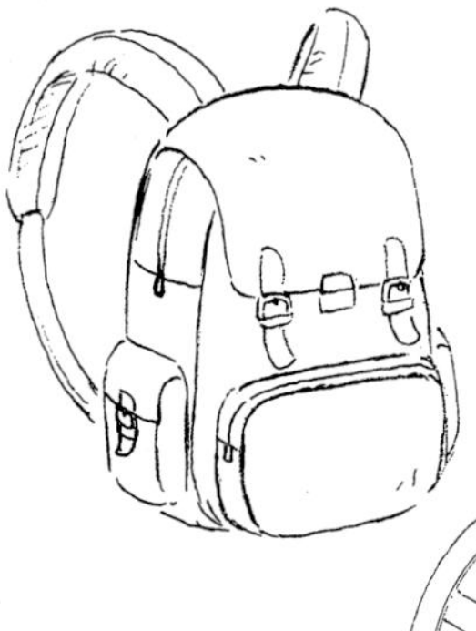

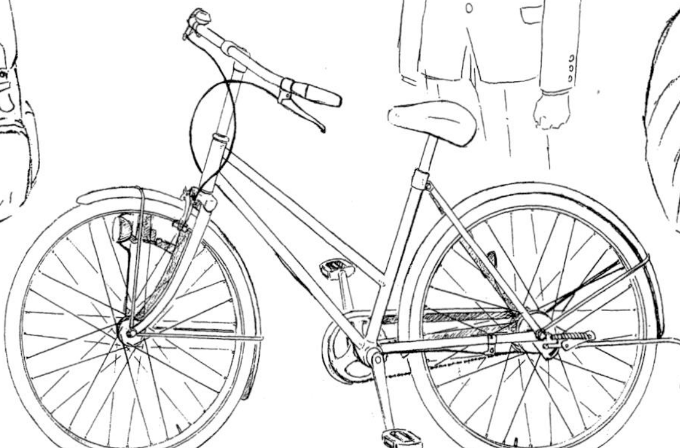

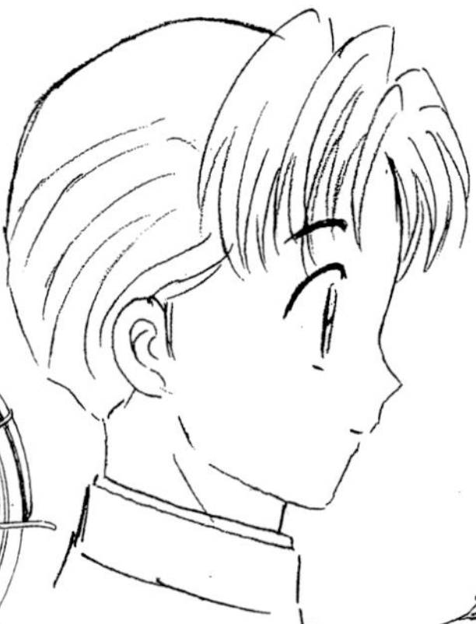

▶ **HOJO'S BICYCLE:** Most students seem to go to school by bike.

◀ HOJO: He is either very tenacious or a little thick, as he keeps trying to go out with Kagome even though she forgets about their dates. Every time he sees her he gives her something for her health.

SESSHOMARU

Unlike Inuyasha, his younger half-brother, Sesshomaru is a pure-blooded demon whose mother was also a demon. He can change into a beast. From his father he inherited Tenseiga, which is useless as a weapon, so he tries to claim Tetsusaiga.

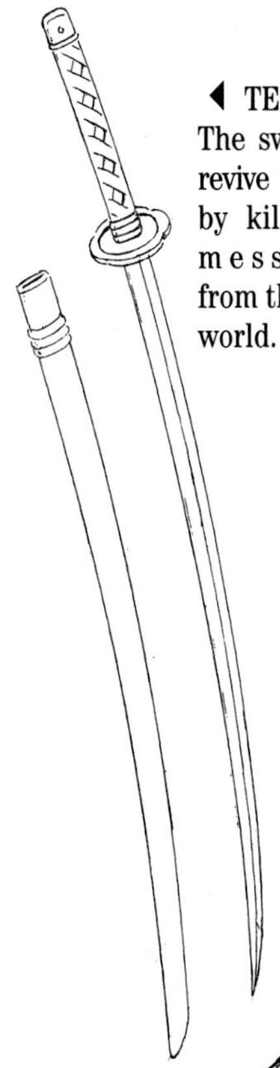

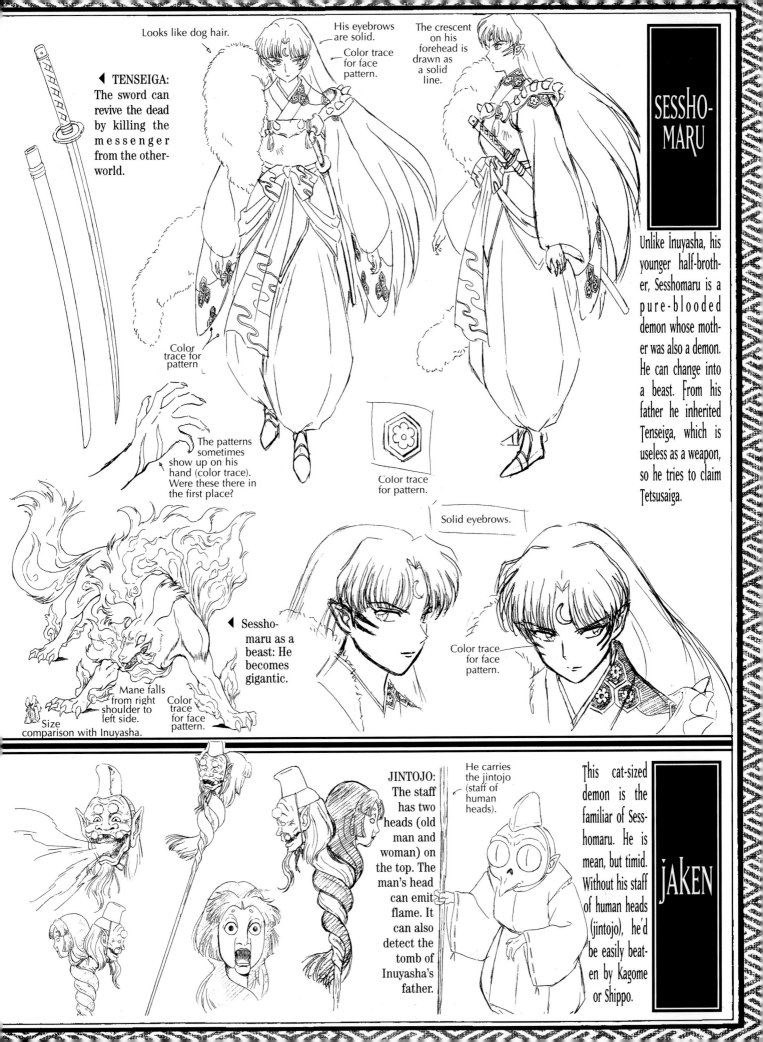

◀ **TENSEIGA:** The sword can revive the dead by killing the messenger from the other-world.

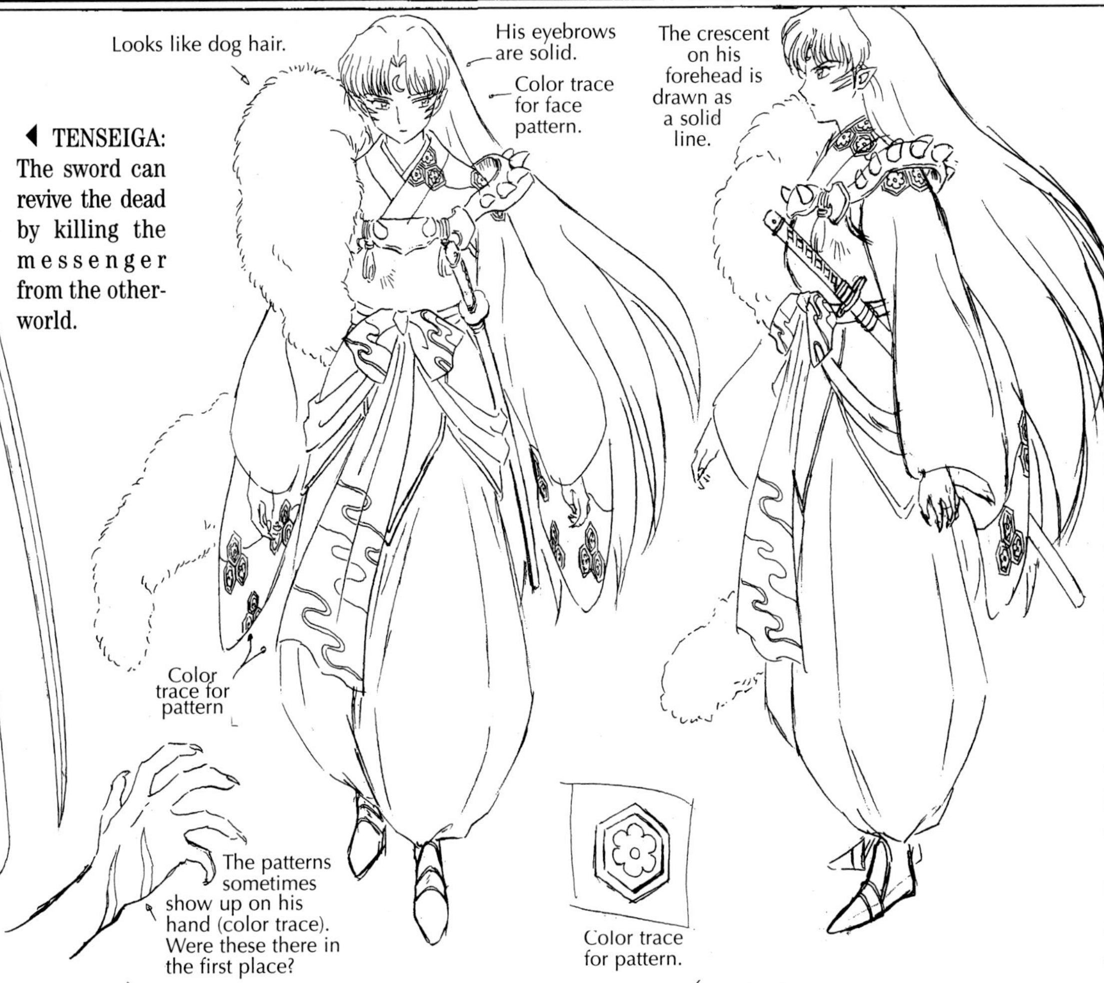

Looks like dog hair.
His eyebrows are solid.
Color trace for face pattern.
The crescent on his forehead is drawn as a solid line.
Color trace for pattern
The patterns sometimes show up on his hand (color trace). Were these there in the first place?
Color trace for pattern.

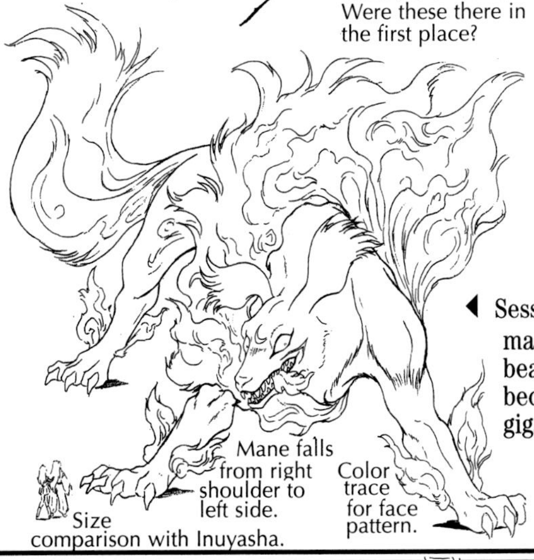

Mane falls from right shoulder to left side.
Color trace for face pattern.
Size comparison with Inuyasha.

◀ Sesshomaru as a beast: He becomes gigantic.

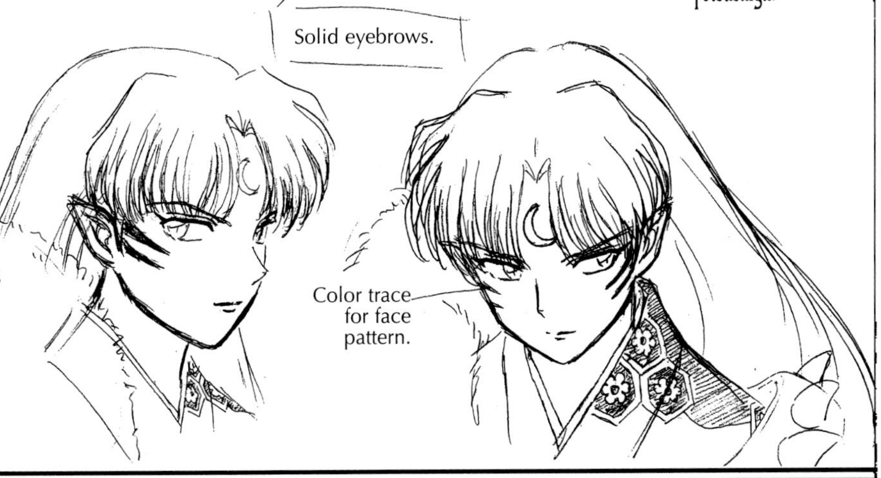

Solid eyebrows.
Color trace for face pattern.

JAKEN

This cat-sized demon is the familiar of Sesshomaru. He is mean, but timid. Without his staff of human heads (jintojo), he'd be easily beaten by Kagome or Shippo.

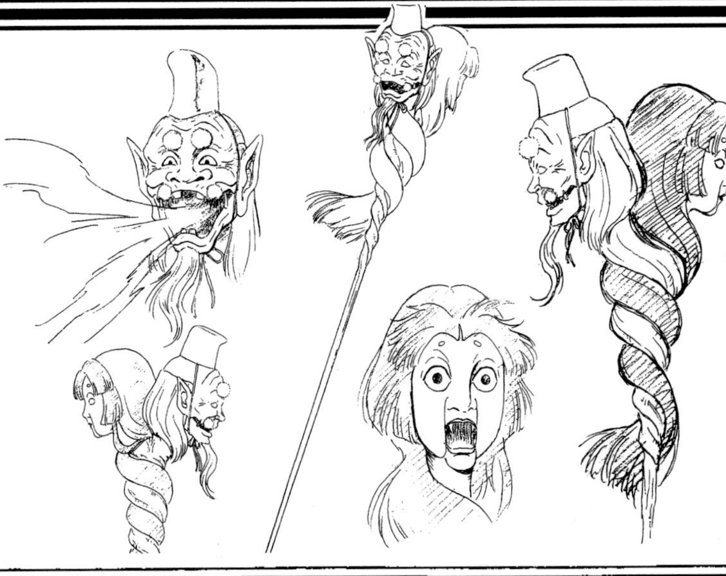

JINTOJO: The staff has two heads (old man and woman) on the top. The man's head can emit flame. It can also detect the tomb of Inuyasha's father.

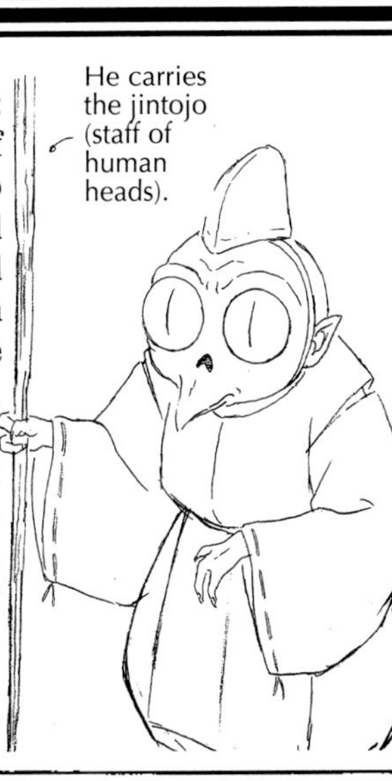

He carries the jintojo (staff of human heads).

ANIMATION SETUP MATERIALS

DEMONS

Many of these inhuman creatures have substance as well as spirit. All are after the jewel because when it is taken inside the body, it increases their supernatural powers and causes metamorphosis.

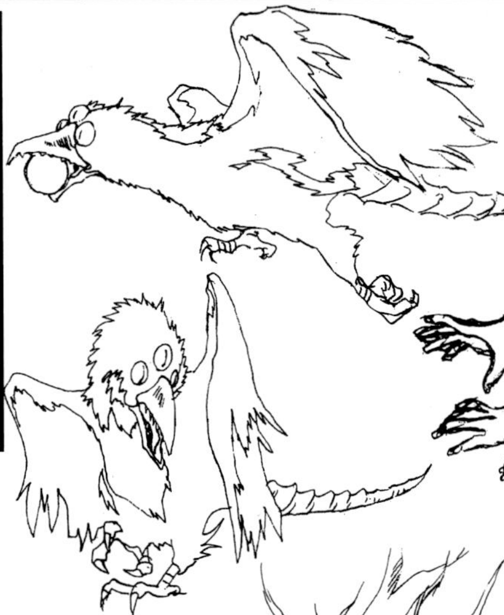

✦ CARRION CROW (SHIBUGARAS)
This demon gets away with the Jewel, which is shattered by Kagome's arrow when she shoots the demon down.

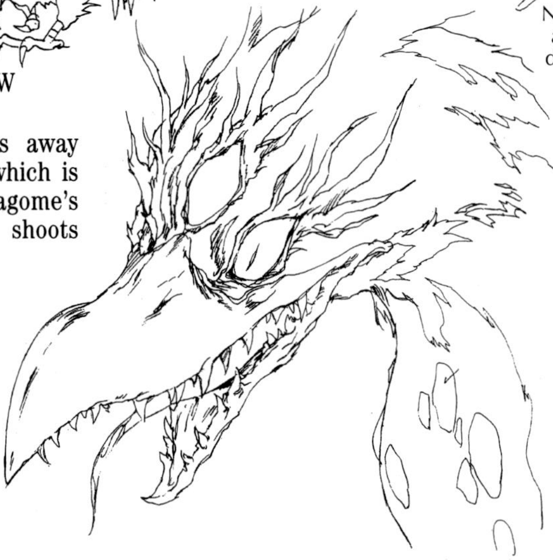

▶ Having eaten the Jewel, the crow turns more vicious.

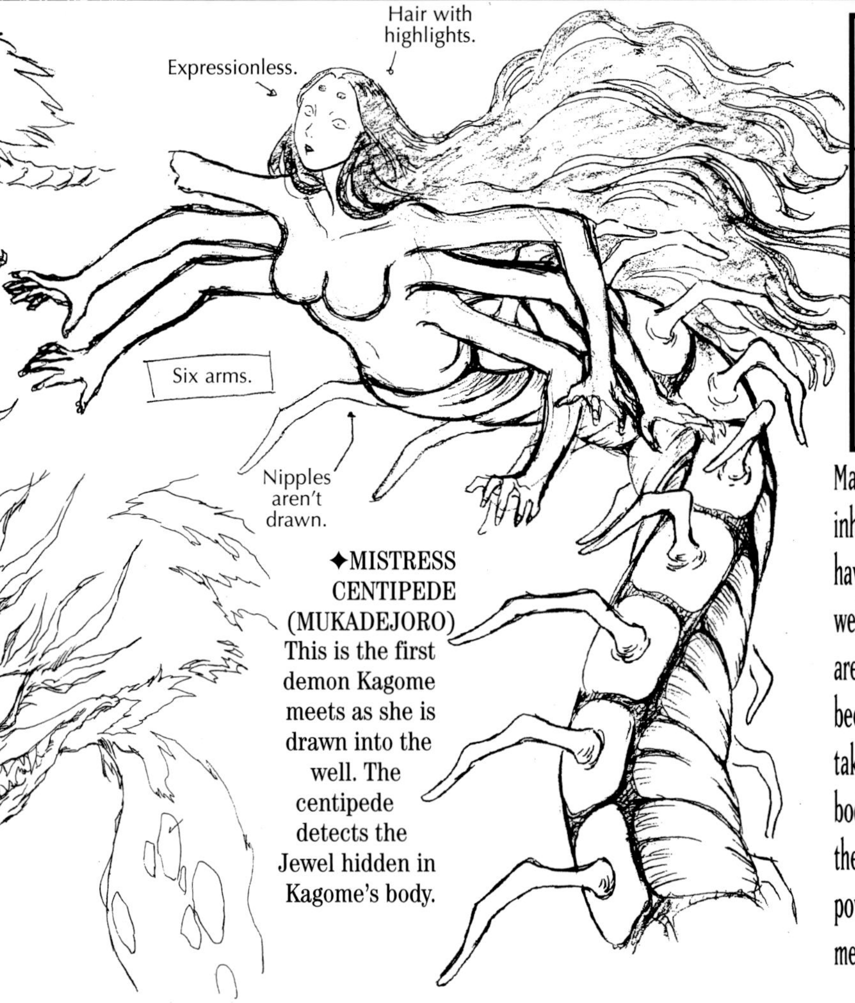
Hair with highlights.
Expressionless.
Six arms.
Nipples aren't drawn.

✦MISTRESS CENTIPEDE (MUKADEJORO)
This is the first demon Kagome meets as she is drawn into the well. The centipede detects the Jewel hidden in Kagome's body.

✦ YURA OF THE DEMON HAIR (SAKAGAMINO YURA)
She manipulates village girls with invisible hairs to attack the Inuyasha party. She never dies, even when she is physically maimed. Her true self is a comb hidden in a red skull.

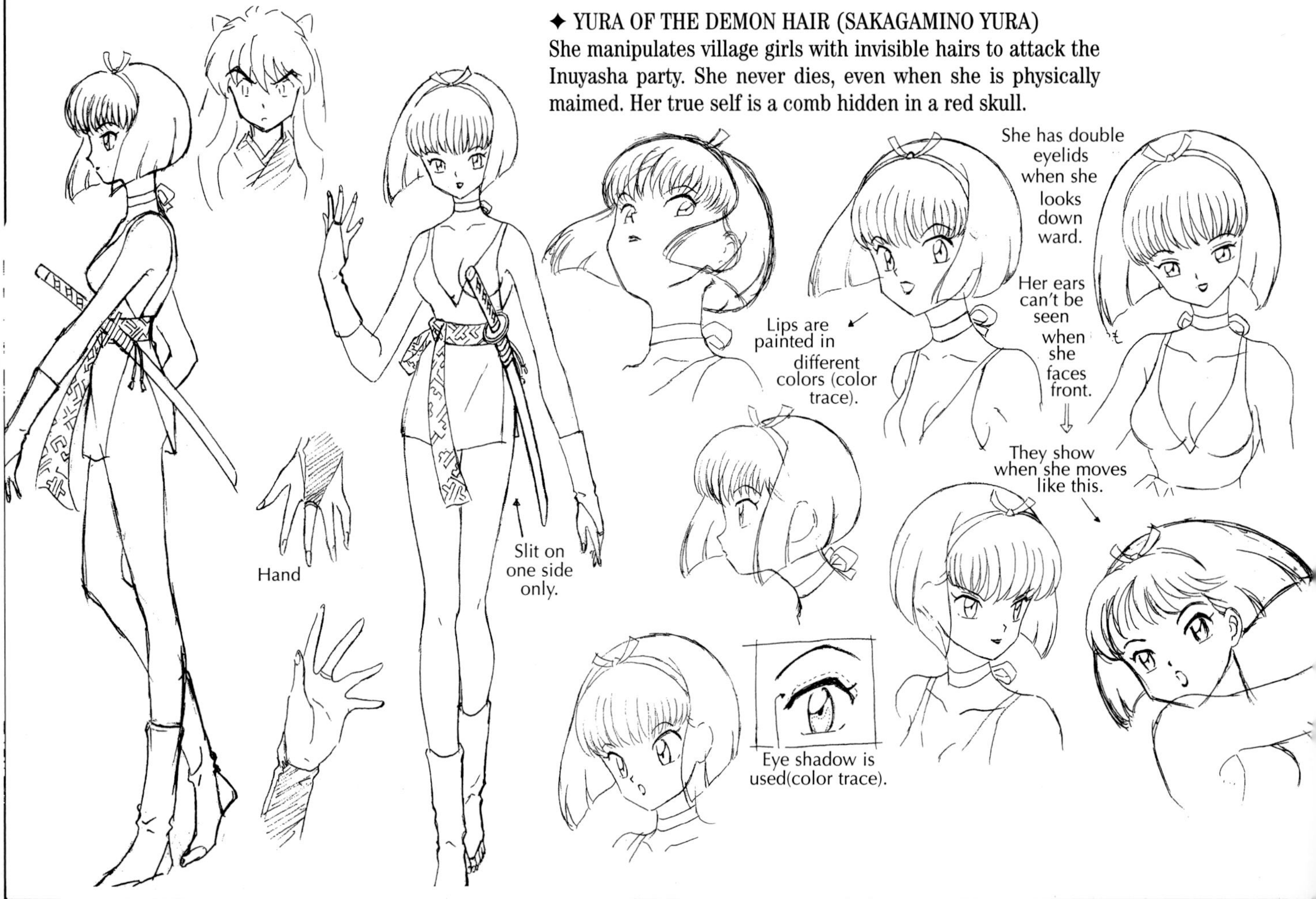
She has double eyelids when she looks down ward.
Lips are painted in different colors (color trace).
Her ears can't be seen when she faces front.
They show when she moves like this.
Hand
Slit on one side only.
Eye shadow is used(color trace).

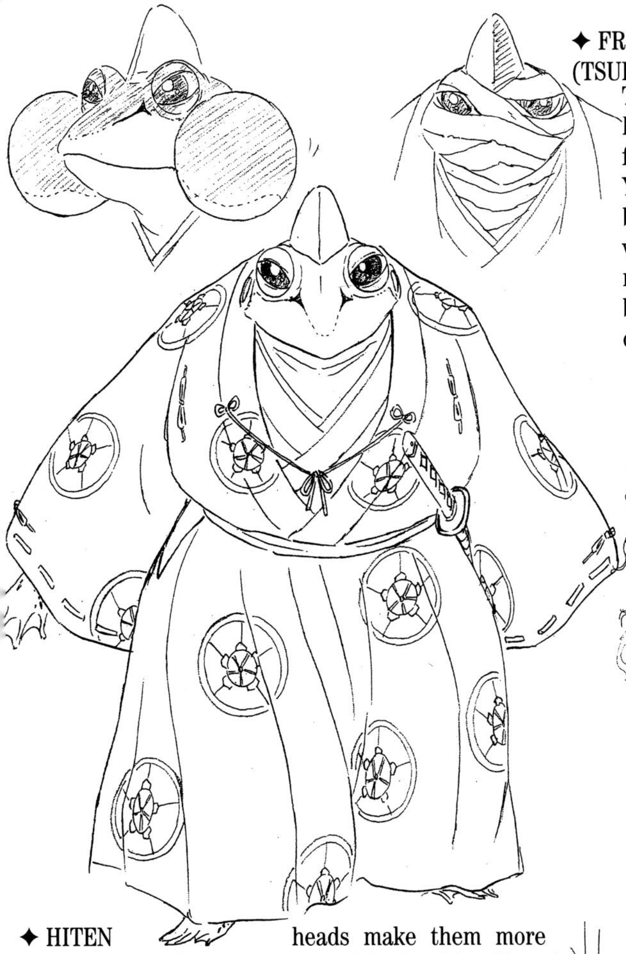

✦ FROG DEMON (TSUKUMO NO GAMA)
This frog demon has possessed a feudal lord in Yamajiro. He breathes poison vapors from his mouth, and lives by eating the souls of young girls.

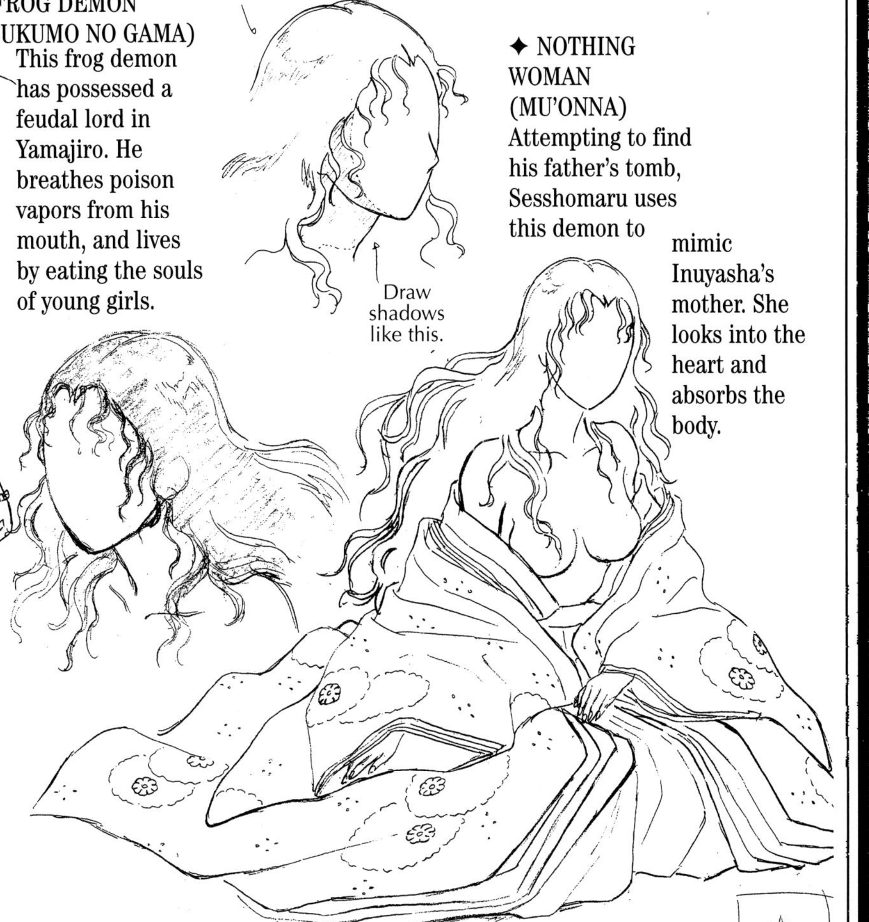
Solid-line highlight acceptable.
Draw shadows like this.

✦ NOTHING WOMAN (MU'ONNA)
Attempting to find his father's tomb, Sesshomaru uses this demon to mimic Inuyasha's mother. She looks into the heart and absorbs the body.

✦ HITEN AND MANTEN ("FLY HEAVEN, FILL HEAVEN")
Demon brothers noted for their violence. The shards of the Jewel buried in their foreheads make them more powerful. The elder, Hiten (right), flies through the sky with flaming wheels at his feet. The younger Manten (left) boasts of enormous physical strength, but is simple-minded.

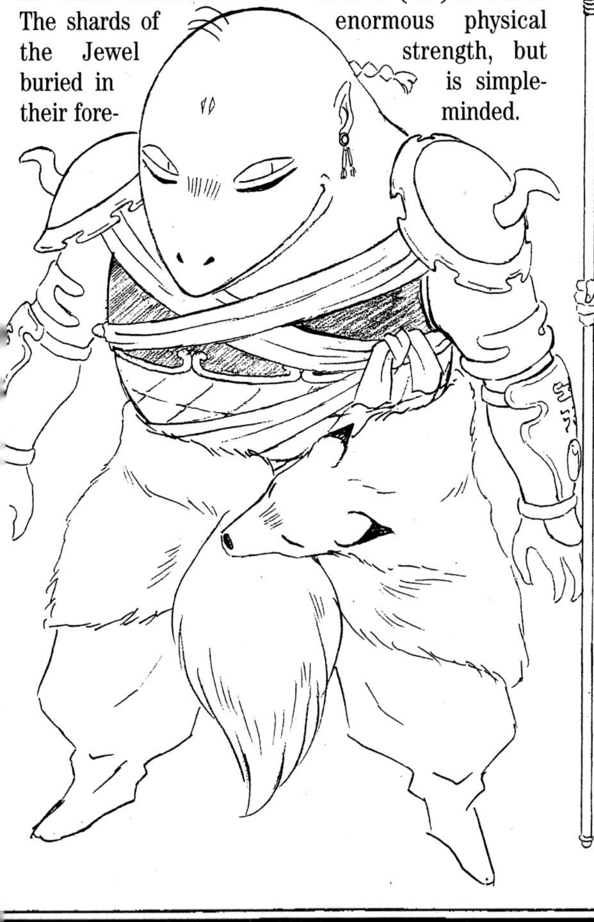

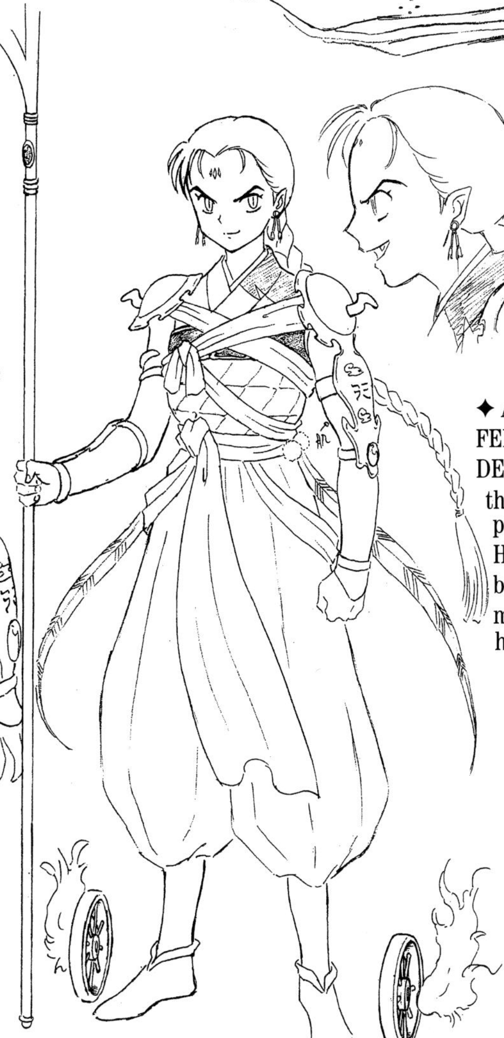
Earrings on both ears.
He has three shards of the Jewel on his forehead.

✦ A FEMALE DEMON
that accompanies Hiten: He brutally murders her.

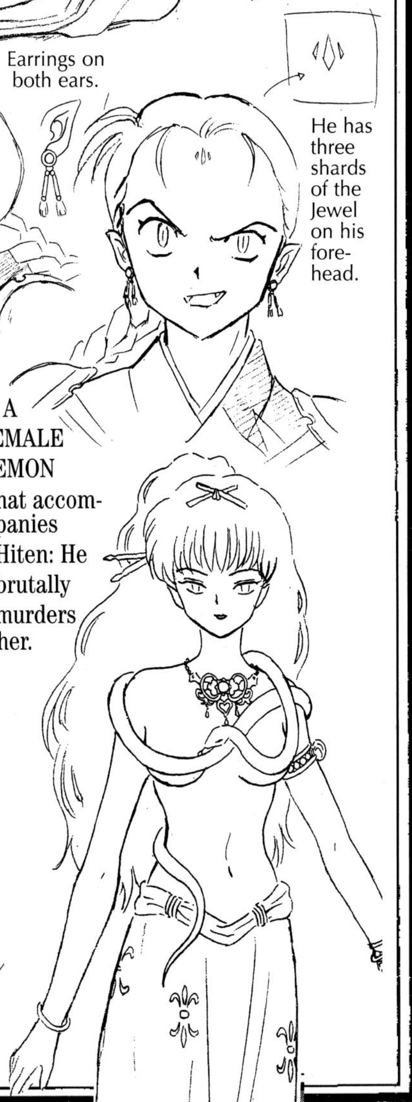

ANIMATION SETUP MATERIALS

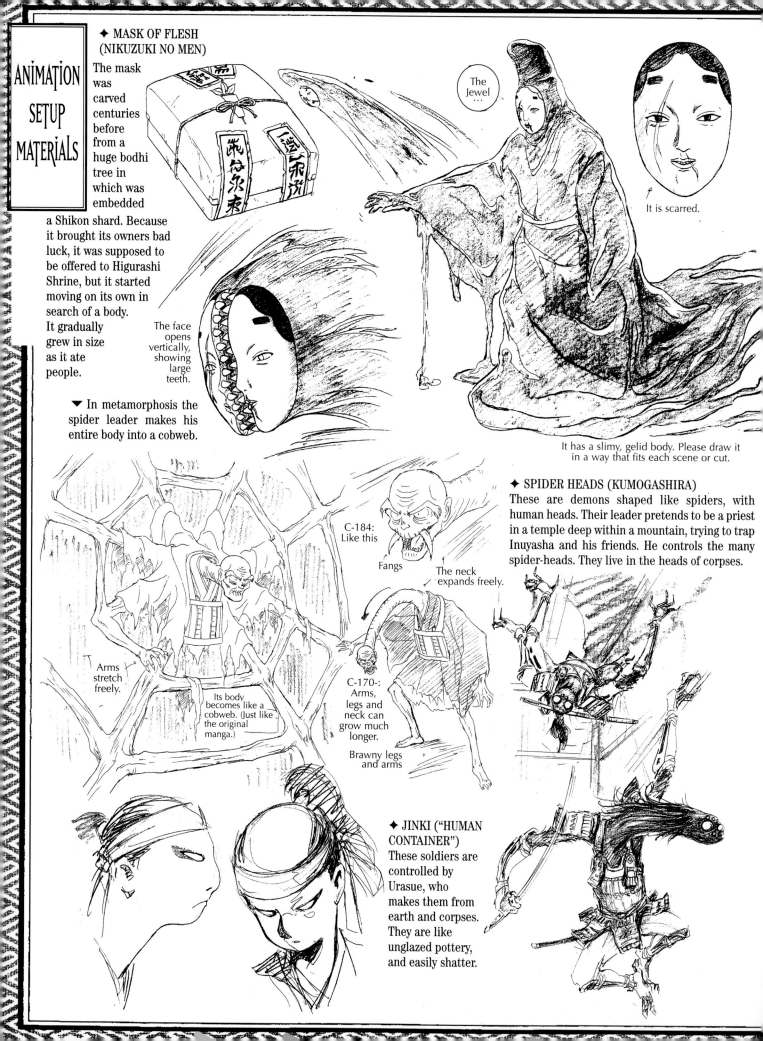

✦ MASK OF FLESH (NIKUZUKI NO MEN)

The mask was carved centuries before from a huge bodhi tree in which was embedded a Shikon shard. Because it brought its owners bad luck, it was supposed to be offered to Higurashi Shrine, but it started moving on its own in search of a body. It gradually grew in size as it ate people.

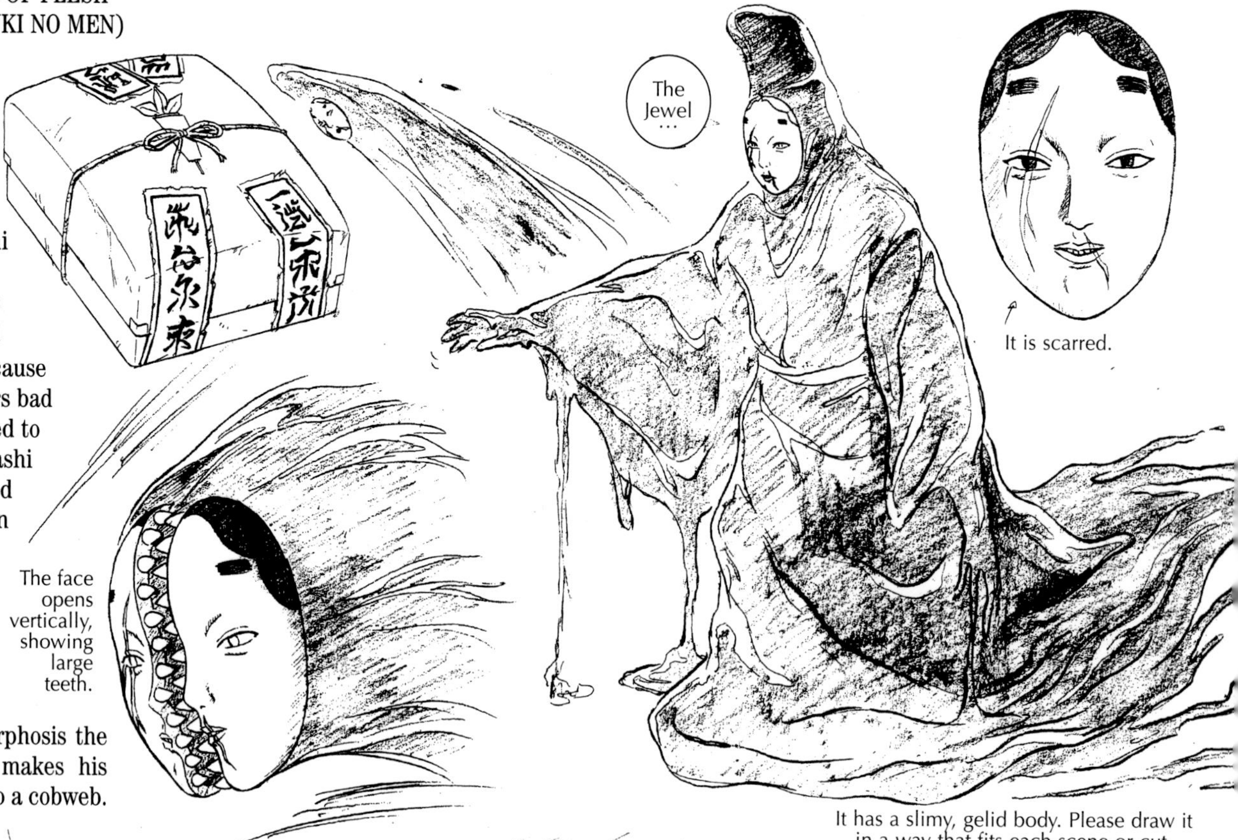
The Jewel . . .
It is scarred.
The face opens vertically, showing large teeth.
It has a slimy, gelid body. Please draw it in a way that fits each scene or cut.

▼ In metamorphosis the spider leader makes his entire body into a cobweb.

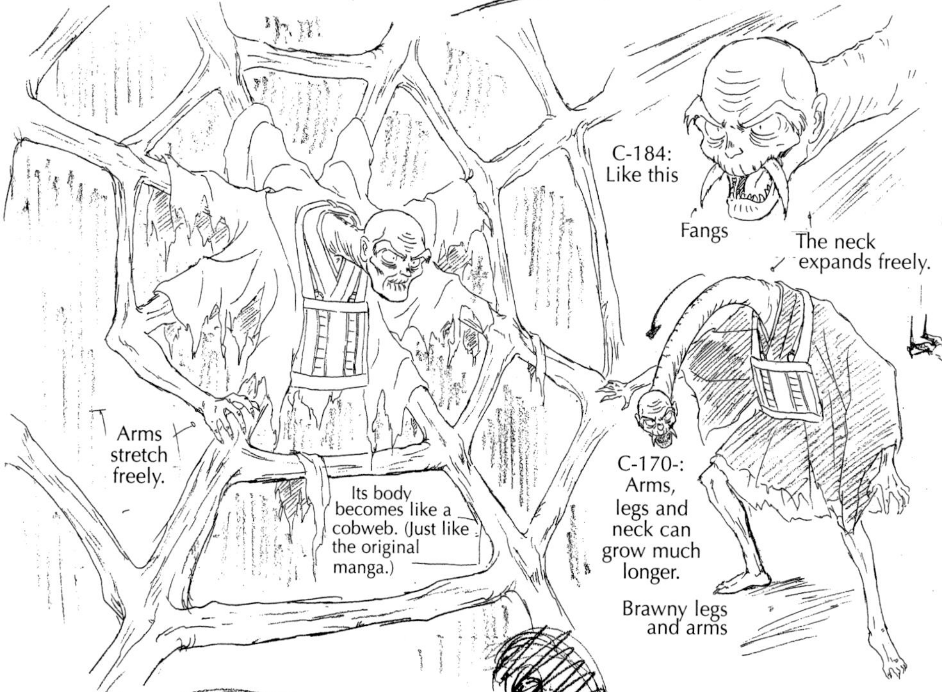
C-184: Like this
Fangs
The neck expands freely.
Arms stretch freely.
Its body becomes like a cobweb. (Just like the original manga.)
C-170-: Arms, legs and neck can grow much longer.
Brawny legs and arms

✦ SPIDER HEADS (KUMOGASHIRA)

These are demons shaped like spiders, with human heads. Their leader pretends to be a priest in a temple deep within a mountain, trying to trap Inuyasha and his friends. He controls the many spider-heads. They live in the heads of corpses.

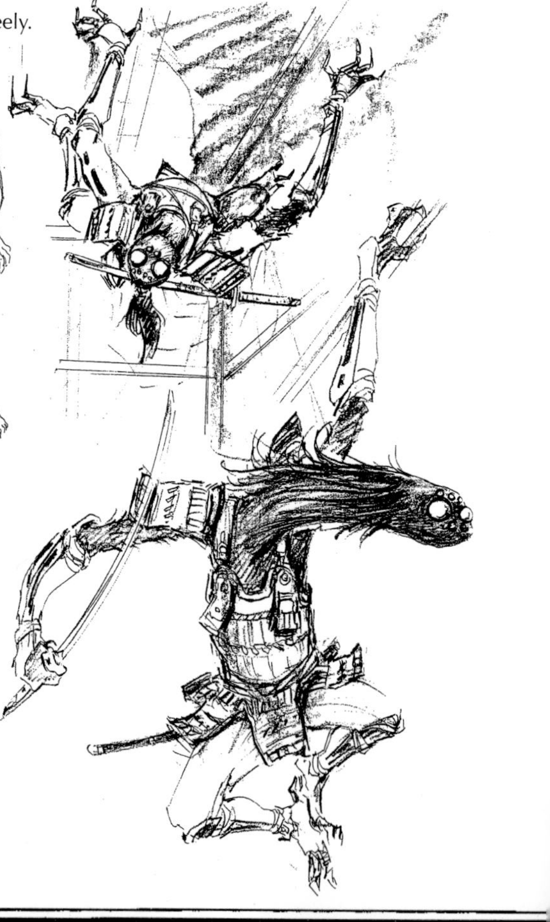

✦ JINKI ("HUMAN CONTAINER")

These soldiers are controlled by Urasue, who makes them from earth and corpses. They are like unglazed pottery, and easily shatter.

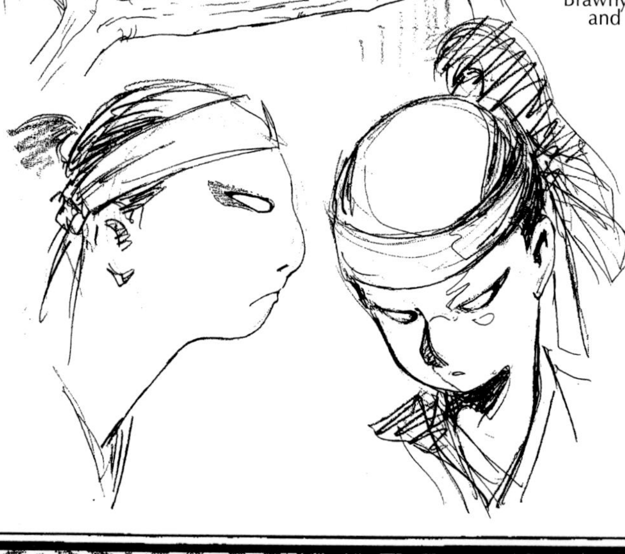

ART SETUP

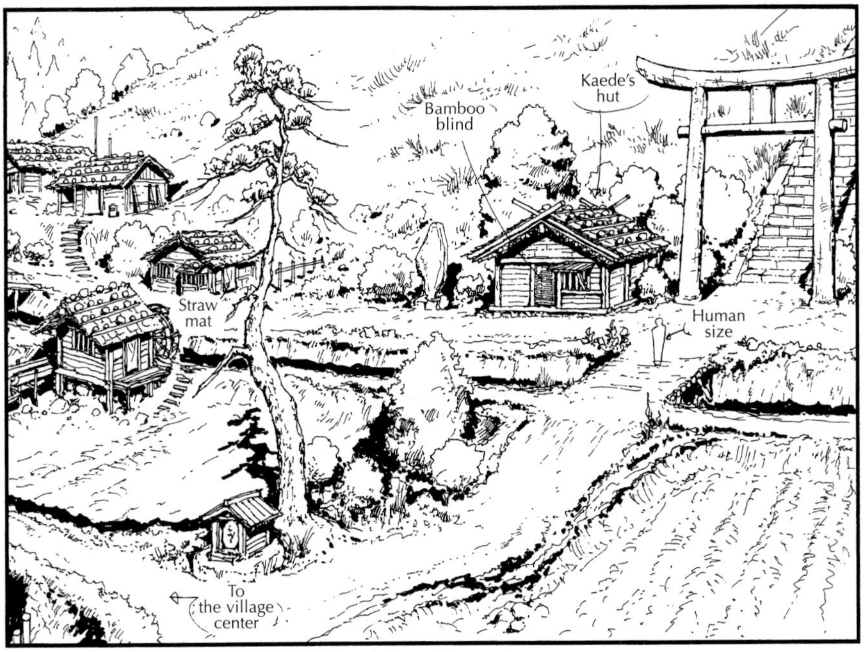

Bamboo blind
Kaede's hut
Straw mat
Human size
To the village center

▲ Kaede's hut beside the shrine and the village view

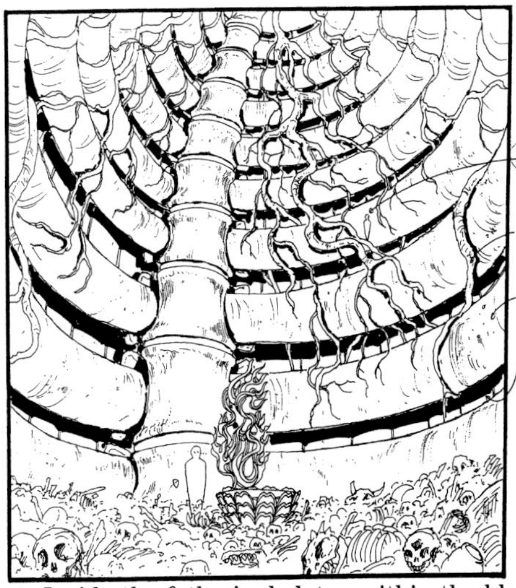

Human size
Tree roots
Ribs
Inside the armor

▲ Inside the father's skeleton within the black pearl. We see gigantic ribs.

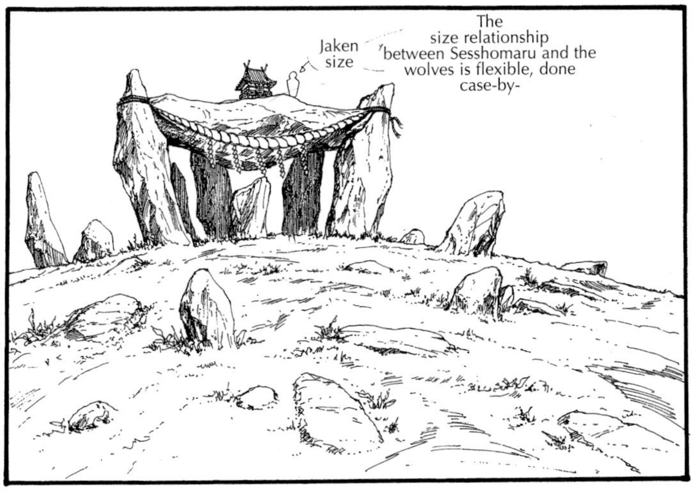

Jaken size
The size relationship between Sesshomaru and the wolves is flexible, done case-by-

▲ THE HIDDEN TOMB OF INUYASHA'S FATHER

The tomb was built like this to hide the real location of Tetsusaiga. Its structure is a stone circle, and a stone platform and small shrine stand at the center of the circle. Discovered by Sesshomaru and Jaken, it is inside a black pearl hidden in Inuyasha's left eye. The pearl is a gate into a different dimension, where they find the massive bones of the canine demon (Inuyasha's father), as in the upper right picture.

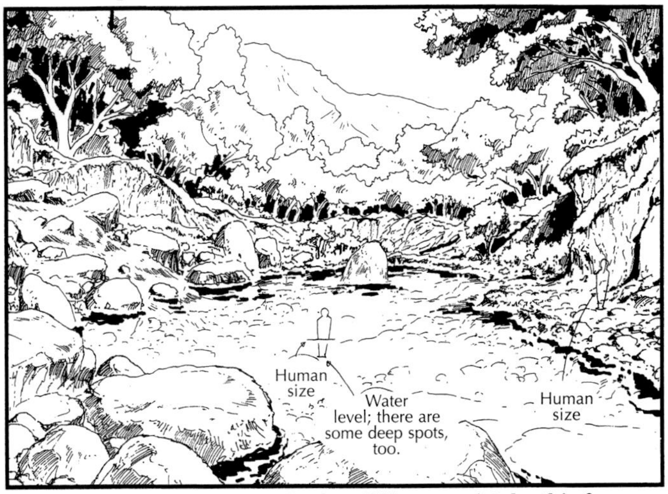

Human size
Water level; there are some deep spots, too.
Human size

▲ The river where Kagome bathes: Villagers mistake this for purifying ritual.

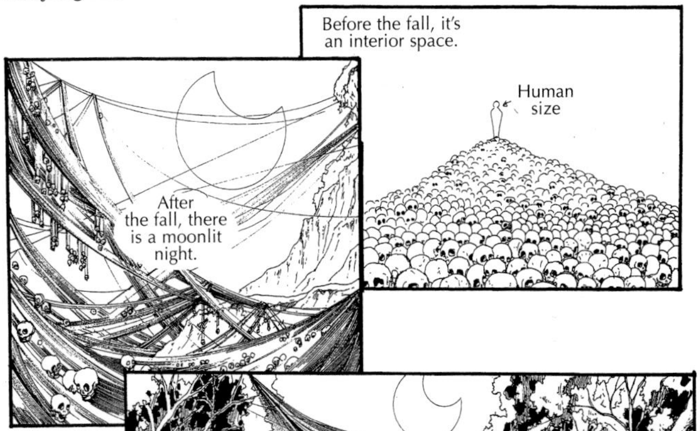

Before the fall, it's an interior space.
Human size
After the fall, there is a moonlit night.

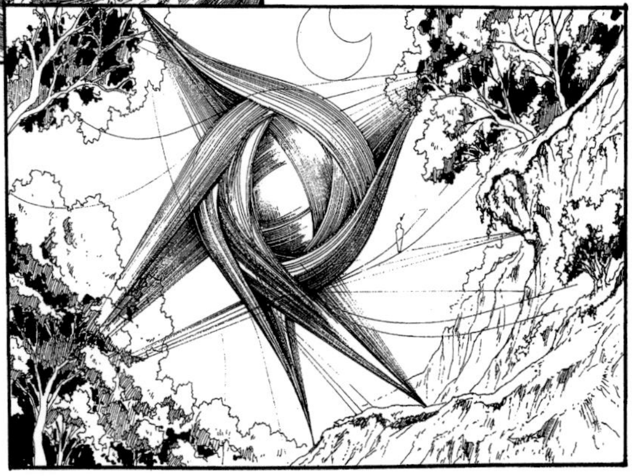

▶ YURA'S NEST (right) and inside view (above right). Scattered skulls are seen after its fall (upper right).

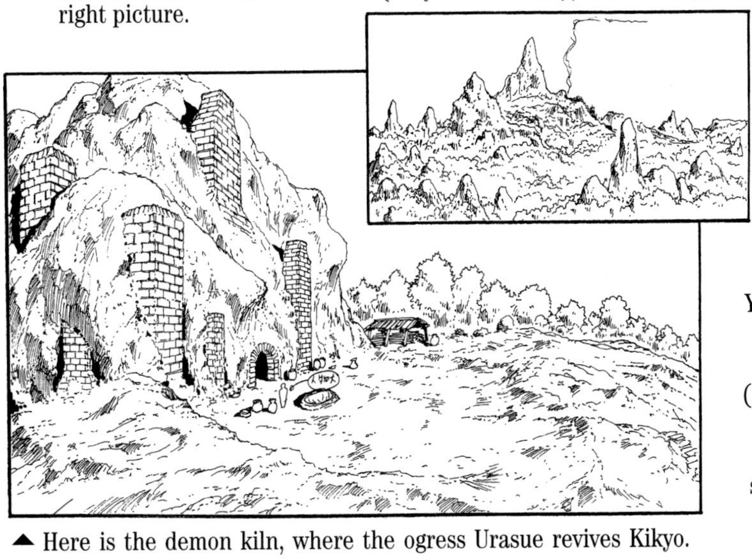

▲ Here is the demon kiln, where the ogress Urasue revives Kikyo. It's inside a certain mountain.

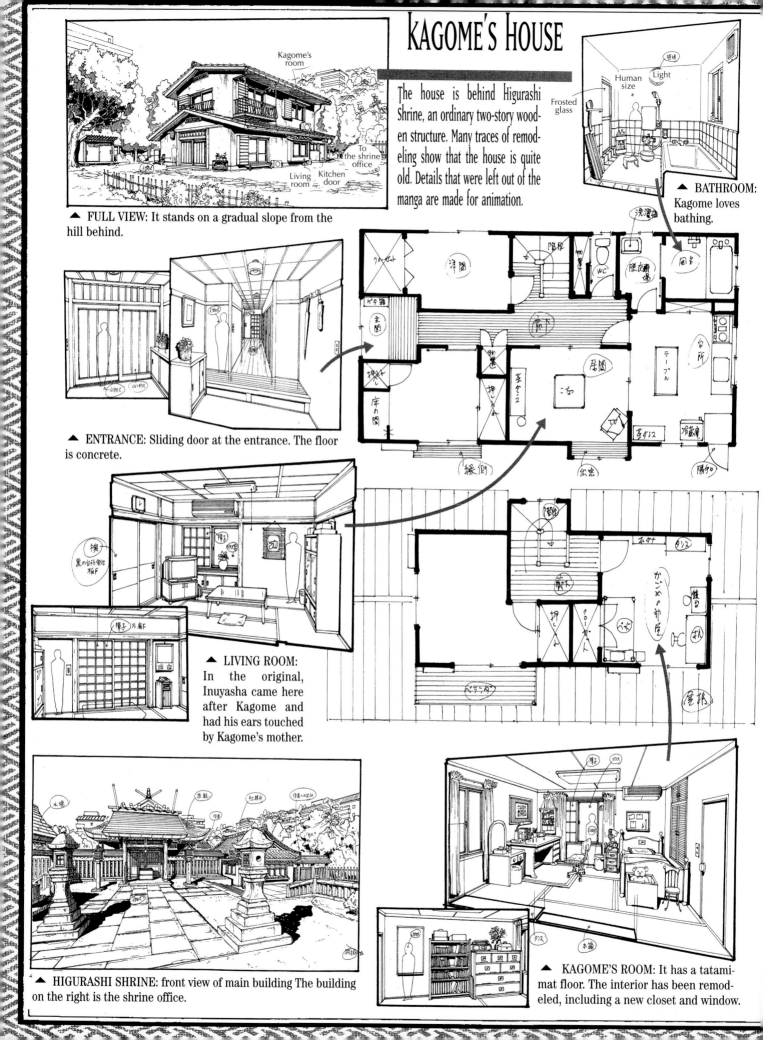

KAGOME'S HOUSE

The house is behind Higurashi Shrine, an ordinary two-story wooden structure. Many traces of remodeling show that the house is quite old. Details that were left out of the manga are made for animation.

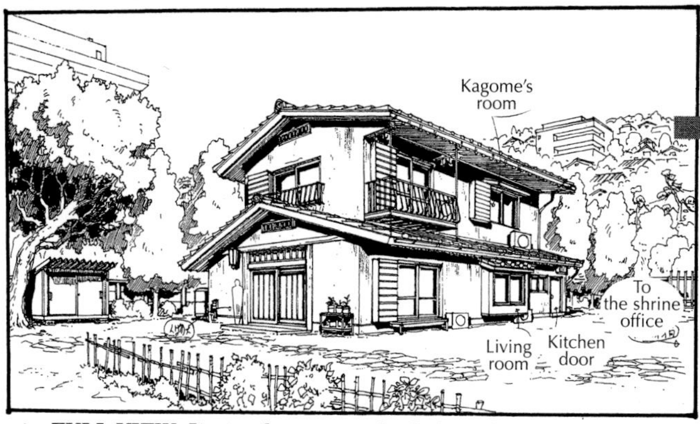
Kagome's room
To the shrine office
Living room
Kitchen door

▲ FULL VIEW: It stands on a gradual slope from the hill behind.

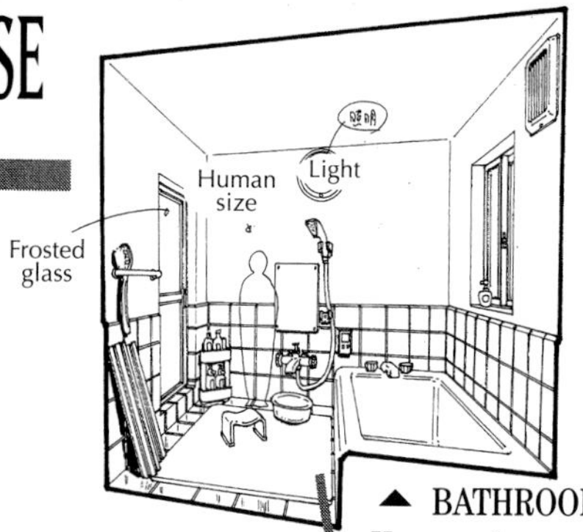
Human size
Light
Frosted glass

▲ BATHROOM: Kagome loves bathing.

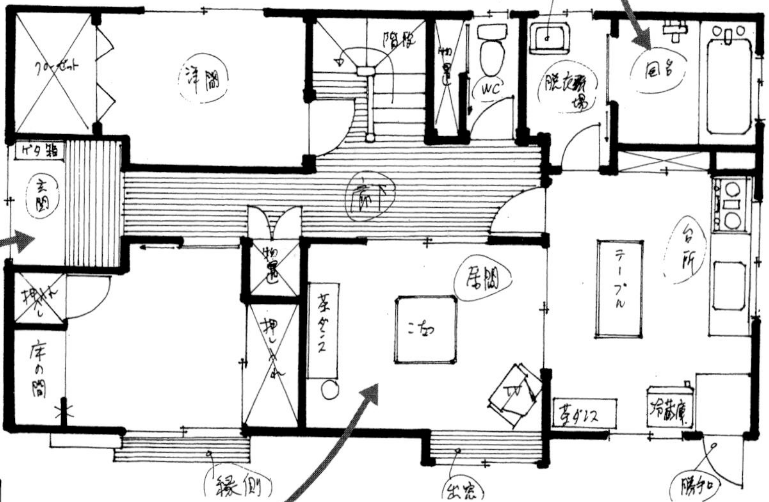

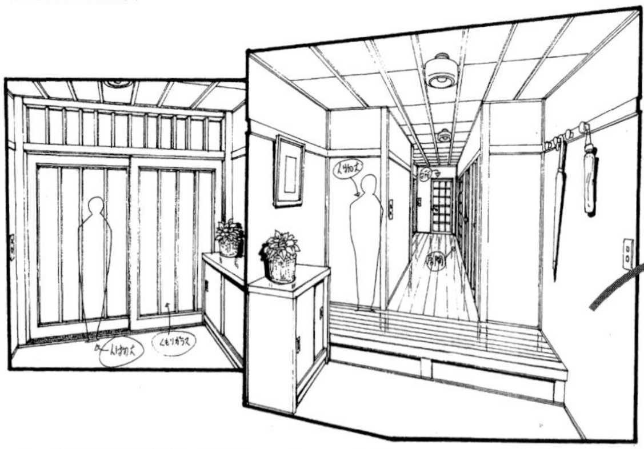

▲ ENTRANCE: Sliding door at the entrance. The floor is concrete.

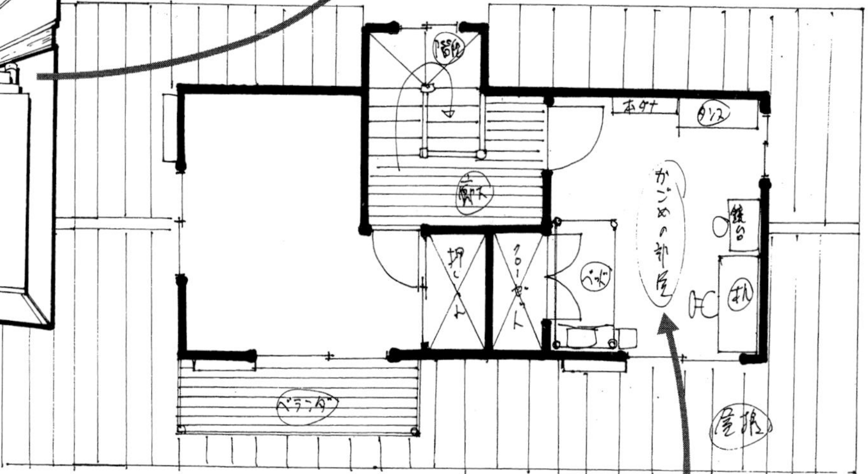

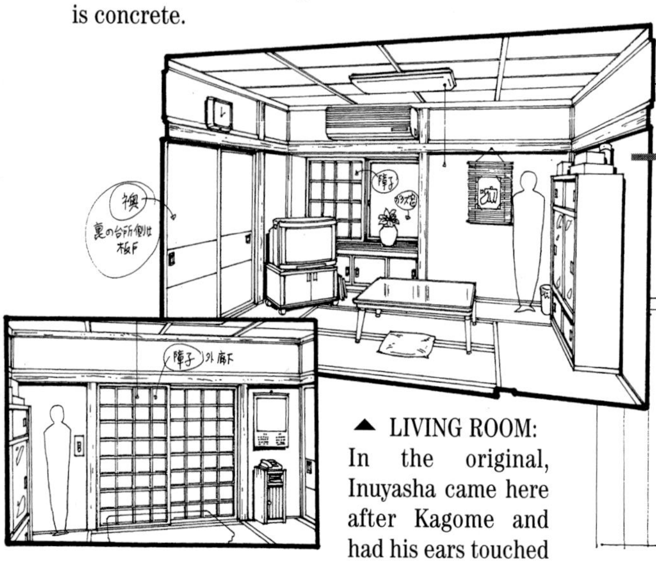

▲ LIVING ROOM: In the original, Inuyasha came here after Kagome and had his ears touched by Kagome's mother.

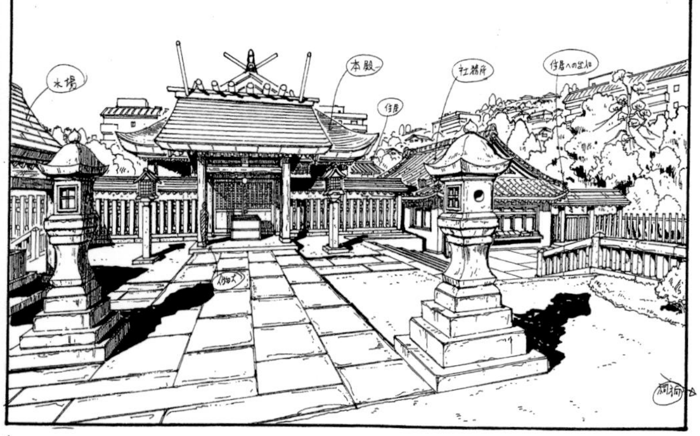

▲ HIGURASHI SHRINE: front view of main building The building on the right is the shrine office.

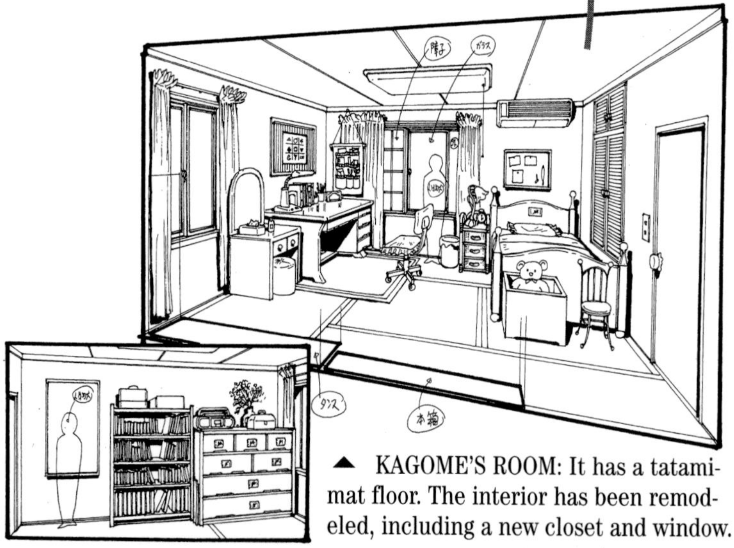

▲ KAGOME'S ROOM: It has a tatami-mat floor. The interior has been remodeled, including a new closet and window.

INUYASHA GLOSSARY

READ THIS WITH THE COLOR PAGES AND YOU'LL HAVE COMPLETE INFORMATION ON "INUYASHA!" IT'S YOUR ULTIMATE GUIDE.

◆ GIANT CENTIPEDE (OOMUKADE)
This is an ordinary centipede that became a monster with the help of a Shikon shard. It is easily beaten by Sango's boomerang. The centipede is often referred to as a monster in anthropological records across the nation. In China the insect is considered stronger than the snake because of it's many legs.

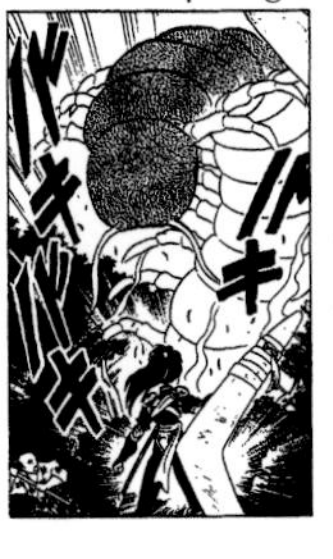

◆ GIANT MANTIS (OOKAMAKIRI)
It seduces Miroku disguised as a noble princess. Swallowed up by Miroku's wind tunnel, it cuts the tunnel bigger. It also has a sister.

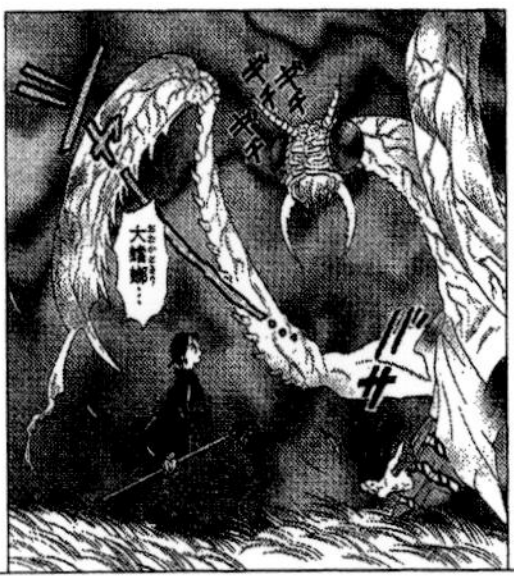

大蟷螂…

◆ INUYASHA'S FATHER
He is a canine monster holding a castle in Saigoku ("Western Nation"). Badly injured in the battle with Ryukotsusei, he died leaving his two sons his swords: Tenseiga to Sesshomaru and Tetsusaiga to Inuyasha. He was said to be very powerful and, according to old Myoga, his blood tasted good. His tomb is hidden in Inuyasha's left eye.

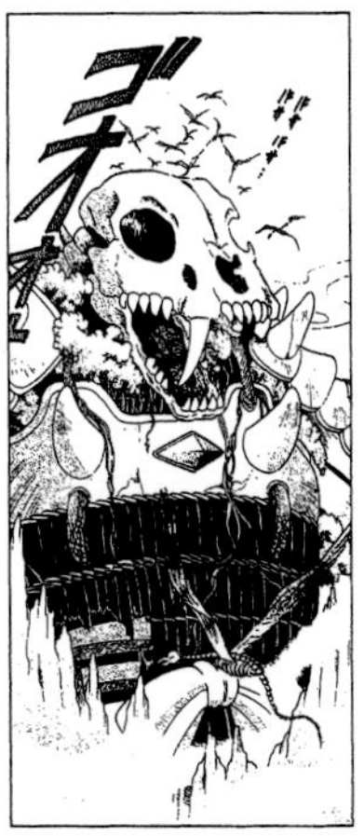

◆ KAGOME'S ILLNESS
Kagome can't go to school when she's in the ancient world, so her grandfather makes excuses for her. He tends to name old men's diseases and excuses, like a strained back, hospitalization for diabetes testing, gout, beri-beri, rheumatism, neuritis, hematemesis (mistake by her friend), difficulty breathing (Kagome's own false excuse), hospitalization for tuberculosis, and a mysterious rash over her entire body.

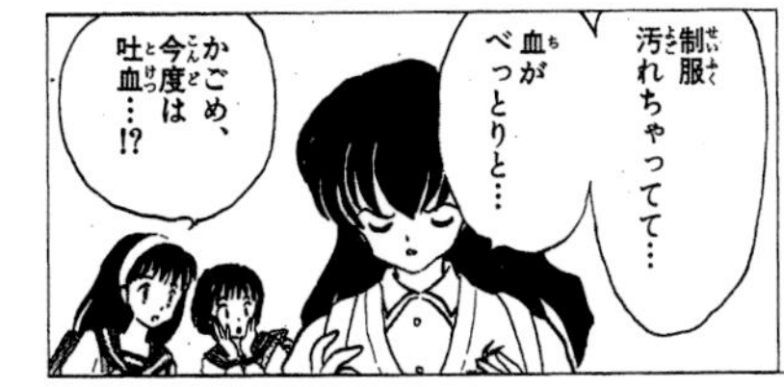

制服汚れちゃってて…
血がべっとりと…
かごめ、今度は吐血…!?

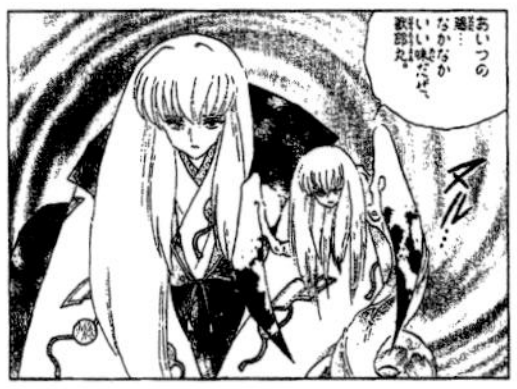

◆KAGEROMARU ("SHADOW MAN")
Alter ego of Naraku and brother of Goshinki. He usually lives inside the body of Juromaru ("beast man"), but emerges in battle. He is killed by Tetsusaiga in battle with the Inuyasha/Koga team.

◆ HUNGRY GHOST (GAKI)
This is the messenger from hell to the person who's just died. Sesshomaru's Tenseiga revives the dead by slashing this messenger. Originally the gaki were the ones who fell into gakido ("way of the hungry ghost"), one of six evil ways described in Buddhism.

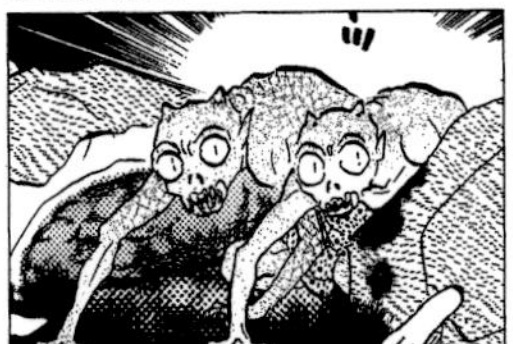

◆ KAEDE ("MAPLE")
She is a priestess who protects the village after her sister Kikyo ("balloon flower"). She acts like a guardian to Kagome and her friends.

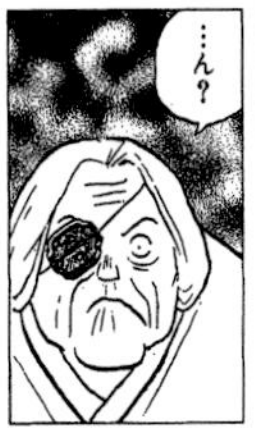

…ん?

◆ ONIGUMO ("DEMON SPIDER")
He was a notorious bandit in a neighboring country. Found with burns all over his body and broken legs, Kikyo saved his life. His evil aura attracted many demons, and his body was consumed by them. The demons fused, and revived as Naraku.

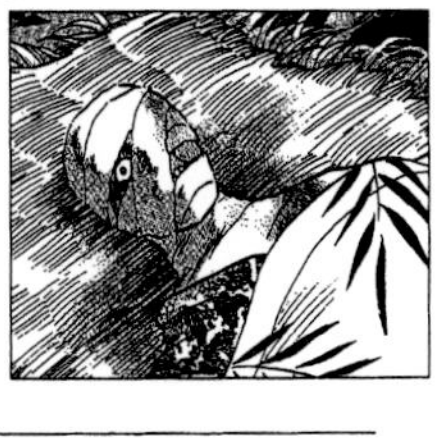

◆ KIRARA ("MICA")
Sango's pet from the exterminator village is a nekomata, an ancient breed of cat with a split tail and supernatural powers. She usually takes the form of a house cat, but in a battle becomes a flying demon with huge, sharp fangs.

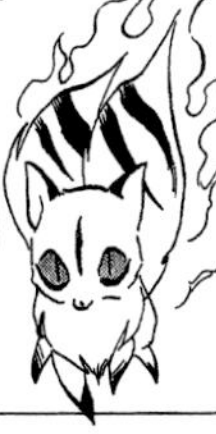

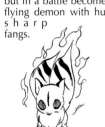

◆ GATENMARU ("MOTH HEAVEN MAN")
This demon leads a group of bandits. He traps Inuyasha and Miroku in a poisonous cocoon. Inuyasha's power grows, and Gatenmaru and his subordinates are torn to pieces.

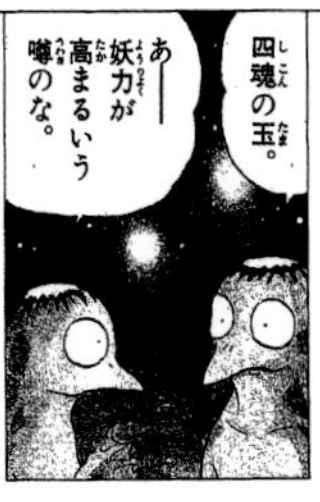

四魂の玉。
あー 妖力が高まるいう噂のな。

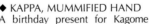

◆ KAPPA ("RIVER IMP")
Inuyasha encounters these imps on his way to the castle of the Immortal Frog (Frog Demon). They speak a Kansai dialect.

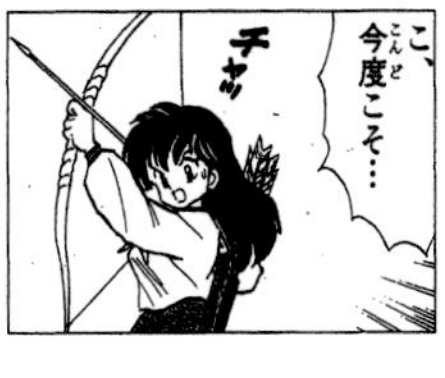

今度こそ…

◆ KAGOME'S BOW
Because Kagome is Kikyo reincarnated, Inuyasha counts on her as a good archer. Her archery is terrible in the beginning, though. With practice she does gets better at it.

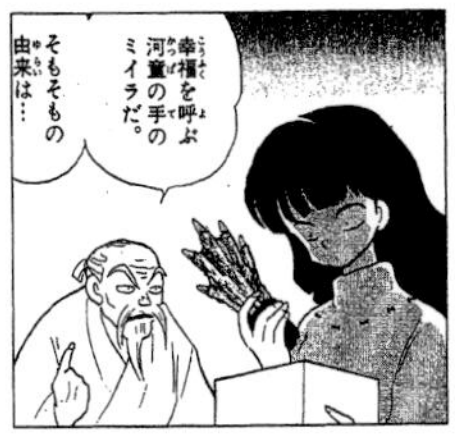

幸福を呼ぶ河童の手のミイラだ。
そもそもの由来は…

◆ KAPPA, MUMMIFIED HAND
A birthday present for Kagome fromGrampa. While Grampa was explaining to her how it would bring good luck, Kagome feeds it to her cat Buyo.

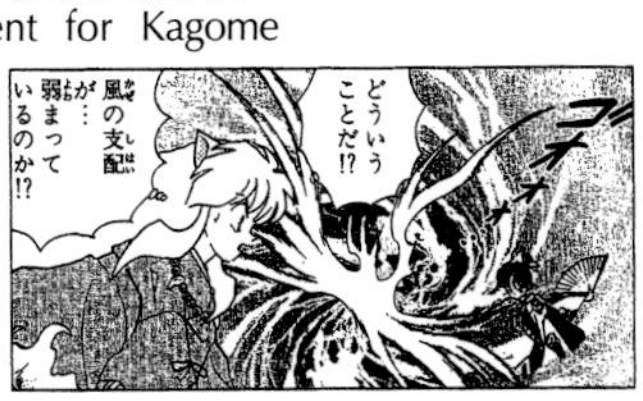

どういうことだ!?
風の支配が…弱まっているのか!?

◆ KAZE NO KIZU ("WIND SCAR")
This is the rift in the flow of demon auras between friend and foe crashing into one another in battle. It offers the right path for Tetsusaiga to work to maximum effect. Slashing along the kaze no kizu is very basic to the mastery of Tetsusaiga. In his battle with Sesshomaru, Inuyasha succeeds in finding the kaze no kizu by smell.

◆ KOARU ("LITTLE SPRING")
A girl who sees her first love, Miroku, for the first time in three years. Miroku had asked Koaru, too, to bear his child.

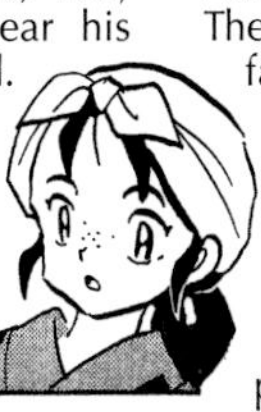

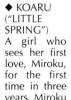

◆ KOHAKU ("AMBER")
Sango's younger brother is killed by archers at Hitomijo castle, but his body is resurrected by Naraku, who puts a shard of the Jewel in his body, and Kohaku becomes Naraku's minion. The memory of his father's murder is suppressed, and he remembers nothing of his past.

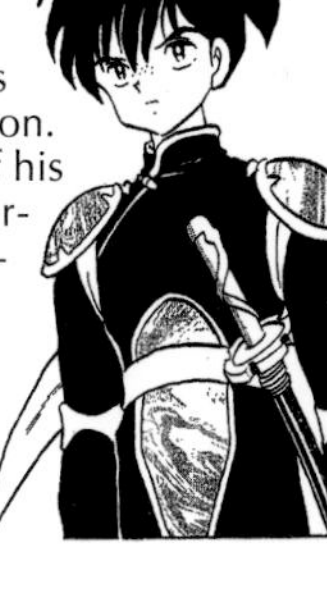

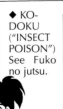

◆ KODOKU ("INSECT POISON")
See Fuko no jutsu.

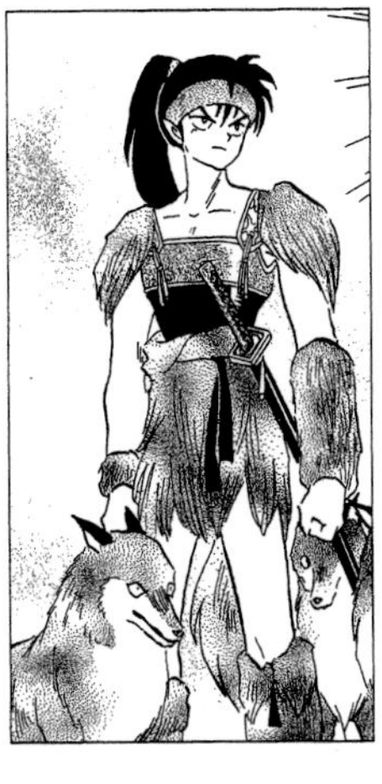

◆ KOGA ("STEEL FANG")
This demon controls man-eating wolves. He has shards of the Jewel in his right arm and feet. He uses Kagome in his battle with the gokurakucho. He falls in love with Kagome at first sight, and makes enough passes at her to anger Inuyasha.

◆ KOTATSU ("RED MASTER")
A painter who picked up a Shikon shard on a battlefield and acquired the skill to manipulate the demons he paints. He paints with ink mixed with blood, liver and the shard. He loses his life when his ink absorbs him.

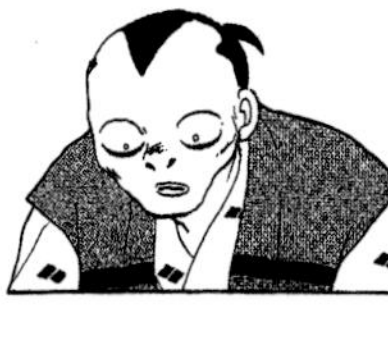

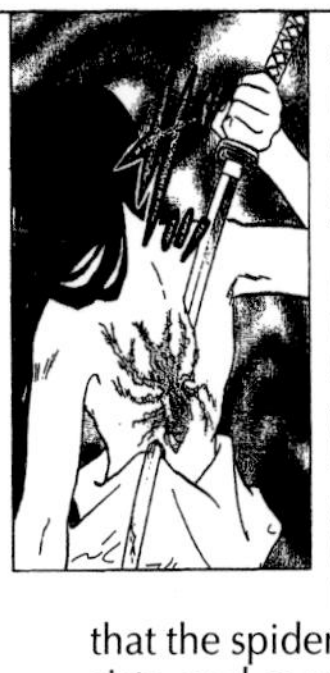

◆ KUMO NO KIZUATO ("SPIDER-SHAPED SCAR")
The scar on Naraku's back identifies him as Onigumo. It is the echo of the burns that Onigumo had over his entire body. Kikyo mentions that the spider-shaped scar persists, and cannot be scraped or burned away, as long as Onigumo's obsession with Kikyo remains.

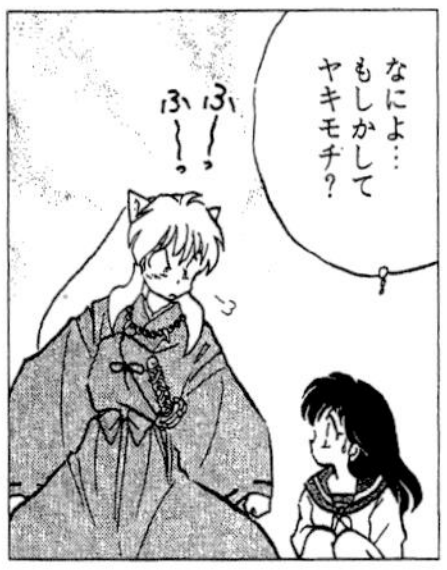

なによ…もしかしてヤキモチ？
ふ～っ ふ～っ

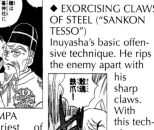

◆ JEALOUSY
Because he "has a tiny heart," says Sota, Inuyasha is green with jealousy of Koga, who makes repeated passes at Kagome. Is Kagome as jealous a type as Inuyasha?

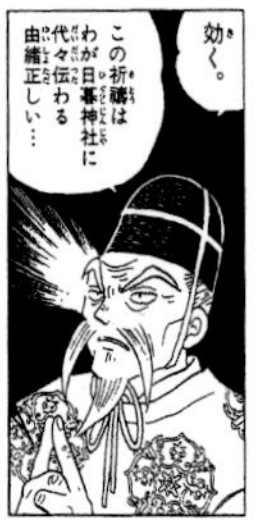

この祈禱はわが日暮神社に代々伝わる由緒正しい…
効く。

◆ GRAMPA
The priest of Higurashi Shrine and Kagome's grandfather. He loves to talk about the origins of things, even the pickles donated by a member of the shrine.

◆ EXORCISING CLAWS OF STEEL ("SANKON TESSO")
Inuyasha's basic offensive technique. He rips the enemy apart with his sharp claws. With this technique he can destroy primitive demons like Mistress Centipede instantly.

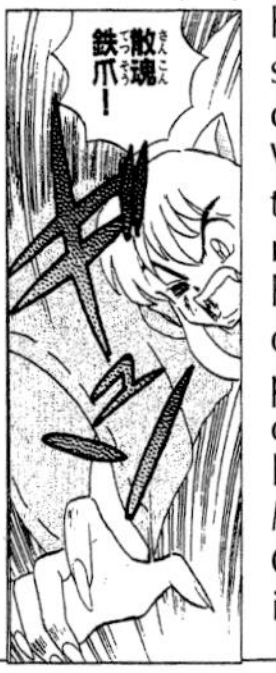

散魂鉄爪！

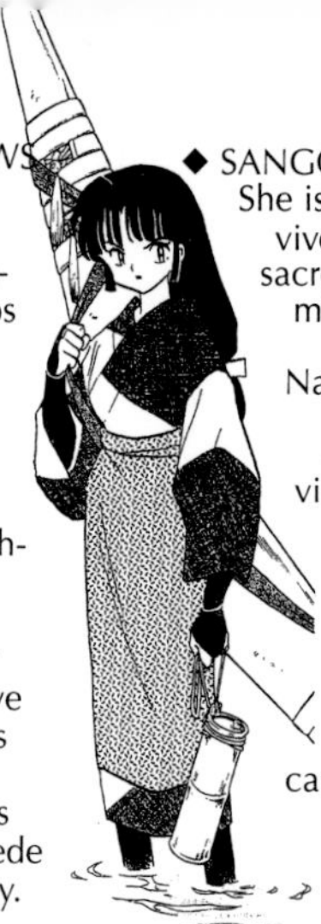

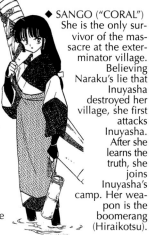

◆ SANGO ("CORAL")
She is the only survivor of the massacre at the exterminator village. Believing Naraku's lie that Inuyasha destroyed her village, she first attacks Inuyasha. After she learns the truth, she joins Inuyasha's camp. Her weapon is the boomerang (Hiraikotsu).

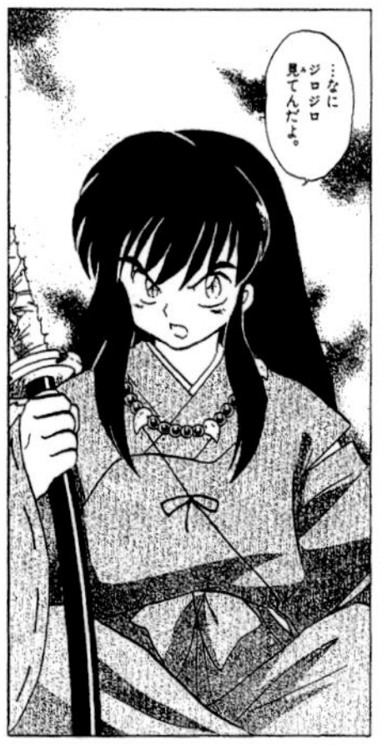

…なにジロジロ見てんだよ。

◆ FIRST DAY OF THE NEW MOON ("SAKU NO HI")
The day of the new moon, also the first day of the ancient calendar month, when Inuyasha loses his supernatural power. On this day Inuyasha looks completely human.

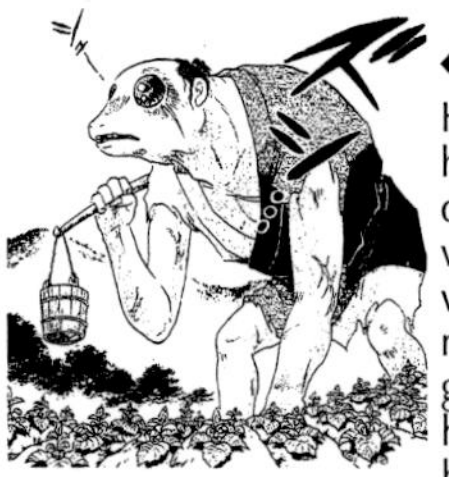

◆ EARTH BOY (JINENJI)
He is a half-demon who, with its mother, grows healing herbs that save the life of Kirara, who is poisoned by Naraku. Kagome and friends find him while passing through a village. Despite his monstrous look, he is very mild and timid. He is accused of killing villagers, but Inuyasha helps prove his innocence. Kagome and friends mistake Jinenji's mother for a yamanba ("mountain witch").

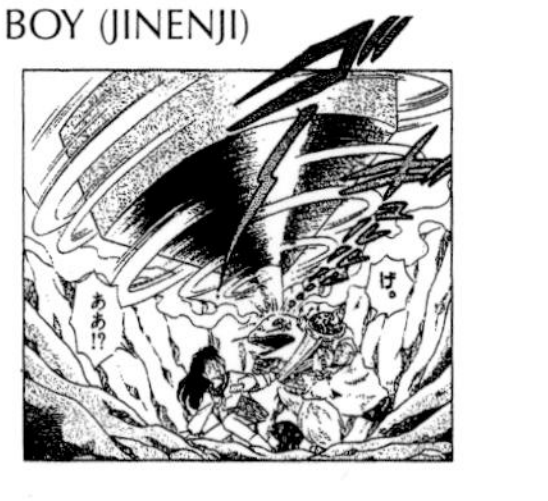

あぁ!?
は…

◆ SHIPPO'S SORCERY
Shippo can do three kinds of sorcery: shape-shifting, signs and illusions. In his first appearance he is a pink demon; later he mimics a princess that Kotatsu is in love with, a mouse and a spider. He is not particularly skilled at using this sorcery, except when he takes on the shape of Kagome. Using signs, including acorns and mushrooms with eyes, he warns of danger. his illusions include the "big top," which breaks off Manten's two last hairs, and a jizo ("children's guardian deity") that grows in weight.

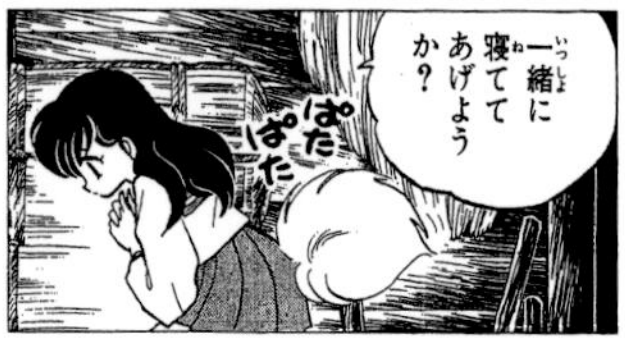

一緒に寝ててあげようか？
ぱた ぱた

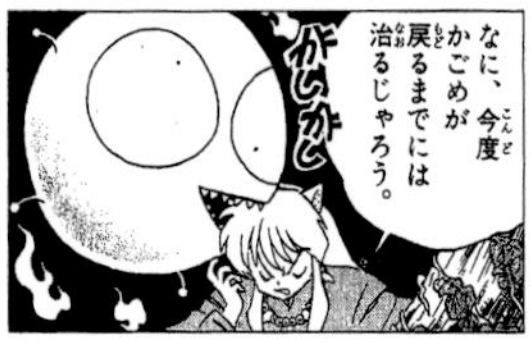

なに、かごめが今度戻るまでには治るじゃろう。

◆ SHIPPO ("SEVEN TREASURES")
He is a baby fox demon who joins Kagome's group to avenge his father. It is ironic that he is the most mature of Kagome's friends.

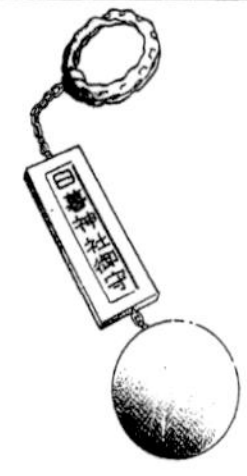

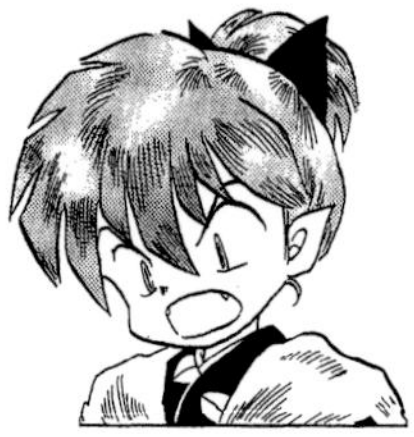

◆ SHIKON JEWEL KEYCHAIN
Grampa makes these good-luck charms to sell at the Higurashi Shrine. He has two boxes of them in stock.

◆ SESSHOMARU ("DESTRUCTION MAN")
Inuyasha's half-brother attacks Inuyasha several times to steal Tetsusaiga, which their father gave Inuyasha. Every battle makes Inuyasha stronger, but Sesshomaru is unaware of this. He has two swords: Tenseiga ("natural fang"), which can preserve the lives of the weak, and Tokijin ("demon-fighting god"), which he makes from Goshinki. Late in the story he takes the little girl Rin as a minion.

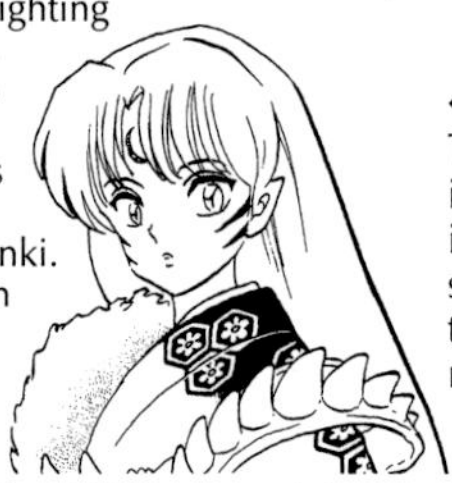

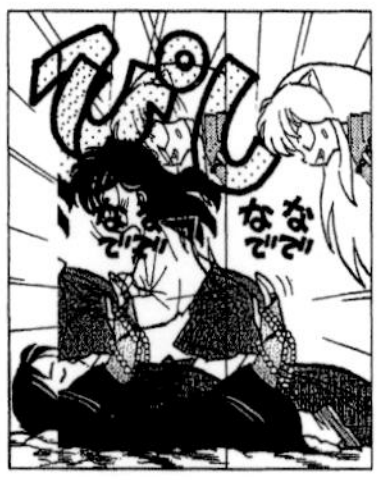

なで なで

◆ SEXUAL HARASSMENT
This is a specialty that Miroku inherited from his womanizing grandfather. Whenever he sees a pretty girl, he asks her to bear his child, and misses no opportunities for a grope. It seems that he does not make his usual requests of Sango.

◆ SUIJIN ("WATER GOD")
This tiny god who guards the lake was tricked by a spirit and confined in a rock. She grows large when she holds the Amakoi Halberd.

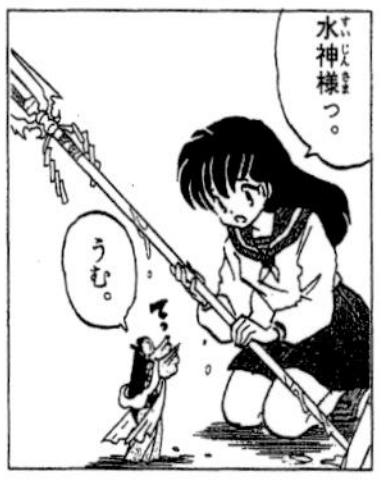

水神様っ。
うむ。

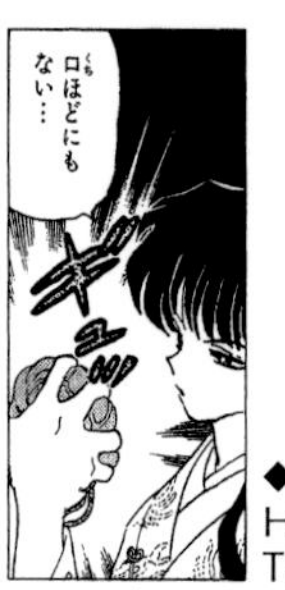

口ほどにもない…

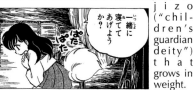

◆ HEARTS
The alter egos that Naraku makes from his body are not always faithful to him. So Naraku removes their hearts to maintain control and prevent rebellion.

◆ JAKEN ("EVIL SIGHT")
This little demon is the familiar of Sesshomaru. His battle skills are poor, and his life is often saved by Sesshomaru. Rin seems to get on Jaken's nerves after she joins Sesshomaru's group, and Jaken sighs a lot. He uses the jintojo, a staff with heads of an old man and woman, to detect the grave of Sesshomaru's father. In Buddhist legend, the jintojo is used by Enma Daio ("king of hell") to measure the weight of sin in the dead. An example from En'ooji Temple in Kamakura is closest to the original drawing used in the story.

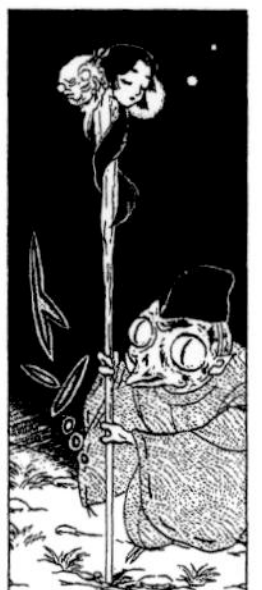

◆ TSUBO TSUKAI ("HIVE HANDLER")
He is a hit-man sent by Naraku to kill Miroku. He uses the Kokochu (hive containing the Hell Wasps) to manipulate Mushin and kill Miroku.

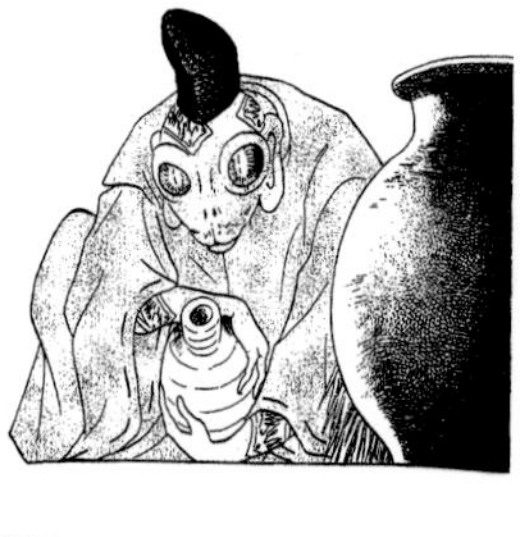

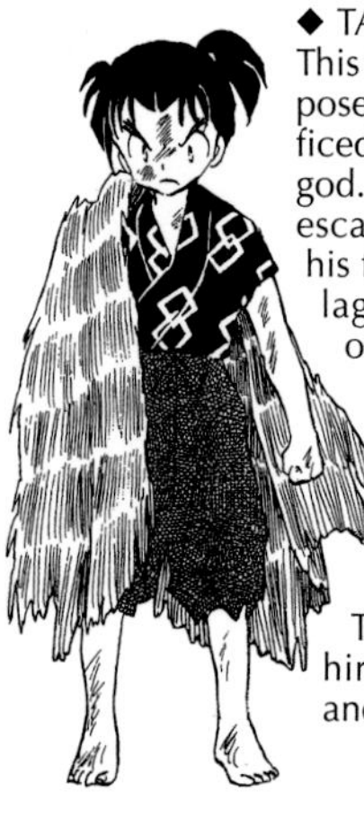

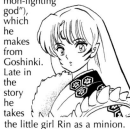

◆ TARO-MARU
This boy was supposed to be sacrificed to the water god. He narrowly escapes because his father, the village headman, offers the servant boy, Suekichi, in his place. To rescue his friend Suekichi, Taro-maru hires Inuyasha and his friends.

◆ SOUL PIPER ("TATARI-MOKKE")
This is a legendary demon from Aomori Prefecture. ("Mokke" means "baby" in the local dialect.) It is given life by the souls of dead children. It plays a requiem on its flute and watches over children's souls until they attain Buddhahood. It watches Mayu, who dies in a fire, and tries to take her away to hell because she fails to achieve peace.

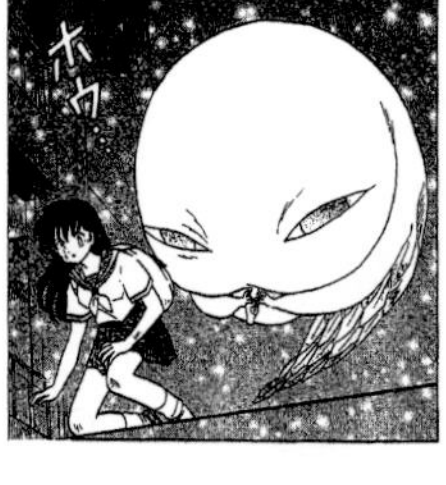

ホウ

◆ WIZARD
The hermit wizard whose body was eaten by his pupil, the Peach Man. His head was kept alive because he did not reveal the knowledge needed to produce the potions which prevent aging and death. Sensing the demon-fighting aura in Kagome's arrows, he spends the last of his energy to change into a bow, and then dies.

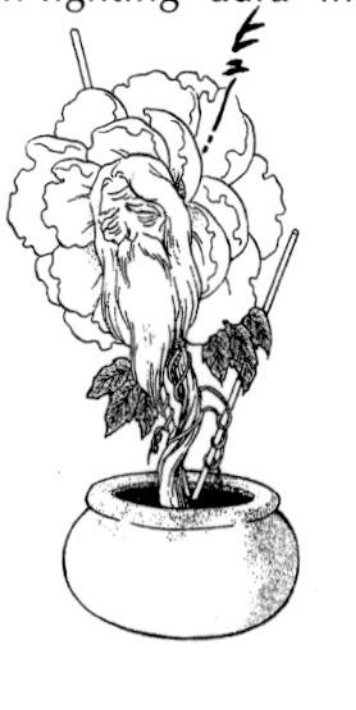

◆ NARAKU'S ALTER EGOS
With the power of the Shikon shards that Kikyo gives him, Naraku creates alter-ego demons, cultured from parts of his body in a mysterious urn. Like Naraku, these demons — Kagura, Goshinki, Juromaru and Kageromaru — have spider-shaped scars on their backs. One demon was repelled and vanished when it touched Kikyo's sanctuary.

◆ NARAKU ("HELL")
The various demons that consumed the body of the evil minded Onigumo, rose up again as Naraku. Onigumo's obsession with Kikyo made Naraku a half-demon. To become a full demon, he seeks shards of the Jewel. He constantly puts Inuyasha, Sango and Miroku in danger, and is the true enemy of Kagome's party.

毒華爪!!

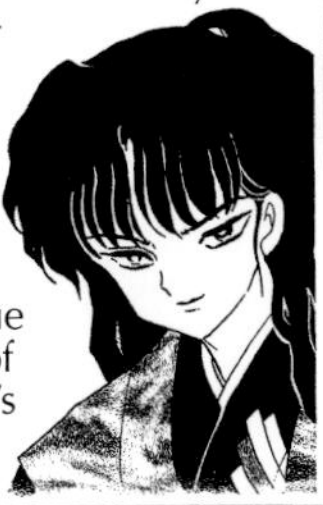

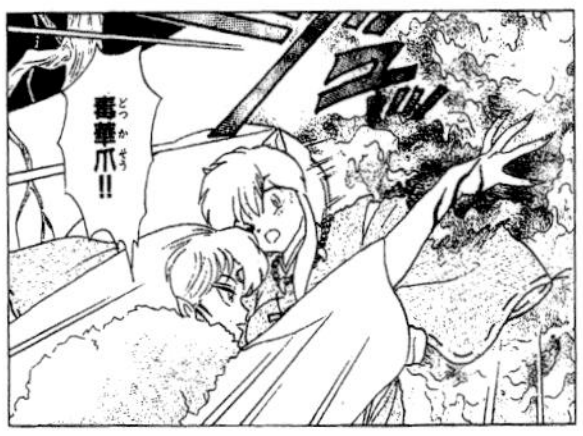

◆ POISON FLOWER CLAWS ("DOKKASO")
Sesshomaru's basic offensive technique. The poison in his claws melts the victim. It is so strong that it can rot Inuyasha's robe of the fire rat.

◆ TOTOSAI ("SWORD CEREMONY-PREPARER")
The demon swordsmith who forged Tenseiga and Tetsusaiga. He is selective about his clients; he turns down Sesshomaru's request for a sword with more power than Tetsusaiga. He shows up with three-eyed cow and gives advice to Inuyasha.

どこに行く…?
せっかく弟子にしてやったというのに。

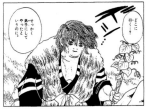

◆ PEACH MAN (TOKAJIN)
Impatient to achieve wizardhood, he eats his master's body. He uses sorcery to put Inuyasha and friends in trouble. Kagome's arrow removes the Shikon shard from his belly and sends him to his death.

◆ BAKURYUHA ("EXPLOSIVE FLOWING WAVE")
The secret of Tetsusaiga. Traps the enemy's spirit in the Wind Scar and makes it flow the opposite way. Even Inuyasha doesn't realize its power. He uses this technique against Ryukotsusei and destroys him.

◆ STEEL BEES: The stings of these demon bees are deadly enough to kill even Inuyasha. He borrows their honey to repair Tetsusaiga, which was bent almost in two in the battle with the Thunder (Raiju) brothers.

◆ HUMAN-FACED FRUIT: People who left the village during the war went to the hermit wizard's mountain, only to be eaten by the Peach Man. He uses them as ingredients in attempts to find the potion to prevent aging and death.

◆ NOH MASK OF FLESH (NIKUZUKI NO MEN)
This mask was carved from a huge bodhi tree that held a shard of the Jewel. Seeking a body of its own, it consumes people. In the modern world it seeks the Shikon shards that Kagome kept with her. The demon was beaten by Inuyasha.

もし…

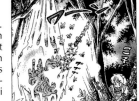

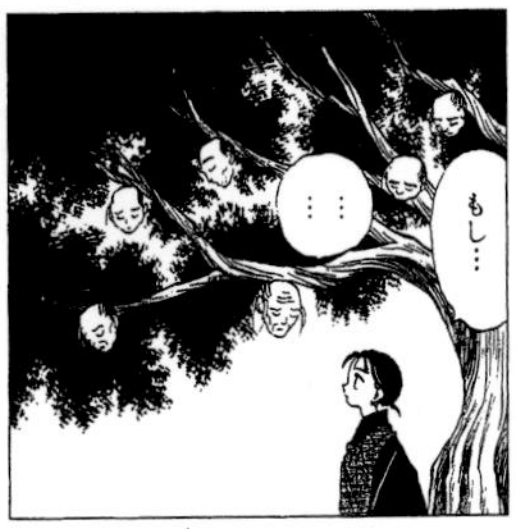

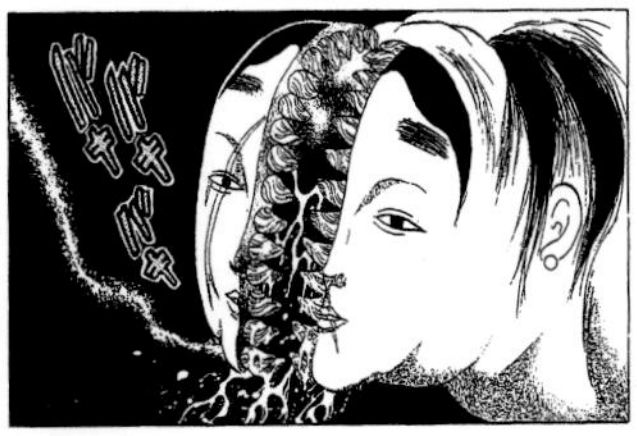

◆ BAKE- (PREFIX INDICATING "DEMON")
Animals can be changed into demons with old age or the power of a shard of Jewel in their bodies, like Oomukade. When the bake-itachi ("demon weasel") that pretended to be a statue of the Buddha was killed by Miroku, the bake-nezumi ("demon mouse") was killed by Sango, and the bake-guma ("demon bear") was killed by the Hell Wasps. Having killed the bear, the Wasps were given the mission of collecting the shards of the jewel as well as being on patrol.

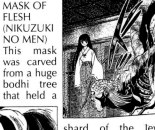

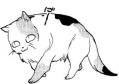

◆ BUYO
Pet cat of the Higurashi family and a bit on the fat side. It triggers Kagome's trips between the modern and ancient worlds. It once ate the mummified hand of a kappa.

◆ BLADES OF BLOOD ("HIJIN KESSO")
This is Inuyasha's second basic offensive technique. He soaks his claws in blood and flicks his hand like a throwing knife to cut his adversary.

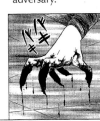

◆ HIGURASHI SOTA
Unlike his sister, Kagome's younger brother is easily frightened. He has a big heart and is the only one who goes to see his classmate Satoru in the hospital when all others are scared away by the strange happenings around him. Although Inuyasha is older, Sota thinks of the half-demon as a peer and friend.

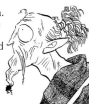

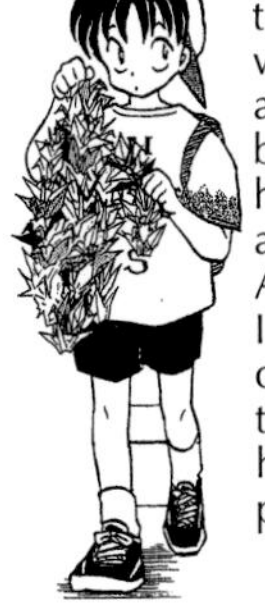

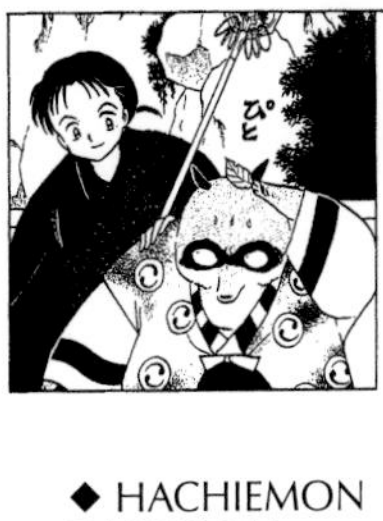

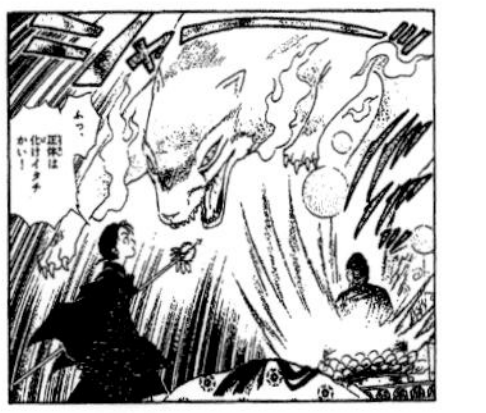

◆ HACHIEMON RACCOON
This little raccoon is threatened, coerced and overused by Miroku. He changes shape using a leaf and flies, with Miroku riding him.

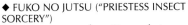

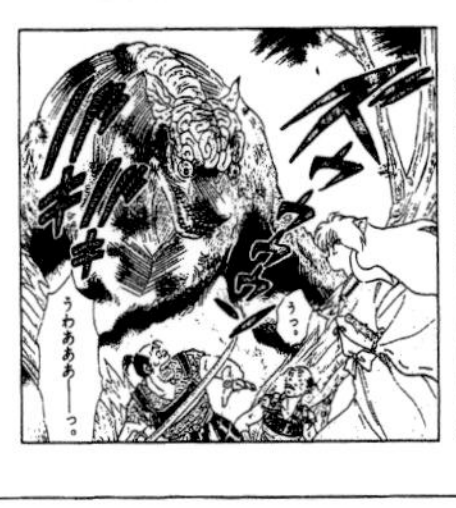

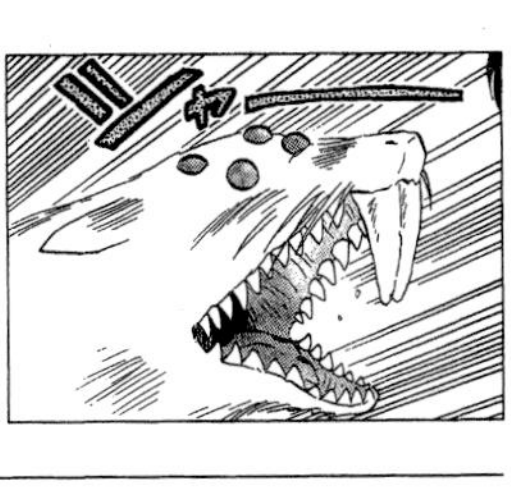

◆ MOM: Kagome's mother, whose name is not mentioned in the story. Mom immediately touches Inuyasha's doglike ears when first encountering him. This happens when he shows up at her house to bring Kagome back to the ancient world to fight Yura. This was exactly what Kagome did when she found Inuyasha enchanted in the tree. Sota expresses interest doing the same. It's a family of curious people.

◆ BOKUSEN'ON ("GRANDFATHER WIZARD NETTLE TREE")
The scabbards of Tenseiga and Tetsusaiga are carved from branches of this 2,000-year-old nettle tree. The tree tells Sesshomaru why their father chose Inuyasha for Tetsusaiga.

◆ HOJO: A pure-hearted boy with a crush on Kagome. Believing Grampa's fibs about her being sick, Hojo gives Kagome all kinds of presents: shiatsu sandals (Vol. 3, Scroll 5), blue bamboo (Vol. 3, Scroll 6), a moxibustion set (Vol. 3, Scroll 9), and a warm poultice (Vol. 4, Scroll 7). In the first episode of Vol. 15 a seventh-grader falls in love with him, but it is unrequited: Hojo sees no other girl than Kagome.

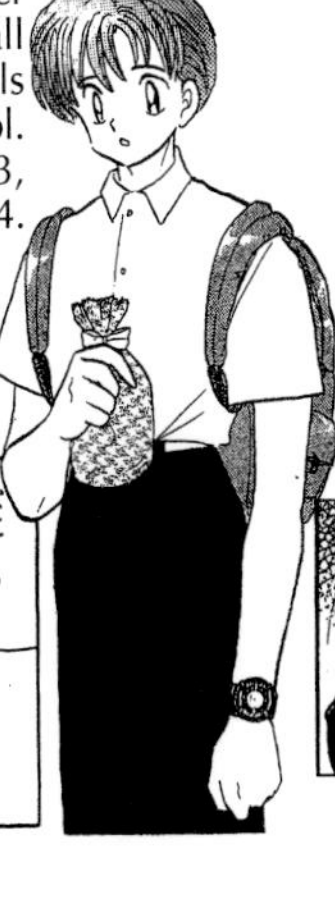

◆ FUKO NO JUTSU ("PRIESTESS INSECT SORCERY")
This sorcery comes from Onmyodo (an ancient Chinese religion), in which poisonous insects, lizards, frogs and other creatures were thrown together into an urn to kill one another. The survivor becomes the Kodoku ("insect poison"). Naraku does the same using demons. He uses the body of the winner to replace his own body which was injured by Kagome's arrow. Inuyasha was nearly used for this, but was

青竹…

かごめは北条くんを忘れていた。
このお姿気にいるかな。

負けた
そいつが
否応なく
おまえの体に
はいり
込んでくる。

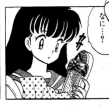

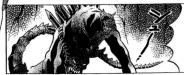

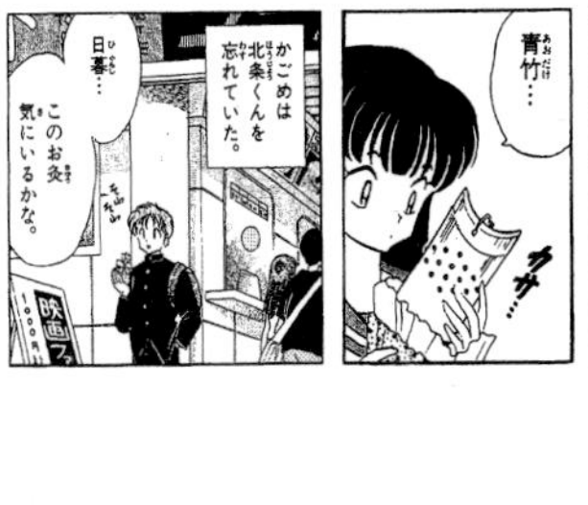

◆ MIDORIKO ("GREEN CHILD")
A priestess of great power. Fighting a legion of demons, she uses the last of her strength to merge the souls of all the demons into hers, which became the Jewel of Four Souls. Her mummified body is found in the village of the exterminators.

◆ BLACK PEARL
Where Inuyasha's father chooses to seal up his bones so they will not turn violent. Inuyasha is unaware of this. Sesshomaru learns of it from the Un-Mother and gouges the pearl out of Inuyasha's eye. When he succeeds in opening the tomb using the Jintojo, he finds the vast alternate dimension where his father's bones rest.

◆ MAYU
Satoru's older sister, who died in the house fire, cannot leave the world for Heaven because she is convinced that her mother hated her and refused to rescue her. Soul Piper nearly takes her to hell.

耳…
本物？
ぐいぐいぐい
ママ、
そんなことしてる場合じゃ…
次ぼくもぼくも。
私もやったけど…

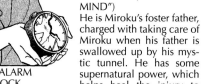

◆ GOODIES FROM THE FUTURE
Kagome brings various things from her world to ancient times: a bicycle, a first-aid kit, camping gear (sleeping bag, rug, kettle), beauty-care products (hairspray, towel), food (instant cup noodles, potato chips). It's as if she's going camping. Inuyasha and friends are surprised at first, but eventually grow so used to them that they immediately turn on the flashlight in the cave where Fuko no Jutsu is taking place.

犬夜叉もなにか食べるー？
いらねーよ。

あっうめえっ。

◆ MIROKU
This rogue Buddhist monk inherited a battle against Naraku that his grandfather began. He has a wind tunnel in his hand, cut by Naraku's curse. The tunnel grows and will eventually swallow him. Like his ancestors, he is a womanizer.

◆ MYOGA ("INVISIBLE DIVINE HELP")
This old flea demon was the keeper of the false grave of Inuyasha's father. He has vast knowledge and a keen sense of danger. No one can escape to a safe place quicker than Myoga.

動けぬ鬼蜘蛛のすさまじき邪念は洞穴の中に籠り、
その邪気が妖怪を呼び集め…

◆ YOKAI ("DEMON")
Demons were part of ordinary life in the medieval period. Most that Inuyasha and friends fight are powerful ones. There are also many other nameless demons of various kinds, including the mountain fairies that Sesshomaru kills with Tetsusaiga, the "soldiers" that Naraku uses, messengers from hell, and the false water god's gang.

◆ ALARM CLOCK
Inuyasha takes it from Kagome's room without telling her. He later uses it to make up to Kagome. They fight over Inuyasha's groundless accusation that Kagome is seeing Koga.

◆ MUSHIN ("DREAM MIND")
He is Miroku's foster father, charged with taking care of Miroku when his father is swallowed up by his mystic tunnel. He has some supernatural power, which helps heal the injury to Miroku's hand. Under the influence of the urn grubs, he attacks Miroku.

◆ MISTRESS CENTIPEDE ("MUKADE JORO")
This is the demon who takes Kagome into the Warring States period. She was seeking shards of the Jewel, but is killed by Inuyasha.

◆ UN MOTHER (MU'ONNA)
To find the true location of his father's tomb, Sesshomaru sends her to Inuyasha disguised as his mother. She is a demon born of the unappeased souls of mothers who lost their children in the war.

坊や…

◆ WACDONALD'S
Kagome and her friends hang out at this burger joint after school. Here Kagome is grilled by her two girlfriends about Hojo and boys. The WacDonald's menu includes the Tamatori Burger and the Teri Cheese Burger. On a date here, Kagome tells Hojo that she doesn't feel well.

白状しなさいよかごめ。
どーゆー男とつきあってるのよっ。
Wacdonal
駅

Surprise, Surprise.

いろいろすまなかった！
じゃっ！

◆ RIN
The girl who cared for Sesshomaru when he was badly injured. After being nearly devoured by the wolves of the Yoro clan, she is revived by the power of Tenseiga. After that the innocent girl becomes attached to Sesshomaru.

This glossary is based on information up to "Tetsuseiga Resurrected" (Vol. 49, Scroll 191, 2000) in Shonen Magazine.

はらはら
はらはら